Great Expectations

Charles Dickens

Great Expectations

Charles Dickens

Trans
Atlantic
Press

This is a Transatlantic Press book
This edition published in 2012

Transatlantic Press
Sky House, Raans Road, Amersham, Bucks, HP6 6JQ, UK

Charles Dickens
asserts the moral right to be identified as the author of this work.

Cover image copyright GettyImages
Author biography copyright Transatlantic Press

All rights reserved. No part of this publication may be reproduced or transmitted
in any form or by any means, electronic or mechanical, including photocopying,
recording, or any information storage and retrieval system, without permission in
writing from the copyright holders.

A catalogue record is available for this book from the British Library

ISBN 978-1-907176-99-9

Printed and bound by CPI Group (UK) Ltd, Croydon, CR0 4YY

CHARLES DICKENS

Charles Dickens was born in Portsmouth on February 7, 1812, the son of a naval clerk whose job required him to uproot the family to several port towns. Never a great provider, John Dickens spent time in Marshalsea debtors' prison in 1824, and 12-year-old Charles found himself set to work in a boot-blacking factory. These events left a lasting mark on the impressionable youngster, the misery and humiliation he suffered manifesting itself time and again in his fictional portraits of maltreated, neglected children.

His formal education was haphazard, but Charles was an avid reader, and after a brief stint as a lawyer's office boy he found employment as a Parliamentary reporter. During his time as a journalist, he produced a series of humorous pieces on English life and character, which were published in book form as *Sketches By Boz* in 1836. That success brought a commission to produce a novel in serial form, and with the publication of *The Posthumous Papers of the Pickwick Club* (1837), Dickens soon established himself as the most popular novelist of the day. It was a position he maintained until his death 33 years later.

Dickens maintained the serial format, his work appearing in periodicals such as *Bentley's Miscellany* and *All The Year Round*. The novelist's hand was often on the editorial tiller of these publications, which gave him a weekly foothold in a large number of households. His output was prodigious, and instalments of two or more novels often ran in tandem. Between 1837 and 1841 Dickens delivered *Oliver Twist*, *Nicholas Nickleby*, *The Old Curiosity Shop* and *Barnaby Rudge*. The last of that quartet was the first of his historical novels, taking the reader back to the days of the Gordon Riots 60 years earlier. The only other time Dickens would dip into the history books for his setting was the French Revolution-based *A Tale of Two Cities* (1859).

On the back of those early triumphs Dickens embarked on his first trip to America in 1842, accompanied by his wife of six years, née Catherine Hogarth. He soon tired of the effusive attention, and the slavery issue was just one of many concerns that made it a somewhat unsuccessful visit. He painted a rather unfavorable picture of the country in *Martin Chuzzlewit* (1844).

During *Chuzzlewit*'s serial run, Dickens published the first of his 'Christmas Books'. Of these, *A Christmas Carol* (1843), the book that launched the series, became a perennial favorite and classic festive-season tale.

Dickens began *Dombey and Son* (1848) during an extensive European sojourn in the mid 1840s. Two years later he published *David Copperfield*, his personal favorite among his novels and yet another depiction of an unhappy childhood. The 1850s, in addition to *A Tale of Two Cities*, brought *Bleak House*, with its interminable legal wrangle, *Hard Times* and *Little Dorrit*. That decade also witnessed domestic upheaval as Dickens fell in love with Ellen Ternan, an actress 27 years his junior. In 1858 he parted from Catherine, who had borne him 10 children during their 22-year marriage.

Dickens's health declined in the final decade of his life. Apart from the energies he devoted to his art, he was a keen amateur thespian, while his public readings—which took in a return trip to America in 1867—were exhausting affairs. A near-fatal train crash also impacted his health. *Great Expectations* (1861) and *Our Mutual Friend* (1865) were his final completed novels, *The Mystery of Edwin Drood* remaining unfinished when he died at his Gads Hill home on June 9, 1870, aged 58. He is buried in Westminster Abbey.

GREAT EXPECTATIONS

Orphaned Philip Pirrip—known as Pip—lives with his tyrannical elder sister and her kindly blacksmith husband. After surviving a terrifying churchyard encounter with an escaped convict, Pip is invited to visit embittered, reclusive spinster Miss Havisham. Jilted on her wedding day, Miss Havisham delights in using the beautiful Estella, whom she has adopted, as an instrument of revenge. Pip falls for the disdainful, cold-hearted Estella, and vows to better himself in the hope of winning her over. A windfall raises his expectations but proves to be no panacea, as wealth alters his values and brings little contentment. Along the path to wisdom and enlightenment, Pip also learns the identity of his mysterious benefactor.

In *Great Expectations*, his penultimate completed novel, Dickens examines class, social mobility, and the corrupting power of money, while adding to his gallery of unforgettable characters.

VOLUME ONE

CHAPTER 1

My father's family name being Pirrip, and my Christian name Philip, my infant tongue could make of both names nothing longer or more explicit than Pip. So, I called myself Pip, and came to be called Pip.

I give Pirrip as my father's family name, on the authority of his tombstone and my sister—Mrs. Joe Gargery, who married the blacksmith. As I never saw my father or my mother, and never saw any likeness of either of them (for their days were long before the days of photographs), my first fancies regarding what they were like were unreasonably derived from their tombstones. The shape of the letters on my father's, gave me an odd idea that he was a square, stout, dark man, with curly black hair. From the character and turn of the inscription, "*Also Georgiana Wife of the Above*," I drew a childish conclusion that my mother was freckled and sickly. To five little stone lozenges, each about a foot and a half long, which were arranged in a neat row beside their grave, and were sacred to the memory of five little brothers of mine—who gave up trying to get a living, exceedingly early in that universal struggle—I am indebted for a belief I religiously entertained that they had all been born on their backs with their hands in their trousers-pockets, and had never taken them out in this state of existence.

Ours was the marsh country, down by the river, within, as

the river wound, twenty miles of the sea. My first most vivid and broad impression of the identity of things seems to me to have been gained on a memorable raw afternoon towards evening. At such a time I found out for certain that this bleak place overgrown with nettles was the churchyard; and that Philip Pirrip, late of this parish, and also Georgiana wife of the above, were dead and buried; and that Alexander, Bartholomew, Abraham, Tobias, and Roger, infant children of the aforesaid, were also dead and buried; and that the dark flat wilderness beyond the churchyard, intersected with dikes and mounds and gates, with scattered cattle feeding on it, was the marshes; and that the low leaden line beyond was the river; and that the distant savage lair from which the wind was rushing was the sea; and that the small bundle of shivers growing afraid of it all and beginning to cry, was Pip.

"Hold your noise!" cried a terrible voice, as a man started up from among the graves at the side of the church porch. "Keep still, you little devil, or I'll cut your throat!"

A fearful man, all in coarse gray, with a great iron on his leg. A man with no hat, and with broken shoes, and with an old rag tied round his head. A man who had been soaked in water, and smothered in mud, and lamed by stones, and cut by flints, and stung by nettles, and torn by briars; who limped, and shivered, and glared, and growled; and whose teeth chattered in his head as he seized me by the chin.

"O! Don't cut my throat, sir," I pleaded in terror. "Pray don't do it, sir."

"Tell us your name!" said the man. "Quick!"

"Pip, sir."

"Once more," said the man, staring at me. "Give it mouth!"

"Pip. Pip, sir."

"Show us where you live," said the man. "Pint out the place!"

I pointed to where our village lay, on the flat in-shore

among the alder-trees and pollards, a mile or more from the church.

The man, after looking at me for a moment, turned me upside down, and emptied my pockets. There was nothing in them but a piece of bread. When the church came to itself—for he was so sudden and strong that he made it go head over heels before me, and I saw the steeple under my feet—when the church came to itself, I say, I was seated on a high tombstone, trembling while he ate the bread ravenously.

"You young dog," said the man, licking his lips, "what fat cheeks you ha' got."

I believe they were fat, though I was at that time undersized for my years, and not strong.

"Darn me if I couldn't eat em," said the man, with a threatening shake of his head, "and if I han't half a mind to't!"

I earnestly expressed my hope that he wouldn't, and held tighter to the tombstone on which he had put me; partly, to keep myself upon it; partly, to keep myself from crying.

"Now lookee here!" said the man. "Where's your mother?"

"There, sir!" said I.

He started, made a short run, and stopped and looked over his shoulder.

"There, sir!" I timidly explained. "Also Georgiana. That's my mother."

"Oh!" said he, coming back. "And is that your father alonger your mother?"

"Yes, sir," said I; "him too; late of this parish."

"Ha!" he muttered then, considering. "Who d'ye live with—supposin' you're kindly let to live, which I han't made up my mind about?"

"My sister sir—Mrs. Joe Gargery—wife of Joe Gargery, the blacksmith, sir."

"Blacksmith, eh?" said he. And looked down at his leg.

After darkly looking at his leg and me several times, he

came closer to my tombstone, took me by both arms, and tilted me back as far as he could hold me; so that his eyes looked most powerfully down into mine, and mine looked most helplessly up into his.

"Now lookee here," he said, "the question being whether you're to be let to live. You know what a file is?"

"Yes, sir."

"And you know what wittles is?"

"Yes, sir."

After each question he tilted me over a little more, so as to give me a greater sense of helplessness and danger.

"You get me a file." He tilted me again. "And you get me wittles." He tilted me again. "You bring 'em both to me." He tilted me again. "Or I'll have your heart and liver out." He tilted me again.

I was dreadfully frightened, and so giddy that I clung to him with both hands, and said, "If you would kindly please to let me keep upright, sir, perhaps I shouldn't be sick, and perhaps I could attend more."

He gave me a most tremendous dip and roll, so that the church jumped over its own weathercock. Then, he held me by the arms, in an upright position on the top of the stone, and went on in these fearful terms:

"You bring me, to-morrow morning early, that file and them wittles. You bring the lot to me, at that old Battery over yonder. You do it, and you never dare to say a word or dare to make a sign concerning your having seen such a person as me, or any person sumever, and you shall be let to live. You fail, or you go from my words in any partickler, no matter how small it is, and your heart and your liver shall be tore out, roasted, and ate. Now, I ain't alone, as you may think I am. There's a young man hid with me, in comparison with which young man I am a Angel. That young man hears the words I speak. That young man has a secret way pecooliar to himself, of getting at a boy, and at his heart, and at his liver. It is in wain for a boy to attempt to hide himself from that young man. A boy may lock his door, may be warm in bed, may tuck himself up, may draw the clothes over his head, may think himself comfortable and safe, but that young man will softly creep and creep his way to him and tear him open. I am a keeping that young man from harming of you at the present moment, with great difficulty. I find it wery hard to hold that young man off of your inside. Now, what do you say?"

I said that I would get him the file, and I would get him what broken bits of food I could, and I would come to him at the Battery, early in the morning.

"Say Lord strike you dead if you don't!" said the man.

I said so, and he took me down.

"Now," he pursued, "you remember what you've undertook, and you remember that young man, and you get home!"

"Goo-good night, sir," I faltered.

"Much of that!" said he, glancing about him over the cold wet flat. "I wish I was a frog. Or a eel!"

At the same time, he hugged his shuddering body in both his arms—clasping himself, as if to hold himself together—and limped towards the low church wall. As I saw him go, picking his way among the nettles, and among the brambles that bound the green mounds, he looked in my young eyes as if he were eluding the hands of the dead people, stretching up cautiously out of their graves, to get a twist upon his ankle and pull him in.

When he came to the low church wall, he got over it, like a man whose legs were numbed and stiff, and then turned round to look for me. When I saw him turning, I set my face towards home, and made the best use of my legs. But presently I looked over my shoulder, and saw him going on again towards the river, still hugging himself in both arms, and picking his way with his sore feet among the great stones dropped into the marshes here and there, for stepping-places when the rains were heavy or the tide was in.

The marshes were just a long black horizontal line then, as I stopped to look after him; and the river was just another horizontal line, not nearly so broad nor yet so black; and the sky was just a row of long angry red lines and dense black lines intermixed. On the edge of the river I could faintly make out the only two black things in all the prospect that seemed to be standing upright; one of these was the beacon by which the sailors steered—like an unhooped cask upon a pole—an ugly thing when you were near it; the other, a gibbet, with some chains hanging to it which had once held a pirate. The man was limping on towards this latter, as if he were the pirate come to life, and come down, and going back to hook himself up again. It gave me a terrible turn when I thought so; and as I saw the cattle lifting their heads to gaze after him, I wondered whether they thought so too. I looked all round for the horrible young man, and could see no signs of him. But now I was frightened again, and ran home without stopping.

CHAPTER 2

My sister, Mrs. Joe Gargery, was more than twenty years older than I, and had established a great reputation with herself and the neighbours because she had brought me up "by hand." Having at that time to find out for myself what the expression meant, and knowing her to have a hard and heavy hand, and to be much in the habit of laying it upon her husband as well as upon me, I supposed that Joe Gargery and I were both brought up by hand.

She was not a good-looking woman, my sister; and I had a general impression that she must have made Joe Gargery marry her by hand. Joe was a fair man, with curls of flaxen hair on each side of his smooth face, and with eyes of such a very undecided blue that they seemed to have somehow got mixed with their own whites. He was a mild, good-natured, sweet-tempered, easy-going, foolish, dear fellow—a sort of Hercules in strength, and also in weakness.

My sister, Mrs. Joe, with black hair and eyes, had such a prevailing redness of skin that I sometimes used to wonder whether it was possible she washed herself with a nutmeg-grater instead of soap. She was tall and bony, and almost always wore a coarse apron, fastened over her figure behind with two loops, and having a square impregnable bib in front, that was stuck full of pins and needles. She made it a powerful merit in herself, and a strong reproach against Joe, that she wore this apron so much. Though I really see no reason why she should have worn it at all; or why, if she did wear it at all, she should not have taken it off, every day of her life.

Joe's forge adjoined our house, which was a wooden house,

as many of the dwellings in our country were—most of them, at that time. When I ran home from the churchyard, the forge was shut up, and Joe was sitting alone in the kitchen. Joe and I being fellow-sufferers, and having confidences as such, Joe imparted a confidence to me, the moment I raised the latch of the door and peeped in at him opposite to it, sitting in the chimney corner.

"Mrs. Joe has been out a dozen times, looking for you, Pip. And she's out now, making it a baker's dozen."

"Is she?"

"Yes, Pip," said Joe; "and what's worse, she's got Tickler with her."

At this dismal intelligence, I twisted the only button on my waistcoat round and round, and looked in great depression at the fire. Tickler was a wax-ended piece of cane, worn smooth by collision with my tickled frame.

"She sot down," said Joe, "and she got up, and she made a grab at Tickler, and she Ram-paged out. That's what she did," said Joe, slowly clearing the fire between the lower bars with the poker, and looking at it; "she Ram-paged out, Pip."

"Has she been gone long, Joe?" I always treated him as a larger species of child, and as no more than my equal.

"Well," said Joe, glancing up at the Dutch clock, "she's been on the Ram-page, this last spell, about five minutes, Pip. She's a coming! Get behind the door, old chap, and have the jack-towel betwixt you."

I took the advice. My sister, Mrs. Joe, throwing the door wide open, and finding an obstruction behind it, immediately divined the cause, and applied Tickler to its further investigation. She concluded by throwing me—I often served as a connubial missile—at Joe, who, glad to get hold of me on any terms, passed me on into the chimney and quietly fenced me up there with his great leg.

"Where have you been, you young monkey?" said Mrs. Joe,

stamping her foot. "Tell me directly what you've been doing to wear me away with fret and fright and worrit, or I'd have you out of that corner if you was fifty Pips, and he was five hundred Gargerys."

"I have only been to the churchyard," said I, from my stool, crying and rubbing myself.

"Churchyard!" repeated my sister. "If it warn't for me you'd have been to the churchyard long ago, and stayed there. Who brought you up by hand?"

"You did," said I.

"And why did I do it, I should like to know?" exclaimed my sister.

I whimpered, "I don't know."

"*I* don't!" said my sister. "I'd never do it again! I know that. I may truly say I've never had this apron of mine off since born you were. It's bad enough to be a blacksmith's wife (and him a Gargery) without being your mother."

My thoughts strayed from that question as I looked disconsolately at the fire. For the fugitive out on the marshes with the ironed leg, the mysterious young man, the file, the food, and the dreadful pledge I was under to commit a larceny on those sheltering premises, rose before me in the avenging coals.

"Hah!" said Mrs. Joe, restoring Tickler to his station. "Churchyard, indeed! You may well say churchyard, you two." One of us, by-the-by, had not said it at all. "You'll drive *me* to the churchyard betwixt you, one of these days, and oh, a pr-r-recious pair you'd be without me!"

As she applied herself to set the tea-things, Joe peeped down at me over his leg, as if he were mentally casting me and himself up, and calculating what kind of pair we practically should make, under the grievous circumstances foreshadowed. After that, he sat feeling his right-side flaxen curls and whisker, and following Mrs. Joe about with his blue eyes, as his manner always was at squally times.

My sister had a trenchant way of cutting our bread and butter for us, that never varied. First, with her left hand she jammed the loaf hard and fast against her bib—where it sometimes got a pin into it, and sometimes a needle, which we afterwards got into our mouths. Then she took some butter (not too much) on a knife and spread it on the loaf, in an apothecary kind of way, as if she were making a plaister—using both sides of the knife with a slapping dexterity, and trimming and moulding the butter off round the crust. Then, she gave the knife a final smart wipe on the edge of the plaster, and then sawed a very thick round off the loaf: which she finally, before separating from the loaf, hewed into two halves, of which Joe got one, and I the other.

On the present occasion, though I was hungry, I dared not eat my slice. I felt that I must have something in reserve for my dreadful acquaintance, and his ally the still more dreadful young man. I knew Mrs. Joe's housekeeping to be of the strictest kind, and that my larcenous researches might find nothing available in the safe. Therefore I resolved to put my hunk of bread and butter down the leg of my trousers.

The effort of resolution necessary to the achievement of this purpose I found to be quite awful. It was as if I had to make up my mind to leap from the top of a high house, or plunge into a great depth of water. And it was made the more difficult by the unconscious Joe. In our already-mentioned freemasonry as fellow-sufferers, and in his good-natured companionship with me, it was our evening habit to compare the way we bit through our slices, by silently holding them up to each other's admiration now and then—which stimulated us to new exertions. To-night, Joe several times invited me, by the display of his fast diminishing slice, to enter upon our usual friendly competition; but he found me, each time, with my yellow mug of tea on one knee, and my untouched bread and butter on the other. At last, I desperately considered that the thing I contemplated must be done, and that it had best be done in the least improbable manner consistent with the circumstances. I took advantage of a moment when Joe had just looked at me, and got my bread and butter down my leg.

Joe was evidently made uncomfortable by what he supposed to be my loss of appetite, and took a thoughtful bite out of his slice, which he didn't seem to enjoy. He turned it about in his mouth much longer than usual, pondering over it a good deal, and after all gulped it down like a pill. He was about to take another bite, and had just got his head on one side for a good purchase on it, when his eye fell on me, and he saw that my bread and butter was gone.

The wonder and consternation with which Joe stopped on the threshold of his bite and stared at me, were too evident to escape my sister's observation.

"What's the matter now?" said she, smartly, as she put down her cup.

"I say, you know!" muttered Joe, shaking his head at me in very serious remonstrance. "Pip, old chap! You'll do yourself a mischief. It'll stick somewhere. You can't have chawed it, Pip."

"What's the matter *now*?" repeated my sister, more sharply than before.

"If you can cough any trifle on it up, Pip, I'd recommend you to do it," said Joe, all aghast. "Manners is manners, but still your elth's your elth."

By this time, my sister was quite desperate, so she pounced on Joe, and, taking him by the two whiskers, knocked his head for a little while against the wall behind him, while I sat in the corner, looking guiltily on.

"Now, perhaps you'll mention what's the matter," said my sister, out of breath, "you staring great stuck pig."

Joe looked at her in a helpless way, then took a helpless bite, and looked at me again.

"You know, Pip," said Joe, solemnly, with his last bite in his cheek, and speaking in a confidential voice, as if we two were quite alone, "you and me is always friends, and I'd be the last to tell upon you, any time. But such a— "he moved his chair and looked about the floor between us, and then again at me— "such a most oncommon Bolt as that!"

"Been bolting his food, has he?" cried my sister.

"You know, old chap," said Joe, looking at me, and not at Mrs. Joe, with his bite still in his cheek, "I Bolted, myself, when I was your age—frequent—and as a boy I've been among a many Bolters; but I never see your Bolting equal yet, Pip, and it's a mercy you ain't Bolted dead."

My sister made a dive at me, and fished me up by the hair, saying nothing more than the awful words, "You come along and be dosed."

Some medical beast had revived Tar-water in those days as a fine medicine, and Mrs. Joe always kept a supply of it in the cupboard; having a belief in its virtues correspondent to its nastiness. At the best of times, so much of this elixir was administered to me as a choice restorative, that I was conscious of going about, smelling like a new fence. On this particular evening the urgency of my case demanded a pint of this mixture, which was poured down my throat, for my greater comfort, while Mrs. Joe held my head under her arm, as a boot would be held in a bootjack. Joe got off with half a pint; but was made to swallow that (much to his disturbance, as he sat slowly munching and meditating before the fire), "because he had had a turn." Judging from myself, I should say he certainly had a turn afterwards, if he had had none before.

Conscience is a dreadful thing when it accuses man or boy; but when, in the case of a boy, that secret burden co-operates with another secret burden down the leg of his trousers, it is (as I can testify) a great punishment. The guilty knowledge that I was going to rob Mrs. Joe—I never thought I was going to rob Joe, for I never thought of any of the housekeeping property as his—united to the necessity of always keeping one hand on my bread-and-butter as I sat, or when I was ordered about the kitchen on any small errand, almost drove me out of my mind. Then, as the marsh winds made the fire glow and flare, I thought I heard the voice outside, of the man with the iron on his leg who had sworn me to secrecy, declaring that he couldn't and wouldn't starve until to-morrow, but must be fed now. At other times, I thought, What if the young man who was with so much difficulty restrained from imbruing his hands in me should yield to a constitutional impatience, or should mistake the time, and should think himself accredited to my heart and liver to-night, instead of to-morrow! If ever anybody's hair stood on end with terror, mine must have done so then. But, perhaps, nobody's ever did.

It was Christmas Eve, and I had to stir the pudding for next day, with a copper-stick, from seven to eight by the Dutch clock. I tried it with the load upon my leg (and that made me think afresh of the man with the load on *his* leg), and found the tendency of exercise to bring the bread and butter out at my ankle, quite unmanageable. Happily I slipped away, and deposited that part of my conscience in my garret bedroom.

"Hark!" said I, when I had done my stirring, and was taking a final warm in the chimney corner before being sent up to bed; "was that great guns, Joe?"

"Ah!" said Joe. "There's another conwict off."

"What does that mean, Joe?" said I.

Mrs. Joe, who always took explanations upon herself, said, snappishly, "Escaped. Escaped." Administering the definition like Tar-water.

While Mrs. Joe sat with her head bending over her needlework, I put my mouth into the forms of saying to Joe, "What's a convict?" Joe put *his* mouth into the forms of returning such a highly elaborate answer, that I could make out nothing of it but the single word "Pip."

"There was a conwict off last night," said Joe, aloud, "after sunset-gun. And they fired warning of him. And now it appears they're firing warning of another."

"*Who's* firing?" said I.

"Drat that boy," interposed my sister, frowning at me over her work, "what a questioner he is. Ask no questions, and you'll be told no lies."

It was not very polite to herself, I thought, to imply that I should be told lies by her even if I did ask questions. But she never was polite unless there was company.

At this point Joe greatly augmented my curiosity by taking the utmost pains to open his mouth very wide, and to put it into the form of a word that looked to me like "sulks." Therefore, I naturally pointed to Mrs. Joe, and put my mouth into the form of saying, "her?" But Joe wouldn't hear of that, at all, and again opened his mouth very wide, and shook the form of a most emphatic word out of it. But I could make nothing of the word.

"Mrs. Joe," said I, as a last resort, "I should like to know—if you wouldn't much mind—where the firing comes from?"

"Lord bless the boy!" exclaimed my sister, as if she didn't quite mean that but rather the contrary. "From the Hulks!"

"Oh-h!" said I, looking at Joe. "Hulks!"

Joe gave a reproachful cough, as much as to say, "Well, I told you so."

"And please, what's Hulks?" said I.

"That's the way with this boy!" exclaimed my sister, pointing me out with her needle and thread, and shaking her head at me. "Answer him one question, and he'll ask you a dozen directly. Hulks are prison-ships, right 'cross th' meshes." We always used that name for marshes, in our country.

"I wonder who's put into prison-ships, and why they're put there?" said I, in a general way, and with quiet desperation.

It was too much for Mrs. Joe, who immediately rose. "I tell

you what, young fellow," said she, "I didn't bring you up by hand to badger people's lives out. It would be blame to me and not praise, if I had. People are put in the Hulks because they murder, and because they rob, and forge, and do all sorts of bad; and they always begin by asking questions. Now, you get along to bed!"

I was never allowed a candle to light me to bed, and, as I went up stairs in the dark, with my head tingling—from Mrs. Joe's thimble having played the tambourine upon it, to accompany her last words—I felt fearfully sensible of the great convenience that the hulks were handy for me. I was clearly on my way there. I had begun by asking questions, and I was going to rob Mrs. Joe.

Since that time, which is far enough away now, I have often thought that few people know what secrecy there is in the young under terror. No matter how unreasonable the terror, so that it be terror. I was in mortal terror of the young man who wanted my heart and liver; I was in mortal terror of my interlocutor with the iron leg; I was in mortal terror of myself, from whom an awful promise had been extracted; I had no hope of deliverance through my all-powerful sister, who repulsed me at every turn; I am afraid to think of what I might have done on requirement, in the secrecy of my terror.

If I slept at all that night, it was only to imagine myself drifting down the river on a strong spring-tide, to the Hulks; a ghostly pirate calling out to me through a speaking-trumpet, as I passed the gibbet-station, that I had better come ashore and be hanged there at once, and not put it off. I was afraid to sleep, even if I had been inclined, for I knew that at the first faint dawn of morning I must rob the pantry. There was no doing it in the night, for there was no getting a light by easy friction then; to have got one I must have struck it out of flint and steel, and have made a noise like the very pirate himself rattling his chains.

As soon as the great black velvet pall outside my little window was shot with gray, I got up and went down stairs; every board upon the way, and every crack in every board calling after me, "Stop thief!" and "Get up, Mrs. Joe!" In the pantry, which was far more abundantly supplied than usual, owing to the season, I was very much alarmed by a hare hanging up by the heels, whom I rather thought I caught when my back was half turned, winking. I had no time for verification, no time for selection, no time for anything, for I had no time to spare. I stole some bread, some rind of cheese, about half a jar of mincemeat (which I tied up in my pocket-handkerchief with my last night's slice), some brandy from a stone bottle (which I decanted into a glass bottle I had secretly used for making that intoxicating fluid, Spanish-liquorice-water, up in my room: diluting the stone bottle from a jug in the kitchen cupboard), a meat bone with very little on it, and a beautiful round compact pork pie. I was nearly going away without the pie, but I was tempted to mount upon a shelf, to look what it was that was put away so carefully in a covered earthen ware dish in a corner, and I found it was the pie, and I took it in the hope that it was not intended for early use, and would not be missed for some time.

There was a door in the kitchen, communicating with the forge; I unlocked and unbolted that door, and got a file from among Joe's tools. Then I put the fastenings as I had found them, opened the door at which I had entered when I ran home last night, shut it, and ran for the misty marshes.

CHAPTER 3

It was a rimy morning, and very damp. I had seen the damp lying on the outside of my little window, as if some goblin had been crying there all night, and using the window for a pocket-handkerchief. Now, I saw the damp lying on the bare hedges and spare grass, like a coarser sort of spiders' webs; hanging itself from twig to twig and blade to blade. On every rail and gate, wet lay clammy, and the marsh mist was so thick, that the wooden finger on the post directing people to our village—a direction which they never accepted, for they never came there—was invisible to me until I was quite close under it. Then, as I looked up at it, while it dripped, it seemed to my oppressed conscience like a phantom devoting me to the Hulks.

The mist was heavier yet when I got out upon the marshes, so that instead of my running at everything, everything seemed to run at me. This was very disagreeable to a guilty mind. The gates and dikes and banks came bursting at me through the mist, as if they cried as plainly as could be, "A boy with Somebody's else's pork pie! Stop him!" The cattle came upon me with like suddenness, staring out of their eyes, and steaming out of their nostrils, "Halloa, young thief!" One black ox, with a white cravat on—who even had to my awakened conscience something of a clerical air—fixed me so obstinately with his eyes, and moved his blunt head round in such an accusatory manner as I moved round, that I blubbered out to him, "I couldn't help it, sir! It wasn't for myself I took it!" Upon which he put down his head, blew a cloud of smoke out of his nose, and vanished with a kick-up of his hind-legs and a flourish of his tail.

All this time, I was getting on towards the river; but however fast I went, I couldn't warm my feet, to which the damp cold seemed riveted, as the iron was riveted to the leg of the man I was running to meet. I knew my way to the Battery, pretty straight, for I had been down there on a Sunday with Joe, and Joe, sitting on an old gun, had told me that when I was 'prentice to him, regularly bound, we would have such Larks there! However, in the confusion of the mist, I found myself at last too far to the right, and consequently had to try back along the river-side, on the bank of loose stones above the mud and the stakes that staked the tide out. Making my way along here with all despatch, I had just crossed a ditch which I knew to be very near the Battery, and had just scrambled up the mound beyond the ditch, when I saw the man sitting before me. His back was towards me, and he had his arms folded, and was nodding forward, heavy with sleep.

I thought he would be more glad if I came upon him with his breakfast, in that unexpected manner, so I went forward softly and touched him on the shoulder. He instantly jumped up, and it was not the same man, but another man!

And yet this man was dressed in coarse graey, too, and had a great iron on his leg, and was lame, and hoarse, and cold, and was everything that the other man was; except that he had not the same face, and had a flat broad-brimmed low-crowned felt hat on. All this I saw in a moment, for I had only a moment to see it in: he swore an oath at me, made a hit at me—it was a round weak blow that missed me and almost knocked himself down, for it made him stumble—and then he ran into the mist, stumbling twice as he went, and I lost him.

"It's the young man!" I thought, feeling my heart shoot as I identified him. I dare say I should have felt a pain in my liver, too, if I had known where it was.

I was soon at the Battery after that, and there was the right man—hugging himself and limping to and fro, as if he had never all night left off hugging and limping—waiting for me. He was awfully cold, to be sure. I half expected to see him drop down before my face and die of deadly cold. His eyes looked so awfully hungry too, that when I handed him the file and he laid it down on the grass, it occurred to me he would have tried to eat it, if he had not seen my bundle. He did not turn me upside down this time to get at what I had, but left me right side upwards while I opened the bundle and emptied my pockets.

"What's in the bottle, boy?" said he.

"Brandy," said I.

He was already handing mincemeat down his throat in the most curious manner—more like a man who was putting it away somewhere in a violent hurry, than a man who was eating it—but he left off to take some of the liquor. He shivered all the while so violently, that it was quite as much as he could do to keep the neck of the bottle between his teeth, without biting it off.

"I think you have got the ague," said I.

"I'm much of your opinion, boy," said he.

"It's bad about here," I told him. "You've been lying out on the meshes, and they're dreadful aguish. Rheumatic too."

"I'll eat my breakfast afore they're the death of me," said he. "I'd do that, if I was going to be strung up to that there gallows as there is over there, directly afterwards. I'll beat the shivers so far, I'll bet you."

He was gobbling mincemeat, meatbone, bread, cheese, and pork pie, all at once: staring distrustfully while he did so at the mist all round us, and often stopping—even stopping his jaws—to listen. Some real or fancied sound, some clink upon the river or breathing of beast upon the marsh, now gave him a start, and he said, suddenly:

"You're not a deceiving imp? You brought no one with you?"

"No, sir! No!"

"Nor giv' no one the office to follow you?"

"No!"

"Well," said he, "I believe you. You'd be but a fierce young hound indeed, if at your time of life you could help to hunt a wretched warmint hunted as near death and dunghill as this poor wretched warmint is!"

Something clicked in his throat as if he had works in him like a clock, and was going to strike. And he smeared his ragged rough sleeve over his eyes.

Pitying his desolation, and watching him as he gradually settled down upon the pie, I made bold to say, "I am glad you enjoy it."

"Did you speak?"

"I said I was glad you enjoyed it."

"Thankee, my boy. I do."

I had often watched a large dog of ours eating his food; and I now noticed a decided similarity between the dog's way of eating, and the man's. The man took strong sharp sudden bites, just like the dog. He swallowed, or rather snapped up, every mouthful, too soon and too fast; and he looked sideways here and there while he ate, as if he thought there was danger in every direction of somebody's coming to take the pie away. He was altogether too unsettled in his mind over it, to appreciate it comfortably I thought, or to have anybody to dine with him, without making a chop with his jaws at the visitor. In all of which particulars he was very like the dog.

"I am afraid you won't leave any of it for him," said I, timidly; after a silence during which I had hesitated as to the politeness of making the remark. "There's no more to be got where that came from." It was the certainty of this fact that impelled me to offer the hint.

"Leave any for him? Who's him?" said my friend, stopping in his crunching of pie-crust.

"The young man. That you spoke of. That was hid with you."

"Oh ah!" he returned, with something like a gruff laugh. "Him? Yes, yes! *He* don't want no wittles."

"I thought he looked as if he did," said I.

The man stopped eating, and regarded me with the keenest scrutiny and the greatest surprise.

"Looked? When?"

"Just now."

"Where?"

"Yonder," said I, pointing; "over there, where I found him nodding asleep, and thought it was you."

He held me by the collar and stared at me so, that I began to think his first idea about cutting my throat had revived.

"Dressed like you, you know, only with a hat," I explained, trembling; "and—and"—I was very anxious to put this delicately— "and with—the same reason for wanting to borrow a file. Didn't you hear the cannon last night?"

"Then there *was* firing!" he said to himself.

"I wonder you shouldn't have been sure of that," I returned, "for we heard it up at home, and that's further away, and we were shut in besides."

"Why, see now!" said he. "When a man's alone on these flats, with a light head and a light stomach, perishing of cold and want, he hears nothin' all night, but guns firing, and voices calling. Hears? He sees the soldiers, with their red coats lighted up by the torches carried afore, closing in round him. Hears his number called, hears himself challenged, hears the rattle of the muskets, hears the orders 'Make ready! Present! Cover him steady, men!' and is laid hands on—and there's nothin'! Why, if I see one pursuing party last night—coming up in order, Damn 'em, with their tramp, tramp—I see a hundred. And as to firing! Why, I see the mist shake with the cannon, arter it was broad day. —But this man"; he had said all the rest, as if he had forgotten my being there; "did you notice anything in him?"

"He had a badly bruised face," said I, recalling what I hardly knew I knew.

"Not here?" exclaimed the man, striking his left cheek mercilessly, with the flat of his hand.

"Yes, there!"

"Where is he?" He crammed what little food was left, into the breast of his gray jacket. "Show me the way he went. I'll pull him down, like a bloodhound. Curse this iron on my sore leg! Give us hold of the file, boy."

I indicated in what direction the mist had shrouded the other man, and he looked up at it for an instant. But he was down on the rank wet grass, filing at his iron like a madman, and not minding me or minding his own leg, which had an old chafe upon it and was bloody, but which he handled as roughly as if it had no more feeling in it than the file. I was very much afraid of him again, now that he had worked himself into this fierce hurry, and I was likewise very much afraid of keeping away from home any longer. I told him I must go, but he took no notice, so I thought the best thing I could do was to slip off. The last I saw of him, his head was bent over his knee and he was working hard at his fetter, muttering impatient imprecations at it and at his leg. The last I heard of him, I stopped in the mist to listen, and the file was still going.

CHAPTER 4

I fully expected to find a Constable in the kitchen, waiting to take me up. But not only was there no Constable there, but no discovery had yet been made of the robbery. Mrs. Joe was prodigiously busy in getting the house ready for the festivities of the day, and Joe had been put upon the kitchen door-step to keep him out of the dustpan, an article into which his destiny always led him, sooner or later, when my sister was vigorously reaping the floors of her establishment.

"And where the deuce ha' *you* been?" was Mrs. Joe's Christmas salutation, when I and my conscience showed ourselves.

I said I had been down to hear the Carols. "Ah! well!" observed Mrs. Joe. "You might ha' done worse." Not a doubt of that I thought.

"Perhaps if I warn't a blacksmith's wife, and (what's the same thing) a slave with her apron never off, *I* should have been to hear the Carols," said Mrs. Joe. "I'm rather partial to Carols, myself, and that's the best of reasons for my never hearing any."

Joe, who had ventured into the kitchen after me as the dustpan had retired before us, drew the back of his hand across his nose with a conciliatory air, when Mrs. Joe darted a look at him, and, when her eyes were withdrawn, secretly crossed his two forefingers, and exhibited them to me, as our token that Mrs. Joe was in a cross temper. This was so much her normal state, that Joe and I would often, for weeks together, be, as to our fingers, like monumental Crusaders as to their legs.

We were to have a superb dinner, consisting of a leg of

pickled pork and greens, and a pair of roast stuffed fowls. A handsome mince-pie had been made yesterday morning (which accounted for the mincemeat not being missed), and the pudding was already on the boil. These extensive arrangements occasioned us to be cut off unceremoniously in respect of breakfast; "for I ain't," said Mrs. Joe, "I ain't a going to have no formal cramming and busting and washing up now, with what I've got before me, I promise you!"

So, we had our slices served out, as if we were two thousand troops on a forced march instead of a man and boy at home; and we took gulps of milk and water, with apologetic countenances, from a jug on the dresser. In the meantime, Mrs. Joe put clean white curtains up, and tacked a new flowered flounce across the wide chimney to replace the old one, and uncovered the little state parlor across the passage, which was never uncovered at any other time, but passed the rest of the year in a cool haze of silver paper, which even extended to the four little white crockery poodles on the mantel-shelf, each with a black nose and a basket of flowers in his mouth, and each the counterpart of the other. Mrs. Joe was a very clean housekeeper, but had an exquisite art of making her cleanliness more uncomfortable and unacceptable than dirt itself. Cleanliness is next to Godliness, and some people do the same by their religion.

My sister, having so much to do, was going to church vicariously, that is to say, Joe and I were going. In his working-clothes, Joe was a well-knit characteristic-looking blacksmith; in his holiday clothes, he was more like a scarecrow in good circumstances, than anything else. Nothing that he wore then fitted him or seemed to belong to him; and everything that he wore then grazed him. On the present festive occasion he emerged from his room, when the blithe bells were going, the picture of misery, in a full suit of Sunday penitentials. As to me, I think my sister must have had some general idea that I was a young offender whom an Accoucheur Policeman had taken up (on my birthday) and delivered over to her, to be dealt with according to the outraged majesty of the law. I was always treated as if I had insisted on being born in opposition to the dictates of reason, religion, and morality, and against the dissuading arguments of my best friends. Even when I was taken to have a new suit of clothes, the tailor had orders to make them like a kind of Reformatory, and on no account to let me have the free use of my limbs.

Joe and I going to church, therefore, must have been a moving spectacle for compassionate minds. Yet, what I suffered outside was nothing to what I underwent within. The terrors that had assailed me whenever Mrs. Joe had gone near the pantry, or out of the room, were only to be equalled by the remorse with which my mind dwelt on what my hands had done. Under the weight of my wicked secret, I pondered whether the Church would be powerful enough to shield me from the vengeance of the terrible young man, if I divulged to that establishment. I conceived the idea that the time when the banns were read and when the clergyman said, "Ye are now to declare it!" would be the time for me to rise and propose a private conference in the vestry. I am far from being sure that I might not have astonished our small congregation by resorting to this extreme measure, but for its being Christmas Day and no Sunday.

Mr. Wopsle, the clerk at church, was to dine with us; and Mr. Hubble the wheelwright and Mrs. Hubble; and Uncle Pumblechook (Joe's uncle, but Mrs. Joe appropriated him), who was a well-to-do cornchandler in the nearest town, and drove his own chaise-cart. The dinner hour was half-past one. When Joe and I got home, we found the table laid, and Mrs. Joe dressed, and the dinner dressing, and the front door unlocked (it never was at any other time) for the company to enter by, and everything most splendid. And still, not a word of the robbery.

The time came, without bringing with it any relief to my feelings, and the company came. Mr. Wopsle, united to a Roman nose and a large shining bald forehead, had a deep voice which he was uncommonly proud of; indeed it was understood among his acquaintance that if you could only give him his head, he would read the clergyman into fits; he himself confessed that if the Church was "thrown open," meaning to competition, he would not despair of making his mark in it. The Church not being "thrown open," he was, as I have said, our clerk. But he punished the Amens tremendously; and when he gave out the psalm—always giving the whole verse—he looked all round the congregation first, as much as to say, "You have heard my friend overhead; oblige me with your opinion of this style!"

I opened the door to the company—making believe that it was a habit of ours to open that door—and I opened it first to Mr. Wopsle, next to Mr. and Mrs. Hubble, and last of all to Uncle Pumblechook. N.B. *I* was not allowed to call him uncle, under the severest penalties.

"Mrs. Joe," said Uncle Pumblechook, a large hard-breathing middle-aged slow man, with a mouth like a fish, dull staring eyes, and sandy hair standing upright on his head, so that he looked as if he had just been all but choked, and had that moment come to, "I have brought you as the compliments of the season—I have brought you, Mum, a bottle of sherry wine—and I have brought you, Mum, a bottle of port wine."

Every Christmas Day he presented himself, as a profound novelty, with exactly the same words, and carrying the two bottles like dumb-bells. Every Christmas Day, Mrs. Joe replied, as she now replied, "Oh, Un—cle Pum-ble—chook! This is kind!" Every Christmas Day, he retorted, as he now retorted, "It's no more than your merits. And now are you all bobbish, and how's Sixpennorth of halfpence?" meaning me.

We dined on these occasions in the kitchen, and adjourned, for the nuts and oranges and apples to the parlor; which was a change very like Joe's change from his working-clothes to his Sunday dress. My sister was uncommonly lively on the present occasion, and indeed was generally more gracious in the society of Mrs. Hubble than in other company. I remember Mrs. Hubble as a little curly sharp-edged person in sky-blue, who held a conventionally juvenile position, because she had married Mr. Hubble—I don't know at what remote period—when she was much younger than he. I remember Mr Hubble as a tough, high-shouldered, stooping old man, of a sawdusty fragrance, with his legs extraordinarily wide apart: so that in my short days I always saw some miles of open country between them when I met him coming up the lane.

Among this good company I should have felt myself, even if I hadn't robbed the pantry, in a false position. Not because I was squeezed in at an acute angle of the tablecloth, with the table in my chest, and the Pumblechookian elbow in my eye, nor because I was not allowed to speak (I didn't want to speak), nor because I was regaled with the scaly tips of the drumsticks of the fowls, and with those obscure corners of pork of which the pig, when living, had had the least reason to be vain. No; I should not have minded that, if they would only have left me alone. But they wouldn't leave me alone. They seemed to think the opportunity lost, if they failed to point the conversation at me, every now and then, and stick the point into me. I might have been an unfortunate little bull in a Spanish arena, I got so smartingly touched up by these moral goads.

It began the moment we sat down to dinner. Mr. Wopsle said grace with theatrical declamation—as it now appears to me, something like a religious cross of the Ghost in Hamlet with Richard the Third—and ended with the very proper aspiration that we might be truly grateful. Upon which my sister fixed me with her eye, and said, in a low reproachful voice, "Do you hear that? Be grateful."

"Especially," said Mr. Pumblechook, "be grateful, boy, to them which brought you up by hand."

Mrs. Hubble shook her head, and contemplating me with a mournful presentiment that I should come to no good, asked, "Why is it that the young are never grateful?" This moral mystery seemed too much for the company until Mr. Hubble tersely solved it by saying, "Naterally wicious." Everybody then murmured "True!" and looked at me in a particularly unpleasant and personal manner.

Joe's station and influence were something feebler (if possible) when there was company than when there was none. But he always aided and comforted me when he could, in some way of his own, and he always did so at dinner-time by giving me gravy, if there were any. There being plenty of gravy to-day, Joe spooned into my plate, at this point, about half a pint.

A little later on in the dinner, Mr. Wopsle reviewed the sermon with some severity, and intimated—in the usual hypothetical case of the Church being "thrown open"—what kind of sermon *he* would have given them. After favoring them with some heads of that discourse, he remarked that he considered the subject of the day's homily, ill chosen; which was the less excusable, he added, when there were so many subjects "going about."

"True again," said Uncle Pumblechook. "You've hit it, sir! Plenty of subjects going about, for them that know how to put salt upon their tails. That's what's wanted. A man needn't go far to find a subject, if he's ready with his salt-box." Mr. Pumblechook added, after a short interval of reflection, "Look at Pork alone. There's a subject! If you want a subject, look at Pork!"

"True, sir. Many a moral for the young," returned Mr. Wopsle; and I knew he was going to lug me in, before he said it; "might be deduced from that text."

("You listen to this," said my sister to me, in a severe parenthesis.)

Joe gave me some more gravy.

"Swine," pursued Mr. Wopsle, in his deepest voice, and pointing his fork at my blushes, as if he were mentioning my christian name; "Swine were the companions of the prodigal. The gluttony of Swine is put before us, as an example to the young." (I thought this pretty well in him who had been praising up the pork for being so plump and juicy.) "What is detestable in a pig is more detestable in a boy."

"Or girl," suggested Mr. Hubble.

"Of course, or girl, Mr. Hubble," assented Mr. Wopsle, rather irritably, "but there is no girl present."

"Besides," said Mr. Pumblechook, turning sharp on me, "think what you've got to be grateful for. If you'd been born a Squeaker—"

"He *was*, if ever a child was," said my sister, most emphatically.

Joe gave me some more gravy.

"Well, but I mean a four-footed Squeaker," said Mr. Pumblechook. "If you had been born such, would you have been here now? Not you—"

"Unless in that form," said Mr. Wopsle, nodding towards the dish.

"But I don't mean in that form, sir," returned Mr. Pumblechook, who had an objection to being interrupted; "I mean, enjoying himself with his elders and betters, and improving himself with their conversation, and rolling in the lap of luxury. Would he have been doing that? No, he wouldn't. And what would have been your destination?" turning on me again. "You would have been disposed of for so many shillings according to the market price of the article, and Dunstable the butcher would have come up to you as you lay in your straw, and he would have whipped you under his left arm, and with his right he would have tucked up his frock to get a penknife from out of his waistcoat-pocket, and he would have shed your blood and had your life. No bringing up by hand then. Not a bit of it!"

Joe offered me more gravy, which I was afraid to take.

"He was a world of trouble to you, ma'am," said Mrs. Hubble, commiserating my sister.

"Trouble?" echoed my sister; "trouble?" and then entered on a fearful catalogue of all the illnesses I had been guilty of, and all the acts of sleeplessness I had committed, and all the high places I had tumbled from, and all the low places I had tumbled into, and all the injuries I had done myself, and all the times she had wished me in my grave, and I had contumaciously refused to go there.

I think the Romans must have aggravated one another very much, with their noses. Perhaps, they became the restless people they were, in consequence. Anyhow, Mr. Wopsle's Roman nose so aggravated me, during the recital of my misdemeanours, that I should have liked to pull it until he howled. But, all I had endured up to this time was nothing in comparison with the awful feelings that took possession of me when the pause was broken which ensued upon my sister's recital, and in which pause everybody had looked at me (as I felt painfully conscious) with indignation and abhorrence.

"Yet," said Mr. Pumblechook, leading the company gently back to the theme from which they had strayed, "Pork—regarded as biled—is rich, too; ain't it?"

"Have a little brandy, uncle," said my sister.

O Heavens, it had come at last! He would find it was weak, he would say it was weak, and I was lost! I held tight to the leg of the table under the cloth, with both hands, and awaited my fate.

My sister went for the stone bottle, came back with the stone bottle, and poured his brandy out: no one else taking any. The wretched man trifled with his glass—took it up, looked at it through the light, put it down—prolonged my misery. All this time Mrs. Joe and Joe were briskly clearing the table for the pie and pudding.

I couldn't keep my eyes off him. Always holding tight by the leg of the table with my hands and feet, I saw the miserable creature finger his glass playfully, take it up, smile, throw his head back, and drink the brandy off. Instantly afterwards, the company were seized with unspeakable consternation, owing to his springing to his feet, turning round several times in an appalling spasmodic whooping-cough dance, and rushing out at the door; he then became visible through the window, violently plunging and expectorating, making the most hideous faces, and apparently out of his mind.

I held on tight, while Mrs. Joe and Joe ran to him. I didn't know how I had done it, but I had no doubt I had murdered him somehow. In my dreadful situation, it was a relief when he was brought back, and surveying the company all round as if *they* had disagreed with him, sank down into his chair with the one significant gasp, "Tar!"

I had filled up the bottle from the tar-water jug. I knew he would be worse by-and-by. I moved the table, like a Medium of the present day, by the vigor of my unseen hold upon it.

"Tar!" cried my sister, in amazement. "Why, how ever could Tar come there?"

But, Uncle Pumblechook, who was omnipotent in that kitchen, wouldn't hear the word, wouldn't hear of the subject, imperiously waved it all away with his hand, and asked for hot gin and water. My sister, who had begun to be alarmingly meditative, had to employ herself actively in getting the gin the hot water, the sugar, and the lemon-peel, and mixing them. For the time being at least, I was saved. I still held on to the leg of the table, but clutched it now with the fervor of gratitude.

By degrees, I became calm enough to release my grasp and partake of pudding. Mr. Pumblechook partook of pudding. All partook of pudding. The course terminated, and Mr.

Pumblechook had begun to beam under the genial influence of gin and water. I began to think I should get over the day, when my sister said to Joe, "Clean plates—cold."

I clutched the leg of the table again immediately, and pressed it to my bosom as if it had been the companion of my youth and friend of my soul. I foresaw what was coming, and I felt that this time I really was gone.

"You must taste," said my sister, addressing the guests with her best grace— "you must taste, to finish with, such a delightful and delicious present of Uncle Pumblechook's!"

Must they! Let them not hope to taste it!

"You must know," said my sister, rising, "it's a pie; a savory pork pie."

The company murmured their compliments. Uncle Pumblechook, sensible of having deserved well of his fellow-creatures, said—quite vivaciously, all things considered— "Well, Mrs. Joe, we'll do our best endeavors; let us have a cut at this same pie."

My sister went out to get it. I heard her steps proceed to the pantry. I saw Mr. Pumblechook balance his knife. I saw reawakening appetite in the Roman nostrils of Mr. Wopsle. I heard Mr. Hubble remark that "a bit of savory pork pie would lay atop of anything you could mention, and do no harm," and I heard Joe say, "You shall have some, Pip." I have never been absolutely certain whether I uttered a shrill yell of terror, merely in spirit, or in the bodily hearing of the company. I felt that I could bear no more, and that I must run away. I released the leg of the table, and ran for my life.

But I ran no farther than the house door, for there I ran head-foremost into a party of soldiers with their muskets, one of whom held out a pair of handcuffs to me, saying, "Here you are, look sharp, come on!"

CHAPTER 5

The apparition of a file of soldiers ringing down the but-ends of their loaded muskets on our door-step, caused the dinner-party to rise from table in confusion, and caused Mrs. Joe re-entering the kitchen empty-handed, to stop short and stare, in her wondering lament of "Gracious goodness gracious me, what's gone—with the—pie!"

The sergeant and I were in the kitchen when Mrs. Joe stood staring; at which crisis I partially recovered the use of my senses. It was the sergeant who had spoken to me, and he was now looking round at the company, with his handcuffs invitingly extended towards them in his right hand, and his left on my shoulder.

"Excuse me, ladies and gentleman," said the sergeant, "but as I have mentioned at the door to this smart young shaver," (which he hadn't), "I am on a chase in the name of the King, and I want the blacksmith."

"And pray what might you want with *him*?" retorted my sister, quick to resent his being wanted at all.

"Missis," returned the gallant sergeant, "speaking for myself, I should reply, the honor and pleasure of his fine wife's acquaintance; speaking for the king, I answer, a little job done."

This was received as rather neat in the sergeant; insomuch that Mr. Pumblechook cried audibly, "Good again!"

"You see, blacksmith," said the sergeant, who had by this time picked out Joe with his eye, "we have had an accident with these, and I find the lock of one of 'em goes wrong, and the coupling don't act pretty. As they are wanted for immediate service, will you throw your eye over them?"

Joe threw his eye over them, and pronounced that the job would necessitate the lighting of his forge fire, and would take nearer two hours than one, "Will it? Then will you set about it at once, blacksmith?" said the off-hand sergeant, "as it's on his Majesty's service. And if my men can bear a hand anywhere, they'll make themselves useful." With that, he called to his men, who came trooping into the kitchen one after another, and piled their arms in a corner. And then they stood about, as soldiers do; now, with their hands loosely clasped before them; now, resting a knee or a shoulder; now, easing a belt or a pouch; now, opening the door to spit stiffly over their high stocks, out into the yard.

All these things I saw without then knowing that I saw them, for I was in an agony of apprehension. But beginning to perceive that the handcuffs were not for me, and that the military had so far got the better of the pie as to put it in the background, I collected a little more of my scattered wits.

"Would you give me the Time?" said the sergeant, addressing himself to Mr. Pumblechook, as to a man whose appreciative powers justified the inference that he was equal to the time.

"It's just gone half-past two."

"That's not so bad," said the sergeant, reflecting; "even if I was forced to halt here nigh two hours, that'll do. How far might you call yourselves from the marshes, hereabouts? Not above a mile, I reckon?"

"Just a mile," said Mrs. Joe.

"That'll do. We begin to close in upon 'em about dusk. A little before dusk, my orders are. That'll do."

"Convicts, sergeant?" asked Mr. Wopsle, in a matter-of-course way.

"Ay!" returned the sergeant, "two. They're pretty well known to be out on the marshes still, and they won't try to get clear of 'em before dusk. Anybody here seen anything of any such game?"

Everybody, myself excepted, said no, with confidence. Nobody thought of me.

"Well!" said the sergeant, "they'll find themselves trapped in a circle, I expect, sooner than they count on. Now, blacksmith! If you're ready, his Majesty the King is."

Joe had got his coat and waistcoat and cravat off, and his leather apron on, and passed into the forge. One of the soldiers opened its wooden windows, another lighted the fire, another turned to at the bellows, the rest stood round the blaze, which was soon roaring. Then Joe began to hammer and clink, hammer and clink, and we all looked on.

The interest of the impending pursuit not only absorbed the general attention, but even made my sister liberal. She drew a pitcher of beer from the cask for the soldiers, and invited the sergeant to take a glass of brandy. But Mr. Pumblechook said, sharply, "Give him wine, Mum. I'll engage there's no Tar in that:" so, the sergeant thanked him and said that as he preferred his drink without Tar, he would take wine, if it was equally convenient. When it was given him, he drank his Majesty's health and Compliments of the Season, and took it all at a mouthful and smacked his lips.

"Good stuff, eh, sergeant?" said Mr. Pumblechook.

"I'll tell you something," returned the sergeant; "I suspect that stuff's of *your* providing."

Mr. Pumblechook, with a fat sort of laugh, said, "Ay, ay? Why?"

"Because," returned the sergeant, clapping him on the shoulder, "you're a man that knows what's what."

"D'ye think so?" said Mr. Pumblechook, with his former laugh. "Have another glass!"

"With you. Hob and nob," returned the sergeant. "The top of mine to the foot of yours—the foot of yours to the top of mine—Ring once, ring twice—the best tune on the Musical Glasses! Your health. May you live a thousand years, and never be a worse judge of the right sort than you are at the present moment of your life!"

The sergeant tossed off his glass again and seemed quite ready for another glass. I noticed that Mr. Pumblechook in his hospitality appeared to forget that he had made a present of the wine, but took the bottle from Mrs. Joe and had all the credit of handing it about in a gush of joviality. Even I got some. And he was so very free of the wine that he even called for the other bottle, and handed that about with the same liberality, when the first was gone.

As I watched them while they all stood clustering about the forge, enjoying themselves so much, I thought what terrible good sauce for a dinner my fugitive friend on the marshes was. They had not enjoyed themselves a quarter so much, before the entertainment was brightened with the excitement he furnished. And now, when they were all in lively anticipation of "the two villains" being taken, and when the bellows seemed to roar for the fugitives, the fire to flare for them, the smoke to hurry away in pursuit of them, Joe to hammer and clink for them, and all the murky shadows on the wall to shake at them in menace as the blaze rose and sank, and the red-hot sparks dropped and died, the pale afternoon outside almost seemed in my pitying young fancy to have turned pale on their account, poor wretches.

At last, Joe's job was done, and the ringing and roaring stopped. As Joe got on his coat, he mustered courage to propose that some of us should go down with the soldiers and see what came of the hunt. Mr. Pumblechook and Mr. Hubble declined, on the plea of a pipe and ladies' society; but Mr. Wopsle said he would go, if Joe would. Joe said he was agreeable, and would take me, if Mrs. Joe approved. We never should have got leave to go, I am sure, but for Mrs. Joe's curiosity to know all about it and how it ended. As it was, she merely stipulated, "If you bring the boy back with his head blown to bits by a musket, don't look to me to put it together again."

The sergeant took a polite leave of the ladies, and parted from Mr. Pumblechook as from a comrade; though I doubt if he were quite as fully sensible of that gentleman's merits under arid conditions, as when something moist was going. His men resumed their muskets and fell in. Mr. Wopsle, Joe, and I, received strict charge to keep in the rear, and to speak no word after we reached the marshes. When we were all out in the raw air and were steadily moving towards our business, I treasonably whispered to Joe, "I hope, Joe, we shan't find them." and Joe whispered to me, "I'd give a shilling if they had cut and run, Pip."

We were joined by no stragglers from the village, for the weather was cold and threatening, the way dreary, the footing bad, darkness coming on, and the people had good fires indoors and were keeping the day. A few faces hurried to glowing windows and looked after us, but none came out. We passed the finger-post, and held straight on to the churchyard. There we were stopped a few minutes by a signal from the sergeant's hand, while two or three of his men dispersed themselves among the graves, and also examined the porch. They came in again without finding anything, and then we struck out on the open marshes, through the gate at the side of the churchyard. A bitter sleet came rattling against us here on the east wind, and Joe took me on his back.

Now that we were out upon the dismal wilderness where they little thought I had been within eight or nine hours and had seen both men hiding, I considered for the first time, with great dread, if we should come upon them, would my particular convict suppose that it was I who had brought the soldiers there? He had asked me if I was a deceiving imp, and he had said I should be a fierce young hound if I joined the hunt against him. Would he believe that I was both imp and hound in treacherous earnest, and had betrayed him?

It was of no use asking myself this question now. There I was, on Joe's back, and there was Joe beneath me, charging at the ditches like a hunter, and stimulating Mr. Wopsle not to tumble on his Roman nose, and to keep up with us. The soldiers were in front of us, extending into a pretty wide line with an interval between man and man. We were taking the course I had begun with, and from which I had diverged in the mist. Either the mist was not out again yet, or the wind had dispelled it. Under the low red glare of sunset, the beacon, and the gibbet, and the mound of the Battery, and the opposite shore of the river, were plain, though all of a watery lead colour.

With my heart thumping like a blacksmith at Joe's broad shoulder, I looked all about for any sign of the convicts. I could see none, I could hear none. Mr. Wopsle had greatly alarmed me more than once, by his blowing and hard breathing; but I knew the sounds by this time, and could dissociate them from the object of pursuit. I got a dreadful start, when I thought I heard the file still going; but it was only a sheep-bell. The sheep stopped in their eating and looked timidly at us; and the cattle, their heads turned from the wind and sleet, stared angrily as if they held us responsible for both annoyances; but, except these things, and the shudder of the dying day in every blade of grass, there was no break in the bleak stillness of the marshes.

The soldiers were moving on in the direction of the old Battery, and we were moving on a little way behind them, when, all of a sudden, we all stopped. For there had reached us on the wings of the wind and rain, a long shout. It was repeated. It was at a distance towards the east, but it was long and loud. Nay, there seemed to be two or more shouts raised together—if one might judge from a confusion in the sound.

To this effect the sergeant and the nearest men were

speaking under their breath, when Joe and I came up. After another moment's listening, Joe (who was a good judge) agreed, and Mr. Wopsle (who was a bad judge) agreed. The sergeant, a decisive man, ordered that the sound should not be answered, but that the course should be changed, and that his men should make towards it "at the double." So we slanted to the right (where the East was), and Joe pounded away so wonderfully, that I had to hold on tight to keep my seat.

It was a run indeed now, and what Joe called, in the only two words he spoke all the time, "a Winder." Down banks and up banks, and over gates, and splashing into dikes, and breaking among coarse rushes: no man cared where he went. As we came nearer to the shouting, it became more and more apparent that it was made by more than one voice. Sometimes, it seemed to stop altogether, and then the soldiers stopped. When it broke out again, the soldiers made for it at a greater rate than ever, and we after them. After a while, we had so run it down, that we could hear one voice calling "Murder!" and another voice, "Convicts! Runaways! Guard! This way for the runaway convicts!" Then both voices would seem to be stifled in a struggle, and then would break out again. And when it had come to this, the soldiers ran like deer, and Joe too.

The sergeant ran in first, when we had run the noise quite down, and two of his men ran in close upon him. Their pieces were cocked and levelled when we all ran in.

"Here are both men!" panted the sergeant, struggling at the bottom of a ditch. "Surrender, you two! and confound you for two wild beasts! Come asunder!"

Water was splashing, and mud was flying, and oaths were being sworn, and blows were being struck, when some more men went down into the ditch to help the sergeant, and dragged out, separately, my convict and the other one. Both were bleeding and panting and execrating and struggling; but of course I knew them both directly.

"Mind!" said my convict, wiping blood from his face with his ragged sleeves, and shaking torn hair from his fingers: "*I* took him! *I* give him up to you! Mind that!"

"It's not much to be particular about," said the sergeant; "it'll do you small good, my man, being in the same plight yourself. Handcuffs there!"

"I don't expect it to do me any good. I don't want it to do me more good than it does now," said my convict, with a greedy laugh. "I took him. He knows it. That's enough for me."

The other convict was livid to look at, and, in addition to the old bruised left side of his face, seemed to be bruised and torn all over. He could not so much as get his breath to speak, until they were both separately handcuffed, but leaned upon a soldier to keep himself from falling.

"Take notice, guard—he tried to murder me," were his first words.

"Tried to murder him?" said my convict, disdainfully. "Try, and not do it? I took him, and giv' him up; that's what I done. I not only prevented him getting off the marshes, but I dragged him here—dragged him this far on his way back. He's a gentleman, if you please, this villain. Now, the Hulks has got its gentleman again, through me. Murder him? Worth my while, too, to murder him, when I could do worse and drag him back!"

The other one still gasped, "He tried—he tried-to—murder me. Bear—bear witness."

"Lookee here!" said my convict to the sergeant. "Single-handed I got clear of the prison-ship; I made a dash and I done it. I could ha' got clear of these death-cold flats likewise—look at my leg: you won't find much iron on it—if I hadn't made the discovery that *he* was here. Let *him* go free? Let *him* profit by the means as I found out? Let *him* make a tool of me afresh and again? Once more? No, no, no. If I had died at the bottom there," and he made an emphatic swing at the ditch with his manacled hands, "I'd have held to him with that grip, that you should have been safe to find him in my hold."

The other fugitive, who was evidently in extreme horror of his companion, repeated, "He tried to murder me. I should have been a dead man if you had not come up."

"He lies!" said my convict, with fierce energy. "He's a liar born, and he'll die a liar. Look at his face; ain't it written there? Let him turn those eyes of his on me. I defy him to do it."

The other, with an effort at a scornful smile—which could not, however, collect the nervous working of his mouth into any set expression—looked at the soldiers, and looked about at the marshes and at the sky, but certainly did not look at the speaker.

"Do you see him?" pursued my convict. "Do you see what a villain he is? Do you see those grovelling and wandering eyes? That's how he looked when we were tried together. He never looked at me."

The other, always working and working his dry lips and turning his eyes restlessly about him far and near, did at last turn them for a moment on the speaker, with the words, "You are not much to look at," and with a half-taunting glance at the bound hands. At that point, my convict became so frantically exasperated, that he would have rushed upon him but for the interposition of the soldiers. "Didn't I tell you," said the other convict then, "that he would murder me, if he could?" And any one could see that he shook with fear, and that there broke out upon his lips curious white flakes, like thin snow.

"Enough of this parley," said the sergeant. "Light those torches."

As one of the soldiers, who carried a basket in lieu of a gun, went down on his knee to open it, my convict looked round him for the first time, and saw me. I had alighted from Joe's back on the brink of the ditch when we came up, and had not moved since. I looked at him eagerly when he looked at me, and slightly moved my hands and shook my head. I had been waiting for him to see me that I might try to assure him of my innocence. It was not at all expressed to me that he even comprehended my intention, for he gave me a look that I did not understand, and it all passed in a moment. But if he had looked at me for an hour or for a day, I could not have remembered his face ever afterwards, as having been more attentive.

The soldier with the basket soon got a light, and lighted three or four torches, and took one himself and distributed the others. It had been almost dark before, but now it seemed quite dark, and soon afterwards very dark. Before we departed from that spot, four soldiers standing in a ring, fired twice into the air. Presently we saw other torches kindled at some distance behind us, and others on the marshes on the opposite bank of the river. "All right," said the sergeant. "March."

We had not gone far when three cannon were fired ahead of us with a sound that seemed to burst something inside my ear. "You are expected on board," said the sergeant to my convict; "they know you are coming. Don't straggle, my man. Close up here."

The two were kept apart, and each walked surrounded by a separate guard. I had hold of Joe's hand now, and Joe carried one of the torches. Mr. Wopsle had been for going back, but Joe was resolved to see it out, so we went on with the party. There was a reasonably good path now, mostly on the edge of the river, with a divergence here and there where a dike came, with a miniature windmill on it and a muddy sluice-gate. When I looked round, I could see the other lights coming in after us. The torches we carried dropped great blotches of fire upon the track, and I could see those, too, lying smoking and flaring. I could see nothing else but black darkness. Our lights warmed the air about us with their pitchy blaze, and the two prisoners seemed rather to like that, as they limped along in the midst of the muskets. We could not go fast, because of their lameness; and they were so spent, that two or three times we had to halt while they rested.

After an hour or so of this travelling, we came to a rough wooden hut and a landing-place. There was a guard in the hut, and they challenged, and the sergeant answered. Then, we went into the hut, where there was a smell of tobacco and whitewash, and a bright fire, and a lamp, and a stand of muskets, and a drum, and a low wooden bedstead, like an overgrown mangle without the machinery, capable of holding about a dozen soldiers all at once. Three or four soldiers who lay upon it in their great-coats were not much interested in us, but just lifted their heads and took a sleepy stare, and then lay down again. The sergeant made some kind of report, and some entry in a book, and then the convict whom I call the other convict was drafted off with his guard, to go on board first.

My convict never looked at me, except that once. While we stood in the hut, he stood before the fire looking thoughtfully at it, or putting up his feet by turns upon the hob, and looking thoughtfully at them as if he pitied them for their recent adventures. Suddenly, he turned to the sergeant, and remarked:

"I wish to say something respecting this escape. It may prevent some persons laying under suspicion alonger me."

"You can say what you like," returned the sergeant, standing coolly looking at him with his arms folded, "but you have no call to say it here. You'll have opportunity enough to say about it, and hear about it, before it's done with, you know."

"I know, but this is another pint, a separate matter. A man can't starve; at least I can't. I took some wittles, up at the willage over yonder—where the church stands a'most out on the marshes."

"You mean stole," said the sergeant.

"And I'll tell you where from. From the blacksmith's."

"Halloa!" said the sergeant, staring at Joe.

"Halloa, Pip!" said Joe, staring at me.

"It was some broken wittles—that's what it was—and a dram of liquor, and a pie."

"Have you happened to miss such an article as a pie, blacksmith?" asked the sergeant, confidentially.

"My wife did, at the very moment when you came in. Don't you know, Pip?"

"So," said my convict, turning his eyes on Joe in a moody manner, and without the least glance at me," so you're the blacksmith, are you? Than I'm sorry to say, I've eat your pie."

"God knows you're welcome to it—so far as it was ever mine," returned Joe, with a saving remembrance of Mrs. Joe. "We don't know what you have done, but we wouldn't have you starved to death for it, poor miserable fellow-creatur.—Would us, Pip?"

The something that I had noticed before, clicked in the man's throat again, and he turned his back. The boat had returned, and his guard were ready, so we followed him to the landing-place made of rough stakes and stones, and saw him put into the boat, which was rowed by a crew of convicts like himself. No one seemed surprised to see him, or interested in seeing him, or glad to see him, or sorry to see him, or spoke a word, except that somebody in the boat growled as if to dogs, "Give way, you!" which was the signal for the dip of the oars. By the light of the torches, we saw the black Hulk lying out a little way from the mud of the shore, like a wicked Noah's ark. Cribbed and barred and moored by massive rusty chains, the prison-ship seemed in my young eyes to be ironed like the prisoners. We saw the boat go alongside, and we saw him taken up the side and disappear. Then, the ends of the torches were flung hissing into the water, and went out, as if it were all over with him.

CHAPTER 6

My state of mind regarding the pilfering from which I had been so unexpectedly exonerated did not impel me to frank disclosure; but I hope it had some dregs of good at the bottom of it.

I do not recal that I felt any tenderness of conscience in reference to Mrs. Joe, when the fear of being found out was lifted off me. But I loved Joe—perhaps for no better reason in those early days than because the dear fellow let me love him—and, as to him, my inner self was not so easily composed. It was much upon my mind (particularly when I first saw him looking about for his file) that I ought to tell Joe the whole truth. Yet I did not, and for the reason that I mistrusted that if I did, he would think me worse than I was. The fear of losing Joe's confidence, and of thenceforth sitting in the chimney corner at night staring drearily at my forever lost companion and friend, tied up my tongue. I morbidly represented to myself that if Joe knew it, I never afterwards could see him at the fireside feeling his fair whisker, without thinking that he was meditating on it. That, if Joe knew it, I never afterwards could see him glance, however casually, at yesterday's meat or pudding when it came on to-day's table, without thinking that he was debating whether I had been in the pantry. That, if Joe knew it, and at any subsequent period of our joint domestic life remarked that his beer was flat or thick, the conviction that he suspected Tar in it, would bring a rush of blood to my face. In a word, I was too cowardly to do what I knew to be right, as I had been too cowardly to avoid doing what I knew to be wrong. I had had no intercourse with the world at that time, and I imitated none of its many inhabitants who act in this manner. Quite an untaught genius, I made the discovery of the line of action for myself.

As I was sleepy before we were far away from the prison-ship, Joe took me on his back again and carried me home. He must have had a tiresome journey of it, for Mr. Wopsle, being knocked up, was in such a very bad temper that if the Church had been thrown open, he would probably have excommunicated the whole expedition, beginning with Joe and myself. In his lay capacity, he persisted in sitting down in the damp to such an insane extent, that when his coat was taken off to be dried at the kitchen fire, the circumstantial evidence on his trousers would have hanged him, if it had been a capital offence.

By that time, I was staggering on the kitchen floor like a little drunkard, through having been newly set upon my feet, and through having been fast asleep, and through waking in the heat and lights and noise of tongues. As I came to myself (with the aid of a heavy thump between the shoulders, and the restorative exclamation "Yah! Was there ever such a boy as this!" from my sister,) I found Joe telling them about the convict's confession, and all the visitors suggesting different ways by which he had got into the pantry. Mr. Pumblechook made out, after carefully surveying the premises, that he had first got upon the roof of the forge, and had then got upon the roof of the house, and had then let himself down the kitchen chimney by a rope made of his bedding cut into strips; and as Mr. Pumblechook was very positive and drove his own chaise-cart—over Everybody—it was agreed that it must be so. Mr. Wopsle, indeed, wildly cried out, "No!" with the feeble malice of a tired man; but, as he had no theory, and no coat on, he was unanimously set at naught—not to mention his smoking hard behind, as he stood with his back to the kitchen fire to draw the damp out: which was not calculated to inspire confidence.

This was all I heard that night before my sister clutched

me, as a slumberous offence to the company's eyesight, and assisted me up to bed with such a strong hand that I seemed to have fifty boots on, and to be dangling them all against the edges of the stairs. My state of mind, as I have described it, began before I was up in the morning, and lasted long after the subject had died out, and had ceased to be mentioned saving on exceptional occasions.

CHAPTER 7

At the time when I stood in the churchyard reading the family tombstones, I had just enough learning to be able to spell them out. My construction even of their simple meaning was not very correct, for I read "wife of the Above" as a complimentary reference to my father's exaltation to a better world; and if any one of my deceased relations had been referred to as "Below," I have no doubt I should have formed the worst opinions of that member of the family. Neither were my notions of the theological positions to which my Catechism bound me, at all accurate; for, I have a lively remembrance that I supposed my declaration that I was to "walk in the same all the days of my life," laid me under an obligation always to go through the village from our house in one particular direction, and never to vary it by turning down by the wheelwright's or up by the mill.

When I was old enough, I was to be apprenticed to Joe, and until I could assume that dignity I was not to be what Mrs. Joe called "Pompeyed," or (as I render it) pampered. Therefore, I was not only odd-boy about the forge, but if any neighbour happened to want an extra boy to frighten birds, or pick up stones, or do any such job, I was favored with the employment. In order, however, that our superior position might not be compromised thereby, a money-box was kept on the kitchen mantel-shelf, in to which it was publicly made known that all my earnings were dropped. I have an impression that they were to be contributed eventually towards the liquidation of the National Debt, but I know I had no hope of any personal participation in the treasure.

Mr. Wopsle's great-aunt kept an evening school in the village; that is to say, she was a ridiculous old woman of limited means and unlimited infirmity, who used to go to sleep from six to seven every evening, in the society of youth who paid two pence per week each, for the improving opportunity of seeing her do it. She rented a small cottage, and Mr. Wopsle had the room up stairs, where we students used to overhear him reading aloud in a most dignified and terrific manner, and occasionally bumping on the ceiling. There was a fiction that Mr. Wopsle "examined" the scholars once a quarter. What he did on those occasions was to turn up his cuffs, stick up his hair, and give us Mark Antony's oration over the body of Caesar. This was always followed by Collins's Ode on the Passions, wherein I particularly venerated Mr. Wopsle as Revenge throwing his blood-stained sword in thunder down, and taking the War-denouncing trumpet with a withering look. It was not with me then, as it was in later life, when I fell into the society of the Passions, and compared them with Collins and Wopsle, rather to the disadvantage of both gentlemen.

Mr. Wopsle's great-aunt, besides keeping this Educational Institution, kept in the same room—a little general shop. She had no idea what stock she had, or what the price of anything in it was; but there was a little greasy memorandum-book kept in a drawer, which served as a Catalogue of Prices, and by this oracle Biddy arranged all the shop transaction. Biddy was Mr. Wopsle's great-aunt's granddaughter; I confess myself quiet unequal to the working out of the problem, what relation she was to Mr. Wopsle. She was an orphan like myself; like me, too, had been brought up by hand. She was most noticeable, I thought, in respect of her extremities; for, her hair always wanted brushing, her hands always wanted washing, and her shoes always wanted mending and pulling up at heel. This description must be received with a week-day limitation. On Sundays, she went to church elaborated.

Much of my unassisted self, and more by the help of Biddy than of Mr. Wopsle's great-aunt, I struggled through the alphabet as if it had been a bramble-bush; getting considerably worried and scratched by every letter. After that I fell among those thieves, the nine figures, who seemed every evening to do something new to disguise themselves and baffle recognition. But, at last I began, in a purblind groping way, to read, write, and cipher, on the very smallest scale.

One night I was sitting in the chimney corner with my slate, expending great efforts on the production of a letter to Joe. I think it must have been a full year after our hunt upon the marshes, for it was a long time after, and it was winter and a hard frost. With an alphabet on the hearth at my feet for reference, I contrived in an hour or two to print and smear this epistle:

"MI DEER JO i OPE U R KR WITE WELL i OPE i SHAL SON B HABELL 4 2 TEEDGE U JO AN THEN WE SHORL B SO GLODD AN WEN iM PRENGTD 2 U JO WOT LARX AN BLEVE ME INF XN PIP."

There was no indispensable necessity for my communicating with Joe by letter, inasmuch as he sat beside me and we were alone. But I delivered this written communication (slate and all) with my own hand, and Joe received it as a miracle of erudition.

"I say, Pip, old chap!" cried Joe, opening his blue eyes wide, "what a scholar you are! An't you?"

"I should like to be," said I, glancing at the slate as he held it; with a misgiving that the writing was rather hilly.

"Why, here's a J," said Joe, "and a O equal to anythink! Here's a J and a O, Pip, and a J-O, Joe."

I had never heard Joe read aloud to any greater extent than this monosyllable, and I had observed at church last Sunday, when I accidentally held our Prayer-Book upside down, that it seemed to suit his convenience quite as well as if it had been all right. Wishing to embrace the present occasion of finding out whether in teaching Joe, I should have to begin quite at the beginning, I said, "Ah! But read the rest, Joe."

"The rest, eh, Pip?" said Joe, looking at it with a slow, searching eye, "One, two, three. Why, here's three Js, and three Os, and three J-O, Joes in it, Pip!"

I leaned over Joe, and, with the aid of my forefinger read him the whole letter.

"Astonishing!" said Joe, when I had finished. "You are a scholar."

"How do you spell Gargery, Joe?" I asked him, with a modest patronage.

"I don't spell it at all," said Joe.

"But supposing you did?"

"It *can't* be supposed," said Joe. "Tho' I'm uncommon fond of reading, too."

"Are you, Joe?"

"On-common. Give me," said Joe, "a good book, or a good newspaper, and sit me down afore a good fire, and I ask no better. Lord!" he continued, after rubbing his knees a little, "when you *do* come to a J and a O, and says you, 'Here, at last, is a J-O, Joe,' how interesting reading is!"

I derived from this, that Joe's education, like Steam, was yet in its infancy. Pursuing the subject, I inquired:

"Didn't you ever go to school, Joe, when you were as little as me?"

"No, Pip."

"Why didn't you ever go to school, Joe, when you were as little as me?"

"Well, Pip," said Joe, taking up the poker, and settling himself to his usual occupation when he was thoughtful, of slowly raking the fire between the lower bars; "I'll tell you. My father, Pip, he were given to drink, and when he were overtook with drink, he hammered away at my mother, most onmerciful. It were a'most the only hammering he did, indeed, 'xcepting at myself. And he hammered at me with a wigor only to be equalled by the wigor with which he didn't hammer at his anwil.—You're a listening and understanding, Pip?"

"Yes, Joe."

"'Consequence, my mother and me we ran away from my father several times; and then my mother she'd go out to work, and she'd say, "Joe," she'd say, "now, please God, you shall have some schooling, child," and she'd put me to school. But my father were that good in his hart that he couldn't abear to be without us. So, he'd come with a most tremenjous crowd and make such a row at the doors of the houses where we was, that they used to be obligated to have no more to do with us and to give us up to him. And then he took us home and hammered us. Which, you see, Pip," said Joe, pausing in his meditative raking of the fire, and looking at me, "were a drawback on my learning."

"Certainly, poor Joe!"

"Though mind you, Pip," said Joe, with a judicial touch or two of the poker on the top bar, "rendering unto all their doo, and maintaining equal justice betwixt man and man, my father were that good in his hart, don't you see?"

I didn't see; but I didn't say so.

"Well!" Joe pursued, "somebody must keep the pot a biling, Pip, or the pot won't bile, don't you know?"

I saw that, and said so.

"'Consequence, my father didn't make objections to my going to work; so I went to work at my present calling, which were his too, if he would have followed it, and I worked tolerable hard, I assure *you*, Pip. In time I were able to keep him, and I kep him till he went off in a purple leptic fit. And it were my intentions to have had put upon his tombstone that, Whatsume'er the failings on his part, Remember reader he were that good in his hart."

Joe recited this couplet with such manifest pride and careful perspicuity, that I asked him if he had made it himself.

"I made it," said Joe, "my own self. I made it in a moment. It was like striking out a horseshoe complete, in a single blow. I never was so much surprised in all my life—couldn't credit my own ed—to tell you the truth, hardly believed it *were* my own ed. As I was saying, Pip, it were my intentions to have had it cut over him; but poetry costs money, cut it how you will, small or large, and it were not done. Not to mention bearers, all the money that could be spared were wanted for my mother. She were in poor elth, and quite broke. She weren't long of following, poor soul, and her share of peace come round at last."

Joe's blue eyes turned a little watery; he rubbed first one of them, and then the other, in a most uncongenial and uncomfortable manner, with the round knob on the top of the poker.

"It were but lonesome then," said Joe, "living here alone, and I got acquainted with your sister. Now, Pip;"—Joe looked firmly at me as if he knew I was not going to agree with him; "your sister is a fine figure of a woman."

I could not help looking at the fire, in an obvious state of doubt.

"Whatever family opinions, or whatever the world's opinions, on that subject may be, Pip, your sister is," Joe tapped the top bar with the poker after every word following, "a-fine-figure—of—a—woman!"

I could think of nothing better to say than "I am glad you think so, Joe."

"So am I," returned Joe, catching me up. "I am glad I think so, Pip. A little redness or a little matter of Bone, here or there, what does it signify to Me?"

I sagaciously observed, if it didn't signify to him, to whom did it signify?

"Certainly!" assented Joe. "That's it. You're right, old chap! When I got acquainted with your sister, it were the talk how she was bringing you up by hand. Very kind of her too, all the folks said, and I said, along with all the folks. As to you," Joe pursued with a countenance expressive of seeing something very nasty indeed, "if you could have been aware how small and flabby and mean you was, dear me, you'd have formed the most contemptible opinion of yourself!"

Not exactly relishing this, I said, "Never mind me, Joe."

"But I did mind you, Pip," he returned with tender simplicity. "When I offered to your sister to keep company, and to be asked in church at such times as she was willing and ready to come to the forge, I said to her, 'And bring the poor little child. God bless the poor little child,' I said to your sister, 'there's room for *him* at the forge!'"

I broke out crying and begging pardon, and hugged Joe round the neck: who dropped the poker to hug me, and to say, "Ever the best of friends; an't us, Pip? Don't cry, old chap!"

When this little interruption was over, Joe resumed:

"Well, you see, Pip, and here we are! That's about where it lights; here we are! Now, when you take me in hand in my learning, Pip (and I tell you beforehand I am awful dull, most awful dull), Mrs. Joe mustn't see too much of what we're up to. It must be done, as I may say, on the sly. And why on the sly? I'll tell you why, Pip."

He had taken up the poker again; without which, I doubt if he could have proceeded in his demonstration.

"Your sister is given to government."

"Given to government, Joe?" I was startled, for I had some shadowy idea (and I am afraid I must add, hope) that Joe had divorced her in a favor of the Lords of the Admiralty, or Treasury.

"Given to government," said Joe. "Which I meantersay the government of you and myself."

"Oh!"

"And she an't over partial to having scholars on the premises," Joe continued, "and in partickler would not be over partial to my being a scholar, for fear as I might rise. Like a sort or rebel, don't you see?"

I was going to retort with an inquiry, and had got as far as "Why—" when Joe stopped me.

"Stay a bit. I know what you're a going to say, Pip; stay a bit! I don't deny that your sister comes the Mo-gul over us, now and again. I don't deny that she do throw us back-falls, and that she do drop down upon us heavy. At such times as when your sister is on the Ram-page, Pip," Joe sank his voice to a whisper and glanced at the door, "candor compels fur to admit that she is a Buster."

Joe pronounced this word, as if it began with at least twelve capital Bs.

"Why don't I rise? That were your observation when I broke it off, Pip?"

"Yes, Joe."

"Well," said Joe, passing the poker into his left hand, that he might feel his whisker; and I had no hope of him whenever he took to that placid occupation; "your sister's a master-mind. A master-mind."

"What's that?" I asked, in some hope of bringing him to a stand. But Joe was readier with his definition than I had expected, and completely stopped me by arguing circularly, and answering with a fixed look, "Her."

"And I an't a master-mind," Joe resumed, when he had unfixed his look, and got back to his whisker. "And last of all, Pip—and this I want to say very serous to you, old chap—I see so much in my poor mother, of a woman drudging and slaving and breaking her honest hart and never getting no peace in her mortal days, that I'm dead afeerd of going wrong in the way of not doing what's right by a woman, and I'd fur rather of the two go wrong the t'other way, and be a little ill-conwenienced myself. I wish it was only me that got put out, Pip; I wish there warn't no Tickler for you, old chap; I wish I could take it all on myself; but this is the up-and-down-and-straight on it, Pip, and I hope you'll overlook shortcomings."

Young as I was, I believe that I dated a new admiration of Joe from that night. We were equals afterwards, as we had been before; but, afterwards at quiet times when I sat looking at Joe and thinking about him, I had a new sensation of feeling conscious that I was looking up to Joe in my heart.

"Howsumever," said Joe, rising to replenish the fire; "here's the Dutch-clock a working himself up to being equal to strike Eight of 'em, and she's not come home yet! I hope Uncle Pumblechook's mare mayn't have set a forefoot on a piece o' ice, and gone down."

Mrs. Joe made occasional trips with Uncle Pumblechook on market-days, to assist him in buying such household stuffs and goods as required a woman's judgment; Uncle Pumblechook being a bachelor and reposing no confidences in his domestic servant. This was market-day, and Mrs. Joe was out on one of these expeditions.

Joe made the fire and swept the hearth, and then we went to the door to listen for the chaise-cart. It was a dry cold night, and the wind blew keenly, and the frost was white and hard. A man would die to-night of lying out on the marshes, I thought. And then I looked at the stars, and considered how awful it would be for a man to turn his face up to them as he froze to death, and see no help or pity in all the glittering multitude.

"Here comes the mare," said Joe, "ringing like a peal of bells!"

The sound of her iron shoes upon the hard road was quite musical, as she came along at a much brisker trot than usual. We got a chair out, ready for Mrs. Joe's alighting, and stirred up the fire that they might see a bright window, and took a final survey of the kitchen that nothing might be out of its place. When we had completed these preparations, they drove up, wrapped to the eyes. Mrs. Joe was soon landed, and Uncle Pumblechook was soon down too, covering the mare with a cloth, and we were soon all in the kitchen, carrying so much cold air in with us that it seemed to drive all the heat out of the fire.

"Now," said Mrs. Joe, unwrapping herself with haste and excitement, and throwing her bonnet back on her shoulders where it hung by the strings, "if this boy an't grateful this night, he never will be!"

I looked as grateful as any boy possibly could, who was wholly uninformed why he ought to assume that expression.

"It's only to be hoped," said my sister, "that he won't be Pompeyed. But I have my fears."

"She ain't in that line, Mum," said Mr. Pumblechook. "She knows better."

She? I looked at Joe, making the motion with my lips and eyebrows, "She?" Joe looked at me, making the motion with *his* lips and eyebrows, "She?" My sister catching him in the act, he drew the back of his hand across his nose with his usual conciliatory air on such occasions, and looked at her.

"Well?" said my sister, in her snappish way. "What are you staring at? Is the house a-fire?"

"—Which some indiwidual," Joe politely hinted, "mentioned—she."

"And she is a she, I suppose?" said my sister. "Unless you call Miss Havisham a he. And I doubt if even you'll go so far as that."

"Miss Havisham, up town?" said Joe.

"Is there any Miss Havisham down town?" returned my sister. "She wants this boy to go and play there. And of course he's going. And he had better play there," said my sister, shaking her head at me as an encouragement to be extremely light and sportive, "or I'll work him."

I had heard of Miss Havisham up town—everybody for miles round had heard of Miss Havisham up town—as an immensely rich and grim lady who lived in a large and dismal house barricaded against robbers, and who led a life of seclusion.

"Well to be sure!" said Joe, astounded. "I wonder how she come to know Pip!"

"Noodle!" cried my sister. "Who said she knew him?"

"—Which some indiwidual," Joe again politely hinted, "mentioned that she wanted him to go and play there."

"And couldn't she ask Uncle Pumblechook if he knew of a boy to go and play there? Isn't it just barely possible that Uncle Pumblechook may be a tenant of hers, and that he may sometimes—we won't say quarterly or half-yearly, for that would be requiring too much of you—but sometimes—go there to pay his rent? And couldn't she then ask Uncle Pumblechook if he knew of a boy to go and play there? And couldn't Uncle Pumblechook, being always considerate and thoughtful for us—though you may not think it, Joseph," in a tone of the deepest reproach, as if he were the most callous of nephews, "then mention this boy, standing Prancing here"—which I solemnly declare I was not doing— "that I have for ever been a willing slave to?"

"Good again!" cried Uncle Pumblechook. "Well put! Prettily pointed! Good indeed! Now Joseph, you know the case."

"No, Joseph," said my sister, still in a reproachful manner, while Joe apologetically drew the back of his hand across and across his nose, "you do not yet—though you may not think it—know the case. You may consider that you do, but you do *not*, Joseph. For you do not know that Uncle Pumblechook, being sensible that for anything we can tell, this boy's fortune may be made by his going to Miss Havisham's, has offered to take him into town to-night in his own chaise-cart, and to keep him to-night, and to take him with his own hands to Miss

Havisham's to-morrow morning. And Lor-a-mussy me!" cried my sister, casting off her bonnet in sudden desperation, "here I stand talking to mere Mooncalfs, with Uncle Pumblechook waiting, and the mare catching cold at the door, and the boy grimed with crock and dirt from the hair of his head to the sole of his foot!"

With that, she pounced upon me, like an eagle on a lamb, and my face was squeezed into wooden bowls in sinks, and my head was put under taps of water-butts, and I was soaped, and kneaded, and towelled, and thumped, and harrowed, and rasped, until I really was quite beside myself. (I may here remark that I suppose myself to be better acquainted than any living authority, with the ridgy effect of a wedding-ring, passing unsympathetically over the human countenance.)

When my ablutions were completed, I was put into clean linen of the stiffest character, like a young penitent into sackcloth, and was trussed up in my tightest and fearfullest suit. I was then delivered over to Mr. Pumblechook, who formally received me as if he were the Sheriff, and who let off upon me the speech that I knew he had been dying to make all along: "Boy, be forever grateful to all friends, but especially unto them which brought you up by hand!"

"Good-bye, Joe!"

"God bless you, Pip, old chap!"

I had never parted from him before, and what with my feelings and what with soapsuds, I could at first see no stars from the chaise-cart. But they twinkled out one by one, without throwing any light on the questions why on earth I was going to play at Miss Havisham's, and what on earth I was expected to play at.

CHAPTER 8

Mr. Pumblechook's premises in the High -street of the market town, were of a peppercorny and farinaceous character, as the premises of a cornchandler and seedsman should be. It appeared to me that he must be a very happy man indeed, to have so many little drawers in his shop; and I wondered when I peeped into one or two on the lower tiers, and saw the tied-up brown paper packets inside, whether the flower-seeds and bulbs ever wanted of a fine day to break out of those jails, and bloom.

It was in the early morning after my arrival that I entertained this speculation. On the previous night, I had been sent straight to bed in an attic with a sloping roof, which was so low in the corner where the bedstead was, that I calculated the tiles as being within a foot of my eyebrows. In the same early morning, I discovered a singular affinity between seeds and corduroys. Mr. Pumblechook wore corduroys, and so did his shopman; and somehow, there was a general air and flavor about the corduroys, so much in the nature of seeds, and a general air and flavor about the seeds, so much in the nature of corduroys, that I hardly knew which was which. The same opportunity served me for noticing that Mr. Pumblechook appeared to conduct *his* business by looking across the street at the saddler, who appeared to transact his business by keeping his eye on the coachmaker, who appeared to get on in life by putting his hands in his pockets and contemplating the baker, who in his turn folded his arms and stared at the grocer, who stood at his door and yawned at the chemist. The watchmaker, always poring over a little desk with a magnifying-glass at his eye, and always inspected by a group of smock-frocks poring over him through the glass of his shop-window, seemed to be about the only person in the High Street whose trade engaged his attention.

Mr. Pumblechook and I breakfasted at eight o'clock in the parlor behind the shop, while the shopman took his mug of tea and hunch of bread and butter on a sack of peas in the front premises. I considered Mr. Pumblechook wretched company. Besides being possessed by my sister's idea that a mortifying and penitential character ought to be imparted to my diet— besides giving me as much crumb as possible in combination with as little butter, and putting such a quantity of warm water into my milk that it would have been more candid to have left the milk out altogether—his conversation consisted of nothing but arithmetic. On my politely bidding him Good morning, he said, pompously, "Seven times nine, boy?" And how should I be able to answer, dodged in that way, in a strange place, on an empty stomach! I was hungry, but before I had swallowed a morsel, he began a running sum that lasted all through the breakfast. "Seven?" "And four?" "And eight?" "And six?" "And two?" "And ten?" And so on. And after each figure was disposed of, it was as much as I could do to get a bite or a sup, before the next came; while he sat at his ease guessing nothing, and eating bacon and hot roll, in (if I may be allowed the expression) a gorging and gormandizing manner.

For such reasons, I was very glad when ten o'clock came and we started for Miss Havisham's; though I was not at all at my ease regarding the manner in which I should acquit myself under that lady's roof. Within a quarter of an hour we came to Miss Havisham's house, which was of old brick, and dismal, and had a great many iron bars to it. Some of the windows had been walled up; of those that remained, all the lower were rustily barred. There was a courtyard in front, and that was barred; so we had to wait, after ringing the bell, until some one should come to open it. While we waited at the gate, I peeped in (even then Mr. Pumblechook said, "And fourteen?" but I pretended not to hear him), and saw that at the side of the house there was a large brewery. No brewing was going on in it, and none seemed to have gone on for a long long time.

A window was raised, and a clear voice demanded "What name?" To which my conductor replied, "Pumblechook." The voice returned, "Quite right," and the window was shut again, and a young lady came across the court-yard, with keys in her hand.

"This," said Mr. Pumblechook, "is Pip."

"This is Pip, is it?" returned the young lady, who was very pretty and seemed very proud; "come in, Pip."

Mr. Pumblechook was coming in also, when she stopped him with the gate.

"Oh!" she said. "Did you wish to see Miss Havisham?"

"If Miss Havisham wished to see me," returned Mr. Pumblechook, discomfited.

"Ah!" said the girl; "but you see she don't."

She said it so finally, and in such an undiscussible way, that Mr. Pumblechook, though in a condition of ruffled dignity, could not protest. But he eyed me severely—as if *I* had done anything to him!—and departed with the words reproachfully delivered: "Boy! Let your behavior here be a credit unto them which brought you up by hand!" I was not free from apprehension that he would come back to propound through the gate, "And sixteen?" But he didn't.

My young conductress locked the gate, and we went across the courtyard. It was paved and clean, but grass was growing in every crevice. The brewery buildings had a little lane of communication with it, and the wooden gates of that lane stood open, and all the brewery beyond stood open, away to the high enclosing wall; and all was empty and disused. The cold wind seemed to blow colder there than outside the gate;

and it made a shrill noise in howling in and out at the open sides of the brewery, like the noise of wind in the rigging of a ship at sea.

She saw me looking at it, and she said, "You could drink without hurt all the strong beer that's brewed there now, boy."

"I should think I could, miss," said I, in a shy way.

"Better not try to brew beer there now, or it would turn out sour, boy; don't you think so?"

"It looks like it, miss."

"Not that anybody means to try," she added, "for that's all done with, and the place will stand as idle as it is till it falls. As to strong beer, there's enough of it in the cellars already, to drown the Manor House."

"Is that the name of this house, miss?"

"One of its names, boy."

"It has more than one, then, miss?"

"One more. Its other name was Satis; which is Greek, or Latin, or Hebrew, or all three—or all one to me—for enough."

"Enough House," said I; "that's a curious name, miss."

"Yes," she replied; "but it meant more than it said. It meant, when it was given, that whoever had this house could want nothing else. They must have been easily satisfied in those days, I should think. But don't loiter, boy."

Though she called me "boy" so often, and with a carelessness that was far from complimentary, she was of about my own age. She seemed much older than I, of course, being a girl, and beautiful and self-possessed; and she was as scornful of me as if she had been one-and-twenty, and a queen.

We went into the house by a side door—the great front entrance had two chains across it outside—and the first thing I noticed was, that the passages were all dark, and that she had left a candle burning there. She took it up, and we went through more passages and up a staircase, and still it was all dark, and only the candle lighted us.

At last we came to the door of a room, and she said, "Go in."

I answered, more in shyness than politeness, "After you, miss."

To this she returned: "Don't be ridiculous, boy; I am not going in." And scornfully walked away, and—what was worse—took the candle with her.

This was very uncomfortable, and I was half afraid. However, the only thing to be done being to knock at the door, I knocked, and was told from within to enter. I entered, therefore, and found myself in a pretty large room, well lighted with wax candles. No glimpse of daylight was to be seen in it. It was a dressing-room, as I supposed from the furniture, though much of it was of forms and uses then quite unknown to me. But prominent in it was a draped table with a gilded looking-glass, and that I made out at first sight to be a fine lady's dressing-table.

Whether I should have made out this object so soon if there had been no fine lady sitting at it, I cannot say. In an arm-chair, with an elbow resting on the table and her head leaning on that hand, sat the strangest lady I have ever seen, or shall ever see.

She was dressed in rich materials—satins, and lace, and silks—all of white. Her shoes were white. And she had a long white veil dependent from her hair, and she had bridal flowers in her hair, but her hair was white. Some bright jewels sparkled on her neck and on her hands, and some other jewels lay sparkling on the table. Dresses, less splendid than the dress she wore, and half-packed trunks, were scattered about. She had not quite finished dressing, for she had but one shoe on—the other was on the table near her hand—her veil was but half arranged, her watch and chain were not put on, and some lace for her bosom lay with those trinkets, and with her handkerchief, and gloves, and some flowers, and a prayer-book all confusedly heaped about the looking-glass.

It was not in the first few moments that I saw all these things, though I saw more of them in the first moments than might be supposed. But I saw that everything within my view which ought to be white, had been white long ago, and had lost its lustre and was faded and yellow. I saw that the bride within the bridal dress had withered like the dress, and like the flowers, and had no brightness left but the brightness of her sunken eyes. I saw that the dress had been put upon the rounded figure of a young woman, and that the figure upon which it now hung loose had shrunk to skin and bone. Once, I had been taken to see some ghastly waxwork at the Fair, representing I know not what impossible personage lying in state. Once, I had been taken to one of our old marsh churches to see a skeleton in the ashes of a rich dress that had been dug out of a vault under the church pavement. Now, waxwork and skeleton seemed to have dark eyes that moved and looked at me. I should have cried out, if I could.

"Who is it?" said the lady at the table.

"Pip, ma'am."

"Pip?"

"Mr. Pumblechook's boy, ma'am. Come—to play."

"Come nearer; let me look at you. Come close."

It was when I stood before her, avoiding her eyes, that I took note of the surrounding objects in detail, and saw that her watch had stopped at twenty minutes to nine, and that a clock in the room had stopped at twenty minutes to nine.

"Look at me," said Miss Havisham. "You are not afraid of a woman who has never seen the sun since you were born?"

I regret to state that I was not afraid of telling the enormous lie comprehended in the answer "No."

"Do you know what I touch here?" she said, laying her hands, one upon the other, on her left side.

"Yes, ma'am." (It made me think of the young man.)

"What do I touch?"

"Your heart."

"Broken!"

She uttered the word with an eager look, and with strong emphasis, and with a weird smile that had a kind of boast in it. Afterwards she kept her hands there for a little while, and slowly took them away as if they were heavy.

"I am tired," said Miss Havisham. "I want diversion, and I have done with men and women. Play."

I think it will be conceded by my most disputatious reader, that she could hardly have directed an unfortunate boy to do anything in the wide world more difficult to be done under the circumstances.

"I sometimes have sick fancies," she went on, "and I have a sick fancy that I want to see some play. There, there!" with an impatient movement of the fingers of her right hand; "play, play, play!"

For a moment, with the fear of my sister's working me before my eyes, I had a desperate idea of starting round the room in the assumed character of Mr. Pumblechook's chaise-cart. But I felt myself so unequal to the performance that I gave it up, and stood looking at Miss Havisham in what I suppose she took for a dogged manner, inasmuch as she said, when we had taken a good look at each other:

"Are you sullen and obstinate?"

"No, ma'am, I am very sorry for you, and very sorry I can't play just now. If you complain of me I shall get into trouble with my sister, so I would do it if I could; but it's so new here, and so strange, and so fine—and melancholy—" I stopped, fearing I might say too much, or had already said it, and we took another look at each other.

Before she spoke again, she turned her eyes from me, and looked at the dress she wore, and at the dressing-table, and finally at herself in the looking-glass.

"So new to him," she muttered, "so old to me; so strange

to him, so familiar to me; so melancholy to both of us! Call Estella."

As she was still looking at the reflection of herself, I thought she was still talking to herself, and kept quiet.

"Call Estella," she repeated, flashing a look at me. "You can do that. Call Estella. At the door."

To stand in the dark in a mysterious passage of an unknown house, bawling Estella to a scornful young lady neither visible nor responsive, and feeling it a dreadful liberty so to roar out her name, was almost as bad as playing to order. But she answered at last, and her light came along the dark passage like a star.

Miss Havisham beckoned her to come close, and took up a jewel from the table, and tried its effect upon her fair young bosom and against her pretty brown hair. "Your own, one day, my dear, and you will use it well. Let me see you play cards with this boy."

"With this boy? Why, he is a common labouring-boy!"

I thought I overheard Miss Havisham answer—only it seemed so unlikely— "Well? You can break his heart."

"What do you play, boy?" asked Estella of myself, with the greatest disdain.

"Nothing but beggar my neighbour, miss."

"Beggar him," said Miss Havisham to Estella. So we sat down to cards.

It was then I began to understand that everything in the room had stopped, like the watch and the clock, a long time ago. I noticed that Miss Havisham put down the jewel exactly on the spot from which she had taken it up. As Estella dealt the cards, I glanced at the dressing-table again, and saw that the shoe upon it, once white, now yellow, had never been worn. I glanced down at the foot from which the shoe was absent, and saw that the silk stocking on it, once white, now yellow, had been trodden ragged. Without this arrest of everything, this standing still of all the pale decayed objects, not even the withered bridal dress on the collapsed form could have looked so like grave-clothes, or the long veil so like a shroud.

So she sat, corpse-like, as we played at cards; the frillings and trimmings on her bridal dress, looking like earthy paper. I knew nothing then of the discoveries that are occasionally made of bodies buried in ancient times, which fall to powder in the moment of being distinctly seen; but, I have often thought since, that she must have looked as if the admission of the natural light of day would have struck her to dust.

"He calls the knaves Jacks, this boy!" said Estella with disdain, before our first game was out. "And what coarse hands he has! And what thick boots!"

I had never thought of being ashamed of my hands before; but I began to consider them a very indifferent pair. Her contempt for me was so strong, that it became infectious, and I caught it.

She won the game, and I dealt. I misdealt, as was only natural, when I knew she was lying in wait for me to do wrong; and she denounced me for a stupid, clumsy labouring-boy.

"You say nothing of her," remarked Miss Havisham to me, as she looked on. "She says many hard things of you, but you say nothing of her. What do you think of her?"

"I don't like to say," I stammered.

"Tell me in my ear," said Miss Havisham, bending down.

"I think she is very proud," I replied, in a whisper.

"Anything else?"

"I think she is very pretty."

"Anything else?"

"I think she is very insulting." (She was looking at me then with a look of supreme aversion.)

"Anything else?"

"I think I should like to go home."

"And never see her again, though she is so pretty?"

"I am not sure that I shouldn't like to see her again, but I should like to go home now."

"You shall go soon," said Miss Havisham, aloud. "Play the game out."

Saving for the one weird smile at first, I should have felt almost sure that Miss Havisham's face could not smile. It had dropped into a watchful and brooding expression—most likely when all the things about her had become transfixed—and it looked as if nothing could ever lift it up again. Her chest had dropped, so that she stooped; and her voice had dropped, so that she spoke low, and with a dead lull upon her; altogether, she had the appearance of having dropped body and soul, within and without, under the weight of a crushing blow.

I played the game to an end with Estella, and she beggared me. She threw the cards down on the table when she had won them all, as if she despised them for having been won of me.

"When shall I have you here again?" said Miss Havisham. "Let me think."

I was beginning to remind her that to-day was Wednesday, when she checked me with her former impatient movement of the fingers of her right hand.

"There, there! I know nothing of days of the week; I know nothing of weeks of the year. Come again after six days. You hear?"

"Yes, ma'am."

"Estella, take him down. Let him have something to eat, and let him roam and look about him while he eats. Go, Pip."

I followed the candle down, as I had followed the candle up, and she stood it in the place where we had found it. Until she opened the side entrance, I had fancied, without thinking about it, that it must necessarily be night-time. The rush of the daylight quite confounded me, and made me feel as if I had been in the candlelight of the strange room many hours.

"You are to wait here, you boy," said Estella; and disappeared and closed the door.

I took the opportunity of being alone in the courtyard to look at my coarse hands and my common boots. My opinion of those accessories was not favorable. They had never troubled me before, but they troubled me now, as vulgar appendages. I determined to ask Joe why he had ever taught me to call those picture-cards Jacks, which ought to be called knaves. I wished Joe had been rather more genteelly brought up, and then I should have been so too.

She came back, with some bread and meat and a little mug of beer. She put the mug down on the stones of the yard, and gave me the bread and meat without looking at me, as insolently as if I were a dog in disgrace. I was so humiliated, hurt, spurned, offended, angry, sorry—I cannot hit upon the right name for the smart—God knows what its name was—that tears started to my eyes. The moment they sprang there, the girl looked at me with a quick delight in having been the cause of them. This gave me power to keep them back and to look at her: so, she gave a contemptuous toss—but with a sense, I thought, of having made too sure that I was so wounded—and left me.

But when she was gone, I looked about me for a place to hide my face in, and got behind one of the gates in the brewery-lane, and leaned my sleeve against the wall there, and leaned my forehead on it and cried. As I cried, I kicked the wall, and took a hard twist at my hair; so bitter were my feelings, and so sharp was the smart without a name, that needed counteraction.

My sister's bringing up had made me sensitive. In the little world in which children have their existence whosoever brings them up, there is nothing so finely perceived and so finely felt as injustice. It may be only small injustice that the child can be exposed to; but the child is small, and its world is small, and its rocking-horse stands as many hands high, according to scale, as a big-boned Irish hunter. Within myself, I had sustained, from my babyhood, a perpetual conflict with injustice. I had known, from the time when I could speak, that my sister, in her capricious and violent coercion, was unjust to me. I had cherished a profound conviction that her bringing me up by hand gave her no right to bring me up by jerks. Through all my punishments, disgraces, fasts, and vigils, and other penitential performances, I had nursed this assurance; and to my communing so much with it, in a solitary and unprotected way, I in great part refer the fact that I was morally timid and very sensitive.

I got rid of my injured feelings for the time by kicking them into the brewery wall, and twisting them out of my hair, and then I smoothed my face with my sleeve, and came from behind the gate. The bread and meat were acceptable, and the beer was warming and tingling, and I was soon in spirits to look about me.

To be sure, it was a deserted place, down to the pigeon-house in the brewery-yard, which had been blown crooked on its pole by some high wind, and would have made the pigeons think themselves at sea, if there had been any pigeons there to be rocked by it. But there were no pigeons in the dove-cot, no horses in the stable, no pigs in the sty, no malt in the storehouse, no smells of grains and beer in the copper or the vat. All the uses and scents of the brewery might have evaporated with its last reek of smoke. In a by-yard, there was a wilderness of empty casks, which had a certain sour remembrance of better days lingering about them; but it was too sour to be accepted as a sample of the beer that was gone—and in this respect I remember those recluses as being like most others.

Behind the furthest end of the brewery, was a rank garden with an old wall; not so high but that I could struggle up and hold on long enough to look over it, and see that the rank garden was the garden of the house, and that it was overgrown with tangled weeds, but that there was a track upon the green and yellow paths, as if some one sometimes walked there, and that Estella was walking away from me even then. But she seemed to be everywhere. For when I yielded to the temptation presented by the casks, and began to walk on them, I saw *her* walking on them at the end of the yard of casks. She had her back towards me, and held her pretty brown hair spread out in her two hands, and never looked round, and passed out of my view directly. So, in the brewery itself—by which I mean the large paved lofty place in which they used to make the beer, and where the brewing utensils still were. When I first went into it, and, rather oppressed by its gloom, stood near the door looking about me, I saw her pass among the extinguished fires, and ascend some light iron stairs, and go out by a gallery high overhead, as if she were going out into the sky.

It was in this place, and at this moment, that a strange thing happened to my fancy. I thought it a strange thing then, and I thought it a stranger thing long afterwards. I turned my eyes—a little dimmed by looking up at the frosty light—towards a great wooden beam in a low nook of the building near me on my right hand, and I saw a figure hanging there by the neck. A figure all in yellow white, with but one shoe to the feet; and it hung so, that I could see that the faded trimmings of the dress were like earthy paper, and that the face was Miss Havisham's, with a movement going over the whole countenance as if she were trying to call to me. In the terror of seeing the figure, and in the terror of being certain that it had not been there a moment before, I at first ran from it, and then ran towards it. And my terror was greatest of all when I found no figure there.

Nothing less than the frosty light of the cheerful sky, the sight of people passing beyond the bars of the court-yard gate, and the reviving influence of the rest of the bread and meat and beer, would have brought me round. Even with those aids, I might not have come to myself as soon as I did, but that I saw Estella approaching with the keys, to let me out. She would have some fair reason for looking down upon me, I thought, if she saw me frightened; and she would have no fair reason.

She gave me a triumphant glance in passing me, as if she rejoiced that my hands were so coarse and my boots were so thick, and she opened the gate, and stood holding it. I was passing out without looking at her, when she touched me with a taunting hand.

"Why don't you cry?"

"Because I don't want to."

"You do," said she. "You have been crying till you are half blind, and you are near crying again now."

She laughed contemptuously, pushed me out, and locked the gate upon me. I went straight to Mr. Pumblechook's, and was immensely relieved to find him not at home. So, leaving word with the shopman on what day I was wanted at Miss Havisham's again, I set off on the four-mile walk to our forge; pondering, as I went along, on all I had seen, and deeply revolving that I was a common laboring-boy; that my hands were coarse; that my boots were thick; that I had fallen into a despicable habit of calling knaves Jacks; that I was much more ignorant than I had considered myself last night, and generally that I was in a low-lived bad way.

CHAPTER 9

When I reached home, my sister was very curious to know all about Miss Havisham's, and asked a number of questions. And I soon found myself getting heavily bumped from behind in the nape of the neck and the small of the back, and having my face ignominiously shoved against the kitchen wall, because I did not answer those questions at sufficient length.

If a dread of not being understood be hidden in the breasts of other young people to anything like the extent to which it used to be hidden in mine—which I consider probable, as I have no particular reason to suspect myself of having been a monstrosity—it is the key to many reservations. I felt convinced that if I described Miss Havisham's as my eyes had seen it, I should not be understood. Not only that, but I felt convinced that Miss Havisham too would not be understood; and although she was perfectly incomprehensible to me, I entertained an impression that there would be something coarse and treacherous in my dragging her as she really was (to say nothing of Miss Estella) before the contemplation of Mrs. Joe. Consequently, I said as little as I could, and had my face shoved against the kitchen wall.

The worst of it was that that bullying old Pumblechook, preyed upon by a devouring curiosity to be informed of all I had seen and heard, came gaping over in his chaise-cart at tea-time, to have the details divulged to him. And the mere sight of the torment, with his fishy eyes and mouth open, his sandy hair inquisitively on end, and his waistcoat heaving with windy arithmetic, made me vicious in my reticence.

"Well, boy," Uncle Pumblechook began, as soon as he was seated in the chair of honor by the fire. "How did you get on up town?"

I answered, "Pretty well, sir," and my sister shook her fist at me.

"Pretty well?" Mr. Pumblechook repeated. "Pretty well is no answer. Tell us what you mean by pretty well, boy?"

Whitewash on the forehead hardens the brain into a state of obstinacy perhaps. Anyhow, with whitewash from the wall on my forehead, my obstinacy was adamantine. I reflected for some time, and then answered as if I had discovered a new idea, "I mean pretty well."

My sister with an exclamation of impatience was going to fly at me—I had no shadow of defence, for Joe was busy in the forge—when Mr. Pumblechook interposed with "No! Don't lose your temper. Leave this lad to me, ma'am; leave this lad to me." Mr. Pumblechook then turned me towards him, as if he were going to cut my hair, and said—

"First (to get our thoughts in order): Forty-three pence"

I calculated the consequences of replying "Four Hundred Pound," and finding them against me, went as near the answer as I could—which was somewhere about eightpence off. Mr. Pumblechook then put me through my pence-table from "twelve pence make one shilling," up to "forty pence make three and fourpence," and then triumphantly demanded, as if he had done for me, "*Now!* How much is forty-three pence?" To which I replied, after a long interval of reflection, "I don't know." And I was so aggravated that I almost doubt if I did know.

Mr. Pumblechook worked his head like a screw to screw it out of me, and said, "Is forty-three pence seven and sixpence three fardens, for instance?"

"Yes!" said I. And although my sister instantly boxed my ears, it was highly gratifying to me to see that the answer spoilt his joke, and brought him to a dead stop.

"Boy! What like is Miss Havisham?" Mr. Pumblechook began again when he had recovered; folding his arms tight on his chest and applying the screw.

"Very tall and dark," I told him.

"Is she, uncle?" asked my sister.

Mr. Pumblechook winked assent; from which I at once inferred that he had never seen Miss Havisham, for she was nothing of the kind.

"Good!" said Mr. Pumblechook conceitedly. ("This is the way to have him! We are beginning to hold our own, I think, Mum?")

"I am sure, uncle," returned Mrs. Joe, "I wish you had him always; you know so well how to deal with him."

"Now, boy! What was she a doing of, when you went in today?" asked Mr. Pumblechook.

"She was sitting," I answered, "in a black velvet coach."

Mr. Pumblechook and Mrs. Joe stared at one another—as they well might—and both repeated, "In a black velvet coach?"

"Yes," said I. "And Miss Estella—that's her niece, I think—handed her in cake and wine at the coach-window, on a gold plate. And we all had cake and wine on gold plates. And I got up behind the coach to eat mine, because she told me to."

"Was anybody else there?" asked Mr. Pumblechook.

"Four dogs," said I.

"Large or small?"

"Immense," said I. "And they fought for veal cutlets out of a silver basket."

Mr. Pumblechook and Mrs. Joe stared at one another again, in utter amazement. I was perfectly frantic—a reckless witness under the torture—and would have told them anything.

"Where *was* this coach, in the name of gracious?" asked my sister.

"In Miss Havisham's room." They stared again. "But there

weren't any horses to it." I added this saving clause, in the moment of rejecting four richly caparisoned coursers which I had had wild thoughts of harnessing.

"Can this be possible, uncle?" asked Mrs. Joe. "What can the boy mean?"

"I'll tell you, Mum," said Mr. Pumblechook. "My opinion is, it's a sedan-chair. She's flighty, you know—very flighty—quite flighty enough to pass her days in a sedan-chair."

"Did you ever see her in it, uncle?" asked Mrs. Joe.

"How could I?" he returned, forced to the admission, "when I never see her in my life? Never clapped eyes upon her!"

"Goodness, uncle! And yet you have spoken to her?"

"Why, don't you know," said Mr. Pumblechook, testily, "that when I have been there, I have been took up to the outside of her door, and the door has stood ajar, and she has spoke to me that way. Don't say you don't know that, Mum. Howsever, the boy went there to play. What did you play at, boy?"

"We played with flags," I said. (I beg to observe that I think of myself with amazement, when I recall the lies I told on this occasion.)

"Flags!" echoed my sister.

"Yes," said I. "Estella waved a blue flag, and I waved a red one, and Miss Havisham waved one sprinkled all over with little gold stars, out at the coach-window. And then we all waved our swords and hurrahed."

"Swords!" repeated my sister. "Where did you get swords from?"

"Out of a cupboard," said I. "And I saw pistols in it—and jam—and pills. And there was no daylight in the room, but it was all lighted up with candles."

"That's true, Mum," said Mr. Pumblechook, with a grave nod. "That's the state of the case, for that much I've seen myself." And then they both stared at me, and I, with an obtrusive show of artlessness on my countenance, stared at them, and plaited the right leg of my trousers with my right hand.

If they had asked me any more questions, I should undoubtedly have betrayed myself, for I was even then on the point of mentioning that there was a balloon in the yard, and should have hazarded the statement but for my invention being divided between that phenomenon and a bear in the brewery. They were so much occupied, however, in discussing the marvels I had already presented for their consideration, that I escaped. The subject still held them when Joe came in from his work to have a cup of tea. To whom my sister, more for the relief of her own mind than for the gratification of his, related my pretended experiences.

Now, when I saw Joe open his blue eyes and roll them all round the kitchen in helpless amazement, I was overtaken by penitence; but only as regarded him—not in the least as regarded the other two. Towards Joe, and Joe only, I considered myself a young monster, while they sat debating what results would come to me from Miss Havisham's acquaintance and favor. They had no doubt that Miss Havisham would "do something" for me; their doubts related to the form that something would take. My sister stood out for "property." Mr. Pumblechook was in favor of a handsome premium for binding me apprentice to some genteel trade—say, the corn and seed trade, for instance. Joe fell into the deepest disgrace with both, for offering the bright suggestion that I might only be presented with one of the dogs who had fought for the veal-cutlets. "If a fool's head can't express better opinions than that," said my sister, "and you have got any work to do, you had better go and do it." So he went.

After Mr. Pumblechook had driven off, and when my sister was washing up, I stole into the forge to Joe, and remained by him until he had done for the night. Then I said, "Before the fire goes out, Joe, I should like to tell you something."

"Should you, Pip?" said Joe, drawing his shoeing-stool near the forge. "Then tell us. What is it, Pip?"

"Joe," said I, taking hold of his rolled-up shirt sleeve, and twisting it between my finger and thumb, "you remember all that about Miss Havisham's?"

"Remember?" said Joe. "I believe you! Wonderful!"

"It's a terrible thing, Joe; it ain't true."

"What are you telling of, Pip?" cried Joe, falling back in the greatest amazement. "You don't mean to say it's—"

"Yes I do; it's lies, Joe."

"But not all of it? Why sure you don't mean to say, Pip, that there was no black welwet co—ch?" For, I stood shaking my head. "But at least there was dogs, Pip? Come, Pip," said Joe, persuasively, "if there warn't no weal-cutlets, at least there was dogs?"

"No, Joe."

"A dog?" said Joe. "A puppy? Come?"

"No, Joe, there was nothing at all of the kind."

As I fixed my eyes hopelessly on Joe, Joe contemplated me in dismay. "Pip, old chap! This won't do, old fellow! I say! Where do you expect to go to?"

"It's terrible, Joe; an't it?"

"Terrible?" cried Joe. "Awful! What possessed you?"

"I don't know what possessed me, Joe," I replied, letting his shirt sleeve go, and sitting down in the ashes at his feet, hanging my head; "but I wish you hadn't taught me to call Knaves at cards Jacks; and I wish my boots weren't so thick nor my hands so coarse."

And then I told Joe that I felt very miserable, and that I hadn't been able to explain myself to Mrs. Joe and Pumblechook, who were so rude to me, and that there had been a beautiful young lady at Miss Havisham's who was dreadfully proud, and that she had said I was common, and that I knew I was common, and that I wished I was not common, and that the lies had come of it somehow, though I didn't know how.

This was a case of metaphysics, at least as difficult for Joe to deal with as for me. But Joe took the case altogether out of the region of metaphysics, and by that means vanquished it.

"There's one thing you may be sure of, Pip," said Joe, after some rumination, "namely, that lies is lies. Howsever they come, they didn't ought to come, and they come from the father of lies, and work round to the same. Don't you tell no more of 'em, Pip. *That* ain't the way to get out of being common, old chap. And as to being common, I don't make it out at all clear. You are oncommon in some things. You're oncommon small. Likewise you're a oncommon scholar."

"No, I am ignorant and backward, Joe."

"Why, see what a letter you wrote last night! Wrote in print even! I've seen letters—Ah! and from gentlefolks!—that I'll swear weren't wrote in print," said Joe.

"I have learnt next to nothing, Joe. You think much of me. It's only that."

"Well, Pip," said Joe, "be it so or be it son't, you must be a common scholar afore you can be a oncommon one, I should hope! The king upon his throne, with his crown upon his ed, can't sit and write his acts of Parliament in print, without having begun, when he were a unpromoted Prince, with the alphabet— Ah!" added Joe, with a shake of the head that was full of meaning, "and begun at A too, and worked his way to Z. And *I* know what that is to do, though I can't say I've exactly done it."

There was some hope in this piece of wisdom, and it rather encouraged me.

"Whether common ones as to callings and earnings," pursued Joe, reflectively, "mightn't be the better of continuing for to keep company with common ones, instead of going out to play with oncommon ones—which reminds me to hope that there were a flag, perhaps?"

"No, Joe."

"(I'm sorry there weren't a flag, Pip). Whether that might be or mightn't be, is a thing as can't be looked into now, without putting your sister on the Rampage; and that's a thing not to be thought of as being done intentional. Lookee here, Pip, at what is said to you by a true friend. Which this to you the true friend say. If you can't get to be oncommon through going straight, you'll never get to do it through going crooked. So don't tell no more on 'em, Pip, and live well and die happy."

"You are not angry with me, Joe?"

"No, old chap. But bearing in mind that them were which I meantersay of a stunning and outdacious sort—alluding to them which bordered on weal-cutlets and dog-fighting—a sincere well-wisher would adwise, Pip, their being dropped into your meditations, when you go up stairs to bed. That's all, old chap, and don't never do it no more."

When I got up to my little room and said my prayers, I did not forget Joe's recommendation, and yet my young mind was in that disturbed and unthankful state, that I thought long after I laid me down, how common Estella would consider Joe, a mere blacksmith; how thick his boots, and how coarse his hands. I thought how Joe and my sister were then sitting in the kitchen, and how I had come up to bed from the kitchen, and how Miss Havisham and Estella never sat in a kitchen, but were far above the level of such common doings. I fell asleep recalling what I "used to do" when I was at Miss Havisham's; as though I had been there weeks or months, instead of hours; and as though it were quite an old subject of remembrance, instead of one that had arisen only that day.

That was a memorable day to me, for it made great changes in me. But it is the same with any life. Imagine one selected day struck out of it, and think how different its course would have been. Pause you who read this, and think for a moment of the long chain of iron or gold, of thorns or flowers, that would never have bound you, but for the formation of the first link on one memorable day.

CHAPTER 10

The felicitous idea occurred to me a morning or two later when I woke, that the best step I could take towards making myself uncommon was to get out of Biddy everything she knew. In pursuance of this luminous conception I mentioned to Biddy when I went to Mr. Wopsle's great-aunt's at night, that I had a particular reason for wishing to get on in life, and that I should feel very much obliged to her if she would impart all her learning to me. Biddy, who was the most obliging of girls, immediately said she would, and indeed began to carry out her promise within five minutes.

The Educational scheme or Course established by Mr. Wopsle's great-aunt may be resolved into the following synopsis. The pupils ate apples and put straws down one another's backs, until Mr. Wopsle's great-aunt collected her energies, and made an indiscriminate totter at them with a birch-rod. After receiving the charge with every mark of derision, the pupils formed in line and buzzingly passed a ragged book from hand to hand. The book had an alphabet in it, some figures and tables, and a little spelling—that is to say, it had had once. As soon as this volume began to circulate, Mr. Wopsle's great-aunt fell into a state of coma; arising either from sleep or a rheumatic paroxysm. The pupils then entered among themselves upon a competitive examination on the subject of Boots, with the view of ascertaining who could tread the hardest upon whose toes. This mental exercise lasted until Biddy made a rush at them and distributed three defaced Bibles (shaped as if they had been unskilfully cut off the chump end of something), more illegibly printed at the best than any curiosities of literature I have since met with, speckled all over with ironmould, and having various specimens of the insect world smashed between their leaves. This part of the Course was usually lightened by several single combats between Biddy and refractory students. When the fights were over, Biddy gave out the number of a page, and then we all read aloud what we could—or what we couldn't—in a frightful chorus; Biddy leading with a high, shrill, monotonous voice, and none of us having the least notion of, or reverence for, what we were reading about. When this horrible din had lasted a certain time, it mechanically awoke Mr. Wopsle's great-aunt, who staggered at a boy fortuitously, and pulled his ears. This was understood to terminate the Course for the evening, and we emerged into the air with shrieks of intellectual victory. It is fair to remark that there was no prohibition against any pupil's entertaining himself with a slate or even with the ink (when there was any), but that it was not easy to pursue that branch of study in the winter season, on account of the little general shop in which the classes were holden—and which was also Mr. Wopsle's great-aunt's sitting-room and bed-chamber—being but faintly illuminated through the agency of one low-spirited dip-candle and no snuffers.

It appeared to me that it would take time to become uncommon, under these circumstances: nevertheless, I resolved to try it, and that very evening Biddy entered on our special agreement, by imparting some information from her little catalogue of Prices, under the head of moist sugar, and lending me, to copy at home, a large old English D which she had imitated from the heading of some newspaper, and which I supposed, until she told me what it was, to be a design for a buckle.

Of course there was a public-house in the village, and of course Joe liked sometimes to smoke his pipe there. I had received strict orders from my sister to call for him at the

Three Jolly Bargemen, that evening, on my way from school, and bring him home at my peril. To the Three Jolly Bargemen, therefore, I directed my steps.

There was a bar at the Jolly Bargemen, with some alarmingly long chalk scores in it on the wall at the side of the door, which seemed to me to be never paid off. They had been there ever since I could remember, and had grown more than I had. But there was a quantity of chalk about our country, and perhaps the people neglected no opportunity of turning it to account.

It being Saturday night, I found the landlord looking rather grimly at these records; but as my business was with Joe and not with him, I merely wished him good evening, and passed into the common room at the end of the passage, where there was a bright large kitchen fire, and where Joe was smoking his pipe in company with Mr. Wopsle and a stranger. Joe greeted me as usual with "Halloa, Pip, old chap!" and the moment he said that, the stranger turned his head and looked at me.

He was a secret-looking man whom I had never seen before. His head was all on one side, and one of his eyes was half shut up, as if he were taking aim at something with an invisible gun. He had a pipe in his mouth, and he took it out, and, after slowly blowing all his smoke away and looking hard at me all the time, nodded. So, I nodded, and then he nodded again, and made room on the settle beside him that I might sit down there.

But as I was used to sit beside Joe whenever I entered that place of resort, I said "No, thank you, sir," and fell into the space Joe made for me on the opposite settle. The strange man, after glancing at Joe, and seeing that his attention was otherwise engaged, nodded to me again when I had taken my seat, and then rubbed his leg—in a very odd way, as it struck me.

"You was saying," said the strange man, turning to Joe, "that you was a blacksmith."

"Yes. I said it, you know," said Joe.

"What'll you drink, Mr.—? You didn't mention your name, by-the-bye."

Joe mentioned it now, and the strange man called him by it. "What'll you drink, Mr. Gargery? At my expense? To top up with?"

"Well," said Joe, "to tell you the truth, I ain't much in the habit of drinking at anybody's expense but my own."

"Habit? No," returned the stranger, "but once and away, and on a Saturday night too. Come! Put a name to it, Mr. Gargery."

"I wouldn't wish to be stiff company," said Joe. "Rum."

"Rum," repeated the stranger. "And will the other gentleman originate a sentiment."

"Rum," said Mr. Wopsle.

"Three Rums!" cried the stranger, calling to the landlord. "Glasses round!"

"This other gentleman," observed Joe, by way of introducing Mr. Wopsle, "is a gentleman that you would like to hear give it out. Our clerk at church."

"Aha!" said the stranger, quickly, and cocking his eye at me. "The lonely church, right out on the marshes, with graves round it!"

"That's it," said Joe.

The stranger, with a comfortable kind of grunt over his pipe, put his legs up on the settle that he had to himself. He wore a flapping broad-brimmed traveller's hat, and under it a handkerchief tied over his head in the manner of a cap: so that he showed no hair. As he looked at the fire, I thought I saw a cunning expression, followed by a half-laugh, come into his face.

"I am not acquainted with this country, gentlemen, but it seems a solitary country towards the river."

"Most marshes is solitary," said Joe.

"No doubt, no doubt. Do you find any gypsies, now, or tramps, or vagrants of any sort, out there?"

"No," said Joe; "none but a runaway convict now and then. And we don't find *them*, easy. Eh, Mr. Wopsle?"

Mr. Wopsle, with a majestic remembrance of old discomfiture, assented; but not warmly.

"Seems you have been out after such?" asked the stranger.

"Once," returned Joe. "Not that we wanted to take them, you understand; we went out as lookers on; me, and Mr. Wopsle, and Pip. Didn't us, Pip?"

"Yes, Joe."

The stranger looked at me again—still cocking his eye, as if he were expressly taking aim at me with his invisible gun—and said, "He's a likely young parcel of bones that. What is it you call him?"

"Pip," said Joe.

"Christened Pip?"

"No, not christened Pip."

"Surname Pip?"

"No," said Joe, "it's a kind of family name what he gave himself when a infant, and is called by."

"Son of yours?"

"Well," said Joe, meditatively, not, of course, that it could be in anywise necessary to consider about it, but because it was the way at the Jolly Bargemen to seem to consider deeply about everything that was discussed over pipes; "well—no. No, he ain't."

"Nevvy?" said the strange man.

"Well," said Joe, with the same appearance of profound cogitation, "he is not—no, not to deceive you, he is *not*—my nevvy."

"What the Blue Blazes is he?" asked the stranger. Which appeared to me to be an inquiry of unnecessary strength.

Mr. Wopsle struck in upon that; as one who knew all about relationships, having professional occasion to bear in mind what female relations a man might not marry; and expounded the ties between me and Joe. Having his hand in, Mr. Wopsle finished off with a most terrifically snarling passage from Richard the Third, and seemed to think he had done quite enough to account for it when he added, "—as the poet says."

And here I may remark that when Mr. Wopsle referred to me, he considered it a necessary part of such reference to rumple my hair and poke it into my eyes. I cannot conceive why everybody of his standing who visited at our house should always have put me through the same inflammatory process under similar circumstances. Yet I do not call to mind that I was ever in my earlier youth the subject of remark in our social family circle, but some large-handed person took some such ophthalmic steps to patronize me.

All this while, the strange man looked at nobody but me, and looked at me as if he were determined to have a shot at me at last, and bring me down. But he said nothing after offering his Blue Blazes observation, until the glasses of rum and water were brought; and then he made his shot, and a most extraordinary shot it was.

It was not a verbal remark, but a proceeding in dumb-show, and was pointedly addressed to me. He stirred his rum and water pointedly at me, and he tasted his rum and water pointedly at me. And he stirred it and he tasted it; not with a spoon that was brought to him, but *with a file.*

He did this so that nobody but I saw the file; and when he had done it he wiped the file and put it in a breast-pocket. I knew it to be Joe's file, and I knew that he knew my convict, the moment I saw the instrument. I sat gazing at him, spell-bound. But he now reclined on his settle, taking very little notice of me, and talking principally about turnips.

There was a delicious sense of cleaning-up and making a quiet pause before going on in life afresh, in our village on Saturday nights, which stimulated Joe to dare to stay out half an hour longer on Saturdays than at other times. The half-hour and the rum and water running out together, Joe got up to go, and took me by the hand.

"Stop half a moment, Mr. Gargery," said the strange man. "I think I've got a bright new shilling somewhere in my pocket, and if I have, the boy shall have it."

He looked it out from a handful of small change, folded it in some crumpled paper, and gave it to me. "Yours!" said he. "Mind! Your own."

I thanked him, staring at him far beyond the bounds of good manners, and holding tight to Joe. He gave Joe good-night, and he gave Mr. Wopsle good-night (who went out with us), and he gave me only a look with his aiming eye—no, not a look, for he shut it up, but wonders may be done with an eye by hiding it.

On the way home, if I had been in a humor for talking, the talk must have been all on my side, for Mr. Wopsle parted from us at the door of the Jolly Bargemen, and Joe went all the way home with his mouth wide open, to rinse the rum out with as much air as possible. But I was in a manner stupefied by this turning up of my old misdeed and old acquaintance, and could think of nothing else.

My sister was not in a very bad temper when we presented ourselves in the kitchen, and Joe was encouraged by that unusual circumstance to tell her about the bright shilling. "A bad un, I'll be bound," said Mrs. Joe triumphantly, "or he wouldn't have given it to the boy! Let's look at it."

I took it out of the paper, and it proved to be a good one. "But what's this?" said Mrs. Joe, throwing down the shilling and catching up the paper. "Two One-Pound notes?"

Nothing less than two fat sweltering one-pound notes that seemed to have been on terms of the warmest intimacy with all the cattle-markets in the county. Joe caught up his hat again, and ran with them to the Jolly Bargemen to restore them to their owner. While he was gone, I sat down on my usual stool and looked vacantly at my sister, feeling pretty sure that the man would not be there.

Presently, Joe came back, saying that the man was gone, but that he, Joe, had left word at the Three Jolly Bargemen concerning the notes. Then my sister sealed them up in a piece of paper, and put them under some dried rose-leaves in an ornamental tea-pot on the top of a press in the state parlor. There they remained, a nightmare to me, many and many a night and day.

I had sadly broken sleep when I got to bed, through thinking of the strange man taking aim at me with his invisible gun, and of the guiltily coarse and common thing it was, to be on secret terms of conspiracy with convicts—a feature in my low career that I had previously forgotten. I was haunted by the file too. A dread possessed me that when I least expected it, the file would reappear. I coaxed myself to sleep by thinking of Miss Havisham's, next Wednesday; and in my sleep I saw the file coming at me out of a door, without seeing who held it, and I screamed myself awake.

CHAPTER 11

At the appointed time I returned to Miss Havisham's, and my hesitating ring at the gate brought out Estella. She locked it after admitting me, as she had done before, and again preceded me into the dark passage where her candle stood. She took no notice of me until she had the candle in her hand, when she looked over her shoulder, superciliously saying, "You are to come this way to-day," and took me to quite another part of the house.

The passage was a long one, and seemed to pervade the whole square basement of the Manor House. We traversed but one side of the square, however, and at the end of it she stopped, and put her candle down and opened a door. Here, the daylight reappeared, and I found myself in a small paved courtyard, the opposite side of which was formed by a detached dwelling-house, that looked as if it had once belonged to the manager or head clerk of the extinct brewery. There was a clock in the outer wall of this house. Like the clock in Miss Havisham's room, and like Miss Havisham's watch, it had stopped at twenty minutes to nine.

We went in at the door, which stood open, and into a gloomy room with a low ceiling, on the ground-floor at the back. There was some company in the room, and Estella said to me as she joined it, "You are to go and stand there boy, till you are wanted." "There", being the window, I crossed to it, and stood "there," in a very uncomfortable state of mind, looking out.

It opened to the ground, and looked into a most miserable corner of the neglected garden, upon a rank ruin of cabbage-stalks, and one box-tree that had been clipped round long ago, like a pudding, and had a new growth at the top of it, out of shape and of a different color, as if that part of the pudding had stuck to the saucepan and got burnt. This was my homely thought, as I contemplated the box-tree. There had been some light snow, overnight, and it lay nowhere else to my knowledge; but, it had not quite melted from the cold shadow of this bit of garden, and the wind caught it up in little eddies and threw it at the window, as if it pelted me for coming there.

I divined that my coming had stopped conversation in the room, and that its other occupants were looking at me. I could see nothing of the room except the shining of the fire in the window-glass, but I stiffened in all my joints with the consciousness that I was under close inspection.

There were three ladies in the room and one gentleman. Before I had been standing at the window five minutes, they somehow conveyed to me that they were all toadies and humbugs, but that each of them pretended not to know that the others were toadies and humbugs: because the admission that he or she did know it, would have made him or her out to be a toady and humbug.

They all had a listless and dreary air of waiting somebody's pleasure, and the most talkative of the ladies had to speak quite rigidly to repress a yawn. This lady, whose name was Camilla, very much reminded me of my sister, with the difference that she was older, and (as I found when I caught sight of her) of a blunter cast of features. Indeed, when I knew her better I began to think it was a Mercy she had any features at all, so very blank and high was the dead wall of her face.

"Poor dear soul!" said this lady, with an abruptness of manner quite my sister's. "Nobody's enemy but his own!"

"It would be much more commendable to be somebody else's enemy," said the gentleman; "far more natural."

"Cousin Raymond," observed another lady, "we are to love our neighbour."

"Sarah Pocket," returned Cousin Raymond, "if a man is not his own neighbour, who is?"

Miss Pocket laughed, and Camilla laughed and said (checking a yawn), "The idea!" But I thought they seemed to think it rather a good idea too. The other lady, who had not spoken yet, said gravely and emphatically, "*Very* true!"

"Poor soul!" Camilla presently went on (I knew they had all been looking at me in the mean time), "he is so very strange! Would anyone believe that when Tom's wife died, he actually could not be induced to see the importance of the children's having the deepest of trimmings to their mourning? 'Good Lord!' says he, 'Camilla, what can it signify so long as the poor bereaved little things are in black?' So like Matthew! The idea!"

"Good points in him, good points in him," said Cousin Raymond; "Heaven forbid I should deny good points in him; but he never had, and he never will have, any sense of the proprieties."

"You know I was obliged," said Camilla, "I was obliged to be firm. I said, 'It will not do, for the credit of the family.' I told him that, without deep trimmings, the family was disgraced. I cried about it from breakfast till dinner. I injured my digestion. And at last he flung out in his violent way, and said, with a D, 'Then do as you like.' Thank Goodness it will always be a consolation to me to know that I instantly went out in a pouring rain and bought the things."

"He paid for them, did he not?" asked Estella.

"It's not the question, my dear child, who paid for them," returned Camilla. "*I* bought them. And I shall often think of that with peace, when I wake up in the night."

The ringing of a distant bell, combined with the echoing of some cry or call along the passage by which I had come, interrupted the conversation and caused Estella to say to me, "Now, boy!" On my turning round, they all looked at me with the utmost contempt, and, as I went out, I heard Sarah Pocket say, "Well I am sure! What next!" and Camilla add, with indignation, "Was there ever such a fancy! The i-de-a!"

As we were going with our candle along the dark passage, Estella stopped all of a sudden, and, facing round, said in her taunting manner, with her face quite close to mine:

"Well?"

"Well, miss?" I answered, almost falling over her and checking myself.

She stood looking at me, and, of course, I stood looking at her.

"Am I pretty?"

"Yes; I think you are very pretty."

"Am I insulting?"

"Not so much so as you were last time," said I.

"Not so much so?"

"No."

She fired when she asked the last question, and she slapped my face with such force as she had, when I answered it.

"Now?" said she. "You little coarse monster, what do you think of me now?"

"I shall not tell you."

"Because you are going to tell up stairs. Is that it?"

"No," said I, "that's not it."

"Why don't you cry again, you little wretch?"

"Because I'll never cry for you again," said I. Which was, I suppose, as false a declaration as ever was made; for I was inwardly crying for her then, and I know what I know of the pain she cost me afterwards.

We went on our way up stairs after this episode; and, as we were going up, we met a gentleman groping his way down.

"Whom have we here?" asked the gentleman, stopping and looking at me.

"A boy," said Estella.

He was a burly man of an exceedingly dark complexion, with an exceedingly large head, and a corresponding large hand. He took my chin in his large hand and turned up my face to have a look at me by the light of the candle. He was prematurely bald on the top of his head, and had bushy black eyebrows that wouldn't lie down but stood up bristling. His eyes were set very deep in his head, and were disagreeably sharp and suspicious. He had a large watch-chain, and strong black dots where his beard and whiskers would have been if he had let them. He was nothing to me, and I could have had no foresight then, that he ever would be anything to me, but it happened that I had this opportunity of observing him well.

"Boy of the neighbourhood? Hey?" said he.

"Yes, sir," said I.

"How do *you* come here?"

"Miss Havisham sent for me, sir," I explained.

"Well! Behave yourself. I have a pretty large experience of boys, and you're a bad set of fellows. Now mind!" said he, biting the side of his great forefinger as he frowned at me, "you behave yourself!"

With those words, he released me—which I was glad of, for his hand smelt of scented soap—and went his way down stairs. I wondered whether he could be a doctor; but no, I thought; he couldn't be a doctor, or he would have a quieter and more persuasive manner. There was not much time to consider the subject, for we were soon in Miss Havisham's room, where she and everything else were just as I had left them. Estella left me standing near the door, and I stood there until Miss Havisham cast her eyes upon me from the dressing-table.

"So!" she said, without being startled or surprised: "the days have worn away, have they?"

"Yes, ma'am. To-day is—"

"There, there, there!" with the impatient movement of her fingers. "I don't want to know. Are you ready to play?"

I was obliged to answer in some confusion, "I don't think I am, ma'am."

"Not at cards again?" she demanded, with a searching look.

"Yes, ma'am; I could do that, if I was wanted."

"Since this house strikes you old and grave, boy," said Miss Havisham, impatiently, "and you are unwilling to play, are you willing to work?"

I could answer this inquiry with a better heart than I had been able to find for the other question, and I said I was quite willing.

"Then go into that opposite room," said she, pointing at the door behind me with her withered hand, "and wait there till I come."

I crossed the staircase landing, and entered the room she indicated. From that room, too, the daylight was completely excluded, and it had an airless smell that was oppressive. A fire had been lately kindled in the damp old-fashioned grate, and it was more disposed to go out than to burn up, and the reluctant smoke which hung in the room seemed colder than the clearer air—like our own marsh mist. Certain wintry branches of candles on the high chimney-piece faintly lighted the chamber; or it would be more expressive to say, faintly troubled its darkness. It was spacious, and I dare say had once been handsome, but every discernible thing in it was covered with dust and mould, and dropping to pieces. The most prominent object was a long table with a tablecloth spread on it, as if a feast had been in preparation when the house and the clocks all stopped together. An epergne or centre-piece of some kind was in the middle of this cloth; it was so heavily overhung with cobwebs that its form was quite undistinguishable; and, as I looked along the yellow expanse out of which I remember its seeming to grow, like a black fungus, I saw speckle-legged spiders with blotchy bodies running home to it, and running out from it, as if some circumstances of the greatest public importance had just transpired in the spider community.

I heard the mice too, rattling behind the panels, as if the same occurrence were important to their interests. But the black beetles took no notice of the agitation, and groped about the hearth in a ponderous elderly way, as if they were short-sighted and hard of hearing, and not on terms with one another.

These crawling things had fascinated my attention, and I was watching them from a distance, when Miss Havisham laid a hand upon my shoulder. In her other hand she had a crutch-headed stick on which she leaned, and she looked like the Witch of the place.

"This," said she, pointing to the long table with her stick, "is where I will be laid when I am dead. They shall come and look at me here."

With some vague misgiving that she might get upon the table then and there and die at once, the complete realization of the ghastly waxwork at the Fair, I shrank under her touch.

"What do you think that is?" she asked me, again pointing with her stick; "that, where those cobwebs are?"

"I can't guess what it is, ma'am."

"It's a great cake. A bride-cake. Mine!"

She looked all round the room in a glaring manner, and then said, leaning on me while her hand twitched my shoulder, "Come, come, come! Walk me, walk me!"

I made out from this, that the work I had to do, was to walk Miss Havisham round and round the room. Accordingly, I started at once, and she leaned upon my shoulder, and we went away at a pace that might have been an imitation (founded on my first impulse under that roof) of Mr. Pumblechook's chaise-cart.

She was not physically strong, and after a little time said, "Slower!" Still, we went at an impatient fitful speed, and as we went, she twitched the hand upon my shoulder, and worked her mouth, and led me to believe that we were going fast because her thoughts went fast. After a while she said, "Call Estella!" so I went out on the landing and roared that name as I had done on the previous occasion. When her light appeared, I returned to Miss Havisham, and we started away again round and round the room.

If only Estella had come to be a spectator of our proceedings, I should have felt sufficiently discontented; but as she brought with her the three ladies and the gentleman whom I had seen below, I didn't know what to do. In my politeness, I would have stopped; but Miss Havisham twitched my shoulder, and we posted on—with a shame-faced consciousness on my part that they would think it was all my doing.

"Dear Miss Havisham," said Miss Sarah Pocket. "How well you look!"

"I do not," returned Miss Havisham. "I am yellow skin and bone."

Camilla brightened when Miss Pocket met with this rebuff; and she murmured, as she plaintively contemplated Miss Havisham, "Poor dear soul! Certainly not to be expected to look well, poor thing. The idea!"

"And how are *you*?" said Miss Havisham to Camilla. As we were close to Camilla then, I would have stopped as a matter of course, only Miss Havisham wouldn't stop. We swept on, and I felt that I was highly obnoxious to Camilla.

"Thank you, Miss Havisham," she returned, "I am as well as can be expected."

"Why, what's the matter with you?" asked Miss Havisham, with exceeding sharpness.

"Nothing worth mentioning," replied Camilla. "I don't wish to make a display of my feelings, but I have habitually thought of you more in the night than I am quite equal to."

"Then don't think of me," retorted Miss Havisham.

"Very easily said!" remarked Camilla, amiably repressing a sob, while a hitch came into her upper lip, and her tears overflowed. "Raymond is a witness what ginger and sal volatile I am obliged to take in the night. Raymond is a witness what nervous jerkings I have in my legs. Chokings and nervous jerkings, however, are nothing new to me when I think with anxiety of those I love. If I could be less affectionate and sensitive, I should have a better digestion and an iron set of nerves. I am sure I wish it could be so. But as to not thinking of you in the night—The idea!" Here, a burst of tears.

The Raymond referred to, I understood to be the gentleman present, and him I understood to be Mr. Camilla. He came to the rescue at this point, and said in a consolatory and complimentary voice, "Camilla, my dear, it is well known that your family feelings are gradually undermining you to the extent of making one of your legs shorter than the other."

"I am not aware," observed the grave lady whose voice I had heard but once, "that to think of any person is to make a great claim upon that person, my dear."

Miss Sarah Pocket, whom I now saw to be a little dry, brown, corrugated old woman, with a small face that might have been made of walnut-shells, and a large mouth like a cat's without the whiskers, supported this position by saying, "No, indeed, my dear. Hem!"

"Thinking is easy enough," said the grave lady.

"What is easier, you know?" assented Miss Sarah Pocket.

"Oh, yes, yes!" cried Camilla, whose fermenting feelings appeared to rise from her legs to her bosom. "It's all very true! It's a weakness to be so affectionate, but I can't help it. No doubt my health would be much better if it was otherwise, still I wouldn't change my disposition if I could. It's the cause of much suffering, but it's a consolation to know I posses it, when I wake up in the night." Here another burst of feeling.

Miss Havisham and I had never stopped all this time, but

kept going round and round the room; now brushing against the skirts of the visitors, now giving them the whole length of the dismal chamber.

"There's Matthew!" said Camilla. "Never mixing with any natural ties, never coming here to see how Miss Havisham is! I have taken to the sofa with my staylace cut, and have lain there hours insensible, with my head over the side, and my hair all down, and my feet I don't know where—"

("Much higher than your head, my love," said Mr. Camilla.)

"I have gone off into that state, hours and hours, on account of Matthew's strange and inexplicable conduct, and nobody has thanked me."

"Really I must say I should think not!" interposed the grave lady.

"You see, my dear," added Miss Sarah Pocket (a blandly vicious personage), "the question to put to yourself is, who did you expect to thank you, my love?"

"Without expecting any thanks, or anything of the sort," resumed Camilla, "I have remained in that state, hours and hours, and Raymond is a witness of the extent to which I have choked, and what the total inefficacy of ginger has been, and I have been heard at the piano-forte tuner's across the street, where the poor mistaken children have even supposed it to be pigeons cooing at a distance—and now to be told—" Here Camilla put her hand to her throat, and began to be quite chemical as to the formation of new combinations there.

When this same Matthew was mentioned, Miss Havisham stopped me and herself, and stood looking at the speaker. This change had a great influence in bringing Camilla's chemistry to a sudden end.

"Matthew will come and see me at last," said Miss Havisham, sternly, "when I am laid on that table. That will be his place—there," striking the table with her stick, "at my head! And yours will be there! And your husband's there! And Sarah Pocket's there! And Georgiana's there! Now you all know where to take your stations when you come to feast upon me. And now go!"

At the mention of each name, she had struck the table with her stick in a new place. She now said, "Walk me, walk me!" and we went on again.

"I suppose there's nothing to be done," exclaimed Camilla, "but comply and depart. It's something to have seen the object of one's love and duty for even so short a time. I shall think of it with a melancholy satisfaction when I wake up in the night. I wish Matthew could have that comfort, but he sets it at defiance. I am determined not to make a display of my feelings, but it's very hard to be told one wants to feast on one's relations—as if one was a Giant—and to be told to go. The bare idea!"

Mr. Camilla interposing, as Mrs. Camilla laid her hand upon her heaving bosom, that lady assumed an unnatural fortitude of manner which I supposed to be expressive of an intention to drop and choke when out of view, and kissing her hand to Miss Havisham, was escorted forth. Sarah Pocket and Georgiana contended who should remain last; but Sarah was too knowing to be outdone, and ambled round Georgiana with that artful slipperiness that the latter was obliged to take precedence. Sarah Pocket then made her separate effect of departing with, "Bless you, Miss Havisham dear!" and with a smile of forgiving pity on her walnut-shell countenance for the weaknesses of the rest.

While Estella was away lighting them down, Miss Havisham still walked with her hand on my shoulder, but more and more slowly. At last she stopped before the fire, and said, after muttering and looking at it some seconds:

"This is my birthday, Pip."

I was going to wish her many happy returns, when she lifted her stick.

"I don't suffer it to be spoken of. I don't suffer those who were here just now, or any one to speak of it. They come here on the day, but they dare not refer to it."

Of course *I* made no further effort to refer to it.

"On this day of the year, long before you were born, this heap of decay," stabbing with her crutched stick at the pile of cobwebs on the table, but not touching it, "was brought here. It and I have worn away together. The mice have gnawed at it, and sharper teeth than teeth of mice have gnawed at me."

She held the head of her stick against her heart as she stood looking at the table; she in her once white dress, all yellow and withered; the once white cloth all yellow and withered; everything around in a state to crumble under a touch.

"When the ruin is complete," said she, with a ghastly look, "and when they lay me dead, in my bride's dress on the bride's table—which shall be done, and which will be the finished curse upon him—so much the better if it is done on this day!"

She stood looking at the table as if she stood looking at her own figure lying there. I remained quiet. Estella returned, and she too remained quiet. It seemed to me that we continued thus for a long time. In the heavy air of the room, and the heavy darkness that brooded in its remoter corners, I even had an alarming fancy that Estella and I might presently begin to decay.

At length, not coming out of her distraught state by degrees, but in an instant, Miss Havisham said, "Let me see you two play cards; why have you not begun?" With that, we returned to her room, and sat down as before; I was beggared, as before; and again, as before, Miss Havisham watched us all the time, directed my attention to Estella's beauty, and made me notice it the more by trying her jewels on Estella's breast and hair.

Estella, for her part, likewise treated me as before, except that she did not condescend to speak. When we had played some half-dozen games, a day was appointed for my return, and I was taken down into the yard to be fed in the former dog-like manner. There, too, I was again left to wander about as I liked.

It is not much to the purpose whether a gate in that garden wall which I had scrambled up to peep over on the last occasion was, on that last occasion, open or shut. Enough that I saw no gate then, and that I saw one now. As it stood open, and as I knew that Estella had let the visitors out—for, she had returned with the keys in her hand—I strolled into the garden, and strolled all over it. It was quite a wilderness, and there were old melon-frames and cucumber-frames in it, which seemed in their decline to have produced a spontaneous growth of weak attempts at pieces of old hats and boots, with now and then a weedy offshoot into the likeness of a battered saucepan.

When I had exhausted the garden and a greenhouse with nothing in it but a fallen-down grape-vine and some bottles, I found myself in the dismal corner upon which I had looked out of the window. Never questioning for a moment that the house was now empty, I looked in at another window, and found myself, to my great surprise, exchanging a broad stare with a pale young gentleman with red eyelids and light hair.

This pale young gentleman quickly disappeared, and reappeared beside me. He had been at his books when I had found myself staring at him, and I now saw that he was inky.

"Halloa!" said he, "young fellow!"

Halloa being a general observation which I had usually observed to be best answered by itself, *I* said, "Halloa!" politely omitting young fellow.

"Who let *you* in?" said he.

"Miss Estella."

"Who gave you leave to prowl about?"

"Miss Estella."

"Come and fight," said the pale young gentleman.

What could I do but follow him? I have often asked myself the question since; but what else could I do? His manner was so final, and I was so astonished, that I followed where he led, as if I had been under a spell.

"Stop a minute, though," he said, wheeling round before we had gone many paces. "I ought to give you a reason for fighting, too. There it is!" In a most irritating manner he instantly slapped his hands against one another, daintily flung one of his legs up behind him, pulled my hair, slapped his hands again, dipped his head, and butted it into my stomach.

The bull-like proceeding last mentioned, besides that it was unquestionably to be regarded in the light of a liberty, was particularly disagreeable just after bread and meat. I therefore hit out at him and was going to hit out again, when he said, "Aha! Would you?" and began dancing backwards and forwards in a manner quite unparalleled within my limited experience.

"Laws of the game!" said he. Here, he skipped from his left leg on to his right. "Regular rules!" Here, he skipped from his right leg on to his left. "Come to the ground, and go through the preliminaries!" Here, he dodged backwards and forwards, and did all sorts of things while I looked helplessly at him.

I was secretly afraid of him when I saw him so dexterous; but I felt morally and physically convinced that his light head of hair could have had no business in the pit of my stomach, and that I had a right to consider it irrelevant when so obtruded on my attention. Therefore, I followed him without a word, to a retired nook of the garden, formed by the junction of two walls and screened by some rubbish. On his asking me if I was satisfied with the ground, and on my replying Yes, he begged my leave to absent himself for a moment, and quickly returned with a bottle of water and a sponge dipped in vinegar. "Available for both," he said, placing these against the wall. And then fell to pulling off, not only his jacket and waistcoat, but his shirt too, in a manner at once light-hearted, business-like, and bloodthirsty.

Although he did not look very healthy—having pimples

on his face, and a breaking out at his mouth—these dreadful preparations quite appalled me. I judged him to be about my own age, but he was much taller, and he had a way of spinning himself about that was full of appearance. For the rest, he was a young gentleman in a gray suit (when not denuded for battle), with his elbows, knees, wrists, and heels considerably in advance of the rest of him as to development.

My heart failed me when I saw him squaring at me with every demonstration of mechanical nicety, and eyeing my anatomy as if he were minutely choosing his bone. I never have been so surprised in my life, as I was when I let out the first blow, and saw him lying on his back, looking up at me with a bloody nose and his face exceedingly fore-shortened.

But, he was on his feet directly, and after sponging himself with a great show of dexterity began squaring again. The second greatest surprise I have ever had in my life was seeing him on his back again, looking up at me out of a black eye.

His spirit inspired me with great respect. He seemed to have no strength, and he never once hit me hard, and he was always knocked down; but he would be up again in a moment, sponging himself or drinking out of the water-bottle, with the greatest satisfaction in seconding himself according to form, and then came at me with an air and a show that made me believe he really was going to do for me at last. He got heavily bruised, for I am sorry to record that the more I hit him, the harder I hit him; but he came up again and again and again, until at last he got a bad fall with the back of his head against the wall. Even after that crisis in our affairs, he got up and turned round and round confusedly a few times, not knowing where I was; but finally went on his knees to his sponge and threw it up: at the same time panting out, "That means you have won."

He seemed so brave and innocent, that although I had not proposed the contest, I felt but a gloomy satisfaction in my victory. Indeed, I go so far as to hope that I regarded myself while dressing as a species of savage young wolf or other wild beast. However, I got dressed, darkly wiping my sanguinary face at intervals, and I said, "Can I help you?" and he said "No thankee," and I said "Good afternoon," and *he* said "Same to you."

When I got into the court-yard, I found Estella waiting with the keys. But she neither asked me where I had been, nor why I had kept her waiting; and there was a bright flush upon her face, as though something had happened to delight her. Instead of going straight to the gate, too, she stepped back into the passage, and beckoned me.

"Come here! You may kiss me, if you like."

I kissed her cheek as she turned it to me. I think I would have gone through a great deal to kiss her cheek. But I felt that the kiss was given to the coarse common boy as a piece of money might have been, and that it was worth nothing.

What with the birthday visitors, and what with the cards, and what with the fight, my stay had lasted so long, that when I neared home the light on the spit of sand off the point on the marshes was gleaming against a black night-sky, and Joe's furnace was flinging a path of fire across the road.

CHAPTER 12

My mind grew very uneasy on the subject of the pale young gentleman. The more I thought of the fight, and recalled the pale young gentleman on his back in various stages of puffy and incrimsoned countenance, the more certain it appeared that something would be done to me. I felt that the pale young gentleman's blood was on my head, and that the Law would avenge it. Without having any definite idea of the penalties I had incurred, it was clear to me that village boys could not go stalking about the country, ravaging the houses of gentlefolks and pitching into the studious youth of England, without laying themselves open to severe punishment. For some days, I even kept close at home, and looked out at the kitchen door with the greatest caution and trepidation before going on an errand, lest the officers of the County Jail should pounce upon me. The pale young gentleman's nose had stained my trousers, and I tried to wash out that evidence of my guilt in the dead of night. I had cut my knuckles against the pale young gentleman's teeth, and I twisted my imagination into a thousand tangles, as I devised incredible ways of accounting for that damnatory circumstance when I should be haled before the judges.

When the day came round for my return to the scene of the deed of violence, my terrors reached their height. Whether myrmidons of Justice, specially sent down from London, would be lying in ambush behind the gate? Whether Miss Havisham, preferring to take personal vengeance for an outrage done to her house, might rise in those grave-clothes of hers, draw a pistol, and shoot me dead? Whether suborned boys—a numerous band of mercenaries—might be engaged to fall upon me in the brewery, and cuff me until I was no more? It was high testimony to my confidence in the spirit of the pale young gentleman, that I never imagined *him* accessory to these retaliations; they always came into my mind as the acts of injudicious relatives of his, goaded on by the state of his visage and an indignant sympathy with the family features.

However, go to Miss Havisham's I must, and go I did. And behold! nothing came of the late struggle. It was not alluded to in any way, and no pale young gentleman was to be discovered on the premises. I found the same gate open, and I explored the garden, and even looked in at the windows of the detached house; but my view was suddenly stopped by the closed shutters within, and all was lifeless. Only in the corner where the combat had taken place could I detect any evidence of the young gentleman's existence. There were traces of his gore in that spot, and I covered them with gardenmould from the eye of man.

On the broad landing between Miss Havisham's own room and that other room in which the long table was laid out, I saw a garden-chair—a light chair on wheels, that you pushed from behind. It had been placed there since my last visit, and I entered, that same day, on a regular occupation of pushing Miss Havisham in this chair (when she was tired of walking with her hand upon my shoulder) round her own room, and across the landing, and round the other room. Over and over and over again, we would make these journeys, and sometimes they would last as long as three hours at a stretch. I insensibly fall into a general mention of these journeys as numerous, because it was at once settled that I should return every alternate day at noon for these purposes, and because I am now going to sum up a period of at least eight or ten months.

As we began to be more used to one another, Miss Havisham talked more to me, and asked me such questions as what had I learnt and what was I going to be? I told her I was going to be apprenticed to Joe, I believed; and I enlarged upon my knowing nothing and wanting to know everything, in the hope that she might offer some help towards that desirable end. But she did not; on the contrary, she seemed to prefer my being ignorant. Neither did she ever give me any money—or anything but my daily dinner—nor ever stipulate that I should be paid for my services.

Estella was always about, and always let me in and out, but never told me I might kiss her again. Sometimes, she would coldly tolerate me; sometimes, she would condescend to me; sometimes, she would be quite familiar with me; sometimes, she would tell me energetically that she hated me. Miss Havisham would often ask me in a whisper, or when we were alone, "Does she grow prettier and prettier, Pip?" And when I said yes (for indeed she did), would seem to enjoy it greedily. Also, when we played at cards Miss Havisham would look on, with a miserly relish of Estella's moods, whatever they were. And sometimes, when her moods were so many and so contradictory of one another that I was puzzled what to say or do, Miss Havisham would embrace her with lavish fondness, murmuring something in her ear that sounded like "Break their hearts my pride and hope, break their hearts and have no mercy!"

There was a song Joe used to hum fragments of at the forge, of which the burden was Old Clem. This was not a very ceremonious way of rendering homage to a patron saint; but I believe Old Clem stood in that relation towards smiths. It was a song that imitated the measure of beating upon iron, and was a mere lyrical excuse for the introduction of Old Clem's respected name. Thus, you were to hammer boys round— Old Clem! With a thump and a sound—Old Clem! Beat it out, beat it out—Old Clem! With a clink for the stout—Old Clem! Blow the fire, blow the fire—Old Clem! Roaring dryer, soaring higher—Old Clem! One day soon after the appearance of the chair, Miss Havisham suddenly saying to me, with the impatient movement of her fingers, "There, there, there! Sing!" I was surprised into crooning this ditty as I pushed her over the floor. It happened so to catch her fancy that she took it up in a low brooding voice as if she were singing in her sleep. After that, it became customary with us to have it as we moved about, and Estella would often join in; though the whole strain was so subdued, even when there were three of us, that it made less noise in the grim old house than the lightest breath of wind.

What could I become with these surroundings? How could my character fail to be influenced by them? Is it to be wondered at if my thoughts were dazed, as my eyes were, when I came out into the natural light from the misty yellow rooms?

Perhaps I might have told Joe about the pale young gentleman, if I had not previously been betrayed into those enormous inventions to which I had confessed. Under the circumstances, I felt that Joe could hardly fail to discern in the pale young gentleman, an appropriate passenger to be put into the black velvet coach; therefore, I said nothing of him. Besides, that shrinking from having Miss Havisham and Estella discussed, which had come upon me in the beginning, grew much more potent as time went on. I reposed complete confidence in no one but Biddy; but I told poor Biddy everything. Why it came natural to me to do so, and why Biddy had a deep concern in everything I told her, I did not know then, though I think I know now.

Meanwhile, councils went on in the kitchen at home, fraught with almost insupportable aggravation to my exasperated spirit. That ass, Pumblechook, used often to come over of a night for the purpose of discussing my prospects with my sister; and I really do believe (to this hour with less penitence than I ought to feel), that if these hands could have taken a linchpin out of his chaise-cart, they would have done it. The miserable man was a man of that confined stolidity of mind, that he could not discuss my prospects without having me before him—as it were, to operate upon—and he would drag me up from my stool (usually by the collar) where I was quiet in a corner, and, putting me before the fire as if I were going to be cooked, would begin by saying, "Now, Mum, here is this boy! Here is this boy which you brought up by hand. Hold up your head, boy, and be forever grateful unto them which so did do. Now, Mum, with respections to this boy!" And then he would rumple my hair the wrong way—which from my earliest remembrance, as already hinted, I have in my soul denied the right of any fellow-creature to do—and would hold me before him by the sleeve: a spectacle of imbecility only to be equalled by himself.

Then, he and my sister would pair off in such nonsensical speculations about Miss Havisham, and about what she would do with me and for me, that I used to want—quite painfully— to burst into spiteful tears, fly at Pumblechook, and pummel him all over. In these dialogues, my sister spoke to me as if she were morally wrenching one of my teeth out at every reference; while Pumblechook himself, self-constituted my patron, would sit supervising me with a depreciatory eye, like the architect of my fortunes who thought himself engaged on a very unremunerative job.

In these discussions, Joe bore no part. But he was often talked at, while they were in progress, by reason of Mrs. Joe's perceiving that he was not favorable to my being taken from the forge. I was fully old enough now to be apprenticed to Joe; and when Joe sat with the poker on his knees thoughtfully raking out the ashes between the lower bars, my sister would so distinctly construe that innocent action into opposition on his part, that she would dive at him, take the poker out of his hands, shake him, and put it away. There was a most irritating end to every one of these debates. All in a moment, with nothing to lead up to it, my sister would stop herself in a yawn, and catching sight of me as it were incidentally, would swoop upon me with, "Come! there's enough of *you! You* get along to bed; *you've* given trouble enough for one night, I hope!" As if I had besought them as a favor to bother my life out.

We went on in this way for a long time, and it seemed likely that we should continue to go on in this way for a long time, when one day Miss Havisham stopped short as she and I were walking, she leaning on my shoulder; and said with some displeasure:

"You are growing tall, Pip!"

I thought it best to hint, through the medium of a meditative look, that this might be occasioned by circumstances over which I had no control.

She said no more at the time; but she presently stopped and looked at me again; and presently again; and after that, looked frowning and moody. On the next day of my attendance, when our usual exercise was over, and I had landed her at her dressing-table, she stayed me with a movement of her impatient fingers:

"Tell me the name again of that blacksmith of yours."

"Joe Gargery, ma'am."

"Meaning the master you were to be apprenticed to?"

"Yes, Miss Havisham."

"You had better be apprenticed at once. Would Gargery come here with you, and bring your indentures, do you think?"

I signified that I had no doubt he would take it as an honor to be asked.

"Then let him come."

"At any particular time, Miss Havisham?"

"There, there! I know nothing about times. Let him come soon, and come along with you."

When I got home at night, and delivered this message for Joe, my sister "went on the Rampage," in a more alarming degree than at any previous period. She asked me and Joe whether we supposed she was door-mats under our feet, and how we dared to use her so, and what company we graciously thought she was fit for? When she had exhausted a torrent of such inquiries, she threw a candlestick at Joe, burst into a loud sobbing, got out the dustpan—which was always a very bad sign—put on her coarse apron, and began cleaning up to a terrible extent. Not satisfied with a dry cleaning, she took to a pail and scrubbing-brush, and cleaned us out of house and home, so that we stood shivering in the back-yard. It was ten o'clock at night before we ventured to creep in again, and then she asked Joe why he hadn't married a Negress Slave at once? Joe offered no answer, poor fellow, but stood feeling his whisker and looking dejectedly at me, as if he thought it really might have been a better speculation.

CHAPTER 13

It was a trial to my feelings, on the next day but one, to see Joe arraying himself in his Sunday clothes to accompany me to Miss Havisham's. However, as he thought his court-suit necessary to the occasion, it was not for me to tell him that he looked far better in his working-dress; the rather, because I knew he made himself so dreadfully uncomfortable, entirely on my account, and that it was for me he pulled up his shirt-collar so very high behind, that it made the hair on the crown of his head stand up like a tuft of feathers.

At breakfast-time my sister declared her intention of going to town with us, and being left at Uncle Pumblechook's and called for "when we had done with our fine ladies"—a way of putting the case, from which Joe appeared inclined to augur the worst. The forge was shut up for the day, and Joe inscribed in chalk upon the door (as it was his custom to do on the very rare occasions when he was not at work) the monosyllable HOUT, accompanied by a sketch of an arrow supposed to be flying in the direction he had taken.

We walked to town, my sister leading the way in a very large beaver bonnet, and carrying a basket like the Great Seal of England in plaited straw, a pair of pattens, a spare shawl, and an umbrella, though it was a fine bright day. I am not quite clear whether these articles were carried penitentially or ostentatiously; but I rather think they were displayed as articles of property—much as Cleopatra or any other sovereign lady on the Rampage might exhibit her wealth in a pageant or procession.

When we came to Pumblechook's, my sister bounced in

and left us. As it was almost noon, Joe and I held straight on to Miss Havisham's house. Estella opened the gate as usual, and, the moment she appeared, Joe took his hat off and stood weighing it by the brim in both his hands; as if he had some urgent reason in his mind for being particular to half a quarter of an ounce.

Estella took no notice of either of us, but led us the way that I knew so well. I followed next to her, and Joe came last. When I looked back at Joe in the long passage, he was still weighing his hat with the greatest care, and was coming after us in long strides on the tips of his toes.

Estella told me we were both to go in, so I took Joe by the coat-cuff and conducted him into Miss Havisham's presence. She was seated at her dressing-table, and looked round at us immediately.

"Oh!" said she to Joe. "You are the husband of the sister of this boy?"

I could hardly have imagined dear old Joe looking so unlike himself or so like some extraordinary bird; standing as he did speechless, with his tuft of feathers ruffled, and his mouth open as if he wanted a worm.

"You are the husband," repeated Miss Havisham, "of the sister of this boy?"

It was very aggravating; but, throughout the interview, Joe persisted in addressing Me instead of Miss Havisham.

"Which I meantersay, Pip," Joe now observed in a manner that was at once expressive of forcible argumentation, strict confidence, and great politeness, "as I hup and married your sister, and I were at the time what you might call (if you was anyways inclined) a single man."

"Well!" said Miss Havisham. "And you have reared the boy, with the intention of taking him for your apprentice; is that so, Mr. Gargery?"

"You know, Pip," replied Joe, "as you and me were ever

friends, and it were looked for'ard to betwixt us, as being calc'lated to lead to larks. Not but what, Pip, if you had ever made objections to the business—such as its being open to black and sut, or such-like—not but what they would have been attended to, don't you see?"

"Has the boy," said Miss Havisham, "ever made any objection? Does he like the trade?"

"Which it is well beknown to yourself, Pip," returned Joe, strengthening his former mixture of argumentation, confidence, and politeness, "that it were the wish of your own hart." (I saw the idea suddenly break upon him that he would adapt his epitaph to the occasion, before he went on to say) "And there weren't no objection on your part, and Pip it were the great wish of your hart!"

It was quite in vain for me to endeavor to make him sensible that he ought to speak to Miss Havisham. The more I made faces and gestures to him to do it, the more confidential, argumentative, and polite, he persisted in being to Me.

"Have you brought his indentures with you?" asked Miss Havisham.

"Well, Pip, you know," replied Joe, as if that were a little unreasonable, "you yourself see me put 'em in my 'at, and therefore you know as they are here." With which he took them out, and gave them, not to Miss Havisham, but to me. I am afraid I was ashamed of the dear good fellow—I *know* I was ashamed of him—when I saw that Estella stood at the back of Miss Havisham's chair, and that her eyes laughed mischievously. I took the indentures out of his hand and gave them to Miss Havisham.

"You expected," said Miss Havisham, as she looked them over, "no premium with the boy?"

"Joe!" I remonstrated, for he made no reply at all. "Why don't you answer—"

"Pip," returned Joe, cutting me short as if he were hurt,

"which I meantersay that were not a question requiring a answer betwixt yourself and me, and which you know the answer to be full well No. You know it to be No, Pip, and wherefore should I say it?"

Miss Havisham glanced at him as if she understood what he really was better than I had thought possible, seeing what he was there; and took up a little bag from the table beside her.

"Pip has earned a premium here," she said, "and here it is. There are five-and-twenty guineas in this bag. Give it to your master, Pip."

As if he were absolutely out of his mind with the wonder awakened in him by her strange figure and the strange room, Joe, even at this pass, persisted in addressing me.

"This is wery liberal on your part, Pip," said Joe, "and it is as such received and grateful welcome, though never looked for, far nor near, nor nowheres. And now, old chap," said Joe, conveying to me a sensation, first of burning and then of freezing, for I felt as if that familiar expression were applied to Miss Havisham— "and now, old chap, may we do our duty! May you and me do our duty, both on us, by one and another, and by them which your liberal present-have-conweyed-to be-for the satisfaction of mind-of-them as never-" here Joe showed that he felt he had fallen into frightful difficulties, until he triumphantly rescued himself with the words, "and from myself far be it!" These words had such a round and convincing sound for him that he said them twice.

"Good by, Pip!" said Miss Havisham. "Let them out, Estella."

"Am I to come again, Miss Havisham?" I asked.

"No. Gargery is your master now. Gargery! One word!"

Thus calling him back as I went out of the door, I heard her say to Joe in a distinct emphatic voice, "The boy has been a good boy here, and that is his reward. Of course, as an honest man, you will expect no other and no more."

How Joe got out of the room, I have never been able to determine; but I know that when he did get out he was steadily proceeding up-stairs instead of coming down, and was deaf to all remonstrances until I went after him and laid hold of him. In another minute we were outside the gate, and it was locked, and Estella was gone.

When we stood in the daylight alone again, Joe backed up against a wall, and said to me, "Astonishing!" And there he remained so long saying, "Astonishing" at intervals, so often, that I began to think his senses were never coming back. At length he prolonged his remark into "Pip, I do assure *you* this is as-ton-ishing!" and so, by degrees, became conversational and able to walk away.

I have reason to think that Joe's intellects were brightened by the encounter they had passed through, and that on our way to Pumblechook's he invented a subtle and deep design. My reason is to be found in what took place in Mr. Pumblechook's parlor: where, on our presenting ourselves, my sister sat in conference with that detested seedsman.

"Well?" cried my sister, addressing us both at once. "And what's happened to *you*? I wonder you condescend to come back to such poor society as this, I am sure I do!"

"Miss Havisham," said Joe, with a fixed look at me, like an effort of remembrance, "made it wery partick'ler that we should give her—were it compliments or respects, Pip?"

"Compliments," I said.

"Which that were my own belief," answered Joe; "her compliments to Mrs. J. Gargery—"

"Much good they'll do me!" observed my sister; but rather gratified too.

"And wishing," pursued Joe, with another fixed look at me, like another effort of remembrance, "that the state of Miss Havisham's elth were sitch as would have—allowed, were it, Pip?"

"Of her having the pleasure," I added.

"Of ladies' company," said Joe. And drew a long breath.

"Well!" cried my sister, with a mollified glance at Mr. Pumblechook. "She might have had the politeness to send that message at first, but it's better late than never. And what did she give young Rantipole here?"

"She giv' him," said Joe, "nothing."

Mrs. Joe was going to break out, but Joe went on.

"What she giv'," said Joe, "she giv' to his friends. 'And by his friends,' were her explanation, 'I mean into the hands of his sister Mrs. J. Gargery.' Them were her words; 'Mrs. J. Gargery.' She mayn't have know'd," added Joe, with an appearance of reflection, "whether it were Joe, or Jorge."

My sister looked at Pumblechook: who smoothed the elbows of his wooden arm-chair, and nodded at her and at the fire, as if he had known all about it beforehand.

"And how much have you got?" asked my sister, laughing. Positively laughing!

"What would present company say to ten pound?" demanded Joe.

"They'd say," returned my sister, curtly, "pretty well. Not too much, but pretty well."

"It's more than that, then," said Joe.

That fearful Impostor, Pumblechook, immediately nodded, and said, as he rubbed the arms of his chair, "It's more than that, Mum."

"Why, you don't mean to say—" began my sister.

"Yes I do, Mum," said Pumblechook; "but wait a bit. Go on, Joseph. Good in you! Go on!"

"What would present company say," proceeded Joe, "to twenty pound?"

"Handsome would be the word," returned my sister.

"Well, then," said Joe, "It's more than twenty pound."

That abject hypocrite, Pumblechook, nodded again, and

said, with a patronizing laugh, "It's more than that, Mum. Good again! Follow her up, Joseph!"

"Then to make an end of it," said Joe, delightedly handing the bag to my sister; "it's five-and-twenty pound."

"It's five-and-twenty pound, Mum," echoed that basest of swindlers, Pumblechook, rising to shake hands with her; "and it's no more than your merits (as I said when my opinion was asked), and I wish you joy of the money!"

If the villain had stopped here, his case would have been sufficiently awful, but he blackened his guilt by proceeding to take me into custody, with a right of patronage that left all his former criminality far behind.

"Now you see, Joseph and wife," said Pumblechook, as he took me by the arm above the elbow, "I am one of them that always go right through with what they've begun. This boy must be bound, out of hand. That's *my* way. Bound out of hand."

"Goodness knows, Uncle Pumblechook," said my sister (grasping the money), "we're deeply beholden to you."

"Never mind me, Mum," returned that diabolical cornchandler. "A pleasure's a pleasure all the world over. But this boy, you know; we must have him bound. I said I'd see to it—to tell you the truth."

The Justices were sitting in the Town Hall near at hand, and we at once went over to have me bound apprentice to Joe in the Magisterial presence. I say we went over, but I was pushed over by Pumblechook, exactly as if I had that moment picked a pocket or fired a rick; indeed, it was the general impression in Court that I had been taken red-handed; for, as Pumblechook shoved me before him through the crowd, I heard some people say, "What's he done?" and others, "He's a young 'un, too, but looks bad, don't he?" One person of mild and benevolent aspect even gave me a tract ornamented with a woodcut of a malevolent young man fitted up with a perfect sausage-shop of fetters, and entitled TO BE READ IN MY CELL.

The Hall was a queer place, I thought, with higher pews in it than a church—and with people hanging over the pews looking on—and with mighty Justices (one with a powdered head) leaning back in chairs, with folded arms, or taking snuff, or going to sleep, or writing, or reading the newspapers—and with some shining black portraits on the walls, which my unartistic eye regarded as a composition of hardbake and sticking-plaster. Here, in a corner my indentures were duly signed and attested, and I was "bound"; Mr. Pumblechook holding me all the while as if we had looked in on our way to the scaffold, to have those little preliminaries disposed of.

When we had come out again, and had got rid of the boys who had been put into great spirits by the expectation of seeing me publicly tortured, and who were much disappointed to find that my friends were merely rallying round me, we went back to Pumblechook's. And there my sister became so excited by the twenty-five guineas, that nothing would serve her but we must have a dinner out of that windfall at the Blue Boar, and that Pumblechook must go over in his chaise-cart, and bring the Hubbles and Mr. Wopsle.

It was agreed to be done; and a most melancholy day I passed. For, it inscrutably appeared to stand to reason, in the minds of the whole company, that I was an excrescence on the entertainment. And to make it worse, they all asked me from time to time,n short, whenever they had nothing else to do,why I didn't enjoy myself? And what could I possibly do then, but say I was enjoying myself,when I wasn't!

However, they were grown up and had their own way, and they made the most of it. That swindling Pumblechook, exalted into the beneficent contriver of the whole occasion, actually took the top of the table; and, when he addressed them on the subject of my being bound, and had fiendishly congratulated them on my being liable to imprisonment if I played at cards, drank strong liquors, kept late hours or bad company, or indulged in other vagaries which the form of my indentures appeared to contemplate as next to inevitable, he placed me standing on a chair beside him to illustrate his remarks.

My only other remembrances of the great festival are, That they wouldn't let me go to sleep, but whenever they saw me dropping off, woke me up and told me to enjoy myself. That, rather late in the evening Mr. Wopsle gave us Collins's ode, and threw his bloodstained sword in thunder down, with such effect, that a waiter came in and said, "The Commercials underneath sent up their compliments, and it wasn't the Tumblers' Arms." That, they were all in excellent spirits on the road home, and sang, O Lady Fair! Mr. Wopsle taking the bass, and asserting with a tremendously strong voice (in reply to the inquisitive bore who leads that piece of music in a most impertinent manner, by wanting to know all about everybody's private affairs) that *he* was the man with his white locks flowing, and that he was upon the whole the weakest pilgrim going.

Finally, I remember that when I got into my little bedroom, I was truly wretched, and had a strong conviction on me that I should never like Joe's trade. I had liked it once, but once was not now.

CHAPTER 14

It is a most miserable thing to feel ashamed of home. There may be black ingratitude in the thing, and the punishment may be retributive and well deserved; but that it is a miserable thing, I can testify.

Home had never been a very pleasant place to me, because of my sister's temper. But, Joe had sanctified it, and I had believed in it. I had believed in the best parlor as a most elegant saloon; I had believed in the front door, as a mysterious portal of the Temple of State whose solemn opening was attended with a sacrifice of roast fowls; I had believed in the kitchen as a chaste though not magnificent apartment; I had believed in the forge as the glowing road to manhood and independence. Within a single year all this was changed. Now it was all coarse and common, and I would not have had Miss Havisham and Estella see it on any account.

How much of my ungracious condition of mind may have been my own fault, how much Miss Havisham's, how much my sister's, is now of no moment to me or to any one. The change was made in me; the thing was done. Well or ill done, excusably or inexcusably, it was done.

Once, it had seemed to me that when I should at last roll up my shirt-sleeves and go into the forge, Joe's 'prentice, I should be distinguished and happy. Now the reality was in my hold, I only felt that I was dusty with the dust of small-coal, and that I had a weight upon my daily remembrance to which the anvil was a feather. There have been occasions in my later life (I suppose as in most lives) when I have felt for a time as if a thick curtain had fallen on all its interest and romance, to shut me out from anything save dull endurance any more. Never has that curtain dropped so heavy and blank, as when my way in life lay stretched out straight before me through the newly entered road of apprenticeship to Joe.

I remember that at a later period of my "time," I used to stand about the churchyard on Sunday evenings when night was falling, comparing my own perspective with the windy marsh view, and making out some likeness between them by thinking how flat and low both were, and how on both there came an unknown way and a dark mist and then the sea. I was quite as dejected on the first working-day of my apprenticeship as in that after-time; but I am glad to know that I never breathed a murmur to Joe while my indentures lasted. It is about the only thing I *am* glad to know of myself in that connection.

For, though it includes what I proceed to add, all the merit of what I proceed to add was Joe's. It was not because I was faithful, but because Joe was faithful, that I never ran away and went for a soldier or a sailor. It was not because I had a strong sense of the virtue of industry, but because Joe had a strong sense of the virtue of industry, that I worked with tolerable zeal against the grain. It is not possible to know how far the influence of any amiable honest-hearted duty-doing man flies out into the world; but it is very possible to know how it has touched one's self in going by, and I know right well that any good that intermixed itself with my apprenticeship came of plain contented Joe, and not of restlessly aspiring discontented me.

What I wanted, who can say? How can *I* say, when I never knew? What I dreaded was, that in some unlucky hour I, being at my grimiest and commonest, should lift up my eyes and see Estella looking in at one of the wooden windows of the forge. I was haunted by the fear that she would, sooner or later, find me out, with a black face and hands, doing the coarsest part of my work, and would exult over me and despise me. Often after dark, when I was pulling the bellows for Joe, and we were singing Old Clem, and when the thought how we used to sing it at Miss Havisham's would seem to show me Estella's face in the fire, with her pretty hair fluttering in the wind and her eyes scorning me,—often at such a time I would look towards those panels of black night in the wall which the wooden windows then were, and would fancy that I saw her just drawing her face away, and would believe that she had come at last.

After that, when we went in to supper, the place and the meal would have a more homely look than ever, and I would feel more ashamed of home than ever, in my own ungracious breast.

CHAPTER 15

As I was getting too big for Mr. Wopsle's great-aunt's room, my education under that preposterous female terminated. Not, however, until Biddy had imparted to me everything she knew, from the little catalogue of prices, to a comic song she had once bought for a half-penny. Although the only coherent part of the latter piece of literature were the opening lines.

> When I went to Lunnon town sirs,
> Too rul loo rul
> Too rul loo rul
> Wasn't I done very brown sirs,
> Too rul loo rul
> Too rul loo rul

—still, in my desire to be wiser, I got this composition by heart with the utmost gravity; nor do I recollect that I questioned its merit, except that I thought (as I still do) the amount of Too rul somewhat in excess of the poetry. In my hunger for information, I made proposals to Mr. Wopsle to bestow some intellectual crumbs upon me, with which he kindly complied. As it turned out, however, that he only wanted me for a dramatic lay-figure, to be contradicted and embraced and wept over and bullied and clutched and stabbed and knocked about in a variety of ways, I soon declined that course of instruction; though not until Mr. Wopsle in his poetic fury had severely mauled me.

Whatever I acquired, I tried to impart to Joe. This statement sounds so well, that I cannot in my conscience let it pass unexplained. I wanted to make Joe less ignorant and common, that he might be worthier of my society and less open to Estella's reproach.

The old Battery out on the marshes was our place of study, and a broken slate and a short piece of slate-pencil were our educational implements: to which Joe always added a pipe of tobacco. I never knew Joe to remember anything from one Sunday to another, or to acquire, under my tuition, any piece of information whatever. Yet he would smoke his pipe at the Battery with a far more sagacious air than anywhere else—even with a learned air—as if he considered himself to be advancing immensely. Dear fellow, I hope he did.

It was pleasant and quiet, out there with the sails on the river passing beyond the earthwork, and sometimes, when the tide was low, looking as if they belonged to sunken ships that were still sailing on at the bottom of the water. Whenever I watched the vessels standing out to sea with their white sails spread, I somehow thought of Miss Havisham and Estella; and whenever the light struck aslant, afar off, upon a cloud or sail or green hillside or water-line, it was just the same—Miss Havisham and Estella and the strange house and the strange life appeared to have something to do with everything that was picturesque.

One Sunday when Joe, greatly enjoying his pipe, had so plumed himself on being "most awful dull," that I had given him up for the day, I lay on the earthwork for some time with my chin on my hand, descrying traces of Miss Havisham and Estella all over the prospect, in the sky and in the water, until at last I resolved to mention a thought concerning them that had been much in my head.

"Joe," said I; "don't you think I ought to make Miss Havisham a visit?"

"Well, Pip," returned Joe, slowly considering. "What for?"

"What for, Joe? What is any visit made for?"

"There is some wisits p'r'aps," said Joe, "as for ever remains open to the question, Pip. But in regard to wisiting Miss Havisham. She might think you wanted something—expected something of her."

"Don't you think I might say that I did not, Joe?"

"You might, old chap," said Joe. "And she might credit it. Similarly she mightn't."

Joe felt, as I did, that he had made a point there, and he pulled hard at his pipe to keep himself from weakening it by repetition.

"You see, Pip," Joe pursued, as soon as he was past that danger, "Miss Havisham done the handsome thing by you. When Miss Havisham done the handsome thing by you, she called me back to say to me as that were all."

"Yes, Joe. I heard her."

"All," Joe repeated, very emphatically.

"Yes, Joe. I tell you, I heard her."

"Which I meantersay, Pip, it might be that her meaning were—Make a end on it!—As you was!—Me to the North, and you to the South!—Keep in sunders!"

I had thought of that too, and it was very far from comforting to me to find that he had thought of it; for it seemed to render it more probable.

"But, Joe."

"Yes, old chap."

"Here am I, getting on in the first year of my time, and, since the day of my being bound, I have never thanked Miss Havisham, or asked after her, or shown that I remember her."

"That's true, Pip; and unless you was to turn her out a set of shoes all four round—and which I meantersay as even a set of shoes all four round might not be acceptable as a present, in a total wacancy of hoofs—"

"I don't mean that sort of remembrance, Joe; I don't mean a present."

But Joe had got the idea of a present in his head and must

harp upon it. "Or even," said he, "if you was helped to knocking her up a new chain for the front door—or say a gross or two of shark-headed screws for general use—or some light fancy article, such as a toasting-fork when she took her muffins—or a gridiron when she took a sprat or such like—"

"I don't mean any present at all, Joe," I interposed.

"Well," said Joe, still harping on it as though I had particularly pressed it, "if I was yourself, Pip, I wouldn't. No, I would *not*. For what's a door-chain when she's got one always up? And shark-headers is open to misrepresentations. And if it was a toasting-fork, you'd go into brass and do yourself no credit. And the oncommonest workman can't show himself oncommon in a gridiron—for a gridiron is a gridiron," said Joe, steadfastly impressing it upon me, as if he were endeavouring to rouse me from a fixed delusion, "and you may haim at what you like, but a gridiron it will come out, either by your leave or again your leave, and you can't help yourself—"

"My dear Joe," I cried, in desperation, taking hold of his coat, "don't go on in that way. I never thought of making Miss Havisham any present."

"No, Pip," Joe assented, as if he had been contending for that, all along; "and what I say to you is, you are right, Pip."

"Yes, Joe; but what I wanted to say, was, that as we are rather slack just now, if you would give me a half-holiday to-morrow, I think I would go up-town and make a call on Miss Est—Havisham."

"Which her name," said Joe, gravely, "ain't Estavisham, Pip, unless she have been rechris'ened."

"I know, Joe, I know. It was a slip of mine. What do you think of it, Joe?"

In brief, Joe thought that if I thought well of it, he thought well of it. But, he was particular in stipulating that if I were not received with cordiality, or if I were not encouraged to repeat my visit as a visit which had no ulterior object but was simply one of gratitude for a favor received, then this experimental trip should have no successor. By these conditions I promised to abide.

Now, Joe kept a journeyman at weekly wages whose name was Orlick. He pretended that his Christian name was Dolge—a clear impossibility—but he was a fellow of that obstinate disposition that I believe him to have been the prey of no delusion in this particular, but wilfully to have imposed that name upon the village as an affront to its understanding. He was a broadshouldered loose-limbed swarthy fellow of great strength, never in a hurry, and always slouching. He never even seemed to come to his work on purpose, but would slouch in as if by mere accident; and when he went to the Jolly Bargemen to eat his dinner, or went away at night, he would slouch out, like Cain or the Wandering Jew, as if he had no idea where he was going and no intention of ever coming back. He lodged at a sluice-keeper's out on the marshes, and on working-days would come slouching from his hermitage, with his hands in his pockets and his dinner loosely tied in a bundle round his neck and dangling on his back. On Sundays he mostly lay all day on the sluice-gates, or stood against ricks and barns. He always slouched, locomotively, with his eyes on the ground; and, when accosted or otherwise required to raise them, he looked up in a half-resentful, half-puzzled way, as though the only thought he ever had was, that it was rather an odd and injurious fact that he should never be thinking.

This morose journeyman had no liking for me. When I was very small and timid, he gave me to understand that the Devil lived in a black corner of the forge, and that he knew the fiend very well: also that it was necessary to make up the fire, once in seven years, with a live boy, and that I might consider myself fuel. When I became Joe's 'prentice, Orlick was perhaps confirmed in some suspicion that I should displace him; howbeit, he liked me still less. Not that he ever said anything, or did anything, openly importing hostility; I only noticed that he always beat his sparks in my direction, and that whenever I sang Old Clem, he came in out of time.

Dolge Orlick was at work and present, next day, when I reminded Joe of my half-holiday. He said nothing at the moment, for he and Joe had just got a piece of hot iron between them, and I was at the bellows; but by and by he said, leaning on his hammer:

"Now, master! Sure you're not a going to favor only one of us. If Young Pip has a half-holiday, do as much for Old Orlick." I suppose he was about five-and-twenty, but he usually spoke of himself as an ancient person.

"Why, what'll you do with a half-holiday, if you get it?" said Joe.

"What'll *I* do with it! What'll *he* do with it! I'll do as much with it as *him*," said Orlick.

"As to Pip, *he's* going up town," said Joe.

"Well then, as to Old Orlick, he's a going up town," retorted that worthy. "Two can go up town. Tan't only one wot can go up town.

"Don't lose your temper," said Joe.

"Shall if I like," growled Orlick. "Some and their up-towning! Now, master! Come. No favoring in this shop. Be a man!"

The master refusing to entertain the subject until the journeyman was in a better temper, Orlick plunged at the furnace, drew out a red-hot bar, made at me with it as if he were going to run it through my body, whisked it round my head, laid it on the anvil, hammered it out—as if it were I, I thought, and the sparks were my spirting blood—and finally said, when he had hammered himself hot and the iron cold, and he again leaned on his hammer:

"Now, master!"

"Are you all right now?" demanded Joe.

"Ah! I am all right," said gruff Old Orlick.

"Then, as in general you stick to your work as well as most men," said Joe, "let it be a half-holiday for all."

My sister had been standing silent in the yard, within hearing—she was a most unscrupulous spy and listener—and she instantly looked in at one of the windows.

"Like you, you fool!" said she to Joe, "giving holidays to great idle hulkers like that. You are a rich man, upon my life, to waste wages in that way. I wish I was his master!"

"You'd be everybody's master, if you durst," retorted Orlick, with an ill-favored grin.

("Let her alone," said Joe.)

"I'd be a match for all noodles and all rogues," returned my sister, beginning to work herself into a mighty rage. "And I couldn't be a match for the noodles, without being a match for your master, who's the dunder-headed king of the noodles. And I couldn't be a match for the rogues, without being a match for you, who are the blackest-looking and the worst rogue between this and France. Now!"

"You're a foul shrew, Mother Gargery," growled the journeyman. "If that makes a judge of rogues, you ought to be a good'un."

("Let her alone, will you?" said Joe.)

"What did you say?" cried my sister, beginning to scream. "What did you say? What did that fellow Orlick say to me, Pip? What did he call me, with my husband standing by? O! O! O!" Each of these exclamations was a shriek; and I must remark of my sister, what is equally true of all the violent women I have ever seen, that passion was no excuse for her, because it is undeniable that instead of lapsing into passion, she consciously and deliberately took extraordinary pains to force herself into it, and became blindly furious by regular stages; "what was the name he gave me before the base man who swore to defend me? O! Hold me! O!"

"Ah-h-h!" growled the journeyman, between his teeth, "I'd hold you, if you was my wife. I'd hold you under the pump, and choke it out of you."

("I tell you, let her alone," said Joe.)

"Oh! To hear him!" cried my sister, with a clap of her hands and a scream together—which was her next stage. "To hear the names he's giving me! That Orlick! In my own house! Me, a married woman! With my husband standing by! O! O!" Here my sister, after a fit of clappings and screamings, beat her hands upon her bosom and upon her knees, and threw her cap off, and pulled her hair down—which were the last stages on her road to frenzy. Being by this time a perfect Fury and a complete success, she made a dash at the door which I had fortunately locked.

What could the wretched Joe do now, after his disregarded parenthetical interruptions, but stand up to his journeyman, and ask him what he meant by interfering betwixt himself and Mrs. Joe; and further whether he was man enough to come on? Old Orlick felt that the situation admitted of nothing less than coming on, and was on his defence straightway; so, without so much as pulling off their singed and burnt aprons, they went at one another, like two giants. But, if any man in that neighbourhood could stand uplong against Joe, I never saw the man. Orlick, as if he had been of no more account than the pale young gentleman, was very soon among the coal-dust, and in no hurry to come out of it. Then Joe unlocked the door and picked up my sister, who had dropped insensible at the window (but who had seen the fight first, I think), and who was carried into the house and laid down, and who was recommended to revive, and would do nothing but struggle and clench her hands in Joe's hair. Then, came that singular calm and silence which succeed all uproars; and then, with the vague sensation which I have always connected with such a lull—namely, that it was

Sunday, and somebody was dead—I went up stairs to dress myself.

When I came down again, I found Joe and Orlick sweeping up, without any other traces of discomposure than a slit in one of Orlick's nostrils, which was neither expressive nor ornamental. A pot of beer had appeared from the Jolly Bargemen, and they were sharing it by turns in a peaceable manner. The lull had a sedative and philosophical influence on Joe, who followed me out into the road to say, as a parting observation that might do me good, "On the Rampage, Pip, and off the Rampage, Pip:— such is Life!

With what absurd emotions (for we think the feelings that are very serious in a man quite comical in a boy) I found myself again going to Miss Havisham's, matters little here. Nor, how I passed and repassed the gate many times before I could make up my mind to ring. Nor, how I debated whether I should go away without ringing; nor, how I should undoubtedly have gone, if my time had been my own, to come back.

Miss Sarah Pocket came to the gate. No Estella.

"How, then? You here again?" said Miss Pocket. "What do you want?"

When I said that I only came to see how Miss Havisham was, Sarah evidently deliberated whether or no she should send me about my business. But unwilling to hazard the responsibility, she let me in, and presently brought the sharp message that I was to "come up."

Everything was unchanged, and Miss Havisham was alone.

"Well?" said she, fixing her eyes upon me. "I hope you want nothing? You'll get nothing."

"No indeed, Miss Havisham. I only wanted you to know that I am doing very well in my apprenticeship, and am always much obliged to you."

"There, there!" with the old restless fingers. "Come now

and then; come on your birthday.—Ay!" she cried suddenly, turning herself and her chair towards me, "You are looking round for Estella? Hey?"

I had been looking round—in fact, for Estella—and I stammered that I hoped she was well.

"Abroad," said Miss Havisham; "educating for a lady; far out of reach; prettier than ever; admired by all who see her. Do you feel that you have lost her?"

There was such a malignant enjoyment in her utterance of the last words, and she broke into such a disagreeable laugh, that I was at a loss what to say. She spared me the trouble of considering, by dismissing me. When the gate was closed upon me by Sarah of the walnut-shell countenance, I felt more than ever dissatisfied with my home and with my trade and with everything; and that was all I took by *that* motion.

As I was loitering along the High Street, looking in disconsolately at the shop windows, and thinking what I would buy if I were a gentleman, who should come out of the bookshop but Mr. Wopsle. Mr. Wopsle had in his hand the affecting tragedy of George Barnwell, in which he had that moment invested sixpence, with the view of heaping every word of it on the head of Pumblechook, with whom he was going to drink tea. No sooner did he see me, than he appeared to consider that a special Providence had put a 'prentice in his way to be read at; and he laid hold of me, and insisted on my accompanying him to the Pumblechookian parlor. As I knew it would be miserable at home, and as the nights were dark and the way was dreary, and almost any companionship on the road was better than none, I made no great resistance; consequently, we turned into Pumblechook's just as the street and the shops were lighting up.

As I never assisted at any other representation of George Barnwell, I don't know how long it may usually take; but I know very well that it took until half-past nine o' clock that night, and that when Mr. Wopsle got into Newgate, I thought he never would go to the scaffold, he became so much slower than at any former period of his disgraceful career. I thought it a little too much that he should complain of being cut short in his flower after all, as if he had not been running to seed, leaf after leaf, ever since his course began. This, however, was a mere question of length and wearisomeness. What stung me, was the identification of the whole affair with my unoffending self. When Barnwell began to go wrong, I declare that I felt positively apologetic, Pumblechook's indignant stare so taxed me with it. Wopsle, too, took pains to present me in the worst light. At once ferocious and maudlin, I was made to murder my uncle with no extenuating circumstances whatever; Millwood put me down in argument, on every occasion; it became sheer monomania in my master's daughter to care a button for me; and all I can say for my gasping and procrastinating conduct on the fatal morning, is, that it was worthy of the general feebleness of my character. Even after I was happily hanged and Wopsle had closed the book, Pumblechook sat staring at me, and shaking his head, and saying, "Take warning, boy, take warning!" as if it were a well-known fact that I contemplated murdering a near relation, provided I could only induce one to have the weakness to become my benefactor.

It was a very dark night when it was all over, and when I set out with Mr. Wopsle on the walk home. Beyond town, we found a heavy mist out, and it fell wet and thick. The turnpike lamp was a blur, quite out of the lamp's usual place apparently, and its rays looked solid substance on the fog. We were noticing this, and saying how that the mist rose with a change of wind from a certain quarter of our marshes, when we came upon a man, slouching under the lee of the turnpike house.

"Halloa!" we said, stopping. "Orlick there?"

"Ah!" he answered, slouching out. "I was standing by a minute, on the chance of company."

"You are late," I remarked.

Orlick not unnaturally answered, "Well? And *you're* late."

"We have been," said Mr. Wopsle, exalted with his late performance,"we have been indulging, Mr. Orlick, in an intellectual evening."

Old Orlick growled, as if he had nothing to say about that, and we all went on together. I asked him presently whether he had been spending his half-holiday up and down town?

"Yes," said he, "all of it. I come in behind yourself. I didn't see you, but I must have been pretty close behind you. By the by, the guns is going again."

"At the Hulks?" said I.

"Ay! There's some of the birds flown from the cages. The guns have been going since dark, about. You'll hear one presently."

In effect, we had not walked many yards further, when the well-remembered boom came towards us, deadened by the mist, and heavily rolled away along the low grounds by the river, as if it were pursuing and threatening the fugitives.

"A good night for cutting off in," said Orlick. "We'd be puzzled how to bring down a jail-bird on the wing, to-night."

The subject was a suggestive one to me, and I thought about it in silence. Mr. Wopsle, as the ill-requited uncle of the evening's tragedy, fell to meditating aloud in his garden at Camberwell. Orlick, with his hands in his pockets, slouched heavily at my side. It was very dark, very wet, very muddy, and so we splashed along. Now and then, the sound of the signal cannon broke upon us again, and again rolled sulkily along the course of the river. I kept myself to myself and my thoughts. Mr. Wopsle died amiably at Camberwell, and exceedingly game on Bosworth Field, and in the greatest agonies at Glastonbury. Orlick sometimes growled, "Beat it out, beat it out—Old Clem! With a clink for the stout—Old Clem!" I thought he had been drinking, but he was not drunk.

Thus, we came to the village. The way by which we approached it took us past the Three Jolly Bargemen, which we were surprised to find—it being eleven o'clock—in a state of commotion, with the door wide open, and unwonted lights that had been hastily caught up and put down scattered about. Mr. Wopsle dropped in to ask what was the matter (surmising that a convict had been taken), but came running out in a great hurry.

"There's something wrong," said he, without stopping, "up at your place, Pip. Run all!"

"What is it?" I asked, keeping up with him. So did Orlick, at my side.

"I can't quite understand. The house seems to have been violently entered when Joe Gargery was out. Supposed by convicts. Somebody has been attacked and hurt."

We were running too fast to admit of more being said, and we made no stop until we got into our kitchen. It was full of people; the whole village was there, or in the yard; and there was a surgeon, and there was Joe, and there were a group of women, all on the floor in the midst of the kitchen. The unemployed bystanders drew back when they saw me, and so I became aware of my sister—lying without sense or movement on the bare boards where she had been knocked down by a tremendous blow on the back of the head, dealt by some unknown hand when her face was turned towards the fire—destined never to be on the Rampage again, while she was the wife of Joe.

CHAPTER 16

With my head full of George Barnwell, I was at first disposed to believe that *I* must have had some hand in the attack upon my sister, or at all events that as her near relation, popularly known to be under obligations to her, I was a more legitimate object of suspicion than any one else. But when, in the clearer light of next morning, I began to reconsider the matter and to hear it discussed around me on all sides, I took another view of the case, which was more reasonable.

Joe had been at the Three Jolly Bargemen, smoking his pipe, from a quarter after eight o'clock to a quarter before ten. While he was there, my sister had been seen standing at the kitchen door, and had exchanged Good Night with a farm-laborer going home. The man could not be more particular as to the time at which he saw her (he got into dense confusion when he tried to be), than that it must have been before nine. When Joe went home at five minutes before ten, he found her struck down on the floor, and promptly called in assistance. The fire had not then burnt unusually low, nor was the snuff of the candle very long; the candle, however, had been blown out.

Nothing had been taken away from any part of the house. Neither, beyond the blowing out of the candle—which stood on a table between the door and my sister, and was behind her when she stood facing the fire and was struck—was there any disarrangement of the kitchen, excepting such as she herself had made, in falling and bleeding. But, there was one remarkable piece of evidence on the spot. She had been struck with something blunt and heavy, on the head and spine; after the blows were dealt, something heavy had been thrown down at her with considerable violence, as she lay on her face. And on the ground beside her, when Joe picked her up, was a convict's leg-iron which had been filed asunder.

Now, Joe, examining this iron with a smith's eye, declared it to have been filed asunder some time ago. The hue and cry going off to the Hulks, and people coming thence to examine the iron, Joe's opinion was corroborated. They did not undertake to say when it had left the prison-ships to which it undoubtedly had once belonged; but they claimed to know for certain that that particular manacle had not been worn by either of the two convicts who had escaped last night. Further, one of those two was already retaken, and had not freed himself of his iron.

Knowing what I knew, I set up an inference of my own here. I believed the iron to be my convict's iron—the iron I had seen and heard him filing at, on the marshes—but my mind did not accuse him of having put it to its latest use. For I believed one of two other persons to have become possessed of it, and to have turned it to this cruel account. Either Orlick, or the strange man who had shown me the file.

Now, as to Orlick; he had gone to town exactly as he told us when we picked him up at the turnpike, he had been seen about town all the evening, he had been in divers companies in several public-houses, and he had come back with myself and Mr. Wopsle. There was nothing against him, save the quarrel; and my sister had quarrelled with him, and with everybody else about her, ten thousand times. As to the strange man; if he had come back for his two bank-notes there could have been no dispute about them, because my sister was fully prepared to restore them. Besides, there had been no altercation; the assailant had come in so silently and suddenly, that she had been felled before she could look round.

It was horrible to think that I had provided the weapon,

however undesignedly, but I could hardly think otherwise. I suffered unspeakable trouble while I considered and reconsidered whether I should at last dissolve that spell of my childhood and tell Joe all the story. For months afterwards, I every day settled the question finally in the negative, and reopened and reargued it next morning. The contention came, after all, to this;—the secret was such an old one now, had so grown into me and become a part of myself, that I could not tear it away. In addition to the dread that, having led up to so much mischief, it would be now more likely than ever to alienate Joe from me if he believed it, I had a further restraining dread that he would not believe it, but would assort it with the fabulous dogs and veal-cutlets as a monstrous invention. However, I temporized with myself, of course—for, was I not wavering between right and wrong, when the thing is always done?—and resolved to make a full disclosure if I should see any such new occasion as a new chance of helping in the discovery of the assailant.

The Constables and the Bow Street men from London—for, this happened in the days of the extinct red-waistcoated police—were about the house for a week or two, and did pretty much what I have heard and read of like authorities doing in other such cases. They took up several obviously wrong people, and they ran their heads very hard against wrong ideas, and persisted in trying to fit the circumstances to the ideas, instead of trying to extract ideas from the circumstances. Also, they stood about the door of the Jolly Bargemen, with knowing and reserved looks that filled the whole neighbourhood with admiration; and they had a mysterious manner of taking their drink, that was almost as good as taking the culprit. But not quite, for they never did it.

Long after these constitutional powers had dispersed, my sister lay very ill in bed. Her sight was disturbed, so that she saw objects multiplied, and grasped at visionary teacups and wineglasses instead of the realities; her hearing was greatly impaired; her memory also; and her speech was unintelligible. When, at last, she came round so far as to be helped down stairs, it was still necessary to keep my slate always by her, that she might indicate in writing what she could not indicate in speech. As she was (very bad handwriting apart) a more than indifferent speller, and as Joe was a more than indifferent reader, extraordinary complications arose between them which I was always called in to solve. The administration of mutton instead of medicine, the substitution of Tea for Joe, and the baker for bacon, were among the mildest of my own mistakes.

However, her temper was greatly improved, and she was patient. A tremulous uncertainty of the action of all her limbs soon became a part of her regular state, and afterwards, at intervals of two or three months, she would often put her hands to her head, and would then remain for about a week at a time in some gloomy aberration of mind. We were at a loss to find a suitable attendant for her, until a circumstance happened conveniently to relieve us. Mr. Wopsle's great-aunt conquered a confirmed habit of living into which she had fallen, and Biddy became a part of our establishment.

It may have been about a month after my sister's reappearance in the kitchen, when Biddy came to us with a small speckled box containing the whole of her worldly effects, and became a blessing to the household. Above all, she was a blessing to Joe, for the dear old fellow was sadly cut up by the constant contemplation of the wreck of his wife, and had been accustomed, while attending on her of an evening, to turn to me every now and then and say, with his blue eyes moistened, "Such a fine figure of a woman as she once were, Pip!" Biddy instantly taking the cleverest charge of her as though she had studied her from infancy; Joe became able in some sort to appreciate the greater quiet of his life, and to get down to the Jolly Bargemen now and then for a change that did him good.

It was characteristic of the police people that they had all more or less suspected poor Joe (though he never knew it), and that they had to a man concurred in regarding him as one of the deepest spirits they had ever encountered.

Biddy's first triumph in her new office, was to solve a difficulty that had completely vanquished me. I had tried hard at it, but had made nothing of it. Thus it was:

Again and again and again, my sister had traced upon the slate, a character that looked like a curious T, and then with the utmost eagerness had called our attention to it as something she particularly wanted. I had in vain tried everything producible that began with a T, from tar to toast and tub. At length it had come into my head that the sign looked like a hammer, and on my lustily calling that word in my sister's ear, she had begun to hammer on the table and had expressed a qualified assent. Thereupon, I had brought in all our hammers, one after another, but without avail. Then I bethought me of a crutch, the shape being much the same, and I borrowed one in the village, and displayed it to my sister with considerable confidence. But she shook her head to that extent when she was shown it, that we were terrified lest in her weak and shattered state she should dislocate her neck.

When my sister found that Biddy was very quick to understand her, this mysterious sign reappeared on the slate. Biddy looked thoughtfully at it, heard my explanation, looked thoughtfully at my sister, looked thoughtfully at Joe (who was always represented on the slate by his initial letter), and ran into the forge, followed by Joe and me.

"Why, of course!" cried Biddy, with an exultant face. "Don't you see? It's *him*!"

Orlick, without a doubt! She had lost his name, and could only signify him by his hammer. We told him why we wanted him to come into the kitchen, and he slowly laid down his hammer, wiped his brow with his arm, took another wipe at it with his apron, and came slouching out, with a curious loose vagabond bend in the knees that strongly distinguished him.

I confess that I expected to see my sister denounce him, and that I was disappointed by the different result. She manifested the greatest anxiety to be on good terms with him, was evidently much pleased by his being at length produced, and motioned that she would have him given something to drink. She watched his countenance as if she were particularly wishful to be assured that he took kindly to his reception, she showed every possible desire to conciliate him, and there was an air of humble propitiation in all she did, such as I have seen pervade the bearing of a child towards a hard master. After that day, a day rarely passed without her drawing the hammer on her slate, and without Orlick's slouching in and standing doggedly before her, as if he knew no more than I did what to make of it.

CHAPTER 17

I now fell into a regular routine of apprenticeship life, which was varied beyond the limits of the village and the marshes, by no more remarkable circumstance than the arrival of my birthday and my paying another visit to Miss Havisham. I found Miss Sarah Pocket still on duty at the gate; I found Miss Havisham just as I had left her, and she spoke of Estella in the very same way, if not in the very same words. The interview lasted but a few minutes, and she gave me a guinea when I was going, and told me to come again on my next birthday. I may mention at once that this became an annual custom. I tried to decline taking the guinea on the first occasion, but with no better effect than causing her to ask me very angrily, if I expected more? Then, and after that, I took it.

So unchanging was the dull old house, the yellow light in the darkened room, the faded spectre in the chair by the dressing-table glass, that I felt as if the stopping of the clocks had stopped Time in that mysterious place, and, while I and everything else outside it grew older, it stood still. Daylight never entered the house as to my thoughts and remembrances of it, any more than as to the actual fact. It bewildered me, and under its influence I continued at heart to hate my trade and to be ashamed of home.

Imperceptibly I became conscious of a change in Biddy, however. Her shoes came up at the heel, her hair grew bright and neat, her hands were always clean. She was not beautiful— she was common, and could not be like Estella—but she was pleasant and wholesome and sweet-tempered. She had not been with us more than a year (I remember her being newly out of mourning at the time it struck me), when I observed to myself one evening that she had curiously thoughtful and attentive eyes; eyes that were very pretty and very good.

It came of my lifting up my own eyes from a task I was poring at—writing some passages from a book, to improve myself in two ways at once by a sort of stratagem—and seeing Biddy observant of what I was about. I laid down my pen, and Biddy stopped in her needlework without laying it down.

"Biddy," said I, "how do you manage it? Either I am very stupid, or you are very clever."

"What is it that I manage? I don't know," returned Biddy, smiling.

She managed our whole domestic life, and wonderfully too; but I did not mean that, though that made what I did mean more surprising.

"How do you manage, Biddy," said I, "to learn everything that I learn, and always to keep up with me?" I was beginning to be rather vain of my knowledge, for I spent my birthday guineas on it, and set aside the greater part of my pocket-money for similar investment; though I have no doubt, now, that the little I knew was extremely dear at the price.

"I might as well ask you," said Biddy, "how *you* manage?"

"No; because when I come in from the forge of a night, any one can see me turning to at it. But you never turn to at it, Biddy."

"I suppose I must catch it - like a cough," said Biddy, quietly; and went on with her sewing.

Pursuing my idea as I leaned back in my wooden chair, and looked at Biddy sewing away with her head on one side, I began to think her rather an extraordinary girl. For I called to mind now, that she was equally accomplished in the terms of our trade, and the names of our different sorts of work, and our various tools. In short, whatever I knew, Biddy knew. Theoretically, she was already as good a blacksmith as I, or better.

"You are one of those, Biddy," said I, "who make the most of every chance. You never had a chance before you came here, and see how improved you are!"

Biddy looked at me for an instant, and went on with her sewing. "I was your first teacher though; wasn't I?" said she, as she sewed.

"Biddy!" I exclaimed, in amazement. "Why, you are crying!"

"No I am not," said Biddy, looking up and laughing. "What put that in your head?"

What could have put it in my head but the glistening of a tear as it dropped on her work? I sat silent, recalling what a drudge she had been until Mr. Wopsle's great-aunt successfully overcame that bad habit of living, so highly desirable to be got rid of by some people. I recalled the hopeless circumstances by which she had been surrounded in the miserable little shop and the miserable little noisy evening school, with that miserable old bundle of incompetence always to be dragged and shouldered. I reflected that even in those untoward times there must have been latent in Biddy what was now developing, for, in my first uneasiness and discontent I had turned to her for help, as a matter of course. Biddy sat quietly sewing, shedding no more tears, and while I looked at her and thought about it all, it occurred to me that perhaps I had not been sufficiently grateful to Biddy. I might have been too reserved, and should have patronized her more (though I did not use that precise word in my meditations) with my confidence.

"Yes, Biddy," I observed, when I had done turning it over, "you were my first teacher, and that at a time when we little thought of ever being together like this, in this kitchen."

"Ah, poor thing!" replied Biddy. It was like her self-forgetfulness to transfer the remark to my sister, and to get up and be busy about her, making her more comfortable; "that's sadly true!"

"Well!" said I, "we must talk together a little more, as we used to do. And I must consult you a little more, as I used to do. Let us have a quiet walk on the marshes next Sunday, Biddy, and a long chat."

My sister was never left alone now; but Joe more than readily undertook the care of her on that Sunday afternoon, and Biddy and I went out together. It was summer-time, and lovely weather. When we had passed the village and the church and the churchyard, and were out on the marshes and began to see the sails of the ships as they sailed on, I began to combine Miss Havisham and Estella with the prospect, in my usual way. When we came to the river-side and sat down on the bank, with the water rippling at our feet, making it all more quiet than it would have been without that sound, I resolved that it was a good time and place for the admission of Biddy into my inner confidence.

"Biddy," said I, after binding her to secrecy, "I want to be a gentleman."

"O, I wouldn't, if I was you!" she returned. "I don't think it would answer."

"Biddy," said I, with some severity, "I have particular reasons for wanting to be a gentleman."

"You know best, Pip; but don't you think you are happier as you are?"

"Biddy," I exclaimed, impatiently, "I am not at all happy as I am. I am disgusted with my calling and with my life. I have never taken to either, since I was bound. Don't be absurd."

"Was I absurd?" said Biddy, quietly raising her eyebrows; "I am sorry for that; I didn't mean to be. I only want you to do well, and to be comfortable."

"Well, then, understand once for all that I never shall or can be comfortable—or anything but miserable—there, Biddy!—unless I can lead a very different sort of life from the life I lead now."

"That's a pity!" said Biddy, shaking her head with a sorrowful air.

Now, I too had so often thought it a pity, that, in the singular kind of quarrel with myself which I was always carrying on, I was half inclined to shed tears of vexation and distress when Biddy gave utterance to her sentiment and my own. I told her she was right, and I knew it was much to be regretted, but still it was not to be helped.

"If I could have settled down," I said to Biddy, plucking up the short grass within reach, much as I had once upon a time pulled my feelings out of my hair and kicked them into the brewery wall: "if I could have settled down and been but half as fond of the forge as I was when I was little, I know it would have been much better for me. You and I and Joe would have wanted nothing then, and Joe and I would perhaps have gone partners when I was out of my time, and I might even have grown up to keep company with you, and we might have sat on this very bank on a fine Sunday, quite different people. I should have been good enough for you; shouldn't I, Biddy?"

Biddy sighed as she looked at the ships sailing on, and returned for answer, "Yes; I am not over-particular." It scarcely sounded flattering, but I knew she meant well.

"Instead of that," said I, plucking up more grass and chewing a blade or two, "see how I am going on. Dissatisfied, and uncomfortable, and—what would it signify to me, being coarse and common, if nobody had told me so!"

Biddy turned her face suddenly towards mine, and looked far more attentively at me than she had looked at the sailing ships.

"It was neither a very true nor a very polite thing to say," she remarked, directing her eyes to the ships again. "Who said it?"

I was disconcerted, for I had broken away without quite seeing where I was going to. It was not to be shuffled off now, however, and I answered, "The beautiful young lady at Miss Havisham's, and she's more beautiful than anybody ever was, and I admire her dreadfully, and I want to be a gentleman on her account." Having made this lunatic confession, I began to throw my torn-up grass into the river, as if I had some thoughts of following it.

"Do you want to be a gentleman, to spite her or to gain her over?" Biddy quietly asked me, after a pause.

"I don't know," I moodily answered.

"Because, if it is to spite her," Biddy pursued, "I should think—but you know best—that might be better and more independently done by caring nothing for her words. And if it is to gain her over, I should think—but you know best—she was not worth gaining over."

Exactly what I myself had thought, many times. Exactly what was perfectly manifest to me at the moment. But how could I, a poor dazed village lad, avoid that wonderful inconsistency into which the best and wisest of men fall every day?

"It may be all quite true," said I to Biddy, "but I admire her dreadfully."

In short, I turned over on my face when I came to that, and got a good grasp on the hair on each side of my head, and wrenched it well. All the while knowing the madness of my heart to be so very mad and misplaced, that I was quite conscious it would have served my face right, if I had lifted it up by my hair, and knocked it against the pebbles as a punishment for belonging to such an idiot.

Biddy was the wisest of girls, and she tried to reason no more with me. She put her hand, which was a comfortable hand though roughened by work, upon my hands, one after another, and gently took them out of my hair. Then she softly patted my shoulder in a soothing way, while with my face upon my sleeve I cried a little—exactly as I had done in the brewery yard—and felt vaguely convinced that I was very much ill-used by somebody, or by everybody; I can't say which.

"I am glad of one thing," said Biddy, "and that is, that you have felt you could give me your confidence, Pip. And I am glad of another thing, and that is, that of course you know you may depend upon my keeping it and always so far deserving it. If your first teacher (dear! such a poor one, and so much in need of being taught herself!) had been your teacher at the present time, she thinks she knows what lesson she would set. But it would be a hard one to learn, and you have got beyond her, and it's of no use now." So, with a quiet sigh for me, Biddy rose from the bank, and said, with a fresh and pleasant change of voice, "Shall we walk a little farther, or go home?"

"Biddy," I cried, getting up, putting my arm round her neck, and giving her a kiss, "I shall always tell you everything."

"Till you're a gentleman," said Biddy.

"You know I never shall be, so that's always. Not that I have any occasion to tell you anything, for you know everything I know—as I told you at home the other night."

"Ah!" said Biddy, quite in a whisper, as she looked away at the ships. And then repeated, with her former pleasant change, "shall we walk a little farther, or go home?"

I said to Biddy we would walk a little farther, and we did so, and the summer afternoon toned down into the summer evening, and it was very beautiful. I began to consider whether I was not more naturally and wholesomely situated, after all, in these circumstances, than playing beggar my neighbour by candle-light in the room with the stopped clocks, and being despised by Estella. I thought it would be very good for me if I could get her out of my head, with all the rest of those remembrances and fancies, and could go to work determined to relish what I had to do, and stick to it, and make the best of it. I asked myself the question whether I did not surely know that if Estella were beside me at that moment instead of Biddy, she would make me miserable? I was obliged to admit that I did know it for a certainty, and I said to myself, "Pip, what a fool you are!"

We talked a good deal as we walked, and all that Biddy said seemed right. Biddy was never insulting, or capricious, or Biddy to-day and somebody else to-morrow; she would have derived only pain, and no pleasure, from giving me pain; she would far rather have wounded her own breast than mine. How could it be, then, that I did not like her much the better of the two?

"Biddy," said I, when we were walking homeward, "I wish you could put me right."

"I wish I could!" said Biddy.

"If I could only get myself to fall in love with you—you don't mind my speaking so openly to such an old acquaintance?"

"Oh dear, not at all!" said Biddy. "Don't mind me."

"If I could only get myself to do it, *that* would be the thing for me."

"But you never will, you see," said Biddy.

It did not appear quite so unlikely to me that evening, as it would have done if we had discussed it a few hours before. I therefore observed I was not quite sure of that. But Biddy said *she* was, and she said it decisively. In my heart I believed her to be right; and yet I took it rather ill, too, that she should be so positive on the point.

When we came near the churchyard, we had to cross an embankment, and get over a stile near a sluice-gate. There started up, from the gate, or from the rushes, or from the ooze (which was quite in his stagnant way), Old Orlick.

"Halloa!" he growled, "where are you two going?"

"Where should we be going, but home?"

"Well, then," said he, "I'm jiggered if I don't see you home!"

This penalty of being jiggered was a favorite supposititious case of his. He attached no definite meaning to the word that

I am aware of, but used it, like his own pretended Christian name, to affront mankind, and convey an idea of something savagely damaging. When I was younger, I had had a general belief that if he had jiggered me personally, he would have done it with a sharp and twisted hook.

Biddy was much against his going with us, and said to me in a whisper, "Don't let him come; I don't like him." As I did not like him either, I took the liberty of saying that we thanked him, but we didn't want seeing home. He received that piece of information with a yell of laughter, and dropped back, but came slouching after us at a little distance.

Curious to know whether Biddy suspected him of having had a hand in that murderous attack of which my sister had never been able to give any account, I asked her why she did not like him.

"Oh!" she replied, glancing over her shoulder as he slouched after us, "because I—I am afraid he likes me."

"Did he ever tell you he liked you?" I asked indignantly.

"No," said Biddy, glancing over her shoulder again, "he never told me so; but he dances at me, whenever he can catch my eye."

However novel and peculiar this testimony of attachment, I did not doubt the accuracy of the interpretation. I was very hot indeed upon Old Orlick's daring to admire her; as hot as if it were an outrage on myself.

"But it makes no difference to you, you know," said Biddy, calmly.

"No, Biddy, it makes no difference to me; only I don't like it; I don't approve of it."

"Nor I neither," said Biddy. "Though *that* makes no difference to you."

"Exactly," said I; "but I must tell you I should have no opinion of you, Biddy, if he danced at you with your own consent."

I kept an eye on Orlick after that night, and, whenever circumstances were favorable to his dancing at Biddy, got before him to obscure that demonstration. He had struck root in Joe's establishment, by reason of my sister's sudden fancy for him, or I should have tried to get him dismissed. He quite understood and reciprocated my good intentions, as I had reason to know thereafter.

And now, because my mind was not confused enough before, I complicated its confusion fifty thousand-fold, by having states and seasons when I was clear that Biddy was immeasurably better than Estella, and that the plain honest working life to which I was born had nothing in it to be ashamed of, but offered me sufficient means of self-respect and happiness. At those times, I would decide conclusively that my disaffection to dear old Joe and the forge was gone, and that I was growing up in a fair way to be partners with Joe and to keep company with Biddy—when all in a moment some confounding remembrance of the Havisham days would fall upon me like a destructive missile, and scatter my wits again. Scattered wits take a long time picking up; and often before I had got them well together, they would be dispersed in all directions by one stray thought, that perhaps after all Miss Havisham was going to make my fortune when my time was out.

If my time had run out, it would have left me still at the height of my perplexities, I dare say. It never did run out, however, but was brought to a premature end, as I proceed to relate.

CHAPTER 18

It was in the fourth year of my apprenticeship to Joe, and it was a Saturday night. There was a group assembled round the fire at the Three Jolly Bargemen, attentive to Mr. Wopsle as he read the newspaper aloud. Of that group I was one.

A highly popular murder had been committed, and Mr. Wopsle was imbrued in blood to the eyebrows. He gloated over every abhorrent adjective in the description, and identified himself with every witness at the Inquest. He faintly moaned, "I am done for," as the victim, and he barbarously bellowed, "I'll serve you out," as the murderer. He gave the medical testimony, in pointed imitation of our local practitioner; and he piped and shook, as the aged turnpike-keeper who had heard blows, to an extent so very paralytic as to suggest a doubt regarding the mental competency of that witness. The coroner, in Mr. Wopsle's hands, became Timon of Athens; the beadle, Coriolanus. He enjoyed himself thoroughly, and we all enjoyed ourselves, and were delightfully comfortable. In this cosey state of mind we came to the verdict Wilful Murder.

Then, and not sooner, I became aware of a strange gentleman leaning over the back of the settle opposite me, looking on. There was an expression of contempt on his face, and he bit the side of a great forefinger as he watched the group of faces.

"Well!" said the stranger to Mr. Wopsle, when the reading was done, "you have settled it all to your own satisfaction, I have no doubt?"

Everybody started and looked up, as if it were the murderer. He looked at everybody coldly and sarcastically.

"Guilty, of course?" said he. "Out with it. Come!"

"Sir," returned Mr. Wopsle, "without having the honor of your acquaintance, I do say Guilty." Upon this we all took courage to unite in a confirmatory murmur.

"I know you do," said the stranger; "I knew you would. I told you so. But now I'll ask you a question. Do you know, or do you not know, that the law of England supposes every man to be innocent, until he is proved-proved—to be guilty?"

"Sir," Mr. Wopsle began to reply, "as an Englishman myself, I—"

"Come!" said the stranger, biting his forefinger at him. "Don't evade the question. Either you know it, or you don't know it. Which is it to be?"

He stood with his head on one side and himself on one side, in a bullying, interrogative manner, and he threw his forefinger at Mr. Wopsle—as it were to mark him out—before biting it again.

"Now!" said he. "Do you know it, or don't you know it?"

"Certainly I know it," replied Mr. Wopsle.

"Certainly you know it. Then why didn't you say so at first? Now, I'll ask you another question;"—taking possession of Mr. Wopsle, as if he had a right to him." *Do* you know that none of these witnesses have yet been cross-examined?"

Mr. Wopsle was beginning, "I can only say—" when the stranger stopped him.

"What? You won't answer the question, yes or no? Now, I'll try you again." Throwing his finger at him again. "Attend to me. Are you aware, or are you not aware, that none of these witnesses have yet been cross-examined? Come, I only want one word from you. Yes, or no?"

Mr. Wopsle hesitated, and we all began to conceive rather a poor opinion of him.

"Come!" said the stranger, "I'll help you. You don't deserve help, but I'll help you. Look at that paper you hold in your hand. What is it?"

"What is it?" repeated Mr. Wopsle, eyeing it, much at a loss.

"Is it," pursued the stranger in his most sarcastic and suspicious manner, "the printed paper you have just been reading from?"

"Undoubtedly."

"Undoubtedly. Now, turn to that paper, and tell me whether it distinctly states that the prisoner expressly said that his legal advisers instructed him altogether to reserve his defence?"

"I read that just now," Mr. Wopsle pleaded.

"Never mind what you read just now, sir; I don't ask you what you read just now. You may read the Lord's Prayer backwards, if you like—and, perhaps, have done it before to-day. Turn to the paper. No, no, no my friend; not to the top of the column; you know better than that; to the bottom, to the bottom." (We all began to think Mr. Wopsle full of subterfuge.) "Well? Have you found it?"

"Here it is," said Mr. Wopsle.

"Now, follow that passage with your eye, and tell me whether it distinctly states that the prisoner expressly said that he was instructed by his legal advisers wholly to reserve his defence? Come! Do you make that of it?"

Mr. Wopsle answered, "Those are not the exact words." "Not the exact words!" repeated the gentleman bitterly. "Is that the exact substance?"

"Yes," said Mr. Wopsle.

"Yes," repeated the stranger, looking round at the rest of the company with his right hand extended towards the witness, Wopsle. "And now I ask you what you say to the conscience of that man who, with that passage before his eyes, can lay his head upon his pillow after having pronounced a fellow-creature guilty, unheard?"

We all began to suspect that Mr. Wopsle was not the man we had thought him, and that he was beginning to be found out.

"And that same man, remember," pursued the gentleman, throwing his finger at Mr. Wopsle heavily; "that same man might be summoned as a juryman upon this very trial, and, having thus deeply committed himself, might return to the bosom of his family and lay his head upon his pillow, after deliberately swearing that he would well and truly try the issue joined between Our Sovereign Lord the King and the prisoner at the bar, and would a true verdict give according to the evidence, so help him God!"

We were all deeply persuaded that the unfortunate Wopsle had gone too far, and had better stop in his reckless career while there was yet time.

The strange gentleman, with an air of authority not to be disputed, and with a manner expressive of knowing something secret about every one of us that would effectually do for each individual if he chose to disclose it, left the back of the settle, and came into the space between the two settles, in front of the fire, where he remained standing, his left hand in his pocket, and he biting the forefinger of his right.

"From information I have received," said he, looking round at us as we all quailed before him, "I have reason to believe there is a blacksmith among you, by name Joseph—or Joe—Gargery. Which is the man?"

"Here is the man," said Joe.

The strange gentleman beckoned him out of his place, and Joe went.

"You have an apprentice," pursued the stranger, "commonly known as Pip? Is he here?"

"I am here!" I cried.

The stranger did not recognize me, but I recognized him as the gentleman I had met on the stairs, on the occasion of my second visit to Miss Havisham. I had known him the moment I saw him looking over the settle, and now that I stood confronting him with his hand upon my shoulder, I checked off again in detail his large head, his dark complexion, his deep-set eyes, his bushy black eyebrows, his large watch-chain, his strong black dots of beard and whisker, and even the smell of scented soap on his great hand.

"I wish to have a private conference with you two," said he, when he had surveyed me at his leisure. "It will take a little time. Perhaps we had better go to your place of residence. I prefer not to anticipate my communication here; you will impart as much or as little of it as you please to your friends afterwards; I have nothing to do with that."

Amidst a wondering silence, we three walked out of the Jolly Bargemen, and in a wondering silence walked home. While going along, the strange gentleman occasionally looked at me, and occasionally bit the side of his finger. As we neared home, Joe vaguely acknowledging the occasion as an impressive and ceremonious one, went on ahead to open the front door. Our conference was held in the state parlor, which was feebly lighted by one candle.

It began with the strange gentleman's sitting down at the table, drawing the candle to him, and looking over some entries in his pocket-book. He then put up the pocket-book and set the candle a little aside, after peering round it into the darkness at Joe and me, to ascertain which was which.

"My name," he said, "is Jaggers, and I am a lawyer in London. I am pretty well known. I have unusual business to transact with you, and I commence by explaining that it is not of my originating. If my advice had been asked, I should not have been here. It was not asked, and you see me here. What I have to do as the confidential agent of another, I do. No less, no more."

Finding that he could not see us very well from where he sat, he got up, and threw one leg over the back of a chair and leaned upon it; thus having one foot on the seat of the chair, and one foot on the ground.

"Now, Joseph Gargery, I am the bearer of an offer to relieve you of this young fellow your apprentice. You would not object to cancel his indentures at his request and for his good? You would want nothing for so doing?"

"Lord forbid that I should want anything for not standing in Pip's way," said Joe, staring.

"Lord forbidding is pious, but not to the purpose," returned Mr. Jaggers. "The question is, Would you want anything? Do you want anything?"

"The answer is," returned Joe, sternly, "No."

I thought Mr. Jaggers glanced at Joe, as if he considered him a fool for his disinterestedness. But I was too much bewildered between breathless curiosity and surprise, to be sure of it.

"Very well," said Mr. Jaggers. "Recollect the admission you have made, and don't try to go from it presently."

"Who's a going to try?" retorted Joe.

"I don't say anybody is. Do you keep a dog?"

"Yes, I do keep a dog."

"Bear in mind then, that Brag is a good dog, but Holdfast is a better. Bear that in mind, will you?" repeated Mr. Jaggers, shutting his eyes and nodding his head at Joe, as if he were forgiving him something. "Now, I return to this young fellow. And the communication I have got to make is, that he has great expectations."

Joe and I gasped, and looked at one another.

"I am instructed to communicate to him," said Mr. Jaggers, throwing his finger at me sideways, "that he will come into a handsome property. Further, that it is the desire of the present possessor of that property, that he be immediately removed from his present sphere of life and from this place, and be brought up as a gentleman—in a word, as a young fellow of great expectations."

My dream was out; my wild fancy was surpassed by sober reality; Miss Havisham was going to make my fortune on a grand scale.

"Now, Mr. Pip," pursued the lawyer, "I address the rest of what I have to say, to you. You are to understand, first, that it is the request of the person from whom I take my instructions that you always bear the name of Pip. You will have no objection, I dare say, to your great expectations being encumbered with that easy condition. But if you have any objection, this is the time to mention it."

My heart was beating so fast, and there was such a singing in my ears, that I could scarcely stammer I had no objection.

"I should think not! Now you are to understand, secondly, Mr. Pip, that the name of the person who is your liberal benefactor remains a profound secret, until the person chooses to reveal it. I am empowered to mention that it is the intention of the person to reveal it at first hand by word of mouth to yourself. When or where that intention may be carried out, I cannot say; no one can say. It may be years hence. Now, you are distinctly to understand that you are most positively prohibited from making any inquiry on this head, or any allusion or reference, however distant, to any individual whomsoever as *the* individual, in all the communications you may have with me. If you have a suspicion in your own breast, keep that suspicion in your own breast. It is not the least to the purpose what the reasons of this prohibition are; they may be the strongest and gravest reasons, or they may be mere whim. This is not for you to inquire into. The condition is laid down. Your acceptance of it, and your observance of it as binding, is the only remaining condition that I am charged with, by the person from whom I take my instructions, and for whom I am not otherwise responsible. That person is the person from whom you derive your expectations, and the secret is solely held by that person and by me. Again, not a very difficult condition with which to encumber such a rise in fortune; but if you have any objection to it, this is the time to mention it. Speak out."

Once more, I stammered with difficulty that I had no objection.

"I should think not! Now, Mr. Pip, I have done with stipulations." Though he called me Mr. Pip, and began rather to make up to me, he still could not get rid of a certain air of bullying suspicion; and even now he occasionally shut his eyes and threw his finger at me while he spoke, as much as to express that he knew all kinds of things to my disparagement, if he only chose to mention them. "We come next, to mere details of arrangement. You must know that, although I have used the term 'expectations' more than once, you are not endowed with expectations only. There is already lodged in my hands a sum of money amply sufficient for your suitable education and maintenance. You will please consider me your guardian. Oh!" for I was going to thank him, "I tell you at once, I am paid for my services, or I shouldn't render them. It is considered that you must be better educated, in accordance with your altered position, and that you will be alive to the importance and necessity of at once entering on that advantage."

I said I had always longed for it.

"Never mind what you have always longed for, Mr. Pip," he retorted; "keep to the record. If you long for it now, that's enough. Am I answered that you are ready to be placed at once under some proper tutor? Is that it?"

I stammered yes, that was it.

"Good. Now, your inclinations are to be consulted. I don't think that wise, mind, but it's my trust. Have you ever heard of any tutor whom you would prefer to another?"

I had never heard of any tutor but Biddy and Mr. Wopsle's great-aunt; so, I replied in the negative.

"There is a certain tutor, of whom I have some knowledge, who I think might suit the purpose," said Mr. Jaggers. "I don't recommend him, observe; because I never recommend anybody. The gentleman I speak of is one Mr. Matthew Pocket."

Ah! I caught at the name directly. Miss Havisham's relation. The Matthew whom Mr. and Mrs. Camilla had spoken of. The Matthew whose place was to be at Miss Havisham's head, when she lay dead, in her bride's dress on the bride's table.

"You know the name?" said Mr. Jaggers, looking shrewdly at me, and then shutting up his eyes while he waited for my answer.

My answer was, that I had heard of the name.

"Oh!" said he. "You have heard of the name. But the question is, what do you say of it?"

I said, or tried to say, that I was much obliged to him for his recommendation—

"No, my young friend!" he interrupted, shaking his great head very slowly. "Recollect yourself!"

Not recollecting myself, I began again that I was much obliged to him for his recommendation—

"No, my young friend," he interrupted, shaking his head and frowning and smiling both at once; "no, no, no; it's very well done, but it won't do; you are too young to fix me with it. Recommendation is not the word, Mr. Pip. Try another."

Correcting myself, I said that I was much obliged to him for his mention of Mr. Matthew Pocket—

"*That's* more like it!" cried Mr. Jaggers.—And (I added), I would gladly try that gentleman.

"Good. You had better try him in his own house. The way shall be prepared for you, and you can see his son first, who is in London. When will you come to London?"

I said (glancing at Joe, who stood looking on, motionless), that I supposed I could come directly.

"First," said Mr. Jaggers, "you should have some new clothes to come in, and they should not be working-clothes. Say this day week. You'll want some money. Shall I leave you twenty guineas?"

He produced a long purse, with the greatest coolness, and

counted them out on the table and pushed them over to me. This was the first time he had taken his leg from the chair. He sat astride of the chair when he had pushed the money over, and sat swinging his purse and eyeing Joe.

"Well, Joseph Gargery? You look dumbfounded?"

"I *am*!" said Joe, in a very decided manner.

"It was understood that you wanted nothing for yourself, remember?"

"It were understood," said Joe. "And it are understood. And it ever will be similar according."

"But what," said Mr. Jaggers, swinging his purse, "what if it was in my instructions to make you a present, as compensation?"

"As compensation what for?" Joe demanded.

"For the loss of his services."

Joe laid his hand upon my shoulder with the touch of a woman. I have often thought him since, like the steam-hammer that can crush a man or pat an egg-shell, in his combination of strength with gentleness. "Pip is that hearty welcome," said Joe, "to go free with his services, to honor and fortun', as no words can tell him. But if you think as money can make compensation to me fur the loss of the little child—what come to the forge—and ever the best of friends!—"

O dear good Joe, whom I was so ready to leave and so unthankful to, I see you again, with your muscular blacksmith's arm before your eyes, and your broad chest heaving, and your voice dying away. O dear good faithful tender Joe, I feel the loving tremble of your hand upon my arm, as solemnly this day as if it had been the rustle of an angel's wing!

But I encouraged Joe at the time. I was lost in the mazes of my future fortunes, and could not retrace the by-paths we had trodden together. I begged Joe to be comforted, for (as he said) we had ever been the best of friends, and (as I said) we ever would be so. Joe scooped his eyes with his disengaged wrist, as if he were bent on gouging himself, but said not another word.

Mr. Jaggers had looked on at this, as one who recognized in Joe the village idiot, and in me his keeper. When it was over, he said, weighing in his hand the purse he had ceased to swing:

"Now, Joseph Gargery, I warn you this is your last chance. No half measures with me. If you mean to take a present that I have it in charge to make you, speak out, and you shall have it. If on the contrary you mean to say—" Here, to his great amazement, he was stopped by Joe's suddenly working round him with every demonstration of a fell pugilistic purpose.

"Which I meantersay," cried Joe, "that if you come into my place bull-baiting and badgering me, come out! Which I meantersay as sech if you're a man, come on! Which I meantersay that what I say, I meantersay and stand or fall by!"

I drew Joe away, and he immediately became placable; merely stating to me, in an obliging manner and as a polite expostulatory notice to any one whom it might happen to concern, that he were not a going to be bull-baited and badgered in his own place. Mr. Jaggers had risen when Joe demonstrated, and had backed near the door. Without evincing any inclination to come in again, he there delivered his valedictory remarks. They were these.

"Well, Mr. Pip, I think the sooner you leave here—as you are to be a gentleman—the better. Let it stand for this day week, and you shall receive my printed address in the meantime. You can take a hackney-coach at the stage-coach office in London, and come straight to me. Understand, that I express no opinion, one way or other, on the trust I undertake. I am paid for undertaking it, and I do so. Now, understand that, finally. Understand that!"

He was throwing his finger at both of us, and I think would have gone on, but for his seeming to think Joe dangerous, and going off.

Something came into my head which induced me to run after him, as he was going down to the Jolly Bargemen, where he had left a hired carriage.

"I beg your pardon, Mr. Jaggers."

"Halloa!" said he, facing round, "what's the matter?"

"I wish to be quite right, Mr. Jaggers, and to keep to your directions; so I thought I had better ask. Would there be any objection to my taking leave of any one I know, about here, before I go away?"

"No," said he, looking as if he hardly understood me.

"I don't mean in the village only, but up town?"

"No," said he. "No objection."

I thanked him and ran home again, and there I found that Joe had already locked the front door and vacated the state parlor, and was seated by the kitchen fire with a hand on each knee, gazing intently at the burning coals. I too sat down before the fire and gazed at the coals, and nothing was said for a long time.

My sister was in her cushioned chair in her corner, and Biddy sat at her needle-work before the fire, and Joe sat next Biddy, and I sat next Joe in the corner opposite my sister. The more I looked into the glowing coals, the more incapable I became of looking at Joe; the longer the silence lasted, the more unable I felt to speak.

At length I got out, "Joe, have you told Biddy?"

"No, Pip," returned Joe, still looking at the fire, and holding his knees tight, as if he had private information that they intended to make off somewhere, "which I left it to yourself, Pip."

"I would rather you told, Joe."

"Pip's a gentleman of fortun' then," said Joe, "and God bless him in it!"

Biddy dropped her work, and looked at me. Joe held his knees and looked at me. I looked at both of them. After a pause, they both heartily congratulated me; but there was a certain touch of sadness in their congratulations that I rather resented.

I took it upon myself to impress Biddy (and through Biddy, Joe) with the grave obligation I considered my friends under, to know nothing and say nothing about the maker of my fortune. It would all come out in good time, I observed, and in the meanwhile nothing was to be said, save that I had come into great expectations from a mysterious patron. Biddy nodded her head thoughtfully at the fire as she took up her work again, and said she would be very particular; and Joe, still detaining his knees, said, "Ay, ay, I'll be ekervally partickler, Pip;" and then they congratulated me again, and went on to express so much wonder at the notion of my being a gentleman that I didn't half like it.

Infinite pains were then taken by Biddy to convey to my sister some idea of what had happened. To the best of my belief, those efforts entirely failed. She laughed and nodded her head a great many times, and even repeated after Biddy, the words "Pip" and "Property." But I doubt if they had more meaning in them than an election cry, and I cannot suggest a darker picture of her state of mind.

I never could have believed it without experience, but as Joe and Biddy became more at their cheerful ease again, I became quite gloomy. Dissatisfied with my fortune, of course I could not be; but it is possible that I may have been, without quite knowing it, dissatisfied with myself.

Anyhow, I sat with my elbow on my knee and my face upon my hand, looking into the fire, as those two talked about my going away, and about what they should do without me, and all that. And whenever I caught one of them looking at me, though never so pleasantly (and they often looked at me—particularly Biddy), I felt offended: as if they were expressing some mistrust of me. Though Heaven knows they never did by word or sign.

At those times I would get up and look out at the door; for our kitchen door opened at once upon the night, and stood open on summer evenings to air the room. The very stars to which I then raised my eyes, I am afraid I took to be but poor and humble stars for glittering on the rustic objects among which I had passed my life.

"Saturday night," said I, when we sat at our supper of bread and cheese and beer. "Five more days, and then the day before *the* day! They'll soon go."

"Yes, Pip," observed Joe, whose voice sounded hollow in his beer-mug. "They'll soon go."

"Soon, soon go," said Biddy.

"I have been thinking, Joe, that when I go down town on Monday, and order my new clothes, I shall tell the tailor that I'll come and put them on there, or that I'll have them sent to Mr. Pumblechook's. It would be very disagreeable to be stared at by all the people here."

"Mr. and Mrs. Hubble might like to see you in your new gen-teel figure too, Pip," said Joe, industriously cutting his bread, with his cheese on it, in the palm of his left hand, and glancing at my untasted supper as if he thought of the time when we used to compare slices. "So might Wopsle. And the Jolly Bargemen might take it as a compliment."

"That's just what I don't want, Joe. They would make such a business of it—such a coarse and common business—that I couldn't bear myself."

"Ah, that indeed, Pip!" said Joe. "If you couldn't abear yourself—"

Biddy asked me here, as she sat holding my sister's plate, "Have you thought about when you'll show yourself to Mr. Gargery, and your sister and me? You will show yourself to us; won't you?"

"Biddy," I returned with some resentment, "you are so exceedingly quick that it's difficult to keep up with you."

("She always were quick," observed Joe.)

"If you had waited another moment, Biddy, you would have heard me say that I shall bring my clothes here in a bundle one evening—most likely on the evening before I go away."

Biddy said no more. Handsomely forgiving her, I soon exchanged an affectionate good night with her and Joe, and went up to bed. When I got into my little room, I sat down and took a long look at it, as a mean little room that I should soon be parted from and raised above, for ever. It was furnished with fresh young remembrances too, and even at the same moment I fell into much the same confused division of mind between it and the better rooms to which I was going, as I had been in so often between the forge and Miss Havisham's, and Biddy and Estella.

The sun had been shining brightly all day on the roof of my attic, and the room was warm. As I put the window open and stood looking out, I saw Joe come slowly forth at the dark door, below, and take a turn or two in the air; and then I saw Biddy come, and bring him a pipe and light it for him. He never smoked so late, and it seemed to hint to me that he wanted comforting, for some reason or other.

He presently stood at the door immediately beneath me, smoking his pipe, and Biddy stood there too, quietly talking to him, and I knew that they talked of me, for I heard my name mentioned in an endearing tone by both of them more than once. I would not have listened for more, if I could have heard more; so I drew away from the window, and sat down in my one chair by the bedside, feeling it very sorrowful and strange that this first night of my bright fortunes should be the loneliest I had ever known.

Looking towards the open window, I saw light wreaths from Joe's pipe floating there, and I fancied it was like a blessing from

Joe—not obtruded on me or paraded before me, but pervading the air we shared together. I put my light out, and crept into bed; and it was an uneasy bed now, and I never slept the old sound sleep in it any more.

CHAPTER 19

Morning made a considerable difference in my general prospect of Life, and brightened it so much that it scarcely seemed the same. What lay heaviest on my mind was, the consideration that six days intervened between me and the day of departure; for I could not divest myself of a misgiving that something might happen to London in the meanwhile, and that, when I got there, it would be either greatly deteriorated or clean gone.

Joe and Biddy were very sympathetic and pleasant when I spoke of our approaching separation; but they only referred to it when I did. After breakfast, Joe brought out my indentures from the press in the best parlor, and we put them in the fire, and I felt that I was free. With all the novelty of my emancipation on me, I went to church with Joe, and thought perhaps the clergyman wouldn't have read that about the rich man and the kingdom of Heaven, if he had known all.

After our early dinner, I strolled out alone, purposing to finish off the marshes at once, and get them done with. As I passed the church, I felt (as I had felt during service in the morning) a sublime compassion for the poor creatures who were destined to go there, Sunday after Sunday, all their lives through, and to lie obscurely at last among the low green mounds. I promised myself that I would do something for them one of these days, and formed a plan in outline for bestowing a dinner of roast-beef and plum-pudding, a pint of ale, and a gallon of condescension, upon everybody in the village.

If I had often thought before, with something allied to shame, of my companionship with the fugitive whom I had once seen limping among those graves, what were my thoughts on this Sunday, when the place recalled the wretch, ragged and shivering, with his felon iron and badge! My comfort was, that it happened a long time ago, and that he had doubtless been transported a long way off, and that he was dead to me, and might be veritably dead into the bargain.

No more low, wet grounds, no more dikes and sluices, no more of these grazing cattle—though they seemed, in their dull manner, to wear a more respectful air now, and to face round, in order that they might stare as long as possible at the possessor of such great expectations—farewell, monotonous acquaintances of my childhood, henceforth I was for London and greatness; not for smith's work in general, and for you! I made my exultant way to the old Battery, and, lying down there to consider the question whether Miss Havisham intended me for Estella, fell asleep.

When I awoke, I was much surprised to find Joe sitting beside me, smoking his pipe. He greeted me with a cheerful smile on my opening my eyes, and said:

"As being the last time, Pip, I thought I'd foller."

"And Joe, I am very glad you did so."

"Thankee, Pip."

"You may be sure, dear Joe," I went on, after we had shaken hands, "that I shall never forget you."

"No, no, Pip!" said Joe, in a comfortable tone, "I'm sure of that. Ay, ay, old chap! Bless you, it were only necessary to get it well round in a man's mind, to be certain on it. But it took a bit of time to get it well round, the change come so oncommon plump; didn't it?"

Somehow, I was not best pleased with Joe's being so mightily secure of me. I should have liked him to have betrayed emotion, or to have said, "It does you credit, Pip," or something of that sort. Therefore, I made no remark on Joe's first head; merely saying as to his second, that the tidings had indeed come suddenly, but that I had always wanted to be a gentleman, and had often and often speculated on what I would do, if I were one.

"Have you though?" said Joe. "Astonishing!"

"It's a pity now, Joe," said I, "that you did not get on a little more, when we had our lessons here; isn't it?"

"Well, I don't know," returned Joe. "I'm so awful dull. I'm only master of my own trade. It were always a pity as I was so awful dull; but it's no more of a pity now, than it was—this day twelvemonth—don't you see?"

What I had meant was, that when I came into my property and was able to do something for Joe, it would have been much more agreeable if he had been better qualified for a rise in station. He was so perfectly innocent of my meaning, however, that I thought I would mention it to Biddy in preference.

So, when we had walked home and had had tea, I took Biddy into our little garden by the side of the lane, and, after throwing out in a general way for the elevation of her spirits, that I should never forget her, said I had a favor to ask of her.

"And it is, Biddy," said I, "that you will not omit any opportunity of helping Joe on, a little."

"How helping him on?" asked Biddy, with a steady sort of glance.

"Well! Joe is a dear good fellow—in fact, I think he is the dearest fellow that ever lived—but he is rather backward in some things. For instance, Biddy, in his learning and his manners."

Although I was looking at Biddy as I spoke, and although she opened her eyes very wide when I had spoken, she did not look at me.

"O, his manners! won't his manners do then?" asked Biddy, plucking a black-currant leaf.

"My dear Biddy, they do very well here—"

"O! they *do* very well here?" interposed Biddy, looking closely at the leaf in her hand.

"Hear me out—but if I were to remove Joe into a higher sphere, as I shall hope to remove him when I fully come into my property, they would hardly do him justice."

"And don't you think he knows that?" asked Biddy.

It was such a very provoking question (for it had never in the most distant manner occurred to me), that I said, snappishly, "Biddy, what do you mean?"

Biddy, having rubbed the leaf to pieces between her hands—and the smell of a black-currant bush has ever since recalled to me that evening in the little garden by the side of the lane—said, "Have you never considered that he may be proud?"

"Proud?" I repeated, with disdainful emphasis.

"Oh! there are many kinds of pride," said Biddy, looking full at me and shaking her head; "pride is not all of one kind—"

"Well? What are you stopping for?" said I.

"Not all of one kind," resumed Biddy. "He may be too proud to let any one take him out of a place that he is competent to fill, and fills well and with respect. To tell you the truth, I think he is; though it sounds bold in me to say so, for you must know him far better than I do."

"Now, Biddy," said I, "I am very sorry to see this in you. I did not expect to see this in you. You are envious, Biddy, and grudging. You are dissatisfied on account of my rise in fortune, and you can't help showing it."

"If you have the heart to think so," returned Biddy, "say so. Say so over and over again, if you have the heart to think so."

"If you have the heart to be so, you mean, Biddy," said I, in a virtuous and superior tone; "don't put it off upon me. I am very sorry to see it, and it's a—it's a bad side of human nature. I did intend to ask you to use any little opportunities you might have after I was gone, of improving dear Joe. But after this I ask you nothing. I am extremely sorry to see this in you, Biddy," I repeated. "It's a—it's a bad side of human nature."

"Whether you scold me or approve of me," returned poor Biddy, "you may equally depend upon my trying to do all that lies in my power, here, at all times. And whatever opinion you take away of me, shall make no difference in my remembrance of you. Yet a gentleman should not be unjust neither," said Biddy, turning away her head.

I again warmly repeated that it was a bad side of human nature (in which sentiment, waiving its application, I have since seen reason to think I was right), and I walked down the little path away from Biddy, and Biddy went into the house, and I went out at the garden gate and took a dejected stroll until supper-time; again feeling it very sorrowful and strange that this, the second night of my bright fortunes, should be as lonely and unsatisfactory as the first.

But, morning once more brightened my view, and I extended my clemency to Biddy, and we dropped the subject. Putting on the best clothes I had, I went into town as early as I could hope to find the shops open, and presented myself before Mr. Trabb, the tailor, who was having his breakfast in the parlor behind his shop, and who did not think it worth his while to come out to me, but called me in to him.

"Well!" said Mr. Trabb, in a hail-fellow-well-met kind of way. "How are you, and what can I do for you?"

Mr. Trabb had sliced his hot roll into three feather-beds, and was slipping butter in between the blankets, and covering it up. He was a prosperous old bachelor, and his open window looked into a prosperous little garden and orchard, and there was a prosperous iron safe let into the wall at the side of his fireplace, and I did not doubt that heaps of his prosperity were put away in it in bags.

"Mr. Trabb," said I, "it's an unpleasant thing to have to mention, because it looks like boasting; but I have come into a handsome property."

A change passed over Mr. Trabb. He forgot the butter in

bed, got up from the bedside, and wiped his fingers on the tablecloth, exclaiming, "Lord bless my soul!"

"I am going up to my guardian in London," said I, casually drawing some guineas out of my pocket and looking at them; "and I want a fashionable suit of clothes to go in. I wish to pay for them," I added—otherwise I thought he might only pretend to make them, "with ready money."

"My dear sir," said Mr. Trabb, as he respectfully bent his body, opened his arms, and took the liberty of touching me on the outside of each elbow, "don't hurt me by mentioning that. May I venture to congratulate you? Would you do me the favor of stepping into the shop?"

Mr. Trabb's boy was the most audacious boy in all that country-side. When I had entered he was sweeping the shop, and he had sweetened his labors by sweeping over me. He was still sweeping when I came out into the shop with Mr. Trabb, and he knocked the broom against all possible corners and obstacles, to express (as I understood it) equality with any blacksmith, alive or dead.

"Hold that noise," said Mr. Trabb, with the greatest sternness, "or I'll knock your head off!—Do me the favor to be seated, sir. Now, this," said Mr. Trabb, taking down a roll of cloth, and tiding it out in a flowing manner over the counter, preparatory to getting his hand under it to show the gloss, "is a very sweet article. I can recommend it for your purpose, sir, because it really is extra super. But you shall see some others. Give me Number Four, you!" (To the boy, and with a dreadfully severe stare; foreseeing the danger of that miscreant's brushing me with it, or making some other sign of familiarity.)

Mr. Trabb never removed his stern eye from the boy until he had deposited number four on the counter and was at a safe distance again. Then he commanded him to bring number five, and number eight. "And let me have none of your tricks here," said Mr. Trabb, "or you shall repent it, you young scoundrel, the longest day you have to live."

Mr. Trabb then bent over number four, and in a sort of deferential confidence recommended it to me as a light article for summer wear, an article much in vogue among the nobility and gentry, an article that it would ever be an honor to him to reflect upon a distinguished fellow-townsman's (if he might claim me for a fellow-townsman) having worn. "Are you bringing numbers five and eight, you vagabond," said Mr. Trabb to the boy after that, "or shall I kick you out of the shop and bring them myself?"

I selected the materials for a suit, with the assistance of Mr. Trabb's judgment, and re-entered the parlor to be measured. For although Mr. Trabb had my measure already, and had previously been quite contented with it, he said apologetically that it "wouldn't do under existing circumstances, sir— wouldn't do at all." So, Mr. Trabb measured and calculated me in the parlor, as if I were an estate and he the finest species of surveyor, and gave himself such a world of trouble that I felt that no suit of clothes could possibly remunerate him for his pains. When he had at last done and had appointed to send the articles to Mr. Pumblechook's on the Thursday evening, he said, with his hand upon the parlor lock, "I know, sir, that London gentlemen cannot be expected to patronize local work, as a rule; but if you would give me a turn now and then in the quality of a townsman, I should greatly esteem it. Good morning, sir, much obliged.—Door!"

The last word was flung at the boy, who had not the least notion what it meant. But I saw him collapse as his master rubbed me out with his hands, and my first decided experience of the stupendous power of money was, that it had morally laid upon his back Trabb's boy.

After this memorable event, I went to the hatter's, and the bootmaker's, and the hosier's, and felt rather like Mother

Hubbard's dog whose outfit required the services of so many trades. I also went to the coach-office and took my place for seven o'clock on Saturday morning. It was not necessary to explain everywhere that I had come into a handsome property; but whenever I said anything to that effect, it followed that the officiating tradesman ceased to have his attention diverted through the window by the High Street, and concentrated his mind upon me. When I had ordered everything I wanted, I directed my steps towards Pumblechook's, and, as I approached that gentleman's place of business, I saw him standing at his door.

He was waiting for me with great impatience. He had been out early with the chaise-cart, and had called at the forge and heard the news. He had prepared a collation for me in the Barnwell parlor, and he too ordered his shopman to "come out of the gangway" as my sacred person passed.

"My dear friend," said Mr. Pumblechook, taking me by both hands, when he and I and the collation were alone, "I give you joy of your good fortune. Well deserved, well deserved!"

This was coming to the point, and I thought it a sensible way of expressing himself.

"To think," said Mr. Pumblechook, after snorting admiration at me for some moments, "that I should have been the humble instrument of leading up to this, is a proud reward."

I begged Mr. Pumblechook to remember that nothing was to be ever said or hinted, on that point.

"My dear young friend," said Mr. Pumblechook; "if you will allow me to call you so—"

I murmured "Certainly," and Mr. Pumblechook took me by both hands again, and communicated a movement to his waistcoat, which had an emotional appearance, though it was rather low down, "My dear young friend, rely upon my doing my little all in your absence, by keeping the fact before the mind of Joseph.—Joseph!" said Mr. Pumblechook, in the way of a compassionate adjuration. "Joseph!! Joseph!!!" Thereupon he shook his head and tapped it, expressing his sense of deficiency in Joseph.

"But my dear young friend," said Mr. Pumblechook, "you must be hungry, you must be exhausted. Be seated. Here is a chicken had round from the Boar, here is a tongue had round from the Boar, here's one or two little things had round from the Boar, that I hope you may not despise. But do I," said Mr. Pumblechook, getting up again the moment after he had sat down, "see afore me, him as I ever sported with in his times of happy infancy? And may I—*may* I—?"

This May I, meant might he shake hands? I consented, and he was fervent, and then sat down again.

"Here is wine," said Mr. Pumblechook. "Let us drink, Thanks to Fortune, and may she ever pick out her favorites with equal judgment! And yet I cannot," said Mr. Pumblechook, getting up again, "see afore me One—and likewise drink to One—without again expressing—May I—*may* I—?"

I said he might, and he shook hands with me again, and emptied his glass and turned it upside down. I did the same; and if I had turned myself upside down before drinking, the wine could not have gone more direct to my head.

Mr. Pumblechook helped me to the liver wing, and to the best slice of tongue (none of those out-of-the-way No Thoroughfares of Pork now), and took, comparatively speaking, no care of himself at all. "Ah! poultry, poultry! You little thought," said Mr. Pumblechook, apostrophizing the fowl in the dish, "when you was a young fledgling, what was in store for you. You little thought you was to be refreshment beneath this humble roof for one as—Call it a weakness, if you will," said Mr. Pumblechook, getting up again, "but may I? *may* I—?"

It began to be unnecessary to repeat the form of saying he might, so he did it at once. How he ever did it so often without wounding himself with my knife, I don't know.

"And your sister," he resumed, after a little steady eating, "which had the honor of bringing you up by hand! It's a sad picter, to reflect that she's no longer equal to fully understanding the honor. May—"

I saw he was about to come at me again, and I stopped him.

"We'll drink her health," said I.

"Ah!" cried Mr. Pumblechook, leaning back in his chair, quite flaccid with admiration, "that's the way you know 'em, sir!" (I don't know who Sir was, but he certainly was not I, and there was no third person present); "that's the way you know the noble-minded, sir! Ever forgiving and ever affable. It might," said the servile Pumblechook, putting down his untasted glass in a hurry and getting up again, "to a common person, have the appearance of repeating—but *may* I—?"

When he had done it, he resumed his seat and drank to my sister. "Let us never be blind," said Mr. Pumblechook, "to her faults of temper, but it is to be hoped she meant well."

At about this time, I began to observe that he was getting flushed in the face; as to myself, I felt all face, steeped in wine and smarting.

I mentioned to Mr. Pumblechook that I wished to have my new clothes sent to his house, and he was ecstatic on my so distinguishing him. I mentioned my reason for desiring to avoid observation in the village, and he lauded it to the skies. There was nobody but himself, he intimated, worthy of my confidence, and—in short, might he? Then he asked me tenderly if I remembered our boyish games at sums, and how we had gone together to have me bound apprentice, and, in effect, how he had ever been my favorite fancy and my chosen friend? If I had taken ten times as many glasses of wine as I had, I should have known that he never had stood in that relation towards me, and should in my heart of hearts have repudiated the idea. Yet for all that, I remember feeling convinced that I had been much mistaken in him, and that he was a sensible, practical, good-hearted prime fellow.

By degrees he fell to reposing such great confidence in me, as to ask my advice in reference to his own affairs. He mentioned that there was an opportunity for a great amalgamation and monopoly of the corn and seed trade on those premises, if enlarged, such as had never occurred before in that or any other neighbourhood. What alone was wanting to the realization of a vast fortune, he considered to be More Capital. Those were the two little words, more capital. Now it appeared to him (Pumblechook) that if that capital were got into the business, through a sleeping partner, sir—which sleeping partner would have nothing to do but walk in, by self or deputy, whenever he pleased, and examine the books—and walk in twice a year and take his profits away in his pocket, to the tune of fifty per cent—it appeared to him that that might be an opening for a young gentleman of spirit combined with property, which would be worthy of his attention. But what did I think? He had great confidence in my opinion, and what did I think? I gave it as my opinion. "Wait a bit!" The united vastness and distinctness of this view so struck him, that he no longer asked if he might shake hands with me, but said he really must—and did.

We drank all the wine, and Mr. Pumblechook pledged himself over and over again to keep Joseph up to the mark (I don't know what mark), and to render me efficient and constant service (I don't know what service). He also made known to me for the first time in my life, and certainly after having kept his secret wonderfully well, that he had always said of me, "That boy is no common boy, and mark me, his fortun' will be no common fortun.'" He said with a tearful smile that it was a singular thing to think of now, and I said so too. Finally, I went out into the air, with a dim perception that there was something unwonted in the conduct of the sunshine, and found that I had slumberously got to the turnpike without having taken any account of the road.

There, I was roused by Mr. Pumblechook's hailing me. He was a long way down the sunny street, and was making expressive gestures for me to stop. I stopped, and he came up breathless.

"No, my dear friend," said he, when he had recovered wind for speech. "Not if I can help it. This occasion shall not entirely pass without that affability on your part.—May I, as an old friend and well-wisher? *May* I?"

We shook hands for the hundredth time at least, and he ordered a young carter out of my way with the greatest indignation. Then, he blessed me and stood waving his hand to me until I had passed the crook in the road; and then I turned into a field and had a long nap under a hedge before I pursued my way home.

I had scant luggage to take with me to London, for little of the little I possessed was adapted to my new station. But I began packing that same afternoon, and wildly packed up things that I knew I should want next morning, in a fiction that there was not a moment to be lost.

So, Tuesday, Wednesday, and Thursday, passed; and on Friday morning I went to Mr. Pumblechook's, to put on my new clothes and pay my visit to Miss Havisham. Mr. Pumblechook's own room was given up to me to dress in, and was decorated with clean towels expressly for the event. My clothes were rather a disappointment, of course. Probably every new and eagerly expected garment ever put on since clothes came in, fell a trifle short of the wearer's expectation. But after I had had my new suit on some half an hour, and had gone through an immensity of posturing with Mr. Pumblechook's very limited dressing-glass, in the futile endeavor to see my legs, it seemed to fit me better. It being market morning at a neighbouring town some ten miles off, Mr. Pumblechook was not at home.

I had not told him exactly when I meant to leave, and was not likely to shake hands with him again before departing. This was all as it should be, and I went out in my new array, fearfully ashamed of having to pass the shopman, and suspicious after all that I was at a personal disadvantage, something like Joe's in his Sunday suit.

I went circuitously to Miss Havisham's by all the back ways, and rang at the bell constrainedly, on account of the stiff long fingers of my gloves. Sarah Pocket came to the gate, and positively reeled back when she saw me so changed; her walnut-shell countenance likewise turned from brown to green and yellow.

"You?" said she. "You? Good gracious! What do you want?"

"I am going to London, Miss Pocket," said I, "and want to say good by to Miss Havisham."

I was not expected, for she left me locked in the yard, while she went to ask if I were to be admitted. After a very short delay, she returned and took me up, staring at me all the way.

Miss Havisham was taking exercise in the room with the long spread table, leaning on her crutch stick. The room was lighted as of yore, and at the sound of our entrance, she stopped and turned. She was then just abreast of the rotted bride-cake.

"Don't go, Sarah," she said. "Well, Pip?"

"I start for London, Miss Havisham, to-morrow," I was exceedingly careful what I said, "and I thought you would kindly not mind my taking leave of you."

"This is a gay figure, Pip," said she, making her crutch stick play round me, as if she, the fairy godmother who had changed me, were bestowing the finishing gift.

"I have come into such good fortune since I saw you last, Miss Havisham," I murmured. "And I am so grateful for it, Miss Havisham!"

"Ay, ay!" said she, looking at the discomfited and envious

Sarah, with delight. "*I* have seen Mr. Jaggers. I have heard about it, Pip. So you go to-morrow?"

"Yes, Miss Havisham."

"And you are adopted by a rich person?"

"Yes, Miss Havisham."

"Not named?"

"No, Miss Havisham."

"And Mr. Jaggers is made your guardian?"

"Yes, Miss Havisham."

She quite gloated on these questions and answers, so keen was her enjoyment of Sarah Pocket's jealous dismay. "Well!" she went on; "you have a promising career before you. Be good—deserve it—and abide by Mr. Jaggers's instructions." She looked at me, and looked at Sarah, and Sarah's countenance wrung out of her watchful face a cruel smile. "Good by, Pip!—you will always keep the name of Pip, you know."

"Yes, Miss Havisham."

"Good by, Pip!"

She stretched out her hand, and I went down on my knee and put it to my lips. I had not considered how I should take leave of her; it came naturally to me at the moment to do this. She looked at Sarah Pocket with triumph in her weird eyes, and so I left my fairy godmother, with both her hands on her crutch stick, standing in the midst of the dimly lighted room beside the rotten bride-cake that was hidden in cobwebs.

Sarah Pocket conducted me down, as if I were a ghost who must be seen out. She could not get over my appearance, and was in the last degree confounded. I said "Good by, Miss Pocket;" but she merely stared, and did not seem collected enough to know that I had spoken. Clear of the house, I made the best of my way back to Pumblechook's, took off my new clothes, made them into a bundle, and went back home in my older dress, carrying it—to speak the truth—much more at my ease too, though I had the bundle to carry.

And now, those six days which were to have run out so slowly, had run out fast and were gone, and to-morrow looked me in the face more steadily than I could look at it. As the six evenings had dwindled away, to five, to four, to three, to two, I had become more and more appreciative of the society of Joe and Biddy. On this last evening, I dressed my self out in my new clothes for their delight, and sat in my splendor until bedtime. We had a hot supper on the occasion, graced by the inevitable roast fowl, and we had some flip to finish with. We were all very low, and none the higher for pretending to be in spirits.

I was to leave our village at five in the morning, carrying my little hand-portmanteau, and I had told Joe that I wished to walk away all alone. I am afraid—sore afraid—that this purpose originated in my sense of the contrast there would be between me and Joe, if we went to the coach together. I had pretended with myself that there was nothing of this taint in the arrangement; but when I went up to my little room on this last night, I felt compelled to admit that it might be so, and had an impulse upon me to go down again and entreat Joe to walk with me in the morning. I did not.

All night there were coaches in my broken sleep, going to wrong places instead of to London, and having in the traces, now dogs, now cats, now pigs, now men—never horses. Fantastic failures of journeys occupied me until the day dawned and the birds were singing. Then, I got up and partly dressed, and sat at the window to take a last look out, and in taking it fell asleep.

Biddy was astir so early to get my breakfast, that, although I did not sleep at the window an hour, I smelt the smoke of the kitchen fire when I started up with a terrible idea that it must be late in the afternoon. But long after that, and long after I had heard the clinking of the teacups and was quite ready, I wanted the resolution to go down stairs. After all, I remained up there, repeatedly unlocking and unstrapping my small portmanteau and locking and strapping it up again, until Biddy called to me that I was late.

It was a hurried breakfast with no taste in it. I got up from the meal, saying with a sort of briskness, as if it had only just occurred to me, "Well! I suppose I must be off!" and then I kissed my sister who was laughing and nodding and shaking in her usual chair, and kissed Biddy, and threw my arms around Joe's neck. Then I took up my little portmanteau and walked out. The last I saw of them was, when I presently heard a scuffle behind me, and looking back, saw Joe throwing an old shoe after me and Biddy throwing another old shoe. I stopped then, to wave my hat, and dear old Joe waved his strong right arm above his head, crying huskily "Hooroar!" and Biddy put her apron to her face.

I walked away at a good pace, thinking it was easier to go than I had supposed it would be, and reflecting that it would never have done to have had an old shoe thrown after the coach, in sight of all the High Street. I whistled and made nothing of going. But the village was very peaceful and quiet, and the light mists were solemnly rising, as if to show me the world, and I had been so innocent and little there, and all beyond was so unknown and great, that in a moment with a strong heave and sob I broke into tears. It was by the finger-post at the end of the village, and I laid my hand upon it, and said, "Good by, O my dear, dear friend!"

Heaven knows we need never be ashamed of our tears, for they are rain upon the blinding dust of earth, overlying our hard hearts. I was better after I had cried than before—more sorry, more aware of my own ingratitude, more gentle. If I had cried before, I should have had Joe with me then.

So subdued I was by those tears, and by their breaking out again in the course of the quiet walk, that when I was on the coach, and it was clear of the town, I deliberated with an aching heart whether I would not get down when we changed horses and walk back, and have another evening at home, and a better parting. We changed, and I had not made up my mind, and still reflected for my comfort that it would be quite practicable to get down and walk back, when we changed again. And while I was occupied with these deliberations, I would fancy an exact resemblance to Joe in some man coming along the road towards us, and my heart would beat high.—As if he could possibly be there!

We changed again, and yet again, and it was now too late and too far to go back, and I went on. And the mists had all solemnly risen now, and the world lay spread before me.

THIS IS THE END OF THE FIRST STAGE OF PIP'S EXPECTATIONS

VOLUME TWO

CHAPTER 1

The journey from our town to the metropolis was a journey of about five hours. It was a little past midday when the four-horse stage-coach by which I was a passenger, got into the ravel of traffic frayed out about the Cross Keys, Wood Street, Cheapside, London.

We Britons had at that time particularly settled that it was treasonable to doubt our having and our being the best of everything: otherwise, while I was scared by the immensity of London, I think I might have had some faint doubts whether it was not rather ugly, crooked, narrow, and dirty.

Mr. Jaggers had duly sent me his address; it was, Little Britain, and he had written after it on his card, "just out of Smithfield, and close by the coach-office." Nevertheless, a hackney-coachman, who seemed to have as many capes to his greasy great-coat as he was years old, packed me up in his coach and hemmed me in with a folding and jingling barrier of steps, as if he were going to take me fifty miles. His getting on his box, which I remember to have been decorated with an old weather-stained pea-green hammercloth moth-eaten into rags, was quite a work of time. It was a wonderful equipage, with six great coronets outside, and ragged things behind for I don't know how many footmen to hold on by, and a harrow below them, to prevent amateur footmen from yielding to the temptation.

I had scarcely had time to enjoy the coach and to think how like a straw-yard it was, and yet how like a rag-shop, and to wonder why the horses' nose-bags were kept inside, when I observed the coachman beginning to get down, as if we were going to stop presently. And stop we presently did, in a gloomy street, at certain offices with an open door, whereon was painted MR. JAGGERS.

"How much?" I asked the coachman.

The coachman answered, "A shilling—unless you wish to make it more."

I naturally said I had no wish to make it more.

"Then it must be a shilling," observed the coachman. "I don't want to get into trouble. I know *him*!" He darkly closed an eye at Mr. Jaggers's name, and shook his head.

When he had got his shilling, and had in course of time completed the ascent to his box, and had got away (which appeared to relieve his mind), I went into the front office with my little portmanteau in my hand and asked, Was Mr. Jaggers at home?

"He is not," returned the clerk. "He is in Court at present. Am I addressing Mr. Pip?"

I signified that he was addressing Mr. Pip.

"Mr. Jaggers left word, would you wait in his room. He couldn't say how long he might be, having a case on. But it stands to reason, his time being valuable, that he won't be longer than he can help."

With those words, the clerk opened a door, and ushered me into an inner chamber at the back. Here, we found a gentleman with one eye, in a velveteen suit and knee-breeches, who wiped his nose with his sleeve on being interrupted in the perusal of the newspaper.

"Go and wait outside, Mike," said the clerk.

I began to say that I hoped I was not interrupting, when the clerk shoved this gentleman out with as little ceremony as

I ever saw used, and tossing his fur cap out after him, left me alone.

Mr. Jaggers's room was lighted by a skylight only, and was a most dismal place; the skylight, eccentrically pitched like a broken head, and the distorted adjoining houses looking as if they had twisted themselves to peep down at me through it. There were not so many papers about, as I should have expected to see; and there were some odd objects about, that I should not have expected to see—such as an old rusty pistol, a sword in a scabbard, several strange-looking boxes and packages, and two dreadful casts on a shelf, of faces peculiarly swollen, and twitchy about the nose. Mr. Jaggers's own high-backed chair was of deadly black horsehair, with rows of brass nails round it, like a coffin; and I fancied I could see how he leaned back in it, and bit his forefinger at the clients. The room was but small, and the clients seemed to have had a habit of backing up against the wall; the wall, especially opposite to Mr. Jaggers's chair, being greasy with shoulders. I recalled, too, that the one-eyed gentleman had shuffled forth against the wall when I was the innocent cause of his being turned out.

I sat down in the cliental chair placed over against Mr. Jaggers's chair, and became fascinated by the dismal atmosphere of the place. I called to mind that the clerk had the same air of knowing something to everybody else's disadvantage, as his master had. I wondered how many other clerks there were up-stairs, and whether they all claimed to have the same detrimental mastery of their fellow-creatures. I wondered what was the history of all the odd litter about the room, and how it came there. I wondered whether the two swollen faces were of Mr. Jaggers's family, and, if he were so unfortunate as to have had a pair of such ill-looking relations, why he stuck them on that dusty perch for the blacks and flies to settle on, instead of giving them a place at home. Of course I had no experience of a London summer day, and my spirits may have been oppressed by the hot exhausted air, and by the dust and grit that lay thick on everything. But I sat wondering and waiting in Mr. Jaggers's close room, until I really could not bear the two casts on the shelf above Mr. Jaggers's chair, and got up and went out.

When I told the clerk that I would take a turn in the air while I waited, he advised me to go round the corner and I should come into Smithfield. So I came into Smithfield; and the shameful place, being all asmear with filth and fat and blood and foam, seemed to stick to me. So, I rubbed it off with all possible speed by turning into a street where I saw the great black dome of Saint Paul's bulging at me from behind a grim stone building which a bystander said was Newgate Prison. Following the wall of the jail, I found the roadway covered with straw to deaden the noise of passing vehicles; and from this, and from the quantity of people standing about smelling strongly of spirits and beer, I inferred that the trials were on.

While I looked about me here, an exceedingly dirty and partially drunk minister of justice asked me if I would like to step in and hear a trial or so: informing me that he could give me a front place for half a crown, whence I should command a full view of the Lord Chief Justice in his wig and robes— mentioning that awful personage like waxwork, and presently offering him at the reduced price of eighteen-pence. As I declined the proposal on the plea of an appointment, he was so good as to take me into a yard and show me where the gallows was kept, and also where people were publicly whipped, and then he showed me the Debtors' Door, out of which culprits came to be hanged; heightening the interest of that dreadful portal by giving me to understand that "four on 'em" would come out at that door the day after to-morrow at eight in the morning, to be killed in a row. This was horrible, and gave me a sickening idea of London; the more so as the Lord Chief Justice's proprietor wore (from his hat down to his boots and up again to his pocket-handkerchief inclusive) mildewed clothes which had evidently not belonged to him originally, and which I took it into my head he had bought cheap of the executioner. Under these circumstances I thought myself well rid of him for a shilling.

I dropped into the office to ask if Mr. Jaggers had come in yet, and I found he had not, and I strolled out again. This time, I made the tour of Little Britain, and turned into Bartholomew Close; and now I became aware that other people were waiting about for Mr. Jaggers, as well as I. There were two men of secret appearance lounging in Bartholomew Close, and thoughtfully fitting their feet into the cracks of the pavement as they talked together, one of whom said to the other when they first passed me, that "Jaggers would do it if it was to be done." There was a knot of three men and two women standing at a corner, and one of the women was crying on her dirty shawl, and the other comforted her by saying, as she pulled her own shawl over her shoulders, "Jaggers is for him, 'Melia, and what more *could* you have?" There was a red-eyed little Jew who came into the Close while I was loitering there, in company with a second little Jew whom he sent upon an errand; and while the messenger was gone, I remarked this Jew, who was of a highly excitable temperament, performing a jig of anxiety under a lamp-post and accompanying himself, in a kind of frenzy, with the words, "O Jaggerth, Jaggerth, Jaggerth! all otherth ith Cag-Maggerth, give me Jaggerth!" These testimonies to the popularity of my guardian made a deep impression on me, and I admired and wondered more than ever.

At length, as I was looking out at the iron gate of Bartholomew Close into Little Britain, I saw Mr. Jaggers coming across the road towards me. All the others who were waiting saw him at the same time, and there was quite a rush at him. Mr. Jaggers, putting a hand on my shoulder and walking me on at his side without saying anything to me, addressed himself to his followers. First, he took the two secret men.

"Now, I have nothing to say to you," said Mr. Jaggers, throwing his finger at them. "I want to know no more than I know. As to the result, it's a toss-up. I told you from the first it was a toss-up. Have you paid Wemmick?"

"We made the money up this morning, sir," said one of the men, submissively, while the other perused Mr. Jaggers's face.

"I don't ask you when you made it up, or where, or whether you made it up at all. Has Wemmick got it?"

"Yes, sir," said both the men together.

"Very well; then you may go. Now, I won't have it!" said Mr Jaggers, waving his hand at them to put them behind him. "If you say a word to me, I'll throw up the case."

"We thought, Mr. Jaggers—" one of the men began, pulling off his hat.

"That's what I told you not to do," said Mr. Jaggers. "*You* thought! I think for you; that's enough for you. If I want you, I know where to find you; I don't want you to find me. Now I won't have it. I won't hear a word."

The two men looked at one another as Mr. Jaggers waved them behind again, and humbly fell back and were heard no more.

"And now *you*!" said Mr. Jaggers, suddenly stopping, and turning on the two women with the shawls, from whom the three men had meekly separated.— "Oh! Amelia, is it?"

"Yes, Mr. Jaggers."

"And do you remember," retorted Mr. Jaggers, "that but for me you wouldn't be here and couldn't be here?"

"O yes, sir!" exclaimed both women together. "Lord bless you, sir, well we knows that!"

"Then why," said Mr. Jaggers, "do you come here?"

"My Bill, sir!" the crying woman pleaded.

"Now, I tell you what!" said Mr. Jaggers. "Once for all.

If you don't know that your Bill's in good hands, I know it. And if you come here bothering about your Bill, I'll make an example of both your Bill and you, and let him slip through my fingers. Have you paid Wemmick?"

"O yes, sir! Every farden."

"Very well. Then you have done all you have got to do. Say another word—one single word—and Wemmick shall give you your money back."

This terrible threat caused the two women to fall off immediately. No one remained now but the excitable Jew, who had already raised the skirts of Mr. Jaggers's coat to his lips several times.

"I don't know this man!" said Mr. Jaggers, in the same devastating strain: "What does this fellow want?"

"Ma thear Mithter Jaggerth. Hown brother to Habraham Latharuth?"

"Who's he?" said Mr. Jaggers. "Let go of my coat."

The suitor, kissing the hem of the garment again before relinquishing it, replied, "Habraham Latharuth, on thuthpithion of plate."

"You're too late," said Mr. Jaggers. "I am over the way."

"Holy father, Mithter Jaggerth!" cried my excitable acquaintance, turning white, "don't thay you're again Habraham Latharuth!"

"I am," said Mr. Jaggers, "and there's an end of it. Get out of the way."

"Mithter Jaggerth! Half a moment! My hown cuthen'th gone to Mithter Wemmick at thith prethent minute, to hoffer him hany termth. Mithter Jaggerth! Half a quarter of a moment! If you'd have the condethenthun to be bought off from the t'other thide—at hany thuperior prithe!—money no object!—Mithter Jaggerth—Mithter—!"

My guardian threw his supplicant off with supreme indifference, and left him dancing on the pavement as if it were red hot. Without further interruption, we reached the front office, where we found the clerk and the man in velveteen with the fur cap.

"Here's Mike," said the clerk, getting down from his stool, and approaching Mr. Jaggers confidentially.

"Oh!" said Mr. Jaggers, turning to the man, who was pulling a lock of hair in the middle of his forehead, like the Bull in Cock Robin pulling at the bell-rope; "your man comes on this afternoon. Well?"

"Well, Mas'r Jaggers," returned Mike, in the voice of a sufferer from a constitutional cold; "arter a deal o' trouble, I've found one, sir, as might do."

"What is he prepared to swear?"

"Well, Mas'r Jaggers," said Mike, wiping his nose on his fur cap this time; "in a general way, anythink."

Mr. Jaggers suddenly became most irate. "Now, I warned you before," said he, throwing his forefinger at the terrified client, "that if you ever presumed to talk in that way here, I'd make an example of you. You infernal scoundrel, how dare you tell ME that?"

The client looked scared, but bewildered too, as if he were unconscious what he had done.

"Spooney!" said the clerk, in a low voice, giving him a stir with his elbow. "Soft Head! Need you say it face to face?"

"Now, I ask you, you blundering booby," said my guardian, very sternly, "once more and for the last time, what the man you have brought here is prepared to swear?"

Mike looked hard at my guardian, as if he were trying to learn a lesson from his face, and slowly replied, "Ayther to character, or to having been in his company and never left him all the night in question."

"Now, be careful. In what station of life is this man?"

Mike looked at his cap, and looked at the floor, and looked at the ceiling, and looked at the clerk, and even looked at me, before beginning to reply in a nervous manner, "We've dressed him up like—" when my guardian blustered out:

"What? You WILL, will you?"

("Spooney!" added the clerk again, with another stir.)

After some helpless casting about, Mike brightened and began again:

"He is dressed like a 'spectable pieman. A sort of a pastry-cook."

"Is he here?" asked my guardian.

"I left him," said Mike, "a setting on some doorsteps round the corner."

"Take him past that window, and let me see him."

The window indicated was the office window. We all three went to it, behind the wire blind, and presently saw the client go by in an accidental manner, with a murderous-looking tall individual, in a short suit of white linen and a paper cap. This guileless confectioner was not by any means sober, and had a black eye in the green stage of recovery, which was painted over.

"Tell him to take his witness away directly," said my guardian to the clerk, in extreme disgust, "and ask him what he means by bringing such a fellow as that."

My guardian then took me into his own room, and while he lunched, standing, from a sandwich-box and a pocket-flask of sherry (he seemed to bully his very sandwich as he ate it), informed me what arrangements he had made for me. I was to go to "Barnard's Inn," to young Mr. Pocket's rooms, where a bed had been sent in for my accommodation; I was to remain with young Mr. Pocket until Monday; on Monday I was to go with him to his father's house on a visit, that I might try how I liked it. Also, I was told what my allowance was to be—it was a very liberal one—and had handed to me from one of my guardian's drawers, the cards of certain tradesmen with whom I was to deal for all kinds of clothes, and such other things as I could in reason want. "You will find your credit good, Mr. Pip," said my guardian, whose flask of sherry smelt like a whole caskful, as he hastily refreshed himself, "but I shall by this means be able to check your bills, and to pull you up if I find you outrunning the constable. Of course you'll go wrong somehow, but that's no fault of mine."

After I had pondered a little over this encouraging sentiment, I asked Mr. Jaggers if I could send for a coach? He said it was not worth while, I was so near my destination; Wemmick should walk round with me, if I pleased.

I then found that Wemmick was the clerk in the next room. Another clerk was rung down from up stairs to take his place while he was out, and I accompanied him into the street, after shaking hands with my guardian. We found a new set of people lingering outside, but Wemmick made a way among them by saying coolly yet decisively, "I tell you it's no use; he won't have a word to say to one of you;" and we soon got clear of them, and went on side by side.

CHAPTER 2

Casting my eyes on Mr. Wemmick as we went along, to see what he was like in the light of day, I found him to be a dry man, rather short in stature, with a square wooden face, whose expression seemed to have been imperfectly chipped out with a dull-edged chisel. There were some marks in it that might have been dimples, if the material had been softer and the instrument finer, but which, as it was, were only dints. The chisel had made three or four of these attempts at embellishment over his nose, but had given them up without an effort to smooth them off. I judged him to be a bachelor from the frayed condition of his linen, and he appeared to have sustained a good many bereavements; for he wore at least four mourning rings, besides a brooch representing a lady and a weeping willow at a tomb with an urn on it. I noticed, too, that several rings and seals hung at his watch-chain, as if he were quite laden with remembrances of departed friends. He had glittering eyes—small, keen, and black—and thin wide mottled lips. He hd had them, to the best of my belief, from forty to fifty years.

"So you were never in London before?" said Mr. Wemmick to me.

"No," said I.

"*I* was new here once," said Mr. Wemmick. "Rum to think of now!"

"You are well acquainted with it now?"

"Why, yes," said Mr. Wemmick. "I know the moves of it."

"Is it a very wicked place?" I asked, more for the sake of saying something than for information.

"You may get cheated, robbed, and murdered in London. But there are plenty of people anywhere, who'll do that for you."

"If there is bad blood between you and them," said I, to soften it off a little.

"O! I don't know about bad blood," returned Mr. Wemmick; "there's not much bad blood about. They'll do it, if there's anything to be got by it."

"That makes it worse."

"You think so?" returned Mr. Wemmick. "Much about the same, I should say."

He wore his hat on the back of his head, and looked straight before him: walking in a self-contained way as if there were nothing in the streets to claim his attention. His mouth was such a post-office of a mouth that he had a mechanical appearance of smiling. We had got to the top of Holborn Hill before I knew that it was merely a mechanical appearance, and that he was not smiling at all.

"Do you know where Mr. Matthew Pocket lives?" I asked Mr. Wemmick.

"Yes," said he, nodding in the direction. "At Hammersmith, west of London."

"Is that far?"

"Well! Say five miles."

"Do you know him?"

"Why, you're a regular cross-examiner!" said Mr. Wemmick, looking at me with an approving air. "Yes, I know him. *I* know him!"

There was an air of toleration or depreciation about his utterance of these words that rather depressed me; and I was still looking sideways at his block of a face in search of any encouraging note to the text, when he said here we were at Barnard's Inn. My depression was not alleviated by the announcement, for, I had supposed that establishment to be an hotel kept by Mr. Barnard, to which the Blue Boar in our town was a mere public-house. Whereas I now found Barnard to be a disembodied spirit, or a fiction, and his inn the dingiest collection of shabby buildings ever squeezed together in a rank corner as a club for Tom-cats.

We entered this haven through a wicket-gate, and were disgorged by an introductory passage into a melancholy little square that looked to me like a flat burying-ground. I thought it had the most dismal trees in it, and the most dismal sparrows, and the most dismal cats, and the most dismal houses (in number half a dozen or so), that I had ever seen. I thought the windows of the sets of chambers into which those houses were divided were in every stage of dilapidated blind and curtain, crippled flower-pot, cracked glass, dusty decay, and miserable makeshift; while To Let, To Let, To Let, glared at me from empty rooms, as if no new wretches ever came there, and the vengeance of the soul of Barnard were being slowly appeased by the gradual suicide of the present occupants and their unholy interment under the gravel. A frowzy mourning of soot and smoke attired this forlorn creation of Barnard, and it had strewn ashes on its head, and was undergoing penance and humiliation as a mere dust-hole. Thus far my sense of sight; while dry rot and wet rot and all the silent rots that rot in neglected roof and cellar—rot of rat and mouse and bug and coaching-stables near at hand besides—addressed themselves faintly to my sense of smell, and moaned, "Try Barnard's Mixture."

So imperfect was this realization of the first of my great expectations, that I looked in dismay at Mr. Wemmick. "Ah!" said he, mistaking me; "the retirement reminds you of the country. So it does me."

He led me into a corner and conducted me up a flight of stairs—which appeared to me to be slowly collapsing into sawdust, so that one of those days the upper lodgers would look out at their doors and find themselves without the means of coming down—to a set of chambers on the top floor. MR. POCKET, JUN., was painted on the door, and there was a label on the letter-box, "Return shortly."

"He hardly thought you'd come so soon," Mr. Wemmick explained. "You don't want me any more?"

"No, thank you," said I.

"As I keep the cash," Mr. Wemmick observed, "we shall most likely meet pretty often. Good day."

"Good day."

I put out my hand, and Mr. Wemmick at first looked at it as if he thought I wanted something. Then he looked at me, and said, correcting himself,

"To be sure! Yes. You're in the habit of shaking hands?"

I was rather confused, thinking it must be out of the London fashion, but said yes.

"I have got so out of it!" said Mr. Wemmick— "except at last. Very glad, I'm sure, to make your acquaintance. Good day!"

When we had shaken hands and he was gone, I opened the staircase window and had nearly beheaded myself, for, the lines had rotted away, and it came down like the guillotine. Happily it was so quick that I had not put my head out. After this escape, I was content to take a foggy view of the Inn through the window's encrusting dirt, and to stand dolefully looking out, saying to myself that London was decidedly overrated.

Mr. Pocket, Junior's, idea of Shortly was not mine, for I had nearly maddened myself with looking out for half an hour, and had written my name with my finger several times in the dirt of every pane in the window, before I heard footsteps on the stairs. Gradually there arose before me the hat, head, neckcloth, waistcoat, trousers, boots, of a member of society of about my own standing. He had a paper-bag under each arm and a pottle of strawberries in one hand, and was out of breath.

"Mr. Pip?" said he.

"Mr. Pocket?" said I.

"Dear me!" he exclaimed. "I am extremely sorry; but I knew there was a coach from your part of the country at midday, and I thought you would come by that one. The fact is, I have been out on your account—not that that is any excuse—for I thought, coming from the country, you might like a little fruit after dinner, and I went to Covent Garden Market to get it good."

For a reason that I had, I felt as if my eyes would start out of my head. I acknowledged his attention incoherently, and began to think this was a dream.

"Dear me!" said Mr. Pocket, Junior. "This door sticks so!"

As he was fast making jam of his fruit by wrestling with the door while the paper-bags were under his arms, I begged him to allow me to hold them. He relinquished them with an agreeable smile, and combated with the door as if it were a wild beast. It yielded so suddenly at last, that he staggered back upon me, and I staggered back upon the opposite door, and we both laughed. But still I felt as if my eyes must start out of my head, and as if this must be a dream.

"Pray come in," said Mr. Pocket, Junior. "Allow me to lead the way. I am rather bare here, but I hope you'll be able to make out tolerably well till Monday. My father thought you would get on more agreeably through to-morrow with me than with him, and might like to take a walk about London. I am sure I shall be very happy to show London to you. As to our table, you won't find that bad, I hope, for it will be supplied from our coffee-house here, and (it is only right I should add) at your expense, such being Mr. Jaggers's directions. As to our lodging, it's not by any means splendid, because I have my own bread to earn, and my father hasn't anything to give me, and I shouldn't be willing to take it, if he had. This is our sitting-room—just such chairs and tables and carpet and so forth, you see, as they could spare from home. You mustn't give me credit for the tablecloth and spoons and castors, because they come for you from the coffee-house. This is my little bedroom; rather musty, but Barnard's is musty. This is your bedroom; the furniture's hired for the occasion, but I trust it will answer the purpose; if you should want anything, I'll go and fetch it. The chambers are retired, and we shall be alone together, but we shan't fight, I dare say. But dear me, I beg your pardon, you're holding the fruit all this time. Pray let me take these bags from you. I am quite ashamed."

As I stood opposite to Mr. Pocket, Junior, delivering him the bags, One, Two, I saw the starting appearance come into his own eyes that I knew to be in mine, and he said, falling back:

"Lord bless me, you're the prowling boy!"

"And you," said I, "are the pale young gentleman!"

CHAPTER 3

The pale young gentleman and I stood contemplating one another in Barnard's Inn, until we both burst out laughing. "The idea of its being you!" said he. "The idea of its being you!" said I. And then we contemplated one another afresh, and laughed again. "Well!" said the pale young gentleman, reaching out his hand good-humoredly, "it's all over now, I hope, and it will be magnanimous in you if you'll forgive me for having knocked you about so."

I derived from this speech that Mr. Herbert Pocket (for Herbert was the pale young gentleman's name) still rather confounded his intention with his execution. But I made a modest reply, and we shook hands warmly.

"You hadn't come into your good fortune at that time?" said Herbert Pocket.

"No," said I.

"No," he acquiesced: "I heard it had happened very lately. I was rather on the lookout for good fortune then."

"Indeed?"

"Yes. Miss Havisham had sent for me, to see if she could take a fancy to me. But she couldn't—at all events, she didn't."

I thought it polite to remark that I was surprised to hear that.

"Bad taste," said Herbert, laughing, "but a fact. Yes, she had sent for me on a trial visit, and if I had come out of it successfully, I suppose I should have been provided for; perhaps I should have been what-you-may-called it to Estella."

"What's that?" I asked, with sudden gravity.

He was arranging his fruit in plates while we talked, which

divided his attention, and was the cause of his having made this lapse of a word. "Affianced," he explained, still busy with the fruit. "Betrothed. Engaged. What's-his-named. Any word of that sort."

"How did you bear your disappointment?" I asked.

"Pooh!" said he, "I didn't care much for it. *She's* a Tartar."

"Miss Havisham?"

"I don't say no to that, but I meant Estella. That girl's hard and haughty and capricious to the last degree, and has been brought up by Miss Havisham to wreak revenge on all the male sex."

"What relation is she to Miss Havisham?"

"None," said he. "Only adopted."

"Why should she wreak revenge on all the male sex? What revenge?"

"Lord, Mr. Pip!" said he. "Don't you know?"

"No," said I.

"Dear me! It's quite a story, and shall be saved till dinner-time. And now let me take the liberty of asking you a question. How did you come there, that day?"

I told him, and he was attentive until I had finished, and then burst out laughing again, and asked me if I was sore afterwards? I didn't ask him if *he* was, for my conviction on that point was perfectly established.

"Mr. Jaggers is your guardian, I understand?" he went on.

"Yes."

"You know he is Miss Havisham's man of business and solicitor, and has her confidence when nobody else has?"

This was bringing me (I felt) towards dangerous ground. I answered with a constraint I made no attempt to disguise, that I had seen Mr. Jaggers in Miss Havisham's house on the very day of our combat, but never at any other time, and that I believed he had no recollection of having ever seen me there.

"He was so obliging as to suggest my father for your tutor,

and he called on my father to propose it. Of course he knew about my father from his connection with Miss Havisham. My father is Miss Havisham's cousin; not that that implies familiar intercourse between them, for he is a bad courtier and will not propitiate her.Herbert Pocket had a frank and easy way with him that was very taking. I had never seen any one then, and I have never seen any one since, who more strongly expressed to me, in every look and tone, a natural incapacity to do anything secret and mean. There was something wonderfully hopeful about his general air, and something that at the same time whispered to me he would never be very successful or rich. I don't know how this was. I became imbued with the notion on that first occasion before we sat down to dinner, but I cannot define by what means.

He was still a pale young gentleman, and had a certain conquered languor about him in the midst of his spirits and briskness, that did not seem indicative of natural strength. He had not a handsome face, but it was better than handsome: being extremely amiable and cheerful. His figure was a little ungainly, as in the days when my knuckles had taken such liberties with it, but it looked as if it would always be light and young. Whether Mr. Trabb's local work would have sat more gracefully on him than on me, may be a question; but I am conscious that he carried off his rather old clothes much better than I carried off my new suit.

As he was so communicative, I felt that reserve on my part would be a bad return unsuited to our years. I therefore told him my small story, and laid stress on my being forbidden to inquire who my benefactor was. I further mentioned that as I had been brought up a blacksmith in a country place, and knew very little of the ways of politeness, I would take it as a great kindness in him if he would give me a hint whenever he saw me at a loss or going wrong.

"With pleasure," said he, "though I venture to prophesy that you'll want very few hints. I dare say we shall be often together, and I should like to banish any needless restraint between us. Will you do me the favour to begin at once to call me by my Christian name, Herbert?"

I thanked him and said I would. I informed him in exchange that my Christian name was Philip.

"I don't take to Philip," said he, smiling, "for it sounds like a moral boy out of the spelling-book, who was so lazy that he fell into a pond, or so fat that he couldn't see out of his eyes, or so avaricious that he locked up his cake till the mice ate it, or so determined to go a bird's-nesting that he got himself eaten by bears who lived handy in the neighbourhood. I tell you what I should like. We are so harmonious, and you have been a blacksmith—would you mind it?"

"I shouldn't mind anything that you propose," I answered, "but I don't understand you."

"Would you mind Handel for a familiar name? There's a charming piece of music by Handel, called the Harmonious Blacksmith."

"I should like it very much."

"Then, my dear Handel," said he, turning round as the door opened, "here is the dinner, and I must beg of you to take the top of the table, because the dinner is of your providing."

This I would not hear of, so he took the top, and I faced him. It was a nice little dinner—seemed to me then a very Lord Mayor's Feast—and it acquired additional relish from being eaten under those independent circumstances, with no old people by, and with London all around us. This again was heightened by a certain gypsy character that set the banquet off; for while the table was, as Mr. Pumblechook might have said, the lap of luxury—being entirely furnished forth from the coffee-house—the circumjacent region of sitting-room was of a comparatively pastureless and shifty character; imposing on the waiter the wandering habits of putting the covers on the floor (where he fell over them), the melted butter in the arm-chair, the bread on the bookshelves, the cheese in the coal-scuttle, and the boiled fowl into my bed in the next room—where I found much of its parsley and butter in a state of congelation when I retired for the night. All this made the feast delightful, and when the waiter was not there to watch me, my pleasure was without alloy.

We had made some progress in the dinner, when I reminded Herbert of his promise to tell me about Miss Havisham.

"True," he replied. "I'll redeem it at once. Let me introduce the topic, Handel, by mentioning that in London it is not the custom to put the knife in the mouth—for fear of accidents—and that while the fork is reserved for that use, it is not put further in than necessary. It is scarcely worth mentioning, only it's as well to do as other people do. Also, the spoon is not generally used over-hand, but under. This has two advantages. You get at your mouth better (which after all is the object), and you save a good deal of the attitude of opening oysters, on the part of the right elbow."

He offered these friendly suggestions in such a lively way, that we both laughed and I scarcely blushed.

"Now," he pursued, "concerning Miss Havisham. Miss Havisham, you must know, was a spoilt child. Her mother died when she was a baby, and her father denied her nothing. Her father was a country gentleman down in your part of the world, and was a brewer. I don't know why it should be a crack thing to be a brewer; but it is indisputable that while you cannot possibly be genteel and bake, you may be as genteel as never was and brew. You see it every day."

"Yet a gentleman may not keep a public-house; may he?" said I.

"Not on any account," returned Herbert; "but a public-house may keep a gentleman. Well! Mr. Havisham was very rich and very proud. So was his daughter."

"Miss Havisham was an only child?" I hazarded.

"Stop a moment, I am coming to that. No, she was not an only child; she had a half-brother. Her father privately married again—his cook, I rather think."

"I thought he was proud," said I.

"My good Handel, so he was. He married his second wife privately, because he was proud, and in course of time *she* died. When she was dead, I apprehend he first told his daughter what he had done, and then the son became a part of the family, residing in the house you are acquainted with. As the son grew a young man, he turned out riotous, extravagant, undutiful—altogether bad. At last his father disinherited him; but he softened when he was dying, and left him well off, though not nearly so well off as Miss Havisham. Take another glass of wine, and excuse my mentioning that society as a body does not expect one to be so strictly conscientious in emptying one's glass, as to turn it bottom upwards with the rim on one's nose."

I had been doing this, in an excess of attention to his recital. I thanked him, and apologized. He said, "Not at all," and resumed.

"Miss Havisham was now an heiress, and you may suppose was looked after as a great match. Her half-brother had now ample means again, but what with debts and what with new madness wasted them most fearfully again. There were stronger differences between him and her than there had been between him and his father, and it is suspected that he cherished a deep and mortal grudge against her as having influenced the father's anger. Now, I come to the cruel part of the story—merely breaking off, my dear Handel, to remark that a dinner-napkin will not go into a tumbler."

Why I was trying to pack mine into my tumbler, I am wholly unable to say. I only know that I found myself, with a perseverance worthy of a much better cause, making the most strenuous exertions to compress it within those limits. Again I thanked him and apologized, and again he said in the cheerfullest manner, "Not at all, I am sure!" and resumed.

"There appeared upon the scene—say at the races, or the public balls, or anywhere else you like—a certain man, who made love to Miss Havisham. I never saw him (for this happened five-and-twenty years ago, before you and I were, Handel), but I have heard my father mention that he was a showy man, and the kind of man for the purpose. But that he was not to be, without ignorance or prejudice, mistaken for a gentleman, my father most strongly asseverates; because it is a principle of his that no man who was not a true gentleman at heart ever was, since the world began, a true gentleman in manner. He says, no varnish can hide the grain of the wood; and that the more varnish you put on, the more the grain will express itself. Well! This man pursued Miss Havisham closely, and professed to be devoted to her. I believe she had not shown much susceptibility up to that time; but all the susceptibility she possessed certainly came out then, and she passionately loved him. There is no doubt that she perfectly idolized him. He practised on her affection in that systematic way, that he got great sums of money from her, and he induced her to buy her brother out of a share in the brewery (which had been weakly left him by his father) at an immense price, on the plea that when he was her husband he must hold and manage it all. Your guardian was not at that time in Miss Havisham's counsels, and she was too haughty and too much in love to be advised by any one. Her relations were poor and scheming, with the exception of my father; he was poor enough, but not time-serving or jealous. The only independent one among them, he warned her that she was doing too much for this man, and was placing herself too unreservedly in his power. She took the first opportunity of angrily ordering my father out of the house, in his presence, and my father has never seen her since."

I thought of her having said, "Matthew will come and see me at last when I am laid dead upon that table;" and I asked Herbert whether his father was so inveterate against her?

"It's not that," said he, "but she charged him, in the presence of her intended husband, with being disappointed in the hope of fawning upon her for his own advancement, and, if he were to go to her now, it would look true—even to him—and even to her. To return to the man and make an end of him. The marriage day was fixed, the wedding dresses were bought, the wedding tour was planned out, the wedding guests were invited. The day came, but not the bridegroom. He wrote her a letter—"

"Which she received," I struck in, "when she was dressing for her marriage? At twenty minutes to nine?"

"At the hour and minute," said Herbert, nodding, "at which she afterwards stopped all the clocks. What was in it, further than that it most heartlessly broke the marriage off, I can't tell you, because I don't know. When she recovered from a bad illness that she had, she laid the whole place waste, as you have seen it, and she has never since looked upon the light of day."

"Is that all the story?" I asked, after considering it.

"All I know of it; and indeed I only know so much, through piecing it out for myself; for my father always avoids it, and, even when Miss Havisham invited me to go there, told me no more of it than it was absolutely requisite I should understand. But I have forgotten one thing. It has been supposed that the man to whom she gave her misplaced confidence acted throughout in concert with her half-brother; that it was a conspiracy between them; and that they shared the profits."

"I wonder he didn't marry her and get all the property," said I.

"He may have been married already, and her cruel mortification may have been a part of her half-brother's scheme," said Herbert. "Mind! I don't know that."

"What became of the two men?" I asked, after again considering the subject.

"They fell into deeper shame and degradation—if there can be deeper—and ruin."

"Are they alive now?"

"I don't know."

"You said just now that Estella was not related to Miss Havisham, but adopted. When adopted?"

Herbert shrugged his shoulders. "There has always been an Estella, since I have heard of a Miss Havisham. I know no more. And now, Handel," said he, finally throwing off the story as it were, "there is a perfectly open understanding between us. All that I know about Miss Havisham, you know."

"And all that I know," I retorted, "you know."

"I fully believe it. So there can be no competition or perplexity between you and me. And as to the condition on which you hold your advancement in life—namely, that you are not to inquire or discuss to whom you owe it—you may be very sure that it will never be encroached upon, or even approached, by me, or by any one belonging to me."

In truth, he said this with so much delicacy, that I felt the subject done with, even though I should be under his father's roof for years and years to come. Yet he said it with so much meaning, too, that I felt he as perfectly understood Miss Havisham to be my benefactress, as I understood the fact myself.

It had not occurred to me before, that he had led up to the theme for the purpose of clearing it out of our way; but we were so much the lighter and easier for having broached it, that I now perceived this to be the case. We were very gay and sociable, and I asked him, in the course of conversation, what he was? He replied, "A capitalist—an Insurer of Ships." I suppose he saw me glancing about the room in search of some tokens of Shipping, or capital, for he added, "In the City."

I had grand ideas of the wealth and importance of Insurers of Ships in the City, and I began to think with awe of having laid a young Insurer on his back, blackened his enterprising eye, and cut his responsible head open. But again there came upon me, for my relief, that odd impression that Herbert Pocket would never be very successful or rich.

"I shall not rest satisfied with merely employing my capital in insuring ships. I shall buy up some good Life Assurance shares, and cut into the Direction. I shall also do a little in the mining way. None of these things will interfere with my chartering a few thousand tons on my own account. I think I shall trade," said he, leaning back in his chair, "to the East Indies, for silks, shawls, spices, dyes, drugs, and precious woods. It's an interesting trade."

"And the profits are large?" said I.

"Tremendous!" said he.

I wavered again, and began to think here were greater expectations than my own.

"I think I shall trade, also," said he, putting his thumbs in his waist-coat pockets, "to the West Indies, for sugar, tobacco, and rum. Also to Ceylon, specially for elephants' tusks."

"You will want a good many ships," said I.

"A perfect fleet," said he.

Quite overpowered by the magnificence of these transactions, I asked him where the ships he insured mostly traded to at present?

"I haven't begun insuring yet," he replied. "I am looking about me."

Somehow, that pursuit seemed more in keeping with Barnard's Inn. I said (in a tone of conviction), "Ah-h!"

"Yes. I am in a counting-house, and looking about me."

"Is a counting-house profitable?" I asked.

"To—do you mean to the young fellow who's in it?" he asked, in reply.

"Yes; to you."

"Why, n-no; not to me." He said this with the air of one carefully reckoning up and striking a balance. "Not directly profitable. That is, it doesn't pay me anything, and I have to—keep myself."

This certainly had not a profitable appearance, and I shook my head as if I would imply that it would be difficult to lay by much accumulative capital from such a source of income.

"But the thing is," said Herbert Pocket, "that you look about you. *That's* the grand thing. You are in a counting-house, you know, and you look about you."

It struck me as a singular implication that you couldn't be out of a counting-house, you know, and look about you; but I silently deferred to his experience.

"Then the time comes," said Herbert, "when you see your opening. And you go in, and you swoop upon it and you make your capital, and then there you are! When you have once made your capital, you have nothing to do but employ it."

This was very like his way of conducting that encounter in the garden; very like. His manner of bearing his poverty, too, exactly corresponded to his manner of bearing that defeat. It seemed to me that he took all blows and buffets now with just the same air as he had taken mine then. It was evident that he had nothing around him but the simplest necessaries, for everything that I remarked upon turned out to have been sent in on my account from the coffee-house or somewhere else.

Yet, having already made his fortune in his own mind, he was so unassuming with it that I felt quite grateful to him for not being puffed up. It was a pleasant addition to his naturally pleasant ways, and we got on famously. In the evening we went out for a walk in the streets, and went half-price to the Theatre; and next day we went to church at Westminster Abbey, and in the afternoon we walked in the Parks; and I wondered who shod all the horses there, and wished Joe did.

On a moderate computation, it was many months, that Sunday, since I had left Joe and Biddy. The space interposed between myself and them partook of that expansion, and our marshes were any distance off. That I could have been at our old church in my old church-going clothes, on the very last Sunday that ever was, seemed a combination of impossibilities, geographical and social, solar and lunar. Yet in the London streets so crowded with people and so brilliantly lighted in the dusk of evening, there were depressing hints of reproaches for that I had put the poor old kitchen at home so far away; and in the dead of night, the footsteps of some incapable impostor of a porter mooning about Barnard's Inn, under pretence of watching it, fell hollow on my heart.

On the Monday morning at a quarter before nine, Herbert went to the counting-house to report himself—to look about him, too, I suppose—and I bore him company. He was to come away in an hour or two to attend me to Hammersmith, and I was to wait about for him. It appeared to me that the eggs from which young Insurers were hatched were incubated in dust and heat, like the eggs of ostriches, judging from the places to which those incipient giants repaired on a Monday morning. Nor did the counting-house where Herbert assisted, show in my eyes as at all a good Observatory; being a back second floor up a yard, of a grimy presence in all particulars, and with a look into another back second floor, rather than a look out.

I waited about until it was noon, and I went upon 'Change, and I saw fluey men sitting there under the bills about shipping, whom I took to be great merchants, though I couldn't understand why they should all be out of spirits. When Herbert came, we went and had lunch at a celebrated house which I then quite venerated, but now believe to have been the most abject superstition in Europe, and where I could not help noticing, even then, that there was much more gravy on the tablecloths and knives and waiters' clothes, than in the steaks.

This collation disposed of at a moderate price (considering the grease, which was not charged for), we went back to Barnard's Inn and got my little portmanteau, and then took coach for Hammersmith. We arrived there at two or three o'clock in the afternoon, and had very little way to walk to Mr. Pocket's house. Lifting the latch of a gate, we passed direct into a little garden overlooking the river, where Mr. Pocket's children were playing about. And unless I deceive myself on a point where my interests or prepossessions are certainly not concerned, I saw that Mr. and Mrs. Pocket's children were not growing up or being brought up, but were tumbling up.

Mrs. Pocket was sitting on a garden chair under a tree, reading, with her legs upon another garden chair; and Mrs. Pocket's two nurse-maids were looking about them while the children played. "Mamma," said Herbert, "this is young Mr. Pip." Upon which Mrs. Pocket received me with an appearance of amiable dignity.

"Master Alick and Miss Jane," cried one of the nurses to two of the children, "if you go a bouncing up against them bushes you'll fall over into the river and be drownded, and what'll your pa say then?"

At the same time this nurse picked up Mrs. Pocket's handkerchief, and said, "If that don't make six times you've dropped it, Mum!" Upon which Mrs. Pocket laughed and said, "Thank you, Flopson," and settling herself in one chair only, resumed her book. Her countenance immediately assumed a knitted and intent expression as if she had been reading for a week, but before she could have read half a dozen lines, she fixed her eyes upon me, and said, "I hope your mamma is quite well?" This unexpected inquiry put me into such a difficulty that I began saying in the absurdest way that if there had been any such person I had no doubt she would have been quite well and would have been very much obliged and would have sent her compliments, when the nurse came to my rescue.

"Well!" she cried, picking up the pocket-handkerchief, "if that don't make seven times! What ARE you a doing of this afternoon, Mum!" Mrs. Pocket received her property, at first with a look of unutterable surprise as if she had never seen it before, and then with a laugh of recognition, and said, "Thank you, Flopson," and forgot me, and went on reading.

I found, now I had leisure to count them, that there were no fewer than six little Pockets present, in various stages of tumbling up. I had scarcely arrived at the total when a seventh was heard, as in the region of air, wailing dolefully.

"If there ain't Baby!" said Flopson, appearing to think it most surprising. "Make haste up, Millers."

Millers, who was the other nurse, retired into the house, and by degrees the child's wailing was hushed and stopped, as if it were a young ventriloquist with something in its mouth. Mrs. Pocket read all the time, and I was curious to know what the book could be.

We were waiting, I supposed, for Mr. Pocket to come out to us; at any rate we waited there, and so I had an opportunity of observing the remarkable family phenomenon that whenever any of the children strayed near Mrs. Pocket in their play, they always tripped themselves up and tumbled over her—always very much to her momentary astonishment, and their own more enduring lamentation. I was at a loss to account for this surprising circumstance, and could not help giving my mind to speculations about it, until by and by Millers came down with the baby, which baby was handed to Flopson, which Flopson was handing it to Mrs. Pocket, when she too went fairly head foremost over Mrs. Pocket, baby and all, and was caught by Herbert and myself.

"Gracious me, Flopson!" said Mrs. Pocket, looking off her book for a moment, "everybody's tumbling!"

"Gracious you, indeed, Mum!" returned Flopson, very red in the face; "what have you got there?"

"*I* got here, Flopson?" asked Mrs. Pocket.

"Why, if it ain't your footstool!" cried Flopson. "And if you keep it under your skirts like that, who's to help tumbling? Here! Take the baby, Mum, and give me your book."

Mrs. Pocket acted on the advice, and inexpertly danced the infant a little in her lap, while the other children played about it. This had lasted but a very short time, when Mrs. Pocket issued summary orders that they were all to be taken into the house for a nap. Thus I made the second discovery on that first occasion, that the nurture of the little Pockets consisted of alternately tumbling up and lying down.

Under these circumstances, when Flopson and Millers had got the children into the house, like a little flock of sheep, and Mr. Pocket came out of it to make my acquaintance, I was not much surprised to find that Mr. Pocket was a gentleman with a rather perplexed expression of face, and with his very gray hair disordered on his head, as if he didn't quite see his way to putting anything straight.

CHAPTER 4

Mr. Pocket said he was glad to see me, and he hoped I was not sorry to see him. "For, I really am not," he added, with his son's smile, "an alarming personage." He was a young-looking man, in spite of his perplexities and his very gray hair, and his manner seemed quite natural. I use the word natural, in the sense of its being unaffected; there was something comic in his distraught way, as though it would have been downright ludicrous but for his own perception that it was very near being so. When he had talked with me a little, he said to Mrs. Pocket, with a rather anxious contraction of his eyebrows, which were black and handsome, "Belinda, I hope you have welcomed Mr. Pip?" And she looked up from her book, and said, "Yes." She then smiled upon me in an absent state of mind, and asked me if I liked the taste of orange-flower water? As the question had no bearing, near or remote, on any foregone or subsequent transaction, I consider it to have been thrown out, like her previous approaches, in general conversational condescension.

I found out within a few hours, and may mention at once, that Mrs. Pocket was the only daughter of a certain quite accidental deceased Knight, who had invented for himself a conviction that his deceased father would have been made a Baronet but for somebody's determined opposition arising out of entirely personal motives—I forget whose, if I ever knew— the Sovereign's, the Prime Minister's, the Lord Chancellor's, the Archbishop of Canterbury's, anybody's—and had tacked himself on to the nobles of the earth in right of this quite supposititious fact. I believe he had been knighted himself for storming the English grammar at the point of the pen, in a desperate address engrossed on vellum, on the occasion of the laying of the first stone of some building or other, and for handing some Royal Personage either the trowel or the mortar. Be that as it may, he had directed Mrs. Pocket to be brought up from her cradle as one who in the nature of things must marry a title, and who was to be guarded from the acquisition of plebeian domestic knowledge. So successful a watch and ward had been established over the young lady by this judicious parent, that she had grown up highly ornamental, but perfectly helpless and useless. With her character thus happily formed, in the first bloom of her youth she had encountered Mr. Pocket: who was also in the first bloom of youth, and not quite decided whether to mount to the Woolsack, or to roof himself in with a mitre. As his doing the one or the other was a mere question of time, he and Mrs. Pocket had taken Time by the forelock (when, to judge from its length, it would seem to have wanted cutting), and had married without the knowledge of the judicious parent. The judicious parent, having nothing to bestow or withhold but his blessing, had handsomely settled that dower upon them after a short struggle, and had informed Mr. Pocket that his wife was "a treasure for a Prince." Mr. Pocket had invested the Prince's treasure in the ways of the world ever since, and it was supposed to have brought him in but indifferent interest. Still, Mrs. Pocket was in general the object of a queer sort of respectful pity, because she had not married a title; while Mr. Pocket was the object of a queer sort of forgiving reproach, because he had never got one.

Mr. Pocket took me into the house and showed me my room: which was a pleasant one, and so furnished as that I could use it with comfort for my own private sitting-room. He then knocked at the doors of two other similar rooms, and introduced me to their occupants, by name Drummle and Startop. Drummle, an old-looking young man of a heavy order of architecture, was whistling. Startop, younger in years and appearance, was reading and holding his head, as if he thought himself in danger of exploding it with too strong a charge of knowledge.

Both Mr. and Mrs. Pocket had such a noticeable air of being in somebody else's hands, that I wondered who really was in possession of the house and let them live there, until I found this unknown power to be the servants. It was a smooth way of going on, perhaps, in respect of saving trouble; but it had the appearance of being expensive, for the servants felt it a duty they owed to themselves to be nice in their eating and drinking, and to keep a deal of company down stairs. They allowed a very liberal table to Mr. and Mrs. Pocket, yet it always appeared to me that by far the best part of the house to have boarded in would have been the kitchen—always supposing the boarder capable of self-defence, for, before I had been there a week, a neighbouring lady with whom the family were personally unacquainted, wrote in to say that she had seen Millers slapping the baby. This greatly distressed Mrs. Pocket, who burst into tears on receiving the note, and said that it was an extraordinary thing that the neighbours couldn't mind their own business.

By degrees I learnt, and chiefly from Herbert, that Mr. Pocket had been educated at Harrow and at Cambridge, where he had distinguished himself; but that when he had had the happiness of marrying Mrs. Pocket very early in life, he had impaired his prospects and taken up the calling of a Grinder. After grinding a number of dull blades—of whom it was remarkable that their fathers, when influential, were always going to help him to preferment, but always forgot to do it when the blades had left the Grindstone—he had wearied of that poor work and had come to London. Here, after gradually failing in loftier hopes, he had "read" with divers who had lacked opportunities or neglected them, and had refurbished divers others for special occasions, and had turned his acquirements to the account of literary compilation and correction, and on such means, added to some very moderate private resources, still maintained the house I saw.

Mr. and Mrs. Pocket had a toady neighbour; a widow lady of that highly sympathetic nature that she agreed with everybody, blessed everybody, and shed smiles and tears on everybody, according to circumstances. This lady's name was Mrs. Coiler, and I had the honor of taking her down to dinner on the day of my installation. She gave me to understand on the stairs, that it was a blow to dear Mrs. Pocket that dear Mr. Pocket should be under the necessity of receiving gentlemen to read with him. That did not extend to me, she told me in a gush of love and confidence (at that time, I had known her something less than five minutes); if they were all like Me, it would be quite another thing.

"But dear Mrs. Pocket," said Mrs. Coiler, "after her early disappointment (not that dear Mr. Pocket was to blame in that), requires so much luxury and elegance—"

"Yes, ma'am," I said, to stop her, for I was afraid she was going to cry.

"And she is of so aristocratic a disposition—"

"Yes, ma'am," I said again, with the same object as before.

"—That it is hard," said Mrs. Coiler, "to have dear Mr. Pocket's time and attention diverted from dear Mrs. Pocket."

I could not help thinking that it might be harder if the butcher's time and attention were diverted from dear Mrs. Pocket; but I said nothing, and indeed had enough to do in keeping a bashful watch upon my company manners.

It came to my knowledge, through what passed between Mrs. Pocket and Drummle while I was attentive to my knife and fork, spoon, glasses, and other instruments of self-destruction, that Drummle, whose Christian name was Bentley, was actually the next heir but one to a baronetcy. It further appeared that the book I had seen Mrs. Pocket reading in the garden was all about titles, and that she knew the exact date at which her grandpapa would have come into the book, if he ever had come at all. Drummle didn't say much, but in his limited way (he struck me as a sulky kind of fellow) he spoke as one of the elect, and recognized Mrs. Pocket as a woman and a sister. No one but themselves and Mrs. Coiler the toady neighbour showed any interest in this part of the conversation, and it appeared to me that it was painful to Herbert; but it promised to last a long time, when the page came in with the announcement of a domestic affliction. It was, in effect, that the cook had mislaid the beef. To my unutterable amazement, I now, for the first time, saw Mr. Pocket relieve his mind by going through a performance that struck me as very extraordinary, but which made no impression on anybody else, and with which I soon became as familiar as the rest. He laid down the carving-knife and fork—being engaged in carving, at the moment—put his two hands into his disturbed hair, and appeared to make an extraordinary effort to lift himself up by it. When he had done this, and had not lifted himself up at all, he quietly went on with what he was about.

Mrs. Coiler then changed the subject and began to flatter me. I liked it for a few moments, but she flattered me so very grossly that the pleasure was soon over. She had a serpentine way of coming close at me when she pretended to be vitally interested in the friends and localities I had left, which was altogether snaky and fork-tongued; and when she made an occasional bounce upon Startop (who said very little to her), or upon Drummle (who said less), I rather envied them for being on the opposite side of the table.

After dinner the children were introduced, and Mrs. Coiler made admiring comments on their eyes, noses, and legs—a sagacious way of improving their minds. There were four little girls, and two little boys, besides the baby who might have been either, and the baby's next successor who was as yet neither.

They were brought in by Flopson and Millers, much as though those two non-commissioned officers had been recruiting somewhere for children and had enlisted these, while Mrs. Pocket looked at the young Nobles that ought to have been as if she rather thought she had had the pleasure of inspecting them before, but didn't quite know what to make of them.

"Here! Give me your fork, Mum, and take the baby," said Flopson. "Don't take it that way, or you'll get its head under the table."

Thus advised, Mrs. Pocket took it the other way, and got its head upon the table; which was announced to all present by a prodigious concussion.

"Dear, dear! Give it me back, Mum," said Flopson; "and Miss Jane, come and dance to baby, do!"

One of the little girls, a mere mite who seemed to have prematurely taken upon herself some charge of the others, stepped out of her place by me, and danced to and from the baby until it left off crying, and laughed. Then, all the children laughed, and Mr. Pocket (who in the meantime had twice endeavored to lift himself up by the hair) laughed, and we all laughed and were glad.

Flopson, by dint of doubling the baby at the joints like a Dutch doll, then got it safely into Mrs. Pocket's lap, and gave it the nut-crackers to play with; at the same time recommending Mrs. Pocket to take notice that the handles of that instrument were not likely to agree with its eyes, and sharply charging Miss Jane to look after the same. Then, the two nurses left the room, and had a lively scuffle on the staircase with a dissipated page who had waited at dinner, and who had clearly lost half his buttons at the gaming-table.

I was made very uneasy in my mind by Mrs. Pocket's falling into a discussion with Drummle respecting two baronetcies, while she ate a sliced orange steeped in sugar and wine, and, forgetting all about the baby on her lap, who did most appalling things with the nut-crackers. At length little Jane, perceiving its young brains to be imperilled, softly left her place, and with many small artifices coaxed the dangerous weapon away. Mrs. Pocket finishing her orange at about the same time, and not approving of this, said to Jane:

"You naughty child, how dAre you? Go and sit down this instant!"

"Mamma dear," lisped the little girl, "baby ood have put hith eyeth out."

"How dare you tell me so?" retorted Mrs. Pocket. "Go and sit down in your chair this moment!"

Mrs. Pocket's dignity was so crushing, that I felt quite abashed, as if I myself had done something to rouse it.

"Belinda," remonstrated Mr. Pocket, from the other end of the table, "how can you be so unreasonable? Jane only interfered for the protection of baby."

"I will not allow anybody to interfere," said Mrs. Pocket. "I am surprised, Matthew, that you should expose me to the affront of interference."

"Good God!" cried Mr. Pocket, in an outbreak of desolate desperation. "Are infants to be nut-crackered into their tombs, and is nobody to save them?"

"I will not be interfered with by Jane," said Mrs. Pocket, with a majestic glance at that innocent little offender. "I hope I know my poor grandpapa's position. Jane, indeed!"

Mr. Pocket got his hands in his hair again, and this time really did lift himself some inches out of his chair. "Hear this!" he helplessly exclaimed to the elements. "Babies are to be nut-crackered dead, for people's poor grandpapa's positions!" Then he let himself down again, and became silent.

We all looked awkwardly at the tablecloth while this was going on. A pause succeeded, during which the honest and irrepressible baby made a series of leaps and crows at little Jane, who appeared to me to be the only member of the family (irrespective of servants) with whom it had any decided acquaintance.

"Mr. Drummle," said Mrs. Pocket, "will you ring for Flopson? Jane, you undutiful little thing, go and lie down. Now, baby darling, come with ma!"

The baby was the soul of honor, and protested with all its might. It doubled itself up the wrong way over Mrs. Pocket's arm, exhibited a pair of knitted shoes and dimpled ankles to the company in lieu of its soft face, and was carried out in the highest state of mutiny. And it gained its point after all, for I saw it through the window within a few minutes, being nursed by little Jane.

It happened that the other five children were left behind at the dinner-table, through Flopson's having some private engagement, and their not being anybody else's business. I thus became aware of the mutual relations between them and Mr. Pocket, which were exemplified in the following manner. Mr. Pocket, with the normal perplexity of his face heightened and his hair rumpled, looked at them for some minutes, as if he couldn't make out how they came to be boarding and lodging in that establishment, and why they hadn't been billeted by Nature on somebody else. Then, in a distant Missionary way he asked them certain questions—as why little Joe had that hole in his frill, who said, Pa, Flopson was going to mend it when she had time—and how little Fanny came by that whitlow, who said, Pa, Millers was going to poultice it when she didn't forget. Then, he melted into parental tenderness, and gave them a shilling apiece and told them to go and play; and then as they went out, with one very strong effort to lift himself up by the hair he dismissed the hopeless subject.

In the evening there was rowing on the river. As Drummle and Startop had each a boat, I resolved to set up mine, and to cut them both out. I was pretty good at most exercises in which country boys are adepts, but as I was conscious of wanting elegance of style for the Thames—not to say for other waters—I at once engaged to place myself under the tuition of the winner of a prize-wherry who plied at our stairs, and to whom I was introduced by my new allies. This practical authority confused me very much by saying I had the arm of a blacksmith. If he could have known how nearly the compliment lost him his pupil, I doubt if he would have paid it.

There was a supper-tray after we got home at night, and I think we should all have enjoyed ourselves, but for a rather disagreeable domestic occurrence. Mr. Pocket was in good spirits, when a housemaid came in, and said, "If you please, sir, I should wish to speak to you."

"Speak to your master?" said Mrs. Pocket, whose dignity was roused again. "How can you think of such a thing? Go and speak to Flopson. Or speak to me—at some other time."

"Begging your pardon, ma'am," returned the housemaid, "I should wish to speak at once, and to speak to master."

Hereupon, Mr. Pocket went out of the room, and we made the best of ourselves until he came back.

"This is a pretty thing, Belinda!" said Mr. Pocket, returning with a countenance expressive of grief and despair. "Here's the cook lying insensibly drunk on the kitchen floor, with a large bundle of fresh butter made up in the cupboard ready to sell for grease!"

Mrs. Pocket instantly showed much amiable emotion, and said, "This is that odious Sophia's doing!"

"What do you mean, Belinda?" demanded Mr. Pocket.

"Sophia has told you," said Mrs. Pocket. "Did I not see her with my own eyes and hear her with my own ears, come into the room just now and ask to speak to you?"

"But has she not taken me down stairs, Belinda," returned Mr. Pocket, "and shown me the woman, and the bundle too?"

"And do you defend her, Matthew," said Mrs. Pocket, "for making mischief?"

Mr. Pocket uttered a dismal groan.

"Am I, grandpapa's granddaughter, to be nothing in the house?" said Mrs. Pocket. "Besides, the cook has always been a very nice respectful woman, and said in the most natural manner when she came to look after the situation, that she felt I was born to be a Duchess."

There was a sofa where Mr. Pocket stood, and he dropped upon it in the attitude of the Dying Gladiator. Still in that attitude he said, with a hollow voice, "Good night, Mr. Pip," when I deemed it advisable to go to bed and leave him.

CHAPTER 5

After two or three days, when I had established myself in my room and had gone backwards and forwards to London several times, and had ordered all I wanted of my tradesmen, Mr. Pocket and I had a long talk together. He knew more of my intended career than I knew myself, for he referred to his having been told by Mr. Jaggers that I was not designed for any profession, and that I should be well enough educated for my destiny if I could "hold my own" with the average of young men in prosperous circumstances. I acquiesced, of course, knowing nothing to the contrary.

He advised my attending certain places in London, for the acquisition of such mere rudiments as I wanted, and my investing him with the functions of explainer and director of all my studies. He hoped that with intelligent assistance I should meet with little to discourage me, and should soon be able to dispense with any aid but his. Through his way of saying this, and much more to similar purpose, he placed himself on confidential terms with me in an admirable manner; and I may state at once that he was always so zealous and honorable in fulfilling his compact with me, that he made me zealous and honorable in fulfilling mine with him. If he had shown indifference as a master, I have no doubt I should have returned the compliment as a pupil; he gave me no such excuse, and each of us did the other justice. Nor did I ever regard him as having anything ludicrous about him—or anything but what was serious, honest, and good—in his tutor communication with me.

When these points were settled, and so far carried out as

that I had begun to work in earnest, it occurred to me that if I could retain my bedroom in Barnard's Inn, my life would be agreeably varied, while my manners would be none the worse for Herbert's society. Mr. Pocket did not object to this arrangement, but urged that before any step could possibly be taken in it, it must be submitted to my guardian. I felt that this delicacy arose out of the consideration that the plan would save Herbert some expense, so I went off to Little Britain and imparted my wish to Mr. Jaggers.

"If I could buy the furniture now hired for me," said I, "and one or two other little things, I should be quite at home there."

"Go it!" said Mr. Jaggers, with a short laugh. "I told you you'd get on. Well! How much do you want?"

I said I didn't know how much.

"Come!" retorted Mr. Jaggers. "How much? Fifty pounds?"

"O, not nearly so much."

"Five pounds?" said Mr. Jaggers.

This was such a great fall, that I said in discomfiture, "O, more than that."

"More than that, eh!" retorted Mr. Jaggers, lying in wait for me, with his hands in his pockets, his head on one side, and his eyes on the wall behind me; "how much more?"

"It is so difficult to fix a sum," said I, hesitating.

"Come!" said Mr. Jaggers. "Let's get at it. Twice five; will that do? Three times five; will that do? Four times five; will that do?"

I said I thought that would do handsomely.

"Four times five will do handsomely, will it?" said Mr. Jaggers, knitting his brows. "Now, what do you make of four times five?"

"What do I make of it?"

"Ah!" said Mr. Jaggers; "how much?"

"I suppose you make it twenty pounds," said I, smiling.

"Never mind what *I* make it, my friend," observed Mr. Jaggers, with a knowing and contradictory toss of his head. "I want to know what *you* make it."

"Twenty pounds, of course."

"Wemmick!" said Mr. Jaggers, opening his office door. "Take Mr. Pip's written order, and pay him twenty pounds."

This strongly marked way of doing business made a strongly marked impression on me, and that not of an agreeable kind. Mr. Jaggers never laughed; but he wore great bright creaking boots, and, in poising himself on these boots, with his large head bent down and his eyebrows joined together, awaiting an answer, he sometimes caused the boots to creak, as if *they* laughed in a dry and suspicious way. As he happened to go out now, and as Wemmick was brisk and talkative, I said to Wemmick that I hardly knew what to make of Mr. Jaggers's manner.

"Tell him that, and he'll take it as a compliment," answered Wemmick; "he don't mean that you *should* know what to make of it.—Oh!" for I looked surprised, "it's not personal; it's professional: only professional."

Wemmick was at his desk, lunching—and crunching—on a dry hard biscuit; pieces of which he threw from time to time into his slit of a mouth, as if he were posting them.

"Always seems to me," said Wemmick, "as if he had set a man-trap and was watching it. Suddenly-click—you're caught!"

Without remarking that man-traps were not among the amenities of life, I said I supposed he was very skilful?

"Deep," said Wemmick, "as Australia." Pointing with his pen at the office floor, to express that Australia was understood, for the purposes of the figure, to be symmetrically on the opposite spot of the globe. "If there was anything deeper," added Wemmick, bringing his pen to paper, "he'd be it."

Then, I said I supposed he had a fine business, and Wemmick said, "Ca-pi-tal!" Then I asked if there were many clerks? to which he replied:

"We don't run much into clerks, because there's only one Jaggers, and people won't have him at second hand. There are only four of us. Would you like to see 'em? You are one of us, as I may say."

I accepted the offer. When Mr. Wemmick had put all the biscuit into the post, and had paid me my money from a cash-box in a safe, the key of which safe he kept somewhere down his back and produced from his coat-collar like an iron-pigtail, we went up stairs. The house was dark and shabby, and the greasy shoulders that had left their mark in Mr. Jaggers's room seemed to have been shuffling up and down the staircase for years. In the front first floor, a clerk who looked something between a publican and a rat-catcher—a large pale, puffed, swollen man—was attentively engaged with three or four people of shabby appearance, whom he treated as unceremoniously as everybody seemed to be treated who contributed to Mr. Jaggers's coffers. "Getting evidence together," said Mr. Wemmick, as we came out, "for the Bailey." In the room over that, a little flabby terrier of a clerk with dangling hair (his cropping seemed to have been forgotten when he was a puppy) was similarly engaged with a man with weak eyes, whom Mr. Wemmick presented to me as a smelter who kept his pot always boiling, and who would melt me anything I pleased—and who was in an excessive white-perspiration, as if he had been trying his art on himself. In a back room, a high-shouldered man with a face-ache tied up in dirty flannel, who was dressed in old black clothes that bore the appearance of having been waxed, was stooping over his work of making fair copies of the notes of the other two gentlemen, for Mr. Jaggers's own use.

This was all the establishment. When we went down stairs

again, Wemmick led me into my guardian's room, and said, "This you've seen already."

"Pray," said I, as the two odious casts with the twitchy leer upon them caught my sight again, "whose likenesses are those?"

"These?" said Wemmick, getting upon a chair, and blowing the dust off the horrible heads before bringing them down. "These are two celebrated ones. Famous clients of ours that got us a world of credit. This chap (why you must have come down in the night and been peeping into the inkstand, to get this blot upon your eyebrow, you old rascal!) murdered his master, and, considering that he wasn't brought up to evidence, didn't plan it badly."

"Is it like him?" I asked, recoiling from the brute, as Wemmick spat upon his eyebrow and gave it a rub with his sleeve.

"Like him? It's himself, you know. The cast was made in Newgate, directly after he was taken down. You had a particular fancy for me, hadn't you, Old Artful?" said Wemmick. He then explained this affectionate apostrophe, by touching his brooch representing the lady and the weeping willow at the tomb with the urn upon it, and saying, "Had it made for me, express!"

"Is the lady anybody?" said I.

"No," returned Wemmick. "Only his game. (You liked your bit of game, didn't you?) No; deuce a bit of a lady in the case, Mr. Pip, except one—and she wasn't of this slender lady-like sort, and you would't have caught *her* looking after this urn, unless there was something to drink in it." Wemmick's attention being thus directed to his brooch, he put down the cast, and polished the brooch with his pocket-handkerchief.

"Did that other creature come to the same end?" I asked. "He has the same look."

"You're right," said Wemmick; "it's the genuine look. Much as if one nostril was caught up with a horse-hair and a little fish-hook. Yes, he came to the same end; quite the natural end here,

I assure you. He forged wills, this blade did, if he didn't also put the supposed testators to sleep too. You were a gentlemanly Cove, though" (Mr. Wemmick was again apostrophizing), "and you said you could write Greek. Yah, Bounceable! What a liar you were! I never met such a liar as you!" Before putting his late friend on his shelf again, Wemmick touched the largest of his mourning rings and said, "Sent out to buy it for me, only the day before."

While he was putting up the other cast and coming down from the chair, the thought crossed my mind that all his personal jewelry was derived from like sources. As he had shown no diffidence on the subject, I ventured on the liberty of asking him the question, when he stood before me, dusting his hands.

"O yes," he returned, "these are all gifts of that kind. One brings another, you see; that's the way of it. I always take 'em. They're curiosities. And they're property. They may not be worth much, but, after all, they're property and portable. It don't signify to you with your brilliant lookout, but as to myself, my guiding-star always is, 'Get hold of portable property.'"

When I had rendered homage to this light, he went on to say, in a friendly manner:

"If at any odd time when you have nothing better to do, you wouldn't mind coming over to see me at Walworth, I could offer you a bed, and I should consider it an honor. I have not much to show you; but such two or three curiosities as I have got you might like to look over; and I am fond of a bit of garden and a summer-house."

I said I should be delighted to accept his hospitality.

"Thankee," said he; "then we'll consider that it's to come off, when convenient to you. Have you dined with Mr. Jaggers yet?"

"Not yet."

"Well," said Wemmick, "he'll give you wine, and good wine. I'll give you punch, and not bad punch. And now I'll tell you something. When you go to dine with Mr. Jaggers, look at his housekeeper."

"Shall I see something very uncommon?"

"Well," said Wemmick, "you'll see a wild beast tamed. Not so very uncommon, you'll tell me. I reply, that depends on the original wildness of the beast, and the amount of taming. It won't lower your opinion of Mr. Jaggers's powers. Keep your eye on it."

I told him I would do so, with all the interest and curiosity that his preparation awakened. As I was taking my departure, he asked me if I would like to devote five minutes to seeing Mr. Jaggers "at it?"

For several reasons, and not least because I didn't clearly know what Mr. Jaggers would be found to be "at," I replied in the affirmative. We dived into the City, and came up in a crowded police-court, where a blood-relation (in the murderous sense) of the deceased, with the fanciful taste in brooches, was standing at the bar, uncomfortably chewing something; while my guardian had a woman under examination or cross-examination—I don't know which—and was striking her, and the bench, and everybody present, with awe. If anybody, of whatsoever degree, said a word that he didn't approve of, he instantly required to have it "taken down." If anybody wouldn't make an admission, he said, "I'll have it out of you!" and if anybody made an admission, he said, "Now I have got you!" The magistrates shivered under a single bite of his finger. Thieves and thief-takers hung in dread rapture on his words, and shrank when a hair of his eyebrows turned in their direction. Which side he was on I couldn't make out, for he seemed to me to be grinding the whole place in a mill; I only know that when I stole out on tiptoe, he was not on the side of the bench; for, he was making the legs of the old gentleman who presided, quite convulsive under the table, by his denunciations of his conduct as the representative of British law and justice in that chair that day.

CHAPTER 6

Bentley Drummle, who was so sulky a fellow that he even took up a book as if its writer had done him an injury, did not take up an acquaintance in a more agreeable spirit. Heavy in figure, movement, and comprehension—in the sluggish complexion of his face, and in the large, awkward tongue that seemed to loll about in his mouth as he himself lolled about in a room—he was idle, proud, niggardly, reserved, and suspicious. He came of rich people down in Somersetshire, who had nursed this combination of qualities until they made the discovery that it was just of age and a blockhead. Thus, Bentley Drummle had come to Mr. Pocket when he was a head taller than that gentleman, and half a dozen heads thicker than most gentlemen.

Startop had been spoilt by a weak mother and kept at home when he ought to have been at school, but he was devotedly attached to her, and admired her beyond measure. He had a woman's delicacy of feature, and was—"as you may see, though you never saw her," said Herbert to me—exactly like his mother." It was but natural that I should take to him much more kindly than to Drummle, and that, even in the earliest evenings of our boating, he and I should pull homeward abreast of one another, conversing from boat to boat, while Bentley Drummle came up in our wake alone, under the overhanging banks and among the rushes. He would always creep in-shore like some uncomfortable amphibious creature, even when the tide would have sent him fast upon his way; and I always think of him as coming after us in the dark or by the back-water, when our own two boats were breaking the sunset or the moonlight in mid-stream.

Herbert was my intimate companion and friend. I presented him with a half-share in my boat, which was the occasion of his often coming down to Hammersmith; and my possession of a half-share in his chambers often took me up to London. We used to walk between the two places at all hours. I have an affection for the road yet (though it is not so pleasant a road as it was then), formed in the impressibility of untried youth and hope.

When I had been in Mr. Pocket's family a month or two, Mr. and Mrs. Camilla turned up. Camilla was Mr. Pocket's sister. Georgiana, whom I had seen at Miss Havisham's on the same occasion, also turned up. She was a cousin—an indigestive single woman, who called her rigidity religion, and her liver love. These people hated me with the hatred of cupidity and disappointment. As a matter of course, they fawned upon me in my prosperity with the basest meanness. Towards Mr. Pocket, as a grown-up infant with no notion of his own interests, they showed the complacent forbearance I had heard them express. Mrs. Pocket they held in contempt; but they allowed the poor soul to have been heavily disappointed in life, because that shed a feeble reflected light upon themselves.

These were the surroundings among which I settled down, and applied myself to my education. I soon contracted expensive habits, and began to spend an amount of money that within a few short months I should have thought almost fabulous; but through good and evil I stuck to my books. There was no other merit in this, than my having sense enough to feel my deficiencies. Between Mr. Pocket and Herbert I got on fast; and, with one or the other always at my elbow to give me the start I wanted, and clear obstructions out of my road, I must have been as great a dolt as Drummle if I had done less.

I had not seen Mr. Wemmick for some weeks, when I thought I would write him a note and propose to go home with him on a certain evening. He replied that it would give him much pleasure, and that he would expect me at the office at six o'clock. Thither I went, and there I found him, putting the key of his safe down his back as the clock struck.

"Did you think of walking down to Walworth?" said he.

"Certainly," said I, "if you approve."

"Very much," was Wemmick's reply, "for I have had my legs under the desk all day, and shall be glad to stretch them. Now, I'll tell you what I have got for supper, Mr. Pip. I have got a stewed steak—which is of home preparation—and a cold roast fowl—which is from the cook's-shop. I think it's tender, because the master of the shop was a Juryman in some cases of ours the other day, and we let him down easy. I reminded him of it when I bought the fowl, and I said, "Pick us out a good one, old Briton, because if we had chosen to keep you in the box another day or two, we could easily have done it." He said to that, "Let me make you a present of the best fowl in the shop." I let him, of course. As far as it goes, it's property and portable. You don't object to an aged parent, I hope?"

I really thought he was still speaking of the fowl, until he added, "Because I have got an aged parent at my place." I then said what politeness required.

"So, you haven't dined with Mr. Jaggers yet?" he pursued, as we walked along.

"Not yet."

"He told me so this afternoon when he heard you were coming. I expect you'll have an invitation to-morrow. He's going to ask your pals, too. Three of 'em; ain't there?"

Although I was not in the habit of counting Drummle as one of my intimate associates, I answered, "Yes."

"Well, he's going to ask the whole gang;"—I hardly felt complimented by the word: "and whatever he gives you, he'll give you good. Don't look forward to variety, but you'll have excellence. And there's another rum thing in his house," proceeded Wemmick, after a moment's pause, as if the remark followed on the housekeeper understood; "he never lets a door or window be fastened at night."

"Is he never robbed?"

"That's it!" returned Wemmick. "He says, and gives it out publicly, "I want to see the man who'll rob *me*." Lord bless you, I have heard him, a hundred times, if I have heard him once, say to regular cracksmen in our front office, "You know where I live; now, no bolt is ever drawn there; why don't you do a stroke of business with me? Come; can't I tempt you?" Not a man of them, sir, would be bold enough to try it on, for love or money."

"They dread him so much?" said I.

"Dread him," said Wemmick. "I believe you they dread him. Not but what he's artful, even in his defiance of them. No silver, sir. Britannia metal, every spoon."

"So they wouldn't have much," I observed, "even if they—"

"Ah! But *he* would have much," said Wemmick, cutting me short, "and they know it. He'd have their lives, and the lives of scores of 'em. He'd have all he could get. And it's impossible to say what he couldn't get, if he gave his mind to it."

I was falling into meditation on my guardian's greatness, when Wemmick remarked:—

"As to the absence of plate, that's only his natural depth, you know. A river's its natural depth, and he's his natural depth. Look at his watch-chain. That's real enough."

"It's very massive," said I.

"Massive?" repeated Wemmick. "I think so. And his watch is a gold repeater, and worth a hundred pound if it's worth a penny. Mr. Pip, there are about seven hundred thieves in this town who know all about that watch; there's not a man, a woman, or a child, among them, who wouldn't identify the smallest link in that chain, and drop it as if it was red hot, if inveigled into touching it."

At first with such discourse, and afterwards with

conversation of a more general nature, did Mr. Wemmick and I beguile the time and the road, until he gave me to understand that we had arrived in the district of Walworth.

It appeared to be a collection of back lanes, ditches, and little gardens, and to present the aspect of a rather dull retirement. Wemmick's house was a little wooden cottage in the midst of plots of garden, and the top of it was cut out and painted like a battery mounted with guns.

"My own doing," said Wemmick. "Looks pretty; don't it?"

I highly commended it, I think it was the smallest house I ever saw; with the queerest gothic windows (by far the greater part of them sham), and a gothic door almost too small to get in at.

"That's a real flagstaff, you see," said Wemmick, "and on Sundays I run up a real flag. Then look here. After I have crossed this bridge, I hoist it up–so–and cut off the communication."

The bridge was a plank, and it crossed a chasm about four feet wide and two deep. But it was very pleasant to see the pride with which he hoisted it up and made it fast; smiling as he did so, with a relish and not merely mechanically.

"At nine o'clock every night, Greenwich time," said Wemmick, "the gun fires. There he is, you see! And when you hear him go, I think you'll say he's a Stinger."

The piece of ordnance referred to, was mounted in a separate fortress, constructed of lattice-work. It was protected from the weather by an ingenious little tarpaulin contrivance in the nature of an umbrella.

"Then, at the back," said Wemmick, "out of sight, so as not to impede the idea of fortifications—for it's a principle with me, if you have an idea, carry it out and keep it up—I don't know whether that's your opinion—"

I said, decidedly.

"—At the back, there's a pig, and there are fowls and rabbits; then, I knock together my own little frame, you see, and grow cucumbers; and you'll judge at supper what sort of a salad I can raise. So, sir," said Wemmick, smiling again, but seriously too, as he shook his head, "if you can suppose the little place besieged, it would hold out a devil of a time in point of provisions."

Then, he conducted me to a bower about a dozen yards off, but which was approached by such ingenious twists of path that it took quite a long time to get at; and in this retreat our glasses were already set forth. Our punch was cooling in an ornamental lake, on whose margin the bower was raised. This piece of water (with an island in the middle which might have been the salad for supper) was of a circular form, and he had constructed a fountain in it, which, when you set a little mill going and took a cork out of a pipe, played to that powerful extent that it made the back of your hand quite wet.

"I am my own engineer, and my own carpenter, and my own plumber, and my own gardener, and my own Jack of all Trades," said Wemmick, in acknowledging my compliments. "Well; it's a good thing, you know. It brushes the Newgate cobwebs away, and pleases the Aged. You wouldn't mind being at once introduced to the Aged, would you? It wouldn't put you out?"

I expressed the readiness I felt, and we went into the castle. There we found, sitting by a fire, a very old man in a flannel coat: clean, cheerful, comfortable, and well cared for, but intensely deaf.

"Well aged parent," said Wemmick, shaking hands with him in a cordial and jocose way, "how am you?"

"All right, John; all right!" replied the old man.

"Here's Mr. Pip, aged parent," said Wemmick, "and I wish you could hear his name. Nod away at him, Mr. Pip; that's what he likes. Nod away at him, if you please, like winking!"

"This is a fine place of my son's, sir," cried the old man, while I nodded as hard as I possibly could. "This is a pretty pleasure-ground, sir. This spot and these beautiful works upon it ought to be kept together by the Nation, after my son's time, for the people's enjoyment."

"You're as proud of it as Punch; ain't you, Aged?" said Wemmick, contemplating the old man, with his hard face really softened; "*there's* a nod for you;" giving him a tremendous one; "*there's* another for you;" giving him a still more tremendous one; "you like that, don't you? If you're not tired, Mr. Pip— though I know it's tiring to strangers—will you tip him one more? You can't think how it pleases him."

I tipped him several more, and he was in great spirits. We left him bestirring himself to feed the fowls, and we sat down to our punch in the arbor; where Wemmick told me, as he smoked a pipe, that it had taken him a good many years to bring the property up to its present pitch of perfection.

"Is it your own, Mr. Wemmick?"

"O yes," said Wemmick, "I have got hold of it, a bit at a time. It's a freehold, by George!"

"Is it indeed? I hope Mr. Jaggers admires it?"

"Never seen it," said Wemmick. "Never heard of it. Never seen the Aged. Never heard of him. No; the office is one thing, and private life is another. When I go into the office, I leave the Castle behind me, and when I come into the Castle, I leave the office behind me. If it's not in any way disagreeable to you, you'll oblige me by doing the same. I don't wish it professionally spoken about."

Of course I felt my good faith involved in the observance of his request. The punch being very nice, we sat there drinking it and talking, until it was almost nine o'clock. "Getting near gun-fire," said Wemmick then, as he laid down his pipe; "it's the Aged's treat."

Proceeding into the Castle again, we found the Aged heating the poker, with expectant eyes, as a preliminary to the performance of this great nightly ceremony. Wemmick stood with his watch in his hand until the moment was come for him to take the red-hot poker from the Aged, and repair to the battery. He took it, and went out, and presently the Stinger went off with a Bang that shook the crazy little box of a cottage as if it must fall to pieces, and made every glass and teacup in it ring. Upon this, the Aged—who I believe would have been blown out of his arm-chair but for holding on by the elbows—cried out exultingly, "He's fired! I heerd him!" and I nodded at the old gentleman until it is no figure of speech to declare that I absolutely could not see him.

The interval between that time and supper Wemmick devoted to showing me his collection of curiosities. They were mostly of a felonious character; comprising the pen with which a celebrated forgery had been committed, a distinguished razor or two, some locks of hair, and several manuscript confessions written under condemnation—upon which Mr. Wemmick set particular value as being, to use his own words, "every one of 'em Lies, sir." These were agreeably dispersed among small specimens of china and glass, various neat trifles made by the proprietor of the museum, and some tobacco-stoppers carved by the Aged. They were all displayed in that chamber of the Castle into which I had been first inducted, and which served, not only as the general sitting-room but as the kitchen too, if I might judge from a saucepan on the hob, and a brazen bijou over the fireplace designed for the suspension of a roasting-jack.

There was a neat little girl in attendance, who looked after the Aged in the day. When she had laid the supper-cloth, the bridge was lowered to give her means of egress, and she withdrew for the night. The supper was excellent; and though the Castle was rather subject to dry-rot insomuch that it tasted like a bad nut, and though the pig might have been farther off, I was heartily pleased with my whole entertainment. Nor was there any drawback on my little turret bedroom, beyond there being such a very thin ceiling between me and the flagstaff, that when I lay down on my back in bed, it seemed as if I had to balance that pole on my forehead all night.

Wemmick was up early in the morning, and I am afraid I heard him cleaning my boots. After that, he fell to gardening, and I saw him from my gothic window pretending to employ the Aged, and nodding at him in a most devoted manner. Our breakfast was as good as the supper, and at half-past eight precisely we started for Little Britain. By degrees, Wemmick got dryer and harder as we went along, and his mouth tightened into a post-office again. At last, when we got to his place of business and he pulled out his key from his coat-collar, he looked as unconscious of his Walworth property as if the Castle and the drawbridge and the arbor and the lake and the fountain and the Aged, had all been blown into space together by the last discharge of the Stinger.

CHAPTER 7

It fell out as Wemmick had told me it would, that I had an early opportunity of comparing my guardian's establishment with that of his cashier and clerk. My guardian was in his room, washing his hands with his scented soap, when I went into the office from Walworth; and he called me to him, and gave me the invitation for myself and friends which Wemmick had prepared me to receive. "No ceremony," he stipulated, "and no dinner dress, and say to-morrow." I asked him where we should come to (for I had no idea where he lived), and I believe it was in his general objection to make anything like an admission, that he replied, "Come here, and I'll take you home with me." I embrace this opportunity of remarking that he washed his clients off, as if he were a surgeon or a dentist. He had a closet in his room, fitted up for the purpose, which smelt of the scented soap like a perfumer's shop. It had an unusually large jack-towel on a roller inside the door, and he would wash his hands, and wipe them and dry them all over this towel, whenever he came in from a police court or dismissed a client from his room. When I and my friends repaired to him at six o'clock next day, he seemed to have been engaged on a case of a darker complexion than usual, for we found him with his head butted into this closet, not only washing his hands, but laving his face and gargling his throat. And even when he had done all that, and had gone all round the jack-towel, he took out his penknife and scraped the case out of his nails before he put his coat on.

There were some people slinking about as usual when we passed out into the street, who were evidently anxious to speak with him; but there was something so conclusive in the halo of scented soap which encircled his presence, that they gave it up for that day. As we walked along westward, he was recognized ever and again by some face in the crowd of the streets, and whenever that happened he talked louder to me; but he never otherwise recognized anybody, or took notice that anybody recognized him.

He conducted us to Gerrard Street, Soho, to a house on the south side of that street. Rather a stately house of its kind, but dolefully in want of painting, and with dirty windows. He took out his key and opened the door, and we all went into a stone hall, bare, gloomy, and little used. So, up a dark brown staircase into a series of three dark brown rooms on the first floor. There were carved garlands on the panelled walls, and as he stood among them giving us welcome, I know what kind of loops I thought they looked like.

Dinner was laid in the best of these rooms; the second was his dressing-room; the third, his bedroom. He told us that he held the whole house, but rarely used more of it than we saw. The table was comfortably laid—no silver in the service, of course—and at the side of his chair was a capacious dumb-waiter, with a variety of bottles and decanters on it, and four dishes of fruit for dessert. I noticed throughout, that he kept everything under his own hand, and distributed everything himself.

There was a bookcase in the room; I saw from the backs of the books, that they were about evidence, criminal law, criminal biography, trials, acts of Parliament, and such things. The furniture was all very solid and good, like his watch-chain. It had an official look, however, and there was nothing merely ornamental to be seen. In a corner was a little table of papers with a shaded lamp: so that he seemed to bring the office home with him in that respect too, and to wheel it out of an evening and fall to work.

As he had scarcely seen my three companions until now—
for he and I had walked together—he stood on the hearth-rug,
after ringing the bell, and took a searching look at them. To
my surprise, he seemed at once to be principally if not solely
interested in Drummle.

"Pip," said he, putting his large hand on my shoulder and
moving me to the window, "I don't know one from the other.
Who's the Spider?"

"The spider?" said I.

"The blotchy, sprawly, sulky fellow."

"That's Bentley Drummle," I replied; "the one with the
delicate face is Startop."

Not making the least account of "the one with the delicate
face," he returned, "Bentley Drummle is his name, is it? I like
the look of that fellow."

He immediately began to talk to Drummle: not at all
deterred by his replying in his heavy reticent way, but apparently
led on by it to screw discourse out of him. I was looking at the
two, when there came between me and them the housekeeper,
with the first dish for the table.

She was a woman of about forty, I supposed—but I may have
thought her younger than she was. Rather tall, of a lithe nimble
figure, extremely pale, with large faded eyes, and a quantity of
streaming hair. I cannot say whether any diseased affection of
the heart caused her lips to be parted as if she were panting, and
her face to bear a curious expression of suddenness and flutter;
but I know that I had been to see Macbeth at the theatre, a
night or two before, and that her face looked to me as if it were
all disturbed by fiery air, like the faces I had seen rise out of the
Witches' caldron.

She set the dish on, touched my guardian quietly on the
arm with a finger to notify that dinner was ready, and vanished.
We took our seats at the round table, and my guardian kept
Drummle on one side of him, while Startop sat on the other. It

was a noble dish of fish that the housekeeper had put on table, and we had a joint of equally choice mutton afterwards, and then an equally choice bird. Sauces, wines, all the accessories we wanted, and all of the best, were given out by our host from his dumb-waiter; and when they had made the circuit of the table, he always put them back again. Similarly, he dealt us clean plates and knives and forks, for each course, and dropped those just disused into two baskets on the ground by his chair. No other attendant than the housekeeper appeared. She set on every dish; and I always saw in her face, a face rising out of the caldron. Years afterwards, I made a dreadful likeness of that woman, by causing a face that had no other natural resemblance to it than it derived from flowing hair to pass behind a bowl of flaming spirits in a dark room.

Induced to take particular notice of the housekeeper, both by her own striking appearance and by Wemmick's preparation, I observed that whenever she was in the room she kept her eyes attentively on my guardian, and that she would remove her hands from any dish she put before him, hesitatingly, as if she dreaded his calling her back, and wanted him to speak when she was nigh, if he had anything to say. I fancied that I could detect in his manner a consciousness of this, and a purpose of always holding her in suspense.

Dinner went off gayly, and although my guardian seemed to follow rather than originate subjects, I knew that he wrenched the weakest part of our dispositions out of us. For myself, I found that I was expressing my tendency to lavish expenditure, and to patronize Herbert, and to boast of my great prospects, before I quite knew that I had opened my lips. It was so with all of us, but with no one more than Drummle: the development of whose inclination to gird in a grudging and suspicious way at the rest, was screwed out of him before the fish was taken off.

It was not then, but when we had got to the cheese, that

our conversation turned upon our rowing feats, and that Drummle was rallied for coming up behind of a night in that slow amphibious way of his. Drummle upon this, informed our host that he much preferred our room to our company, and that as to skill he was more than our master, and that as to strength he could scatter us like chaff. By some invisible agency, my guardian wound him up to a pitch little short of ferocity about this trifle; and he fell to baring and spanning his arm to show how muscular it was, and we all fell to baring and spanning our arms in a ridiculous manner.

Now the housekeeper was at that time clearing the table; my guardian, taking no heed of her, but with the side of his face turned from her, was leaning back in his chair biting the side of his forefinger and showing an interest in Drummle, that, to me, was quite inexplicable. Suddenly, he clapped his large hand on the housekeeper's, like a trap, as she stretched it across the table. So suddenly and smartly did he do this, that we all stopped in our foolish contention.

"If you talk of strength," said Mr. Jaggers, "I'll show you a wrist. Molly, let them see your wrist."

Her entrapped hand was on the table, but she had already put her other hand behind her waist. "Master," she said, in a low voice, with her eyes attentively and entreatingly fixed upon him. "Don't."

"*I'll* show you a wrist," repeated Mr. Jaggers, with an immovable determination to show it. "Molly, let them see your wrist."

"Master," she again murmured. "Please!"

"Molly," said Mr. Jaggers, not looking at her, but obstinately looking at the opposite side of the room, "let them see *both* your wrists. Show them. Come!"

He took his hand from hers, and turned that wrist up on the table. She brought her other hand from behind her, and held the two out side by side. The last wrist was much disfigured—

deeply scarred and scarred across and across. When she held her hands out she took her eyes from Mr. Jaggers, and turned them watchfully on every one of the rest of us in succession.

"There's power here," said Mr. Jaggers, coolly tracing out the sinews with his forefinger. "Very few men have the power of wrist that this woman has. It's remarkable what mere force of grip there is in these hands. I have had occasion to notice many hands; but I never saw stronger in that respect, man's or woman's, than these."

While he said these words in a leisurely, critical style, she continued to look at every one of us in regular succession as we sat. The moment he ceased, she looked at him again. "That'll do, Molly," said Mr. Jaggers, giving her a slight nod; "you have been admired, and can go." She withdrew her hands and went out of the room, and Mr. Jaggers, putting the decanters on from his dumb-waiter, filled his glass and passed round the wine.

"At half-past nine, gentlemen," said he, "we must break up. Pray make the best use of your time. I am glad to see you all. Mr. Drummle, I drink to you."

If his object in singling out Drummle were to bring him out still more, it perfectly succeeded. In a sulky triumph, Drummle showed his morose depreciation of the rest of us, in a more and more offensive degree, until he became downright intolerable. Through all his stages, Mr. Jaggers followed him with the same strange interest. He actually seemed to serve as a zest to Mr. Jaggers's wine.

In our boyish want of discretion I dare say we took too much to drink, and I know we talked too much. We became particularly hot upon some boorish sneer of Drummle's, to the effect that we were too free with our money. It led to my remarking, with more zeal than discretion, that it came with a bad grace from him, to whom Startop had lent money in my presence but a week or so before.

"Well," retorted Drummle; "he'll be paid."

"I don't mean to imply that he won't," said I, "but it might make you hold your tongue about us and our money, I should think."

"You should think!" retorted Drummle. "Oh Lord!"

"I dare say," I went on, meaning to be very severe, "that you wouldn't lend money to any of us if we wanted it."

"You are right," said Drummle. "I wouldn't lend one of you a sixpence. I wouldn't lend anybody a sixpence."

"Rather mean to borrow under those circumstances, I should say."

"*You* should say," repeated Drummle. "Oh Lord!"

This was so very aggravating—the more especially as I found myself making no way against his surly obtuseness—that I said, disregarding Herbert's efforts to check me:

"Come, Mr. Drummle, since we are on the subject, I'll tell you what passed between Herbert here and me, when you borrowed that money."

"*I* don't want to know what passed between Herbert there and you," growled Drummle. And I think he added in a lower growl, that we might both go to the devil and shake ourselves. "I'll tell you, however," said I, "whether you want to know or not. We said that as you put it in your pocket very glad to get it, you seemed to be immensely amused at his being so weak as to lend it."

Drummle laughed outright, and sat laughing in our faces, with his hands in his pockets and his round shoulders raised; plainly signifying that it was quite true, and that he despised us as asses all.

Hereupon Startop took him in hand, though with a much better grace than I had shown, and exhorted him to be a little more agreeable. Startop, being a lively, bright young fellow, and Drummle being the exact opposite, the latter was always disposed to resent him as a direct personal affront. He now retorted in a coarse, lumpish way, and Startop tried to turn the discussion aside with some small pleasantry that made us all laugh. Resenting this little success more than anything, Drummle, without any threat or warning, pulled his hands out of his pockets, dropped his round shoulders, swore, took up a large glass, and would have flung it at his adversary's head, but for our entertainer's dexterously seizing it at the instant when it was raised for that purpose.

"Gentlemen," said Mr. Jaggers, deliberately putting down the glass, and hauling out his gold repeater by its massive chain, "I am exceedingly sorry to announce that it's half past nine."

On this hint we all rose to depart. Before we got to the street door, Startop was cheerily calling Drummle "old boy," as if nothing had happened. But the old boy was so far from responding, that he would not even walk to Hammersmith on the same side of the way; so Herbert and I, who remained in town, saw them going down the street on opposite sides; Startop leading, and Drummle lagging behind in the shadow of the houses, much as he was wont to follow in his boat.

As the door was not yet shut, I thought I would leave Herbert there for a moment, and run up stairs again to say a word to my guardian. I found him in his dressing-room surrounded by his stock of boots, already hard at it, washing his hands of us.

I told him I had come up again to say how sorry I was that anything disagreeable should have occurred, and that I hoped he would not blame me much.

"Pooh!" said he, sluicing his face, and speaking through the water-drops; "it's nothing, Pip. I like that Spider though."

He had turned towards me now, and was shaking his head, and blowing, and towelling himself.

"I am glad you like him, sir," said I— "but I don't."

"No, no," my guardian assented; "don't have too much to do with him. Keep as clear of him as you can. But I like the fellow, Pip; he is one of the true sort. Why, if I was a fortune-teller—"

Looking out of the towel, he caught my eye.

"But I am not a fortune-teller," he said, letting his head drop into a festoon of towel, and towelling away at his two ears. "You know what I am, don't you? Good night, Pip."

"Good night, sir."

In about a month after that, the Spider's time with Mr. Pocket was up for good, and, to the great relief of all the house but Mrs. Pocket, he went home to the family hole.

CHAPTER 8

"MY DEAR MR PIP:—
"I write this by request of Mr. Gargery, for
to let you know that he is going to London in company
with Mr. Wopsle and would be glad if agreeable to be
allowed to see you. He would call at Barnard's Hotel
Tuesday morning at nine o'clock, when if not agreeable
please leave word. Your poor sister is much the same
as when you left. We talk of you in the kitchen every
night, and wonder what you are saying and doing. If
now considered in the light of a liberty, excuse it for
the love of poor old days. No more, dear Mr. Pip, from
your ever obliged, and affectionate servant,
       "BIDDY."
       "P.S. He wishes me most particular to write what
larks. He says you will understand. I hope and do not
doubt it will be agreeable to see him, even though a
gentleman, for you had ever a good heart, and he is
a worthy, worthy man. I have read him all, excepting
only the last little sentence, and he wishes me most
particular to write again what larks."

I received this letter by the post on Monday morning, and
therefore its appointment was for next day. Let me confess
exactly with what feelings I looked forward to Joe's coming.

Not with pleasure, though I was bound to him by so many
ties; no; with considerable disturbance, some mortification,
and a keen sense of incongruity. If I could have kept him
away by paying money, I certainly would have paid money.

My greatest reassurance was that he was coming to Barnard's Inn, not to Hammersmith, and consequently would not fall in Bentley Drummle's way. I had little objection to his being seen by Herbert or his father, for both of whom I had a respect; but I had the sharpest sensitiveness as to his being seen by Drummle, whom I held in contempt. So, throughout life, our worst weaknesses and meannesses are usually committed for the sake of the people whom we most despise.

I had begun to be always decorating the chambers in some quite unnecessary and inappropriate way or other, and very expensive those wrestles with Barnard proved to be. By this time, the rooms were vastly different from what I had found them, and I enjoyed the honor of occupying a few prominent pages in the books of a neighbouring upholsterer. I had got on so fast of late, that I had even started a boy in boots—top boots—in bondage and slavery to whom I might have been said to pass my days. For, after I had made the monster (out of the refuse of my washerwoman's family), and had clothed him with a blue coat, canary waistcoat, white cravat, creamy breeches, and the boots already mentioned, I had to find him a little to do and a great deal to eat; and with both of those horrible requirements he haunted my existence.

This avenging phantom was ordered to be on duty at eight on Tuesday morning in the hall, (it was two feet square, as charged for floorcloth,) and Herbert suggested certain things for breakfast that he thought Joe would like. While I felt sincerely obliged to him for being so interested and considerate, I had an odd half-provoked sense of suspicion upon me, that if Joe had been coming to see *him*, he wouldn't have been quite so brisk about it.

However, I came into town on the Monday night to be ready for Joe, and I got up early in the morning, and caused the sitting-room and breakfast-table to assume their most splendid appearance. Unfortunately the morning was drizzly, and an angel could not have concealed the fact that Barnard was shedding sooty tears outside the window, like some weak giant of a Sweep.

As the time approached I should have liked to run away, but the Avenger pursuant to orders was in the hall, and presently I heard Joe on the staircase. I knew it was Joe, by his clumsy manner of coming up stairs—his state boots being always too big for him—and by the time it took him to read the names on the other floors in the course of his ascent. When at last he stopped outside our door, I could hear his finger tracing over the painted letters of my name, and I afterwards distinctly heard him breathing in at the keyhole. Finally he gave a faint single rap, and Pepper—such was the compromising name of the avenging boy—announced "Mr. Gargery!" I thought he never would have done wiping his feet, and that I must have gone out to lift him off the mat, but at last he came in.

"Joe, how are you, Joe?"

"Pip, how AIR you, Pip?"

With his good honest face all glowing and shining, and his hat put down on the floor between us, he caught both my hands and worked them straight up and down, as if I had been the last-patented Pump.

"I am glad to see you, Joe. Give me your hat."

But Joe, taking it up carefully with both hands, like a bird's-nest with eggs in it, wouldn't hear of parting with that piece of property, and persisted in standing talking over it in a most uncomfortable way.

"Which you have that growed," said Joe, "and that swelled, and that gentle-folked;" Joe considered a little before he discovered this word; "as to be sure you are a honor to your king and country."

"And you, Joe, look wonderfully well."

"Thank God," said Joe, "I'm ekerval to most. And your sister, she's no worse than she were. And Biddy, she's ever right and ready. And all friends is no backerder, if not no forarder. 'Ceptin Wopsle; he's had a drop."

All this time (still with both hands taking great care of the bird's-nest), Joe was rolling his eyes round and round the room, and round and round the flowered pattern of my dressing-gown.

"Had a drop, Joe?"

"Why yes," said Joe, lowering his voice, "he's left the Church and went into the playacting. Which the playacting have likeways brought him to London along with me. And his wish were," said Joe, getting the bird's-nest under his left arm for the moment, and groping in it for an egg with his right; "if no offence, as I would 'and you that."

I took what Joe gave me, and found it to be the crumpled play-bill of a small metropolitan theatre, announcing the first appearance, in that very week, of "the celebrated Provincial Amateur of Roscian renown, whose unique performance in the highest tragic walk of our National Bard has lately occasioned so great a sensation in local dramatic circles."

"Were you at his performance, Joe?" I inquired.

"I *were*," said Joe, with emphasis and solemnity.

"Was there a great sensation?"

"Why," said Joe, "yes, there certainly were a peck of orange-peel. Partickler when he see the ghost. Though I put it to yourself, sir, whether it were calc'lated to keep a man up to his work with a good hart, to be continiwally cutting in betwixt him and the Ghost with "Amen!" A man may have had a misfortun' and been in the Church," said Joe, lowering his voice to an argumentative and feeling tone, "but that is no reason why you should put him out at such a time. Which I meantersay, if the ghost of a man's own father cannot be allowed to claim his attention, what can, Sir? Still more, when his mourning 'at is unfortunately made so small as that the weight of the black feathers brings it off, try to keep it on how you may."

A ghost-seeing effect in Joe's own countenance informed me that Herbert had entered the room. So, I presented Joe to Herbert, who held out his hand; but Joe backed from it, and held on by the bird's-nest.

"Your servant, Sir," said Joe, "which I hope as you and Pip"—here his eye fell on the Avenger, who was putting some toast on table, and so plainly denoted an intention to make that young gentleman one of the family, that I frowned it down and confused him more— "I meantersay, you two gentlemen—which I hope as you get your elths in this close spot? For the present may be a werry good inn, according to London opinions," said Joe, confidentially, "and I believe its character do stand i; but I wouldn't keep a pig in it myself—not in the case that I wished him to fatten wholesome and to eat with a meller flavor on him."

Having borne this flattering testimony to the merits of our dwelling-place, and having incidentally shown this tendency to call me "sir," Joe, being invited to sit down to table, looked all round the room for a suitable spot on which to deposit his hat—as if it were only on some very few rare substances in nature that it could find a resting place—and ultimately stood it on an extreme corner of the chimney-piece, from which it ever afterwards fell off at intervals.

"Do you take tea, or coffee, Mr. Gargery?" asked Herbert, who always presided of a morning.

"Thankee, Sir," said Joe, stiff from head to foot, "I'll take whichever is most agreeable to yourself."

"What do you say to coffee?"

"Thankee, Sir," returned Joe, evidently dispirited by the proposal, "since you *are* so kind as make chice of coffee, I will not run contrairy to your own opinions. But don't you never find it a little 'eating?"

"Say tea then," said Herbert, pouring it out.

Here Joe's hat tumbled off the mantel-piece, and he started

out of his chair and picked it up, and fitted it to the same exact spot. As if it were an absolute point of good breeding that it should tumble off again soon.

"When did you come to town, Mr. Gargery?"

"Were it yesterday afternoon?" said Joe, after coughing behind his hand, as if he had had time to catch the whooping-cough since he came. "No it were not. Yes it were. Yes. It were yesterday afternoon" (with an appearance of mingled wisdom, relief, and strict impartiality).

"Have you seen anything of London yet?"

"Why, yes, Sir," said Joe, "me and Wopsle went off straight to look at the Blacking Ware'us. But we didn't find that it come up to its likeness in the red bills at the shop doors; which I meantersay," added Joe, in an explanatory manner, "as it is there drawd too architectooralooral."

I really believe Joe would have prolonged this word (mightily expressive to my mind of some architecture that I know) into a perfect Chorus, but for his attention being providentially attracted by his hat, which was toppling. Indeed, it demanded from him a constant attention, and a quickness of eye and hand, very like that exacted by wicket-keeping. He made extraordinary play with it, and showed the greatest skill; now, rushing at it and catching it neatly as it dropped; now, merely stopping it midway, beating it up, and humoring it in various parts of the room and against a good deal of the pattern of the paper on the wall, before he felt it safe to close with it; finally splashing it into the slop-basin, where I took the liberty of laying hands upon it.

As to his shirt-collar, and his coat-collar, they were perplexing to reflect upon—insoluble mysteries both. Why should a man scrape himself to that extent, before he could consider himself full dressed? Why should he suppose it necessary to be purified by suffering for his holiday clothes? Then he fell into such unaccountable fits of meditation, with his fork midway between his plate and his mouth; had his eyes attracted in such strange directions; was afflicted with such remarkable coughs; sat so far from the table, and dropped so much more than he ate, and pretended that he hadn't dropped it; that I was heartily glad when Herbert left us for the City.

I had neither the good sense nor the good feeling to know that this was all my fault, and that if I had been easier with Joe, Joe would have been easier with me. I felt impatient of him and out of temper with him; in which condition he heaped coals of fire on my head.

"Us two being now alone, Sir,"—began Joe.

"Joe," I interrupted, pettishly, "how can you call me, Sir?"

Joe looked at me for a single instant with something faintly like reproach. Utterly preposterous as his cravat was, and as his collars were, I was conscious of a sort of dignity in the look.

"Us two being now alone," resumed Joe, "and me having the intentions and abilities to stay not many minutes more, I will now conclude—leastways begin—to mention what have led to my having had the present honor. For was it not," said Joe, with his old air of lucid exposition, "that my only wish were to be useful to you, I should not have had the honor of breaking wittles in the company and abode of gentlemen."

I was so unwilling to see the look again, that I made no remonstrance against this tone.

"Well, Sir," pursued Joe, "this is how it were. I were at the Bargemen t'other night, Pip;"—whenever he subsided into affection, he called me Pip, and whenever he relapsed into politeness he called me Sir; "when there come up in his shay-cart, Pumblechook. Which that same identical," said Joe, going down a new track, "do comb my 'air the wrong way sometimes, awful, by giving out up and down town as it were him which ever had your infant companionation and were looked upon as a playfellow by yourself."

"Nonsense. It was you, Joe."

"Which I fully believed it were, Pip," said Joe, slightly tossing his head, "though it signify little now, sir. Well, Pip; this same identical, which his manners is given to blusterous, come to me at the Bargemen (wot a pipe and a pint of beer do give refreshment to the workingman, sir, and do not over stimilate), and his word were, 'Joseph, Miss Havisham she wish to speak to you.'"

"Miss Havisham, Joe?"

"'She wish,' were Pumblechook's word, 'to speak to you.'" Joe sat and rolled his eyes at the ceiling.

"Yes, Joe? Go on, please."

"Next day, Sir," said Joe, looking at me as if I were a long way off, "having cleaned myself, I go and I see Miss A."

"Miss A., Joe? Miss Havisham?"

"Which I say, sir," replied Joe, with an air of legal formality, as if he were making his will, "Miss A., or otherways Havisham. Her expression air then as follering: 'Mr. Gargery. You air in correspondence with Mr. Pip?' Having had a letter from you, I were able to say 'I am.' (When I married your sister, sir, I said 'I will;' and when I answered your friend, Pip, I said 'I am.') 'Would you tell him, then,' said she, 'that which Estella has come home and would be glad to see him.'"

I felt my face fire up as I looked at Joe. I hope one remote cause of its firing may have been my consciousness that if I had known his errand, I should have given him more encouragement.

"Biddy," pursued Joe, "when I got home and asked her fur to write the message to you, a little hung back. Biddy says, 'I know he will be very glad to have it by word of mouth, it is holiday time, you want to see him, go!' I have now concluded, Sir," said Joe, rising from his chair, "and, Pip, I wish you ever well and ever prospering to a greater and a greater height."

"But you are not going now, Joe?"

"Yes I am," said Joe.

"But you are coming back to dinner, Joe?"

"No I am not," said Joe.

Our eyes met, and all the "Sir" melted out of that manly heart as he gave me his hand.

"Pip, dear old chap, life is made of ever so many partings welded together, as I may say, and one man's a blacksmith, and one's a whitesmith, and one's a goldsmith, and one's a coppersmith. Diwisions among such must come, and must be met as they come. If there's been any fault at all to-day, it's mine. You and me is not two figures to be together in London; nor yet anywheres else but what is private, and beknown, and understood among friends. It ain't that I am proud, but that I want to be right, as you shall never see me no more in these clothes. I'm wrong in these clothes. I'm wrong out of the forge, the kitchen, or off th' meshes. You won't find half so much fault in me if you think of me in my forge dress, with my hammer in my hand, or even my pipe. You won't find half so much fault in me if, supposing as you should ever wish to see me, you come and put your head in at the forge window and see Joe the blacksmith, there, at the old anvil, in the old burnt apron, sticking to the old work. I'm awful dull, but I hope I've beat out something nigh the rights of this at last. And so God bless you, dear old Pip, old chap, God bless you!"

I had not been mistaken in my fancy that there was a simple dignity in him. The fashion of his dress could no more come in its way when he spoke these words than it could come in its way in Heaven. He touched me gently on the forehead, and went out. As soon as I could recover myself sufficiently, I hurried out after him and looked for him in the neighbouring streets; but he was gone.

CHAPTER 9

It was clear that I must repair to our town next day, and in the first flow of my repentance, it was equally clear that I must stay at Joe's. But, when I had secured my box-place by to-morrow's coach, and had been down to Mr. Pocket's and back, I was not by any means convinced on the last point, and began to invent reasons and make excuses for putting up at the Blue Boar. I should be an inconvenience at Joe's; I was not expected, and my bed would not be ready; I should be too far from Miss Havisham's, and she was exacting and mightn't like it. All other swindlers upon earth are nothing to the self-swindlers, and with such pretences did I cheat myself. Surely a curious thing. That I should innocently take a bad half-crown of somebody else's manufacture is reasonable enough; but that I should knowingly reckon the spurious coin of my own make as good money! An obliging stranger, under pretence of compactly folding up my bank-notes for security's sake, abstracts the notes and gives me nutshells; but what is his sleight of hand to mine, when I fold up my own nutshells and pass them on myself as notes!

Having settled that I must go to the Blue Boar, my mind was much disturbed by indecision whether or not to take the Avenger. It was tempting to think of that expensive Mercenary publicly airing his boots in the archway of the Blue Boar's posting-yard; it was almost solemn to imagine him casually produced in the tailor's shop, and confounding the disrespectful senses of Trabb's boy. On the other hand, Trabb's boy might worm himself into his intimacy and tell him things; or, reckless and desperate wretch as I knew he could be, might hoot him in the High Street. My patroness, too, might hear of him, and not approve. On the whole, I resolved to leave the Avenger behind.

It was the afternoon coach by which I had taken my place, and, as winter had now come round, I should not arrive at my destination until two or three hours after dark. Our time of starting from the Cross Keys was two o'clock. I arrived on the ground with a quarter of an hour to spare, attended by the Avenger—if I may connect that expression with one who never attended on me if he could possibly help it.

At that time it was customary to carry Convicts down to the dock-yards by stage-coach. As I had often heard of them in the capacity of outside passengers, and had more than once seen them on the high road dangling their ironed legs over the coach roof, I had no cause to be surprised when Herbert, meeting me in the yard, came up and told me there were two convicts going down with me. But I had a reason that was an old reason now for constitutionally faltering whenever I heard the word "convict."

"You don't mind them, Handel?" said Herbert.

"Oh no!"

"I thought you seemed as if you didn't like them?"

"I can't pretend that I do like them, and I suppose you don't particularly. But I don't mind them."

"See! There they are," said Herbert, "coming out of the Tap. What a degraded and vile sight it is!"

They had been treating their guard, I suppose, for they had a gaoler with them, and all three came out wiping their mouths on their hands. The two convicts were handcuffed together, and had irons on their legs—irons of a pattern that I knew well. They wore the dress that I likewise knew well. Their keeper had a brace of pistols, and carried a thick-knobbed bludgeon under his arm; but he was on terms of good understanding with them, and stood with them beside him, looking on at the putting-to of the horses, rather with an air as if the convicts were an interesting Exhibition not formally open at the moment, and he the Curator. One was a taller and stouter man than the other, and appeared as a matter of course, according to the mysterious ways of the world, both convict and free, to have had allotted to him the smaller suit of clothes. His arms and legs were like great pincushions of those shapes, and his attire disguised him absurdly; but I knew his half-closed eye at one glance. There stood the man whom I had seen on the settle at the Three Jolly Bargemen on a Saturday night, and who had brought me down with his invisible gun!

It was easy to make sure that as yet he knew me no more than if he had never seen me in his life. He looked across at me, and his eye appraised my watch-chain, and then he incidentally spat and said something to the other convict, and they laughed and slued themselves round with a clink of their coupling manacle, and looked at something else. The great numbers on their backs, as if they were street doors; their coarse mangy ungainly outer surface, as if they were lower animals; their ironed legs, apologetically garlanded with pocket-handkerchiefs; and the way in which all present looked at them and kept from them; made them (as Herbert had said) a most disagreeable and degraded spectacle.

But this was not the worst of it. It came out that the whole of the back of the coach had been taken by a family removing from London, and that there were no places for the two prisoners but on the seat in front behind the coachman. Hereupon, a choleric gentleman, who had taken the fourth place on that seat, flew into a most violent passion, and said that it was a breach of contract to mix him up with such villainous company, and that it was poisonous, and pernicious, and infamous, and shameful, and I don't know what else. At this time the coach was ready and the coachman impatient, and we were all preparing to get up, and the prisoners had come over with their keeper—bringing with them that curious flavor of bread-poultice, baize, rope-yarn, and hearthstone, which attends the convict presence.

"Don't take it so much amiss, sir," pleaded the keeper to the angry passenger; "I'll sit next you myself. I'll put 'em on the outside of the row. They won't interfere with you, sir. You needn't know they're there."

"And don't blame *me*," growled the convict I had recognized. "I don't want to go. I *am* quite ready to stay behind. As fur as I am concerned any one's welcome to *my* place."

"Or mine," said the other, gruffly. "*I* wouldn't have incommoded none of you, if I'd had *my* way." Then they both laughed, and began cracking nuts, and spitting the shells about.—As I really think I should have liked to do myself, if I had been in their place and so despised.

At length, it was voted that there was no help for the angry gentleman, and that he must either go in his chance company or remain behind. So he got into his place, still making complaints, and the keeper got into the place next him, and the convicts hauled themselves up as well as they could, and the convict I had recognized sat behind me with his breath on the hair of my head.

"Good by, Handel!" Herbert called out as we started. I thought what a blessed fortune it was, that he had found another name for me than Pip.

It is impossible to express with what acuteness I felt the convict's breathing, not only on the back of my head, but all along my spine. The sensation was like being touched in the marrow with some pungent and searching acid, it set my very teeth on edge. He seemed to have more breathing business to do than another man, and to make more noise in doing it; and I was conscious of growing high-shouldered on one side, in my shrinking endeavors to fend him off.

The weather was miserably raw, and the two cursed the

cold. It made us all lethargic before we had gone far, and when we had left the Half-way House behind, we habitually dozed and shivered and were silent. I dozed off, myself, in considering the question whether I ought to restore a couple of pounds sterling to this creature before losing sight of him, and how it could best be done. In the act of dipping forward as if I were going to bathe among the horses, I woke in a fright and took the question up again.

But I must have lost it longer than I had thought, since, although I could recognize nothing in the darkness and the fitful lights and shadows of our lamps, I traced marsh country in the cold damp wind that blew at us. Cowering forward for warmth and to make me a screen against the wind, the convicts were closer to me than before. The very first words I heard them interchange as I became conscious, were the words of my own thought, "Two One Pound notes."

"How did he get 'em?" said the convict I had never seen.

"How should I know?" returned the other. "He had 'em stowed away somehows. Giv him by friends, I expect."

"I wish," said the other, with a bitter curse upon the cold, "that I had 'em here."

"Two one pound notes, or friends?"

"Two one pound notes. I'd sell all the friends I ever had for one, and think it a blessed good bargain. Well? So he says—?"

"So he says," resumed the convict I had recognized— "it was all said and done in half a minute, behind a pile of timber in the Dock-yard— 'You're a going to be discharged?' Yes, I was. Would I find out that boy that had fed him and kep his secret, and give him them two one pound notes? Yes, I would. And I did."

"More fool you," growled the other. "I'd have spent 'em on a Man, in wittles and drink. He must have been a green one. Mean to say he knowed nothing of you?"

"Not a ha'porth. Different gangs and different ships. He was tried again for prison breaking, and got made a Lifer."

"And was that—Honor!—the only time you worked out, in this part of the country?"

"The only time."

"What might have been your opinion of the place?"

"A most beastly place. Mudbank, mist, swamp, and work; work, swamp, mist, and mudbank."

They both execrated the place in very strong language, and gradually growled themselves out, and had nothing left to say.

After overhearing this dialogue, I should assuredly have got down and been left in the solitude and darkness of the highway, but for feeling certain that the man had no suspicion of my identity. Indeed, I was not only so changed in the course of nature, but so differently dressed and so differently circumstanced, that it was not at all likely he could have known me without accidental help. Still, the coincidence of our being together on the coach, was sufficiently strange to fill me with a dread that some other coincidence might at any moment connect me, in his hearing, with my name. For this reason, I resolved to alight as soon as we touched the town, and put myself out of his hearing. This device I executed successfully. My little portmanteau was in the boot under my feet; I had but to turn a hinge to get it out; I threw it down before me, got down after it, and was left at the first lamp on the first stones of the town pavement. As to the convicts, they went their way with the coach, and I knew at what point they would be spirited off to the river. In my fancy, I saw the boat with its convict crew waiting for them at the slime-washed stairs—again heard the gruff "Give way, you!" like and order to dogs—again saw the wicked Noah's Ark lying out on the black water.

I could not have said what I was afraid of, for my fear was altogether undefined and vague, but there was great fear upon me. As I walked on to the hotel, I felt that a dread, much exceeding the mere apprehension of a painful or disagreeable

recognition, made me tremble. I am confident that it took
no distinctness of shape, and that it was the revival for a few
minutes of the terror of childhood.

The coffee-room at the Blue Boar was empty, and I had not
only ordered my dinner there, but had sat down to it, before
the waiter knew me. As soon as he had apologized for the
remissness of his memory, he asked me if he should send Boots
for Mr. Pumblechook?

"No," said I, "certainly not."

The waiter (it was he who had brought up the Great
Remonstrance from the Commercials, on the day when I was
bound) appeared surprised, and took the earliest opportunity
of putting a dirty old copy of a local newspaper so directly in
my way, that I took it up and read this paragraph:—

> "Our readers will learn, not altogether without
> interest, in reference to the recent romantic rise in fortune
> of a young artificer in iron of this neighbourhood (what
> a theme, by the way, for the magic pen of our as yet
> not universally acknowledged townsman TOOBY, the
> poet of our columns!) that the youth's earliest patron,
> companion, and friend, was a highly respected individual
> not entirely unconnected with the corn and seed trade,
> and whose eminently convenient and commodious
> business premises are situate within a hundred miles
> of the High Street. It is not wholly irrespective of our
> personal feelings that we record HIM as the Mentor
> of our young Telemachus, for it is good to know that
> our town produced the founder of the latter's fortunes.
> Does the thought-contracted brow of the local Sage or
> the lustrous eye of local Beauty inquire whose fortunes?
> We believe that Quintin Matsys was the BLACKSMITH
> of Antwerp. VERB. SAP."

I entertain a conviction, based upon large experience, that if in the days of my prosperity I had gone to the North Pole, I should have met somebody there, wandering Esquimaux or civilized man, who would have told me that Pumblechook was my earliest patron and the founder of my fortunes.

CHAPTER 10

Betimes in the morning I was up and out. It was too early yet to go to Miss Havisham's, so I loitered into the country on Miss Havisham's side of town—which was not Joe's side; I could go there to-morrow—thinking about my patroness, and painting brilliant pictures of her plans for me.

She had adopted Estella, she had as good as adopted me, and it could not fail to be her intention to bring us together. She reserved it for me to restore the desolate house, admit the sunshine into the dark rooms, set the clocks a-going and the cold hearths a-blazing, tear down the cobwebs, destroy the vermin—in short, do all the shining deeds of the young Knight of romance, and marry the Princess. I had stopped to look at the house as I passed; and its seared red brick walls, blocked windows, and strong green ivy clasping even the stacks of chimneys with its twigs and tendons, as if with sinewy old arms, had made up a rich attractive mystery, of which I was the hero. Estella was the inspiration of it, and the heart of it, of course. But, though she had taken such strong possession of me, though my fancy and my hope were so set upon her, though her influence on my boyish life and character had been all-powerful, I did not, even that romantic morning, invest her with any attributes save those she possessed. I mention this in this place, of a fixed purpose, because it is the clew by which I am to be followed into my poor labyrinth. According to my experience, the conventional notion of a lover cannot be always true. The unqualified truth is, that when I loved Estella with the love of a man, I loved her simply because I found her irresistible. Once for all; I knew to my sorrow, often and often, if not always, that I loved her against reason, against promise, against peace, against hope, against happiness, against all discouragement that could be. Once for all; I loved her none the less because I knew it, and it had no more influence in restraining me than if I had devoutly believed her to be human perfection.

I so shaped out my walk as to arrive at the gate at my old time. When I had rung at the bell with an unsteady hand, I turned my back upon the gate, while I tried to get my breath and keep the beating of my heart moderately quiet. I heard the side-door open, and steps come across the courtyard; but I pretended not to hear, even when the gate swung on its rusty hinges.

Being at last touched on the shoulder, I started and turned. I started much more naturally then, to find myself confronted by a man in a sober gray dress. The last man I should have expected to see in that place of porter at Miss Havisham's door.

"Orlick!"

"Ah, young master, there's more changes than yours. But come in, come in. It's opposed to my orders to hold the gate open."

I entered and he swung it, and locked it, and took the key out. "Yes!" said he, facing round, after doggedly preceding me a few steps towards the house. "Here I am!"

"How did you come here?"

"I come her," he retorted, "on my legs. I had my box brought alongside me in a barrow."

"Are you here for good?"

"I ain't here for harm, young master, I suppose?"

I was not so sure of that. I had leisure to entertain the retort in my mind, while he slowly lifted his heavy glance from the pavement, up my legs and arms, to my face.

"Then you have left the forge?" I said.

"Do this look like a forge?" replied Orlick, sending his glance all round him with an air of injury. "Now, do it look like it?"

I asked him how long he had left Gargery's forge?

"One day is so like another here," he replied, "that I don't know without casting it up. However, I come here some time since you left."

"I could have told you that, Orlick."

"Ah!" said he, dryly. "But then you've got to be a scholar."

By this time we had come to the house, where I found his room to be one just within the side-door, with a little window in it looking on the courtyard. In its small proportions, it was not unlike the kind of place usually assigned to a gate-porter in Paris. Certain keys were hanging on the wall, to which he now added the gate key; and his patchwork-covered bed was in a little inner division or recess. The whole had a slovenly, confined, and sleepy look, like a cage for a human dormouse; while he, looming dark and heavy in the shadow of a corner by the window, looked like the human dormouse for whom it was fitted up—as indeed he was.

"I never saw this room before," I remarked; "but there used to be no Porter here."

"No," said he; "not till it got about that there was no protection on the premises, and it come to be considered dangerous, with convicts and Tag and Rag and Bobtail going up and down. And then I was recommended to the place as a man who could give another man as good as he brought, and I took it. It's easier than bellowsing and hammering.—That's loaded, that is."

My eye had been caught by a gun with a brass-bound stock over the chimney-piece, and his eye had followed mine.

"Well," said I, not desirous of more conversation, "shall I go up to Miss Havisham?"

"Burn me, if I know!" he retorted, first stretching himself

and then shaking himself; "my orders ends here, young master. I give this here bell a rap with this here hammer, and you go on along the passage till you meet somebody."

"I am expected, I believe?"

"Burn me twice over, if I can say!" said he.

Upon that, I turned down the long passage which I had first trodden in my thick boots, and he made his bell sound. At the end of the passage, while the bell was still reverberating, I found Sarah Pocket, who appeared to have now become constitutionally green and yellow by reason of me.

"Oh!" said she. "You, is it, Mr. Pip?"

"It is, Miss Pocket. I am glad to tell you that Mr. Pocket and family are all well."

"Are they any wiser?" said Sarah, with a dismal shake of the head; "they had better be wiser, than well. Ah, Matthew, Matthew! You know your way, sir?"

Tolerably, for I had gone up the staircase in the dark, many a time. I ascended it now, in lighter boots than of yore, and tapped in my old way at the door of Miss Havisham's room. "Pip's rap," I heard her say, immediately; "come in, Pip."

She was in her chair near the old table, in the old dress, with her two hands crossed on her stick, her chin resting on them, and her eyes on the fire. Sitting near her, with the white shoe, that had never been worn, in her hand, and her head bent as she looked at it, was an elegant lady whom I had never seen.

"Come in, Pip," Miss Havisham continued to mutter, without looking round or up; "come in, Pip, how do you do, Pip? so you kiss my hand as if I were a queen, eh?—Well?"

She looked up at me suddenly, only moving her eyes, and repeated in a grimly playful manner.

"Well?"

"I heard, Miss Havisham," said I, rather at a loss, "that you were so kind as to wish me to come and see you, and I came directly."

"Well?"

The lady whom I had never seen before, lifted up her eyes and looked archly at me, and then I saw that the eyes were Estella's eyes. But she was so much changed, was so much more beautiful, so much more womanly, in all things winning admiration, had made such wonderful advance, that I seemed to have made none. I fancied, as I looked at her, that I slipped hopelessly back into the coarse and common boy again. O the sense of distance and disparity that came upon me, and the inaccessibility that came about her!

She gave me her hand. I stammered something about the pleasure I felt in seeing her again, and about my having looked forward to it, for a long, long time.

"Do you find her much changed, Pip?" asked Miss Havisham, with her greedy look, and striking her stick upon a chair that stood between them, as a sign to me to sit down there.

"When I came in, Miss Havisham, I thought there was nothing of Estella in the face or figure; but now it all settles down so curiously into the old—"

"What? You are not going to say into the old Estella?" Miss Havisham interrupted. "She was proud and insulting, and you wanted to go away from her. Don't you remember?"

I said confusedly that that was long ago, and that I knew no better then, and the like. Estella smiled with perfect composure, and said she had no doubt of my having been quite right, and of her having been very disagreeable.

"Is *he* changed?" Miss Havisham asked her.

"Very much," said Estella, looking at me.

"Less coarse and common?" said Miss Havisham, playing with Estella's hair.

Estella laughed, and looked at the shoe in her hand, and laughed again, and looked at me, and put the shoe down. She treated me as a boy still, but she lured me on.

We sat in the dreamy room among the old strange influences which had so wrought upon me, and I learnt that she had but just come home from France, and that she was going to London. Proud and wilful as of old, she had brought those qualities into such subjection to her beauty that it was impossible and out of nature—or I thought so—to separate them from her beauty. Truly it was impossible to dissociate her presence from all those wretched hankerings after money and gentility that had disturbed my boyhood—from all those ill-regulated aspirations that had first made me ashamed of home and Joe—from all those visions that had raised her face in the glowing fire, struck it out of the iron on the anvil, extracted it from the darkness of night to look in at the wooden window of the forge, and flit away. In a word, it was impossible for me to separate her, in the past or in the present, from the innermost life of my life.

It was settled that I should stay there all the rest of the day, and return to the hotel at night, and to London to-morrow. When we had conversed for a while, Miss Havisham sent us two out to walk in the neglected garden: on our coming in by and by, she said, I should wheel her about a little, as in times of yore.

So, Estella and I went out into the garden by the gate through which I had strayed to my encounter with the pale young gentleman, now Herbert; I, trembling in spirit and worshipping the very hem of her dress; she, quite composed and most decidedly not worshipping the hem of mine. As we drew near to the place of encounter, she stopped and said:

"I must have been a singular little creature to hide and see that fight that day; but I did, and I enjoyed it very much."

"You rewarded me very much."

"Did I?" she replied, in an incidental and forgetful way. "I remember I entertained a great objection to your adversary, because I took it ill that he should be brought here to pester me with his company."

"He and I are great friends now."

"Are you? I think I recollect though, that you read with his father?"

"Yes."

I made the admission with reluctance, for it seemed to have a boyish look, and she already treated me more than enough like a boy.

"Since your change of fortune and prospects, you have changed your companions," said Estella.

"Naturally," said I.

"And necessarily," she added, in a haughty tone; "what was fit company for you once, would be quite unfit company for you now."

In my conscience, I doubt very much whether I had any lingering intention left of going to see Joe; but if I had, this observation put it to flight.

"You had no idea of your impending good fortune, in those times?" said Estella, with a slight wave of her hand, signifying in the fighting times.

"Not the least."

The air of completeness and superiority with which she walked at my side, and the air of youthfulness and submission with which I walked at hers, made a contrast that I strongly felt. It would have rankled in me more than it did, if I had not regarded myself as eliciting it by being so set apart for her and assigned to her.

The garden was too overgrown and rank for walking in with ease, and after we had made the round of it twice or thrice, we came out again into the brewery yard. I showed her to a nicety where I had seen her walking on the casks, that first old day, and she said, with a cold and careless look in that direction, "Did I?" I reminded her where she had come out of the house and given me my meat and drink, and she said, "I don't remember." "Not remember that you made me cry?" said I. "No," said she, and shook her head and looked about her. I verily believe that her not remembering and not minding in the least, made me cry again, inwardly—and that is the sharpest crying of all.

"You must know," said Estella, condescending to me as a brilliant and beautiful woman might, "that I have no heart—if that has anything to do with my memory."

I got through some jargon to the effect that I took the liberty of doubting that. That I knew better. That there could be no such beauty without it.

"Oh! I have a heart to be stabbed in or shot in, I have no doubt," said Estella, "and of course if it ceased to beat I should cease to be. But you know what I mean. I have no softness there, no—sympathy—sentiment—nonsense."

What *was* it that was borne in upon my mind when she stood still and looked attentively at me? Anything that I had seen in Miss Havisham? No. In some of her looks and gestures there was that tinge of resemblance to Miss Havisham which may often be noticed to have been acquired by children, from grown person with whom they have been much associated and secluded, and which, when childhood is passed, will produce a remarkable occasional likeness of expression between faces that are otherwise quite different. And yet I could not trace this to Miss Havisham. I looked again, and though she was still looking at me, the suggestion was gone.

What *was* it?

"I am serious," said Estella, not so much with a frown (for her brow was smooth) as with a darkening of her face; "if we are to be thrown much together, you had better believe it at once. No!" imperiously stopping me as I opened my lips. "I have not bestowed my tenderness anywhere. I have never had any such thing."

In another moment we were in the brewery, so long disused, and she pointed to the high gallery where I had seen her going out on that same first day, and told me she remembered to have been up there, and to have seen me standing scared below. As my eyes followed her white hand, again the same dim suggestion that I could not possibly grasp crossed me. My involuntary start occasioned her to lay her hand upon my arm. Instantly the ghost passed once more and was gone.

What *was* it?

"What is the matter?" asked Estella. "Are you scared again?"

"I should be, if I believed what you said just now," I replied, to turn it off.

"Then you don't? Very well. It is said, at any rate. Miss Havisham will soon be expecting you at your old post, though I think that might be laid aside now, with other old belongings. Let us make one more round of the garden, and then go in. Come! You shall not shed tears for my cruelty to-day; you shall be my Page, and give me your shoulder."

Her handsome dress had trailed upon the ground. She held it in one hand now, and with the other lightly touched my shoulder as we walked. We walked round the ruined garden twice or thrice more, and it was all in bloom for me. If the green and yellow growth of weed in the chinks of the old wall had been the most precious flowers that ever blew, it could not have been more cherished in my remembrance.

There was no discrepancy of years between us to remove her far from me; we were of nearly the same age, though of course the age told for more in her case than in mine; but the air of inaccessibility which her beauty and her manner gave her, tormented me in the midst of my delight, and at the height of the assurance I felt that our patroness had chosen us for one another. Wretched boy!

At last we went back into the house, and there I heard, with surprise, that my guardian had come down to see Miss Havisham on business, and would come back to dinner. The old wintry branches of chandeliers in the room where the mouldering table was spread had been lighted while we were out, and Miss Havisham was in her chair and waiting for me.

It was like pushing the chair itself back into the past, when we began the old slow circuit round about the ashes of the bridal feast. But, in the funereal room, with that figure of the grave fallen back in the chair fixing its eyes upon her, Estella looked more bright and beautiful than before, and I was under stronger enchantment.

The time so melted away, that our early dinner-hour drew close at hand, and Estella left us to prepare herself. We had stopped near the centre of the long table, and Miss Havisham, with one of her withered arms stretched out of the chair, rested that clenched hand upon the yellow cloth. As Estella looked back over her shoulder before going out at the door, Miss Havisham kissed that hand to her, with a ravenous intensity that was of its kind quite dreadful.

Then, Estella being gone and we two left alone, she turned to me, and said in a whisper:

"Is she beautiful, graceful, well-grown? Do you admire her?"

"Everybody must who sees her, Miss Havisham."

She drew an arm round my neck, and drew my head close down to hers as she sat in the chair. "Love her, love her, love her! How does she use you?"

Before I could answer (if I could have answered so difficult a question at all) she repeated, "Love her, love her, love her! If she favors you, love her. If she wounds you, love her. If she tears your heart to pieces—and as it gets older and stronger it will tear deeper—love her, love her, love her!"

Never had I seen such passionate eagerness as was joined to her utterance of these words. I could feel the muscles of the thin arm round my neck swell with the vehemence that possessed her.

"Hear me, Pip! I adopted her, to be loved. I bred her and

educated her, to be loved. I developed her into what she is, that she might be loved. Love her!"

She said the word often enough, and there could be no doubt that she meant to say it; but if the often repeated word had been hate instead of love—despair—revenge—dire death—it could not have sounded from her lips more like a curse.

"I'll tell you," said she, in the same hurried passionate whisper, "what real love is. It is blind devotion, unquestioning self-humiliation, utter submission, trust and belief against yourself and against the whole world, giving up your whole heart and soul to the smiter—as I did!"

When she came to that, and to a wild cry that followed that, I caught her round the waist. For she rose up in the chair, in her shroud of a dress, and struck at the air as if she would as soon have struck herself against the wall and fallen dead.

All this passed in a few seconds. As I drew her down into her chair, I was conscious of a scent that I knew, and turning, saw my guardian in the room.

He always carried (I have not yet mentioned it, I think) a pocket-handkerchief of rich silk and of imposing proportions, which was of great value to him in his profession. I have seen him so terrify a client or a witness by ceremoniously unfolding this pocket-handkerchief as if he were immediately going to blow his nose, and then pausing, as if he knew he should not have time to do it before such client or witness committed himself, that the self-committal has followed directly, quite as a matter of course. When I saw him in the room he had this expressive pocket-handkerchief in both hands, and was looking at us. On meeting my eye, he said plainly, by a momentary and silent pause in that attitude, "Indeed? Singular!" and then put the handkerchief to its right use with wonderful effect.

Miss Havisham had seen him as soon as I, and was (like everybody else) afraid of him. She made a strong attempt to compose herself, and stammered that he was as punctual as ever.

"As punctual as ever," he repeated, coming up to us. "(How do you do, Pip? Shall I give you a ride, Miss Havisham? Once round?) And so you are here, Pip?"

I told him when I had arrived, and how Miss Havisham had wished me to come and see Estella. To which he replied, "Ah! Very fine young lady!" Then he pushed Miss Havisham in her chair before him, with one of his large hands, and put the other in his trousers-pocket as if the pocket were full of secrets.

"Well, Pip! How often have you seen Miss Estella before?" said he, when he came to a stop.

"How often?"

"Ah! How many times? Ten thousand times?"

"Oh! Certainly not so many."

"Twice?"

"Jaggers," interposed Miss Havisham, much to my relief, "leave my Pip alone, and go with him to your dinner."

He complied, and we groped our way down the dark stairs together. While we were still on our way to those detached apartments across the paved yard at the back, he asked me how often I had seen Miss Havisham eat and drink; offering me a breadth of choice, as usual, between a hundred times and once.

I considered, and said, "Never."

"And never will, Pip," he retorted, with a frowning smile. "She has never allowed herself to be seen doing either, since she lived this present life of hers. She wanders about in the night, and then lays hands on such food as she takes."

"Pray, sir," said I, "may I ask you a question?"

"You may," said he, "and I may decline to answer it. Put your question."

"Estella's name. Is it Havisham or—?" I had nothing to add.

"Or what?" said he.

"Is it Havisham?"

"It is Havisham."

This brought us to the dinner-table, where she and Sarah Pocket awaited us. Mr. Jaggers presided, Estella sat opposite to him, I faced my green and yellow friend. We dined very well, and were waited on by a maid-servant whom I had never seen in all my comings and goings, but who, for anything I know, had been in that mysterious house the whole time. After dinner a bottle of choice old port was placed before my guardian (he was evidently well acquainted with the vintage), and the two ladies left us.

Anything to equal the determined reticence of Mr. Jaggers under that roof I never saw elsewhere, even in him. He kept his very looks to himself, and scarcely directed his eyes to Estella's face once during dinner. When she spoke to him, he listened, and in due course answered, but never looked at her, that I could see. On the other hand, she often looked at him, with interest and curiosity, if not distrust, but his face never showed the least consciousness. Throughout dinner he took a dry delight in making Sarah Pocket greener and yellower, by often referring in conversation with me to my expectations; but here, again, he showed no consciousness, and even made it appear that he extorted—and even did extort, though I don't know how—those references out of my innocent self.

And when he and I were left alone together, he sat with an air upon him of general lying by in consequence of information he possessed, that really was too much for me. He cross-examined his very wine when he had nothing else in hand. He held it between himself and the candle, tasted the port, rolled it in his mouth, swallowed it, looked at his glass again, smelt the port, tried it, drank it, filled again, and cross-examined the glass again, until I was as nervous as if I had known the wine to be telling him something to my disadvantage. Three or four times I feebly thought I would start conversation; but whenever he saw me going to ask him anything, he looked at me with his glass in his hand, and rolling his wine about in his mouth, as if requesting me to take notice that it was of no use, for he couldn't answer.

I think Miss Pocket was conscious that the sight of me involved her in the danger of being goaded to madness, and perhaps tearing off her cap—which was a very hideous one, in the nature of a muslin mop—and strewing the ground with her hair—which assuredly had never grown on *her* head. She did not appear when we afterwards went up to Miss Havisham's room, and we four played at whist. In the interval, Miss Havisham, in a fantastic way, had put some of the most beautiful jewels from her dressing-table into Estella's hair, and about her bosom and arms; and I saw even my guardian look at her from under his thick eyebrows, and raise them a little, when her loveliness was before him, with those rich flushes of glitter and color in it.

Of the manner and extent to which he took our trumps into custody, and came out with mean little cards at the ends of hands, before which the glory of our Kings and Queens was utterly abased, I say nothing; nor, of the feeling that I had, respecting his looking upon us personally in the light of three very obvious and poor riddles that he had found out long ago. What I suffered from, was the incompatibility between his cold presence and my feelings towards Estella. It was not that I knew I could never bear to speak to him about her, that I knew I could never bear to hear him creak his boots at her, that I knew I could never bear to see him wash his hands of her; it was, that my admiration should be within a foot or two of him—it was, that my feelings should be in the same place with him—that, was the agonizing circumstance.

We played until nine o'clock, and then it was arranged that when Estella came to London I should be forewarned of her coming and should meet her at the coach; and then I took leave of her, and touched her and left her.

My guardian lay at the Boar in the next room to mine. Far into the night, Miss Havisham's words, "Love her, love her, love her!" sounded in my ears. I adapted them for my own repetition, and said to my pillow, "I love her, I love her, I love her!" hundreds of times. Then, a burst of gratitude came upon me, that she should be destined for me, once the blacksmith's boy. Then I thought if she were, as I feared, by no means rapturously grateful for that destiny yet, when would she begin to be interested in me? When should I awaken the heart within her that was mute and sleeping now?

Ah me! I thought those were high and great emotions. But I never thought there was anything low and small in my keeping away from Joe, because I knew she would be contemptuous of him. It was but a day gone, and Joe had brought the tears into my eyes; they had soon dried, God forgive me! soon dried.

CHAPTER 11

After well considering the matter while I was dressing at the Blue Boar in the morning, I resolved to tell my guardian that I doubted Orlick's being the right sort of man to fill a post of trust at Miss Havisham's. "Why of course he is not the right sort of man, Pip," said my guardian, comfortably satisfied beforehand on the general head, "because the man who fills the post of trust never is the right sort of man." It seemed quite to put him into spirits to find that this particular post was not exceptionally held by the right sort of man, and he listened in a satisfied manner while I told him what knowledge I had of Orlick. "Very good, Pip," he observed, when I had concluded, "I'll go round presently, and pay our friend off." Rather alarmed by this summary action, I was for a little delay, and even hinted that our friend himself might be difficult to deal with. "Oh no he won't," said my guardian, making his pocket-handkerchief-point, with perfect confidence; "I should like to see him argue the question with *me*."

As we were going back together to London by the midday coach, and as I breakfasted under such terrors of Pumblechook that I could scarcely hold my cup, this gave me an opportunity of saying that I wanted a walk, and that I would go on along the London road while Mr. Jaggers was occupied, if he would let the coachman know that I would get into my place when overtaken. I was thus enabled to fly from the Blue Boar immediately after breakfast. By then making a loop of about a couple of miles into the open country at the back of Pumblechook's premises, I got round into the High Street again, a little beyond that pitfall, and felt myself in comparative security.

It was interesting to be in the quiet old town once more, and it was not disagreeable to be here and there suddenly recognized and stared after. One or two of the tradespeople even darted out of their shops and went a little way down the street before me, that they might turn, as if they had forgotten something, and pass me face to face—on which occasions I don't know whether they or I made the worse pretence; they of not doing it, or I of not seeing it. Still my position was a distinguished one, and I was not at all dissatisfied with it, until Fate threw me in the way of that unlimited miscreant, Trabb's boy.

Casting my eyes along the street at a certain point of my progress, I beheld Trabb's boy approaching, lashing himself with an empty blue bag. Deeming that a serene and unconscious contemplation of him would best beseem me, and would be most likely to quell his evil mind, I advanced with that expression of countenance, and was rather congratulating myself on my success, when suddenly the knees of Trabb's boy smote together, his hair uprose, his cap fell off, he trembled violently in every limb, staggered out into the road, and crying to the populace, "Hold me! I'm so frightened!" feigned to be in a paroxysm of terror and contrition, occasioned by the dignity of my appearance. As I passed him, his teeth loudly chattered in his head, and with every mark of extreme humiliation, he prostrated himself in the dust.

This was a hard thing to bear, but this was nothing. I had not advanced another two hundred yards when, to my inexpressible terror, amazement, and indignation, I again beheld Trabb's boy approaching. He was coming round a narrow corner. His blue bag was slung over his shoulder, honest industry beamed in his eyes, a determination to proceed to Trabb's with cheerful briskness was indicated in his gait. With a shock he became aware of me, and was severely visited as before; but this time his motion was rotatory, and he staggered round and round me with knees more afflicted, and with uplifted hands as if beseeching for mercy. His sufferings were hailed with the greatest joy by a knot of spectators, and I felt utterly confounded.

I had not got as much further down the street as the post-office, when I again beheld Trabb's boy shooting round by a back way. This time, he was entirely changed. He wore the blue bag in the manner of my great-coat, and was strutting along the pavement towards me on the opposite side of the street, attended by a company of delighted young friends to whom he from time to time exclaimed, with a wave of his hand, "Don't know yah!" Words cannot state the amount of aggravation and injury wreaked upon me by Trabb's boy, when passing abreast of me, he pulled up his shirt-collar, twined his side-hair, stuck an arm akimbo, and smirked extravagantly by, wriggling his elbows and body, and drawling to his attendants, "Don't know yah, don't know yah, 'pon my soul don't know yah!" The disgrace attendant on his immediately afterwards taking to crowing and pursuing me across the bridge with crows, as from an exceedingly dejected fowl who had known me when I was a blacksmith, culminated the disgrace with which I left the town, and was, so to speak, ejected by it into the open country.

But unless I had taken the life of Trabb's boy on that occasion, I really do not even now see what I could have done save endure. To have struggled with him in the street, or to have exacted any lower recompense from him than his heart's best blood, would have been futile and degrading. Moreover, he was a boy whom no man could hurt; an invulnerable and dodging serpent who, when chased into a corner, flew out again between his captor's legs, scornfully yelping. I wrote, however, to Mr. Trabb by next day's post, to say that Mr. Pip must decline to deal further with one who could so far forget what he owed to the best interests of society, as to employ a boy who excited Loathing in every respectable mind.

The coach, with Mr. Jaggers inside, came up in due time, and I took my box-seat again, and arrived in London safe—but not sound, for my heart was gone. As soon as I arrived, I sent a penitential codfish and barrel of oysters to Joe (as reparation for not having gone myself), and then went on to Barnard's Inn.

I found Herbert dining on cold meat, and delighted to welcome me back. Having despatched The Avenger to the coffee-house for an addition to the dinner, I felt that I must open my breast that very evening to my friend and chum. As confidence was out of the question with The Avenger in the hall, which could merely be regarded in the light of an antechamber to the keyhole, I sent him to the Play. A better proof of the severity of my bondage to that taskmaster could scarcely be afforded, than the degrading shifts to which I was constantly driven to find him employment. So mean is extremity, that I sometimes sent him to Hyde Park corner to see what o'clock it was.

Dinner done and we sitting with our feet upon the fender, I said to Herbert, "My dear Herbert, I have something very particular to tell you."

"My dear Handel," he returned, "I shall esteem and respect your confidence."

"It concerns myself, Herbert," said I, "and one other person."

Herbert crossed his feet, looked at the fire with his head on one side, and having looked at it in vain for some time, looked at me because I didn't go on.

"Herbert," said I, laying my hand upon his knee, "I love—I adore—Estella."

Instead of being transfixed, Herbert replied in an easy matter-of-course way, "Exactly. Well?"

"Well, Herbert? Is that all you say? Well?"

"What next, I mean?" said Herbert. "Of course I know *that.*"

"How do you know it?" said I.

"How do I know it, Handel? Why, from you."

"I never told you."

"Told me! You have never told me when you have got your hair cut, but I have had senses to perceive it. You have always adored her, ever since I have known you. You brought your adoration and your portmanteau here together. Told me! Why, you have always told me all day long. When you told me your own story, you told me plainly that you began adoring her the first time you saw her, when you were very young indeed."

"Very well, then," said I, to whom this was a new and not unwelcome light, "I have never left off adoring her. And she has come back, a most beautiful and most elegant creature. And I saw her yesterday. And if I adored her before, I now doubly adore her."

"Lucky for you then, Handel," said Herbert, "that you are picked out for her and allotted to her. Without encroaching on forbidden ground, we may venture to say that there can be no doubt between ourselves of that fact. Have you any idea yet, of Estella's views on the adoration question?"

I shook my head gloomily. "Oh! She is thousands of miles away, from me," said I.

"Patience, my dear Handel: time enough, time enough. But you have something more to say?"

"I am ashamed to say it," I returned, "and yet it's no worse to say it than to think it. You call me a lucky fellow. Of course, I am. I was a blacksmith's boy but yesterday; I am—what shall I say I am—to-day?"

"Say a good fellow, if you want a phrase," returned Herbert, smiling, and clapping his hand on the back of mine— "a good fellow, with impetuosity and hesitation, boldness and diffidence, action and dreaming, curiously mixed in him."

I stopped for a moment to consider whether there really was this mixture in my character. On the whole, I by no means recognized the analysis, but thought it not worth disputing.

"When I ask what I am to call myself to-day, Herbert," I went on, "I suggest what I have in my thoughts. You say I am lucky. I know I have done nothing to raise myself in life, and that Fortune alone has raised me; that is being very lucky. And yet, when I think of Estella—"

("And when don't you, you know?" Herbert threw in, with his eyes on the fire; which I thought kind and sympathetic of him.)

"—Then, my dear Herbert, I cannot tell you how dependent and uncertain I feel, and how exposed to hundreds of chances. Avoiding forbidden ground, as you did just now, I may still say that on the constancy of one person (naming no person) all my expectations depend. And at the best, how indefinite and unsatisfactory, only to know so vaguely what they are!" In saying this, I relieved my mind of what had always been there, more or less, though no doubt most since yesterday.

"Now, Handel," Herbert replied, in his gay, hopeful way, "it seems to me that in the despondency of the tender passion, we are looking into our gift-horse's mouth with a magnifying-glass. Likewise, it seems to me that, concentrating our attention on the examination, we altogether overlook one of the best points of the animal. Didn't you tell me that your guardian, Mr. Jaggers, told you in the beginning, that you were not endowed with expectations only? And even if he had not told you so— though that is a very large If, I grant—could you believe that of all men in London, Mr. Jaggers is the man to hold his present relations towards you unless he were sure of his ground?"

I said I could not deny that this *was* a strong point. I said it (people often do so, in such cases) like a rather reluctant concession to truth and justice;—as if I wanted to deny it!

"I should think it was a strong point," said Herbert, "and I should think you would be puzzled to imagine a stronger; as to the rest, you must bide your guardian's time, and he must bide his client's time. You'll be one-and-twenty before you know where you are, and then perhaps you'll get some further enlightenment. At all events, you'll be nearer getting it, for it must come at last."

"What a hopeful disposition you have!" said I, gratefully admiring his cheery ways.

"I ought to have," said Herbert, "for I have not much else. I must acknowledge, by the by, that the good sense of what I have just said is not my own, but my father's. The only remark I ever heard him make on your story, was the final one, "The thing is settled and done, or Mr. Jaggers would not be in it." And now before I say anything more about my father, or my father's son, and repay confidence with confidence, I want to make myself seriously disagreeable to you for a moment— positively repulsive."

"You won't succeed," said I.

"O yes I shall!" said he. "One, two, three, and now I am in for it. Handel, my good fellow;"—though he spoke in this light tone, he was very much in earnest; "I have been thinking since we have been talking with our feet on this fender, that Estella surely cannot be a condition of your inheritance, if she was never referred to by your guardian. Am I right in so understanding what you have told me, as that he never referred to her, directly or indirectly, in any way? Never even hinted, for instance, that your patron might have views as to your marriage ultimately?"

"Never."

"Now, Handel, I am quite free from the flavor of sour grapes, upon my soul and honor! Not being bound to her, can you not detach yourself from her?—I told you I should be disagreeable."

I turned my head aside, for, with a rush and a sweep, like the old marsh winds coming up from the sea, a feeling like that which had subdued me on the morning when I left the forge, when the mists were solemnly rising, and when I laid my hand upon the village finger-post, smote upon my heart again. There was silence between us for a little while.

"Yes; but my dear Handel," Herbert went on, as if we had been talking, instead of silent, "its having been so strongly rooted in the breast of a boy whom nature and circumstances made so romantic, renders it very serious. Think of her bringing-up, and think of Miss Havisham. Think of what she is herself (now I am repulsive and you abominate me). This may lead to miserable things."

"I know it, Herbert," said I, with my head still turned away, "but I can't help it."

"You can't detach yourself?"

"No. Impossible!"

"You can't try, Handel?"

"No. Impossible!"

"Well!" said Herbert, getting up with a lively shake as if he had been asleep, and stirring the fire, "now I'll endeavor to make myself agreeable again!"

So he went round the room and shook the curtains out, put the chairs in their places, tidied the books and so forth that were lying about, looked into the hall, peeped into the letter-box, shut the door, and came back to his chair by the fire: where he sat down, nursing his left leg in both arms.

"I was going to say a word or two, Handel, concerning my father and my father's son. I am afraid it is scarcely necessary for my father's son to remark that my father's establishment is not particularly brilliant in its housekeeping."

"There is always plenty, Herbert," said I, to say something encouraging.

"O yes! and so the dustman says, I believe, with the strongest approval, and so does the marine-store shop in the back street. Gravely, Handel, for the subject is grave enough, you know how it is as well as I do. I suppose there was a time once when my father had not given matters up; but if ever there was, the time is gone. May I ask you if you have ever had an opportunity of remarking, down in your part of the country, that the children of not exactly suitable marriages are always most particularly anxious to be married?"

This was such a singular question, that I asked him in return, "Is it so?"

"I don't know," said Herbert, "that's what I want to know. Because it is decidedly the case with us. My poor sister Charlotte, who was next me and died before she was fourteen, was a striking example. Little Jane is the same. In her desire to be matrimonially established, you might suppose her to have passed her short existence in the perpetual contemplation of domestic bliss. Little Alick in a frock has already made arrangements for his union with a suitable young person at Kew. And indeed, I think we are all engaged, except the baby."

"Then you are?" said I.

"I am," said Herbert; "but it's a secret."

I assured him of my keeping the secret, and begged to be favored with further particulars. He had spoken so sensibly and feelingly of my weakness that I wanted to know something about his strength.

"May I ask the name?" I said.

"Name of Clara," said Herbert.

"Live in London?"

"Yes, perhaps I ought to mention," said Herbert, who had become curiously crestfallen and meek, since we entered on the interesting theme, "that she is rather below my mother's nonsensical family notions. Her father had to do with the victualling of passenger-ships. I think he was a species of purser."

"What is he now?" said I.

"He's an invalid now," replied Herbert.

"Living on—?"

"On the first floor," said Herbert. Which was not at all what I meant, for I had intended my question to apply to his means. "I have never seen him, for he has always kept his room overhead, since I have known Clara. But I have heard him constantly. He makes tremendous rows—roars, and pegs at the floor with some frightful instrument." In looking at me and then laughing heartily, Herbert for the time recovered his usual lively manner.

"Don't you expect to see him?" said I.

"O yes, I constantly expect to see him," returned Herbert, "because I never hear him, without expecting him to come tumbling through the ceiling. But I don't know how long the rafters may hold."

When he had once more laughed heartily, he became meek again, and told me that the moment he began to realize Capital, it was his intention to marry this young lady. He added as a self-evident proposition, engendering low spirits, "But you *can't* marry, you know, while you're looking about you."

As we contemplated the fire, and as I thought what a difficult vision to realize this same Capital sometimes was, I put my hands in my pockets. A folded piece of paper in one of them attracting my attention, I opened it and found it to be the play-bill I had received from Joe, relative to the celebrated provincial amateur of Roscian renown. "And bless my heart," I involuntarily added aloud, "it's to-night!"

This changed the subject in an instant, and made us hurriedly resolve to go to the play. So, when I had pledged myself to comfort and abet Herbert in the affair of his heart by all practicable and impracticable means, and when Herbert had told me that his affianced already knew me by reputation and that I should be presented to her, and when we had warmly shaken hands upon our mutual confidence, we blew out our candles, made up our fire, locked our door, and issued forth in quest of Mr. Wopsle and Denmark.

CHAPTER 12

On our arrival in Denmark, we found the king and queen of that country elevated in two arm-chairs on a kitchen-table, holding a Court. The whole of the Danish nobility were in attendance; consisting of a noble boy in the wash-leather boots of a gigantic ancestor, a venerable Peer with a dirty face who seemed to have risen from the people late in life, and the Danish chivalry with a comb in its hair and a pair of white silk legs, and presenting on the whole a feminine appearance. My gifted townsman stood gloomily apart, with folded arms, and I could have wished that his curls and forehead had been more probable.

Several curious little circumstances transpired as the action proceeded. The late king of the country not only appeared to have been troubled with a cough at the time of his decease, but to have taken it with him to the tomb, and to have brought it back. The royal phantom also carried a ghostly manuscript round its truncheon, to which it had the appearance of occasionally referring, and that too, with an air of anxiety and a tendency to lose the place of reference which were suggestive of a state of mortality. It was this, I conceive, which led to the Shade's being advised by the gallery to "turn over!"—a recommendation which it took extremely ill. It was likewise to be noted of this majestic spirit, that whereas it always appeared with an air of having been out a long time and walked an immense distance, it perceptibly came from a closely contiguous wall. This occasioned its terrors to be received derisively. The Queen of Denmark, a very buxom lady, though no doubt historically brazen, was considered by the public to have too much brass about her; her chin being attached to her diadem by a broad band of that metal (as if she had a gorgeous toothache), her waist being encircled by another, and each of her arms by another, so that she was openly mentioned as "the kettle-drum." The noble boy in the ancestral boots was inconsistent, representing himself, as it were in one breath, as an able seaman, a strolling actor, a grave-digger, a clergyman, and a person of the utmost importance at a Court fencing-match, on the authority of whose practised eye and nice discrimination the finest strokes were judged. This gradually led to a want of toleration for him, and even—on his being detected in holy orders, and declining to perform the funeral service—to the general indignation taking the form of nuts. Lastly, Ophelia was a prey to such slow musical madness, that when, in course of time, she had taken off her white muslin scarf, folded it up, and buried it, a sulky man who had been long cooling his impatient nose against an iron bar in the front row of the gallery, growled, "Now the baby's put to bed let's have supper!" Which, to say the least of it, was out of keeping.

Upon my unfortunate townsman all these incidents accumulated with playful effect. Whenever that undecided Prince had to ask a question or state a doubt, the public helped him out with it. As for example; on the question whether 'twas nobler in the mind to suffer, some roared yes, and some no, and some inclining to both opinions said "Toss up for it;" and quite a Debating Society arose. When he asked what should such fellows as he do crawling between earth and heaven, he was encouraged with loud cries of "Hear, hear!" When he appeared with his stocking disordered (its disorder expressed, according to usage, by one very neat fold in the top, which I suppose to be always got up with a flat iron), a conversation took place in the gallery respecting the paleness of his leg, and whether it was occasioned by the turn the ghost had given him. On his taking the recorders—very like a little black flute that had just been played in the orchestra and handed out at the door—he was called upon unanimously for Rule Britannia. When he recommended the player not to saw the air thus, the sulky man said, "And don't *you* do it, neither; you're a deal worse than *him*!" And I grieve to add that peals of laughter greeted Mr. Wopsle on every one of these occasions.

But his greatest trials were in the churchyard, which had the appearance of a primeval forest, with a kind of small ecclesiastical wash-house on one side, and a turnpike gate on the other. Mr. Wopsle in a comprehensive black cloak, being descried entering at the turnpike, the gravedigger was admonished in a friendly way, "Look out! Here's the undertaker a coming, to see how you're a getting on with your work!" I believe it is well known in a constitutional country that Mr. Wopsle could not possibly have returned the skull, after moralizing over it, without dusting his fingers on a white napkin taken from his breast; but even that innocent and indispensable action did not pass without the comment, "Wai-ter!" The arrival of the body for interment (in an empty black box with the lid tumbling open), was the signal for a general joy, which was much enhanced by the discovery, among the bearers, of an individual obnoxious to identification. The joy attended Mr. Wopsle through his struggle with Laertes on the brink of the orchestra and the grave, and slackened no more until he had tumbled the king off the kitchen-table, and had died by inches from the ankles upward.

We had made some pale efforts in the beginning to applaud Mr. Wopsle; but they were too hopeless to be persisted in. Therefore we had sat, feeling keenly for him, but laughing, nevertheless, from ear to ear. I laughed in spite of myself all the time, the whole thing was so droll; and yet I had a latent impression that there was something decidedly fine in Mr. Wopsle's elocution—not for old associations' sake, I am afraid, but because it was very slow, very dreary, very up-hill and down-hill, and very unlike any way in which any man in any natural circumstances of life or death ever expressed himself about anything. When the tragedy was over, and he had been called for and hooted, I said to Herbert, "Let us go at once, or perhaps we shall meet him."

We made all the haste we could down stairs, but we were not quick enough either. Standing at the door was a Jewish man with an unnatural heavy smear of eyebrow, who caught my eyes as we advanced, and said, when we came up with him:

"Mr. Pip and friend?"

Identity of Mr. Pip and friend confessed.

"Mr. Waldengarver," said the man, "would be glad to have the honor."

"Waldengarver?" I repeated—when Herbert murmured in my ear, "Probably Wopsle."

"Oh!" said I. "Yes. Shall we follow you?"

"A few steps, please." When we were in a side alley, he turned and asked, "How did you think he looked?—*I* dressed him."

I don't know what he had looked like, except a funeral; with the addition of a large Danish sun or star hanging round his neck by a blue ribbon, that had given him the appearance of being insured in some extraordinary Fire Office. But I said he had looked very nice.

"When he come to the grave," said our conductor, "he showed his cloak beautiful. But, judging from the wing, it looked to me that when he see the ghost in the queen's apartment, he might have made more of his stockings."

I modestly assented, and we all fell through a little dirty swing door, into a sort of hot packing-case immediately behind it. Here Mr. Wopsle was divesting himself of his Danish garments, and here there was just room for us to look at him over one another's shoulders, by keeping the packing-case door, or lid, wide open.

"Gentlemen," said Mr. Wopsle, "I am proud to see you. I hope, Mr. Pip, you will excuse my sending round. I had the happiness to know you in former times, and the Drama has ever had a claim which has ever been acknowledged, on the noble and the affluent."

Meanwhile, Mr. Waldengarver, in a frightful perspiration, was trying to get himself out of his princely sables.

"Skin the stockings off Mr. Waldengarver," said the owner of that property, "or you'll bust 'em. Bust 'em, and you'll bust five-and-thirty shillings. Shakspeare never was complimented with a finer pair. Keep quiet in your chair now, and leave 'em to me."

With that, he went upon his knees, and began to flay his victim; who, on the first stocking coming off, would certainly have fallen over backward with his chair, but for there being no room to fall anyhow.

I had been afraid until then to say a word about the play. But then, Mr. Waldengarver looked up at us complacently, and said:

"Gentlemen, how did it seem to you, to go, in front?"

Herbert said from behind (at the same time poking me), "capitally." So I said "capitally."

"How did you like my reading of the character, gentlemen?" said Mr. Waldengarver, almost, if not quite, with patronage.

Herbert said from behind (again poking me), "Massive and concrete." So I said boldly, as if I had originated it, and must beg to insist upon it, "Massive and concrete."

"I am glad to have your approbation, gentlemen," said Mr. Waldengarver, with an air of dignity, in spite of his being ground against the wall at the time, and holding on by the seat of the chair.

"But I'll tell you one thing, Mr. Waldengarver," said the man who was on his knees, "in which you're out in your reading. Now mind! I don't care who says contrary; I tell you so. You're out in your reading of Hamlet when you get your legs in profile. The last Hamlet as I dressed, made the same mistakes in his reading at rehearsal, till I got him to put a large red wafer on each of his shins, and then at that rehearsal (which was the last) I went in front, sir, to the back of the pit, and whenever his reading brought him into profile, I called out "I don't see no wafers!" And at night his reading was lovely."

Mr. Waldengarver smiled at me, as much as to say "a faithful dependent—I overlook his folly;" and then said aloud, "My view is a little classic and thoughtful for them here; but they will improve, they will improve."

Herbert and I said together, O, no doubt they would improve.

"Did you observe, gentlemen," said Mr. Waldengarver, "that there was a man in the gallery who endeavored to cast derision on the service—I mean, the representation?"

We basely replied that we rather thought we had noticed such a man. I added, "He was drunk, no doubt."

"O dear no, sir," said Mr. Wopsle, "not drunk. His employer would see to that, sir. His employer would not allow him to be drunk."

"You know his employer?" said I.

Mr. Wopsle shut his eyes, and opened them again; performing both ceremonies very slowly. "You must have observed, gentlemen," said he, "an ignorant and a blatant ass, with a rasping throat and a countenance expressive of low malignity, who went through—I will not say sustained—the rôle (if I may use a French expression) of Claudius, King of Denmark. That is his employer, gentlemen. Such is the profession!"

Without distinctly knowing whether I should have been more sorry for Mr. Wopsle if he had been in despair, I was so sorry for him as it was, that I took the opportunity of his turning round to have his braces put on—which jostled us out at the doorway—to ask Herbert what he thought of having him home to supper? Herbert said he thought it would be kind to do so; therefore I invited him, and he went to Barnard's with us, wrapped up to the eyes, and we did our best for him, and he sat until two o'clock in the morning, reviewing his success and developing his plans. I forget in detail what they were, but I have a general recollection that he was to begin with reviving the Drama, and to end with crushing it; inasmuch as his decease would leave it utterly bereft and without a chance or hope.

Miserably I went to bed after all, and miserably thought of Estella, and miserably dreamed that my expectations were all cancelled, and that I had to give my hand in marriage to Herbert's Clara, or play Hamlet to Miss Havisham's Ghost, before twenty thousand people, without knowing twenty words of it.

CHAPTER 13

One day when I was busy with my books and Mr. Pocket, I received a note by the post, the mere outside of which threw me into a great flutter; for, though I had never seen the handwriting in which it was addressed, I divined whose hand it was. It had no set beginning, as Dear Mr. Pip, or Dear Pip, or Dear Sir, or Dear Anything, but ran thus:

"I am to come to London the day after to-morrow by the midday coach. I believe it was settled you should meet me? At all events Miss Havisham has that impression, and I write in obedience to it. She sends you her regard.

"Yours, ESTELLA."

If there had been time, I should probably have ordered several suits of clothes for this occasion; but as there was not, I was fain to be content with those I had. My appetite vanished instantly, and I knew no peace or rest until the day arrived. Not that its arrival brought me either; for, then I was worse than ever, and began haunting the coach-office in Wood Street, Cheapside, before the coach had left the Blue Boar in our town. For all that I knew this perfectly well, I still felt as if it were not safe to let the coach-office be out of my sight longer than five minutes at a time; and in this condition of unreason I had performed the first half-hour of a watch of four or five hours, when Wemmick ran against me.

"Halloa, Mr. Pip," said he; "how do you do? I should hardly have thought this was *your* beat."

I explained that I was waiting to meet somebody who was

coming up by coach, and I inquired after the Castle and the Aged.

"Both flourishing thankye," said Wemmick, "and particularly the Aged. He's in wonderful feather. He'll be eighty-two next birthday. I have a notion of firing eighty-two times, if the neighbourhood shouldn't complain, and that cannon of mine should prove equal to the pressure. However, this is not London talk. Where do you think I am going to?"

"To the office?" said I, for he was tending in that direction.

"Next thing to it," returned Wemmick, "I am going to Newgate. We are in a banker's-parcel case just at present, and I have been down the road taking a squint at the scene of action, and thereupon must have a word or two with our client."

"Did your client commit the robbery?" I asked.

"Bless your soul and body, no," answered Wemmick, very drily. "But he is accused of it. So might you or I be. Either of us might be accused of it, you know."

"Only neither of us is," I remarked.

"Yah!" said Wemmick, touching me on the breast with his forefinger; "you're a deep one, Mr. Pip! Would you like to have a look at Newgate? Have you time to spare?"

I had so much time to spare, that the proposal came as a relief, notwithstanding its irreconcilability with my latent desire to keep my eye on the coach-office. Muttering that I would make the inquiry whether I had time to walk with him, I went into the office, and ascertained from the clerk with the nicest precision and much to the trying of his temper, the earliest moment at which the coach could be expected—which I knew beforehand, quite as well as he. I then rejoined Mr. Wemmick, and affecting to consult my watch, and to be surprised by the information I had received, accepted his offer.

We were at Newgate in a few minutes, and we passed through the lodge where some fetters were hanging up on the bare walls among the prison rules, into the interior of the jail. At that time jails were much neglected, and the period of exaggerated reaction consequent on all public wrongdoing—and which is always its heaviest and longest punishment—was still far off. So felons were not lodged and fed better than soldiers, (to say nothing of paupers,) and seldom set fire to their prisons with the excusable object of improving the flavor of their soup. It was visiting time when Wemmick took me in, and a potman was going his rounds with beer; and the prisoners, behind bars in yards, were buying beer, and talking to friends; and a frowzy, ugly, disorderly, depressing scene it was.

It struck me that Wemmick walked among the prisoners much as a gardener might walk among his plants. This was first put into my head by his seeing a shoot that had come up in the night, and saying, "What, Captain Tom? Are *you* there? Ah, indeed!" and also, "Is that Black Bill behind the cistern? Why I didn't look for you these two months; how do you find yourself?" Equally in his stopping at the bars and attending to anxious whisperers—always singly—Wemmick with his post-office in an immovable state, looked at them while in conference, as if he were taking particular notice of the advance they had made, since last observed, towards coming out in full blow at their trial.

He was highly popular, and I found that he took the familiar department of Mr. Jaggers's business; though something of the state of Mr. Jaggers hung about him too, forbidding approach beyond certain limits. His personal recognition of each successive client was comprised in a nod, and in his settling his hat a little easier on his head with both hands, and then tightening the post-office, and putting his hands in his pockets. In one or two instances there was a difficulty respecting the raising of fees, and then Mr. Wemmick, backing as far as possible from the insufficient money produced, said, "it's no use, my boy. I'm only a subordinate. I can't take it. Don't go on in that way with a subordinate. If you are unable to make up your quantum, my boy, you had better address yourself to a principal; there are plenty of principals in the profession, you know, and what is not worth the while of one, may be worth the while of another; that's my recommendation to you, speaking as a subordinate. Don't try on useless measures. Why should you? Now, who's next?"

Thus, we walked through Wemmick's greenhouse, until he turned to me and said, "Notice the man I shall shake hands with." I should have done so, without the preparation, as he had shaken hands with no one yet.

Almost as soon as he had spoken, a portly upright man (whom I can see now, as I write) in a well-worn olive-colored frock-coat, with a peculiar pallor overspreading the red in his complexion, and eyes that went wandering about when he tried to fix them, came up to a corner of the bars, and put his hand to his hat—which had a greasy and fatty surface like cold broth—with a half-serious and half-jocose military salute.

"Colonel, to you!" said Wemmick; "how are you, Colonel?"

"All right, Mr. Wemmick."

"Everything was done that could be done, but the evidence was too strong for us, Colonel."

"Yes, it was too strong, sir—but *I* don't care."

"No, no," said Wemmick, coolly, "*you* don't care." Then, turning to me, "Served His Majesty this man. Was a soldier in the line and bought his discharge."

I said, "Indeed?" and the man's eyes looked at me, and then looked over my head, and then looked all round me, and then he drew his hand across his lips and laughed.

"I think I shall be out of this on Monday, sir," he said to Wemmick.

"Perhaps," returned my friend, "but there's no knowing."

"I am glad to have the chance of bidding you good by, Mr. Wemmick," said the man, stretching out his hand between two bars.

"Thankye," said Wemmick, shaking hands with him. "Same to you, Colonel."

"If what I had upon me when taken had been real, Mr. Wemmick," said the man, unwilling to let his hand go, "I should have asked the favor of your wearing another ring—in acknowledgment of your attentions."

"I'll accept the will for the deed," said Wemmick. "By the by; you were quite a pigeon-fancier." The man looked up at the sky. "I am told you had a remarkable breed of tumblers. *Could* you commission any friend of yours to bring me a pair, of you've no further use for 'em?"

"It shall be done, sir?"

"All right," said Wemmick, "they shall be taken care of. Good afternoon, Colonel. Good by!" They shook hands again, and as we walked away Wemmick said to me, "A Coiner, a very good workman. The Recorder's report is made to-day, and he is sure to be executed on Monday. Still you see, as far as it goes, a pair of pigeons are portable property all the same." With that, he looked back, and nodded at this dead plant, and then cast his eyes about him in walking out of the yard, as if he were considering what other pot would go best in its place.

As we came out of the prison through the lodge, I found that the great importance of my guardian was appreciated by the turnkeys, no less than by those whom they held in charge. "Well, Mr. Wemmick," said the turnkey, who kept us between the two studded and spiked lodge gates, and who carefully locked one before he unlocked the other, "what's Mr. Jaggers going to do with that water-side murder? Is he going to make it manslaughter, or what's he going to make of it?"

"Why don't you ask him?" returned Wemmick.

"O yes, I dare say!" said the turnkey.

"Now, that's the way with them here, Mr. Pip," remarked Wemmick, turning to me with his post-office elongated. "They don't mind what they ask of me, the subordinate; but you'll never catch 'em asking any questions of my principal."

"Is this young gentleman one of the 'prentices or articled ones of your office?" asked the turnkey, with a grin at Mr. Wemmick's humor.

"There he goes again, you see!" cried Wemmick, "I told you so! Asks another question of the subordinate before his first is dry! Well, supposing Mr. Pip is one of them?"

"Why then," said the turnkey, grinning again, "he knows what Mr. Jaggers is."

"Yah!" cried Wemmick, suddenly hitting out at the turnkey in a facetious way, "you're dumb as one of your own keys when you have to do with my principal, you know you are. Let us out, you old fox, or I'll get him to bring an action against you for false imprisonment."

The turnkey laughed, and gave us good day, and stood laughing at us over the spikes of the wicket when we descended the steps into the street.

"Mind you, Mr. Pip," said Wemmick, gravely in my ear, as he took my arm to be more confidential; "I don't know that Mr. Jaggers does a better thing than the way in which he keeps himself so high. He's always so high. His constant height is of a piece with his immense abilities. That Colonel durst no more take leave of *him*, than that turnkey durst ask him his intentions respecting a case. Then, between his height and them, he slips in his subordinate—don't you see?—and so he has 'em, soul and body."

I was very much impressed, and not for the first time, by my guardian's subtlety. To confess the truth, I very heartily wished, and not for the first time, that I had had some other guardian of minor abilities.

Mr. Wemmick and I parted at the office in Little Britain, where suppliants for Mr. Jaggers's notice were lingering about as usual, and I returned to my watch in the street of the coach-office, with some three hours on hand. I consumed the whole time in thinking how strange it was that I should be encompassed by all this taint of prison and crime; that, in my childhood out on our lonely marshes on a winter evening, I should have first encountered it; that, it should have reappeared on two occasions, starting out like a stain that was faded but not gone; that, it should in this new way pervade my fortune and advancement. While my mind was thus engaged, I thought of the beautiful young Estella, proud and refined, coming towards me, and I thought with absolute abhorrence of the contrast between the jail and her. I wished that Wemmick had not met me, or that I had not yielded to him and gone with him, so that, of all days in the year on this day, I might not have had Newgate in my breath and on my clothes. I beat the prison dust off my feet as I sauntered to and fro, and I shook it out of my dress, and I exhaled its air from my lungs. So contaminated did I feel, remembering who was coming, that the coach came quickly after all, and I was not yet free from the soiling consciousness of Mr. Wemmick's conservatory, when I saw her face at the coach window and her hand waving to me.

What *was* the nameless shadow which again in that one instant had passed?

CHAPTER 14

In her furred travelling-dress, Estella seemed more delicately beautiful than she had ever seemed yet, even in my eyes. Her manner was more winning than she had cared to let it be to me before, and I thought I saw Miss Havisham's influence in the change.

We stood in the Inn Yard while she pointed out her luggage to me, and when it was all collected I remembered—having forgotten everything but herself in the meanwhile—that I knew nothing of her destination.

"I am going to Richmond," she told me. "Our lesson is, that there are two Richmonds, one in Surrey and one in Yorkshire, and that mine is the Surrey Richmond. The distance is ten miles. I am to have a carriage, and you are to take me. This is my purse, and you are to pay my charges out of it. O, you must take the purse! We have no choice, you and I, but to obey our instructions. We are not free to follow our own devices, you and I."

As she looked at me in giving me the purse, I hoped there was an inner meaning in her words. She said them slightingly, but not with displeasure.

"A carriage will have to be sent for, Estella. Will you rest here a little?"

"Yes, I am to rest here a little, and I am to drink some tea, and you are to take care of me the while."

She drew her arm through mine, as if it must be done, and I requested a waiter who had been staring at the coach like a man who had never seen such a thing in his life, to show us a private sitting-room. Upon that, he pulled out a napkin, as if it were a magic clew without which he couldn't find the way up stairs, and led us to the black hole of the establishment, fitted up with a diminishing mirror (quite a superfluous article, considering the hole's proportions), an anchovy sauce-cruet, and somebody's pattens. On my objecting to this retreat, he took us into another room with a dinner-table for thirty, and in the grate a scorched leaf of a copy-book under a bushel of coal-dust. Having looked at this extinct conflagration and shaken his head, he took my order; which, proving to be merely, "Some tea for the lady," sent him out of the room in a very low state of mind.

I was, and I am, sensible that the air of this chamber, in its strong combination of stable with soup-stock, might have led one to infer that the coaching department was not doing well, and that the enterprising proprietor was boiling down the horses for the refreshment department. Yet the room was all in all to me, Estella being in it. I thought that with her I could have been happy there for life. (I was not at all happy there at the time, observe, and I knew it well.)

"Where are you going to, at Richmond?" I asked Estella.

"I am going to live," said she, "at a great expense, with a lady there, who has the power—or says she has—of taking me about, and introducing me, and showing people to me and showing me to people."

"I suppose you will be glad of variety and admiration?"

"Yes, I suppose so."

She answered so carelessly, that I said, "You speak of yourself as if you were some one else."

"Where did you learn how I speak of others? Come, come," said Estella, smiling delightfully, "you must not expect me to go to school to *you*; I must talk in my own way. How do you thrive with Mr. Pocket?"

"I live quite pleasantly there; at least—" It appeared to me that I was losing a chance"At least?" repeated Estella.

"As pleasantly as I could anywhere, away from you."

"You silly boy," said Estella, quite composedly, "how can you talk such nonsense? Your friend Mr. Matthew, I believe, is superior to the rest of his family?"

"Very superior indeed. He is nobody's enemy—"

"Don't add but his own," interposed Estella, "for I hate that class of man. But he really is disinterested, and above small jealousy and spite, I have heard?"

"I am sure I have every reason to say so."

"You have not every reason to say so of the rest of his people," said Estella, nodding at me with an expression of face that was at once grave and rallying, "for they beset Miss Havisham with reports and insinuations to your disadvantage. They watch you, misrepresent you, write letters about you (anonymous sometimes), and you are the torment and the occupation of their lives. You can scarcely realize to yourself the hatred those people feel for you."

"They do me no harm, I hope?"

Instead of answering, Estella burst out laughing. This was very singular to me, and I looked at her in considerable perplexity. When she left off—and she had not laughed languidly, but with real enjoyment—I said, in my diffident way with her:

"I hope I may suppose that you would not be amused if they did me any harm."

"No, no you may be sure of that," said Estella. "You may be certain that I laugh because they fail. O, those people with Miss Havisham, and the tortures they undergo!" She laughed again, and even now when she had told me why, her laughter was very singular to me, for I could not doubt its being genuine, and yet it seemed too much for the occasion. I thought there must really be something more here than I knew; she saw the thought in my mind, and answered it.

"It is not easy for even you." said Estella, "to know what

satisfaction it gives me to see those people thwarted, or what an enjoyable sense of the ridiculous I have when they are made ridiculous. For *you* were not brought up in that strange house from a mere baby. I was. You had not your little wits sharpened by their intriguing against you, suppressed and defenceless, under the mask of sympathy and pity and what not that is soft and soothing. I had. You did not gradually open your round childish eyes wider and wider to the discovery of that impostor of a woman who calculates *her* stores of peace of mind for when she wakes up in the night. I did."

It was no laughing matter with Estella now, nor was she summoning these remembrances from any shallow place. I would not have been the cause of that look of hers for all my expectations in a heap.

"Two things I can tell you," said Estella. "First, notwithstanding the proverb that constant dropping will wear away a stone, you may set your mind at rest that these people never will—never would, in hundred years—impair your ground with Miss Havisham, in any particular, great or small. Second, I am beholden to you as the cause of their being so busy and so mean in vain, and there is my hand upon it."

As she gave it to me playfully—for her darker mood had been but momentary—I held it and put it to my lips. "You ridiculous boy," said Estella, "will you never take warning? Or do you kiss my hand in the same spirit in which I once let you kiss my cheek?"

"What spirit was that?" said I.

"I must think a moment. A spirit of contempt for the fawners and plotters."

"If I say yes, may I kiss the cheek again?"

"You should have asked before you touched the hand. But, yes, if you like."

I leaned down, and her calm face was like a statue's. "Now," said Estella, gliding away the instant I touched her cheek, "you are to take care that I have some tea, and you are to take me to Richmond."

Her reverting to this tone as if our association were forced upon us, and we were mere puppets, gave me pain; but everything in our intercourse did give me pain. Whatever her tone with me happened to be, I could put no trust in it, and build no hope on it; and yet I went on against trust and against hope. Why repeat it a thousand times? So it always was.

I rang for the tea, and the waiter, reappearing with his magic clew, brought in by degrees some fifty adjuncts to that refreshment, but of tea not a glimpse. A teaboard, cups and saucers, plates, knives and forks (including carvers), spoons (various), saltcellars, a meek little muffin confined with the utmost precaution under a strong iron cover, Moses in the bulrushes typified by a soft bit of butter in a quantity of parsley, a pale loaf with a powdered head, two proof impressions of the bars of the kitchen fireplace on triangular bits of bread, and ultimately a fat family urn; which the waiter staggered in with, expressing in his countenance burden and suffering. After a prolonged absence at this stage of the entertainment, he at length came back with a casket of precious appearance containing twigs. These I steeped in hot water, and so from the whole of these appliances extracted one cup of I don't know what for Estella.

The bill paid, and the waiter remembered, and the ostler not forgotten, and the chambermaid taken into consideration—in a word, the whole house bribed into a state of contempt and animosity, and Estella's purse much lightened—we got into our post-coach and drove away. Turning into Cheapside and rattling up Newgate Street, we were soon under the walls of which I was so ashamed.

"What place is that?" Estella asked me.

I made a foolish pretence of not at first recognizing it, and then told her. As she looked at it, and drew in her head again, murmuring, "Wretches!" I would not have confessed to my visit for any consideration.

"Mr. Jaggers," said I, by way of putting it neatly on somebody else, "has the reputation of being more in the secrets of that dismal place than any man in London."

"He is more in the secrets of every place, I think," said Estella, in a low voice.

"You have been accustomed to see him often, I suppose?"

"I have been accustomed to see him at uncertain intervals, ever since I can remember. But I know him no better now, than I did before I could speak plainly. What is your own experience of him? Do you advance with him?"

"Once habituated to his distrustful manner," said I, "I have done very well."

"Are you intimate?"

"I have dined with him at his private house."

"I fancy," said Estella, shrinking "that must be a curious place."

"It is a curious place."

I should have been chary of discussing my guardian too freely even with her; but I should have gone on with the subject so far as to describe the dinner in Gerrard Street, if we had not then come into a sudden glare of gas. It seemed, while it lasted, to be all alight and alive with that inexplicable feeling I had had before; and when we were out of it, I was as much dazed for a few moments as if I had been in Lightning.

So we fell into other talk, and it was principally about the way by which we were travelling, and about what parts of London lay on this side of it, and what on that. The great city was almost new to her, she told me, for she had never left Miss Havisham's neighbourhood until she had gone to France, and she had merely passed through London then in going and returning. I asked her if my guardian had any charge of her while she remained here? To that she emphatically said "God forbid!" and no more.

It was impossible for me to avoid seeing that she cared to attract me; that she made herself winning, and would have won me even if the task had needed pains. Yet this made me none the happier, for even if she had not taken that tone of our being disposed of by others, I should have felt that she held my heart in her hand because she wilfully chose to do it, and not because it would have wrung any tenderness in her to crush it and throw it away.

When we passed through Hammersmith, I showed her where Mr. Matthew Pocket lived, and said it was no great way from Richmond, and that I hoped I should see her sometimes.

"O yes, you are to see me; you are to come when you think proper; you are to be mentioned to the family; indeed you are already mentioned."

I inquired was it a large household she was going to be a member of?

"No; there are only two; mother and daughter. The mother is a lady of some station, though not averse to increasing her income."

"I wonder Miss Havisham could part with you again so soon."

"It is a part of Miss Havisham's plans for me, Pip," said Estella, with a sigh, as if she were tired; "I am to write to her constantly and see her regularly and report how I go on—I and the jewels—for they are nearly all mine now."

It was the first time she had ever called me by my name. Of course she did so purposely, and knew that I should treasure it up.

We came to Richmond all too soon, and our destination there was a house by the Green: a staid old house, where hoops and powder and patches, embroidered coats, rolled stockings, ruffles and swords, had had their court days many a time. Some ancient trees before the house were still cut into fashions as formal and unnatural as the hoops and wigs and stiff skirts; but their own allotted places in the great procession of the dead were not far off, and they would soon drop into them and go the silent way of the rest.

A bell with an old voice—which I dare say in its time had often said to the house, Here is the green farthingale, Here is the diamond-hilted sword, Here are the shoes with red heels and the blue solitaire,—sounded gravely in the moonlight, and two cherry-colored maids came fluttering out to receive Estella. The doorway soon absorbed her boxes, and she gave me her hand and a smile, and said good night, and was absorbed likewise. And still I stood looking at the house, thinking how happy I should be if I lived there with her, and knowing that I never was happy with her, but always miserable.

I got into the carriage to be taken back to Hammersmith, and I got in with a bad heart-ache, and I got out with a worse heart-ache. At our own door, I found little Jane Pocket coming home from a little party escorted by her little lover; and I envied her little lover, in spite of his being subject to Flopson.

Mr. Pocket was out lecturing; for, he was a most delightful lecturer on domestic economy, and his treatises on the management of children and servants were considered the very best text-books on those themes. But Mrs. Pocket was at home, and was in a little difficulty, on account of the baby's having been accommodated with a needle-case to keep him quiet during the unaccountable absence (with a relative in the Foot Guards) of Millers. And more needles were missing than it could be regarded as quite wholesome for a patient of such tender years either to apply externally or to take as a tonic.

Mr. Pocket being justly celebrated for giving most excellent practical advice, and for having a clear and sound perception of things and a highly judicious mind, I had some notion in my heart-ache of begging him to accept my confidence. But happening to look up at Mrs. Pocket as she sat reading her book of dignities after prescribing Bed as a sovereign remedy for baby, I thought—Well—No, I wouldn't.

CHAPTER 15

As I had grown accustomed to my expectations, I had insensibly begun to notice their effect upon myself and those around me. Their influence on my own character I disguised from my recognition as much as possible, but I knew very well that it was not all good. I lived in a state of chronic uneasiness respecting my behavior to Joe. My conscience was not by any means comfortable about Biddy. When I woke up in the night—like Camilla—I used to think, with a weariness on my spirits, that I should have been happier and better if I had never seen Miss Havisham's face, and had risen to manhood content to be partners with Joe in the honest old forge. Many a time of an evening, when I sat alone looking at the fire, I thought, after all there was no fire like the forge fire and the kitchen fire at home.

Yet Estella was so inseparable from all my restlessness and disquiet of mind, that I really fell into confusion as to the limits of my own part in its production. That is to say, supposing I had had no expectations, and yet had had Estella to think of, I could not make out to my satisfaction that I should have done much better. Now, concerning the influence of my position on others, I was in no such difficulty, and so I perceived—though dimly enough perhaps—that it was not beneficial to anybody, and, above all, that it was not beneficial to Herbert. My lavish habits led his easy nature into expenses that he could not afford, corrupted the simplicity of his life, and disturbed his peace with anxieties and regrets. I was not at all remorseful for having unwittingly set those other branches of the Pocket family to the poor arts they practised; because such littlenesses were their natural bent, and would have been evoked by anybody else, if I had left them slumbering. But Herbert's was a very different case, and it often caused me a twinge to think that I had done him evil service in crowding his sparely furnished chambers with incongruous upholstery work, and placing the Canary-breasted Avenger at his disposal.

So now, as an infallible way of making little ease great ease, I began to contract a quantity of debt. I could hardly begin but Herbert must begin too, so he soon followed. At Startop's suggestion, we put ourselves down for election into a club called The Finches of the Grove: the object of which institution I have never divined, if it were not that the members should dine expensively once a fortnight, to quarrel among themselves as much as possible after dinner, and to cause six waiters to get drunk on the stairs. I know that these gratifying social ends were so invariably accomplished, that Herbert and I understood nothing else to be referred to in the first standing toast of the society: which ran "Gentlemen, may the present promotion of good feeling ever reign predominant among the Finches of the Grove."

The Finches spent their money foolishly (the Hotel we dined at was in Covent Garden), and the first Finch I saw when I had the honor of joining the Grove was Bentley Drummle, at that time floundering about town in a cab of his own, and doing a great deal of damage to the posts at the street corners. Occasionally, he shot himself out of his equipage headforemost over the apron; and I saw him on one occasion deliver himself at the door of the Grove in this unintentional way—like coals. But here I anticipate a little, for I was not a Finch, and could not be, according to the sacred laws of the society, until I came of age.

In my confidence in my own resources, I would willingly have taken Herbert's expenses on myself; but Herbert was proud, and I could make no such proposal to him. So he got into difficulties in every direction, and continued to look about him. When we gradually fell into keeping late hours and late company, I noticed that he looked about him with a desponding eye at breakfast-time; that he began to look about him more hopefully about mid-day; that he drooped when he came into dinner; that he seemed to descry Capital in the distance, rather clearly, after dinner; that he all but realized Capital towards midnight; and that at about two o'clock in the morning, he became so deeply despondent again as to talk of buying a rifle and going to America, with a general purpose of compelling buffaloes to make his fortune.

I was usually at Hammersmith about half the week, and when I was at Hammersmith I haunted Richmond, whereof separately by and by. Herbert would often come to Hammersmith when I was there, and I think at those seasons his father would occasionally have some passing perception that the opening he was looking for, had not appeared yet. But in the general tumbling up of the family, his tumbling out in life somewhere, was a thing to transact itself somehow. In the meantime Mr. Pocket grew grayer, and tried oftener to lift himself out of his perplexities by the hair. While Mrs. Pocket tripped up the family with her footstool, read her book of dignities, lost her pocket-handkerchief, told us about her grandpapa, and taught the young idea how to shoot, by shooting it into bed whenever it attracted her notice.

As I am now generalizing a period of my life with the object of clearing my way before me, I can scarcely do so better than by at once completing the description of our usual manners and customs at Barnard's Inn.

We spent as much money as we could, and got as little for it as people could make up their minds to give us. We were always more or less miserable, and most of our acquaintance were in the same condition. There was a gay fiction among us that we were constantly enjoying ourselves, and a skeleton truth that we never did. To the best of my belief, our case was in the last aspect a rather common one.

Every morning, with an air ever new, Herbert went into the City to look about him. I often paid him a visit in the dark back-room in which he consorted with an ink-jar, a hat-peg, a coal-box, a string-box, an almanac, a desk and stool, and a ruler; and I do not remember that I ever saw him do anything else but look about him. If we all did what we undertake to do, as faithfully as Herbert did, we might live in a Republic of the Virtues. He had nothing else to do, poor fellow, except at a certain hour of every afternoon to "go to Lloyd's"—in observance of a ceremony of seeing his principal, I think. He never did anything else in connection with Lloyd's that I could find out, except come back again. When he felt his case unusually serious, and that he positively must find an opening, he would go on 'Change at a busy time, and walk in and out, in a kind of gloomy country dance figure, among the assembled magnates. "For," says Herbert to me, coming home to dinner on one of those special occasions, "I find the truth to be, Handel, that an opening won't come to one, but one must go to it—so I have been."

If we had been less attached to one another, I think we must have hated one another regularly every morning. I detested the chambers beyond expression at that period of repentance, and could not endure the sight of the Avenger's livery; which had a more expensive and a less remunerative appearance then than at any other time in the four-and-twenty hours. As we got more and more into debt, breakfast became a hollower and hollower form, and, being on one occasion at breakfast-time threatened (by letter) with legal proceedings, "not unwholly unconnected," as my local paper might put it, "with jewelery," I went so far as to seize the Avenger by his blue collar and shake him off his feet—so that he was actually in the air, like a booted Cupid—for presuming to suppose that we wanted a roll.

At certain times—meaning at uncertain times, for they depended on our humor—I would say to Herbert, as if it were a remarkable discovery:

"My dear Herbert, we are getting on badly."

"My dear Handel," Herbert would say to me, in all sincerity, "if you will believe me, those very words were on my lips, by a strange coincidence."

"Then, Herbert," I would respond, "let us look into out affairs."

We always derived profound satisfaction from making an appointment for this purpose. I always thought this was business, this was the way to confront the thing, this was the way to take the foe by the throat. And I know Herbert thought so too.

We ordered something rather special for dinner, with a bottle of something similarly out of the common way, in order that our minds might be fortified for the occasion, and we might come well up to the mark. Dinner over, we produced a bundle of pens, a copious supply of ink, and a goodly show of writing and blotting paper. For there was something very comfortable in having plenty of stationery.

I would then take a sheet of paper, and write across the top of it, in a neat hand, the heading, "Memorandum of Pip's debts"; with Barnard's Inn and the date very carefully added. Herbert would also take a sheet of paper, and write across it with similar formalities, "Memorandum of Herbert's debts."

Each of us would then refer to a confused heap of papers at his side, which had been thrown into drawers, worn into holes in pockets, half burnt in lighting candles, stuck for weeks into the looking-glass, and otherwise damaged. The sound of our pens going refreshed us exceedingly, insomuch that I sometimes found it difficult to distinguish between this edifying business proceeding and actually paying the money. In point of meritorious character, the two things seemed about equal.

When we had written a little while, I would ask Herbert how he got on? Herbert probably would have been scratching his head in a most rueful manner at the sight of his accumulating figures.

"They are mounting up, Handel," Herbert would say; "upon my life, they are mounting up."

"Be firm, Herbert," I would retort, plying my own pen with great assiduity. "Look the thing in the face. Look into your affairs. Stare them out of countenance."

"So I would, Handel, only they are staring me out of countenance."

However, my determined manner would have its effect, and Herbert would fall to work again. After a time he would give up once more, on the plea that he had not got Cobbs's bill, or Lobbs's, or Nobbs's, as the case might be.

"Then, Herbert, estimate; estimate it in round numbers, and put it down."

"What a fellow of resource you are!" my friend would reply, with admiration. "Really your business powers are very remarkable."

I thought so too. I established with myself, on these occasions, the reputation of a first-rate man of business—prompt, decisive, energetic, clear, cool-headed. When I had got all my responsibilities down upon my list, I compared each with the bill, and ticked it off. My self-approval when I ticked an entry was quite a luxurious sensation. When I had no more ticks to make, I folded all my bills up uniformly, docketed each on the back, and tied the whole into a symmetrical bundle. Then I did the same for Herbert (who modestly said he had not my administrative genius), and felt that I had brought his affairs into a focus for him.

My business habits had one other bright feature, which I called "leaving a Margin." For example; supposing Herbert's debts to be one hundred and sixty-four pounds four-and-twopence, I would say, "Leave a margin, and put them down at two hundred." Or, supposing my own to be four times as much, I would leave a margin, and put them down at seven hundred. I had the highest opinion of the wisdom of this same Margin, but I am bound to acknowledge that on looking back, I deem it to have been an expensive device. For, we always ran into new debt immediately, to the full extent of the margin, and sometimes, in the sense of freedom and solvency it imparted, got pretty far on into another margin.

But there was a calm, a rest, a virtuous hush, consequent on these examinations of our affairs that gave me, for the time, an admirable opinion of myself. Soothed by my exertions, my method, and Herbert's compliments, I would sit with his symmetrical bundle and my own on the table before me among the stationary, and feel like a Bank of some sort, rather than a private individual.

We shut our outer door on these solemn occasions, in order that we might not be interrupted. I had fallen into my serene state one evening, when we heard a letter dropped through the slit in the said door, and fall on the ground. "It's for you, Handel," said Herbert, going out and coming back with it, "and I hope there is nothing the matter." This was in allusion to its heavy black seal and border.

The letter was signed Trabb & Co., and its contents were simply, that I was an honored sir, and that they begged to inform me that Mrs. J. Gargery had departed this life on Monday last at twenty minutes past six in the evening, and that my attendance was requested at the interment on Monday next at three o'clock in the afternoon.

CHAPTER 16

It was the first time that a grave had opened in my road of life, and the gap it made in the smooth ground was wonderful. The figure of my sister in her chair by the kitchen fire, haunted me night and day. That the place could possibly be, without her, was something my mind seemed unable to compass; and whereas she had seldom or never been in my thoughts of late, I had now the strangest ideas that she was coming towards me in the street, or that she would presently knock at the door. In my rooms too, with which she had never been at all associated, there was at once the blankness of death and a perpetual suggestion of the sound of her voice or the turn of her face or figure, as if she were still alive and had been often there.

Whatever my fortunes might have been, I could scarcely have recalled my sister with much tenderness. But I suppose there is a shock of regret which may exist without much tenderness. Under its influence (and perhaps to make up for the want of the softer feeling) I was seized with a violent indignation against the assailant from whom she had suffered so much; and I felt that on sufficient proof I could have revengefully pursued Orlick, or any one else, to the last extremity.

Having written to Joe, to offer him consolation, and to assure him that I would come to the funeral, I passed the intermediate days in the curious state of mind I have glanced at. I went down early in the morning, and alighted at the Blue Boar in good time to walk over to the forge.

It was fine summer weather again, and, as I walked along, the times when I was a little helpless creature, and my sister did not spare me, vividly returned. But they returned with a gentle tone upon them that softened even the edge of Tickler. For now, the very breath of the beans and clover whispered to my heart that the day must come when it would be well for my memory that others walking in the sunshine should be softened as they thought of me.

At last I came within sight of the house, and saw that Trabb and Co. had put in a funereal execution and taken possession. Two dismally absurd persons, each ostentatiously exhibiting a crutch done up in a black bandage—as if that instrument could possibly communicate any comfort to anybody—were posted at the front door; and in one of them I recognized a postboy discharged from the Boar for turning a young couple into a sawpit on their bridal morning, in consequence of intoxication rendering it necessary for him to ride his horse clasped round the neck with both arms. All the children of the village, and most of the women, were admiring these sable warders and the closed windows of the house and forge; and as I came up, one of the two warders (the postboy) knocked at the door— implying that I was far too much exhausted by grief to have strength remaining to knock for myself.

Another sable warder (a carpenter, who had once eaten two geese for a wager) opened the door, and showed me into the best parlor. Here, Mr. Trabb had taken unto himself the best table, and had got all the leaves up, and was holding a kind of black Bazaar, with the aid of a quantity of black pins. At the moment of my arrival, he had just finished putting somebody's hat into black long-clothes, like an African baby; so he held out his hand for mine. But I, misled by the action, and confused by the occasion, shook hands with him with every testimony of warm affection.

Poor dear Joe, entangled in a little black cloak tied in a large bow under his chin, was seated apart at the upper end of the room; where, as chief mourner, he had evidently been stationed by Trabb. When I bent down and said to him, "Dear

Joe, how are you?" he said, "Pip, old chap, you knowed her when she were a fine figure of a—" and clasped my hand and said no more.

Biddy, looking very neat and modest in her black dress, went quietly here and there, and was very helpful. When I had spoken to Biddy, as I thought it not a time for talking I went and sat down near Joe, and there began to wonder in what part of the house it—she—my sister—was. The air of the parlor being faint with the smell of sweet-cake, I looked about for the table of refreshments; it was scarcely visible until one had got accustomed to the gloom, but there was a cut-up plum cake upon it, and there were cut-up oranges, and sandwiches, and biscuits, and two decanters that I knew very well as ornaments, but had never seen used in all my life; one full of port, and one of sherry. Standing at this table, I became conscious of the servile Pumblechook in a black cloak and several yards of hatband, who was alternately stuffing himself, and making obsequious movements to catch my attention. The moment he succeeded, he came over to me (breathing sherry and crumbs), and said in a subdued voice, "May I, dear sir?" and did. I then descried Mr. and Mrs. Hubble; the last-named in a decent speechless paroxysm in a corner. We were all going to "follow," and were all in course of being tied up separately (by Trabb) into ridiculous bundles.

"Which I meantersay, Pip," Joe whispered me, as we were being what Mr. Trabb called "formed" in the parlor, two and two—and it was dreadfully like a preparation for some grim kind of dance; "which I meantersay, sir, as I would in preference have carried her to the church myself, along with three or four friendly ones wot come to it with willing harts and arms, but it were considered wot the neighbours would look down on such and would be of opinions as it were wanting in respect."

"Pocket-handkerchiefs out, all!" cried Mr. Trabb at this point, in a depressed business-like voice. "Pocket-handkerchiefs out! We are ready!"

So we all put our pocket-handkerchiefs to our faces, as if our noses were bleeding, and filed out two and two; Joe and I; Biddy and Pumblechook; Mr. and Mrs. Hubble. The remains of my poor sister had been brought round by the kitchen door, and, it being a point of Undertaking ceremony that the six bearers must be stifled and blinded under a horrible black velvet housing with a white border, the whole looked like a blind monster with twelve human legs, shuffling and blundering along, under the guidance of two keepers—the postboy and his comrade.

The neighbourhood, however, highly approved of these arrangements, and we were much admired as we went through the village; the more youthful and vigorous part of the community making dashes now and then to cut us off, and lying in wait to intercept us at points of vantage. At such times the more exuberant among them called out in an excited manner on our emergence round some corner of expectancy, "*Here* they come!" "*Here* they are!" and we were all but cheered. In this progress I was much annoyed by the abject Pumblechook, who, being behind me, persisted all the way as a delicate attention in arranging my streaming hatband, and smoothing my cloak. My thoughts were further distracted by the excessive pride of Mr. and Mrs. Hubble, who were surpassingly conceited and vainglorious in being members of so distinguished a procession.

And now the range of marshes lay clear before us, with the sails of the ships on the river growing out of it; and we went into the churchyard, close to the graves of my unknown parents, Philip Pirrip, late of this parish, and Also Georgiana, Wife of the Above. And there, my sister was laid quietly in the earth, while the larks sang high above it, and the light wind strewed it with beautiful shadows of clouds and trees.

Of the conduct of the worldly minded Pumblechook while

GREAT EXPECTATIONS   337

this was doing, I desire to say no more than it was all addressed
to me; and that even when those noble passages were read which
remind humanity how it brought nothing into the world and
can take nothing out, and how it fleeth like a shadow and never
continueth long in one stay, I heard him cough a reservation
of the case of a young gentleman who came unexpectedly into
large property. When we got back, he had the hardihood to tell
me that he wished my sister could have known I had done her
so much honor, and to hint that she would have considered
it reasonably purchased at the price of her death. After that,
he drank all the rest of the sherry, and Mr. Hubble drank the
port, and the two talked (which I have since observed to be
customary in such cases) as if they were of quite another race
from the deceased, and were notoriously immortal. Finally, he
went away with Mr. and Mrs. Hubble—to make an evening
of it, I felt sure, and to tell the Jolly Bargemen that he was the
founder of my fortunes and my earliest benefactor.

When they were all gone, and when Trabb and his men—but
not his Boy; I looked for him—had crammed their mummery
into bags, and were gone too, the house felt wholesomer. Soon
afterwards, Biddy, Joe, and I, had a cold dinner together; but
we dined in the best parlor, not in the old kitchen, and Joe was
so exceedingly particular what he did with his knife and fork
and the saltcellar and what not, that there was great restraint
upon us. But after dinner, when I made him take his pipe, and
when I had loitered with him about the forge, and when we sat
down together on the great block of stone outside it, we got on
better. I noticed that after the funeral Joe changed his clothes
so far, as to make a compromise between his Sunday dress and
working dress; in which the dear fellow looked natural, and
like the Man he was.

He was very much pleased by my asking if I might sleep
in my own little room, and I was pleased too; for I felt that I
had done rather a great thing in making the request. When the

shadows of evening were closing in, I took an opportunity of getting into the garden with Biddy for a little talk.

"Biddy," said I, "I think you might have written to me about these sad matters."

"Do you, Mr. Pip?" said Biddy. "I should have written if I had thought that."

"Don't suppose that I mean to be unkind, Biddy, when I say I consider that you ought to have thought that."

"Do you, Mr. Pip?"

She was so quiet, and had such an orderly, good, and pretty way with her, that I did not like the thought of making her cry again. After looking a little at her downcast eyes as she walked beside me, I gave up that point.

"I suppose it will be difficult for you to remain here now, Biddy dear?"

"Oh! I can't do so, Mr. Pip," said Biddy, in a tone of regret but still of quiet conviction. "I have been speaking to Mrs. Hubble, and I am going to her to-morrow. I hope we shall be able to take some care of Mr. Gargery, together, until he settles down."

"How are you going to live, Biddy? If you want any mo—"

"How am I going to live?" repeated Biddy, striking in, with a momentary flush upon her face. "I'll tell you, Mr. Pip. I am going to try to get the place of mistress in the new school nearly finished here. I can be well recommended by all the neighbours, and I hope I can be industrious and patient, and teach myself while I teach others. You know, Mr. Pip," pursued Biddy, with a smile, as she raised her eyes to my face, "the new schools are not like the old, but I learnt a good deal from you after that time, and have had time since then to improve."

"I think you would always improve, Biddy, under any circumstances."

"Ah! Except in my bad side of human nature," murmured Biddy.

It was not so much a reproach as an irresistible thinking aloud. Well! I thought I would give up that point too. So, I walked a little further with Biddy, looking silently at her downcast eyes.

"I have not heard the particulars of my sister's death, Biddy."

"They are very slight, poor thing. She had been in one of her bad states—though they had got better of late, rather than worse—for four days, when she came out of it in the evening, just at tea-time, and said quite plainly, 'Joe.' As she had never said any word for a long while, I ran and fetched in Mr. Gargery from the forge. She made signs to me that she wanted him to sit down close to her, and wanted me to put her arms round his neck. So I put them round his neck, and she laid her head down on his shoulder quite content and satisfied. And so she presently said 'Joe' again, and once 'Pardon,' and once 'Pip.' And so she never lifted her head up any more, and it was just an hour later when we laid it down on her own bed, because we found she was gone."

Biddy cried; the darkening garden, and the lane, and the stars that were coming out, were blurred in my own sight.

"Nothing was ever discovered, Biddy?"

"Nothing."

"Do you know what is become of Orlick?"

"I should think from the color of his clothes that he is working in the quarries."

"Of course you have seen him then?—Why are you looking at that dark tree in the lane?"

"I saw him there, on the night she died."

"That was not the last time either, Biddy?"

"No; I have seen him there, since we have been walking here—It is of no use," said Biddy, laying her hand upon my arm, as I was for running out, "you know I would not deceive you; he was not there a minute, and he is gone."

It revived my utmost indignation to find that she was still pursued by this fellow, and I felt inveterate against him. I told her so, and told her that I would spend any money or take any pains to drive him out of that country. By degrees she led me into more temperate talk, and she told me how Joe loved me, and how Joe never complained of anything—she didn't say, of me; she had no need; I knew what she meant—but ever did his duty in his way of life, with a strong hand, a quiet tongue, and a gentle heart.

"Indeed, it would be hard to say too much for him," said I; "and Biddy, we must often speak of these things, for of course I shall be often down here now. I am not going to leave poor Joe alone."

Biddy said never a single word.

"Biddy, don't you hear me?"

"Yes, Mr. Pip."

"Not to mention your calling me Mr. Pip—which appears to me to be in bad taste, Biddy—what do you mean?"

"What do I mean?" asked Biddy, timidly.

"Biddy," said I, in a virtuously self-asserting manner, "I must request to know what you mean by this?"

"By this?" said Biddy.

"Now, don't echo," I retorted. "You used not to echo, Biddy."

"Used not!" said Biddy. "O Mr. Pip! Used!"

Well! I rather thought I would give up that point too. After another silent turn in the garden, I fell back on the main position.

"Biddy," said I, "I made a remark respecting my coming down here often, to see Joe, which you received with a marked silence. Have the goodness, Biddy, to tell me why."

"Are you quite sure, then, that you WILL come to see him often?" asked Biddy, stopping in the narrow garden walk, and looking at me under the stars with a clear and honest eye.

"O dear me!" said I, as if I found myself compelled to give up Biddy in despair. "This really is a very bad side of human nature! Don't say any more, if you please, Biddy. This shocks me very much."

For which cogent reason I kept Biddy at a distance during supper, and when I went up to my own old little room, took as stately a leave of her as I could, in my murmuring soul, deem reconcilable with the churchyard and the event of the day. As often as I was restless in the night, and that was every quarter of an hour, I reflected what an unkindness, what an injury, what an injustice, Biddy had done me.

Early in the morning I was to go. Early in the morning I was out, and looking in, unseen, at one of the wooden windows of the forge. There I stood, for minutes, looking at Joe, already at work with a glow of health and strength upon his face that made it show as if the bright sun of the life in store for him were shining on it.

"Good by, dear Joe!—No, don't wipe it off—for God's sake, give me your blackened hand!—I shall be down soon and often."

"Never too soon, sir," said Joe, "and never too often, Pip!"

Biddy was waiting for me at the kitchen door, with a mug of new milk and a crust of bread. "Biddy," said I, when I gave her my hand at parting, "I am not angry, but I am hurt."

"No, don't be hurt," she pleaded quite pathetically; "let only me be hurt, if I have been ungenerous."

Once more, the mists were rising as I walked away. If they disclosed to me, as I suspect they did, that I should not come back, and that Biddy was quite right, all I can say is—they were quite right too.

CHAPTER 17

Herbert and I went on from bad to worse, in the way of increasing our debts, looking into our affairs, leaving Margins, and the like exemplary transactions; and Time went on, whether or no, as he has a way of doing; and I came of age—in fulfilment of Herbert's prediction, that I should do so before I knew where I was.

Herbert himself had come of age eight months before me. As he had nothing else than his majority to come into, the event did not make a profound sensation in Barnard's Inn. But we had looked forward to my one-and-twentieth birthday, with a crowd of speculations and anticipations, for we had both considered that my guardian could hardly help saying something definite on that occasion.

I had taken care to have it well understood in Little Britain when my birthday was. On the day before it, I received an official note from Wemmick, informing me that Mr. Jaggers would be glad if I would call upon him at five in the afternoon of the auspicious day. This convinced us that something great was to happen, and threw me into an unusual flutter when I repaired to my guardian's office, a model of punctuality.

In the outer office Wemmick offered me his congratulations, and incidentally rubbed the side of his nose with a folded piece of tissue-paper that I liked the look of. But he said nothing respecting it, and motioned me with a nod into my guardian's room. It was November, and my guardian was standing before his fire leaning his back against the chimney-piece, with his hands under his coat-tails.

"Well, Pip," said he, "I must call you Mr. Pip to-day.

Congratulations, Mr. Pip."

We shook hands—he was always a remarkably short shaker—and I thanked him.

"Take a chair, Mr. Pip," said my guardian.

As I sat down, and he preserved his attitude and bent his brows at his boots, I felt at a disadvantage, which reminded me of that old time when I had been put upon a tombstone. The two ghastly casts on the shelf were not far from him, and their expression was as if they were making a stupid apoplectic attempt to attend to the conversation.

"Now my young friend," my guardian began, as if I were a witness in the box, "I am going to have a word or two with you."

"If you please, sir."

"What do you suppose," said Mr. Jaggers, bending forward to look at the ground, and then throwing his head back to look at the ceiling, "what do you suppose you are living at the rate of?"

"At the rate of, sir?"

"At," repeated Mr. Jaggers, still looking at the ceiling, "the—rate—of?" And then looked all round the room, and paused with his pocket-handkerchief in his hand, half-way to his nose.

I had looked into my affairs so often, that I had thoroughly destroyed any slight notion I might ever have had of their bearings. Reluctantly, I confessed myself quite unable to answer the question. This reply seemed agreeable to Mr. Jaggers, who said, "I thought so!" and blew his nose with an air of satisfaction.

"Now, I have asked *you* a question, my friend," said Mr. Jaggers. "Have you anything to ask *me*?"

"Of course it would be a great relief to me to ask you several questions, sir; but I remember your prohibition."

"Ask one," said Mr. Jaggers.

"Is my benefactor to be made known to me to-day?"

"No. Ask another."

"Is that confidence to be imparted to me soon?"

"Waive that, a moment," said Mr. Jaggers, "and ask another."

I looked about me, but there appeared to be now no possible escape from the inquiry, "Have-I-anything to receive, sir?" On that, Mr. Jaggers said, triumphantly, "I thought we should come to it!" and called to Wemmick to give him that piece of paper. Wemmick appeared, handed it in, and disappeared.

"Now, Mr. Pip," said Mr. Jaggers, "attend, if you please. You have been drawing pretty freely here; your name occurs pretty often in Wemmick's cash-book; but you are in debt, of course?"

"I am afraid I must say yes, sir."

"You know you must say yes; don't you?" said Mr. Jaggers.

"Yes, sir."

"I don't ask you what you owe, because you don't know; and if you did know, you wouldn't tell me; you would say less. Yes, yes, my friend," cried Mr. Jaggers, waving his forefinger to stop me as I made a show of protesting: "it's likely enough that you think you wouldn't, but you would. You'll excuse me, but I know better than you. Now, take this piece of paper in your hand. You have got it? Very good. Now, unfold it and tell me what it is."

"This is a bank-note," said I, "for five hundred pounds."

"That is a bank-note," repeated Mr. Jaggers, "for five hundred pounds. And a very handsome sum of money too, I think. You consider it so?"

"How could I do otherwise!"

"Ah! But answer the question," said Mr. Jaggers.

"Undoubtedly."

"You consider it, undoubtedly, a handsome sum of money. Now, that handsome sum of money, Pip, is your own. It is a present to you on this day, in earnest of your expectations.

And at the rate of that handsome sum of money per annum, and at no higher rate, you are to live until the donor of the whole appears. That is to say, you will now take your money affairs entirely into your own hands, and you will draw from Wemmick one hundred and twenty-five pounds per quarter, until you are in communication with the fountain-head, and no longer with the mere agent. As I have told you before, I am the mere agent. I execute my instructions, and I am paid for doing so. I think them injudicious, but I am not paid for giving any opinion on their merits."

I was beginning to express my gratitude to my benefactor for the great liberality with which I was treated, when Mr. Jaggers stopped me. "I am not paid, Pip," said he, coolly, "to carry your words to any one;" and then gathered up his coat-tails, as he had gathered up the subject, and stood frowning at his boots as if he suspected them of designs against him.

After a pause, I hinted:

"There was a question just now, Mr. Jaggers, which you desired me to waive for a moment. I hope I am doing nothing wrong in asking it again?"

"What is it?" said he.

I might have known that he would never help me out; but it took me aback to have to shape the question afresh, as if it were quite new. "Is it likely," I said, after hesitating, "that my patron, the fountain-head you have spoken of, Mr. Jaggers, will soon—" there I delicately stopped.

"Will soon what?" asked Mr. Jaggers. "That's no question as it stands, you know."

"Will soon come to London," said I, after casting about for a precise form of words, "or summon me anywhere else?"

"Now, here," replied Mr. Jaggers, fixing me for the first time with his dark deep-set eyes, "we must revert to the evening when we first encountered one another in your village. What did I tell you then, Pip?"

"You told me, Mr. Jaggers, that it might be years hence when that person appeared."

"Just so," said Mr. Jaggers, "that's my answer."

As we looked full at one another, I felt my breath come quicker in my strong desire to get something out of him. And as I felt that it came quicker, and as I felt that he saw that it came quicker, I felt that I had less chance than ever of getting anything out of him.

"Do you suppose it will still be years hence, Mr. Jaggers?"

Mr. Jaggers shook his head—not in negativing the question, but in altogether negativing the notion that he could anyhow be got to answer it—and the two horrible casts of the twitched faces looked, when my eyes strayed up to them, as if they had come to a crisis in their suspended attention, and were going to sneeze.

"Come!" said Mr. Jaggers, warming the backs of his legs with the backs of his warmed hands, "I'll be plain with you, my friend Pip. That's a question I must not be asked. You'll understand that better, when I tell you it's a question that might compromise *me*. Come! I'll go a little further with you; I'll say something more."

He bent down so low to frown at his boots, that he was able to rub the calves of his legs in the pause he made.

"When that person discloses," said Mr. Jaggers, straightening himself, "you and that person will settle your own affairs. When that person discloses, my part in this business will cease and determine. When that person discloses, it will not be necessary for me to know anything about it. And that's all I have got to say."

We looked at one another until I withdrew my eyes, and looked thoughtfully at the floor. From this last speech I derived the notion that Miss Havisham, for some reason or no reason, had not taken him into her confidence as to her designing me for Estella; that he resented this, and felt a jealousy about it;

or that he really did object to that scheme, and would have nothing to do with it. When I raised my eyes again, I found that he had been shrewdly looking at me all the time, and was doing so still.

"If that is all you have to say, sir," I remarked, "there can be nothing left for me to say."

He nodded assent, and pulled out his thief-dreaded watch, and asked me where I was going to dine? I replied at my own chambers, with Herbert. As a necessary sequence, I asked him if he would favor us with his company, and he promptly accepted the invitation. But he insisted on walking home with me, in order that I might make no extra preparation for him, and first he had a letter or two to write, and (of course) had his hands to wash. So I said I would go into the outer office and talk to Wemmick.

The fact was, that when the five hundred pounds had come into my pocket, a thought had come into my head which had been often there before; and it appeared to me that Wemmick was a good person to advise with concerning such thought.

He had already locked up his safe, and made preparations for going home. He had left his desk, brought out his two greasy office candlesticks and stood them in line with the snuffers on a slab near the door, ready to be extinguished; he had raked his fire low, put his hat and great-coat ready, and was beating himself all over the chest with his safe-key, as an athletic exercise after business.

"Mr. Wemmick," said I, "I want to ask your opinion. I am very desirous to serve a friend."

Wemmick tightened his post-office and shook his head, as if his opinion were dead against any fatal weakness of that sort.

"This friend," I pursued, "is trying to get on in commercial life, but has no money, and finds it difficult and disheartening to make a beginning. Now I want somehow to help him to a beginning."

"With money down?" said Wemmick, in a tone drier than any sawdust.

"With *some* money down," I replied, for an uneasy remembrance shot across me of that symmetrical bundle of papers at home— "with *some* money down, and perhaps some anticipation of my expectations."

"Mr. Pip," said Wemmick, "I should like just to run over with you on my fingers, if you please, the names of the various bridges up as high as Chelsea Reach. Let's see; there's London, one; Southwark, two; Blackfriars, three; Waterloo, four; Westminster, five; Vauxhall, six." He had checked off each bridge in its turn, with the handle of his safe-key on the palm of his hand. "There's as many as six, you see, to choose from."

"I don't understand you," said I.

"Choose your bridge, Mr. Pip," returned Wemmick, "and take a walk upon your bridge, and pitch your money into the Thames over the centre arch of your bridge, and you know the end of it. Serve a friend with it, and you may know the end of it too—but it's a less pleasant and profitable end."

I could have posted a newspaper in his mouth, he made it so wide after saying this.

"This is very discouraging," said I.

"Meant to be so," said Wemmick.

"Then is it your opinion," I inquired, with some little indignation, "that a man should never—"

"—Invest portable property in a friend?" said Wemmick. "Certainly he should not. Unless he wants to get rid of the friend—and then it becomes a question how much portable property it may be worth to get rid of him."

"And that," said I, "is your deliberate opinion, Mr. Wemmick?"

"That," he returned, "is my deliberate opinion in this office."

"Ah!" said I, pressing him, for I thought I saw him near a

loophole here; "but would that be your opinion at Walworth?"

"Mr. Pip," he replied, with gravity, "Walworth is one place, and this office is another. Much as the Aged is one person, and Mr. Jaggers is another. They must not be confounded together. My Walworth sentiments must be taken at Walworth; none but my official sentiments can be taken in this office."

"Very well," said I, much relieved, "then I shall look you up at Walworth, you may depend upon it."

"Mr. Pip," he returned, "you will be welcome there, in a private and personal capacity."

We had held this conversation in a low voice, well knowing my guardian's ears to be the sharpest of the sharp. As he now appeared in his doorway, towelling his hands, Wemmick got on his great-coat and stood by to snuff out the candles. We all three went into the street together, and from the door-step Wemmick turned his way, and Mr. Jaggers and I turned ours.

I could not help wishing more than once that evening, that Mr. Jaggers had had an Aged in Gerrard Street, or a Stinger, or a Something, or a Somebody, to unbend his brows a little. It was an uncomfortable consideration on a twenty-first birthday, that coming of age at all seemed hardly worth while in such a guarded and suspicious world as he made of it. He was a thousand times better informed and cleverer than Wemmick, and yet I would a thousand times rather have had Wemmick to dinner. And Mr. Jaggers made not me alone intensely melancholy, because, after he was gone, Herbert said of himself, with his eyes fixed on the fire, that he thought he must have committed a felony and forgotten the details of it, he felt so dejected and guilty.

CHAPTER 18

Deeming Sunday the best day for taking Mr. Wemmick's Walworth sentiments, I devoted the next ensuing Sunday afternoon to a pilgrimage to the Castle. On arriving before the battlements, I found the Union Jack flying and the drawbridge up; but undeterred by this show of defiance and resistance, I rang at the gate, and was admitted in a most pacific manner by the Aged.

"My son, sir," said the old man, after securing the drawbridge, "rather had it in his mind that you might happen to drop in, and he left word that he would soon be home from his afternoon's walk. He is very regular in his walks, is my son. Very regular in everything, is my son."

I nodded at the old gentleman as Wemmick himself might have nodded, and we went in and sat down by the fireside.

"You made acquaintance with my son, sir," said the old man, in his chirping way, while he warmed his hands at the blaze, "at his office, I expect?" I nodded. "Hah! I have heerd that my son is a wonderful hand at his business, sir?" I nodded hard. "Yes; so they tell me. His business is the Law?" I nodded harder. "Which makes it more surprising in my son," said the old man, "for he was not brought up to the Law, but to the Wine-Coopering."

Curious to know how the old gentleman stood informed concerning the reputation of Mr. Jaggers, I roared that name at him. He threw me into the greatest confusion by laughing heartily and replying in a very sprightly manner, "No, to be sure; you're right." And to this hour I have not the faintest notion what he meant, or what joke he thought I had made.

As I could not sit there nodding at him perpetually, without making some other attempt to interest him, I shouted at inquiry whether his own calling in life had been "the Wine-Coopering." By dint of straining that term out of myself several times and tapping the old gentleman on the chest to associate it with him, I at last succeeded in making my meaning understood.

"No," said the old gentleman; "the warehousing, the warehousing. First, over yonder;" he appeared to mean up the chimney, but I believe he intended to refer me to Liverpool; "and then in the City of London here. However, having an infirmity—for I am hard of hearing, sir—"

I expressed in pantomime the greatest astonishment.

"—Yes, hard of hearing; having that infirmity coming upon me, my son he went into the Law, and he took charge of me, and he by little and little made out this elegant and beautiful property. But returning to what you said, you know," pursued the old man, again laughing heartily, "what I say is, No to be sure; you're right."

I was modestly wondering whether my utmost ingenuity would have enabled me to say anything that would have amused him half as much as this imaginary pleasantry, when I was startled by a sudden click in the wall on one side of the chimney, and the ghostly tumbling open of a little wooden flap with "John" upon it. The old man, following my eyes, cried with great triumph, "My son's come home!" and we both went out to the drawbridge.

It was worth any money to see Wemmick waving a salute to me from the other side of the moat, when we might have shaken hands across it with the greatest ease. The Aged was so delighted to work the drawbridge, that I made no offer to assist him, but stood quiet until Wemmick had come across, and had presented me to Miss Skiffins; a lady by whom he was accompanied.

Miss Skiffins was of a wooden appearance, and was, like

her escort, in the post-office branch of the service. She might have been some two or three years younger than Wemmick, and I judged her to stand possessed of portable property. The cut of her dress from the waist upward, both before and behind, made her figure very like a boy's kite; and I might have pronounced her gown a little too decidedly orange, and her gloves a little too intensely green. But she seemed to be a good sort of fellow, and showed a high regard for the Aged. I was not long in discovering that she was a frequent visitor at the Castle; for, on our going in, and my complimenting Wemmick on his ingenious contrivance for announcing himself to the Aged, he begged me to give my attention for a moment to the other side of the chimney, and disappeared. Presently another click came, and another little door tumbled open with "Miss Skiffins" on it; then Miss Skiffins shut up and John tumbled open; then Miss Skiffins and John both tumbled open together, and finally shut up together. On Wemmick's return from working these mechanical appliances, I expressed the great admiration with which I regarded them, and he said, "Well, you know, they're both pleasant and useful to the Aged. And by George, sir, it's a thing worth mentioning, that of all the people who come to this gate, the secret of those pulls is only known to the Aged, Miss Skiffins, and me!"

"And Mr. Wemmick made them," added Miss Skiffins, "with his own hands out of his own head."

While Miss Skiffins was taking off her bonnet (she retained her green gloves during the evening as an outward and visible sign that there was company), Wemmick invited me to take a walk with him round the property, and see how the island looked in wintertime. Thinking that he did this to give me an opportunity of taking his Walworth sentiments, I seized the opportunity as soon as we were out of the Castle.

Having thought of the matter with care, I approached my subject as if I had never hinted at it before. I informed Wemmick that I was anxious in behalf of Herbert Pocket, and I told him how we had first met, and how we had fought. I glanced at Herbert's home, and at his character, and at his having no means but such as he was dependent on his father for; those, uncertain and unpunctual. I alluded to the advantages I had derived in my first rawness and ignorance from his society, and I confessed that I feared I had but ill repaid them, and that he might have done better without me and my expectations. Keeping Miss Havisham in the background at a great distance, I still hinted at the possibility of my having competed with him in his prospects, and at the certainty of his possessing a generous soul, and being far above any mean distrusts, retaliations, or designs. For all these reasons (I told Wemmick), and because he was my young companion and friend, and I had a great affection for him, I wished my own good fortune to reflect some rays upon him, and therefore I sought advice from Wemmick's experience and knowledge of men and affairs, how I could best try with my resources to help Herbert to some present income—say of a hundred a year, to keep him in good hope and heart—and gradually to buy him on to some small partnership. I begged Wemmick, in conclusion, to understand that my help must always be rendered without Herbert's knowledge or suspicion, and that there was no one else in the world with whom I could advise. I wound up by laying my hand upon his shoulder, and saying, "I can't help confiding in you, though I know it must be troublesome to you; but that is your fault, in having ever brought me here."

Wemmick was silent for a little while, and then said with a kind of start, "Well you know, Mr. Pip, I must tell you one thing. This is devilish good of you."

"Say you'll help me to be good then," said I.

"Ecod," replied Wemmick, shaking his head, "that's not my trade."

"Nor is this your trading-place," said I.

"You are right," he returned. "You hit the nail on the head. Mr. Pip, I'll put on my considering-cap, and I think all you want to do may be done by degrees. Skiffins (that's her brother) is an accountant and agent. I'll look him up and go to work for you."

"I thank you ten thousand times.""On the contrary," said he, "I thank you, for though we are strictly in our private and personal capacity, still it may be mentioned that there *are* Newgate cobwebs about, and it brushes them away."

After a little further conversation to the same effect, we returned into the Castle where we found Miss Skiffins preparing tea. The responsible duty of making the toast was delegated to the Aged, and that excellent old gentleman was so intent upon it that he seemed to me in some danger of melting his eyes. It was no nominal meal that we were going to make, but a vigorous reality. The Aged prepared such a hay-stack of buttered toast, that I could scarcely see him over it as it simmered on an iron stand hooked on to the top-bar; while Miss Skiffins brewed such a jorum of tea, that the pig in the back premises became strongly excited, and repeatedly expressed his desire to participate in the entertainment.

The flag had been struck, and the gun had been fired, at the right moment of time, and I felt as snugly cut off from the rest of Walworth as if the moat were thirty feet wide by as many deep. Nothing disturbed the tranquillity of the Castle, but the occasional tumbling open of John and Miss Skiffins: which little doors were a prey to some spasmodic infirmity that made me sympathetically uncomfortable until I got used to it. I inferred from the methodical nature of Miss Skiffins's arrangements that she made tea there every Sunday night; and I rather suspected that a classic brooch she wore, representing the profile of an undesirable female with a very straight nose and a very new moon, was a piece of portable property that had been given her by Wemmick.

We ate the whole of the toast, and drank tea in proportion, and it was delightful to see how warm and greasy we all got after it. The Aged especially, might have passed for some clean old chief of a savage tribe, just oiled. After a short pause of repose, Miss Skiffins—in the absence of the little servant who, it seemed, retired to the bosom of her family on Sunday afternoons—washed up the tea-things, in a trifling lady-like amateur manner that compromised none of us. Then, she put on her gloves again, and we drew round the fire, and Wemmick said, "Now, Aged Parent, tip us the paper."

Wemmick explained to me while the Aged got his spectacles out, that this was according to custom, and that it gave the old gentleman infinite satisfaction to read the news aloud. "I won't offer an apology," said Wemmick, "for he isn't capable of many pleasures—are you, Aged P.?"

"All right, John, all right," returned the old man, seeing himself spoken to.

"Only tip him a nod every now and then when he looks off his paper," said Wemmick, "and he'll be as happy as a king. We are all attention, Aged One."

"All right, John, all right!" returned the cheerful old man, so busy and so pleased, that it really was quite charming.

The Aged's reading reminded me of the classes at Mr. Wopsle's great-aunt's, with the pleasanter peculiarity that it seemed to come through a keyhole. As he wanted the candles close to him, and as he was always on the verge of putting either his head or the newspaper into them, he required as much watching as a powder-mill. But Wemmick was equally untiring and gentle in his vigilance, and the Aged read on, quite unconscious of his many rescues. Whenever he looked at us, we all expressed the greatest interest and amazement, and nodded until he resumed again.

As Wemmick and Miss Skiffins sat side by side, and as I sat in a shadowy corner, I observed a slow and gradual elongation of Mr. Wemmick's mouth, powerfully suggestive of his slowly and gradually stealing his arm round Miss Skiffins's waist. In course of time I saw his hand appear on the other side of Miss Skiffins; but at that moment Miss Skiffins neatly stopped him with the green glove, unwound his arm again as if it were an article of dress, and with the greatest deliberation laid it on the table before her. Miss Skiffins's composure while she did this was one of the most remarkable sights I have ever seen, and if I could have thought the act consistent with abstraction of mind, I should have deemed that Miss Skiffins performed it mechanically.

By and by, I noticed Wemmick's arm beginning to disappear again, and gradually fading out of view. Shortly afterwards, his mouth began to widen again. After an interval of suspense on my part that was quite enthralling and almost painful, I saw his hand appear on the other side of Miss Skiffins. Instantly, Miss Skiffins stopped it with the neatness of a placid boxer, took off that girdle or cestus as before, and laid it on the table. Taking the table to represent the path of virtue, I am justified in stating that during the whole time of the Aged's reading, Wemmick's arm was straying from the path of virtue and being recalled to it by Miss Skiffins. At last, the Aged read himself into a light slumber. This was the time for Wemmick to produce a little kettle, a tray of glasses, and a black bottle with a porcelain-topped cork, representing some clerical dignitary of a rubicund and social aspect. With the aid of these appliances we all had something warm to drink, including the Aged, who was soon awake again. Miss Skiffins mixed, and I observed that she and Wemmick drank out of one glass. Of course I knew better than to offer to see Miss Skiffins home, and under the circumstances I thought I had best go first; which I did, taking a cordial leave of the Aged, and having passed a pleasant evening.

Before a week was out, I received a note from Wemmick, dated Walworth, stating that he hoped he had made some advance in that matter appertaining to our private and personal capacities, and that he would be glad if I could come and see him again upon it. So, I went out to Walworth again, and yet again, and yet again, and I saw him by appointment in the City several times, but never held any communication with him on the subject in or near Little Britain. The upshot was, that we found a worthy young merchant or shipping-broker, not long established in business, who wanted intelligent help, and who wanted capital, and who in due course of time and receipt would want a partner. Between him and me, secret articles were signed of which Herbert was the subject, and I paid him half of my five hundred pounds down, and engaged for sundry other payments: some, to fall due at certain dates out of my income: some, contingent on my coming into my property. Miss Skiffins's brother conducted the negotiation. Wemmick pervaded it throughout, but never appeared in it.

The whole business was so cleverly managed, that Herbert had not the least suspicion of my hand being in it. I never shall forget the radiant face with which he came home one afternoon, and told me, as a mighty piece of news, of his having fallen in with one Clarriker (the young merchant's name), and of Clarriker's having shown an extraordinary inclination towards him, and of his belief that the opening had come at last. Day by day as his hopes grew stronger and his face brighter, he must have thought me a more and more affectionate friend, for I had the greatest difficulty in restraining my tears of triumph when I saw him so happy. At length, the thing being done, and he having that day entered Clarriker's House, and he having talked to me for a whole evening in a flush of pleasure and success, I did really cry in good earnest when I went to bed, to think that my expectations had done some good to somebody.

A great event in my life, the turning point of my life, now opens on my view. But, before I proceed to narrate it, and before I pass on to all the changes it involved, I must give one chapter to Estella. It is not much to give to the theme that so long filled my heart.

CHAPTER 19

If that staid old house near the Green at Richmond should ever come to be haunted when I am dead, it will be haunted, surely, by my ghost. O the many, many nights and days through which the unquiet spirit within me haunted that house when Estella lived there! Let my body be where it would, my spirit was always wandering, wandering, wandering, about that house.

The lady with whom Estella was placed, Mrs. Brandley by name, was a widow, with one daughter several years older than Estella. The mother looked young, and the daughter looked old; the mother's complexion was pink, and the daughter's was yellow; the mother set up for frivolity, and the daughter for theology. They were in what is called a good position, and visited, and were visited by, numbers of people. Little, if any, community of feeling subsisted between them and Estella, but the understanding was established that they were necessary to her, and that she was necessary to them. Mrs. Brandley had been a friend of Miss Havisham's before the time of her seclusion.

In Mrs. Brandley's house and out of Mrs. Brandley's house, I suffered every kind and degree of torture that Estella could cause me. The nature of my relations with her, which placed me on terms of familiarity without placing me on terms of favor, conduced to my distraction. She made use of me to tease other admirers, and she turned the very familiarity between herself and me to the account of putting a constant slight on my devotion to her. If I had been her secretary, steward, half-brother, poor relation—if I had been a younger brother of her appointed husband—I could not have seemed to myself further from my hopes when I was nearest to her. The privilege of calling her by her name and hearing her call me by mine became, under the circumstances an aggravation of my trials; and while I think it likely that it almost maddened her other lovers, I know too certainly that it almost maddened me.

She had admirers without end. No doubt my jealousy made an admirer of every one who went near her; but there were more than enough of them without that.

I saw her often at Richmond, I heard of her often in town, and I used often to take her and the Brandleys on the water; there were picnics, fête days, plays, operas, concerts, parties, all sorts of pleasures, through which I pursued her—and they were all miseries to me. I never had one hour's happiness in her society, and yet my mind all round the four-and-twenty hours was harping on the happiness of having her with me unto death.

Throughout this part of our intercourse—and it lasted, as will presently be seen, for what I then thought a long time— she habitually reverted to that tone which expressed that our association was forced upon us. There were other times when she would come to a sudden check in this tone and in all her many tones, and would seem to pity me.

"Pip, Pip," she said one evening, coming to such a check, when we sat apart at a darkening window of the house in Richmond; "will you never take warning?"

"Of what?"

"Of me."

"Warning not to be attracted by you, do you mean, Estella?"

"Do I mean! If you don't know what I mean, you are blind."

I should have replied that Love was commonly reputed blind, but for the reason that I always was restrained—and this was not the least of my miseries—by a feeling that it was ungenerous to press myself upon her, when she knew that she could not choose but obey Miss Havisham. My dread always was, that this knowledge on her part laid me under a heavy disadvantage with her pride, and made me the subject of a rebellious struggle in her bosom.

"At any rate," said I, "I have no warning given me just now, for you wrote to me to come to you, this time."

"That's true," said Estella, with a cold careless smile that always chilled me.

After looking at the twilight without, for a little while, she went on to say:

"The time has come round when Miss Havisham wishes to have me for a day at Satis. You are to take me there, and bring me back, if you will. She would rather I did not travel alone, and objects to receiving my maid, for she has a sensitive horror of being talked of by such people. Can you take me?"

"Can I take you, Estella!"

"You can then? The day after to-morrow, if you please. You are to pay all charges out of my purse. You hear the condition of your going?"

"And must obey," said I.

This was all the preparation I received for that visit, or for others like it; Miss Havisham never wrote to me, nor had I ever so much as seen her handwriting. We went down on the next day but one, and we found her in the room where I had first beheld her, and it is needless to add that there was no change in Satis House.

She was even more dreadfully fond of Estella than she had been when I last saw them together; I repeat the word advisedly, for there was something positively dreadful in the energy of her looks and embraces. She hung upon Estella's beauty, hung upon her words, hung upon her gestures, and sat mumbling her own trembling fingers while she looked at her, as though she were devouring the beautiful creature she had reared.

From Estella she looked at me, with a searching glance that seemed to pry into my heart and probe its wounds. "How does she use you, Pip; how does she use you?" she asked me again, with her witch-like eagerness, even in Estella's hearing. But, when we sat by her flickering fire at night, she was most weird; for then, keeping Estella's hand drawn through her arm and clutched in her own hand, she extorted from her, by dint of referring back to what Estella had told her in her regular letters, the names and conditions of the men whom she had fascinated; and as Miss Havisham dwelt upon this roll, with the intensity of a mind mortally hurt and diseased, she sat with her other hand on her crutch stick, and her chin on that, and her wan bright eyes glaring at me, a very spectre.

I saw in this, wretched though it made me, and bitter the sense of dependence and even of degradation that it awakened—I saw in this that Estella was set to wreak Miss Havisham's revenge on men, and that she was not to be given to me until she had gratified it for a term. I saw in this, a reason for her being beforehand assigned to me. Sending her out to attract and torment and do mischief, Miss Havisham sent her with the malicious assurance that she was beyond the reach of all admirers, and that all who staked upon that cast were secured to lose. I saw in this that I, too, was tormented by a perversion of ingenuity, even while the prize was reserved for me. I saw in this the reason for my being staved off so long and the reason for my late guardian's declining to commit himself to the formal knowledge of such a scheme. In a word, I saw in this Miss Havisham as I had her then and there before my eyes, and always had had her before my eyes; and I saw in this, the distinct shadow of the darkened and unhealthy house in which her life was hidden from the sun.

The candles that lighted that room of hers were placed in sconces on the wall. They were high from the ground, and they burnt with the steady dulness of artificial light in air that is seldom renewed. As I looked round at them, and at the pale gloom they made, and at the stopped clock, and at the withered articles of bridal dress upon the table and the ground, and at her own awful figure with its ghostly reflection thrown large by the fire upon the ceiling and the wall, I saw in everything the construction that my mind had come to, repeated and thrown back to me. My thoughts passed into the great room across the landing where the table was spread, and I saw it written, as it were, in the falls of the cobwebs from the centre-piece, in the crawlings of the spiders on the cloth, in the tracks of the mice as they betook their little quickened hearts behind the panels, and in the gropings and pausings of the beetles on the floor.

It happened on the occasion of this visit that some sharp words arose between Estella and Miss Havisham. It was the first time I had ever seen them opposed.

We were seated by the fire, as just now described, and Miss Havisham still had Estella's arm drawn through her own, and still clutched Estella's hand in hers, when Estella gradually began to detach herself. She had shown a proud impatience more than once before, and had rather endured that fierce affection than accepted or returned it.

"What!" said Miss Havisham, flashing her eyes upon her, "are you tired of me?"

"Only a little tired of myself," replied Estella, disengaging her arm, and moving to the great chimney-piece, where she stood looking down at the fire.

"Speak the truth, you ingrate!" cried Miss Havisham, passionately striking her stick upon the floor; "you are tired of me."

Estella looked at her with perfect composure, and again looked down at the fire. Her graceful figure and her beautiful face expressed a self-possessed indifference to the wild heat of the other, that was almost cruel.

"You stock and stone!" exclaimed Miss Havisham. "You cold, cold heart!"

"What?" said Estella, preserving her attitude of indifference as she leaned against the great chimney-piece and only moving her eyes; "do you reproach me for being cold? You?"

"Are you not?" was the fierce retort.

"You should know," said Estella. "I am what you have made me. Take all the praise, take all the blame; take all the success, take all the failure; in short, take me."

"O, look at her, look at her!" cried Miss Havisham, bitterly; "Look at her so hard and thankless, on the hearth where she was reared! Where I took her into this wretched breast when it was first bleeding from its stabs, and where I have lavished years of tenderness upon her!"

"At least I was no party to the compact," said Estella, "for if I could walk and speak, when it was made, it was as much as I could do. But what would you have? You have been very good to me, and I owe everything to you. What would you have?"

"Love," replied the other.

"You have it."

"I have not," said Miss Havisham.

"Mother by adoption," retorted Estella, never departing from the easy grace of her attitude, never raising her voice as the other did, never yielding either to anger or tenderness— "Mother by adoption, I have said that I owe everything to you. All I possess is freely yours. All that you have given me, is at your command to have again. Beyond that, I have nothing. And if you ask me to give you, what you never gave me, my gratitude and duty cannot do impossibilities."

"Did I never give her love!" cried Miss Havisham, turning wildly to me. "Did I never give her a burning love, inseparable from jealousy at all times, and from sharp pain, while she speaks thus to me! Let her call me mad, let her call me mad!"

"Why should I call you mad," returned Estella, "I, of all

people? Does any one live, who knows what set purposes you have, half as well as I do? Does any one live, who knows what a steady memory you have, half as well as I do? I who have sat on this same hearth on the little stool that is even now beside you there, learning your lessons and looking up into your face, when your face was strange and frightened me!"

"Soon forgotten!" moaned Miss Havisham. "Times soon forgotten!"

"No, not forgotten," retorted Estella. "Not forgotten, but treasured up in my memory. When have you found me false to your teaching? When have you found me unmindful of your lessons? When have you found me giving admission here," she touched her bosom with her hand, "to anything that you excluded? Be just to me."

"So proud, so proud!" moaned Miss Havisham, pushing away her gray hair with both her hands.

"Who taught me to be proud?" returned Estella. "Who praised me when I learnt my lesson?"

"So hard, so hard!" moaned Miss Havisham, with her former action.

"Who taught me to be hard?" returned Estella. "Who praised me when I learnt my lesson?"

"But to be proud and hard to *me*!" Miss Havisham quite shrieked, as she stretched out her arms. "Estella, Estella, Estella, to be proud and hard to *me*!"

Estella looked at her for a moment with a kind of calm wonder, but was not otherwise disturbed; when the moment was past, she looked down at the fire again.

"I cannot think," said Estella, raising her eyes after a silence "why you should be so unreasonable when I come to see you after a separation. I have never forgotten your wrongs and their causes. I have never been unfaithful to you or your schooling. I have never shown any weakness that I can charge myself with."

"Would it be weakness to return my love?" exclaimed Miss Havisham. "But yes, yes, she would call it so!"

"I begin to think," said Estella, in a musing way, after another moment of calm wonder, "that I almost understand how this comes about. If you had brought up your adopted daughter wholly in the dark confinement of these rooms, and had never let her know that there was such a thing as the daylight by which she had never once seen your face—if you had done that, and then, for a purpose had wanted her to understand the daylight and know all about it, you would have been disappointed and angry?"

Miss Havisham, with her head in her hands, sat making a low moaning, and swaying herself on her chair, but gave no answer.

"Or," said Estella— "which is a nearer case—if you had taught her, from the dawn of her intelligence, with your utmost energy and might, that there was such a thing as daylight, but that it was made to be her enemy and destroyer, and she must always turn against it, for it had blighted you and would else blight her;—if you had done this, and then, for a purpose, had wanted her to take naturally to the daylight and she could not do it, you would have been disappointed and angry?"

Miss Havisham sat listening (or it seemed so, for I could not see her face), but still made no answer.

"So," said Estella, "I must be taken as I have been made. The success is not mine, the failure is not mine, but the two together make me."

Miss Havisham had settled down, I hardly knew how, upon the floor, among the faded bridal relics with which it was strewn. I took advantage of the moment—I had sought one from the first—to leave the room, after beseeching Estella's attention to her, with a movement of my hand. When I left, Estella was yet standing by the great chimney-piece, just as she had stood throughout. Miss Havisham's gray hair was all adrift upon the ground, among the other bridal wrecks, and was a miserable sight to see.

It was with a depressed heart that I walked in the starlight for an hour and more, about the courtyard, and about the brewery, and about the ruined garden. When I at last took courage to return to the room, I found Estella sitting at Miss Havisham's knee, taking up some stitches in one of those old articles of dress that were dropping to pieces, and of which I have often been reminded since by the faded tatters of old banners that I have seen hanging up in cathedrals. Afterwards, Estella and I played at cards, as of yore—only we were skilful now, and played French games—and so the evening wore away, and I went to bed.

I lay in that separate building across the courtyard. It was the first time I had ever lain down to rest in Satis House, and sleep refused to come near me. A thousand Miss Havishams haunted me. She was on this side of my pillow, on that, at the head of the bed, at the foot, behind the half-opened door of the dressing-room, in the dressing-room, in the room overhead, in the room beneath—everywhere. At last, when the night was slow to creep on towards two o'clock, I felt that I absolutely could no longer bear the place as a place to lie down in, and that I must get up. I therefore got up and put on my clothes, and went out across the yard into the long stone passage, designing to gain the outer courtyard and walk there for the relief of my mind. But I was no sooner in the passage than I extinguished my candle; for I saw Miss Havisham going along it in a ghostly manner, making a low cry. I followed her at a distance, and saw her go up the staircase. She carried a bare candle in her hand, which she had probably taken from one of the sconces in her own room, and was a most unearthly object by its light. Standing at the bottom of the staircase, I felt the mildewed air of the feast-chamber, without seeing her open the door, and I heard her walking there, and so across into her own room, and so across again into that, never ceasing the low cry. After a time, I tried in the dark both to get out, and to go back, but I could do neither until some streaks of day strayed in and showed me where to lay my hands. During the whole interval, whenever I went to the bottom of the staircase, I heard her footstep, saw her light pass above, and heard her ceaseless low cry.

Before we left next day, there was no revival of the difference between her and Estella, nor was it ever revived on any similar occasion; and there were four similar occasions, to the best of my remembrance. Nor, did Miss Havisham's manner towards Estella in anywise change, except that I believed it to have something like fear infused among its former characteristics.

It is impossible to turn this leaf of my life, without putting Bentley Drummle's name upon it; or I would, very gladly.

On a certain occasion when the Finches were assembled in force, and when good feeling was being promoted in the usual manner by nobody's agreeing with anybody else, the presiding Finch called the Grove to order, forasmuch as Mr. Drummle had not yet toasted a lady; which, according to the solemn constitution of the society, it was the brute's turn to do that day. I thought I saw him leer in an ugly way at me while the decanters were going round, but as there was no love lost between us, that might easily be. What was my indignant surprise when he called upon the company to pledge him to "Estella!"

"Estella who?" said I.

"Never you mind," retorted Drummle.

"Estella of where?" said I. "You are bound to say of where." Which he was, as a Finch.

"Of Richmond, gentlemen," said Drummle, putting me out of the question, "and a peerless beauty."

Much he knew about peerless beauties, a mean, miserable idiot! I whispered Herbert.

"I know that lady," said Herbert, across the table, when the toast had been honored.

"*Do* you?" said Drummle.

"And so do I," I added, with a scarlet face.

"*Do* you?" said Drummle. "*Oh*, Lord!"

This was the only retort—except glass or crockery—that the heavy creature was capable of making; but, I became as highly incensed by it as if it had been barbed with wit, and I immediately rose in my place and said that I could not but regard it as being like the honorable Finch's impudence to come down to that Grove—we always talked about coming down to that Grove, as a nea Parliamentary turn of expression—down to that Grove, proposing a lady of whom he knew nothing. Mr. Drummle, upon this, starting up, demanded what I meant by that? Whereupon I made him the extreme reply that I believed he knew where I was to be found.

Whether it was possible in a Christian country to get on without blood, after this, was a question on which the Finches were divided. The debate upon it grew so lively, indeed, that at least six more honorable members told six more, during the discussion, that they believed *they* knew where *they* were to be found. However, it was decided at last (the Grove being a Court of Honor) that if Mr. Drummle would bring never so slight a certificate from the lady, importing that he had the honor of her acquaintance, Mr. Pip must express his regret, as a gentleman and a Finch, for "having been betrayed into a warmth which." Next day was appointed for the production (lest our honor should take cold from delay), and next day Drummle appeared with a polite little avowal in Estella's hand, that she had had the honor of dancing with him several times. This left me no course but to regret that I had been "betrayed into a warmth which," and on the whole to repudiate, as untenable, the idea that I was to be found anywhere. Drummle and I then sat snorting at one another for an hour, while the

Grove engaged in indiscriminate contradiction, and finally the promotion of good feeling was declared to have gone ahead at an amazing rate.

I tell this lightly, but it was no light thing to me. For, I cannot adequately express what pain it gave me to think that Estella should show any favor to a contemptible, clumsy, sulky booby, so very far below the average. To the present moment, I believe it to have been referable to some pure fire of generosity and disinterestedness in my love for her, that I could not endure the thought of her stooping to that hound. No doubt I should have been miserable whomsoever she had favored; but a worthier object would have caused me a different kind and degree of distress.

It was easy for me to find out, and I did soon find out, that Drummle had begun to follow her closely, and that she allowed him to do it. A little while, and he was always in pursuit of her, and he and I crossed one another every day. He held on, in a dull persistent way, and Estella held him on; now with encouragement, now with discouragement, now almost flattering him, now openly despising him, now knowing him very well, now scarcely remembering who he was.

The Spider, as Mr. Jaggers had called him, was used to lying in wait, however, and had the patience of his tribe. Added to that, he had a blockhead confidence in his money and in his family greatness, which sometimes did him good service— almost taking the place of concentration and determined purpose. So, the Spider, doggedly watching Estella, outwatched many brighter insects, and would often uncoil himself and drop at the right nick of time.

At a certain Assembly Ball at Richmond (there used to be Assembly Balls at most places then), where Estella had outshone all other beauties, this blundering Drummle so hung about her, and with so much toleration on her part, that I resolved to speak to her concerning him. I took the next opportunity;

which was when she was waiting for Mrs. Blandley to take her home, and was sitting apart among some flowers, ready to go. I was with her, for I almost always accompanied them to and from such places.

"Are you tired, Estella?"

"Rather, Pip."

"You should be."

"Say rather, I should not be; for I have my letter to Satis House to write, before I go to sleep."

"Recounting to-night's triumph?" said I. "Surely a very poor one, Estella."

"What do you mean? I didn't know there had been any."

"Estella," said I, "do look at that fellow in the corner yonder, who is looking over here at us."

"Why should I look at him?" returned Estella, with her eyes on me instead. "What is there in that fellow in the corner yonder—to use your words—that I need look at?"

"Indeed, that is the very question I want to ask you," said I. "For he has been hovering about you all night."

"Moths, and all sorts of ugly creatures," replied Estella, with a glance towards him, "hover about a lighted candle. Can the candle help it?"

"No," I returned; "but cannot the Estella help it?"

"Well!" said she, laughing, after a moment, "perhaps. Yes. Anything you like."

"But, Estella, do hear me speak. It makes me wretched that you should encourage a man so generally despised as Drummle. You know he is despised."

"Well?" said she.

"You know he is as ungainly within as without. A deficient, ill-tempered, lowering, stupid fellow."

"Well?" said she.

"You know he has nothing to recommend him but money and a ridiculous roll of addle-headed predecessors; now, don't you?"

"Well?" said she again; and each time she said it, she opened her lovely eyes the wider.

To overcome the difficulty of getting past that monosyllable, I took it from her, and said, repeating it with emphasis, "Well! Then, that is why it makes me wretched."

Now, if I could have believed that she favored Drummle with any idea of making me-me-wretched, I should have been in better heart about it; but in that habitual way of hers, she put me so entirely out of the question, that I could believe nothing of the kind.

"Pip," said Estella, casting her glance over the room, "don't be foolish about its effect on you. It may have its effect on others, and may be meant to have. It's not worth discussing."

"Yes it is," said I, "because I cannot bear that people should say, 'she throws away her graces and attractions on a mere boor, the lowest in the crowd.'"

"I can bear it," said Estella.

"Oh! don't be so proud, Estella, and so inflexible."

"Calls me proud and inflexible in this breath!" said Estella, opening her hands. "And in his last breath reproached me for stooping to a boor!"

"There is no doubt you do," said I, something hurriedly, "for I have seen you give him looks and smiles this very night, such as you never give to—me."

"Do you want me then," said Estella, turning suddenly with a fixed and serious, if not angry, look, "to deceive and entrap you?"

"Do you deceive and entrap him, Estella?"

"Yes, and many others—all of them but you. Here is Mrs. Brandley. I'll say no more."

And now that I have given the one chapter to the theme that so filled my heart, and so often made it ache and ache again, I pass on unhindered, to the event that had impended over me longer yet; the event that had begun to be prepared for, before I knew that the world held Estella, and in the days when her baby intelligence was receiving its first distortions from Miss Havisham's wasting hands.

In the Eastern story, the heavy slab that was to fall on the bed of state in the flush of conquest was slowly wrought out of the quarry, the tunnel for the rope to hold it in its place was slowly carried through the leagues of rock, the slab was slowly raised and fitted in the roof, the rope was rove to it and slowly taken through the miles of hollow to the great iron ring. All being made ready with much labor, and the hour come, the sultan was aroused in the dead of the night, and the sharpened axe that was to sever the rope from the great iron ring was put into his hand, and he struck with it, and the rope parted and rushed away, and the ceiling fell. So, in my case; all the work, near and afar, that tended to the end, had been accomplished; and in an instant the blow was struck, and the roof of my stronghold dropped upon me.

CHAPTER 20

I was three-and-twenty years of age. Not another word had I heard to enlighten me on the subject of my expectations, and my twenty-third birthday was a week gone. We had left Barnard's Inn more than a year, and lived in the Temple. Our chambers were in Garden-court, down by the river.

Mr. Pocket and I had for some time parted company as to our original relations, though we continued on the best terms. Notwithstanding my inability to settle to anything—which I hope arose out of the restless and incomplete tenure on which I held my means—I had a taste for reading, and read regularly so many hours a day. That matter of Herbert's was still progressing, and everything with me was as I have brought it down to the close of the last preceding chapter.

Business had taken Herbert on a journey to Marseilles. I was alone, and had a dull sense of being alone. Dispirited and anxious, long hoping that to-morrow or next week would clear my way, and long disappointed, I sadly missed the cheerful face and ready response of my friend.

It was wretched weather; stormy and wet, stormy and wet; and mud, mud, mud, deep in all the streets. Day after day, a vast heavy veil had been driving over London from the East, and it drove still, as if in the East there were an Eternity of cloud and wind. So furious had been the gusts, that high buildings in town had had the lead stripped off their roofs; and in the country, trees had been torn up, and sails of windmills carried away; and gloomy accounts had come in from the coast, of shipwreck and death. Violent blasts of rain had accompanied these rages of wind, and the day just closed as I sat down to read had been the worst of all.

Alterations have been made in that part of the Temple since that time, and it has not now so lonely a character as it had then, nor is it so exposed to the river. We lived at the top of the last house, and the wind rushing up the river shook the house that night, like discharges of cannon, or breakings of a sea. When the rain came with it and dashed against the windows, I thought, raising my eyes to them as they rocked, that I might have fancied myself in a storm-beaten lighthouse. Occasionally, the smoke came rolling down the chimney as though it could not bear to go out into such a night; and when I set the doors open and looked down the staircase, the staircase lamps were blown out; and when I shaded my face with my hands and looked through the black windows (opening them ever so little was out of the question in the teeth of such wind and rain), I saw that the lamps in the court were blown out, and that the lamps on the bridges and the shore were shuddering, and that the coal-fires in barges on the river were being carried away before the wind like red-hot splashes in the rain.

I read with my watch upon the table, purposing to close my book at eleven o'clock. As I shut it, Saint Paul's, and all the many church-clocks in the City—some leading, some accompanying, some following—struck that hour. The sound was curiously flawed by the wind; and I was listening, and thinking how the wind assailed and tore it, when I heard a footstep on the stair.

What nervous folly made me start, and awfully connect it with the footstep of my dead sister, matters not. It was past in a moment, and I listened again, and heard the footstep stumble in coming on. Remembering then, that the staircase-lights were blown out, I took up my reading-lamp and went out to the stair-head. Whoever was below had stopped on seeing my lamp, for all was quiet.

"There is some one down there, is there not?" I called out, looking down.

"Yes," said a voice from the darkness beneath.

"What floor do you want?"

"The top. Mr. Pip."

"That is my name—There is nothing the matter?"

"Nothing the matter," returned the voice. And the man came on.

I stood with my lamp held out over the stair-rail, and he came slowly within its light. It was a shaded lamp, to shine upon a book, and its circle of light was very contracted; so that he was in it for a mere instant, and then out of it. In the instant, I had seen a face that was strange to me, looking up with an incomprehensible air of being touched and pleased by the sight of me.

Moving the lamp as the man moved, I made out that he was substantially dressed, but roughly, like a voyager by sea. That he had long iron-gray hair. That his age was about sixty. That he was a muscular man, strong on his legs, and that he was browned and hardened by exposure to weather. As he ascended the last stair or two, and the light of my lamp included us both, I saw, with a stupid kind of amazement, that he was holding out both his hands to me.

"Pray what is your business?" I asked him.

"My business?" he repeated, pausing. "Ah! Yes. I will explain my business, by your leave."

"Do you wish to come in?"

"Yes," he replied; "I wish to come in, master."

I had asked him the question inhospitably enough, for I resented the sort of bright and gratified recognition that still shone in his face. I resented it, because it seemed to imply that he expected me to respond to it. But I took him into the room I had just left, and, having set the lamp on the table, asked him as civilly as I could to explain himself.

He looked about him with the strangest air—an air of wondering pleasure, as if he had some part in the things he admired—and he pulled off a rough outer coat, and his hat. Then, I saw that his head was furrowed and bald, and that the long iron-gray hair grew only on its sides. But, I saw nothing that in the least explained him. On the contrary, I saw him next moment, once more holding out both his hands to me.

"What do you mean?" said I, half suspecting him to be mad.

He stopped in his looking at me, and slowly rubbed his right hand over his head. "It's disapinting to a man," he said, in a coarse broken voice, "arter having looked for'ard so distant, and come so fur; but you're not to blame for that—neither on us is to blame for that. I'll speak in half a minute. Give me half a minute, please."

He sat down on a chair that stood before the fire, and covered his forehead with his large brown veinous hands. I looked at him attentively then, and recoiled a little from him; but I did not know him.

"There's no one nigh," said he, looking over his shoulder; "is there?"

"Why do you, a stranger coming into my rooms at this time of the night, ask that question?" said I. "You're a game one," he returned, shaking his head at me with a deliberate affection, at once most unintelligible and most exasperating; "I'm glad you've grow'd up, a game one! But don't catch hold of me. You'd be sorry arterwards to have done it."

I relinquished the intention he had detected, for I knew him! Even yet I could not recall a single feature, but I knew him! If the wind and the rain had driven away the intervening years, had scattered all the intervening objects, had swept us to the churchyard where we first stood face to face on such different levels, I could not have known my convict more distinctly than I knew him now as he sat in the chair before the fire. No need to take a file from his pocket and show it to me; no need to take the handkerchief from his neck and twist it round his head; no need to hug himself with both his arms, and take a shivering turn across the room, looking back at me for recognition. I knew him before he gave me one of those aids, though, a moment before, I had not been conscious of remotely suspecting his identity.

He came back to where I stood, and again held out both his hands. Not knowing what to do—for, in my astonishment I had lost my self-possession—I reluctantly gave him my hands. He grasped them heartily, raised them to his lips, kissed them, and still held them.

"You acted noble, my boy," said he. "Noble, Pip! And I have never forgot it!"

At a change in his manner as if he were even going to embrace me, I laid a hand upon his breast and put him away.

"Stay!" said I. "Keep off! If you are grateful to me for what I did when I was a little child, I hope you have shown your gratitude by mending your way of life. If you have come here to thank me, it was not necessary. Still, however you have found me out, there must be something good in the feeling that has brought you here, and I will not repulse you; but surely you must understand that—I—"

My attention was so attracted by the singularity of his fixed look at me, that the words died away on my tongue.

"You was a saying," he observed, when we had confronted one another in silence, "that surely I must understand. What, surely must I understand?"

"That I cannot wish to renew that chance intercourse with you of long ago, under these different circumstances. I am glad to believe you have repented and recovered yourself. I am glad to tell you so. I am glad that, thinking I deserve to be thanked, you have come to thank me. But our ways are different ways, none the less. You are wet, and you look weary. Will you drink something before you go?"

He had replaced his neckerchief loosely, and had stood,

keenly observant of me, biting a long end of it. "I think," he answered, still with the end at his mouth and still observant of me, "that I *will* drink (I thank you) afore I go."

There was a tray ready on a side-table. I brought it to the table near the fire, and asked him what he would have? He touched one of the bottles without looking at it or speaking, and I made him some hot rum and water. I tried to keep my hand steady while I did so, but his look at me as he leaned back in his chair with the long draggled end of his neckerchief between his teeth—evidently forgotten—made my hand very difficult to master. When at last I put the glass to him, I saw with amazement that his eyes were full of tears.

Up to this time I had remained standing, not to disguise that I wished him gone. But I was softened by the softened aspect of the man, and felt a touch of reproach. "I hope," said I, hurriedly putting something into a glass for myself, and drawing a chair to the table, "that you will not think I spoke harshly to you just now. I had no intention of doing it, and I am sorry for it if I did. I wish you well and happy!"

As I put my glass to my lips, he glanced with surprise at the end of his neckerchief, dropping from his mouth when he opened it, and stretched out his hand. I gave him mine, and then he drank, and drew his sleeve across his eyes and forehead.

"How are you living?" I asked him.

"I've been a sheep-farmer, stock-breeder, other trades besides, away in the new world," said he; "many a thousand mile of stormy water off from this."

"I hope you have done well?"

"I've done wonderfully well. There's others went out alonger me as has done well too, but no man has done nigh as well as me. I'm famous for it."

"I am glad to hear it."

"I hope to hear you say so, my dear boy."

Without stopping to try to understand those words or the tone in which they were spoken, I turned off to a point that had just come into my mind.

"Have you ever seen a messenger you once sent to me," I inquired, "since he undertook that trust?"

"Never set eyes upon him. I warn't likely to it."

"He came faithfully, and he brought me the two one-pound notes. I was a poor boy then, as you know, and to a poor boy they were a little fortune. But, like you, I have done well since, and you must let me pay them back. You can put them to some other poor boy's use." I took out my purse.

He watched me as I laid my purse upon the table and opened it, and he watched me as I separated two one-pound notes from its contents. They were clean and new, and I spread them out and handed them over to him. Still watching me, he laid them one upon the other, folded them long-wise, gave them a twist, set fire to them at the lamp, and dropped the ashes into the tray.

"May I make so bold," he said then, with a smile that was like a frown, and with a frown that was like a smile, "as ask you *how* you have done well, since you and me was out on them lone shivering marshes?"

"How?"

"Ah!"

He emptied his glass, got up, and stood at the side of the fire, with his heavy brown hand on the mantel-shelf. He put a foot up to the bars, to dry and warm it, and the wet boot began to steam; but, he neither looked at it, nor at the fire, but steadily looked at me. It was only now that I began to tremble.

When my lips had parted, and had shaped some words that were without sound, I forced myself to tell him (though I could not do it distinctly), that I had been chosen to succeed to some property.

"Might a mere warmint ask what property?" said he.

I faltered, "I don't know."

"Might a mere warmint ask whose property?" said he.

I faltered again, "I don't know."

"Could I make a guess, I wonder," said the Convict, "at your income since you come of age! As to the first figure now. Five?"

With my heart beating like a heavy hammer of disordered action, I rose out of my chair, and stood with my hand upon the back of it, looking wildly at him.

"Concerning a guardian," he went on. "There ought to have been some guardian, or such-like, whiles you was a minor. Some lawyer, maybe. As to the first letter of that lawyer's name now. Would it be J?"

All the truth of my position came flashing on me; and its disappointments, dangers, disgraces, consequences of all kinds, rushed in in such a multitude that I was borne down by them and had to struggle for every breath I drew.

"Put it," he resumed, "as the employer of that lawyer whose name begun with a J, and might be Jaggers—put it as he had come over sea to Portsmouth, and had landed there, and had wanted to come on to you. 'However, you have found me out,' you says just now. Well! However, did I find you out? Why, I wrote from Portsmouth to a person in London, for particulars of your address. That person's name? Why, Wemmick."

I could not have spoken one word, though it had been to save my life. I stood, with a hand on the chair-back and a hand on my breast, where I seemed to be suffocating—I stood so, looking wildly at him, until I grasped at the chair, when the room began to surge and turn. He caught me, drew me to the sofa, put me up against the cushions, and bent on one knee before me, bringing the face that I now well remembered, and that I shuddered at, very near to mine.

"Yes, Pip, dear boy, I've made a gentleman on you! It's me wot has done it! I swore that time, sure as ever I earned a guinea, that guinea should go to you. I swore arterwards, sure as ever I spec'lated and got rich, you should get rich. I lived rough, that you should live smooth; I worked hard, that you should be above work. What odds, dear boy? Do I tell it, fur you to feel a obligation? Not a bit. I tell it, fur you to know as that there hunted dunghill dog wot you kep life in, got his head so high that he could make a gentleman—and, Pip, you're him!"

The abhorrence in which I held the man, the dread I had of him, the repugnance with which I shrank from him, could not have been exceeded if he had been some terrible beast.

"Look'ee here, Pip. I'm your second father. You're my son— more to me nor any son. I've put away money, only for you to spend. When I was a hired-out shepherd in a solitary hut, not seeing no faces but faces of sheep till I half forgot wot men's and women's faces wos like, I see yourn. I drops my knife many a time in that hut when I was a-eating my dinner or my supper, and I says, 'Here's the boy again, a looking at me whiles I eats and drinks!' I see you there a many times, as plain as ever I see you on them misty marshes. 'Lord strike me dead!' I says each time—and I goes out in the air to say it under the open heavens— 'but wot, if I gets liberty and money, I'll make that boy a gentleman!' And I done it. Why, look at you, dear boy! Look at these here lodgings o'yourn, fit for a lord! A lord? Ah! You shall show money with lords for wagers, and beat 'em!"

In his heat and triumph, and in his knowledge that I had been nearly fainting, he did not remark on my reception of all this. It was the one grain of relief I had.

"Look'ee here!" he went on, taking my watch out of my pocket, and turning towards him a ring on my finger, while I recoiled from his touch as if he had been a snake, "a gold 'un and a beauty: *that's* a gentleman's, I hope! A diamond all set round with rubies; *that's* a gentleman's, I hope! Look at your linen; fine and beautiful! Look at your clothes; better ain't to be got! And your books too," turning his eyes round the room, "mounting up, on their shelves, by hundreds! And you read 'em; don't you? I see you'd been a reading of 'em when I come in. Ha, ha, ha! You shall read 'em to me, dear boy! And if they're in foreign languages wot I don't understand, I shall be just as proud as if I did."

Again he took both my hands and put them to his lips, while my blood ran cold within me.

"Don't you mind talking, Pip," said he, after again drawing his sleeve over his eyes and forehead, as the click came in his throat which I well remembered—and he was all the more horrible to me that he was so much in earnest; "you can't do better nor keep quiet, dear boy. You ain't looked slowly forward to this as I have; you wosn't prepared for this as I wos. But didn't you never think it might be me?"

"O no, no, no," I returned, "Never, never!"

"Well, you see it *wos* me, and single-handed. Never a soul in it but my own self and Mr. Jaggers."

"Was there no one else?" I asked.

"No," said he, with a glance of surprise: "who else should there be? And, dear boy, how good looking you have growed! There's bright eyes somewheres—eh? Isn't there bright eyes somewheres, wot you love the thoughts on?"

O Estella, Estella!

"They shall be yourn, dear boy, if money can buy 'em. Not that a gentleman like you, so well set up as you, can't win 'em off of his own game; but money shall back you! Let me finish wot I was a telling you, dear boy. From that there hut and that there hiring-out, I got money left me by my master (which died, and had been the same as me), and got my liberty and went for myself. In every single thing I went for, I went for you. 'Lord strike a blight upon it,' I says, wotever it was I went for, 'if it ain't for him!' It all prospered wonderful. As I giv' you to understand just now, I'm famous for it. It was the money left me, and the gains of the first few year wot I sent home to Mr.

Jaggers—all for you—when he first come arter you, agreeable to my letter."

O that he had never come! That he had left me at the forge—far from contented, yet, by comparison happy!

"And then, dear boy, it was a recompense to me, look'ee here, to know in secret that I was making a gentleman. The blood horses of them colonists might fling up the dust over me as I was walking; what do I say? I says to myself, 'I'm making a better gentleman nor ever *you*'ll be!' When one of 'em says to another, 'He was a convict, a few year ago, and is a ignorant common fellow now, for all he's lucky,' what do I say? I says to myself, 'If I ain't a gentleman, nor yet ain't got no learning, I'm the owner of such. All on you owns stock and land; which on you owns a brought-up London gentleman?' This way I kep myself a going. And this way I held steady afore my mind that I would for certain come one day and see my boy, and make myself known to him, on his own ground."

He laid his hand on my shoulder. I shuddered at the thought that for anything I knew, his hand might be stained with blood.

"It warn't easy, Pip, for me to leave them parts, nor yet it warn't safe. But I held to it, and the harder it was, the stronger I held, for I was determined, and my mind firm made up. At last I done it. Dear boy, I done it!"

I tried to collect my thoughts, but I was stunned. Throughout, I had seemed to myself to attend more to the wind and the rain than to him; even now, I could not separate his voice from those voices, though those were loud and his was silent.

"Where will you put me?" he asked, presently. "I must be put somewheres, dear boy."

"To sleep?" said I.

"Yes. And to sleep long and sound," he answered; "for I've been sea-tossed and sea-washed, months and months."

"My friend and companion," said I, rising from the sofa, "is absent; you must have his room."

"He won't come back to-morrow; will he?"

"No," said I, answering almost mechanically, in spite of my utmost efforts; "not to-morrow."

"Because, look'ee here, dear boy," he said, dropping his voice, and laying a long finger on my breast in an impressive manner, "caution is necessary."

"How do you mean? Caution?"

"By G——, it's Death!"

"What's death?"

"I was sent for life. It's death to come back. There's been overmuch coming back of late years, and I should of a certainty be hanged if took."

Nothing was needed but this; the wretched man, after loading wretched me with his gold and silver chains for years, had risked his life to come to me, and I held it there in my keeping! If I had loved him instead of abhorring him; if I had been attracted to him by the strongest admiration and affection, instead of shrinking from him with the strongest repugnance; it could have been no worse. On the contrary, it would have been better, for his preservation would then have naturally and tenderly addressed my heart.

My first care was to close the shutters, so that no light might be seen from without, and then to close and make fast the doors. While I did so, he stood at the table drinking rum and eating biscuit; and when I saw him thus engaged, I saw my convict on the marshes at his meal again. It almost seemed to me as if he must stoop down presently, to file at his leg.

When I had gone into Herbert's room, and had shut off any other communication between it and the staircase than through the room in which our conversation had been held, I asked him if he would go to bed? He said yes, but asked me for some of my "gentleman's linen" to put on in the morning.

I brought it out, and laid it ready for him, and my blood again ran cold when he again took me by both hands to give me good night.

I got away from him, without knowing how I did it, and mended the fire in the room where we had been together, and sat down by it, afraid to go to bed. For an hour or more, I remained too stunned to think; and it was not until I began to think, that I began fully to know how wrecked I was, and how the ship in which I had sailed was gone to pieces.

Miss Havisham's intentions towards me, all a mere dream; Estella not designed for me; I only suffered in Satis House as a convenience, a sting for the greedy relations, a model with a mechanical heart to practise on when no other practice was at hand; those were the first smarts I had. But, sharpest and deepest pain of all—it was for the convict, guilty of I knew not what crimes, and liable to be taken out of those rooms where I sat thinking, and hanged at the Old Bailey door, that I had deserted Joe.

I would not have gone back to Joe now, I would not have gone back to Biddy now, for any consideration; simply, I suppose, because my sense of my own worthless conduct to them was greater than every consideration. No wisdom on earth could have given me the comfort that I should have derived from their simplicity and fidelity; but I could never, never, undo what I had done.

In every rage of wind and rush of rain, I heard pursuers. Twice, I could have sworn there was a knocking and whispering at the outer door. With these fears upon me, I began either to imagine or recall that I had had mysterious warnings of this man's approach. That, for weeks gone by, I had passed faces in the streets which I had thought like his. That these likenesses had grown more numerous, as he, coming over the sea, had drawn nearer. That his wicked spirit had somehow sent these messengers to mine, and that now on this stormy night he was as good as his word, and with me.

Crowding up with these reflections came the reflection that I had seen him with my childish eyes to be a desperately violent man; that I had heard that other convict reiterate that he had tried to murder him; that I had seen him down in the ditch tearing and fighting like a wild beast. Out of such remembrances I brought into the light of the fire a half-formed terror that it might not be safe to be shut up there with him in the dead of the wild solitary night. This dilated until it filled the room, and impelled me to take a candle and go in and look at my dreadful burden.

He had rolled a handkerchief round his head, and his face was set and lowering in his sleep. But he was asleep, and quietly too, though he had a pistol lying on the pillow. Assured of this, I softly removed the key to the outside of his door, and turned it on him before I again sat down by the fire. Gradually I slipped from the chair and lay on the floor. When I awoke without having parted in my sleep with the perception of my wretchedness, the clocks of the Eastward churches were striking five, the candles were wasted out, the fire was dead, and the wind and rain intensified the thick black darkness.

THIS IS THE END OF THE SECOND STAGE OF PIP'S EXPECTATIONS

VOLUME THREE

CHAPTER 1

It was fortunate for me that I had to take precautions to ensure (so far as I could) the safety of my dreaded visitor; for, this thought pressing on me when I awoke, held other thoughts in a confused concourse at a distance.

The impossibility of keeping him concealed in the chambers was self-evident. It could not be done, and the attempt to do it would inevitably engender suspicion. True, I had no Avenger in my service now, but I was looked after by an inflammatory old female, assisted by an animated rag-bag whom she called her niece, and to keep a room secret from them would be to invite curiosity and exaggeration. They both had weak eyes, which I had long attributed to their chronically looking in at keyholes, and they were always at hand when not wanted; indeed that was their only reliable quality besides larceny. Not to get up a mystery with these people, I resolved to announce in the morning that my uncle had unexpectedly come from the country.

This course I decided on while I was yet groping about in the darkness for the means of getting a light. Not stumbling on the means after all, I was fain to go out to the adjacent Lodge and get the watchman there to come with his lantern. Now, in groping my way down the black staircase I fell over something, and that something was a man crouching in a corner.

As the man made no answer when I asked him what he did there, but eluded my touch in silence, I ran to the Lodge and urged the watchman to come quickly; telling him of the incident on the way back. The wind being as fierce as ever, we did not care to endanger the light in the lantern by rekindling the extinguished lamps on the staircase, but we examined the staircase from the bottom to the top and found no one there. It then occurred to me as possible that the man might have slipped into my rooms; so, lighting my candle at the watchman's, and leaving him standing at the door, I examined them carefully, including the room in which my dreaded guest lay asleep. All was quiet, and assuredly no other man was in those chambers.

It troubled me that there should have been a lurker on the stairs, on that night of all nights in the year, and I asked the watchman, on the chance of eliciting some hopeful explanation as I handed him a dram at the door, whether he had admitted at his gate any gentleman who had perceptibly been dining out? Yes, he said; at different times of the night, three. One lived in Fountain Court, and the other two lived in the Lane, and he had seen them all go home. Again, the only other man who dwelt in the house of which my chambers formed a part had been in the country for some weeks, and he certainly had not returned in the night, because we had seen his door with his seal on it as we came up-stairs."

The night being so bad, sir," said the watchman, as he gave me back my glass, "uncommon few have come in at my gate. Besides them three gentlemen that I have named, I don't call to mind another since about eleven o'clock, when a stranger asked for you."

"My uncle," I muttered. "Yes."

"You saw him, sir?"

"Yes. Oh yes."

"Likewise the person with him?"

"Person with him!" I repeated.

"I judged the person to be with him," returned the watchman. "The person stopped, when he stopped to make inquiry of me, and the person took this way when he took this way."

"What sort of person?"

The watchman had not particularly noticed; he should say a working person; to the best of his belief, he had a dust-colored kind of clothes on, under a dark coat. The watchman made more light of the matter than I did, and naturally; not having my reason for attaching weight to it.

When I had got rid of him, which I thought it well to do without prolonging explanations, my mind was much troubled by these two circumstances taken together. Whereas they were easy of innocent solution apart—as, for instance, some diner out or diner at home, who had not gone near this watchman's gate, might have strayed to my staircase and dropped asleep there—and my nameless visitor might have brought some one with him to show him the way—still, joined, they had an ugly look to one as prone to distrust and fear as the changes of a few hours had made me.

I lighted my fire, which burnt with a raw pale flare at that time of the morning, and fell into a doze before it. I seemed to have been dozing a whole night when the clocks struck six. As there was full an hour and a half between me and daylight, I dozed again; now, waking up uneasily, with prolix conversations about nothing, in my ears; now, making thunder of the wind in the chimney; at length, falling off into a profound sleep from which the daylight woke me with a start.

All this time I had never been able to consider my own situation, nor could I do so yet. I had not the power to attend to it. I was greatly dejected and distressed, but in an incoherent wholesale sort of way. As to forming any plan for the future, I could as soon have formed an elephant. When I opened the shutters and looked out at the wet wild morning, all of a leaden hue; when I walked from room to room; when I sat down again shivering, before the fire, waiting for my laundress to appear; I thought how miserable I was, but hardly knew why, or how long I had been so, or on what day of the week I made the reflection, or even who I was that made it.

At last, the old woman and the niece came in—the latter with a head not easily distinguishable from her dusty broom—and testified surprise at sight of me and the fire. To whom I imparted how my uncle had come in the night and was then asleep, and how the breakfast preparations were to be modified accordingly. Then I washed and dressed while they knocked the furniture about and made a dust; and so, in a sort of dream or sleep-waking, I found myself sitting by the fire again, waiting for—Him—to come to breakfast.

By-and-by, his door opened and he came out. I could not bring myself to bear the sight of him, and I thought he had a worse look by daylight.

"I do not even know," said I, speaking low as he took his seat at the table, "by what name to call you. I have given out that you are my uncle."

"That's it, dear boy! Call me uncle."

"You assumed some name, I suppose, on board ship?"

"Yes, dear boy. I took the name of Provis."

"Do you mean to keep that name?"

"Why, yes, dear boy, it's as good as another—unless you'd like another."

"What is your real name?" I asked him in a whisper.

"Magwitch," he answered, in the same tone; "chrisen'd Abel."

"What were you brought up to be?"

"A warmint, dear boy."

He answered quite seriously, and used the word as if it denoted some profession.

"When you came into the Temple last night—" said I, pausing to wonder whether that could really have been last night, which seemed so long ago.

"Yes, dear boy?"

"When you came in at the gate and asked the watchman the way here, had you any one with you?"

"With me? No, dear boy."

"But there was some one there?"

"I didn't take particular notice," he said, dubiously, "not knowing the ways of the place. But I think there *was* a person, too, come in alonger me."

"Are you known in London?"

"I hope not!" said he, giving his neck a jerk with his forefinger that made me turn hot and sick.

"Were you known in London, once?"

"Not over and above, dear boy. I was in the provinces mostly."

"Were you—tried—in London?"

"Which time?" said he, with a sharp look.

"The last time."

He nodded. "First knowed Mr. Jaggers that way. Jaggers was for me."

It was on my lips to ask him what he was tried for, but he took up a knife, gave it a flourish, and with the words, "And what I done is worked out and paid for!" fell to at his breakfast.

He ate in a ravenous way that was very disagreeable, and all his actions were uncouth, noisy, and greedy. Some of his teeth had failed him since I saw him eat on the marshes, and as he turned his food in his mouth, and turned his head sideways to bring his strongest fangs to bear upon it, he looked terribly like a hungry old dog. If I had begun with any appetite, he would have taken it away, and I should have sat much as I did—repelled from him by an insurmountable aversion, and gloomily looking at the cloth.

"I'm a heavy grubber, dear boy," he said, as a polite kind of apology when he made an end of his meal, "but I always was. If it had been in my constitution to be a lighter grubber, I might ha' got into lighter trouble. Similarly, I must have my smoke. When I was first hired out as shepherd t'other side the world, it's my belief I should ha' turned into a molloncolly-mad sheep myself, if I hadn't a had my smoke."

As he said so, he got up from table, and putting his hand into the breast of the pea-coat he wore, brought out a short black pipe, and a handful of loose tobacco of the kind that is called Negro-head. Having filled his pipe, he put the surplus tobacco back again, as if his pocket were a drawer. Then, he took a live coal from the fire with the tongs, and lighted his pipe at it, and then turned round on the hearth-rug with his back to the fire, and went through his favorite action of holding out both his hands for mine.

"And this," said he, dandling my hands up and down in his, as he puffed at his pipe— "and this is the gentleman what I made! The real genuine One! It does me good fur to look at you, Pip. All I stip'late, is, to stand by and look at you, dear boy!"

I released my hands as soon as I could, and found that I was beginning slowly to settle down to the contemplation of my condition. What I was chained to, and how heavily, became intelligible to me, as I heard his hoarse voice, and sat looking up at his furrowed bald head with its iron gray hair at the sides.

"I mustn't see my gentleman a footing it in the mire of the streets; there mustn't be no mud on *his* boots. My gentleman must have horses, Pip! Horses to ride, and horses to drive, and horses for his servant to ride and drive as well. Shall colonists have their horses (and blood 'uns, if you please, good Lord!) and not my London gentleman? No, no. We'll show 'em another pair of shoes than that, Pip; won't us?"

He took out of his pocket a great thick pocket-book, bursting with papers, and tossed it on the table.

"There's something worth spending in that there book, dear boy. It's yourn. All I've got ain't mine; it's yourn. Don't you be afeerd on it. There's more where that come from. I've come to the old country fur to see my gentleman spend his money *like* a gentleman. That'll be *my* pleasure. My pleasure 'ull be fur to see him do it. And blast you all!" he wound up, looking round the room and snapping his fingers once with a loud snap, "blast you every one, from the judge in his wig, to the colonist a stirring up the dust, I'll show a better gentleman than the whole kit on you put together!"

"Stop!" said I, almost in a frenzy of fear and dislike, "I want to speak to you. I want to know what is to be done. I want to know how you are to be kept out of danger, how long you are going to stay, what projects you have."

"Look'ee here, Pip," said he, laying his hand on my arm in a suddenly altered and subdued manner; "first of all, look'ee here. I forgot myself half a minute ago. What I said was low; that's what it was; low. Look'ee here, Pip. Look over it. I ain't a going to be low."

"First," I resumed, half groaning, "what precautions can be taken against your being recognized and seized?"

"No, dear boy," he said, in the same tone as before, "that don't go first. Lowness goes first. I ain't took so many year to make a gentleman, not without knowing what's due to him. Look'ee here, Pip. I was low; that's what I was; low. Look over it, dear boy."

Some sense of the grimly-ludicrous moved me to a fretful laugh, as I replied, "I *have* looked over it. In Heaven's name, don't harp upon it!"

"Yes, but look'ee here," he persisted. "Dear boy, I ain't come so fur, not fur to be low. Now, go on, dear boy. You was a saying—"

"How are you to be guarded from the danger you have incurred?"

"Well, dear boy, the danger ain't so great. Without I was informed agen, the danger ain't so much to signify. There's Jaggers, and there's Wemmick, and there's you. Who else is there to inform?"

"Is there no chance person who might identify you in the street?" said I.

"Well," he returned, "there ain't many. Nor yet I don't intend to advertise myself in the newspapers by the name of A.M. come back from Botany Bay; and years have rolled away, and who's to gain by it? Still, look'ee here, Pip. If the danger had been fifty times as great, I should ha' come to see you, mind you, just the same."

"And how long do you remain?"

"How long?" said he, taking his black pipe from his mouth, and dropping his jaw as he stared at me. "I'm not a going back. I've come for good."

"Where are you to live?" said I. "What is to be done with you? Where will you be safe?"

"Dear boy," he returned, "there's disguising wigs can be bought for money, and there's hair powder, and spectacles, and black clothes—shorts and what not. Others has done it safe afore, and what others has done afore, others can do agen. As to the where and how of living, dear boy, give me your own opinions on it."

"You take it smoothly now," said I, "but you were very serious last night, when you swore it was Death."

"And so I swear it is Death," said he, putting his pipe back in his mouth, "and Death by the rope, in the open street not fur from this, and it's serious that you should fully understand it to be so. What then, when that's once done? Here I am. To go back now 'ud be as bad as to stand ground—worse. Besides, Pip, I'm here, because I've meant it by you, years and years. As to what I dare, I'm a old bird now, as has dared all manner of traps since first he was fledged, and I'm not afeerd to perch upon a scarecrow. If there's Death hid inside of it, there is, and let him come out, and I'll face him, and then I'll believe in him and not afore. And now let me have a look at my gentleman agen."

Once more, he took me by both hands and surveyed me with an air of admiring proprietorship: smoking with great complacency all the while.

It appeared to me that I could do no better than secure him some quiet lodging hard by, of which he might take possession when Herbert returned: whom I expected in two or three days. That the secret must be confided to Herbert as a matter of unavoidable necessity, even if I could have put the immense relief I should derive from sharing it with him out of the question, was plain to me. But it was by no means so plain to Mr. Provis (I resolved to call him by that name), who reserved his consent to Herbert's participation until he should have seen him and formed a favorable judgment of his physiognomy. "And even then, dear boy," said he, pulling a greasy little clasped black Testament out of his pocket, "we'll have him on his oath."

To state that my terrible patron carried this little black book about the world solely to swear people on in cases of emergency, would be to state what I never quite established— but this I can say, that I never knew him put it to any other use. The book itself had the appearance of having been stolen from some court of justice, and perhaps his knowledge of its antecedents, combined with his own experience in that wise, gave him a reliance on its powers as a sort of legal spell or charm. On this first occasion of his producing it, I recalled how he had made me swear fidelity in the churchyard long ago, and how he had described himself last night as always swearing to his resolutions in his solitude.

As he was at present dressed in a seafaring slop suit, in which he looked as if he had some parrots and cigars to dispose of, I next discussed with him what dress he should wear. He cherished an extraordinary belief in the virtues of "shorts" as a disguise, and had in his own mind sketched a dress for himself that would have made him something between a dean and a dentist. It was with considerable difficulty that I won him over to the assumption of a dress more like a prosperous farmer's; and we arranged that he should cut his hair close, and wear a little powder. Lastly, as he had not yet been seen by the laundress or her niece, he was to keep himself out of their view until his change of dress was made.

It would seem a simple matter to decide on these precautions; but in my dazed, not to say distracted, state, it took so long, that I did not get out to further them until two or three in the afternoon. He was to remain shut up in the chambers while I was gone, and was on no account to open the door.

There being to my knowledge a respectable lodging-house in Essex Street, the back of which looked into the Temple, and was almost within hail of my windows, I first of all repaired to that house, and was so fortunate as to secure the second floor for my uncle, Mr. Provis. I then went from shop to shop, making such purchases as were necessary to the change in his appearance. This business transacted, I turned my face, on my own account, to Little Britain. Mr. Jaggers was at his desk, but, seeing me enter, got up immediately and stood before his fire.

"Now, Pip," said he, "be careful."

"I will, sir," I returned. For, coming along I had thought well of what I was going to say.

"Don't commit yourself," said Mr. Jaggers, "and don't commit any one. You understand—any one. Don't tell me anything: I don't want to know anything; I am not curious."

Of course I saw that he knew the man was come.

"I merely want, Mr. Jaggers," said I, "to assure myself that what I have been told is true. I have no hope of its being untrue, but at least I may verify it."

Mr. Jaggers nodded. "But did you say 'told' or 'informed'?" he asked me, with his head on one side, and not looking at me, but looking in a listening way at the floor. "Told would seem to imply verbal communication. You can't have verbal communication with a man in New South Wales, you know."

"I will say, informed, Mr. Jaggers."

"Good."

"I have been informed by a person named Abel Magwitch, that he is the benefactor so long unknown to me."

"That is the man," said Mr. Jaggers, "—in New South Wales."

"And only he?" said I.

"And only he," said Mr. Jaggers.

"I am not so unreasonable, sir, as to think you at all responsible for my mistakes and wrong conclusions; but I always supposed it was Miss Havisham."

"As you say, Pip," returned Mr. Jaggers, turning his eyes upon me coolly, and taking a bite at his forefinger, "I am not at all responsible for that."

"And yet it looked so like it, sir," I pleaded with a downcast heart.

"Not a particle of evidence, Pip," said Mr. Jaggers, shaking his head and gathering up his skirts. "Take nothing on its looks; take everything on evidence. There's no better rule."

"I have no more to say," said I, with a sigh, after standing silent for a little while. "I have verified my information, and there's an end."

"And Magwitch—in New South Wales—having at last disclosed himself," said Mr. Jaggers, "you will comprehend, Pip, how rigidly throughout my communication with you, I have always adhered to the strict line of fact. There has never been the least departure from the strict line of fact. You are quite aware of that?"

"Quite, sir."

"I communicated to Magwitch—in New South Wales— when he first wrote to me—from New South Wales—the caution that he must not expect me ever to deviate from the strict line of fact. I also communicated to him another caution. He appeared to me to have obscurely hinted in his letter at some distant idea he had of seeing you in England here. I cautioned him that I must hear no more of that; that he was not at all likely to obtain a pardon; that he was expatriated for the term of his natural life; and that his presenting himself in this country would be an act of felony, rendering him liable to the extreme penalty of the law. I gave Magwitch that caution," said Mr. Jaggers, looking hard at me; "I wrote it to New South Wales. He guided himself by it, no doubt."

"No doubt," said I.

"I have been informed by Wemmick," pursued Mr. Jaggers, still looking hard at me, "that he has received a letter, under date Portsmouth, from a colonist of the name of Purvis, or—"

"Or Provis," I suggested.

"Or Provis—thank you, Pip. Perhaps it is Provis? Perhaps you know it's Provis?"

"Yes," said I.

"You know it's Provis. A letter, under date Portsmouth, from a colonist of the name of Provis, asking for the particulars of your address, on behalf of Magwitch. Wemmick sent him the particulars, I understand, by return of post. Probably it is through Provis that you have received the explanation of Magwitch—in New South Wales?"

"It came through Provis," I replied.

"Good day, Pip," said Mr. Jaggers, offering his hand; "glad to have seen you. In writing by post to Magwitch—in New South Wales—or in communicating with him through Provis, have the goodness to mention that the particulars and vouchers of our long account shall be sent to you, together with the balance; for there is still a balance remaining. Good day, Pip!"

We shook hands, and he looked hard at me as long as he could see me. I turned at the door, and he was still looking hard at me, while the two vile casts on the shelf seemed to be trying to get their eyelids open, and to force out of their swollen throats, "O, what a man he is!"

Wemmick was out, and though he had been at his desk he could have done nothing for me. I went straight back to the Temple, where I found the terrible Provis drinking rum and water and smoking negro-head, in safety.

Next day the clothes I had ordered all came home, and he put them on. Whatever he put on, became him less (it dismally seemed to me) than what he had worn before. To my thinking, there was something in him that made it hopeless to attempt to disguise him. The more I dressed him and the better I dressed him, the more he looked like the slouching fugitive on the marshes. This effect on my anxious fancy was partly referable, no doubt, to his old face and manner growing more familiar to me; but I believe too that he dragged one of his legs as if there were still a weight of iron on it, and that from head to foot there was Convict in the very grain of the man.

The influences of his solitary hut-life were upon him besides, and gave him a savage air that no dress could tame; added to these were the influences of his subsequent branded life among men, and, crowning all, his consciousness that he was dodging and hiding now. In all his ways of sitting and standing, and eating and drinking—of brooding about in a high-shouldered reluctant style—of taking out his great horn-handled jackknife and wiping it on his legs and cutting his food—of lifting light glasses and cups to his lips, as if they were clumsy pannikins—of chopping a wedge off his bread, and soaking up with it the last fragments of gravy round and round his plate, as if to make the most of an allowance, and then drying his finger-ends on it, and then swallowing it—in these ways and a thousand other small nameless instances arising every minute in the day, there was Prisoner, Felon, Bondsman, plain as plain could be.

It had been his own idea to wear that touch of powder, and I had conceded the powder after overcoming the shorts. But I can compare the effect of it, when on, to nothing but the probable effect of rouge upon the dead; so awful was the manner in which everything in him that it was most desirable to repress, started through that thin layer of pretence, and seemed to come blazing out at the crown of his head. It was abandoned as soon as tried, and he wore his grizzled hair cut short.

Words cannot tell what a sense I had, at the same time, of the dreadful mystery that he was to me. When he fell asleep of an evening, with his knotted hands clenching the sides of the easy-chair, and his bald head tattooed with deep wrinkles falling forward on his breast, I would sit and look at him, wondering what he had done, and loading him with all the crimes in the Calendar, until the impulse was powerful on me to start up and fly from him. Every hour so increased my abhorrence of him, that I even think I might have yielded to this impulse in the first agonies of being so haunted, notwithstanding all he had done for me and the risk he ran, but for the knowledge that Herbert must soon come back. Once, I actually did start out of bed in the night, and begin to dress myself in my worst clothes, hurriedly intending to leave him there with everything else I possessed, and enlist for India as a private soldier.

I doubt if a ghost could have been more terrible to me, up in those lonely rooms in the long evenings and long nights, with the wind and the rain always rushing by. A ghost could not have been taken and hanged on my account, and the consideration that he could be, and the dread that he would be, were no small addition to my horrors. When he was not asleep, or playing a complicated kind of Patience with a ragged pack of cards of his own—a game that I never saw before or since, and in which he recorded his winnings by sticking his jackknife into the table—when he was not engaged in either of these pursuits, he would ask me to read to him— "Foreign language, dear boy!" While I complied, he, not comprehending a single word, would stand before the fire surveying me with the air of an Exhibitor, and I would see him, between the fingers of the hand with which I shaded my face, appealing in dumb show to the furniture to take notice of my proficiency. The imaginary student pursued by the misshapen creature he had impiously made, was not more wretched than I, pursued by the creature who had made me, and recoiling from him with a stronger repulsion, the more he admired me and the fonder he was of me.

This is written of, I am sensible, as if it had lasted a year. It lasted about five days. Expecting Herbert all the time, I dared not go out, except when I took Provis for an airing after dark. At length, one evening when dinner was over and I had dropped into a slumber quite worn out—for my nights had been agitated and my rest broken by fearful dreams—I was roused by the welcome footstep on the staircase. Provis, who had been asleep too, staggered up at the noise I made, and in an instant I saw his jackknife shining in his hand.

"Quiet! It's Herbert!" I said; and Herbert came bursting in, with the airy freshness of six hundred miles of France upon him.

"Handel, my dear fellow, how are you, and again how are you, and again how are you? I seem to have been gone a twelvemonth! Why, so I must have been, for you have grown quite thin and pale! Handel, my—Halloa! I beg your pardon."

He was stopped in his running on and in his shaking hands with me, by seeing Provis. Provis, regarding him with a fixed attention, was slowly putting up his jackknife, and groping in another pocket for something else.

"Herbert, my dear friend," said I, shutting the double doors, while Herbert stood staring and wondering, "something very strange has happened. This is—a visitor of mine."

"It's all right, dear boy!" said Provis coming forward, with his little clasped black book, and then addressing himself to Herbert. "Take it in your right hand. Lord strike you dead on the spot, if ever you split in any way sumever! Kiss it!"

"Do so, as he wishes it," I said to Herbert. So, Herbert, looking at me with a friendly uneasiness and amazement, complied, and Provis immediately shaking hands with him, said, "Now you're on your oath, you know. And never believe me on mine, if Pip shan't make a gentleman on you!"

CHAPTER 2

In vain should I attempt to describe the astonishment and disquiet of Herbert, when he and I and Provis sat down before the fire, and I recounted the whole of the secret. Enough, that I saw my own feelings reflected in Herbert's face, and not least among them, my repugnance towards the man who had done so much for me.

What would alone have set a division between that man and us, if there had been no other dividing circumstance, was his triumph in my story. Saving his troublesome sense of having been "low" on one occasion since his return—on which point he began to hold forth to Herbert, the moment my revelation was finished—he had no perception of the possibility of my finding any fault with my good fortune. His boast that he had made me a gentleman, and that he had come to see me support the character on his ample resources, was made for me quite as much as for himself. And that it was a highly agreeable boast to both of us, and that we must both be very proud of it, was a conclusion quite established in his own mind.

"Though, look'ee here, Pip's comrade," he said to Herbert, after having discoursed for some time, "I know very well that once since I come back—for half a minute—I've been low. I said to Pip, I knowed as I had been low. But don't you fret yourself on that score. I ain't made Pip a gentleman, and Pip ain't a going to make you a gentleman, not fur me not to know what's due to ye both. Dear boy, and Pip's comrade, you two may count upon me always having a gen-teel muzzle on. Muzzled I have been since that half a minute when I was betrayed into lowness, muzzled I am at the present time, muzzled I ever will be."

Herbert said, "Certainly," but looked as if there were no specific consolation in this, and remained perplexed and dismayed. We were anxious for the time when he would go to his lodging and leave us together, but he was evidently jealous of leaving us together, and sat late. It was midnight before I took him round to Essex Street, and saw him safely in at his own dark door. When it closed upon him, I experienced the first moment of relief I had known since the night of his arrival.

Never quite free from an uneasy remembrance of the man on the stairs, I had always looked about me in taking my guest out after dark, and in bringing him back; and I looked about me now. Difficult as it is in a large city to avoid the suspicion of being watched, when the mind is conscious of danger in that regard, I could not persuade myself that any of the people within sight cared about my movements. The few who were passing passed on their several ways, and the street was empty when I turned back into the Temple. Nobody had come out at the gate with us, nobody went in at the gate with me. As I crossed by the fountain, I saw his lighted back windows looking bright and quiet, and, when I stood for a few moments in the doorway of the building where I lived, before going up the stairs, Garden Court was as still and lifeless as the staircase was when I ascended it.

Herbert received me with open arms, and I had never felt before so blessedly what it is to have a friend. When he had spoken some sound words of sympathy and encouragement, we sat down to consider the question, What was to be done?

The chair that Provis had occupied still remaining where it had stood—for he had a barrack way with him of hanging about one spot, in one unsettled manner, and going through one round of observances with his pipe and his negro-head and his jackknife and his pack of cards, and what not, as if it were all put down for him on a slate—I say his chair remaining where it had stood, Herbert unconsciously took it, but next moment started out of it, pushed it away, and took another. He had no occasion to say after that that he had conceived an aversion for my patron, neither had I occasion to confess my own. We interchanged that confidence without shaping a syllable.

"What," said I to Herbert, when he was safe in another chair, "what is to be done?"

"My poor dear Handel," he replied, holding his head, "I am too stunned to think."

"So was I, Herbert, when the blow first fell. Still, something must be done. He is intent upon various new expenses—horses, and carriages, and lavish appearances of all kinds. He must be stopped somehow."

"You mean that you can't accept—"

"How can I?" I interposed, as Herbert paused. "Think of him! Look at him!"

An involuntary shudder passed over both of us.

"Yet I am afraid the dreadful truth is, Herbert, that he is attached to me, strongly attached to me. Was there ever such a fate!"

"My poor dear Handel," Herbert repeated.

"Then," said I, "after all, stopping short here, never taking another penny from him, think what I owe him already! Then again: I am heavily in debt—very heavily for me, who have now no expectations—and I have been bred to no calling, and I am fit for nothing."

"Well, well, well!" Herbert remonstrated. "Don't say fit for nothing."

"What am I fit for? I know only one thing that I am fit for, and that is, to go for a soldier. And I might have gone, my dear Herbert, but for the prospect of taking counsel with your friendship and affection."

Of course I broke down there: and of course Herbert, beyond seizing a warm grip of my hand, pretended not to know it.

"Anyhow, my dear Handel," said he presently, "soldiering won't do. If you were to renounce this patronage and these favors, I suppose you would do so with some faint hope of one day repaying what you have already had. Not very strong, that hope, if you went soldiering! Besides, it's absurd. You would be infinitely better in Clarriker's house, small as it is. I am working up towards a partnership, you know."

Poor fellow! He little suspected with whose money.

"But there is another question," said Herbert. "This is an ignorant, determined man, who has long had one fixed idea. More than that, he seems to me (I may misjudge him) to be a man of a desperate and fierce character."

"I know he is," I returned. "Let me tell you what evidence I have seen of it." And I told him what I had not mentioned in my narrative, of that encounter with the other convict.

"See, then," said Herbert; "think of this! He comes here at the peril of his life, for the realization of his fixed idea. In the moment of realization, after all his toil and waiting, you cut the ground from under his feet, destroy his idea, and make his gains worthless to him. Do you see nothing that he might do, under the disappointment?"

"I have seen it, Herbert, and dreamed of it, ever since the fatal night of his arrival. Nothing has been in my thoughts so distinctly as his putting himself in the way of being taken."

"Then you may rely upon it," said Herbert, "that there would be great danger of his doing it. That is his power over you as long as he remains in England, and that would be his reckless course if you forsook him."

I was so struck by the horror of this idea, which had weighed upon me from the first, and the working out of which would make me regard myself, in some sort, as his murderer, that I could not rest in my chair, but began pacing to and fro. I said to Herbert, meanwhile, that even if Provis were recognized and taken, in spite of himself, I should be wretched as the cause, however innocently. Yes; even though I was so wretched in having him at large and near me, and even though I would far rather have worked at the forge all the days of my life than I would ever have come to this!

But there was no staving off the question, What was to be done?

"The first and the main thing to be done," said Herbert, "is to get him out of England. You will have to go with him, and then he may be induced to go."

"But get him where I will, could I prevent his coming back?"

"My good Handel, is it not obvious that with Newgate in the next street, there must be far greater hazard in your breaking your mind to him and making him reckless, here, than elsewhere. If a pretext to get him away could be made out of that other convict, or out of anything else in his life, now."

"There, again!" said I, stopping before Herbert, with my open hands held out, as if they contained the desperation of the case. "I know nothing of his life. It has almost made me mad to sit here of a night and see him before me, so bound up with my fortunes and misfortunes, and yet so unknown to me, except as the miserable wretch who terrified me two days in my childhood!"

Herbert got up, and linked his arm in mine, and we slowly walked to and fro together, studying the carpet.

"Handel," said Herbert, stopping, "you feel convinced that you can take no further benefits from him; do you?"

"Fully. Surely you would, too, if you were in my place?"

"And you feel convinced that you must break with him?"

"Herbert, can you ask me?"

"And you have, and are bound to have, that tenderness for the life he has risked on your account, that you must save him, if possible, from throwing it away. Then you must get him out of England before you stir a finger to extricate yourself. That done, extricate yourself, in Heaven's name, and we'll see it out together, dear old boy."

It was a comfort to shake hands upon it, and walk up and down again, with only that done.

"Now, Herbert," said I, "with reference to gaining some knowledge of his history. There is but one way that I know of. I must ask him point-blank."

"Yes. Ask him," said Herbert, "when we sit at breakfast in the morning." For he had said, on taking leave of Herbert, that he would come to breakfast with us.

With this project formed, we went to bed. I had the wildest dreams concerning him, and woke unrefreshed; I woke, too, to recover the fear which I had lost in the night, of his being found out as a returned transport. Waking, I never lost that fear.

He came round at the appointed time, took out his jackknife, and sat down to his meal. He was full of plans "for his gentleman's coming out strong, and like a gentleman," and urged me to begin speedily upon the pocket-book which he had left in my possession. He considered the chambers and his own lodging as temporary residences, and advised me to look out at once for a "fashionable crib" near Hyde Park, in which he could have "a shake-down." When he had made an end of his breakfast, and was wiping his knife on his leg, I said to him, without a word of preface:

"After you were gone last night, I told my friend of the struggle that the soldiers found you engaged in on the marshes, when we came up. You remember?"

"Remember!" said he. "I think so!"

"We want to know something about that man—and about you. It is strange to know no more about either, and particularly you, than I was able to tell last night. Is not this as good a time as another for our knowing more?"

"Well!" he said, after consideration. "You're on your oath, you know, Pip's comrade?"

"Assuredly," replied Herbert.

"As to anything I say, you know," he insisted. "The oath applies to all."

"I understand it to do so."

"And look'ee here! Wotever I done is worked out and paid for," he insisted again.

"So be it."

He took out his black pipe and was going to fill it with negro-head, when, looking at the tangle of tobacco in his hand, he seemed to think it might perplex the thread of his narrative. He put it back again, stuck his pipe in a button-hole of his coat, spread a hand on each knee, and after turning an angry eye on the fire for a few silent moments, looked round at us and said what follows.

CHAPTER 3

"Dear boy and Pip's comrade. I am not a going fur to tell you my life like a song, or a story-book. But to give it you short and handy, I'll put it at once into a mouthful of English. In jail and out of jail, in jail and out of jail, in jail and out of jail. There, you've got it. That's *my* life pretty much, down to such times as I got shipped off, arter Pip stood my friend.

"I've been done everything to, pretty well—except hanged. I've been locked up as much as a silver tea-kittle. I've been carted here and carted there, and put out of this town, and put out of that town, and stuck in the stocks, and whipped and worried and drove. I've no more notion where I was born than you have—if so much. I first become aware of myself down in Essex, a thieving turnips for my living. Summun had run away from me—a man—a tinker—and he'd took the fire with him, and left me wery cold.

"I know'd my name to be Magwitch, chrisen'd Abel. How did I know it? Much as I know'd the birds' names in the hedges to be chaffinch, sparrer, thrush. I might have thought it was all lies together, only as the birds' names come out true, I supposed mine did.

"So fur as I could find, there warn't a soul that see young Abel Magwitch, with us little on him as in him, but wot caught fright at him, and either drove him off, or took him up. I was took up, took up, took up, to that extent that I reg'larly grow'd up took up.

"This is the way it was, that when I was a ragged little creetur as much to be pitied as ever I see (not that I looked in the glass, for there warn't many insides of furnished houses known to me), I got the name of being hardened. 'This is a terrible hardened one,' they says to prison wisitors, picking out me. 'May be said to live in jails, this boy.' Then they looked at me, and I looked at them, and they measured my head, some on 'em—they had better a measured my stomach—and others on 'em giv me tracts what I couldn't read, and made me speeches what I couldn't understand. They always went on agen me about the Devil. But what the Devil was I to do? I must put something into my stomach, mustn't I?—Howsomever, I'm a getting low, and I know what's due. Dear boy and Pip's comrade, don't you be afeerd of me being low.

"Tramping, begging, thieving, working sometimes when I could—though that warn't as often as you may think, till you put the question whether you would ha' been over-ready to give me work yourselves—a bit of a poacher, a bit of a laborer, a bit of a wagoner, a bit of a haymaker, a bit of a hawker, a bit of most things that don't pay and lead to trouble, I got to be a man. A deserting soldier in a Traveller's Rest, what lay hid up to the chin under a lot of taturs, learnt me to read; and a travelling Giant what signed his name at a penny a time learnt me to write. I warn't locked up as often now as formerly, but I wore out my good share of key-metal still.

"At Epsom races, a matter of over twenty years ago, I got acquainted wi' a man whose skull I'd crack wi' this poker, like the claw of a lobster, if I'd got it on this hob. His right name was Compeyson; and that's the man, dear boy, what you see me a pounding in the ditch, according to what you truly told your comrade arter I was gone last night.

"He set up fur a gentleman, this Compeyson, and he'd been to a public boarding-school and had learning. He was a smooth one to talk, and was a dab at the ways of gentlefolks. He was good-looking too. It was the night afore the great race, when I found him on the heath, in a booth that I know'd on. Him and some more was a sitting among the tables when I went in, and the landlord (which had a knowledge of me, and was a sporting one) called him out, and said, 'I think this is a man that might suit you,'—meaning I was.

"Compeyson, he looks at me very noticing, and I look at him. He has a watch and a chain and a ring and a breast-pin and a handsome suit of clothes.

"'To judge from appearances, you're out of luck,' says Compeyson to me.

"'Yes, master, and I've never been in it much.' (I had come out of Kingston Jail last on a vagrancy committal. Not but what it might have been for something else; but it warn't.)

"'Luck changes,' says Compeyson; 'perhaps yours is going to change.'

"I says, 'I hope it may be so. There's room.'

"'What can you do?' says Compeyson.

"'Eat and drink,' I says; 'if you'll find the materials.'

"Compeyson laughed, looked at me again very noticing, giv me five shillings, and appointed me for next night. Same place.

"I went to Compeyson next night, same place, and Compeyson took me on to be his man and pardner. And what was Compeyson's business in which we was to go pardners? Compeyson's business was the swindling, handwriting forging, stolen bank-note passing, and such-like. All sorts of traps as Compeyson could set with his head, and keep his own legs out of and get the profits from and let another man in for, was Compeyson's business. He'd no more heart than a iron file, he was as cold as death, and he had the head of the Devil afore mentioned.

"There was another in with Compeyson, as was called Arthur—not as being so chrisen'd, but as a surname. He was in a Decline, and was a shadow to look at. Him and Compeyson had been in a bad thing with a rich lady some years afore, and they'd made a pot of money by it; but Compeyson betted and gamed, and he'd have run through the king's taxes. So, Arthur was a dying, and a dying poor and with the horrors on him, and Compeyson's wife (which Compeyson kicked mostly) was a having pity on him when she could, and Compeyson was a having pity on nothing and nobody.

"I might a took warning by Arthur, but I didn't; and I won't pretend I was partick'ler—for where 'ud be the good on it, dear boy and comrade? So I begun wi' Compeyson, and a poor tool I was in his hands. Arthur lived at the top of Compeyson's house (over nigh Brentford it was), and Compeyson kept a careful account agen him for board and lodging, in case he should ever get better to work it out. But Arthur soon settled the account. The second or third time as ever I see him, he come a tearing down into Compeyson's parlor late at night, in only a flannel gown, with his hair all in a sweat, and he says to Compeyson's wife, 'Sally, she really is upstairs alonger me, now, and I can't get rid of her. She's all in white,' he says, 'wi' white flowers in her hair, and she's awful mad, and she's got a shroud hanging over her arm, and she says she'll put it on me at five in the morning.'

"Says Compeyson: 'Why, you fool, don't you know she's got a living body? And how should she be up there, without coming through the door, or in at the window, and up the stairs?'

"'I don't know how she's there,' says Arthur, shivering dreadful with the horrors, 'but she's standing in the corner at the foot of the bed, awful mad. And over where her heart's broke—*you* broke it!—there's drops of blood.'

"Compeyson spoke hardy, but he was always a coward. 'Go up alonger this drivelling sick man,' he says to his wife, 'and Magwitch, lend her a hand, will you?' But he never come nigh himself.

"Compeyson's wife and me took him up to bed agen, and he raved most dreadful. 'Why look at her!' he cries out. 'She's a shaking the shroud at me! Don't you see her? Look at her eyes!

Ain't it awful to see her so mad?' Next he cries, 'She'll put it on me, and then I'm done for! Take it away from her, take it away!' And then he catched hold of us, and kep on a talking to her, and answering of her, till I half believed I see her myself.

"Compeyson's wife, being used to him, giv him some liquor to get the horrors off, and by and by he quieted. 'O, she's gone! Has her keeper been for her?' he says. 'Yes,' says Compeyson's wife. 'Did you tell him to lock her and bar her in?' 'Yes.' 'And to take that ugly thing away from her?' 'Yes, yes, all right.' 'You're a good creetur,' he says, 'don't leave me, whatever you do, and thank you!'

"He rested pretty quiet till it might want a few minutes of five, and then he starts up with a scream, and screams out, 'Here she is! She's got the shroud again. She's unfolding it. She's coming out of the corner. She's coming to the bed. Hold me, both on you—one of each side—don't let her touch me with it. Hah! she missed me that time. Don't let her throw it over my shoulders. Don't let her lift me up to get it round me. She's lifting me up. Keep me down!' Then he lifted himself up hard, and was dead.

"Compeyson took it easy as a good riddance for both sides. Him and me was soon busy, and first he swore me (being ever artful) on my own book—this here little black book, dear boy, what I swore your comrade on.

"Not to go into the things that Compeyson planned, and I done—which 'ud take a week—I'll simply say to you, dear boy, and Pip's comrade, that that man got me into such nets as made me his black slave. I was always in debt to him, always under his thumb, always a working, always a getting into danger. He was younger than me, but he'd got craft, and he'd got learning, and he overmatched me five hundred times told and no mercy. My Missis as I had the hard time wi'—Stop though! I ain't brought *her* in—"

He looked about him in a confused way, as if he had lost

his place in the book of his remembrance; and he turned his face to the fire, and spread his hands broader on his knees, and lifted them off and put them on again.

"There ain't no need to go into it," he said, looking round once more. "The time wi' Compeyson was a'most as hard a time as ever I had; that said, all's said. Did I tell you as I was tried, alone, for misdemeanor, while with Compeyson?"

I answered, No.

"Well!" he said, "I was, and got convicted. As to took up on suspicion, that was twice or three times in the four or five year that it lasted; but evidence was wanting. At last, me and Compeyson was both committed for felony—on a charge of putting stolen notes in circulation—and there was other charges behind. Compeyson says to me, 'Separate defences, no communication,' and that was all. And I was so miserable poor, that I sold all the clothes I had, except what hung on my back, afore I could get Jaggers.

"When we was put in the dock, I noticed first of all what a gentleman Compeyson looked, wi' his curly hair and his black clothes and his white pocket-handkercher, and what a common sort of a wretch I looked. When the prosecution opened and the evidence was put short, aforehand, I noticed how heavy it all bore on me, and how light on him. When the evidence was giv in the box, I noticed how it was always me that had come for'ard, and could be swore to, how it was always me that the money had been paid to, how it was always me that had seemed to work the thing and get the profit. But when the defence come on, then I see the plan plainer; for, says the counsellor for Compeyson, 'My lord and gentlemen, here you has afore you, side by side, two persons as your eyes can separate wide; one, the younger, well brought up, who will be spoke to as such; one, the elder, ill brought up, who will be spoke to as such; one, the younger, seldom if ever seen in these here transactions, and only suspected; t'other, the elder, always seen in 'em and always wi'his guilt brought home. Can you doubt, if there is but one in it, which is the one, and, if there is two in it, which is much the worst one?' And such-like. And when it come to character, warn't it Compeyson as had been to the school, and warn't it his schoolfellows as was in this position and in that, and warn't it him as had been know'd by witnesses in such clubs and societies, and nowt to his disadvantage? And warn't it me as had been tried afore, and as had been know'd up hill and down dale in Bridewells and Lock-Ups! And when it come to speech-making, warn't it Compeyson as could speak to 'em wi' his face dropping every now and then into his white pocket-handkercher—ah! and wi' verses in his speech, too—and warn't it me as could only say, 'Gentlemen, this man at my side is a most precious rascal'? And when the verdict come, warn't it Compeyson as was recommended to mercy on account of good character and bad company, and giving up all the information he could agen me, and warn't it me as got never a word but Guilty? And when I says to Compeyson, 'Once out of this court, I'll smash that face of yourn!' ain't it Compeyson as prays the Judge to be protected, and gets two turnkeys stood betwixt us? And when we're sentenced, ain't it him as gets seven year, and me fourteen, and ain't it him as the Judge is sorry for, because he might a done so well, and ain't it me as the Judge perceives to be a old offender of wiolent passion, likely to come to worse?"

He had worked himself into a state of great excitement, but he checked it, took two or three short breaths, swallowed as often, and stretching out his hand towards me said, in a reassuring manner, "I ain't a going to be low, dear boy!"

He had so heated himself that he took out his handkerchief and wiped his face and head and neck and hands, before he could go on.

"I had said to Compeyson that I'd smash that face of his, and I swore Lord smash mine! to do it. We was in the same prison-ship, but I couldn't get at him for long, though I tried. At last I come behind him and hit him on the cheek to turn him round and get a smashing one at him, when I was seen and seized. The black-hole of that ship warn't a strong one, to a judge of black-holes that could swim and dive. I escaped to the shore, and I was a hiding among the graves there, envying them as was in 'em and all over, when I first see my boy!"

He regarded me with a look of affection that made him almost abhorrent to me again, though I had felt great pity for him.

"By my boy, I was giv to understand as Compeyson was out on them marshes too. Upon my soul, I half believe he escaped in his terror, to get quit of me, not knowing it was me as had got ashore. I hunted him down. I smashed his face. 'And now,' says I 'as the worst thing I can do, caring nothing for myself, I'll drag you back.' And I'd have swum off, towing him by the hair, if it had come to that, and I'd a got him aboard without the soldiers.

"Of course he'd much the best of it to the last—his character was so good. He had escaped when he was made half wild by me and my murderous intentions; and his punishment was light. I was put in irons, brought to trial again, and sent for life. I didn't stop for life, dear boy and Pip's comrade, being here."

"He wiped himself again, as he had done before, and then slowly took his tangle of tobacco from his pocket, and plucked his pipe from his button-hole, and slowly filled it, and began to smoke.

"Is he dead?" I asked, after a silence.

"Is who dead, dear boy?"

"Compeyson."

"He hopes *I* am, if he's alive, you may be sure," with a fierce look. "I never heerd no more of him."

Herbert had been writing with his pencil in the cover of a book. He softly pushed the book over to me, as Provis stood smoking with his eyes on the fire, and I read in it:

"Young Havisham's name was Arthur. Compeyson is the man who professed to be Miss Havisham's lover."

I shut the book and nodded slightly to Herbert, and put the book by; but we neither of us said anything, and both looked at Provis as he stood smoking by the fire.

CHAPTER 4

Why should I pause to ask how much of my shrinking from Provis might be traced to Estella? Why should I loiter on my road, to compare the state of mind in which I had tried to rid myself of the stain of the prison before meeting her at the coach-office, with the state of mind in which I now reflected on the abyss between Estella in her pride and beauty, and the returned transport whom I harboured? The road would be none the smoother for it, the end would be none the better for it, he would not be helped, nor I extenuated.

A new fear had been engendered in my mind by his narrative; or rather, his narrative had given form and purpose to the fear that was already there. If Compeyson were alive and should discover his return, I could hardly doubt the consequence. That Compeyson stood in mortal fear of him, neither of the two could know much better than I; and that any such man as that man had been described to be would hesitate to release himself for good from a dreaded enemy by the safe means of becoming an informer was scarcely to be imagined.

Never had I breathed, and never would I breathe—or so I resolved—a word of Estella to Provis. But, I said to Herbert that, before I could go abroad, I must see both Estella and Miss Havisham. This was when we were left alone on the night of the day when Provis told us his story. I resolved to go out to Richmond next day, and I went.

On my presenting myself at Mrs. Brandley's, Estella's maid was called to tell that Estella had gone into the country. Where? To Satis House, as usual. Not as usual, I said, for she had never yet gone there without me; when was she coming back? There was an air of reservation in the answer which increased my perplexity, and the answer was, that her maid believed she was only coming back at all for a little while. I could make nothing of this, except that it was meant that I should make nothing of it, and I went home again in complete discomfiture.

Another night consultation with Herbert after Provis was gone home (I always took him home, and always looked well about me), led us to the conclusion that nothing should be said about going abroad until I came back from Miss Havisham's. In the mean time, Herbert and I were to consider separately what it would be best to say; whether we should devise any pretence of being afraid that he was under suspicious observation; or whether I, who had never yet been abroad, should propose an expedition. We both knew that I had but to propose anything, and he would consent. We agreed that his remaining many days in his present hazard was not to be thought of.

Next day I had the meanness to feign that I was under a binding promise to go down to Joe; but I was capable of almost any meanness towards Joe or his name. Provis was to be strictly careful while I was gone, and Herbert was to take the charge of him that I had taken. I was to be absent only one night, and, on my return, the gratification of his impatience for my starting as a gentleman on a greater scale was to be begun. It occurred to me then, and as I afterwards found to Herbert also, that he might be best got away across the water, on that pretence—as, to make purchases, or the like.

Having thus cleared the way for my expedition to Miss Havisham's, I set off by the early morning coach before it was yet light, and was out on the open country road when the day came creeping on, halting and whimpering and shivering, and wrapped in patches of cloud and rags of mist, like a beggar. When we drove up to the Blue Boar after a drizzly ride, whom should I see come out under the gateway, toothpick in hand, to look at the coach, but Bentley Drummle!

As he pretended not to see me, I pretended not to see him. It was a very lame pretence on both sides; the lamer, because we both went into the coffee-room, where he had just finished his breakfast, and where I ordered mine. It was poisonous to me to see him in the town, for I very well knew why he had come there.

Pretending to read a smeary newspaper long out of date, which had nothing half so legible in its local news, as the foreign matter of coffee, pickles, fish sauces, gravy, melted butter, and wine with which it was sprinkled all over, as if it had taken the measles in a highly irregular form, I sat at my table while he stood before the fire. By degrees it became an enormous injury to me that he stood before the fire. And I got up, determined to have my share of it. I had to put my hand behind his legs for the poker when I went up to the fireplace to stir the fire, but still pretended not to know him.

"Is this a cut?" said Mr. Drummle.

"Oh!" said I, poker in hand; "it's you, is it? How do you do? I was wondering who it was, who kept the fire off."

With that, I poked tremendously, and having done so, planted myself side by side with Mr. Drummle, my shoulders squared and my back to the fire.

"You have just come down?" said Mr. Drummle, edging me a little away with his shoulder.

"Yes," said I, edging *him* a little away with *my* shoulder.

"Beastly place," said Drummle. "Your part of the country, I think?"

"Yes," I assented. "I am told it's very like your Shropshire."

"Not in the least like it," said Drummle.

Here Mr. Drummle looked at his boots and I looked at mine, and then Mr. Drummle looked at my boots, and I looked at his.

"Have you been here long?" I asked, determined not to yield an inch of the fire.

"Long enough to be tired of it," returned Drummle, pretending to yawn, but equally determined.

"Do you stay here long?"

"Can't say," answered Mr. Drummle. "Do you?"

"Can't say," said I.

I felt here, through a tingling in my blood, that if Mr. Drummle's shoulder had claimed another hair's breadth of room, I should have jerked him into the window; equally, that if my own shoulder had urged a similar claim, Mr. Drummle would have jerked me into the nearest box. He whistled a little. So did I.

"Large tract of marshes about here, I believe?" said Drummle.

"Yes. What of that?" said I.

Mr. Drummle looked at me, and then at my boots, and then said, "Oh!" and laughed.

"Are you amused, Mr. Drummle?"

"No," said he, "not particularly. I am going out for a ride in the saddle. I mean to explore those marshes for amusement. Out-of-the-way villages there, they tell me. Curious little public-houses—and smithies—and that. Waiter!"

"Yes, sir."

"Is that horse of mine ready?"

"Brought round to the door, sir."

"I say. Look here, you sir. The lady won't ride to-day; the weather won't do."

"Very good, sir."

"And I don't dine, because I'm going to dine at the lady's."

"Very good, sir."

Then, Drummle glanced at me, with an insolent triumph on his great-jowled face that cut me to the heart, dull as he was, and so exasperated me, that I felt inclined to take him in my arms (as the robber in the story-book is said to have taken the old lady) and seat him on the fire.

One thing was manifest to both of us, and that was, that until relief came, neither of us could relinquish the fire. There we stood, well squared up before it, shoulder to shoulder and foot to foot, with our hands behind us, not budging an inch. The horse was visible outside in the drizzle at the door, my breakfast was put on the table, Drummle's was cleared away, the waiter invited me to begin, I nodded, we both stood our ground.

"Have you been to the Grove since?" said Drummle.

"No," said I, "I had quite enough of the Finches the last time I was there."

"Was that when we had a difference of opinion?"

"Yes," I replied, very shortly.

"Come, come! They let you off easily enough," sneered Drummle. "You shouldn't have lost your temper."

"Mr. Drummle," said I, "you are not competent to give advice on that subject. When I lose my temper (not that I admit having done so on that occasion), I don't throw glasses."

"I do," said Drummle.

After glancing at him once or twice, in an increased state of smouldering ferocity, I said:

"Mr. Drummle, I did not seek this conversation, and I don't think it an agreeable one."

"I am sure it's not," said he, superciliously over his shoulder; "I don't think anything about it."

"And therefore," I went on, "with your leave, I will suggest that we hold no kind of communication in future."

"Quite my opinion," said Drummle, "and what I should have suggested myself, or done—more likely—without suggesting. But don't lose your temper. Haven't you lost enough without that?"

"What do you mean, sir?"

"Wai-ter!" said Drummle, by way of answering me.

The waiter reappeared.

"Look here, you sir. You quite understand that the young lady don't ride to-day, and that I dine at the young lady's?"

"Quite so, sir!"

When the waiter had felt my fast-cooling teapot with the palm of his hand, and had looked imploringly at me, and had gone out, Drummle, careful not to move the shoulder next me, took a cigar from his pocket and bit the end off, but showed no sign of stirring. Choking and boiling as I was, I felt that we could not go a word further, without introducing Estella's name, which I could not endure to hear him utter; and therefore I looked stonily at the opposite wall, as if there were no one present, and forced myself to silence. How long we might have remained in this ridiculous position it is impossible to say, but for the incursion of three thriving farmers—laid on by the waiter, I think—who came into the coffee-room unbuttoning their great-coats and rubbing their hands, and before whom, as they charged at the fire, we were obliged to give way.

I saw him through the window, seizing his horse's mane, and mounting in his blundering brutal manner, and sidling and backing away. I thought he was gone, when he came back, calling for a light for the cigar in his mouth, which he had forgotten. A man in a dust-colored dress appeared with what was wanted—I could not have said from where: whether from the inn yard, or the street, or where not—and as Drummle leaned down from the saddle and lighted his cigar and laughed, with a jerk of his head towards the coffee-room windows, the slouching shoulders and ragged hair of this man whose back was towards me reminded me of Orlick.

Too heavily out of sorts to care much at the time whether it were he or no, or after all to touch the breakfast, I washed the weather and the journey from my face and hands, and went out to the memorable old house that it would have been so much the better for me never to have entered, never to have seen.

CHAPTER 5

In the room where the dressing-table stood, and where the wax-candles burnt on the wall, I found Miss Havisham and Estella; Miss Havisham seated on a settee near the fire, and Estella on a cushion at her feet. Estella was knitting, and Miss Havisham was looking on. They both raised their eyes as I went in, and both saw an alteration in me. I derived that, from the look they interchanged.

"And what wind," said Miss Havisham, "blows you here, Pip?"

Though she looked steadily at me, I saw that she was rather confused. Estella, pausing a moment in her knitting with her eyes upon me, and then going on, I fancied that I read in the action of her fingers, as plainly as if she had told me in the dumb alphabet, that she perceived I had discovered my real benefactor.

"Miss Havisham," said I, "I went to Richmond yesterday, to speak to Estella; and finding that some wind had blown her here, I followed."

Miss Havisham motioning to me for the third or fourth time to sit down, I took the chair by the dressing-table, which I had often seen her occupy. With all that ruin at my feet and about me, it seemed a natural place for me, that day.

"What I had to say to Estella, Miss Havisham, I will say before you, presently—in a few moments. It will not surprise you, it will not displease you. I am as unhappy as you can ever have meant me to be."

Miss Havisham continued to look steadily at me. I could see in the action of Estella's fingers as they worked that she attended to what I said; but she did not look up.

"I have found out who my patron is. It is not a fortunate discovery, and is not likely ever to enrich me in reputation, station, fortune, anything. There are reasons why I must say no more of that. It is not my secret, but another's."

As I was silent for a while, looking at Estella and considering how to go on, Miss Havisham repeated, "It is not your secret, but another's. Well?"

"When you first caused me to be brought here, Miss Havisham, when I belonged to the village over yonder, that I wish I had never left, I suppose I did really come here, as any other chance boy might have come—as a kind of servant, to gratify a want or a whim, and to be paid for it?"

"Ay, Pip," replied Miss Havisham, steadily nodding her head; "you did."

"And that Mr. Jaggers—"

"Mr. Jaggers," said Miss Havisham, taking me up in a firm tone, "had nothing to do with it, and knew nothing of it. His being my lawyer, and his being the lawyer of your patron is a coincidence. He holds the same relation towards numbers of people, and it might easily arise. Be that as it may, it did arise, and was not brought about by any one."

Any one might have seen in her haggard face that there was no suppression or evasion so far.

"But when I fell into the mistake I have so long remained in, at least you led me on?" said I.

"Yes," she returned, again nodding steadily, "I let you go on."

"Was that kind?"

"Who am I," cried Miss Havisham, striking her stick upon the floor and flashing into wrath so suddenly that Estella glanced up at her in surprise, "who am I, for God's sake, that I should be kind?"

It was a weak complaint to have made, and I had not

meant to make it. I told her so, as she sat brooding after this outburst.

"Well, well, well!" she said. "What else?"

"I was liberally paid for my old attendance here," I said, to soothe her, "in being apprenticed, and I have asked these questions only for my own information. What follows has another (and I hope more disinterested) purpose. In humoring my mistake, Miss Havisham, you punished—practised on—perhaps you will supply whatever term expresses your intention, without offence—your self-seeking relations?"

"I did. Why, they would have it so! So would you. What has been my history, that I should be at the pains of entreating either them or you not to have it so! You made your own snares. *I* never made them."

Waiting until she was quiet again—for this, too, flashed out of her in a wild and sudden way—I went on.

"I have been thrown among one family of your relations, Miss Havisham, and have been constantly among them since I went to London. I know them to have been as honestly under my delusion as I myself. And I should be false and base if I did not tell you, whether it is acceptable to you or no, and whether you are inclined to give credence to it or no, that you deeply wrong both Mr. Matthew Pocket and his son Herbert, if you suppose them to be otherwise than generous, upright, open, and incapable of anything designing or mean."

"They are your friends," said Miss Havisham.

"They made themselves my friends," said I, "when they supposed me to have superseded them; and when Sarah Pocket, Miss Georgiana, and Mistress Camilla were not my friends, I think."

This contrasting of them with the rest seemed, I was glad to see, to do them good with her. She looked at me keenly for a little while, and then said quietly:

"What do you want for them?"

"Only," said I, "that you would not confound them with the others. They may be of the same blood, but, believe me, they are not of the same nature."

Still looking at me keenly, Miss Havisham repeated:

"What do you want for them?"

"I am not so cunning, you see," I said, in answer, conscious that I reddened a little, "as that I could hide from you, even if I desired, that I do want something. Miss Havisham, if you would spare the money to do my friend Herbert a lasting service in life, but which from the nature of the case must be done without his knowledge, I could show you how."

"Why must it be done without his knowledge?" she asked, settling her hands upon her stick, that she might regard me the more attentively.

"Because," said I, "I began the service myself, more than two years ago, without his knowledge, and I don't want to be betrayed. Why I fail in my ability to finish it, I cannot explain. It is a part of the secret which is another person's and not mine."

She gradually withdrew her eyes from me, and turned them on the fire. After watching it for what appeared in the silence and by the light of the slowly wasting candles to be a long time, she was roused by the collapse of some of the red coals, and looked towards me again—at first, vacantly—then, with a gradually concentrating attention. All this time Estella knitted on. When Miss Havisham had fixed her attention on me, she said, speaking as if there had been no lapse in our dialogue:

"What else?"

"Estella," said I, turning to her now, and trying to command my trembling voice, "you know I love you. You know that I have loved you long and dearly."

She raised her eyes to my face, on being thus addressed, and her fingers plied their work, and she looked at me with an unmoved countenance. I saw that Miss Havisham glanced from me to her, and from her to me.

"I should have said this sooner, but for my long mistake. It induced me to hope that Miss Havisham meant us for one another. While I thought you could not help yourself, as it were, I refrained from saying it. But I must say it now."

Preserving her unmoved countenance, and with her fingers still going, Estella shook her head.

"I know," said I, in answer to that action; "I know. I have no hope that I shall ever call you mine, Estella. I am ignorant what may become of me very soon, how poor I may be, or where I may go. Still, I love you. I have loved you ever since I first saw you in this house."

Looking at me perfectly unmoved and with her fingers busy, she shook her head again.

"It would have been cruel in Miss Havisham, horribly cruel, to practise on the susceptibility of a poor boy, and to torture me through all these years with a vain hope and an idle pursuit, if she had reflected on the gravity of what she did. But I think she did not. I think that, in the endurance of her own trial, she forgot mine, Estella."

I saw Miss Havisham put her hand to her heart and hold it there, as she sat looking by turns at Estella and at me.

"It seems," said Estella, very calmly, "that there are sentiments, fancies—I don't know how to call them—which I am not able to comprehend. When you say you love me, I know what you mean, as a form of words; but nothing more. You address nothing in my breast, you touch nothing there. I don't care for what you say at all. I have tried to warn you of this; now, have I not?"

I said in a miserable manner, "Yes."

"Yes. But you would not be warned, for you thought I did not mean it. Now, did you not think so?"

"I thought and hoped you could not mean it. You, so young, untried, and beautiful, Estella! Surely it is not in Nature."

"It is in *my* nature," she returned. And then she added, with a stress upon the words, "It is in the nature formed within me. I make a great difference between you and all other people when I say so much. I can do no more."

"Is it not true," said I, "that Bentley Drummle is in town here, and pursuing you?"

"It is quite true," she replied, referring to him with the indifference of utter contempt.

"That you encourage him, and ride out with him, and that he dines with you this very day?"

She seemed a little surprised that I should know it, but again replied, "Quite true."

"You cannot love him, Estella!"

Her fingers stopped for the first time, as she retorted rather angrily, "What have I told you? Do you still think, in spite of it, that I do not mean what I say?"

"You would never marry him, Estella?"

She looked towards Miss Havisham, and considered for a moment with her work in her hands. Then she said, "Why not tell you the truth? I am going to be married to him."

I dropped my face into my hands, but was able to control myself better than I could have expected, considering what agony it gave me to hear her say those words. When I raised my face again, there was such a ghastly look upon Miss Havisham's, that it impressed me, even in my passionate hurry and grief.

"Estella, dearest Estella, do not let Miss Havisham lead you into this fatal step. Put me aside for ever—you have done so, I well know—but bestow yourself on some worthier person than Drummle. Miss Havisham gives you to him, as the greatest slight and injury that could be done to the many far better men who admire you, and to the few who truly love you. Among those few there may be one who loves you even as dearly, though he has not loved you as long, as I. Take him, and I can bear it better, for your sake!"

My earnestness awoke a wonder in her that seemed as if it

would have been touched with compassion, if she could have rendered me at all intelligible to her own mind.

"I am going," she said again, in a gentler voice, "to be married to him. The preparations for my marriage are making, and I shall be married soon. Why do you injuriously introduce the name of my mother by adoption? It is my own act."

"Your own act, Estella, to fling yourself away upon a brute?"

"On whom should I fling myself away?" she retorted, with a smile.

"Should I fling myself away upon the man who would the soonest feel (if people do feel such things) that I took nothing to him? There! It is done. I shall do well enough, and so will my husband. As to leading me into what you call this fatal step, Miss Havisham would have had me wait, and not marry yet; but I am tired of the life I have led, which has very few charms for me, and I am willing enough to change it. Say no more. We shall never understand each other."

"Such a mean brute, such a stupid brute!" I urged, in despair.

"Don't be afraid of my being a blessing to him," said Estella; "I shall not be that. Come! Here is my hand. Do we part on this, you visionary boy—or man?"

"O Estella!" I answered, as my bitter tears fell fast on her hand, do what I would to restrain them; "even if I remained in England and could hold my head up with the rest, how could I see you Drummle's wife?"

"Nonsense," she returned, "nonsense. This will pass in no time."

"Never, Estella!"

"You will get me out of your thoughts in a week."

"Out of my thoughts! You are part of my existence, part of myself. You have been in every line I have ever read since I first came here, the rough common boy whose poor heart you wounded even then. You have been in every prospect I have ever seen since—on the river, on the sails of the ships, on the marshes, in the clouds, in the light, in the darkness, in the wind, in the woods, in the sea, in the streets. You have been the embodiment of every graceful fancy that my mind has ever become acquainted with. The stones of which the strongest London buildings are made are not more real, or more impossible to be displaced by your hands, than your presence and influence have been to me, there and everywhere, and will be. Estella, to the last hour of my life, you cannot choose but remain part of my character, part of the little good in me, part of the evil. But, in this separation, I associate you only with the good; and I will faithfully hold you to that always, for you must have done me far more good than harm, let me feel now what sharp distress I may. O God bless you, God forgive you!"

In what ecstasy of unhappiness I got these broken words out of myself, I don't know. The rhapsody welled up within me, like blood from an inward wound, and gushed out. I held her hand to my lips some lingering moments, and so I left her. But ever afterwards, I remembered—and soon afterwards with stronger reason—that while Estella looked at me merely with incredulous wonder, the spectral figure of Miss Havisham, her hand still covering her heart, seemed all resolved into a ghastly stare of pity and remorse.

All done, all gone! So much was done and gone, that when I went out at the gate, the light of the day seemed of a darker color than when I went in. For a while, I hid myself among some lanes and by-paths, and then struck off to walk all the way to London. For, I had by that time come to myself so far as to consider that I could not go back to the inn and see Drummle there; that I could not bear to sit upon the coach and be spoken to; that I could do nothing half so good for myself as tire myself out.

It was past midnight when I crossed London Bridge.

Pursuing the narrow intricacies of the streets which at that time tended westward near the Middlesex shore of the river, my readiest access to the Temple was close by the river-side, through Whitefriars. I was not expected till to-morrow; but I had my keys, and, if Herbert were gone to bed, could get to bed myself without disturbing him.

As it seldom happened that I came in at that Whitefriars gate after the Temple was closed, and as I was very muddy and weary, I did not take it ill that the night-porter examined me with much attention as he held the gate a little way open for me to pass in. To help his memory I mentioned my name.

"I was not quite sure, sir, but I thought so. Here's a note, sir. The messenger that brought it, said would you be so good as read it by my lantern?"

Much surprised by the request, I took the note. It was directed to Philip Pip, Esquire, and on the top of the superscription were the words, "Please read this, here." I opened it, the watchman holding up his light, and read inside, in Wemmick's writing:

"DON'T GO HOME."

CHAPTER 6

Turning from the Temple gate as soon as I had read the warning, I made the best of my way to Fleet Street, and there got a late hackney chariot and drove to the Hummums in Covent Garden. In those times a bed was always to be got there at any hour of the night, and the chamberlain, letting me in at his ready wicket, lighted the candle next in order on his shelf, and showed me straight into the bedroom next in order on his list. It was a sort of vault on the ground floor at the back, with a despotic monster of a four-post bedstead in it, straddling over the whole place, putting one of his arbitrary legs into the fireplace and another into the doorway, and squeezing the wretched little washing-stand in quite a Divinely Righteous manner.

As I had asked for a night-light, the chamberlain had brought me in, before he left me, the good old constitutional rushlight of those virtuous days—an object like the ghost of a walking-cane, which instantly broke its back if it were touched, which nothing could ever be lighted at, and which was placed in solitary confinement at the bottom of a high tin tower, perforated with round holes that made a staringly wide-awake pattern on the walls. When I had got into bed, and lay there footsore, weary, and wretched, I found that I could no more close my own eyes than I could close the eyes of this foolish Argus. And thus, in the gloom and death of the night, we stared at one another.

What a doleful night! How anxious, how dismal, how long! There was an inhospitable smell in the room, of cold soot and hot dust; and, as I looked up into the corners of the tester over my head, I thought what a number of blue-bottle flies from the butchers', and earwigs from the market, and grubs from the country, must be holding on up there, lying by for next summer. This led me to speculate whether any of them ever tumbled down, and then I fancied that I felt light falls on my face—a disagreeable turn of thought, suggesting other and more objectionable approaches up my back. When I had lain awake a little while, those extraordinary voices with which silence teems began to make themselves audible. The closet whispered, the fireplace sighed, the little washing-stand ticked, and one guitar-string played occasionally in the chest of drawers. At about the same time, the eyes on the wall acquired a new expression, and in every one of those staring rounds I saw written, DON'T GO HOME.

Whatever night-fancies and night-noises crowded on me, they never warded off this DON'T GO HOME. It plaited itself into whatever I thought of, as a bodily pain would have done. Not long before, I had read in the newspapers, how a gentleman unknown had come to the Hummums in the night, and had gone to bed, and had destroyed himself, and had been found in the morning weltering in blood. It came into my head that he must have occupied this very vault of mine, and I got out of bed to assure myself that there were no red marks about; then opened the door to look out into the passages, and cheer myself with the companionship of a distant light, near which I knew the chamberlain to be dozing. But all this time, why I was not to go home, and what had happened at home, and when I should go home, and whether Provis was safe at home, were questions occupying my mind so busily, that one might have supposed there could be no more room in it for any other theme. Even when I thought of Estella, and how we had parted that day forever, and when I recalled all the circumstances of our parting, and all her looks and tones, and the action of her fingers while she knitted—even then I was pursuing, here and there and everywhere, the caution, Don't go home. When at last I dozed, in sheer exhaustion of mind and body, it became a vast shadowy verb which I had to conjugate. Imperative mood, present tense: Do not thou go home, let him not go home, let us not go home, do not ye or you go home, let not them go home. Then potentially: I may not and I cannot go home; and I might not, could not, would not, and should not go home; until I felt that I was going distracted, and rolled over on the pillow, and looked at the staring rounds upon the wall again.

I had left directions that I was to be called at seven; for it was plain that I must see Wemmick before seeing any one else, and equally plain that this was a case in which his Walworth sentiments only could be taken. It was a relief to get out of the room where the night had been so miserable, and I needed no second knocking at the door to startle me from my uneasy bed.

The Castle battlements arose upon my view at eight o'clock. The little servant happening to be entering the fortress with two hot rolls, I passed through the postern and crossed the drawbridge in her company, and so came without announcement into the presence of Wemmick as he was making tea for himself and the Aged. An open door afforded a perspective view of the Aged in bed.

"Halloa, Mr. Pip!" said Wemmick. "You did come home, then?""Yes," I returned; "but I didn't go home."

"That's all right," said he, rubbing his hands. "I left a note for you at each of the Temple gates, on the chance. Which gate did you come to?"

I told him.

"I'll go round to the others in the course of the day and destroy the notes," said Wemmick; "it's a good rule never to leave documentary evidence if you can help it, because you don't know when it may be put in. I'm going to take a liberty with you. – *Would* you mind toasting this sausage for the Aged P.?"

I said I should be delighted to do it.

"Then you can go about your work, Mary Anne," said Wemmick to the little servant; "which leaves us to ourselves, don't you see, Mr. Pip?" he added, winking, as she disappeared.

I thanked him for his friendship and caution, and our discourse proceeded in a low tone, while I toasted the Aged's sausage and he buttered the crumb of the Aged's roll.

"Now, Mr. Pip, you know," said Wemmick, "you and I understand one another. We are in our private and personal capacities, and we have been engaged in a confidential transaction before to-day. Official sentiments are one thing. We are extra official."

I cordially assented. I was so very nervous, that I had already lighted the Aged's sausage like a torch, and been obliged to blow it out.

"I accidentally heard, yesterday morning," said Wemmick, "being in a certain place where I once took you—even between you and me, it's as well not to mention names when avoidable—"

"Much better not," said I. "I understand you."

"I heard there by chance, yesterday morning," said Wemmick, "that a certain person not altogether of uncolonial pursuits, and not unpossessed of portable property—I don't know who it may really be—we won't name this person—"

"Not necessary," said I.

"—had made some little stir in a certain part of the world where a good many people go, not always in gratification of their own inclinations, and not quite irrespective of the government expense—"

In watching his face, I made quite a firework of the Aged's sausage, and greatly discomposed both my own attention and Wemmick's; for which I apologized.

"—by disappearing from such place, and being no

more heard of thereabouts. From which," said Wemmick, "conjectures had been raised and theories formed. I also heard that you at your chambers in Garden Court, Temple, had been watched, and might be watched again."

"By whom?" said I.

"I wouldn't go into that," said Wemmick, evasively, "it might clash with official responsibilities. I heard it, as I have in my time heard other curious things in the same place. I don't tell it you on information received. I heard it."

He took the toasting-fork and sausage from me as he spoke, and set forth the Aged's breakfast neatly on a little tray. Previous to placing it before him, he went into the Aged's room with a clean white cloth, and tied the same under the old gentleman's chin, and propped him up, and put his nightcap on one side, and gave him quite a rakish air. Then he placed his breakfast before him with great care, and said, "All right, ain't you, Aged P.?" To which the cheerful Aged replied, "All right, John, my boy, all right!" As there seemed to be a tacit understanding that the Aged was not in a presentable state, and was therefore to be considered invisible, I made a pretence of being in complete ignorance of these proceedings.

"This watching of me at my chambers (which I have once had reason to suspect)," I said to Wemmick when he came back, "is inseparable from the person to whom you have adverted; is it?"

Wemmick looked very serious. "I couldn't undertake to say that, of my own knowledge. I mean, I couldn't undertake to say it was at first. But it either is, or it will be, or it's in great danger of being."

As I saw that he was restrained by fealty to Little Britain from saying as much as he could, and as I knew with thankfulness to him how far out of his way he went to say what he did, I could not press him. But I told him, after a little meditation over the fire, that I would like to ask him a question, subject to his answering or not answering, as he deemed right, and sure that his course would be right. He paused in his breakfast, and crossing his arms, and pinching his shirt-sleeves (his notion of in-door comfort was to sit without any coat), he nodded to me once, to put my question.

"You have heard of a man of bad character, whose true name is Compeyson?"

He answered with one other nod.

"Is he living?"

One other nod.

"Is he in London?"

He gave me one other nod, compressed the post-office exceedingly, gave me one last nod, and went on with his breakfast.

"Now," said Wemmick, "questioning being over," which he emphasized and repeated for my guidance, "I come to what I did, after hearing what I heard. I went to Garden Court to find you; not finding you, I went to Clarriker's to find Mr. Herbert."

"And him you found?" said I, with great anxiety.

"And him I found. Without mentioning any names or going into any details, I gave him to understand that if he was aware of anybody—Tom, Jack, or Richard—being about the chambers, or about the immediate neighbourhood, he had better get Tom, Jack, or Richard out of the way while you were out of the way."

"He would be greatly puzzled what to do?"

"He *was* puzzled what to do; not the less, because I gave him my opinion that it was not safe to try to get Tom, Jack, or Richard too far out of the way at present. Mr. Pip, I'll tell you something. Under existing circumstances, there is no place like a great city when you are once in it. Don't break cover too soon. Lie close. Wait till things slacken, before you try the open, even for foreign air."

I thanked him for his valuable advice, and asked him what Herbert had done?

"Mr. Herbert," said Wemmick, "after being all of a heap for half an hour, struck out a plan. He mentioned to me as a secret, that he is courting a young lady who has, as no doubt you are aware, a bedridden Pa. Which Pa, having been in the Purser line of life, lies a-bed in a bow-window where he can see the ships sail up and down the river. You are acquainted with the young lady, most probably?"

"Not personally," said I.

The truth was, that she had objected to me as an expensive companion who did Herbert no good, and that, when Herbert had first proposed to present me to her, she had received the proposal with such very moderate warmth, that Herbert had felt himself obliged to confide the state of the case to me, with a view to the lapse of a little time before I made her acquaintance. When I had begun to advance Herbert's prospects by stealth, I had been able to bear this with cheerful philosophy: he and his affianced, for their part, had naturally not been very anxious to introduce a third person into their interviews; and thus, although I was assured that I had risen in Clara's esteem, and although the young lady and I had long regularly interchanged messages and remembrances by Herbert, I had never seen her. However, I did not trouble Wemmick with these particulars.

"The house with the bow-window," said Wemmick, "being by the river-side, down the Pool there between Limehouse and Greenwich, and being kept, it seems, by a very respectable widow who has a furnished upper floor to let, Mr. Herbert put it to me, what did I think of that as a temporary tenement for Tom, Jack, or Richard? Now, I thought very well of it, for three reasons I'll give you. That is to say: Firstly. It's altogether out of all your beats, and is well away from the usual heap of streets great and small. Secondly. Without going near it yourself, you could always hear of the safety of Tom, Jack, or Richard, through Mr. Herbert. Thirdly. After a while and when it might be prudent, if you should want to slip Tom, Jack, or Richard on board a foreign packet-boat, there he is—ready."

Much comforted by these considerations, I thanked Wemmick again and again, and begged him to proceed.

"Well, sir! Mr. Herbert threw himself into the business with a will, and by nine o'clock last night he housed Tom, Jack, or Richard—whichever it may be—you and I don't want to know—quite successfully. At the old lodgings it was understood that he was summoned to Dover, and, in fact, he was taken down the Dover road and cornered out of it. Now, another great advantage of all this is, that it was done without you, and when, if any one was concerning himself about your movements, you must be known to be ever so many miles off and quite otherwise engaged. This diverts suspicion and confuses it; and for the same reason I recommended that, even if you came back last night, you should not go home. It brings in more confusion, and you want confusion."

Wemmick, having finished his breakfast, here looked at his watch, and began to get his coat on.

"And now, Mr. Pip," said he, with his hands still in the sleeves, "I have probably done the most I can do; but if I can ever do more—from a Walworth point of view and in a strictly private and personal capacity—I shall be glad to do it. Here's the address. There can be no harm in your going here to-night, and seeing for yourself that all is well with Tom, Jack, or Richard, before you go home—which is another reason for your not going home last night. But, after you have gone home, don't go back here. You are very welcome, I am sure, Mr. Pip"; his hands were now out of his sleeves, and I was shaking them; "and let me finally impress one important point upon you." He laid his hands upon my shoulders, and added in a solemn whisper: "Avail yourself of this evening to lay hold of his portable property. You don't know what may happen to him. Don't let anything happen to the portable property."

Quite despairing of making my mind clear to Wemmick on this point, I forbore to try.

"Time's up," said Wemmick, "and I must be off. If you had nothing more pressing to do than to keep here till dark, that's what I should advise. You look very much worried, and it would do you good to have a perfectly quiet day with the Aged—he'll be up presently—and a little bit of—you remember the pig?"

"Of course," said I.

"Well; and a little bit of *him*. That sausage you toasted was his, and he was in all respects a first-rater. Do try him, if it is only for old acquaintance sake. Good by, Aged Parent!" in a cheery shout.

"All right, John; all right, my boy!" piped the old man from within.

I soon fell asleep before Wemmick's fire, and the Aged and I enjoyed one another's society by falling asleep before it more or less all day. We had loin of pork for dinner, and greens grown on the estate; and I nodded at the Aged with a good intention whenever I failed to do it drowsily. When it was quite dark, I left the Aged preparing the fire for toast; and I inferred from the number of teacups, as well as from his glances at the two little doors in the wall, that Miss Skiffins was expected.

CHAPTER 7

Eight o'clock had struck before I got into the air, that was scented, not disagreeably, by the chips and shavings of the long-shore boat-builders, and mast, oar, and block makers. All that water-side region of the upper and lower Pool below Bridge was unknown ground to me; and when I struck down by the river, I found that the spot I wanted was not where I had supposed it to be, and was anything but easy to find. It was called Mill Pond Bank, Chinks's Basin; and I had no other guide to Chinks's Basin than the Old Green Copper Rope-Walk.

It matters not what stranded ships repairing in dry docks I lost myself among, what old hulls of ships in course of being knocked to pieces, what ooze and slime and other dregs of tide, what yards of ship-builders and ship-breakers, what rusty anchors blindly biting into the ground, though for years off duty, what mountainous country of accumulated casks and timber, how many rope-walks that were not the Old Green Copper. After several times falling short of my destination and as often overshooting it, I came unexpectedly round a corner, upon Mill Pond Bank. It was a fresh kind of place, all circumstances considered, where the wind from the river had room to turn itself round; and there were two or three trees in it, and there was the stump of a ruined windmill, and there was the Old Green Copper Rope-walk—whose long and narrow vista I could trace in the moonlight, along a series of wooden frames set in the ground, that looked like superannuated haymaking-rakes which had grown old and lost most of their teeth.

Selecting from the few queer houses upon Mill Pond Bank a house with a wooden front and three stories of bow-window (not bay-window, which is another thing), I looked at the plate upon the door, and read there, Mrs. Whimple. That being the name I wanted, I knocked, and an elderly woman of a pleasant and thriving appearance responded. She was immediately deposed, however, by Herbert, who silently led me into the parlor and shut the door. It was an odd sensation to see his very familiar face established quite at home in that very unfamiliar room and region; and I found myself looking at him, much as I looked at the corner-cupboard with the glass and china, the shells upon the chimney-piece, and the coloured engravings on the wall, representing the death of Captain Cook, a ship-launch, and his Majesty King George the Third in a state coachman's wig, leather-breeches, and top-boots, on the terrace at Windsor.

"All is well, Handel," said Herbert, "and he is quite satisfied, though eager to see you. My dear girl is with her father; and if you'll wait till she comes down, I'll make you known to her, and then we'll go up stairs. —*That's* her father."

I had become aware of an alarming growling overhead, and had probably expressed the fact in my countenance.

"I am afraid he is a sad old rascal," said Herbert, smiling, "but I have never seen him. Don't you smell rum? He is always at it."

"At rum?" said I.

"Yes," returned Herbert, "and you may suppose how mild it makes his gout. He persists, too, in keeping all the provisions up stairs in his room, and serving them out. He keeps them on shelves over his head, and *will* weigh them all. His room must be like a chandler's shop."

While he thus spoke, the growling noise became a prolonged roar, and then died away.

"What else can be the consequence," said Herbert, in

explanation, "if he *will* cut the cheese? A man with the gout in his right hand—and everywhere else—can't expect to get through a Double Gloucester without hurting himself."

He seemed to have hurt himself very much, for he gave another furious roar.

"To have Provis for an upper lodger is quite a godsend to Mrs. Whimple," said Herbert, "for of course people in general won't stand that noise. A curious place, Handel; isn't it?"

It was a curious place, indeed; but remarkably well kept and clean.

"Mrs. Whimple," said Herbert, when I told him so, "is the best of housewives, and I really do not know what my Clara would do without her motherly help. For, Clara has no mother of her own, Handel, and no relation in the world but old Gruffandgrim."

"Surely that's not his name, Herbert?"

"No, no," said Herbert, "that's my name for him. His name is Mr. Barley. But what a blessing it is for the son of my father and mother to love a girl who has no relations, and who can never bother herself or anybody else about her family!"

Herbert had told me on former occasions, and now reminded me, that he first knew Miss Clara Barley when she was completing her education at an establishment at Hammersmith, and that on her being recalled home to nurse her father, he and she had confided their affection to the motherly Mrs. Whimple, by whom it had been fostered and regulated with equal kindness and discretion, ever since. It was understood that nothing of a tender nature could possibly be confided to old Barley, by reason of his being totally unequal to the consideration of any subject more psychological than Gout, Rum, and Purser's stores.

As we were thus conversing in a low tone while Old Barley's sustained growl vibrated in the beam that crossed the ceiling, the room door opened, and a very pretty, slight, dark-eyed girl of twenty or so came in with a basket in her hand: whom Herbert tenderly relieved of the basket, and presented, blushing, as "Clara." She really was a most charming girl, and might have passed for a captive fairy, whom that truculent Ogre, Old Barley, had pressed into his service.

"Look here," said Herbert, showing me the basket, with a compassionate and tender smile, after we had talked a little; "here's poor Clara's supper, served out every night. Here's her allowance of bread, and here's her slice of cheese, and here's her rum—which I drink. This is Mr. Barley's breakfast for to-morrow, served out to be cooked. Two mutton-chops, three potatoes, some split peas, a little flour, two ounces of butter, a pinch of salt, and all this black pepper. It's stewed up together, and taken hot, and it's a nice thing for the gout, I should think!"

There was something so natural and winning in Clara's resigned way of looking at these stores in detail, as Herbert pointed them out; and something so confiding, loving, and innocent in her modest manner of yielding herself to Herbert's embracing arm—and something so gentle in her, so much needing protection on Mill Pond Bank, by Chinks's Basin, and the Old Green Copper Rope-Walk, with Old Barley growling in the beam—that I would not have undone the engagement between her and Herbert for all the money in the pocket-book I had never opened.

I was looking at her with pleasure and admiration, when suddenly the growl swelled into a roar again, and a frightful bumping noise was heard above, as if a giant with a wooden leg were trying to bore it through the ceiling to come at us. Upon this Clara said to Herbert, "Papa wants me, darling!" and ran away.

"There is an unconscionable old shark for you!" said Herbert. "What do you suppose he wants now, Handel?"

"I don't know," said I. "Something to drink?"

"That's it!" cried Herbert, as if I had made a guess of extraordinary merit. "He keeps his grog ready mixed in a little tub on the table. Wait a moment, and you'll hear Clara lift him up to take some.—There he goes!" Another roar, with a prolonged shake at the end. "Now," said Herbert, as it was succeeded by silence, "he's drinking. Now," said Herbert, as the growl resounded in the beam once more, "he's down again on his back!"

Clara returned soon afterwards, and Herbert accompanied me up stairs to see our charge. As we passed Mr. Barley's door, he was heard hoarsely muttering within, in a strain that rose and fell like wind, the following Refrain, in which I substitute good wishes for something quite the reverse:—

"Ahoy! Bless your eyes, here's old Bill Barley. Here's old Bill Barley, bless your eyes. Here's old Bill Barley on the flat of his back, by the Lord. Lying on the flat of his back like a drifting old dead flounder, here's your old Bill Barley, bless your eyes. Ahoy! Bless you."

In this strain of consolation, Herbert informed me the invisible Barley would commune with himself by the day and night together; Often, while it was light, having, at the same time, one eye at a telescope which was fitted on his bed for the convenience of sweeping the river.

In his two cabin rooms at the top of the house, which were fresh and airy, and in which Mr. Barley was less audible than below, I found Provis comfortably settled. He expressed no alarm, and seemed to feel none that was worth mentioning; but it struck me that he was softened—indefinably, for I could not have said how, and could never afterwards recall how when I tried, but certainly.

The opportunity that the day's rest had given me for reflection had resulted in my fully determining to say nothing to him respecting Compeyson. For anything I knew, his animosity towards the man might otherwise lead to his seeking him out and rushing on his own destruction. Therefore, when Herbert and I sat down with him by his fire, I asked him first of all whether he relied on Wemmick's judgment and sources of information?

"Ay, ay, dear boy!" he answered, with a grave nod, "Jaggers knows."

"Then, I have talked with Wemmick," said I, "and have come to tell you what caution he gave me and what advice."

This I did accurately, with the reservation just mentioned; and I told him how Wemmick had heard, in Newgate prison (whether from officers or prisoners I could not say), that he was under some suspicion, and that my chambers had been watched; how Wemmick had recommended his keeping close for a time, and my keeping away from him; and what Wemmick had said about getting him abroad. I added, that of course, when the time came, I should go with him, or should follow close upon him, as might be safest in Wemmick's judgment. What was to follow that I did not touch upon; neither, indeed, was I at all clear or comfortable about it in my own mind, now that I saw him in that softer condition, and in declared peril for my sake. As to altering my way of living by enlarging my expenses, I put it to him whether in our present unsettled and difficult circumstances, it would not be simply ridiculous, if it were no worse?

He could not deny this, and indeed was very reasonable throughout. His coming back was a venture, he said, and he had always known it to be a venture. He would do nothing to make it a desperate venture, and he had very little fear of his safety with such good help.

Herbert, who had been looking at the fire and pondering, here said that something had come into his thoughts arising out of Wemmick's suggestion, which it might be worth while to pursue. "We are both good watermen, Handel, and could take him down the river ourselves when the right time comes.

No boat would then be hired for the purpose, and no boatmen; that would save at least a chance of suspicion, and any chance is worth saving. Never mind the season; don't you think it might be a good thing if you began at once to keep a boat at the Temple stairs, and were in the habit of rowing up and down the river? You fall into that habit, and then who notices or minds? Do it twenty or fifty times, and there is nothing special in your doing it the twenty-first or fifty-first."

I liked this scheme, and Provis was quite elated by it. We agreed that it should be carried into execution, and that Provis should never recognize us if we came below Bridge, and rowed past Mill Pond Bank. But we further agreed that he should pull down the blind in that part of his window which gave upon the east, whenever he saw us and all was right.

Our conference being now ended, and everything arranged, I rose to go; remarking to Herbert that he and I had better not go home together, and that I would take half an hour's start of him. "I don't like to leave you here," I said to Provis, "though I cannot doubt your being safer here than near me. Good-by!"

"Dear boy," he answered, clasping my hands, "I don't know when we may meet again, and I don't like Good-by. Say Good Night!"

"Good-night! Herbert will go regularly between us, and when the time comes you may be certain I shall be ready. Good night, good night!"

We thought it best that he should stay in his own rooms; and we left him on the landing outside his door, holding a light over the stair-rail to light us down stairs. Looking back at him, I thought of the first night of his return, when our positions were reversed, and when I little supposed my heart could ever be as heavy and anxious at parting from him as it was now.

Old Barley was growling and swearing when we repassed his door, with no appearance of having ceased or of meaning to cease. When we got to the foot of the stairs, I asked Herbert whether he had preserved the name of Provis. He replied, certainly not, and that the lodger was Mr. Campbell. He also explained that the utmost known of Mr. Campbell there was, that he (Herbert) had Mr. Campbell consigned to him, and felt a strong personal interest in his being well cared for, and living a secluded life. So, when we went into the parlor where Mrs. Whimple and Clara were seated at work, I said nothing of my own interest in Mr. Campbell, but kept it to myself.

When I had taken leave of the pretty, gentle, dark-eyed girl, and of the motherly woman who had not outlived her honest sympathy with a little affair of true love, I felt as if the Old Green Copper Rope-walk had grown quite a different place. Old Barley might be as old as the hills, and might swear like a whole field of troopers, but there were redeeming youth and trust and hope enough in Chinks's Basin to fill it to overflowing. And then I thought of Estella, and of our parting, and went home very sadly.

All things were as quiet in the Temple as ever I had seen them. The windows of the rooms on that side, lately occupied by Provis, were dark and still, and there was no lounger in Garden Court. I walked past the fountain twice or thrice before I descended the steps that were between me and my rooms, but I was quite alone. Herbert, coming to my bedside when he came in—for I went straight to bed, dispirited and fatigued—made the same report. Opening one of the windows after that, he looked out into the moonlight, and told me that the pavement was a solemnly empty as the pavement of any cathedral at that same hour.

Next day I set myself to get the boat. It was soon done, and the boat was brought round to the Temple stairs, and lay where I could reach her within a minute or two. Then, I began to go out as for training and practice: sometimes alone, sometimes with Herbert. I was often out in cold, rain, and sleet, but nobody took much note of me after I had been out a few times.

At first, I kept above Blackfriars Bridge; but as the hours of the tide changed, I took towards London Bridge. It was Old London Bridge in those days, and at certain states of the tide there was a race and fall of water there which gave it a bad reputation. But I knew well enough how to 'shoot' the bridge after seeing it done, and so began to row about among the shipping in the Pool, and down to Erith. The first time I passed Mill Pond Bank, Herbert and I were pulling a pair of oars; and, both in going and returning, we saw the blind towards the east come down. Herbert was rarely there less frequently than three times in a week, and he never brought me a single word of intelligence that was at all alarming. Still, I knew that there was cause for alarm, and I could not get rid of the notion of being watched. Once received, it is a haunting idea; how many undesigning persons I suspected of watching me, it would be hard to calculate.

In short, I was always full of fears for the rash man who was in hiding. Herbert had sometimes said to me that he found it pleasant to stand at one of our windows after dark, when the tide was running down, and to think that it was flowing, with everything it bore, towards Clara. But I thought with dread that it was flowing towards Magwitch, and that any black mark on its surface might be his pursuers, going swiftly, silently, and surely, to take him.

CHAPTER 8

Some weeks passed without bringing any change. We waited for Wemmick, and he made no sign. If I had never known him out of Little Britain, and had never enjoyed the privilege of being on a familiar footing at the Castle, I might have doubted him; not so for a moment, knowing him as I did.

My worldly affairs began to wear a gloomy appearance, and I was pressed for money by more than one creditor. Even I myself began to know the want of money (I mean of ready money in my own pocket), and to relieve it by converting some easily spared articles of jewelery into cash. But I had quite determined that it would be a heartless fraud to take more money from my patron in the existing state of my uncertain thoughts and plans. Therefore, I had sent him the unopened pocket-book by Herbert, to hold in his own keeping, and I felt a kind of satisfaction—whether it was a false kind or a true, I hardly know—in not having profited by his generosity since his revelation of himself.

As the time wore on, an impression settled heavily upon me that Estella was married. Fearful of having it confirmed, though it was all but a conviction, I avoided the newspapers, and begged Herbert (to whom I had confided the circumstances of our last interview) never to speak of her to me. Why I hoarded up this last wretched little rag of the robe of hope that was rent and given to the winds, how do I know? Why did you who read this, commit that not dissimilar inconsistency of your own last year, last month, last week?

It was an unhappy life that I lived; and its one dominant anxiety, towering over all its other anxieties, like a high mountain above a range of mountains, never disappeared from my view. Still, no new cause for fear arose. Let me start from my bed as I would, with the terror fresh upon me that he was discovered; let me sit listening, as I would with dread, for Herbert's returning step at night, lest it should be fleeter than ordinary, and winged with evil news; for all that, and much more to like purpose, the round of things went on. Condemned to inaction and a state of constant restlessness and suspense, I rowed about in my boat, and waited, waited, waited, as I best could.

There were states of the tide when, having been down the river, I could not get back through the eddy-chafed arches and starlings of old London Bridge; then, I left my boat at a wharf near the Custom House, to be brought up afterwards to the Temple stairs. I was not averse to doing this, as it served to make me and my boat a commoner incident among the water-side people there. From this slight occasion sprang two meetings that I have now to tell of.

One afternoon, late in the month of February, I came ashore at the wharf at dusk. I had pulled down as far as Greenwich with the ebb tide, and had turned with the tide. It had been a fine bright day, but had become foggy as the sun dropped, and I had had to feel my way back among the shipping, pretty carefully. Both in going and returning, I had seen the signal in his window, All well.

As it was a raw evening, and I was cold, I thought I would comfort myself with dinner at once; and as I had hours of dejection and solitude before me if I went home to the Temple, I thought I would afterwards go to the play. The theatre where Mr. Wopsle had achieved his questionable triumph was in that water-side neighbourhood (it is nowhere now), and to that theatre I resolved to go. I was aware that Mr. Wopsle had not succeeded in reviving the Drama, but, on the contrary, had rather partaken of its decline. He had been ominously heard of, through the play-bills, as a faithful Black, in connection with a little girl of noble birth, and a monkey. And Herbert had seen him as a predatory Tartar of comic propensities, with a face like a red brick, and an outrageous hat all over bells.

I dined at what Herbert and I used to call a Geographical chop-house—where there were maps of the world in porter-pot rims on every half-yard of the tablecloths, and charts of gravy on every one of the knives—to this day there is scarcely a single chop-house within the Lord Mayor's dominions which is not geographical—and wore out the time in dozing over crumbs, staring at gas, and baking in a hot blast of dinners. By and by, I roused myself, and went to the play.

There, I found a virtuous boatswain in His Majesty's service—a most excellent man, though I could have wished his trousers not quite so tight in some places, and not quite so loose in others—who knocked all the little men's hats over their eyes, though he was very generous and brave, and who wouldn't hear of anybody's paying taxes, though he was very patriotic. He had a bag of money in his pocket, like a pudding in the cloth, and on that property married a young person in bed-furniture, with great rejoicings; the whole population of Portsmouth (nine in number at the last census) turning out on the beach to rub their own hands and shake everybody else's, and sing "Fill, fill!" A certain dark-complexioned Swab, however, who wouldn't fill, or do anything else that was proposed to him, and whose heart was openly stated (by the boatswain) to be as black as his figure-head, proposed to two other Swabs to get all mankind into difficulties; which was so effectually done (the Swab family having considerable political influence) that it took half the evening to set things right, and then it was only brought about through an honest little grocer with a white hat, black gaiters, and red nose, getting into a clock, with a gridiron, and listening, and coming out, and knocking everybody down from behind with the gridiron whom he couldn't confute with what he had overheard. This led to Mr. Wopsle's (who had never been heard of before) coming in with a star and garter on, as a plenipotentiary of great power direct from the Admiralty, to say that the Swabs were all to go to prison on the spot, and that he had brought the boatswain down the Union Jack, as a slight acknowledgment of his public services. The boatswain, unmanned for the first time, respectfully dried his eyes on the Jack, and then cheering up, and addressing Mr. Wopsle as Your Honor, solicited permission to take him by the fin. Mr. Wopsle, conceding his fin with a gracious dignity, was immediately shoved into a dusty corner, while everybody danced a hornpipe; and from that corner, surveying the public with a discontented eye, became aware of me.

The second piece was the last new grand comic Christmas pantomime, in the first scene of which, it pained me to suspect that I detected Mr. Wopsle with red worsted legs under a highly magnified phosphoric countenance and a shock of red curtain-fringe for his hair, engaged in the manufacture of thunderbolts in a mine, and displaying great cowardice when his gigantic master came home (very hoarse) to dinner. But he presently presented himself under worthier circumstances; for, the Genius of Youthful Love being in want of assistance—on account of the parental brutality of an ignorant farmer who opposed the choice of his daughter's heart, by purposely falling upon the object, in a flour-sack, out of the first-floor window—summoned a sententious Enchanter; and he, coming up from the antipodes rather unsteadily, after an apparently violent journey, proved to be Mr. Wopsle in a high-crowned hat, with a necromantic work in one volume under his arm. The business of this enchanter on earth being principally to be talked at, sung at, butted at, danced at, and flashed at with fires of various colors, he had a good deal of time on his hands. And I observed, with great surprise, that he devoted it to staring in my direction as if he were lost in amazement.

There was something so remarkable in the increasing glare of Mr. Wopsle's eye, and he seemed to be turning so many things over in his mind and to grow so confused, that I could not make it out. I sat thinking of it long after he had ascended to the clouds in a large watch-case, and still I could not make it out. I was still thinking of it when I came out of the theatre an hour afterwards, and found him waiting for me near the door.

"How do you do?" said I, shaking hands with him as we turned down the street together. "I saw that you saw me."

"Saw you, Mr. Pip!" he returned. "Yes, of course I saw you. But who else was there?"

"Who else?"

"It is the strangest thing," said Mr. Wopsle, drifting into his lost look again; "and yet I could swear to him."

Becoming alarmed, I entreated Mr. Wopsle to explain his meaning.

"Whether I should have noticed him at first but for your being there," said Mr. Wopsle, going on in the same lost way, "I can't be positive; yet I think I should."

Involuntarily I looked round me, as I was accustomed to look round me when I went home; for these mysterious words gave me a chill.

"Oh! He can't be in sight," said Mr. Wopsle. "He went out before I went off. I saw him go."

Having the reason that I had for being suspicious, I even suspected this poor actor. I mistrusted a design to entrap me into some admission. Therefore I glanced at him as we walked on together, but said nothing.

"I had a ridiculous fancy that he must be with you, Mr. Pip, till I saw that you were quite unconscious of him, sitting behind you there like a ghost."

My former chill crept over me again, but I was resolved not to speak yet, for it was quite consistent with his words that he might be set on to induce me to connect these references with

Provis. Of course, I was perfectly sure and safe that Provis had not been there.

"I dare say you wonder at me, Mr. Pip; indeed, I see you do. But it is so very strange! You'll hardly believe what I am going to tell you. I could hardly believe it myself, if you told me."

"Indeed?" said I.

"No, indeed. Mr. Pip, you remember in old times a certain Christmas Day, when you were quite a child, and I dined at Gargery's, and some soldiers came to the door to get a pair of hand-cuffs mended?"

"I remember it very well."

"And you remember that there was a chase after two convicts, and that we joined in it, and that Gargery took you on his back, and that I took the lead, and you kept up with me as well as you could?"

"I remember it all very well." Better than he thought—except the last clause.

"And you remember that we came up with the two in a ditch, and that there was a scuffle between them, and that one of them had been severely handled and much mauled about the face by the other?"

"I see it all before me."

"And that the soldiers lighted torches, and put the two in the centre, and that we went on to see the last of them, over the black marshes, with the torchlight shining on their faces—I am particular about that—with the torchlight shining on their faces, when there was an outer ring of dark night all about us?"

"Yes," said I. "I remember all that."

"Then, Mr. Pip, one of those two prisoners sat behind you tonight. I saw him over your shoulder."

"Steady!" I thought. I asked him then, "Which of the two do you suppose you saw?"

"The one who had been mauled," he answered readily, "and

I'll swear I saw him! The more I think of him, the more certain I am of him."

"This is very curious!" said I, with the best assumption I could put on of its being nothing more to me. "Very curious indeed!"

I cannot exaggerate the enhanced disquiet into which this conversation threw me, or the special and peculiar terror I felt at Compeyson's having been behind me "like a ghost." For if he had ever been out of my thoughts for a few moments together since the hiding had begun, it was in those very moments when he was closest to me; and to think that I should be so unconscious and off my guard after all my care was as if I had shut an avenue of a hundred doors to keep him out, and then had found him at my elbow. I could not doubt, either, that he was there, because I was there, and that, however slight an appearance of danger there might be about us, danger was always near and active.

I put such questions to Mr. Wopsle as, When did the man come in? He could not tell me that; he saw me, and over my shoulder he saw the man. It was not until he had seen him for some time that he began to identify him; but he had from the first vaguely associated him with me, and known him as somehow belonging to me in the old village time. How was he dressed? Prosperously, but not noticeably otherwise; he thought, in black. Was his face at all disfigured? No, he believed not. I believed not too, for, although in my brooding state I had taken no especial notice of the people behind me, I thought it likely that a face at all disfigured would have attracted my attention.

When Mr. Wopsle had imparted to me all that he could recall or I extract, and when I had treated him to a little appropriate refreshment, after the fatigues of the evening, we parted. It was between twelve and one o'clock when I reached the Temple, and the gates were shut. No one was near me when I went in and went home.

Herbert had come in, and we held a very serious council by the fire. But there was nothing to be done, saving to communicate to Wemmick what I had that night found out, and to remind him that we waited for his hint. As I thought that I might compromise him if I went too often to the Castle, I made this communication by letter. I wrote it before I went to bed, and went out and posted it; and again no one was near me. Herbert and I agreed that we could do nothing else but be very cautious. And we were very cautious indeed—more cautious than before, if that were possible—and I for my part never went near Chinks's Basin, except when I rowed by, and then I only looked at Mill Pond Bank as I looked at anything else.

CHAPTER 9

The second of the two meetings referred to in the last chapter occurred about a week after the first. I had again left my boat at the wharf below Bridge; the time was an hour earlier in the afternoon; and, undecided where to dine, I had strolled up into Cheapside, and was strolling along it, surely the most unsettled person in all the busy concourse, when a large hand was laid upon my shoulder by some one overtaking me. It was Mr. Jaggers's hand, and he passed it through my arm.

"As we are going in the same direction, Pip, we may walk together. Where are you bound for?"

"For the Temple, I think," said I.

"Don't you know?" said Mr. Jaggers.

"Well," I returned, glad for once to get the better of him in cross-examination, "I do *not* know, for I have not made up my mind."

"You are going to dine?" said Mr. Jaggers. "You don't mind admitting that, I suppose?"

"No," I returned, "I don't mind admitting that."

"And are not engaged?"

"I don't mind admitting also that I am not engaged."

"Then," said Mr. Jaggers, "come and dine with me."

I was going to excuse myself, when he added, "Wemmick's coming." So I changed my excuse into an acceptance—the few words I had uttered, serving for the beginning of either—and we went along Cheapside and slanted off to Little Britain, while the lights were springing up brilliantly in the shop windows, and the street lamp-lighters, scarcely finding ground enough to plant their ladders on in the midst of the afternoon's bustle, were skipping up and down and running in and out, opening more red eyes in the gathering fog than my rushlight tower at the Hummums had opened white eyes in the ghostly wall.

At the office in Little Britain there was the usual letter-writing, hand-washing, candle-snuffing, and safe-locking, that closed the business of the day. As I stood idle by Mr. Jaggers's fire, its rising and falling flame made the two casts on the shelf look as if they were playing a diabolical game at bo-peep with me; while the pair of coarse, fat office candles that dimly lighted Mr. Jaggers as he wrote in a corner were decorated with dirty winding-sheets, as if in remembrance of a host of hanged clients.

We went to Gerrard Street, all three together, in a hackney-coach: And, as soon as we got there, dinner was served. Although I should not have thought of making, in that place, the most distant reference by so much as a look to Wemmick's Walworth sentiments, yet I should have had no objection to catching his eye now and then in a friendly way. But it was not to be done. He turned his eyes on Mr. Jaggers whenever he raised them from the table, and was as dry and distant to me as if there were twin Wemmicks, and this was the wrong one.

"Did you send that note of Miss Havisham's to Mr. Pip, Wemmick?" Mr. Jaggers asked, soon after we began dinner.

"No, sir," returned Wemmick; "it was going by post, when you brought Mr. Pip into the office. Here it is." He handed it to his principal instead of to me.

"It's a note of two lines, Pip," said Mr. Jaggers, handing it on, "sent up to me by Miss Havisham on account of her not being sure of your address. She tells me that she wants to see you on a little matter of business you mentioned to her. You'll go down?"

"Yes," said I, casting my eyes over the note, which was exactly in those terms.

"When do you think of going down?"

"I have an impending engagement," said I, glancing at Wemmick, who was putting fish into the post-office, "that renders me rather uncertain of my time. At once, I think."

"If Mr. Pip has the intention of going at once," said Wemmick to Mr. Jaggers, "he needn't write an answer, you know."

Receiving this as an intimation that it was best not to delay, I settled that I would go to-morrow, and said so. Wemmick drank a glass of wine, and looked with a grimly satisfied air at Mr. Jaggers, but not at me.

"So, Pip! Our friend the Spider," said Mr. Jaggers, "has played his cards. He has won the pool."

It was as much as I could do to assent.

"Hah! He is a promising fellow—in his way—but he may not have it all his own way. The stronger will win in the end, but the stronger has to be found out first. If he should turn to, and beat her—"

"Surely," I interrupted, with a burning face and heart, "you do not seriously think that he is scoundrel enough for that, Mr. Jaggers?"

"I didn't say so, Pip. I am putting a case. If he should turn to and beat her, he may possibly get the strength on his side; if it should be a question of intellect, he certainly will not. It would be chance work to give an opinion how a fellow of that sort will turn out in such circumstances, because it's a toss-up between two results."

"May I ask what they are?"

"A fellow like our friend the Spider," answered Mr. Jaggers, "either beats or cringes. He may cringe and growl, or cringe and not growl; but he either beats or cringes. Ask Wemmick *his* opinion."

"Either beats or cringes," said Wemmick, not at all addressing himself to me.

"So here's to Mrs. Bentley Drummle," said Mr. Jaggers,

taking a decanter of choicer wine from his dumb-waiter, and filling for each of us and for himself, "and may the question of supremacy be settled to the lady's satisfaction! To the satisfaction of the lady *and* the gentleman, it never will be. Now, Molly, Molly, Molly, Molly, how slow you are to-day!"

She was at his elbow when he addressed her, putting a dish upon the table. As she withdrew her hands from it, she fell back a step or two, nervously muttering some excuse. And a certain action of her fingers, as she spoke, arrested my attention.

"What's the matter?" said Mr. Jaggers.

"Nothing. Only the subject we were speaking of," said I, "was rather painful to me."

The action of her fingers was like the action of knitting. She stood looking at her master, not understanding whether she was free to go, or whether he had more to say to her and would call her back if she did go. Her look was very intent. Surely, I had seen exactly such eyes and such hands on a memorable occasion very lately!

He dismissed her, and she glided out of the room. But she remained before me as plainly as if she were still there. I looked at those hands, I looked at those eyes, I looked at that flowing hair; and I compared them with other hands, other eyes, other hair, that I knew of, and with what those might be after twenty years of a brutal husband and a stormy life. I looked again at those hands and eyes of the housekeeper, and thought of the inexplicable feeling that had come over me when I last walked—not alone—in the ruined garden, and through the deserted brewery. I thought how the same feeling had come back when I saw a face looking at me, and a hand waving to me from a stage-coach window; and how it had come back again and had flashed about me like lightning, when I had passed in a carriage—not alone—through a sudden glare of light in a dark street. I thought how one link of association had helped that identification in the theatre, and how such a link, wanting before, had been riveted for me now, when I had passed by a chance swift from Estella's name to the fingers with their knitting action, and the attentive eyes. And I felt absolutely certain that this woman was Estella's mother.

Mr. Jaggers had seen me with Estella, and was not likely to have missed the sentiments I had been at no pains to conceal. He nodded when I said the subject was painful to me, clapped me on the back, put round the wine again, and went on with his dinner.

Only twice more did the housekeeper reappear, and then her stay in the room was very short, and Mr. Jaggers was sharp with her. But her hands were Estella's hands, and her eyes were Estella's eyes, and if she had reappeared a hundred times I could have been neither more sure nor less sure that my conviction was the truth.

It was a dull evening, for Wemmick drew his wine, when it came round, quite as a matter of business—just as he might have drawn his salary when that came round—and with his eyes on his chief, sat in a state of perpetual readiness for cross-examination. As to the quantity of wine, his post-office was as indifferent and ready as any other post-office for its quantity of letters. From my point of view, he was the wrong twin all the time, and only externally like the Wemmick of Walworth.

We took our leave early, and left together. Even when we were groping among Mr. Jaggers's stock of boots for our hats, I felt that the right twin was on his way back; and we had not gone half a dozen yards down Gerrard Street in the Walworth direction, before I found that I was walking arm in arm with the right twin, and that the wrong twin had evaporated into the evening air.

"Well!" said Wemmick, "that's over! He's a wonderful man, without his living likeness; but I feel that I have to screw myself up when I dine with him—and I dine more comfortably unscrewed."

I felt that this was a good statement of the case, and told him so.

"Wouldn't say it to anybody but yourself," he answered. "I know that what is said between you and me goes no further."

I asked him if he had ever seen Miss Havisham's adopted daughter, Mrs. Bentley Drummle. He said no. To avoid being too abrupt, I then spoke of the Aged and of Miss Skiffins. He looked rather sly when I mentioned Miss Skiffins, and stopped in the street to blow his nose, with a roll of the head, and a flourish not quite free from latent boastfulness.

"Wemmick," said I, "do you remember telling me, before I first went to Mr. Jaggers's private house, to notice that housekeeper?"

"Did I?" he replied. "Ah, I dare say I did. Deuce take me," he added, suddenly, "I know I did. I find I am not quite unscrewed yet."

"A wild beast tamed, you called her."

"And what do *you* call her?"

"The same. How did Mr. Jaggers tame her, Wemmick?"

"That's his secret. She has been with him many a long year."

"I wish you would tell me her story. I feel a particular interest in being acquainted with it. You know that what is said between you and me goes no further."

"Well!" Wemmick replied, "I don't know her story—that is, I don't know all of it. But what I do know I'll tell you. We are in our private and personal capacities, of course."

"Of course."

"A score or so of years ago, that woman was tried at the Old Bailey for murder, and was acquitted. She was a very handsome young woman, and I believe had some gypsy blood in her. Anyhow, it was hot enough when it was up, as you may suppose."

"But she was acquitted."

"Mr. Jaggers was for her," pursued Wemmick, with a look full of meaning, "and worked the case in a way quite astonishing. It was a desperate case, and it was comparatively early days with him then, and he worked it to general admiration; in fact, it may almost be said to have made him. He worked it himself at the police-office, day after day for many days, contending against even a committal; and at the trial where he couldn't work it himself, sat under counsel, and—every one knew—put in all the salt and pepper. The murdered person was a woman—a woman a good ten years older, very much larger, and very much stronger. It was a case of jealousy. They both led tramping lives, and this woman in Gerrard Street here had been married very young, over the broomstick (as we say), to a tramping man, and was a perfect fury in point of jealousy. The murdered woman—more a match for the man, certainly, in point of years—was found dead in a barn near Hounslow Heath. There had been a violent struggle, perhaps a fight. She was bruised and scratched and torn, and had been held by the throat, at last, and choked. Now, there was no reasonable evidence to implicate any person but this woman, and on the improbabilities of her having been able to do it Mr. Jaggers principally rested his case. You may be sure," said Wemmick, touching me on the sleeve, "that he never dwelt upon the strength of her hands then, though he sometimes does now."

I had told Wemmick of his showing us her wrists, that day of the dinner party.

"Well, sir!" Wemmick went on; "it happened—happened, don't you see?—that this woman was so very artfully dressed from the time of her apprehension, that she looked much slighter than she really was; in particular, her sleeves are always remembered to have been so skilfully contrived that her arms had quite a delicate look. She had only a bruise or two about her—nothing for a tramp—but the backs of her hands were lacerated, and the question was, Was it with finger-nails? Now, Mr. Jaggers showed that she had struggled through a great lot of brambles which were not as high as her face; but which she could not have got through and kept her hands out of; and bits of those brambles were actually found in her skin and put in evidence, as well as the fact that the brambles in question were found on examination to have been broken through, and to have little shreds of her dress and little spots of blood upon them here and there. But the boldest point he made was this: it was attempted to be set up, in proof of her jealousy, that she was under strong suspicion of having, at about the time of the murder, frantically destroyed her child by this man—some three years old—to revenge herself upon him. Mr. Jaggers worked that in this way: "We say these are not marks of finger-nails, but marks of brambles, and we show you the brambles. You say they are marks of finger-nails, and you set up the hypothesis that she destroyed her child. You must accept all consequences of that hypothesis. For anything we know, she may have destroyed her child, and the child in clinging to her may have scratched her hands. What then? You are not trying her for the murder of her child; why don't you? As to this case, if you *will* have scratches, we say that, for anything we know, you may have accounted for them, assuming for the sake of argument that you have not invented them?" "To sum up, sir," said Wemmick, "Mr. Jaggers was altogether too many for the jury, and they gave in."

"Has she been in his service ever since?"

"Yes; but not only that," said Wemmick, "she went into his service immediately after her acquittal, tamed as she is now. She has since been taught one thing and another in the way of her duties, but she was tamed from the beginning."

"Do you remember the sex of the child?"

"Said to have been a girl."

"You have nothing more to say to me to-night?"

"Nothing. I got your letter and destroyed it. Nothing."

We exchanged a cordial good-night, and I went home, with new matter for my thoughts, though with no relief from the old.

CHAPTER 10

Putting Miss Havisham's note in my pocket, that it might serve as my credentials for so soon reappearing at Satis House, in case her waywardness should lead her to express any surprise at seeing me, I went down again by the coach next day. But I alighted at the Halfway House, and breakfasted there, and walked the rest of the distance; for I sought to get into the town quietly by the unfrequented ways, and to leave it in the same manner.

The best light of the day was gone when I passed along the quiet echoing courts behind the High Street. The nooks of ruin where the old monks had once had their refectories and gardens, and where the strong walls were now pressed into the service of humble sheds and stables, were almost as silent as the old monks in their graves. The cathedral chimes had at once a sadder and a more remote sound to me, as I hurried on avoiding observation, than they had ever had before; so, the swell of the old organ was borne to my ears like funeral music; and the rooks, as they hovered about the gray tower and swung in the bare high trees of the priory garden, seemed to call to me that the place was changed, and that Estella was gone out of it for ever.

An elderly woman, whom I had seen before as one of the servants who lived in the supplementary house across the back courtyard, opened the gate. The lighted candle stood in the dark passage within, as of old, and I took it up and ascended the staircase alone. Miss Havisham was not in her own room, but was in the larger room across the landing. Looking in at the door, after knocking in vain, I saw her sitting on the hearth in a ragged chair, close before, and lost in the contemplation of, the ashy fire.

Doing as I had often done, I went in, and stood touching the old chimney-piece, where she could see me when she raised her eyes. There was an air or utter loneliness upon her, that would have moved me to pity though she had wilfully done me a deeper injury than I could charge her with. As I stood compassionating her, and thinking how, in the progress of time, I too had come to be a part of the wrecked fortunes of that house, her eyes rested on me. She stared, and said in a low voice, "Is it real?"

"It is I, Pip. Mr. Jaggers gave me your note yesterday, and I have lost no time."

"Thank you. Thank you."

As I brought another of the ragged chairs to the hearth and sat down, I remarked a new expression on her face, as if she were afraid of me.

"I want," she said, "to pursue that subject you mentioned to me when you were last here, and to show you that I am not all stone. But perhaps you can never believe, now, that there is anything human in my heart?"

When I said some reassuring words, she stretched out her tremulous right hand, as though she was going to touch me; but she recalled it again before I understood the action, or knew how to receive it.

"You said, speaking for your friend, that you could tell me how to do something useful and good. Something that you would like done, is it not?"

"Something that I would like done very much."

"What is it?"

I began explaining to her that secret history of the partnership. I had not got far into it, when I judged from her looks that she was thinking in a discursive way of me, rather than of what I said. It seemed to be so; for, when I stopped speaking, many moments passed before she showed that she was conscious of the fact.

"Do you break off," she asked then, with her former air of being afraid of me, "because you hate me too much to bear to speak to me?"

"No, no," I answered, "how can you think so, Miss Havisham! I stopped because I thought you were not following what I said."

"Perhaps I was not," she answered, putting a hand to her head. "Begin again, and let me look at something else. Stay! Now tell me."

She set her hand upon her stick in the resolute way that sometimes was habitual to her, and looked at the fire with a strong expression of forcing herself to attend. I went on with my explanation, and told her how I had hoped to complete the transaction out of my means, but how in this I was disappointed. That part of the subject (I reminded her) involved matters which could form no part of my explanation, for they were the weighty secrets of another.

"So!" said she, assenting with her head, but not looking at me. "And how much money is wanting to complete the purchase?"

I was rather afraid of stating it, for it sounded a large sum. "Nine hundred pounds."

"If I give you the money for this purpose, will you keep my secret as you have kept your own?"

"Quite as faithfully."

"And your mind will be more at rest?"

"Much more at rest."

"Are you very unhappy now?"

She asked this question, still without looking at me, but in an unwonted tone of sympathy. I could not reply at the moment, for my voice failed me. She put her left arm across the head of her stick, and softly laid her forehead on it.

"I am far from happy, Miss Havisham; but I have other causes of disquiet than any you know of. They are the secrets I have mentioned."

After a little while, she raised her head, and looked at the fire Again.

"It is noble in you to tell me that you have other causes of unhappiness, Is it true?"

"Too true."

"Can I only serve you, Pip, by serving your friend? Regarding that as done, is there nothing I can do for you yourself?"

"Nothing. I thank you for the question. I thank you even more for the tone of the question. But there is nothing."

She presently rose from her seat, and looked about the blighted room for the means of writing. There were none there, and she took from her pocket a yellow set of ivory tablets, mounted in tarnished gold, and wrote upon them with a pencil in a case of tarnished gold that hung from her neck.

"You are still on friendly terms with Mr. Jaggers?""Quite. I dined with him yesterday."

"This is an authority to him to pay you that money, to lay out at your irresponsible discretion for your friend. I keep no money here; but if you would rather Mr. Jaggers knew nothing of the matter, I will send it to you."

"Thank you, Miss Havisham; I have not the least objection to receiving it from him."

She read me what she had written; and it was direct and clear, and evidently intended to absolve me from any suspicion of profiting by the receipt of the money. I took the tablets from her hand, and it trembled again, and it trembled more as she took off the chain to which the pencil was attached, and put it in mine. All this she did without looking at me.

"My name is on the first leaf. If you can ever write under my name, "I forgive her," though ever so long after my broken heart is dust—pray do it!"

"O Miss Havisham," said I, "I can do it now. There have been sore mistakes; and my life has been a blind and thankless one; and I want forgiveness and direction far too much, to be bitter with you."

She turned her face to me for the first time since she had averted it, and, to my amazement, I may even add to my terror, dropped on her knees at my feet; with her folded hands raised to me in the manner in which, when her poor heart was young and fresh and whole, they must often have been raised to heaven from her mother's side.

To see her with her white hair and her worn face kneeling at my feet gave me a shock through all my frame. I entreated her to rise, and got my arms about her to help her up; but she only pressed that hand of mine which was nearest to her grasp, and hung her head over it and wept. I had never seen her shed a tear before, and, in the hope that the relief might do her good, I bent over her without speaking. She was not kneeling now, but was down upon the ground.

"O!" she cried, despairingly. "What have I done! What have I done!"

"If you mean, Miss Havisham, what have you done to injure me, let me answer. Very little. I should have loved her under any circumstances.—Is she married?"

"Yes."

It was a needless question, for a new desolation in the desolate house had told me so.

"What have I done! What have I done!" She wrung her hands, and crushed her white hair, and returned to this cry over and over again. "What have I done!"

I knew not how to answer, or how to comfort her. That she had done a grievous thing in taking an impressionable child to mould into the form that her wild resentment, spurned affection, and wounded pride found vengeance in, I knew full well. But that, in shutting out the light of day, she had shut out infinitely more; that, in seclusion, she had secluded herself from a thousand natural and healing influences; that, her mind, brooding solitary, had grown diseased, as all minds do and must and will that reverse the appointed order of their Maker, I knew equally well. And could I look upon her without compassion, seeing her punishment in the ruin she was, in her profound unfitness for this earth on which she was placed, in the vanity of sorrow which had become a master mania, like the vanity of penitence, the vanity of remorse, the vanity of unworthiness, and other monstrous vanities that have been curses in this world?

"Until you spoke to her the other day, and until I saw in you a looking-glass that showed me what I once felt myself, I did not know what I had done. What have I done! What have I done!" And so again, twenty, fifty times over, What had she done!

"Miss Havisham," I said, when her cry had died away, "you may dismiss me from your mind and conscience. But Estella is a different case, and if you can ever undo any scrap of what you have done amiss in keeping a part of her right nature away from her, it will be better to do that than to bemoan the past through a hundred years."

"Yes, yes, I know it. But, Pip—my Dear!" There was an earnest womanly compassion for me in her new affection. "My Dear! Believe this: when she first came to me, I meant to save her from misery like my own. At first, I meant no more."

"Well, well!" said I. "I hope so."

"But as she grew, and promised to be very beautiful, I gradually did worse, and with my praises, and with my jewels, and with my teachings, and with this figure of myself always before her, a warning to back and point my lessons, I stole her heart away, and put ice in its place."

"Better," I could not help saying, "to have left her a natural heart, even to be bruised or broken."

With that, Miss Havisham looked distractedly at me for a while, and then burst out again, What had she done!

"If you knew all my story," she pleaded, "you would have some compassion for me and a better understanding of me."

"Miss Havisham," I answered, as delicately as I could, "I believe I may say that I do know your story, and have known it ever since I first left this neighbourhood. It has inspired me with great commiseration, and I hope I understand it and its influences. Does what has passed between us give me any excuse for asking you a question relative to Estella? Not as she is, but as she was when she first came here?"

She was seated on the ground, with her arms on the ragged chair, and her head leaning on them. She looked full at me when I said this, and replied, "Go on."

"Whose child was Estella?"

She shook her head.

"You don't know?"

She shook her head again.

"But Mr. Jaggers brought her here, or sent her here?"

"Brought her here."

"Will you tell me how that came about?"

She answered in a low whisper and with caution: "I had been shut up in these rooms a long time (I don't know how long; you know what time the clocks keep here), when I told him that I wanted a little girl to rear and love, and save from my fate. I had first seen him when I sent for him to lay this place waste for me; having read of him in the newspapers, before I and the world parted. He told me that he would look about him for such an orphan child. One night he brought her here asleep, and I called her Estella."

"Might I ask her age then?"

"Two or three. She herself knows nothing, but that she was left an orphan and I adopted her."

So convinced I was of that woman's being her mother, that

I wanted no evidence to establish the fact in my own mind. But, to any mind, I thought, the connection here was clear and straight.

What more could I hope to do by prolonging the interview? I had succeeded on behalf of Herbert, Miss Havisham had told me all she knew of Estella, I had said and done what I could to ease her mind. No matter with what other words we parted; we parted.

Twilight was closing in when I went down stairs into the natural air. I called to the woman who had opened the gate when I entered, that I would not trouble her just yet, but would walk round the place before leaving. For I had a presentiment that I should never be there again, and I felt that the dying light was suited to my last view of it.

By the wilderness of casks that I had walked on long ago, and on which the rain of years had fallen since, rotting them in many places, and leaving miniature swamps and pools of water upon those that stood on end, I made my way to the ruined garden. I went all round it; round by the corner where Herbert and I had fought our battle; round by the paths where Estella and I had walked. So cold, so lonely, so dreary all!

Taking the brewery on my way back, I raised the rusty latch of a little door at the garden end of it, and walked through. I was going out at the opposite door—not easy to open now, for the damp wood had started and swelled, and the hinges were yielding, and the threshold was encumbered with a growth of fungus—when I turned my head to look back. A childish association revived with wonderful force in the moment of the slight action, and I fancied that I saw Miss Havisham hanging to the beam. So strong was the impression, that I stood under the beam shuddering from head to foot before I knew it was a fancy—though to be sure I was there in an instant.

The mournfulness of the place and time, and the great terror of this illusion, though it was but momentary, caused me to feel an indescribable awe as I came out between the open wooden gates where I had once wrung my hair after Estella had wrung my heart. Passing on into the front courtyard, I hesitated whether to call the woman to let me out at the locked gate of which she had the key, or first to go up stairs and assure myself that Miss Havisham was as safe and well as I had left her. I took the latter course and went up.

I looked into the room where I had left her, and I saw her seated in the ragged chair upon the hearth close to the fire, with her back towards me. In the moment when I was withdrawing my head to go quietly away, I saw a great flaming light spring up. In the same moment I saw her running at me, shrieking, with a whirl of fire blazing all about her, and soaring at least as many feet above her head as she was high.

I had a double-caped great-coat on, and over my arm another thick coat. That I got them off, closed with her, threw her down, and got them over her; that I dragged the great cloth from the table for the same purpose, and with it dragged down the heap of rottenness in the midst, and all the ugly things that sheltered there; that we were on the ground struggling like desperate enemies, and that the closer I covered her, the more wildly she shrieked and tried to free herself; that this occurred I knew through the result, but not through anything I felt, or thought, or knew I did. I knew nothing until I knew that we were on the floor by the great table, and that patches of tinder yet alight were floating in the smoky air, which, a moment ago, had been her faded bridal dress.

Then, I looked round and saw the disturbed beetles and spiders running away over the floor, and the servants coming in with breathless cries at the door. I still held her forcibly down with all my strength, like a prisoner who might escape; and I doubt if I even knew who she was, or why we had struggled, or that she had been in flames, or that the flames were out, until I saw the patches of tinder that had been her garments no longer alight but falling in a black shower around us.

She was insensible, and I was afraid to have her moved, or even touched. Assistance was sent for, and I held her until it came, as if I unreasonably fancied (I think I did) that, if I let her go, the fire would break out again and consume her. When I got up, on the surgeon's coming to her with other aid, I was astonished to see that both my hands were burnt; for, I had no knowledge of it through the sense of feeling.

On examination it was pronounced that she had received serious hurts, but that they of themselves were far from hopeless; the danger lay mainly in the nervous shock. By the surgeon's directions, her bed was carried into that room and laid upon the great table, which happened to be well suited to the dressing of her injuries. When I saw her again, an hour afterwards, she lay, indeed, where I had seen her strike her stick, and had heard her say that she would lie one day.

Though every vestige of her dress was burnt, as they told me, she still had something of her old ghastly bridal appearance; for, they had covered her to the throat with white cotton-wool, and as she lay with a white sheet loosely overlying that, the phantom air of something that had been and was changed was still upon her.

I found, on questioning the servants, that Estella was in Paris, and I got a promise from the surgeon that he would write to her by the next post. Miss Havisham's family I took upon myself; intending to communicate with Mr. Matthew Pocket only, and leave him to do as he liked about informing the rest. This I did next day, through Herbert, as soon as I returned to town.

There was a stage, that evening, when she spoke collectedly of what had happened, though with a certain terrible vivacity. Towards midnight she began to wander in her speech; and after that it gradually set in that she said innumerable times in a low solemn voice, "What have I done!" And then, "When she first came, I meant to save her from misery like mine." And then, "Take the pencil and write under my name, 'I forgive her!'" She never changed the order of these three sentences, but she sometimes left out a word in one or other of them; never putting in another word, but always leaving a blank and going on to the next word.

As I could do no service there, and as I had, nearer home, that pressing reason for anxiety and fear which even her wanderings could not drive out of my mind, I decided, in the course of the night that I would return by the early morning coach, walking on a mile or so, and being taken up clear of the town. At about six o'clock of the morning, therefore, I leaned over her and touched her lips with mine, just as they said, not stopping for being touched, "Take the pencil and write under my name, 'I forgive her.'"

CHAPTER 11

My hands had been dressed twice or thrice in the night, and again in the morning. My left arm was a good deal burned to the elbow, and, less severely, as high as the shoulder; it was very painful, but the flames had set in that direction, and I felt thankful it was no worse. My right hand was not so badly burnt but that I could move the fingers. It was bandaged, of course, but much less inconveniently than my left hand and arm; those I carried in a sling; and I could only wear my coat like a cloak, loose over my shoulders and fastened at the neck. My hair had been caught by the fire, but not my head or face.

When Herbert had been down to Hammersmith and seen his father, he came back to me at our chambers, and devoted the day to attending on me. He was the kindest of nurses, and at stated times took off the bandages, and steeped them in the cooling liquid that was kept ready, and put them on again, with a patient tenderness that I was deeply grateful for.

At first, as I lay quiet on the sofa, I found it painfully difficult, I might say impossible, to get rid of the impression of the glare of the flames, their hurry and noise, and the fierce burning smell. If I dozed for a minute, I was awakened by Miss Havisham's cries, and by her running at me with all that height of fire above her head. This pain of the mind was much harder to strive against than any bodily pain I suffered; and Herbert, seeing that, did his utmost to hold my attention engaged.

Neither of us spoke of the boat, but we both thought of it. That was made apparent by our avoidance of the subject, and by our agreeing—without agreement—to make my recovery of the use of my hands a question of so many hours, not of so many weeks.

My first question when I saw Herbert had been of course, whether all was well down the river? As he replied in the affirmative, with perfect confidence and cheerfulness, we did not resume the subject until the day was wearing away. But then, as Herbert changed the bandages, more by the light of the fire than by the outer light, he went back to it spontaneously.

"I sat with Provis last night, Handel, two good hours."

"Where was Clara?"

"Dear little thing!" said Herbert. "She was up and down with Gruffandgrim all the evening. He was perpetually pegging at the floor the moment she left his sight. I doubt if he can hold out long, though. What with rum and pepper—and pepper and rum—I should think his pegging must be nearly over."

"And then you will be married, Herbert?"

"How can I take care of the dear child otherwise?—Lay your arm out upon the back of the sofa, my dear boy, and I'll sit down here, and get the bandage off so gradually that you shall not know when it comes. I was speaking of Provis. Do you know, Handel, he improves?"

"I said to you I thought he was softened when I last saw him."

"So you did. And so he is. He was very communicative last night, and told me more of his life. You remember his breaking off here about some woman that he had had great trouble with.—Did I hurt you?"

I had started, but not under his touch. His words had given me a start.

"I had forgotten that, Herbert, but I remember it now you speak of it."

"Well! He went into that part of his life, and a dark wild part it is. Shall I tell you? Or would it worry you just now?"

"Tell me by all means. Every word."

Herbert bent forward to look at me more nearly, as if my reply had been rather more hurried or more eager than he could quite account for. "Your head is cool?" he said, touching it.

"Quite," said I. "Tell me what Provis said, my dear Herbert."

"It seems," said Herbert, "—there's a bandage off most charmingly, and now comes the cool one—makes you shrink at first, my poor dear fellow, don't it? but it will be comfortable presently—it seems that the woman was a young woman, and a jealous woman, and a revengeful woman; revengeful, Handel, to the last degree."

"To what last degree?"

"Murder.—Does it strike too cold on that sensitive place?"

"I don't feel it. How did she murder? Whom did she murder?"

"Why, the deed may not have merited quite so terrible a name," said Herbert, "but, she was tried for it, and Mr. Jaggers defended her, and the reputation of that defence first made his name known to Provis. It was another and a stronger woman who was the victim, and there had been a struggle—in a barn. Who began it, or how fair it was, or how unfair, may be doubtful; but how it ended is certainly not doubtful, for the victim was found throttled."

"Was the woman brought in guilty?"

"No; she was acquitted.—My poor Handel, I hurt you!"

"It is impossible to be gentler, Herbert. Yes? What else?"

"This acquitted young woman and Provis had a little child; a little child of whom Provis was exceedingly fond. On the evening of the very night when the object of her jealousy was strangled as I tell you, the young woman presented herself before Provis for one moment, and swore that she would destroy the child (which was in her possession), and he should never see it again; then she vanished.—There's the worst arm comfortably in the sling once more, and now there remains but the right hand, which is a far easier job. I can do it better by this light than by a stronger, for my hand is steadiest when I don't see the poor blistered patches too distinctly.—You don't think your breathing is affected, my dear boy? You seem to breathe quickly."

"Perhaps I do, Herbert. Did the woman keep her oath?"

"There comes the darkest part of Provis's life. She did."

"That is, he says she did."

"Why, of course, my dear boy," returned Herbert, in a tone of surprise, and again bending forward to get a nearer look at me. "He says it all. I have no other information."

"No, to be sure."

"Now, whether," pursued Herbert, "he had used the child's mother ill, or whether he had used the child's mother well, Provis doesn't say; but she had shared some four or five years of the wretched life he described to us at this fireside, and he seems to have felt pity for her, and forbearance towards her. Therefore, fearing he should be called upon to depose about this destroyed child, and so be the cause of her death, he hid himself (much as he grieved for the child), kept himself dark, as he says, out of the way and out of the trial, and was only vaguely talked of as a certain man called Abel, out of whom the jealousy arose. After the acquittal she disappeared, and thus he lost the child and the child's mother."

"I want to ask—"

"A moment, my dear boy, and I have done. That evil genius, Compeyson, the worst of scoundrels among many scoundrels, knowing of his keeping out of the way at that time and of his reasons for doing so, of course afterwards held the knowledge over his head as a means of keeping him poorer and working him harder. It was clear last night that this barbed the point of Provis's animosity."

"I want to know," said I, "and particularly, Herbert, whether he told you when this happened?"

"Particularly? Let me remember, then, what he said as to that. His expression was, 'a round score o' year ago, and a'most directly after I took up wi' Compeyson.' How old were you when you came upon him in the little churchyard?"

"I think in my seventh year.""Ay. It had happened some three or four years then, he said, and you brought into his mind the little girl so tragically lost, who would have been about your age."

"Herbert," said I, after a short silence, in a hurried way, "can you see me best by the light of the window, or the light of the fire?"

"By the firelight," answered Herbert, coming close again.

"Look at me."

"I do look at you, my dear boy."

"Touch me."

"I do touch you, my dear boy."

"You are not afraid that I am in any fever, or that my head is much disordered by the accident of last night?"

"N-no, my dear boy," said Herbert, after taking time to examine me. "You are rather excited, but you are quite yourself."

"I know I am quite myself. And the man we have in hiding down the river, is Estella's Father."

CHAPTER 12

What purpose I had in view when I was hot on tracing out and proving Estella's parentage, I cannot say. It will presently be seen that the question was not before me in a distinct shape until it was put before me by a wiser head than my own.

But when Herbert and I had held our momentous conversation, I was seized with a feverish conviction that I ought to hunt the matter down—that I ought not to let it rest, but that I ought to see Mr. Jaggers, and come at the bare truth. I really do not know whether I felt that I did this for Estella's sake, or whether I was glad to transfer to the man in whose preservation I was so much concerned some rays of the romantic interest that had so long surrounded me. Perhaps the latter possibility may be the nearer to the truth.

Any way, I could scarcely be withheld from going out to Gerrard Street that night. Herbert's representations that, if I did, I should probably be laid up and stricken useless, when our fugitive's safety would depend upon me, alone restrained my impatience. On the understanding, again and again reiterated, that, come what would, I was to go to Mr. Jaggers to-morrow, I at length submitted to keep quiet, and to have my hurts looked after, and to stay at home. Early next morning we went out together, and at the corner of Giltspur Street by Smithfield, I left Herbert to go his way into the City, and took my way to Little Britain.

There were periodical occasions when Mr. Jaggers and Wemmick went over the office accounts, and checked off the vouchers, and put all things straight. On these occasions,

Wemmick took his books and papers into Mr. Jaggers's room, and one of the up-stairs clerks came down into the outer office. Finding such clerk on Wemmick's post that morning, I knew what was going on; but I was not sorry to have Mr. Jaggers and Wemmick together, as Wemmick would then hear for himself that I said nothing to compromise him.

My appearance, with my arm bandaged and my coat loose over my shoulders, favored my object. Although I had sent Mr. Jaggers a brief account of the accident as soon as I had arrived in town, yet I had to give him all the details now; and the speciality of the occasion caused our talk to be less dry and hard, and less strictly regulated by the rules of evidence, than it had been before. While I described the disaster, Mr. Jaggers stood, according to his wont, before the fire. Wemmick leaned back in his chair, staring at me, with his hands in the pockets of his trousers, and his pen put horizontally into the post. The two brutal casts, always inseparable in my mind from the official proceedings, seemed to be congestively considering whether they didn't smell fire at the present moment.

My narrative finished, and their questions exhausted, I then produced Miss Havisham's authority to receive the nine hundred pounds for Herbert. Mr. Jaggers's eyes retired a little deeper into his head when I handed him the tablets, but he presently handed them over to Wemmick, with instructions to draw the check for his signature. While that was in course of being done, I looked on at Wemmick as he wrote, and Mr. Jaggers, poising and swaying himself on his well-polished boots, looked on at me. "I am sorry, Pip," said he, as I put the check in my pocket, when he had signed it, "that we do nothing for *you*."

"Miss Havisham was good enough to ask me," I returned, "whether she could do nothing for me, and I told her No."

"Everybody should know his own business," said Mr. Jaggers. And I saw Wemmick's lips form the words "portable property."

"I should *not* have told her No, if I had been you," said Mr Jaggers; "but every man ought to know his own business best."

"Every man's business," said Wemmick, rather reproachfully towards me, "is portable property."

As I thought the time was now come for pursuing the theme I had at heart, I said, turning on Mr. Jaggers:—

"I did ask something of Miss Havisham, however, sir. I asked her to give me some information relative to her adopted daughter, and she gave me all she possessed."

"Did she?" said Mr. Jaggers, bending forward to look at his boots and then straightening himself. "Hah! I don't think I should have done so, if I had been Miss Havisham. But *she* ought to know her own business best."

"I know more of the history of Miss Havisham's adopted child than Miss Havisham herself does, sir. I know her mother."

Mr. Jaggers looked at me inquiringly, and repeated "Mother?"

"I have seen her mother within these three days."

"Yes?" said Mr. Jaggers.

"And so have you, sir. And you have seen her still more recently."

"Yes?" said Mr. Jaggers.

"Perhaps I know more of Estella's history than even you do," said I. "I know her father too."

A certain stop that Mr. Jaggers came to in his manner—he was too self-possessed to change his manner, but he could not help its being brought to an indefinably attentive stop—assured me that he did not know who her father was. This I had strongly suspected from Provis's account (as Herbert had repeated it) of his having kept himself dark; which I pieced on to the fact that he himself was not Mr. Jaggers's client until some four years later, and when he could have no reason for claiming his identity. But, I could not be sure of this unconsciousness on Mr. Jaggers's part before, though I was quite sure of it now.

"So! You know the young lady's father, Pip?" said Mr. Jaggers.

"Yes," I replied, "and his name is Provis—from New South Wales."

Even Mr. Jaggers started when I said those words. It was the slightest start that could escape a man, the most carefully repressed and the sooner checked, but he did start, though he made it a part of the action of taking out his pocket-handkerchief. How Wemmick received the announcement I am unable to say; for I was afraid to look at him just then, lest Mr. Jaggers's sharpness should detect that there had been some communication unknown to him between us.

"And on what evidence, Pip," asked Mr. Jaggers, very coolly, as he paused with his handkerchief half way to his nose, "does Provis make this claim?"

"He does not make it," said I, "and has never made it, and has no knowledge or belief that his daughter is in existence."

For once, the powerful pocket-handkerchief failed. My reply was so Unexpected, that Mr. Jaggers put the handkerchief back into his pocket without completing the usual performance, folded his arms, and looked with stern attention at me, though with an immovable face.

Then I told him all I knew, and how I knew it; with the one reservation that I left him to infer that I knew from Miss Havisham what I in fact knew from Wemmick. I was very careful indeed as to that. Nor did I look towards Wemmick until I had finished all I had to tell, and had been for some time silently meeting Mr. Jaggers's look. When I did at last turn my eyes in Wemmick's direction, I found that he had unposted his pen, and was intent upon the table before him.

"Hah!" said Mr. Jaggers at last, as he moved towards the papers on the table. "—What item was it you were at, Wemmick, when Mr. Pip came in?"

But I could not submit to be thrown off in that way, and I made a passionate, almost an indignant appeal, to him to be more frank and manly with me. I reminded him of the false hopes into which I had lapsed, the length of time they had lasted, and the discovery I had made: and I hinted at the danger that weighed upon my spirits. I represented myself as being surely worthy of some little confidence from him, in return for the confidence I had just now imparted. I said that I did not blame him, or suspect him, or mistrust him, but I wanted assurance of the truth from him. And if he asked me why I wanted it, and why I thought I had any right to it, I would tell him, little as he cared for such poor dreams, that I had loved Estella dearly and long, and that although I had lost her, and must live a bereaved life, whatever concerned her was still nearer and dearer to me than anything else in the world. And seeing that Mr. Jaggers stood quite still and silent, and apparently quite obdurate, under this appeal, I turned to Wemmick, and said, "Wemmick, I know you to be a man with a gentle heart. I have seen your pleasant home, and your old father, and all the innocent, cheerful playful ways with which you refresh your business life. And I entreat you to say a word for me to Mr. Jaggers, and to represent to him that, all circumstances considered, he ought to be more open with me!"

I have never seen two men look more oddly at one another than Mr. Jaggers and Wemmick did after this apostrophe. At first, a misgiving crossed me that Wemmick would be instantly dismissed from his employment; but it melted as I saw Mr. Jaggers relax into something like a smile, and Wemmick become bolder.

"What's all this?" said Mr. Jaggers. "You with an old father, and you with pleasant and playful ways?"

"Well!" returned Wemmick. "If I don't bring 'em here, what does it matter?"

"Pip," said Mr. Jaggers, laying his hand upon my arm, and

smiling openly, "this man must be the most cunning impostor in all London."

"Not a bit of it," returned Wemmick, growing bolder and bolder. "I think you're another."

Again they exchanged their former odd looks, each apparently still distrustful that the other was taking him in.

"*You* with a pleasant home?" said Mr. Jaggers.

"Since it don't interfere with business," returned Wemmick, "let it be so. Now, I look at you, sir, I shouldn't wonder if *you* might be planning and contriving to have a pleasant home of your own one of these days, when you're tired of all this work."

Mr. Jaggers nodded his head retrospectively two or three times, and actually drew a sigh. "Pip," said he, "we won't talk about 'poor dreams;' you know more about such things than I, having much fresher experience of that kind. But now about this other matter. I'll put a case to you. Mind! I admit nothing."

He waited for me to declare that I quite understood that he expressly said that he admitted nothing.

"Now, Pip," said Mr. Jaggers, "put this case. Put the case that a woman, under such circumstances as you have mentioned, held her child concealed, and was obliged to communicate the fact to her legal adviser, on his representing to her that he must know, with an eye to the latitude of his defence, how the fact stood about that child. Put the case that, at the same time he held a trust to find a child for an eccentric rich lady to adopt and bring up."

"I follow you, sir."

"Put the case that he lived in an atmosphere of evil, and that all he saw of children was their being generated in great numbers for certain destruction. Put the case that he often saw children solemnly tried at a criminal bar, where they were held up to be seen; put the case that he habitually knew of their being imprisoned, whipped, transported, neglected, cast out, qualified in all ways for the hangman, and growing up to be hanged. Put the case that pretty nigh all the children he saw in his daily business life he had reason to look upon as so much spawn, to develop into the fish that were to come to his net—to be prosecuted, defended, forsworn, made orphans, bedevilled somehow."

"I follow you, sir."

"Put the case, Pip, that here was one pretty little child out of the heap who could be saved; whom the father believed dead, and dared make no stir about; as to whom, over the mother, the legal adviser had this power: "I know what you did, and how you did it. You came so and so, you did such and such things to divert suspicion. I have tracked you through it all, and I tell it you all. Part with the child, unless it should be necessary to produce it to clear you, and then it shall be produced. Give the child into my hands, and I will do my best to bring you off. If you are saved, your child is saved too; if you are lost, your child is still saved." Put the case that this was done, and that the woman was cleared."

"I understand you perfectly."

"But that I make no admissions?"

"That you make no admissions." And Wemmick repeated, "No admissions."

"Put the case, Pip, that passion and the terror of death had a little shaken the woman's intellects, and that when she was set at liberty, she was scared out of the ways of the world, and went to him to be sheltered. Put the case that he took her in, and that he kept down the old, wild, violent nature whenever he saw an inkling of its breaking out, by asserting his power over her in the old way. Do you comprehend the imaginary case?"

"Quite."

"Put the case that the child grew up, and was married for money. That the mother was still living. That the father was still living. That the mother and father, unknown to one another, were dwelling within so many miles, furlongs, yards if you like, of one another. That the secret was still a secret, except that you had got wind of it. Put that last case to yourself very carefully."

"I do."

"I ask Wemmick to put it to *himself* very carefully."

And Wemmick said, "I do."

"For whose sake would you reveal the secret? For the father's? I think he would not be much the better for the mother. For the mother's? I think if she had done such a deed she would be safer where she was. For the daughter's? I think it would hardly serve her to establish her parentage for the information of her husband, and to drag her back to disgrace, after an escape of twenty years, pretty secure to last for life. But add the case that you had loved her, Pip, and had made her the subject of those 'poor dreams' which have, at one time or another, been in the heads of more men than you think likely, then I tell you that you had better—and would much sooner when you had thought well of it—chop off that bandaged left hand of yours with your bandaged right hand, and then pass the chopper on to Wemmick there, to cut *that* off too."

I looked at Wemmick, whose face was very grave. He gravely touched his lips with his forefinger. I did the same. Mr. Jaggers did the same. "Now, Wemmick," said the latter then, resuming his usual manner, "what item was it you were at when Mr. Pip came in?"

Standing by for a little, while they were at work, I observed that the odd looks they had cast at one another were repeated several times: with this difference now, that each of them seemed suspicious, not to say conscious, of having shown himself in a weak and unprofessional light to the other. For this reason, I suppose, they were now inflexible with one another; Mr. Jaggers being highly dictatorial, and Wemmick obstinately justifying himself whenever there was the smallest point in abeyance for a moment. I had never seen them on such ill terms; for generally they got on very well indeed together.

But they were both happily relieved by the opportune appearance of Mike, the client with the fur cap and the habit of wiping his nose on his sleeve, whom I had seen on the very first day of my appearance within those walls. This individual, who, either in his own person or in that of some member of his family, seemed to be always in trouble (which in that place meant Newgate), called to announce that his eldest daughter was taken up on suspicion of shoplifting. As he imparted this melancholy circumstance to Wemmick, Mr. Jaggers standing magisterially before the fire and taking no share in the proceedings, Mike's eye happened to twinkle with a tear.

"What are you about?" demanded Wemmick, with the utmost indignation. "What do you come snivelling here for?"

"I didn't go to do it, Mr. Wemmick."

"You did," said Wemmick. "How dare you? You're not in a fit state to come here, if you can't come here without spluttering like a bad pen. What do you mean by it?"

"A man can't help his feelings, Mr. Wemmick," pleaded Mike.

"His what?" demanded Wemmick, quite savagely. "Say that again!"

"Now look here my man," said Mr. Jaggers, advancing a step, and pointing to the door. "Get out of this office. I'll have no feelings here. Get out."

"It serves you right," said Wemmick, "Get out."

So, the unfortunate Mike very humbly withdrew, and Mr. Jaggers and Wemmick appeared to have re-established their good understanding, and went to work again with an air of refreshment upon them as if they had just had lunch.

CHAPTER 13

From Little Britain I went, with my check in my pocket, to Miss Skiffins's brother, the accountant; and Miss Skiffins's brother, the accountant, going straight to Clarriker's and bringing Clarriker to me, I had the great satisfaction of concluding that arrangement. It was the only good thing I had done, and the only completed thing I had done, since I was first apprised of my great expectations.

Clarriker informing me on that occasion that the affairs of the House were steadily progressing, that he would now be able to establish a small branch-house in the East which was much wanted for the extension of the business, and that Herbert in his new partnership capacity would go out and take charge of it, I found that I must have prepared for a separation from my friend, even though my own affairs had been more settled. And now, indeed, I felt as if my last anchor were loosening its hold, and I should soon be driving with the winds and waves.

But there was recompense in the joy with which Herbert would come home of a night and tell me of these changes, little imagining that he told me no news, and would sketch airy pictures of himself conducting Clara Barley to the land of the Arabian Nights, and of me going out to join them (with a caravan of camels, I believe), and of our all going up the Nile and seeing wonders. Without being sanguine as to my own part in those bright plans, I felt that Herbert's way was clearing fast, and that old Bill Barley had but to stick to his pepper and rum, and his daughter would soon be happily provided for.

We had now got into the month of March. My left arm, though it presented no bad symptoms, took, in the natural course, so long to heal that I was still unable to get a coat on. My right arm was tolerably restored; —disfigured, but fairly serviceable.

On a Monday morning, when Herbert and I were at breakfast, I received the following letter from Wemmick by the post.

"Walworth. Burn this as soon as read. Early in the week, or say Wednesday, you might do what you know of, if you felt disposed to try it. Now burn."

When I had shown this to Herbert and had put it in the fire—but not before we had both got it by heart—we considered what to do. For, of course my being disabled could now be no longer kept out of view.

"I have thought it over again and again," said Herbert, "and I think I know a better course than taking a Thames waterman. Take Startop. A good fellow, a skilled hand, fond of us, and enthusiastic and honorable."

I had thought of him more than once.

"But how much would you tell him, Herbert?"

"It is necessary to tell him very little. Let him suppose it a mere freak, but a secret one, until the morning comes: then let him know that there is urgent reason for your getting Provis aboard and away. You go with him?"

"No doubt."

"Where?"

It seemed to me, in the many anxious considerations I had given the point, almost indifferent what port we made for— Hamburg, Rotterdam, Antwerp—the place signified little, so that he was out of England. Any foreign steamer that fell in our way and would take us up would do. I had always proposed to myself to get him well down the river in the boat; certainly well beyond Gravesend, which was a critical place for search or inquiry if suspicion were afoot. As foreign steamers would leave London at about the time of high-water, our plan would be to get down the river by a previous ebb-tide, and lie by in some quiet spot until we could pull off to one. The time when one would be due where we lay, wherever that might be, could be calculated pretty nearly, if we made inquiries beforehand.

Herbert assented to all this, and we went out immediately after breakfast to pursue our investigations. We found that a steamer for Hamburg was likely to suit our purpose best, and we directed our thoughts chiefly to that vessel. But we noted down what other foreign steamers would leave London with the same tide, and we satisfied ourselves that we knew the build and color of each. We then separated for a few hours: I, to get at once such passports as were necessary; Herbert, to see Startop at his lodgings. We both did what we had to do without any hindrance, and when we met again at one o'clock reported it done. I, for my part, was prepared with passports; Herbert had seen Startop, and he was more than ready to join.

Those two should pull a pair of oars, we settled, and I would steer; our charge would be sitter, and keep quiet; as speed was not our object, we should make way enough. We arranged that Herbert should not come home to dinner before going to Mill Pond Bank that evening; that he should not go there at all to-morrow evening, Tuesday; that he should prepare Provis to come down to some stairs hard by the house, on Wednesday, when he saw us approach, and not sooner; that all the arrangements with him should be concluded that Monday night; and that he should be communicated with no more in any way, until we took him on board.

These precautions well understood by both of us, I went home.

On opening the outer door of our chambers with my key, I found a letter in the box, directed to me; a very dirty letter, though not ill-written. It had been delivered by hand (of course, since I left home), and its contents were these:—

"If you are not afraid to come to the old marshes to-night or to-morrow night at nine, and to come to the little sluice-house by the limekiln, you had better come. If you want information regarding your uncle Provis, you had much better come and tell no one, and lose no time. You must come alone. Bring this with you."

I had had load enough upon my mind before the receipt of this strange letter. What to do now, I could not tell. And the worst was, that I must decide quickly, or I should miss the afternoon coach, which would take me down in time for to-night. To-morrow night I could not think of going, for it would be too close upon the time of the flight. And again, for anything I knew, the proffered information might have some important bearing on the flight itself.

If I had had ample time for consideration, I believe I should still have gone. Having hardly any time for consideration—my watch showing me that the coach started within half an hour—I resolved to go. I should certainly not have gone, but for the reference to my Uncle Provis. That, coming on Wemmick's letter and the morning's busy preparation, turned the scale.

It is so difficult to become clearly possessed of the contents of almost any letter, in a violent hurry, that I had to read this mysterious epistle again twice, before its injunction to me to be secret got mechanically into my mind. Yielding to it in the same mechanical kind of way, I left a note in pencil for Herbert, telling him that as I should be so soon going away, I knew not for how long, I had decided to hurry down and back, to ascertain for myself how Miss Havisham was faring. I had then barely time to get my great-coat, lock up the chambers, and make for the coach-office by the short by-ways. If I had taken a hackney-chariot and gone by the streets, I should have missed my aim; going as I did, I caught the coach just as it came out of the yard. I was the only inside passenger, jolting away knee-deep in straw, when I came to myself.

For I really had not been myself since the receipt of the letter; it had so bewildered me, ensuing on the hurry of the morning. The morning hurry and flutter had been great; for, long and anxiously as I had waited for Wemmick, his hint had come like a surprise at last. And now I began to wonder at myself for being in the coach, and to doubt whether I had sufficient reason for being there, and to consider whether I should get out presently and go back, and to argue against ever heeding an anonymous communication, and, in short, to pass through all those phases of contradiction and indecision to which I suppose very few hurried people are strangers. Still, the reference to Provis by name mastered everything. I reasoned as I had reasoned already without knowing it—if that be reasoning—in case any harm should befall him through my not going, how could I ever forgive myself!

It was dark before we got down, and the journey seemed long and dreary to me, who could see little of it inside, and who could not go outside in my disabled state. Avoiding the Blue Boar, I put up at an inn of minor reputation down the town, and ordered some dinner. While it was preparing, I went to Satis House and inquired for Miss Havisham; she was still very ill, though considered something better.

My inn had once been a part of an ancient ecclesiastical house, and I dined in a little octagonal common-room, like a font. As I was not able to cut my dinner, the old landlord with a shining bald head did it for me. This bringing us into conversation, he was so good as to entertain me with my own story—of course with the popular feature that Pumblechook was my earliest benefactor and the founder of my fortunes.

"Do you know the young man?" said I.

"Know him!" repeated the landlord. "Ever since he was—no height at all."

"Does he ever come back to this neighbourhood?"

"Ay, he comes back," said the landlord, "to his great friends, now and again, and gives the cold shoulder to the man that made him."

"What man is that?"

"Him that I speak of," said the landlord. "Mr. Pumblechook."

"Is he ungrateful to no one else?"

"No doubt he would be, if he could," returned the landlord, "but he can't. And why? Because Pumblechook done everything for him."

"Does Pumblechook say so?"

"Say so!" replied the landlord. "He han't no call to say so."

"But does he say so?"

"It would turn a man's blood to white wine winegar to hear him tell of it, sir," said the landlord.

I thought, "Yet Joe, dear Joe, *you* never tell of it. Long-suffering and loving Joe, *you* never complain. Nor you, sweet-tempered Biddy!"

"Your appetite's been touched like by your accident," said the landlord, glancing at the bandaged arm under my coat. "Try a tenderer bit."

"No, thank you," I replied, turning from the table to brood over the fire. "I can eat no more. Please take it away."

I had never been struck at so keenly, for my thanklessness to Joe, as through the brazen impostor Pumblechook. The falser he, the truer Joe; the meaner he, the nobler Joe.

My heart was deeply and most deservedly humbled as I mused over the fire for an hour or more. The striking of the clock aroused me, but not from my dejection or remorse, and I got up and had my coat fastened round my neck, and went out. I had previously sought in my pockets for the letter, that I might refer to it again; but I could not find it, and was uneasy to think that it must have been dropped in the straw of the coach. I knew very well, however, that the appointed place was the little sluice-house by the limekiln on the marshes, and the hour nine. Towards the marshes I now went straight, having no time to spare.

CHAPTER 14

It was a dark night, though the full moon rose as I left the enclosed lands, and passed out upon the marshes. Beyond their dark line there was a ribbon of clear sky, hardly broad enough to hold the red large moon. In a few minutes she had ascended out of that clear field, in among the piled mountains of cloud.

There was a melancholy wind, and the marshes were very dismal. A stranger would have found them insupportable, and even to me they were so oppressive that I hesitated, half inclined to go back. But I knew them well, and could have found my way on a far darker night, and had no excuse for returning, being there. So, having come there against my inclination, I went on against it.

The direction that I took was not that in which my old home lay, nor that in which we had pursued the convicts. My back was turned towards the distant Hulks as I walked on, and, though I could see the old lights away on the spits of sand, I saw them over my shoulder. I knew the limekiln as well as I knew the old Battery, but they were miles apart; so that, if a light had been burning at each point that night, there would have been a long strip of the blank horizon between the two bright specks.

At first, I had to shut some gates after me, and now and then to stand still while the cattle that were lying in the banked-up pathway arose and blundered down among the grass and reeds. But after a little while I seemed to have the whole flats to myself.

It was another half-hour before I drew near to the kiln. The lime was burning with a sluggish stifling smell, but the fires were made up and left, and no workmen were visible. Hard by was a small stone-quarry. It lay directly in my way, and had been worked that day, as I saw by the tools and barrows that were lying about.

Coming up again to the marsh level out of this excavation—for the rude path lay through it—I saw a light in the old sluice-house. I quickened my pace, and knocked at the door with my hand. Waiting for some reply, I looked about me, noticing how the sluice was abandoned and broken, and how the house—of wood with a tiled roof—would not be proof against the weather much longer, if it were so even now, and how the mud and ooze were coated with lime, and how the choking vapor of the kiln crept in a ghostly way towards me. Still there was no answer, and I knocked again. No answer still, and I tried the latch.

It rose under my hand, and the door yielded. Looking in, I saw a lighted candle on a table, a bench, and a mattress on a truckle bedstead. As there was a loft above, I called, "Is there any one here?" but no voice answered. Then I looked at my watch, and, finding that it was past nine, called again, "Is there any one here?" There being still no answer, I went out at the door, irresolute what to do.

It was beginning to rain fast. Seeing nothing save what I had seen already, I turned back into the house, and stood just within the shelter of the doorway, looking out into the night. While I was considering that some one must have been there lately and must soon be coming back, or the candle would not be burning, it came into my head to look if the wick were long. I turned round to do so, and had taken up the candle in my hand, when it was extinguished by some violent shock; and the next thing I comprehended was, that I had been caught in a strong running noose, thrown over my head from behind.

"Now," said a suppressed voice with an oath, "I've got you!"

"What is this?" I cried, struggling. "Who is it? Help, help, help!"

Not only were my arms pulled close to my sides, but the pressure on my bad arm caused me exquisite pain. Sometimes, a strong man's hand, sometimes a strong man's breast, was set against my mouth to deaden my cries, and with a hot breath always close to me, I struggled ineffectually in the dark, while I was fastened tight to the wall. "And now," said the suppressed voice with another oath, "call out again, and I'll make short work of you!"

Faint and sick with the pain of my injured arm, bewildered by the surprise, and yet conscious how easily this threat could be put in execution, I desisted, and tried to ease my arm were it ever so little. But, it was bound too tight for that. I felt as if, having been burnt before, it were now being boiled.

The sudden exclusion of the night, and the substitution of black darkness in its place, warned me that the man had closed a shutter. After groping about for a little, he found the flint and steel he wanted, and began to strike a light. I strained my sight upon the sparks that fell among the tinder, and upon which he breathed and breathed, match in hand, but I could only see his lips, and the blue point of the match; even those but fitfully. The tinder was damp—no wonder there—and one after another the sparks died out.

The man was in no hurry, and struck again with the flint and steel. As the sparks fell thick and bright about him, I could see his hands, and touches of his face, and could make out that he was seated and bending over the table; but nothing more. Presently I saw his blue lips again, breathing on the tinder, and then a flare of light flashed up, and showed me Orlick.

Whom I had looked for, I don't know. I had not looked for him. Seeing him, I felt that I was in a dangerous strait indeed, and I kept my eyes upon him.

He lighted the candle from the flaring match with great

deliberation, and dropped the match, and trod it out. Then he put the candle away from him on the table, so that he could see me, and sat with his arms folded on the table and looked at me. I made out that I was fastened to a stout perpendicular ladder a few inches from the wall—a fixture there—the means of ascent to the loft above.

"Now," said he, when we had surveyed one another for some time, "I've got you."

"Unbind me. Let me go!"

"Ah!" he returned, "I'll let you go. I'll let you go to the moon, I'll let you go to the stars. All in good time."

"Why have you lured me here?"

"Don't you know?" said he, with a deadly look.

"Why have you set upon me in the dark?"

"Because I mean to do it all myself. One keeps a secret better than two. O you enemy, you enemy!"

His enjoyment of the spectacle I furnished, as he sat with his arms folded on the table, shaking his head at me and hugging himself, had a malignity in it that made me tremble. As I watched him in silence, he put his hand into the corner at his side, and took up a gun with a brass-bound stock.

"Do you know this?" said he, making as if he would take aim at me. "Do you know where you saw it afore? Speak, wolf!"

"Yes," I answered.

"You cost me that place. You did. Speak!"

"What else could I do?"

"You did that, and that would be enough, without more. How dared you to come betwixt me and a young woman I liked?"

"When did I?"

"When didn't you? It was you as always give Old Orlick a bad name to her."

"You gave it to yourself; you gained it for yourself. I could have done you no harm, if you had done yourself none."

"You're a liar. And you'll take any pains, and spend any money, to drive me out of this country, will you?" said he, repeating my words to Biddy in the last interview I had with her. "Now, I'll tell you a piece of information. It was never so well worth your while to get me out of this country as it is to-night. Ah! If it was all your money twenty times told, to the last brass farden!" As he shook his heavy hand at me, with his mouth snarling like a tiger's, I felt that it was true.

"What are you going to do to me?"

"I'm a going," said he, bringing his fist down upon the table with a heavy blow, and rising as the blow fell to give it greater force, "I'm a going to have your life!"

He leaned forward staring at me, slowly unclenched his hand and drew it across his mouth as if his mouth watered for me, and sat down again.

"You was always in Old Orlick's way since ever you was a child. You goes out of his way this present night. He'll have no more on you. You're dead."

I felt that I had come to the brink of my grave. For a moment I looked wildly round my trap for any chance of escape; but there was none.

"More than that," said he, folding his arms on the table again, "I won't have a rag of you, I won't have a bone of you, left on earth. I'll put your body in the kiln—I'd carry two such to it, on my shoulders—and, let people suppose what they may of you, they shall never know nothing."

My mind, with inconceivable rapidity followed out all the consequences of such a death. Estella's father would believe I had deserted him, would be taken, would die accusing me; even Herbert would doubt me, when he compared the letter I had left for him with the fact that I had called at Miss Havisham's gate for only a moment; Joe and Biddy would never know how sorry I had been that night, none would ever know what I had suffered, how true I had meant to be, what an agony I had passed through. The death close before me was terrible, but far more terrible than death was the dread of being misremembered after death. And so quick were my thoughts, that I saw myself despised by unborn generations—Estella's children, and their children—while the wretch's words were yet on his lips.

"Now, wolf," said he, "afore I kill you like any other beast— which is wot I mean to do and wot I have tied you up for—I'll have a good look at you and a good goad at you. Oh you enemy!"

It had passed through my thoughts to cry out for help again; though few could know better than I, the solitary nature of the spot, and the hopelessness of aid. But as he sat gloating over me, I was supported by a scornful detestation of him that sealed my lips. Above all things, I resolved that I would not entreat him, and that I would die making some last poor resistance to him. Softened as my thoughts of all the rest of men were in that dire extremity; humbly beseeching pardon, as I did, of Heaven; melted at heart, as I was, by the thought that I had taken no farewell, and never now could take farewell of those who were dear to me, or could explain myself to them, or ask for their compassion on my miserable errors; still, if I could have killed him, even in dying, I would have done it.

He had been drinking, and his eyes were red and bloodshot. Around his neck was slung a tin bottle, as I had often seen his meat and drink slung about him in other days. He brought the bottle to his lips, and took a fiery drink from it; and I smelt the strong spirits that I saw flash into his face.

"Wolf!" said he, folding his arms again, "Old Orlick's a going to tell you somethink. It was you as did for your shrew sister."

Again my mind, with its former inconceivable rapidity, had exhausted the whole subject of the attack upon my sister, her illness, and her death, before his slow and hesitating speech had formed these words.

"It was you, villain," said I.

"I tell you it was your doing—I tell you it was done through you," he retorted, catching up the gun, and making a blow with the stock at the vacant air between us. "I come upon her from behind, as I come upon you to-night. *I* giv' it her! I left her for dead, and if there had been a limekiln as nigh her as there is now nigh you, she shouldn't have come to life again. But it warn't Old Orlick as did it; it was you. You was favored, and he was bullied and beat. Old Orlick bullied and beat, eh? Now you pays for it. You done it; now you pays for it."

He drank again, and became more ferocious. I saw by his tilting of the bottle that there was no great quantity left in it. I distinctly understood that he was working himself up with its contents to make an end of me. I knew that every drop it held was a drop of my life. I knew that when I was changed into a part of the vapor that had crept towards me but a little while before, like my own warning ghost, he would do as he had done in my sister's case—make all haste to the town, and be seen slouching about there drinking at the alehouses. My rapid mind pursued him to the town, made a picture of the street with him in it, and contrasted its lights and life with the lonely marsh and the white vapor creeping over it, into which I should have dissolved.

It was not only that I could have summed up years and years and years while he said a dozen words, but that what he did say presented pictures to me, and not mere words. In the excited and exalted state of my brain, I could not think of a place without seeing it, or of persons without seeing them. It is impossible to overstate the vividness of these images, and yet I was so intent, all the time, upon him himself—who would not be intent on the tiger crouching to spring!—that I knew of the slightest action of his fingers.

When he had drunk this second time, he rose from the bench on which he sat, and pushed the table aside. Then, he took up the candle, and, shading it with his murderous hand so as to throw its light on me, stood before me, looking at me and enjoying the sight.

"Wolf, I'll tell you something more. It was Old Orlick as you tumbled over on your stairs that night."

I saw the staircase with its extinguished lamps. I saw the shadows of the heavy stair-rails, thrown by the watchman's lantern on the wall. I saw the rooms that I was never to see again; here, a door half open; there, a door closed; all the articles of furniture around.

"And why was Old Orlick there? I'll tell you something more, wolf. You and her *have* pretty well hunted me out of this country, so far as getting a easy living in it goes, and I've took up with new companions, and new masters. Some of 'em writes my letters when I wants 'em wrote—do you mind?—writes my letters, wolf! They writes fifty hands; they're not like sneaking you, as writes but one. I've had a firm mind and a firm will to have your life, since you was down here at your sister's burying. I han't seen a way to get you safe, and I've looked arter you to know your ins and outs. For, says Old Orlick to himself, 'Somehow or another I'll have him!' What! When I looks for you, I finds your uncle Provis, eh?"

Mill Pond Bank, and Chinks's Basin, and the Old Green Copper Rope-walk, all so clear and plain! Provis in his rooms, the signal whose use was over, pretty Clara, the good motherly woman, old Bill Barley on his back, all drifting by, as on the swift stream of my life fast running out to sea!"

"You with a uncle too! Why, I know'd you at Gargery's when you was so small a wolf that I could have took your weazen betwixt this finger and thumb and chucked you away dead (as I'd thoughts o' doing, odd times, when I see you loitering amongst the pollards on a Sunday), and you hadn't found no uncles then. No, not you! But when Old Orlick come for to hear that your uncle Provis had most like wore the leg-iron wot

Old Orlick had picked up, filed asunder, on these meshes ever so many year ago, and wot he kep by him till he dropped your sister with it, like a bullock, as he means to drop you—hey?—when he come for to hear that—hey?"

In his savage taunting, he flared the candle so close at me that I turned my face aside to save it from the flame.

"Ah!" he cried, laughing, after doing it again, "the burnt child dreads the fire! Old Orlick knowed you was burnt, Old Orlick knowed you was smuggling your uncle Provis away, Old Orlick's a match for you and know'd you'd come to-night! Now I'll tell you something more, wolf, and this ends it. There's them that's as good a match for your uncle Provis as Old Orlick has been for you. Let him 'ware them, when he's lost his nevvy! Let him 'ware them, when no man can't find a rag of his dear relation's clothes, nor yet a bone of his body. There's them that can't and that won't have Magwitch—yes, *I* know the name!—alive in the same land with them, and that's had such sure information of him when he was alive in another land, as that he couldn't and shouldn't leave it unbeknown and put them in danger. P'raps it's them that writes fifty hands, and that's not like sneaking you as writes but one. 'Ware Compeyson, Magwitch, and the gallows!"

He flared the candle at me again, smoking my face and hair, and for an instant blinding me, and turned his powerful back as he replaced the light on the table. I had thought a prayer, and had been with Joe and Biddy and Herbert, before he turned towards me again.

There was a clear space of a few feet between the table and the opposite wall. Within this space, he now slouched backwards and forwards. His great strength seemed to sit stronger upon him than ever before, as he did this with his hands hanging loose and heavy at his sides, and with his eyes scowling at me. I had no grain of hope left. Wild as my inward hurry was, and wonderful the force of the pictures that rushed by me instead of thoughts, I could yet clearly understand that, unless he had resolved that I was within a few moments of surely perishing out of all human knowledge, he would never have told me what he had told.

Of a sudden, he stopped, took the cork out of his bottle, and tossed it away. Light as it was, I heard it fall like a plummet. He swallowed slowly, tilting up the bottle by little and little, and now he looked at me no more. The last few drops of liquor he poured into the palm of his hand, and licked up. Then, with a sudden hurry of violence and swearing horribly, he threw the bottle from him, and stooped; and I saw in his hand a stone-hammer with a long heavy handle.

The resolution I had made did not desert me, for, without uttering one vain word of appeal to him, I shouted out with all my might, and struggled with all my might. It was only my head and my legs that I could move, but to that extent I struggled with all the force, until then unknown, that was within me. In the same instant I heard responsive shouts, saw figures and a gleam of light dash in at the door, heard voices and tumult, and saw Orlick emerge from a struggle of men, as if it were tumbling water, clear the table at a leap, and fly out into the night.

After a blank, I found that I was lying unbound, on the floor, in the same place, with my head on some one's knee. My eyes were fixed on the ladder against the wall, when I came to myself—had opened on it before my mind saw it—and thus as I recovered consciousness, I knew that I was in the place where I had lost it.

Too indifferent at first, even to look round and ascertain who supported me, I was lying looking at the ladder, when there came between me and it a face. The face of Trabb's boy!

"I think he's all right!" said Trabb's boy, in a sober voice; "but ain't he just pale though!"

At these words, the face of him who supported me looked

over into mine, and I saw my supporter to be—

"Herbert! Great Heaven!"

"Softly," said Herbert. "Gently, Handel. Don't be too eager."

"And our old comrade, Startop!" I cried, as he too bent over me.

"Remember what he is going to assist us in," said Herbert, "and be calm."

The allusion made me spring up; though I dropped again from the pain in my arm. "The time has not gone by, Herbert, has it? What night is to-night? How long have I been here?" For, I had a strange and strong misgiving that I had been lying there a long time—a day and a night—two days and nights—more.

"The time has not gone by. It is still Monday night."

"Thank God!"

"And you have all to-morrow, Tuesday, to rest in," said Herbert. "But you can't help groaning, my dear Handel. What hurt have you got? Can you stand?"

"Yes, yes," said I, "I can walk. I have no hurt but in this throbbing arm."

They laid it bare, and did what they could. It was violently swollen and inflamed, and I could scarcely endure to have it touched. But, they tore up their handkerchiefs to make fresh bandages, and carefully replaced it in the sling, until we could get to the town and obtain some cooling lotion to put upon it. In a little while we had shut the door of the dark and empty sluice-house, and were passing through the quarry on our way back. Trabb's boy—Trabb's overgrown young man now—went before us with a lantern, which was the light I had seen come in at the door. But, the moon was a good two hours higher than when I had last seen the sky, and the night, though rainy, was much lighter. The white vapor of the kiln was passing from us as we went by, and as I had thought a prayer before, I thought a thanksgiving now.

Entreating Herbert to tell me how he had come to my rescue—which at first he had flatly refused to do, but had insisted on my remaining quiet—I learnt that I had in my hurry dropped the letter, open, in our chambers, where he, coming home to bring with him Startop whom he had met in the street on his way to me, found it, very soon after I was gone. Its tone made him uneasy, and the more so because of the inconsistency between it and the hasty letter I had left for him. His uneasiness increasing instead of subsiding, after a quarter of an hour's consideration, he set off for the coach-office with Startop, who volunteered his company, to make inquiry when the next coach went down. Finding that the afternoon coach was gone, and finding that his uneasiness grew into positive alarm, as obstacles came in his way, he resolved to follow in a post-chaise. So he and Startop arrived at the Blue Boar, fully expecting there to find me, or tidings of me; but, finding neither, went on to Miss Havisham's, where they lost me. Hereupon they went back to the hotel (doubtless at about the time when I was hearing the popular local version of my own story) to refresh themselves and to get some one to guide them out upon the marshes. Among the loungers under the Boar's archway happened to be Trabb's Boy—true to his ancient habit of happening to be everywhere where he had no business—and Trabb's boy had seen me passing from Miss Havisham's in the direction of my dining-place. Thus Trabb's boy became their guide, and with him they went out to the sluice-house, though by the town way to the marshes, which I had avoided. Now, as they went along, Herbert reflected, that I might, after all, have been brought there on some genuine and serviceable errand tending to Provis's safety, and, bethinking himself that in that case interruption must be mischievous, left his guide and Startop on the edge of the quarry, and went on by himself, and stole round the house two or three times, endeavouring to ascertain whether all was right within. As he could hear nothing but indistinct sounds of one deep rough voice (this was while my mind was so busy), he even at last began to doubt whether I was there, when suddenly I cried out loudly, and he answered the cries, and rushed in, closely followed by the other two.

When I told Herbert what had passed within the house, he was for our immediately going before a magistrate in the town, late at night as it was, and getting out a warrant. But, I had already considered that such a course, by detaining us there, or binding us to come back, might be fatal to Provis. There was no gainsaying this difficulty, and we relinquished all thoughts of pursuing Orlick at that time. For the present, under the circumstances, we deemed it prudent to make rather light of the matter to Trabb's boy; who, I am convinced, would have been much affected by disappointment, if he had known that his intervention saved me from the limekiln. Not that Trabb's boy was of a malignant nature, but that he had too much spare vivacity, and that it was in his constitution to want variety and excitement at anybody's expense. When we parted, I presented him with two guineas (which seemed to meet his views), and told him that I was sorry ever to have had an ill opinion of him (which made no impression on him at all).

Wednesday being so close upon us, we determined to go back to London that night, three in the post-chaise; the rather, as we should then be clear away before the night's adventure began to be talked of. Herbert got a large bottle of stuff for my arm; and by dint of having this stuff dropped over it all the night through, I was just able to bear its pain on the journey. It was daylight when we reached the Temple, and I went at once to bed, and lay in bed all day.

My terror, as I lay there, of falling ill, and being unfitted for to-morrow, was so besetting, that I wonder it did not disable me of itself. It would have done so, pretty surely, in conjunction with the mental wear and tear I had suffered, but for the unnatural strain upon me that to-morrow was. So anxiously looked forward to, charged with such consequences, its results so impenetrably hidden, though so near.

No precaution could have been more obvious than our refraining from communication with him that day; yet this again increased my restlessness. I started at every footstep and every sound, believing that he was discovered and taken, and this was the messenger to tell me so. I persuaded myself that I knew he was taken; that there was something more upon my mind than a fear or a presentiment; that the fact had occurred, and I had a mysterious knowledge of it. As the days wore on, and no ill news came, as the day closed in and darkness fell, my overshadowing dread of being disabled by illness before to-morrow morning altogether mastered me. My burning arm throbbed, and my burning head throbbed, and I fancied I was beginning to wander. I counted up to high numbers, to make sure of myself, and repeated passages that I knew in prose and verse. It happened sometimes that in the mere escape of a fatigued mind, I dozed for some moments or forgot; then I would say to myself with a start, "Now it has come, and I am turning delirious!"

They kept me very quiet all day, and kept my arm constantly dressed, and gave me cooling drinks. Whenever I fell asleep, I awoke with the notion I had had in the sluice-house, that a long time had elapsed and the opportunity to save him was gone. About midnight I got out of bed and went to Herbert, with the conviction that I had been asleep for four-and-twenty hours, and that Wednesday was past. It was the last self-exhausting effort of my fretfulness, for after that I slept soundly.

Wednesday morning was dawning when I looked out of window. The winking lights upon the bridges were already pale, the coming sun was like a marsh of fire on the horizon. The river, still dark and mysterious, was spanned by bridges that were turning coldly gray, with here and there at top a warm touch from the burning in the sky. As I looked along the clustered roofs, with church-towers and spires shooting into the unusually clear air, the sun rose up, and a veil seemed to be drawn from the river, and millions of sparkles burst out upon its waters. From me too, a veil seemed to be drawn, and I felt strong and well.

Herbert lay asleep in his bed, and our old fellow-student lay asleep on the sofa. I could not dress myself without help; but I made up the fire, which was still burning, and got some coffee ready for them. In good time they too started up strong and well, and we admitted the sharp morning air at the windows, and looked at the tide that was still flowing towards us.

"When it turns at nine o'clock," said Herbert, cheerfully, "look out for us, and stand ready, you over there at Mill Pond Bank!"

CHAPTER 15

It was one of those March days when the sun shines hot and the wind blows cold: when it is summer in the light, and winter in the shade. We had our pea-coats with us, and I took a bag. Of all my worldly possessions I took no more than the few necessaries that filled the bag. Where I might go, what I might do, or when I might return, were questions utterly unknown to me; nor did I vex my mind with them, for it was wholly set on Provis's safety. I only wondered for the passing moment, as I stopped at the door and looked back, under what altered circumstances I should next see those rooms, if ever.

We loitered down to the Temple stairs, and stood loitering there, as if we were not quite decided to go upon the water at all. Of course, I had taken care that the boat should be ready and everything in order. After a little show of indecision, which there were none to see but the two or three amphibious creatures belonging to our Temple stairs, we went on board and cast off; Herbert in the bow, I steering. It was then about high-water—half-past eight.

Our plan was this. The tide, beginning to run down at nine, and being with us until three, we intended still to creep on after it had turned, and row against it until dark. We should then be well in those long reaches below Gravesend, between Kent and Essex, where the river is broad and solitary, where the water-side inhabitants are very few, and where lone public-houses are scattered here and there, of which we could choose one for a resting-place. There, we meant to lie by all night. The steamer for Hamburg and the steamer for Rotterdam would start from London at about nine on Thursday morning. We should know at what time to expect them, according to where we were, and would hail the first; so that, if by any accident we were not taken abroad, we should have another chance. We knew the distinguishing marks of each vessel.

The relief of being at last engaged in the execution of the purpose was so great to me that I felt it difficult to realize the condition in which I had been a few hours before. The crisp air, the sunlight, the movement on the river, and the moving river itself—the road that ran with us, seeming to sympathize with us, animate us, and encourage us on—freshened me with new hope. I felt mortified to be of so little use in the boat; but, there were few better oarsmen than my two friends, and they rowed with a steady stroke that was to last all day.

At that time, the steam-traffic on the Thames was far below its present extent, and watermen's boats were far more numerous. Of barges, sailing colliers, and coasting-traders, there were perhaps, as many as now; but of steam-ships, great and small, not a tithe or a twentieth part so many. Early as it was, there were plenty of scullers going here and there that morning, and plenty of barges dropping down with the tide; the navigation of the river between bridges, in an open boat, was a much easier and commoner matter in those days than it is in these; and we went ahead among many skiffs and wherries briskly.

Old London Bridge was soon passed, and old Billingsgate Market with its oyster-boats and Dutchmen, and the White Tower and Traitor's Gate, and we were in among the tiers of shipping. Here were the Leith, Aberdeen, and Glasgow steamers, loading and unloading goods, and looking immensely high out of the water as we passed alongside; here, were colliers by the score and score, with the coal-whippers plunging off stages on deck, as counterweights to measures of coal swinging up, which were then rattled over the side into barges; here, at her moorings was to-morrow's steamer for Rotterdam, of which we took good notice; and here to-morrow's for Hamburg, under whose bowsprit we crossed. And now I, sitting in the stern, could see, with a faster beating heart, Mill Pond Bank and Mill Pond stairs.

"Is he there?" said Herbert.

"Not yet."

"Right! He was not to come down till he saw us. Can you see his signal?"

"Not well from here; but I think I see it.—Now I see him! Pull both. Easy, Herbert. Oars!"

We touched the stairs lightly for a single moment, and he was on board, and we were off again. He had a boat-cloak with him, and a black canvas bag; and he looked as like a river-pilot as my heart could have wished.

"Dear boy!" he said, putting his arm on my shoulder, as he took his seat. "Faithful dear boy, well done. Thankye, thankye!"

Again among the tiers of shipping, in and out, avoiding rusty chain-cables frayed hempen hawsers and bobbing buoys, sinking for the moment floating broken baskets, scattering floating chips of wood and shaving, cleaving floating scum of coal, in and out, under the figure-head of the John of Sunderland making a speech to the winds (as is done by many Johns), and the Betsy of Yarmouth with a firm formality of bosom and her knobby eyes starting two inches out of her head; in and out, hammers going in ship-builders' yards, saws going at timber, clashing engines going at things unknown, pumps going in leaky ships, capstans going, ships going out to sea, and unintelligible sea-creatures roaring curses over the bulwarks at respondent lightermen, in and out—out at last upon the clearer river, where the ships' boys might take their fenders in, no longer fishing in troubled waters with them over the side, and where the festooned sails might fly out to the wind.

At the Stairs where we had taken him abroad, and ever

since, I had looked warily for any token of our being suspected. I had seen none. We certainly had not been, and at that time as certainly we were not either attended or followed by any boat. If we had been waited on by any boat, I should have run in to shore, and have obliged her to go on, or to make her purpose evident. But we held our own without any appearance of molestation.

He had his boat-cloak on him, and looked, as I have said, a natural part of the scene. It was remarkable (but perhaps the wretched life he had led accounted for it) that he was the least anxious of any of us. He was not indifferent, for he told me that he hoped to live to see his gentleman one of the best of gentlemen in a foreign country; he was not disposed to be passive or resigned, as I understood it; but he had no notion of meeting danger half way. When it came upon him, he confronted it, but it must come before he troubled himself.

"If you knowed, dear boy," he said to me, "what it is to sit here alonger my dear boy and have my smoke, arter having been day by day betwixt four walls, you'd envy me. But you don't know what it is."

"I think I know the delights of freedom," I answered.

"Ah," said he, shaking his head gravely. "But you don't know it equal to me. You must have been under lock and key, dear boy, to know it equal to me—but I ain't a going to be low."

It occurred to me as inconsistent, that, for any mastering idea, he should have endangered his freedom, and even his life. But I reflected that perhaps freedom without danger was too much apart from all the habit of his existence to be to him what it would be to another man. I was not far out, since he said, after smoking a little:—

"You see, dear boy, when I was over yonder, t'other side the world, I was always a looking to this side; and it come flat to be there, for all I was a growing rich. Everybody knowed Magwitch, and Magwitch could come, and Magwitch could go, and nobody's head would be troubled about him. They ain't so easy concerning me here, dear boy—wouldn't be, leastwise, if they knowed where I was."

"If all goes well," said I, "you will be perfectly free and safe again within a few hours." "Well," he returned, drawing a long breath, "I hope so."

"And think so?"

He dipped his hand in the water over the boat's gunwale, and said, smiling with that softened air upon him which was not new to me:—

"Ay, I s'pose I think so, dear boy. We'd be puzzled to be more quiet and easy-going than we are at present. But—it's a flowing so soft and pleasant through the water, p'raps, as makes me think it—I was a thinking through my smoke just then, that we can no more see to the bottom of the next few hours than we can see to the bottom of this river what I catches hold of. Nor yet we can't no more hold their tide than I can hold this. And it's run through my fingers and gone, you see!" holding up his dripping hand.

"But for your face I should think you were a little despondent," said I.

"Not a bit on it, dear boy! It comes of flowing on so quiet, and of that there rippling at the boat's head making a sort of a Sunday tune. Maybe I'm a growing a trifle old besides."

He put his pipe back in his mouth with an undisturbed expression of face, and sat as composed and contented as if we were already out of England. Yet he was as submissive to a word of advice as if he had been in constant terror; for, when we ran ashore to get some bottles of beer into the boat, and he was stepping out, I hinted that I thought he would be safest where he was, and he said. "Do you, dear boy?" and quietly sat down again.

The air felt cold upon the river, but it was a bright day, and the sunshine was very cheering. The tide ran strong, I took care to lose none of it, and our steady stroke carried us on thoroughly well. By imperceptible degrees, as the tide ran out, we lost more and more of the nearer woods and hills, and dropped lower and lower between the muddy banks, but the tide was yet with us when we were off Gravesend. As our charge was wrapped in his cloak, I purposely passed within a boat or two's length of the floating Custom House, and so out to catch the stream, alongside of two emigrant ships, and under the bows of a large transport with troops on the forecastle looking down at us. And soon the tide began to slacken, and the craft lying at anchor to swing, and presently they had all swung round, and the ships that were taking advantage of the new tide to get up to the Pool began to crowd upon us in a fleet, and we kept under the shore, as much out of the strength of the tide now as we could, standing carefully off from low shallows and mud-banks.

Our oarsmen were so fresh, by dint of having occasionally let her drive with the tide for a minute or two, that a quarter of an hour's rest proved full as much as they wanted. We got ashore among some slippery stones while we ate and drank what we had with us, and looked about. It was like my own marsh country, flat and monotonous, and with a dim horizon; while the winding river turned and turned, and the great floating buoys upon it turned and turned, and everything else seemed stranded and still. For now the last of the fleet of ships was round the last low point we had headed; and the last green barge, straw-laden, with a brown sail, had followed; and some ballast-lighters, shaped like a child's first rude imitation of a boat, lay low in the mud; and a little squat shoal-lighthouse on open piles stood crippled in the mud on stilts and crutches; and slimy stakes stuck out of the mud, and slimy stones stuck out of the mud, and red landmarks and tidemarks stuck out of the mud, and an old landing-stage and an old roofless building slipped into the mud, and all about us was stagnation and mud.

We pushed off again, and made what way we could. It was much harder work now, but Herbert and Startop persevered, and rowed and rowed and rowed until the sun went down. By that time the river had lifted us a little, so that we could see above the bank. There was the red sun, on the low level of the shore, in a purple haze, fast deepening into black; and there was the solitary flat marsh; and far away there were the rising grounds, between which and us there seemed to be no life, save here and there in the foreground a melancholy gull.

As the night was fast falling, and as the moon, being past the full, would not rise early, we held a little council; a short one, for clearly our course was to lie by at the first lonely tavern we could find. So, they plied their oars once more, and I looked out for anything like a house. Thus we held on, speaking little, for four or five dull miles. It was very cold, and, a collier coming by us, with her galley-fire smoking and flaring, looked like a comfortable home. The night was as dark by this time as it would be until morning; and what light we had, seemed to come more from the river than the sky, as the oars in their dipping struck at a few reflected stars.

At this dismal time we were evidently all possessed by the idea that we were followed. As the tide made, it flapped heavily at irregular intervals against the shore; and whenever such a sound came, one or other of us was sure to start, and look in that direction. Here and there, the set of the current had worn down the bank into a little creek, and we were all suspicious of such places, and eyed them nervously. Sometimes, "What was that ripple?" one of us would say in a low voice. Or another, "Is that a boat yonder?" And afterwards we would fall into a dead silence, and I would sit impatiently thinking with what an unusual amount of noise the oars worked in the thowels.

At length we descried a light and a roof, and presently afterwards ran alongside a little causeway made of stones that had been picked up hard by. Leaving the rest in the boat, I stepped ashore, and found the light to be in a window of a public-house. It was a dirty place enough, and I dare say not unknown to smuggling adventurers; but there was a good fire in the kitchen, and there were eggs and bacon to eat, and various liquors to drink. Also, there were two double-bedded rooms— "such as they were," the landlord said. No other company was in the house than the landlord, his wife, and a grizzled male creature, the "Jack" of the little causeway, who was as slimy and smeary as if he had been low-water mark too.

With this assistant, I went down to the boat again, and we all came ashore, and brought out the oars, and rudder and boat-hook, and all else, and hauled her up for the night. We made a very good meal by the kitchen fire, and then apportioned the bedrooms: Herbert and Startop were to occupy one; I and our charge the other. We found the air as carefully excluded from both, as if air were fatal to life; and there were more dirty clothes and bandboxes under the beds than I should have thought the family possessed. But we considered ourselves well off, notwithstanding, for a more solitary place we could not have found.

While we were comforting ourselves by the fire after our meal, the Jack—who was sitting in a corner, and who had a bloated pair of shoes on, which he had exhibited while we were eating our eggs and bacon, as interesting relics that he had taken a few days ago from the feet of a drowned seaman washed ashore—asked me if we had seen a four-oared galley going up with the tide? When I told him No, he said she must have gone down then, and yet she "took up too," when she left there.

"They must ha' thought better on't for some reason or another," said the Jack, "and gone down."

"A four-oared galley, did you say?" said I.

"A four," said the Jack, "and two sitters."

"Did they come ashore here?"

"They put in with a stone two-gallon jar for some beer. I'd ha' been glad to pison the beer myself," said the Jack, "or put some rattling physic in it."

"Why?"

"*I* know why," said the Jack. He spoke in a slushy voice, as if much mud had washed into his throat.

"He thinks," said the landlord, a weakly meditative man with a pale eye, who seemed to rely greatly on his Jack: "he thinks they was, what they wasn't."

"*I* knows what I thinks," observed the Jack.

"*You* thinks Custum 'Us, Jack?" said the landlord.

"I do," said the Jack.

"Then you're wrong, Jack."

"AM I!"

In the infinite meaning of his reply and his boundless confidence in his views, the Jack took one of his bloated shoes off, looked into it, knocked a few stones out of it on the kitchen floor, and put it on again. He did this with the air of a Jack who was so right that he could afford to do anything.

"Why, what do you make out that they done with their buttons then, Jack?" asked the landlord, vacillating weakly.

"Done with their buttons?" returned the Jack. "Chucked 'em overboard. Swallered 'em. Sowed 'em, to come up small salad. Done with their buttons!"

"Don't be cheeky, Jack," remonstrated the landlord, in a melancholy and pathetic way.

"A Custum 'Us officer knows what to do with his Buttons," said the Jack, repeating the obnoxious word with the greatest contempt, "when they comes betwixt him and his own light. A four and two sitters don't go hanging and hovering, up with one tide and down with another, and both with and against another, without there being Custum 'Us at the bottom of it." Saying which he went out in disdain; and the landlord, having no one to reply upon, found it impracticable to pursue the subject.

This dialogue made us all uneasy, and me very uneasy. The dismal wind was muttering round the house, the tide was flapping at the shore, and I had a feeling that we were caged and threatened. A four-oared galley hovering about in so unusual a way as to attract this notice was an ugly circumstance that I could not get rid of. When I had induced Provis to go up to bed, I went outside with my two companions (Startop by this time knew the state of the case), and held another council. Whether we should remain at the house until near the steamer's time, which would be about one in the afternoon, or whether we should put off early in the morning, was the question we discussed. On the whole we deemed it the better course to lie where we were, until within an hour or so of the steamer's time, and then to get out in her track, and drift easily with the tide. Having settled to do this, we returned into the house and went to bed.

I lay down with the greater part of my clothes on, and slept well for a few hours. When I awoke, the wind had risen, and the sign of the house (the Ship) was creaking and banging about, with noises that startled me. Rising softly, for my charge lay fast asleep, I looked out of the window. It commanded the causeway where we had hauled up our boat, and, as my eyes adapted themselves to the light of the clouded moon, I saw two men looking into her. They passed by under the window, looking at nothing else, and they did not go down to the landing-place which I could discern to be empty, but struck across the marsh in the direction of the Nore.

My first impulse was to call up Herbert, and show him the two men going away. But reflecting, before I got into his room, which was at the back of the house and adjoined mine, that he and Startop had had a harder day than I, and were fatigued, I forbore. Going back to my window, I could see the two men moving over the marsh. In that light, however, I soon lost them, and, feeling very cold, lay down to think of the matter, and fell asleep again.

We were up early. As we walked to and fro, all four together, before breakfast, I deemed it right to recount what I had seen. Again our charge was the least anxious of the party. It was very likely that the men belonged to the Custom House, he said quietly, and that they had no thought of us. I tried to persuade myself that it was so—as, indeed, it might easily be. However, I proposed that he and I should walk away together to a distant point we could see, and that the boat should take us aboard there, or as near there as might prove feasible, at about noon. This being considered a good precaution, soon after breakfast he and I set forth, without saying anything at the tavern.

He smoked his pipe as we went along, and sometimes stopped to clap me on the shoulder. One would have supposed that it was I who was in danger, not he, and that he was reassuring me. We spoke very little. As we approached the point, I begged him to remain in a sheltered place, while I went on to reconnoitre; for it was towards it that the men had passed in the night. He complied, and I went on alone. There was no boat off the point, nor any boat drawn up anywhere near it, nor were there any signs of the men having embarked there. But, to be sure, the tide was high, and there might have been some footpints under water.

When he looked out from his shelter in the distance, and saw that I waved my hat to him to come up, he rejoined me, and there we waited; sometimes lying on the bank, wrapped in our coats, and sometimes moving about to warm ourselves, until we saw our boat coming round. We got aboard easily, and rowed out into the track of the steamer. By that time it wanted but ten minutes of one o'clock, and we began to look out for her smoke.

But, it was half-past one before we saw her smoke, and soon afterwards we saw behind it the smoke of another steamer.

As they were coming on at full speed, we got the two bags ready, and took that opportunity of saying good by to Herbert and Startop. We had all shaken hands cordially, and neither Herbert's eyes nor mine were quite dry, when I saw a four-oared galley shoot out from under the bank but a little way ahead of us, and row out into the same track.

A stretch of shore had been as yet between us and the steamer's smoke, by reason of the bend and wind of the river; but now she was visible, coming head on. I called to Herbert and Startop to keep before the tide, that she might see us lying by for her, and I adjured Provis to sit quite still, wrapped in his cloak. He answered cheerily, "Trust to me, dear boy," and sat like a statue. Meantime the galley, which was very skilfully handled, had crossed us, let us come up with her, and fallen alongside. Leaving just room enough for the play of the oars, she kept alongside, drifting when we drifted, and pulling a stroke or two when we pulled. Of the two sitters one held the rudder-lines, and looked at us attentively—as did all the rowers; the other sitter was wrapped up, much as Provis was, and seemed to shrink, and whisper some instruction to the steerer as he looked at us. Not a word was spoken in either boat.

Startop could make out, after a few minutes, which steamer was first, and gave me the word "Hamburg," in a low voice, as we sat face to face. She was nearing us very fast, and the beating of her peddles grew louder and louder. I felt as if her shadow were absolutely upon us, when the galley hailed us. I answered.

"You have a returned Transport there," said the man who held the lines. "That's the man, wrapped in the cloak. His name is Abel Magwitch, otherwise Provis. I apprehend that man, and call upon him to surrender, and you to assist."

At the same moment, without giving any audible direction to his crew, he ran the galley abroad of us. They had pulled one sudden stroke ahead, had got their oars in, had run athwart us, and were holding on to our gunwale, before we knew what they were doing. This caused great confusion on board the steamer, and I heard them calling to us, and heard the order given to stop the paddles, and heard them stop, but felt her driving down upon us irresistibly. In the same moment, I saw the steersman of the galley lay his hand on his prisoner's shoulder, and saw that both boats were swinging round with the force of the tide, and saw that all hands on board the steamer were running forward quite frantically. Still, in the same moment, I saw the prisoner start up, lean across his captor, and pull the cloak from the neck of the shrinking sitter in the galley. Still in the same moment, I saw that the face disclosed, was the face of the other convict of long ago. Still, in the same moment, I saw the face tilt backward with a white terror on it that I shall never forget, and heard a great cry on board the steamer, and a loud splash in the water, and felt the boat sink from under me.

It was but for an instant that I seemed to struggle with a thousand mill-weirs and a thousand flashes of light; that instant past, I was taken on board the galley. Herbert was there, and Startop was there; but our boat was gone, and the two convicts were gone.

What with the cries aboard the steamer, and the furious blowing off of her steam, and her driving on, and our driving on, I could not at first distinguish sky from water or shore from shore; but the crew of the galley righted her with great speed, and, pulling certain swift strong strokes ahead, lay upon their oars, every man looking silently and eagerly at the water astern. Presently a dark object was seen in it, bearing towards us on the tide. No man spoke, but the steersman held up his hand, and all softly backed water, and kept the boat straight and true before it. As it came nearer, I saw it to be Magwitch, swimming, but not swimming freely. He was taken on board, and instantly manacled at the wrists and ankles.

The galley was kept steady, and the silent, eager look-out at the water was resumed. But, the Rotterdam steamer now came up, and apparently not understanding what had happened, came on at speed. By the time she had been hailed and stopped, both steamers were drifting away from us, and we were rising and falling in a troubled wake of water. The look-out was kept, long after all was still again and the two steamers were gone; but everybody knew that it was hopeless now.

At length we gave it up, and pulled under the shore towards the tavern we had lately left, where we were received with no little surprise. Here I was able to get some comforts for Magwitch—Provis no longer—who had received some very severe injury in the Chest, and a deep cut in the head.

He told me that he believed himself to have gone under the keel of the steamer, and to have been struck on the head in rising. The injury to his chest (which rendered his breathing extremely painful) he thought he had received against the side of the galley. He added that he did not pretend to say what he might or might not have done to Compeyson, but that, in the moment of his laying his hand on his cloak to identify him, that villain had staggered up and staggered back, and they had both gone overboard together, when the sudden wrenching of him (Magwitch) out of our boat, and the endeavor of his captor to keep him in it, had capsized us. He told me in a whisper that they had gone down fiercely locked in each other's arms, and that there had been a struggle under water, and that he had disengaged himself, struck out, and swum away.

I never had any reason to doubt the exact truth of what he thus told me. The officer who steered the galley gave the same account of their going overboard.

When I asked this officer's permission to change the prisoner's wet clothes by purchasing any spare garments I could get at the public-house, he gave it readily: merely observing that he must take charge of everything his prisoner had about him. So the pocket-book which had once been in my hands passed into the officer's. He further gave me leave to accompany the prisoner to London; but declined to accord that grace to my two friends.

The Jack at the Ship was instructed where the drowned man had gone down, and undertook to search for the body in the places where it was likeliest to come ashore. His interest in its recovery seemed to me to be much heightened when he heard that it had stockings on. Probably, it took about a dozen drowned men to fit him out completely; and that may have been the reason why the different articles of his dress were in various stages of decay.

We remained at the public-house until the tide turned, and then Magwitch was carried down to the galley and put on board. Herbert and Startop were to get to London by land, as soon as they could. We had a doleful parting, and when I took my place by Magwitch's side, I felt that that was my place henceforth while he lived.

For now, my repugnance to him had all melted away; and in the hunted, wounded, shackled creature who held my hand in his, I only saw a man who had meant to be my benefactor, and who had felt affectionately, gratefully, and generously, towards me with great constancy through a series of years. I only saw in him a much better man than I had been to Joe.

His breathing became more difficult and painful as the night drew on, and often he could not repress a groan. I tried to rest him on the arm I could use, in any easy position; but it was dreadful to think that I could not be sorry at heart for his being badly hurt, since it was unquestionably best that he should die. That there were, still living, people enough who were able and willing to identify him, I could not doubt. That he would be leniently treated, I could not hope. He who had been presented in the worst light at his trial, who had since broken prison and had been tried again, who had returned from transportation under a life sentence, and who had occasioned the death of the man who was the cause of his arrest.

As we returned towards the setting sun we had yesterday left behind us, and as the stream of our hopes seemed all running back, I told him how grieved I was to think that he had come home for my sake.

"Dear boy," he answered, "I'm quite content to take my chance. I've seen my boy, and he can be a gentleman without me."

No. I had thought about that, while we had been there side by side. No. Apart from any inclinations of my own, I understood Wemmick's hint now. I foresaw that, being convicted, his possessions would be forfeited to the Crown.

"Look'ee here, dear boy," said he "It's best as a gentleman should not be knowed to belong to me now. Only come to see me as if you come by chance alonger Wemmick. Sit where I can see you when I am swore to, for the last o' many times, and I don't ask no more."

"I will never stir from your side," said I, "when I am suffered to be near you. Please God, I will be as true to you as you have been to me!"

I felt his hand tremble as it held mine, and he turned his face away as he lay in the bottom of the boat, and I heard that old sound in his throat—softened now, like all the rest of him. It was a good thing that he had touched this point, for it put into my mind what I might not otherwise have thought of until too late: That he need never know how his hopes of enriching me had perished.

CHAPTER 16

He was taken to the Police Court next day, and would have been immediately committed for trial, but that it was necessary to send down for an old officer of the prison-ship from which he had once escaped, to speak to his identity. Nobody doubted it; but Compeyson, who had meant to depose to it, was tumbling on the tides, dead, and it happened that there was not at that time any prison officer in London who could give the required evidence. I had gone direct to Mr. Jaggers at his private house, on my arrival over night, to retain his assistance, and Mr. Jaggers on the prisoner's behalf would admit nothing. It was the sole resource; for he told me that the case must be over in five minutes when the witness was there, and that no power on earth could prevent its going against us.

I imparted to Mr. Jaggers my design of keeping him in ignorance of the fate of his wealth. Mr. Jaggers was querulous and angry with me for having "let it slip through my fingers," and said we must memorialize by and by, and try at all events for some of it. But he did not conceal from me that, although there might be many cases in which the forfeiture would not be exacted, there were no circumstances in this case to make it one of them. I understood that very well. I was not related to the outlaw, or connected with him by any recognizable tie; he had put his hand to no writing or settlement in my favor before his apprehension, and to do so now would be idle. I had no claim, and I finally resolved, and ever afterwards abided by the resolution, that my heart should never be sickened with the hopeless task of attempting to establish one.

There appeared to be reason for supposing that the drowned

informer had hoped for a reward out of this forfeiture, and had obtained some accurate knowledge of Magwitch's affairs. When his body was found, many miles from the scene of his death, and so horribly disfigured that he was only recognizable by the contents of his pockets, notes were still legible, folded in a case he carried. Among these were the name of a banking-house in New South Wales, where a sum of money was, and the designation of certain lands of considerable value. Both these heads of information were in a list that Magwitch, while in prison, gave to Mr. Jaggers, of the possessions he supposed I should inherit. His ignorance, poor fellow, at last served him; he never mistrusted but that my inheritance was quite safe, with Mr. Jaggers's aid.

After three days' delay, during which the crown prosecution stood over for the production of the witness from the prison-ship, the witness came, and completed the easy case. He was committed to take his trial at the next Sessions, which would come on in a month.

It was at this dark time of my life that Herbert returned home one evening, a good deal cast down, and said:

"My dear Handel, I fear I shall soon have to leave you."

His partner having prepared me for that, I was less surprised than he thought.

"We shall lose a fine opportunity if I put off going to Cairo, and I am very much afraid I must go, Handel, when you most need me."

"Herbert, I shall always need you, because I shall always love you; but my need is no greater now than at another time."

"You will be so lonely."

"I have not leisure to think of that," said I. "You know that I am always with him to the full extent of the time allowed, and that I should be with him all day long, if I could. And when I come away from him, you know that my thoughts are with him."

The dreadful condition to which he was brought, was so appalling to both of us, that we could not refer to it in plainer words.

"My dear fellow," said Herbert, "let the near prospect of our separation—for, it is very near—be my justification for troubling you about yourself. Have you thought of your future?"

"No, for I have been afraid to think of any future."

"But yours cannot be dismissed; indeed, my dear dear Handel, it must not be dismissed. I wish you would enter on it now, as far as a few friendly words go, with me."

"I will," said I.

"In this branch house of ours, Handel, we must have a—"

I saw that his delicacy was avoiding the right word, so I said, "A clerk."

"A clerk. And I hope it is not at all unlikely that he may expand (as a clerk of your acquaintance has expanded) into a partner. Now, Handel—in short, my dear boy, will you come to me?"

There was something charmingly cordial and engaging in the manner in which after saying "Now, Handel," as if it were the grave beginning of a portentous business exordium, he had suddenly given up that tone, stretched out his honest hand, and spoken like a schoolboy.

"Clara and I have talked about it again and again," Herbert pursued, "and the dear little thing begged me only this evening, with tears in her eyes, to say to you that, if you will live with us when we come together, she will do her best to make you happy, and to convince her husband's friend that he is her friend too. We should get on so well, Handel!"

I thanked her heartily, and I thanked him heartily, but said I could not yet make sure of joining him as he so kindly offered. Firstly, my mind was too preoccupied to be able to take in the subject clearly. Secondly—Yes! Secondly, there was a vague something lingering in my thoughts that will come out very near the end of this slight narrative.

"But if you thought, Herbert, that you could, without doing any injury to your business, leave the question open for a little while—"

"For any while," cried Herbert. "Six months, a year!"

"Not so long as that," said I. "Two or three months at most."

Herbert was highly delighted when we shook hands on this arrangement, and said he could now take courage to tell me that he believed he must go away at the end of the week.

"And Clara?" said I.

"The dear little thing," returned Herbert, "holds dutifully to her father as long as he lasts; but he won't last long. Mrs. Whimple confides to me that he is certainly going."

"Not to say an unfeeling thing," said I, "he cannot do better than go."

"I am afraid that must be admitted," said Herbert; "and then I shall come back for the dear little thing, and the dear little thing and I will walk quietly into the nearest church. Remember! The blessed darling comes of no family, my dear Handel, and never looked into the red book, and hasn't a notion about her grandpapa. What a fortune for the son of my mother!"

On the Saturday in that same week, I took my leave of Herbert—full of bright hope, but sad and sorry to leave me—as he sat on one of the seaport mail coaches. I went into a coffee-house to write a little note to Clara, telling her he had gone off, sending his love to her over and over again, and then went to my lonely home—if it deserved the name; for it was now no home to me, and I had no home anywhere.

On the stairs I encountered Wemmick, who was coming down, after an unsuccessful application of his knuckles to my door. I had not seen him alone since the disastrous issue of the attempted flight; and he had come, in his private and personal capacity, to say a few words of explanation in reference to that failure.

"The late Compeyson," said Wemmick, "had by little and little got at the bottom of half of the regular business now transacted; and it was from the talk of some of his people in trouble (some of his people being always in trouble) that I heard what I did. I kept my ears open, seeming to have them shut, until I heard that he was absent, and I thought that would be the best time for making the attempt. I can only suppose now, that it was a part of his policy, as a very clever man, habitually to deceive his own instruments. You don't blame me, I hope, Mr. Pip? I am sure I tried to serve you, with all my heart."

"I am as sure of that, Wemmick, as you can be, and I thank you most earnestly for all your interest and friendship."

"Thank you, thank you very much. It's a bad job," said Wemmick, scratching his head, "and I assure you I haven't been so cut up for a long time. What I look at is the sacrifice of so much portable property. Dear me!"

"What *I* think of, Wemmick, is the poor owner of the property."

"Yes, to be sure," said Wemmick. "Of course, there can be no objection to your being sorry for him, and I'd put down a five-pound note myself to get him out of it. But what I look at is this. The late Compeyson having been beforehand with him in intelligence of his return, and being so determined to bring him to book, I do not think he could have been saved. Whereas, the portable property certainly could have been saved. That's the difference between the property and the owner, don't you see?"

I invited Wemmick to come up stairs, and refresh himself with a glass of grog before walking to Walworth. He accepted the invitation. While he was drinking his moderate allowance, he said, with nothing to lead up to it, and after having appeared rather fidgety:

"What do you think of my meaning to take a holiday on Monday, Mr. Pip?"

"Why, I suppose you have not done such a thing these twelve months."

"These twelve years, more likely," said Wemmick. "Yes. I'm going to take a holiday. More than that; I'm going to take a walk. More than that; I'm going to ask you to take a walk with me."

I was about to excuse myself, as being but a bad companion just then, when Wemmick anticipated me.

"I know your engagements," said he, "and I know you are out of sorts, Mr. Pip. But if you *could* oblige me, I should take it as a kindness. It ain't a long walk, and it's an early one. Say it might occupy you (including breakfast on the walk) from eight to twelve. Couldn't you stretch a point and manage it?"

He had done so much for me at various times, that this was very little to do for him. I said I could manage it—would manage it—and he was so very much pleased by my acquiescence, that I was pleased too. At his particular request, I appointed to call for him at the Castle at half past eight on Monday morning, and so we parted for the time.

Punctual to my appointment, I rang at the Castle gate on the Monday morning, and was received by Wemmick himself, who struck me as looking tighter than usual, and having a sleeker hat on. Within, there were two glasses of rum and milk prepared, and two biscuits. The Aged must have been stirring with the lark, for, glancing into the perspective of his bedroom, I observed that his bed was empty.

When we had fortified ourselves with the rum and milk and biscuits, and were going out for the walk with that training preparation on us, I was considerably surprised to see Wemmick take up a fishing-rod, and put it over his shoulder. "Why, we are not going fishing!" said I. "No," returned Wemmick, "but I like to walk with one."

I thought this odd; however, I said nothing, and we set off. We went towards Camberwell Green, and when we were thereabouts, Wemmick said suddenly:

"Halloa! Here's a church!"

There was nothing very surprising in that; but again, I was rather surprised, when he said, as if he were animated by a brilliant idea:

"Let's go in!"

We went in, Wemmick leaving his fishing-rod in the porch, and looked all round. In the mean time, Wemmick was diving into his coat-pockets, and getting something out of paper there.

"Halloa!" said he. "Here's a couple of pair of gloves! Let's put 'em on!"

As the gloves were white kid gloves, and as the post-office was widened to its utmost extent, I now began to have my strong suspicions. They were strengthened into certainty when I beheld the Aged enter at a side door, escorting a lady.

"Halloa!" said Wemmick. "Here's Miss Skiffins! Let's have a wedding."

That discreet damsel was attired as usual, except that she was now engaged in substituting for her green kid gloves a pair of white. The Aged was likewise occupied in preparing a similar sacrifice for the altar of Hymen. The old gentleman, however, experienced so much difficulty in getting his gloves on, that Wemmick found it necessary to put him with his back against a pillar, and then to get behind the pillar himself and pull away at them, while I for my part held the old gentleman round the waist, that he might present and equal and safe resistance. By dint of this ingenious scheme, his gloves were got on to perfection.

The clerk and clergyman then appearing, we were ranged in order at those fatal rails. True to his notion of seeming to do it all without preparation, I heard Wemmick say to himself, as he took something out of his waistcoat-pocket before the service began, "Halloa! Here's a ring!"

I acted in the capacity of backer, or best-man, to the bridegroom; while a little limp pew-opener in a soft bonnet like a baby's, made a feint of being the bosom friend of Miss Skiffins. The responsibility of giving the lady away devolved upon the Aged, which led to the clergyman's being unintentionally scandalized, and it happened thus. When he said, "Who giveth this woman to be married to this man?" the old gentlemen, not in the least knowing what point of the ceremony we had arrived at, stood most amiably beaming at the ten commandments. Upon which, the clergyman said again, "who giveth this woman to be married to this man?" The old gentleman being still in a state of most estimable unconsciousness, the bridegroom cried out in his accustomed voice, "Now Aged P. you know; who giveth?" To which the Aged replied with great briskness, before saying that *he* gave, "All right, John, all right, my boy!" And the clergyman came to so gloomy a pause upon it, that I had doubts for the moment whether we should get completely married that day.

It was completely done, however, and when we were going out of church Wemmick took the cover off the font, and put his white gloves in it, and put the cover on again. Mrs. Wemmick, more heedful of the future, put her white gloves in her pocket and assumed her green. "Now, Mr. Pip," said Wemmick, triumphantly shouldering the fishing-rod as we came out, "let me ask you whether anybody would suppose this to be a wedding-party!"

Breakfast had been ordered at a pleasant little tavern, a mile or so away upon the rising ground beyond the green; and there was a bagatelle board in the room, in case we should desire to unbend our minds after the solemnity. It was pleasant to observe that Mrs. Wemmick no longer unwound Wemmick's arm when it adapted itself to her figure, but sat in a high-backed chair against the wall, like a violoncello in its case, and submitted to be embraced as that melodious instrument might have done.

We had an excellent breakfast, and when any one declined anything on table, Wemmick said, "Provided by contract, you know; don't be afraid of it!" I drank to the new couple, drank to the Aged, drank to the Castle, saluted the bride at parting, and made myself as agreeable as I could.

Wemmick came down to the door with me, and I again shook hands with him, and wished him joy.

"Thankee!" said Wemmick, rubbing his hands. "She's such a manager of fowls, you have no idea. You shall have some eggs, and judge for yourself. I say, Mr. Pip!" calling me back, and speaking low. "This is altogether a Walworth sentiment, please."

"I understand. Not to be mentioned in Little Britain," said I.

Wemmick nodded. "After what you let out the other day, Mr. Jaggers may as well not know of it. He might think my brain was softening, or something of the kind."

CHAPTER 17

He lay in prison very ill, during the whole interval between his committal for trial and the coming round of the Sessions. He had broken two ribs, they had wounded one of his lungs, and he breathed with great pain and difficulty, which increased daily. It was a consequence of his hurt that he spoke so low as to be scarcely audible; therefore he spoke very little. But he was ever ready to listen to me; and it became the first duty of my life to say to him, and read to him, what I knew he ought to hear.

Being far too ill to remain in the common prison, he was removed, after the first day or so, into the infirmary. This gave me opportunities of being with him that I could not otherwise have had. And but for his illness he would have been put in irons, for he was regarded as a determined prison-breaker, and I know not what else.

Although I saw him every day, it was for only a short time; hence, the regularly recurring spaces of our separation were long enough to record on his face any slight changes that occurred in his physical state. I do not recollect that I once saw any change in it for the better; he wasted, and became slowly weaker and worse, day by day, from the day when the prison door closed upon him.

The kind of submission or resignation that he showed was that of a man who was tired out. I sometimes derived an impression, from his manner or from a whispered word or two which escaped him, that he pondered over the question whether he might have been a better man under better circumstances. But he never justified himself by a hint tending that way, or tried to bend the past out of its eternal shape.

It happened on two or three occasions in my presence, that his desperate reputation was alluded to by one or other of the people in attendance on him. A smile crossed his face then, and he turned his eyes on me with a trustful look, as if he were confident that I had seen some small redeeming touch in him, even so long ago as when I was a little child. As to all the rest, he was humble and contrite, and I never knew him complain.

When the Sessions came round, Mr. Jaggers caused an application to be made for the postponement of his trial until the following Sessions. It was obviously made with the assurance that he could not live so long, and was refused. The trial came on at once, and, when he was put to the bar, he was seated in a chair. No objection was made to my getting close to the dock, on the outside of it, and holding the hand that he stretched forth to me.

The trial was very short and very clear. Such things as could be said for him were said—how he had taken to industrious habits, and had thriven lawfully and reputably. But nothing could unsay the fact that he had returned, and was there in presence of the Judge and Jury. It was impossible to try him for that, and do otherwise than find him guilty.

At that time, it was the custom (as I learnt from my terrible experience of that Sessions) to devote a concluding day to the passing of Sentences, and to make a finishing effect with the Sentence of Death. But for the indelible picture that my remembrance now holds before me, I could scarcely believe, even as I write these words, that I saw two-and-thirty men and women put before the Judge to receive that sentence together. Foremost among the two-and-thirty was he; seated, that he might get breath enough to keep life in him.

The whole scene starts out again in the vivid colors of the moment, down to the drops of April rain on the windows of the court, glittering in the rays of April sun. Penned in the dock, as I again stood outside it at the corner with his hand in mine, were the two-and-thirty men and women; some defiant, some stricken with terror, some sobbing and weeping, some covering their faces, some staring gloomily about. There had been shrieks from among the women convicts; but they had been stilled, and a hush had succeeded. The sheriffs with their great chains and nosegays, other civic gewgaws and monsters, criers, ushers, a great gallery full of people—a large theatrical audience—looked on, as the two-and-thirty and the Judge were solemnly confronted. Then the Judge addressed them. Among the wretched creatures before him whom he must single out for special address was one who almost from his infancy had been an offender against the laws; who, after repeated imprisonments and punishments, had been at length sentenced to exile for a term of years; and who, under circumstances of great violence and daring, had made his escape and been re-sentenced to exile for life. That miserable man would seem for a time to have become convinced of his errors, when far removed from the scenes of his old offences, and to have lived a peaceable and honest life. But in a fatal moment, yielding to those propensities and passions, the indulgence of which had so long rendered him a scourge to society, he had quitted his haven of rest and repentance, and had come back to the country where he was proscribed. Being here presently denounced, he had for a time succeeded in evading the officers of Justice, but being at length seized while in the act of flight, he had resisted them, and had—he best knew whether by express design, or in the blindness of his hardihood—caused the death of his denouncer, to whom his whole career was known. The appointed punishment for his return to the land that had cast him out, being Death, and his case being this aggravated case, he must prepare himself to Die.

The sun was striking in at the great windows of the court, through the glittering drops of rain upon the glass, and it made a broad shaft of light between the two-and-thirty and the Judge, linking both together, and perhaps reminding some among the audience how both were passing on, with absolute equality, to the greater Judgment that knoweth all things, and cannot err. Rising for a moment, a distinct speck of face in this way of light, the prisoner said, "My Lord, I have received my sentence of Death from the Almighty, but I bow to yours," and sat down again. There was some hushing, and the Judge went on with what he had to say to the rest. Then they were all formally doomed, and some of them were supported out, and some of them sauntered out with a haggard look of bravery, and a few nodded to the gallery, and two or three shook hands, and others went out chewing the fragments of herb they had taken from the sweet herbs lying about. He went last of all, because of having to be helped from his chair, and to go very slowly; and he held my hand while all the others were removed, and while the audience got up (putting their dresses right, as they might at church or elsewhere), and pointed down at this criminal or at that, and most of all at him and me.

I earnestly hoped and prayed that he might die before the Recorder's Report was made; but, in the dread of his lingering on, I began that night to write out a petition to the Home Secretary of State, setting forth my knowledge of him, and how it was that he had come back for my sake. I wrote it as fervently and pathetically as I could; and when I had finished it and sent it in, I wrote out other petitions to such men in authority as I hoped were the most merciful, and drew up one to the Crown itself. For several days and nights after he was sentenced I took no rest except when I fell asleep in my chair, but was wholly absorbed in these appeals. And after I had sent them in, I could not keep away from the places where they were, but felt as if they were more hopeful and less desperate when I was near them. In this unreasonable restlessness and pain of mind I would roam the streets of an evening, wandering by those offices and houses where I had left the petitions. To the present hour, the weary western streets of London on a cold, dusty spring night, with their ranges of stern, shut-up mansions, and their long rows of lamps, are melancholy to me from this association.

The daily visits I could make him were shortened now, and he was more strictly kept. Seeing, or fancying, that I was suspected of an intention of carrying poison to him, I asked to be searched before I sat down at his bedside, and told the officer who was always there, that I was willing to do anything that would assure him of the singleness of my designs. Nobody was hard with him or with me. There was duty to be done, and it was done, but not harshly. The officer always gave me the assurance that he was worse, and some other sick prisoners in the room, and some other prisoners who attended on them as sick nurses, (malefactors, but not incapable of kindness, God be thanked!) always joined in the same report.

As the days went on, I noticed more and more that he would lie placidly looking at the white ceiling, with an absence of light in his face until some word of mine brightened it for an instant, and then it would subside again. Sometimes he was almost or quite unable to speak, then he would answer me with slight pressures on my hand, and I grew to understand his meaning very well.

The number of the days had risen to ten, when I saw a greater change in him than I had seen yet. His eyes were turned towards the door, and lighted up as I entered.

"Dear boy," he said, as I sat down by his bed: "I thought you was late. But I knowed you couldn't be that."

"It is just the time," said I. "I waited for it at the gate."

"You always waits at the gate; don't you, dear boy?"

"Yes. Not to lose a moment of the time."

"Thank'ee dear boy, thank'ee. God bless you! You've never deserted me, dear boy."

I pressed his hand in silence, for I could not forget that I had once meant to desert him.

"And what's the best of all," he said, "you've been more comfortable alonger me, since I was under a dark cloud, than when the sun shone. That's best of all."

He lay on his back, breathing with great difficulty. Do what he would, and love me though he did, the light left his face ever and again, and a film came over the placid look at the white ceiling.

"Are you in much pain to-day?"

"I don't complain of none, dear boy."

"You never do complain."

He had spoken his last words. He smiled, and I understood his touch to mean that he wished to lift my hand, and lay it on his breast. I laid it there, and he smiled again, and put both his hands upon it.

The allotted time ran out, while we were thus; but, looking round, I found the governor of the prison standing near me, and he whispered, "You needn't go yet." I thanked him gratefully, and asked, "Might I speak to him, if he can hear me?"

The governor stepped aside, and beckoned the officer away. The change, though it was made without noise, drew back the film from the placid look at the white ceiling, and he looked most affectionately at me.

"Dear Magwitch, I must tell you now, at last. You understand what I say?"

A gentle pressure on my hand.

"You had a child once, whom you loved and lost."

A stronger pressure on my hand.

"She lived, and found powerful friends. She is living now. She is a lady and very beautiful. And I love her!"

With a last faint effort, which would have been powerless but for my yielding to it and assisting it, he raised my hand to his lips. Then, he gently let it sink upon his breast again, with his own hands lying on it. The placid look at the white ceiling came back, and passed away, and his head dropped quietly on his breast.

Mindful, then, of what we had read together, I thought of the two men who went up into the Temple to pray, and I knew there were no better words that I could say beside his bed, than "O Lord, be merciful to him a sinner!"

CHAPTER 18

Now that I was left wholly to myself, I gave notice of my intention to quit the chambers in the Temple as soon as my tenancy could legally determine, and in the meanwhile to underlet them. At once I put bills up in the windows; for, I was in debt, and had scarcely any money, and began to be seriously alarmed by the state of my affairs. I ought rather to write that I should have been alarmed if I had had energy and concentration enough to help me to the clear perception of any truth beyond the fact that I was falling very ill. The late stress upon me had enabled me to put off illness, but not to put it away; I knew that it was coming on me now, and I knew very little else, and was even careless as to that.

For a day or two, I lay on the sofa, or on the floor—anywhere, according as I happened to sink down—with a heavy head and aching limbs, and no purpose, and no power. Then there came, one night which appeared of great duration, and which teemed with anxiety and horror; and when in the morning I tried to sit up in my bed and think of it, I found I could not do so.

Whether I really had been down in Garden Court in the dead of the night, groping about for the boat that I supposed to be there; whether I had two or three times come to myself on the staircase with great terror, not knowing how I had got out of bed; whether I had found myself lighting the lamp, possessed by the idea that he was coming up the stairs, and that the lights were blown out; whether I had been inexpressibly harassed by the distracted talking, laughing, and groaning of some one, and had half suspected those sounds to be of my own making; whether there had been a closed iron furnace in a dark corner of the room, and a voice had called out, over and over again, that Miss Havisham was consuming within it; these were things that I tried to settle with myself and get into some order, as I lay that morning on my bed. But the vapor of a limekiln would come between me and them, disordering them all, and it was through the vapor at last that I saw two men looking at me.

"What do you want?" I asked, starting; "I don't know you."

"Well, sir," returned one of them, bending down and touching me on the shoulder, "this is a matter that you'll soon arrange, I dare say, but you're arrested."

"What is the debt?"

"Hundred and twenty-three pound, fifteen, six. Jeweller's account, I think."

"What is to be done?"

"You had better come to my house," said the man. "I keep a very nice house."

I made some attempt to get up and dress myself. When I next attended to them, they were standing a little off from the bed, looking at me. I still lay there.

"You see my state," said I. "I would come with you if I could; but indeed I am quite unable. If you take me from here, I think I shall die by the way."

Perhaps they replied, or argued the point, or tried to encourage me to believe that I was better than I thought. Forasmuch as they hang in my memory by only this one slender thread, I don't know what they did, except that they forbore to remove me.

That I had a fever and was avoided, that I suffered greatly, that I often lost my reason, that the time seemed interminable, that I confounded impossible existences with my own identity; that I was a brick in the house-wall, and yet entreating to be released from the giddy place where the builders had set me; that I was a steel beam of a vast engine, clashing and whirling over a gulf, and yet that I implored in my own person to have the engine stopped, and my part in it hammered off; that I passed through these phases of disease, I know of my own remembrance, and did in some sort know at the time. That I sometimes struggled with real people, in the belief that they were murderers, and that I would all at once comprehend that they meant to do me good, and would then sink exhausted in their arms, and suffer them to lay me down, I also knew at the time. But, above all, I knew that there was a constant tendency in all these people—who, when I was very ill, would present all kinds of extraordinary transformations of the human face, and would be much dilated in size—above all, I say, I knew that there was an extraordinary tendency in all these people, sooner or later, to settle down into the likeness of Joe.

After I had turned the worst point of my illness, I began to notice that while all its other features changed, this one consistent feature did not change. Whoever came about me, still settled down into Joe. I opened my eyes in the night, and I saw, in the great chair at the bedside, Joe. I opened my eyes in the day, and, sitting on the window-seat, smoking his pipe in the shaded open window, still I saw Joe. I asked for cooling drink, and the dear hand that gave it me was Joe's. I sank back on my pillow after drinking, and the face that looked so hopefully and tenderly upon me was the face of Joe.

At last, one day, I took courage, and said, "*Is* it Joe?"

And the dear old home-voice answered, "Which it air, old chap."

"O Joe, you break my heart! Look angry at me, Joe. Strike me, Joe. Tell me of my ingratitude. Don't be so good to me!"

For Joe had actually laid his head down on the pillow at my side, and put his arm round my neck, in his joy that I knew him.

"Which dear old Pip, old chap," said Joe, "you and me was

ever friends. And when you're well enough to go out for a ride—what larks!"

After which, Joe withdrew to the window, and stood with his back towards me, wiping his eyes. And as my extreme weakness prevented me from getting up and going to him, I lay there, penitently whispering, "O God bless him! O God bless this gentle Christian man!"

Joe's eyes were red when I next found him beside me; but I was holding his hand, and we both felt happy.

"How long, dear Joe?"

"Which you meantersay, Pip, how long have your illness lasted, dear old chap?"

"Yes, Joe."

"It's the end of May, Pip. To-morrow is the first of June."

"And have you been here all that time, dear Joe?"

"Pretty nigh, old chap. For, as I says to Biddy when the news of your being ill were brought by letter, which it were brought by the post, and being formerly single he is now married though underpaid for a deal of walking and shoe-leather, but wealth were not a object on his part, and marriage were the great wish of his hart—"

"It is so delightful to hear you, Joe! But I interrupt you in what you said to Biddy."

"Which it were," said Joe, "that how you might be amongst strangers, and that how you and me having been ever friends, a wisit at such a moment might not prove unacceptabobble. And Biddy, her word were, 'Go to him, without loss of time.' That," said Joe, summing up with his judicial air, "were the word of Biddy. 'Go to him,' Biddy say, 'without loss of time.' In short, I shouldn't greatly deceive you," Joe added, after a little grave reflection, "if I represented to you that the word of that young woman were, 'without a minute's loss of time.'"

There Joe cut himself short, and informed me that I was to be talked to in great moderation, and that I was to take a little nourishment at stated frequent times, whether I felt inclined for it or not, and that I was to submit myself to all his orders. So I kissed his hand, and lay quiet, while he proceeded to indite a note to Biddy, with my love in it.

Evidently Biddy had taught Joe to write. As I lay in bed looking at him, it made me, in my weak state, cry again with pleasure to see the pride with which he set about his letter. My bedstead, divested of its curtains, had been removed, with me upon it, into the sitting-room, as the airiest and largest, and the carpet had been taken away, and the room kept always fresh and wholesome night and day. At my own writing-table, pushed into a corner and cumbered with little bottles, Joe now sat down to his great work, first choosing a pen from the pen-tray as if it were a chest of large tools, and tucking up his sleeves as if he were going to wield a crow-bar or sledgehammer. It was necessary for Joe to hold on heavily to the table with his left elbow, and to get his right leg well out behind him, before he could begin; and when he did begin he made every down-stroke so slowly that it might have been six feet long, while at every up-stroke I could hear his pen spluttering extensively. He had a curious idea that the inkstand was on the side of him where it was not, and constantly dipped his pen into space, and seemed quite satisfied with the result. Occasionally, he was tripped up by some orthographical stumbling-block; but on the whole he got on very well indeed; and when he had signed his name, and had removed a finishing blot from the paper to the crown of his head with his two forefingers, he got up and hovered about the table, trying the effect of his performance from various points of view, as it lay there, with unbounded satisfaction.

Not to make Joe uneasy by talking too much, even if I had been able to talk much, I deferred asking him about Miss Havisham until next day. He shook his head when I then asked him if she had recovered.

"Is she dead, Joe?"

"Why you see, old chap," said Joe, in a tone of remonstrance, and by way of getting at it by degrees, "I wouldn't go so far as to say that, for that's a deal to say; but she ain't—"

"Living, Joe?"

"That's nigher where it is," said Joe; "she ain't living."

"Did she linger long, Joe?"

"Arter you was took ill, pretty much about what you might call (if you was put to it) a week," said Joe; still determined, on my account, to come at everything by degrees.

"Dear Joe, have you heard what becomes of her property?"

"Well, old chap," said Joe, "it do appear that she had settled the most of it, which I meantersay tied it up, on Miss Estella. But she had wrote out a little coddleshell in her own hand a day or two afore the accident, leaving a cool four thousand to Mr. Matthew Pocket. And why, do you suppose, above all things, Pip, she left that cool four thousand unto him? 'Because of Pip's account of him, the said Matthew.' I am told by Biddy, that air the writing," said Joe, repeating the legal turn as if it did him infinite good, "'account of him the said Matthew.' And a cool four thousand, Pip!"

I never discovered from whom Joe derived the conventional temperature of the four thousand pounds; but it appeared to make the sum of money more to him, and he had a manifest relish in insisting on its being cool.

This account gave me great joy, as it perfected the only good thing I had done. I asked Joe whether he had heard if any of the other relations had any legacies?

"Miss Sarah," said Joe, "she have twenty-five pound perannium fur to buy pills, on account of being bilious. Miss Georgiana, she have twenty pound down. Mrs.—what's the name of them wild beasts with humps, old chap?"

"Camels?" said I, wondering why he could possibly want to know.

Joe nodded. "Mrs. Camels," by which I presently understood he meant Camilla, "she have five pound fur to buy rushlights to put her in spirits when she wake up in the night."

The accuracy of these recitals was sufficiently obvious to me, to give me great confidence in Joe's information. "And now," said Joe, "you ain't that strong yet, old chap, that you can take in more nor one additional shovelful to-day. Old Orlick he's been a bustin' open a dwelling-ouse."

"Whose?" said I.

"Not, I grant you, but what his manners is given to blusterous," said Joe, apologetically; "still, a Englishman's ouse is his Castle, and castles must not be busted 'cept when done in war time. And wotsume'er the failings on his part, he were a corn and seedsman in his hart."

"Is it Pumblechook's house that has been broken into, then?"

"That's it, Pip," said Joe; "and they took his till, and they took his cash-box, and they drinked his wine, and they partook of his wittles, and they slapped his face, and they pulled his nose, and they tied him up to his bedpust, and they giv' him a dozen, and they stuffed his mouth full of flowering annuals to prewent his crying out. But he knowed Orlick, and Orlick's in the county jail."

By these approaches we arrived at unrestricted conversation. I was slow to gain strength, but I did slowly and surely become less weak, and Joe stayed with me, and I fancied I was little Pip again.

For the tenderness of Joe was so beautifully proportioned to my need, that I was like a child in his hands. He would sit and talk to me in the old confidence, and with the old simplicity, and in the old unassertive protecting way, so that I would half believe that all my life since the days of the old kitchen was one of the mental troubles of the fever that was gone. He did everything for me except the household work, for which he had engaged a very decent woman, after paying off the laundress on his first arrival. "Which I do assure you, Pip," he would often say, in explanation of that liberty; "I found her a tapping the spare bed, like a cask of beer, and drawing off the feathers in a bucket, for sale. Which she would have tapped yourn next, and draw'd it off with you a laying on it, and was then a carrying away the coals gradiwally in the soup-tureen and wegetable-dishes, and the wine and spirits in your Wellington boots."

We looked forward to the day when I should go out for a ride, as we had once looked forward to the day of my apprenticeship. And when the day came, and an open carriage was got into the Lane, Joe wrapped me up, took me in his arms, carried me down to it, and put me in, as if I were still the small helpless creature to whom he had so abundantly given of the wealth of his great nature.

And Joe got in beside me, and we drove away together into the country, where the rich summer growth was already on the trees and on the grass, and sweet summer scents filled all the air. The day happened to be Sunday, and when I looked on the loveliness around me, and thought how it had grown and changed, and how the little wild-flowers had been forming, and the voices of the birds had been strengthening, by day and by night, under the sun and under the stars, while poor I lay burning and tossing on my bed, the mere remembrance of having burned and tossed there came like a check upon my peace. But when I heard the Sunday bells, and looked around a little more upon the outspread beauty, I felt that I was not nearly thankful enough—that I was too weak yet to be even that—and I laid my head on Joe's shoulder, as I had laid it long ago when he had taken me to the Fair or where not, and it was too much for my young senses.

More composure came to me after a while, and we talked as we used to talk, lying on the grass at the old Battery. There was no change whatever in Joe. Exactly what he had been in my eyes then, he was in my eyes still; just as simply faithful, and as simply right.

When we got back again, and he lifted me out, and carried me—so easily!—across the court and up the stairs, I thought of that eventful Christmas Day when he had carried me over the marshes. We had not yet made any allusion to my change of fortune, nor did I know how much of my late history he was acquainted with. I was so doubtful of myself now, and put so much trust in him, that I could not satisfy myself whether I ought to refer to it when he did not.

"Have you heard, Joe," I asked him that evening, upon further consideration, as he smoked his pipe at the window, "who my patron was?"

"I heerd," returned Joe, "as it were not Miss Havisham, old chap."

"Did you hear who it was, Joe?"

"Well! I heerd as it were a person what sent the person what giv' you the bank-notes at the Jolly Bargemen, Pip."

"So it was."

"Astonishing!" said Joe, in the placidest way.

"Did you hear that he was dead, Joe?" I presently asked, with increasing diffidence.

"Which? Him as sent the bank-notes, Pip?"

"Yes."

"I think," said Joe, after meditating a long time, and looking rather evasively at the window-seat, "as I *did* hear tell that how he were something or another in a general way in that direction."

"Did you hear anything of his circumstances, Joe?"

"Not partickler, Pip."

"If you would like to hear, Joe—" I was beginning, when Joe got up and came to my sofa.

"Lookee here, old chap," said Joe, bending over me. "Ever

the best of friends; ain't us, Pip?"

I was ashamed to answer him.

"Wery good, then," said Joe, as if I *had* answered; "that's all right; that's agreed upon. Then why go into subjects, old chap, which as betwixt two sech must be for ever onnecessary? There's subjects enough as betwixt two sech, without onnecessary ones. Lord! To think of your poor sister and her Rampages! And don't you remember Tickler?"

"I do indeed, Joe."

"Lookee here, old chap," said Joe. "I done what I could to keep you and Tickler in sunders, but my power were not always fully equal to my inclinations. For when your poor sister had a mind to drop into you, it were not so much," said Joe, in his favorite argumentative way, "that she dropped into me too, if I put myself in opposition to her, but that she dropped into you always heavier for it. I noticed that. It ain't a grab at a man's whisker, not yet a shake or two of a man (to which your sister was quite welcome), that 'ud put a man off from getting a little child out of punishment. But when that little child is dropped into heavier for that grab of whisker or shaking, then that man naterally up and says to himself, 'Where is the good as you are a doing? I grant you I see the 'arm,' says the man, 'but I don't see the good. I call upon you, sir, therefore, to pint out the good.'"

"The man says?" I observed, as Joe waited for me to speak.

"The man says," Joe assented. "Is he right, that man?"

"Dear Joe, he is always right."

"Well, old chap," said Joe, "then abide by your words. If he's always right (which in general he's more likely wrong), he's right when he says this: —Supposing ever you kep any little matter to yourself, when you was a little child, you kep it mostly because you know'd as J. Gargery's power to part you and Tickler in sunders were not fully equal to his inclinations. Theerfore, think no more of it as betwixt two sech, and do not let us pass remarks upon onnecessary subjects. Biddy giv' herself a deal o' trouble with me afore I left (for I am almost awful dull), as I should view it in this light, and, viewing it in this light, as I should so put it. Both of which," said Joe, quite charmed with his logical arrangement, "being done, now this to you a true friend, say. Namely. You mustn't go a overdoing on it, but you must have your supper and your wine and water, and you must be put betwixt the sheets."

The delicacy with which Joe dismissed this theme, and the sweet tact and kindness with which Biddy—who with her woman's wit had found me out so soon—had prepared him for it, made a deep impression on my mind. But whether Joe knew how poor I was, and how my great expectations had all dissolved, like our own marsh mists before the sun, I could not understand.

Another thing in Joe that I could not understand when it first began to develop itself, but which I soon arrived at a sorrowful comprehension of, was this: As I became stronger and better, Joe became a little less easy with me. In my weakness and entire dependence on him, the dear fellow had fallen into the old tone, and called me by the old names, the dear "old Pip, old chap," that now were music in my ears. I too had fallen into the old ways, only happy and thankful that he let me. But, imperceptibly, though I held by them fast, Joe's hold upon them began to slacken; and whereas I wondered at this, at first, I soon began to understand that the cause of it was in me, and that the fault of it was all mine.

Ah! Had I given Joe no reason to doubt my constancy, and to think that in prosperity I should grow cold to him and cast him off? Had I given Joe's innocent heart no cause to feel instinctively that as I got stronger, his hold upon me would be weaker, and that he had better loosen it in time and let me go, before I plucked myself away?

It was on the third or fourth occasion of my going out

walking in the Temple Gardens leaning on Joe's arm, that I saw this change in him very plainly. We had been sitting in the bright warm sunlight, looking at the river, and I chanced to say as we got up:

"See, Joe! I can walk quite strongly. Now, you shall see me walk back by myself."

"Which do not overdo it, Pip," said Joe; "but I shall be happy fur to see you able, sir."

The last word grated on me; but how could I remonstrate! I walked no further than the gate of the gardens, and then pretended to be weaker than I was, and asked Joe for his arm. Joe gave it me, but was thoughtful.

I, for my part, was thoughtful too; for, how best to check this growing change in Joe was a great perplexity to my remorseful thoughts. That I was ashamed to tell him exactly how I was placed, and what I had come down to, I do not seek to conceal; but I hope my reluctance was not quite an unworthy one. He would want to help me out of his little savings, I knew, and I knew that he ought not to help me, and that I must not suffer him to do it.

It was a thoughtful evening with both of us. But, before we went to bed, I had resolved that I would wait over to-morrow, to-morrow being Sunday, and would begin my new course with the new week. On Monday morning I would speak to Joe about this change, I would lay aside this last vestige of reserve, I would tell him what I had in my thoughts (that Secondly, not yet arrived at), and why I had not decided to go out to Herbert, and then the change would be conquered for ever. As I cleared, Joe cleared, and it seemed as though he had sympathetically arrived at a resolution too.

We had a quiet day on the Sunday, and we rode out into the country, and then walked in the fields.

"I feel thankful that I have been ill, Joe," I said.

"Dear old Pip, old chap, you're a'most come round, sir."

"It has been a memorable time for me, Joe."

"Likeways for myself, sir," Joe returned.

"We have had a time together, Joe, that I can never forget. There were days once, I know, that I did for a while forget; but I never shall forget these."

"Pip," said Joe, appearing a little hurried and troubled, "there has been larks. And, dear sir, what have been betwixt us—have been."

At night, when I had gone to bed, Joe came into my room, as he had done all through my recovery. He asked me if I felt sure that I was as well as in the morning?

"Yes, dear Joe, quite."

"And are always a getting stronger, old chap?"

"Yes, dear Joe, steadily."

Joe patted the coverlet on my shoulder with his great good hand, and said, in what I thought a husky voice, "Good night!"

When I got up in the morning, refreshed and stronger yet, I was full of my resolution to tell Joe all, without delay. I would tell him before breakfast. I would dress at once and go to his room and surprise him; for, it was the first day I had been up early. I went to his room, and he was not there. Not only was he not there, but his box was gone.

I hurried then to the breakfast-table, and on it found a letter. These were its brief contents:—

"Not wishful to intrude I have departured fur you are well again dear Pip and will do better without Jo.
"P.S. Ever the best of friends."

Enclosed in the letter was a receipt for the debt and costs on which I had been arrested. Down to that moment, I had vainly supposed that my creditor had withdrawn, or suspended proceedings until I should be quite recovered. I had never dreamed of Joe's having paid the money; but Joe had paid it, and the receipt was in his name.

What remained for me now, but to follow him to the dear old forge, and there to have out my disclosure to him, and my penitent remonstrance with him, and there to relieve my mind and heart of that reserved Secondly, which had begun as a vague something lingering in my thoughts, and had formed into a settled purpose?

The purpose was, that I would go to Biddy, that I would show her how humbled and repentant I came back, that I would tell her how I had lost all I once hoped for, that I would remind her of our old confidences in my first unhappy time. Then I would say to her, "Biddy, I think you once liked me very well, when my errant heart, even while it strayed away from you, was quieter and better with you than it ever has been since. If you can like me only half as well once more, if you can take me with all my faults and disappointments on my head, if you can receive me like a forgiven child (and indeed I am as sorry, Biddy, and have as much need of a hushing voice and a soothing hand), I hope I am a little worthier of you that I was—not much, but a little. And, Biddy, it shall rest with you to say whether I shall work at the forge with Joe, or whether I shall try for any different occupation down in this country, or whether we shall go away to a distant place where an opportunity awaits me which I set aside, when it was offered, until I knew your answer. And now, dear Biddy, if you can tell me that you will go through the world with me, you will surely make it a better world for me, and me a better man for it, and I will try hard to make it a better world for you."

Such was my purpose. After three days more of recovery, I went down to the old place to put it in execution. And how I sped in it is all I have left to tell.

CHAPTER 19

The tidings of my high fortunes having had a heavy fall had got down to my native place and its neighbourhood before I got there. I found the Blue Boar in possession of the intelligence, and I found that it made a great change in the Boar's demeanour. Whereas the Boar had cultivated my good opinion with warm assiduity when I was coming into property, the Boar was exceedingly cool on the subject now that I was going out of property.

It was evening when I arrived, much fatigued by the journey I had so often made so easily. The Boar could not put me into my usual bedroom, which was engaged (probably by some one who had expectations), and could only assign me a very indifferent chamber among the pigeons and post-chaises up the yard. But I had as sound a sleep in that lodging as in the most superior accommodation the Boar could have given me, and the quality of my dreams was about the same as in the best bedroom.

Early in the morning, while my breakfast was getting ready, I strolled round by Satis House. There were printed bills on the gate and on bits of carpet hanging out of the windows, announcing a sale by auction of the Household Furniture and Effects, next week. The House itself was to be sold as old building materials, and pulled down. LOT 1 was marked in whitewashed knock-knee letters on the brew house; LOT 2 on that part of the main building which had been so long shut up. Other lots were marked off on other parts of the structure, and the ivy had been torn down to make room for the inscriptions, and much of it trailed low in the dust and was withered already. Stepping in for a moment at the open gate, and looking around me with the uncomfortable air of a stranger who had no business there, I saw the auctioneer's clerk walking on the casks and telling them off for the information of a catalogue-compiler, pen in hand, who made a temporary desk of the wheeled chair I had so often pushed along to the tune of Old Clem.

When I got back to my breakfast in the Boar's coffee-room, I found Mr. Pumblechook conversing with the landlord. Mr. Pumblechook (not improved in appearance by his late nocturnal adventure) was waiting for me, and addressed me in the following terms:

"Young man, I am sorry to see you brought low. But what else could be expected! what else could be expected!"

As he extended his hand with a magnificently forgiving air, and as I was broken by illness and unfit to quarrel, I took it.

"William," said Mr. Pumblechook to the waiter, "put a muffin on table. And has it come to this! Has it come to this!"

I frowningly sat down to my breakfast. Mr. Pumblechook stood over me and poured out my tea—before I could touch the teapot—with the air of a benefactor who was resolved to be true to the last.

"William," said Mr. Pumblechook, mournfully, "put the salt on. In happier times," addressing me, "I think you took sugar? And did you take milk? You did. Sugar and milk. William, bring a watercress."

"Thank you," said I, shortly, "but I don't eat watercresses."

"You don't eat 'em," returned Mr. Pumblechook, sighing and nodding his head several times, as if he might have expected that, and as if abstinence from watercresses were consistent with my downfall. "True. The simple fruits of the earth. No. You needn't bring any, William."

I went on with my breakfast, and Mr. Pumblechook continued to stand over me, staring fishily and breathing noisily, as he always did.

"Little more than skin and bone!" mused Mr. Pumblechook, aloud. "And yet when he went from here (I may say with my blessing), and I spread afore him my humble store, like the Bee, he was as plump as a Peach!"

This reminded me of the wonderful difference between the servile manner in which he had offered his hand in my new prosperity, saying, "May I?" and the ostentatious clemency with which he had just now exhibited the same fat five fingers.

"Hah!" he went on, handing me the bread and butter. "And air you a going to Joseph?"

"In Heaven's name," said I, firing in spite of myself, "what does it matter to you where I am going? Leave that tea-pot alone."

It was the worst course I could have taken, because it gave Pumblechook the opportunity he wanted.

"Yes, young man," said he, releasing the handle of the article in question, retiring a step or two from my table, and speaking for the behoof of the landlord and waiter at the door, "I *will* leave that tea-pot alone. You are right, young man. For once you are right. I forgit myself when I take such an interest in your breakfast, as to wish your frame, exhausted by the debilitating effects of prodigygality, to be stimilated by the 'olesome nourishment of your forefathers. And yet," said Pumblechook, turning to the landlord and waiter, and pointing me out at arm's length, "this is him as I ever sported with in his days of happy infancy! Tell me not it cannot be; I tell you this is him!"

A low murmur from the two replied. The waiter appeared to be particularly affected.

"This is him," said Pumblechook, "as I have rode in my shay-cart. This is him as I have seen brought up by hand. This is him untoe the sister of which I was uncle by marriage, as her name was Georgiana M'ria from her own mother, let him deny it if he can!"

The waiter seemed convinced that I could not deny it, and that it gave the case a black look.

"Young man," said Pumblechook, screwing his head at me in the old fashion, "you air a going to Joseph. What does it matter to me, you ask me, where you air a going? I say to you, Sir, you air a going to Joseph."

The waiter coughed, as if he modestly invited me to get over that.

"Now," said Pumblechook, and all this with a most exasperating air of saying in the cause of virtue what was perfectly convincing and conclusive, "I will tell you what to say to Joseph. Here is Squires of the Boar present, known and respected in this town, and here is William, which his father's name was Potkins if I do not deceive myself."

"You do not, sir," said William.

"In their presence," pursued Pumblechook, "I will tell you, young man, what to say to Joseph. Says you, "Joseph, I have this day seen my earliest benefactor and the founder of my fortun's. I will name no names, Joseph, but so they are pleased to call him up town, and I have seen that man.""

"I swear I don't see him here," said I.

"Say that likewise," retorted Pumblechook. "Say you said that, and even Joseph will probably betray surprise."

"There you quite mistake him," said I. "I know better."

"Says you," Pumblechook went on, "'Joseph, I have seen that man, and that man bears you no malice and bears me no malice. He knows your character, Joseph, and is well acquainted with your pig-headedness and ignorance; and he knows my character, Joseph, and he knows my want of gratitoode. Yes, Joseph,' says you," here Pumblechook shook his head and hand at me, "'he knows my total deficiency of common human gratitoode. *He* knows it, Joseph, as none can. *You* do not know it, Joseph, having no call to know it, but that man do.'"

Windy donkey as he was, it really amazed me that he could have the face to talk thus to mine.

"Says you, 'Joseph, he gave me a little message, which I will now repeat. It was that, in my being brought low, he saw the finger of Providence. He knowed that finger when he saw Joseph, and he saw it plain. It pinted out this writing, Joseph. *Reward of ingratitoode to his earliest benefactor, and founder of fortun's.* But that man said he did not repent of what he had done, Joseph. Not at all. It was right to do it, it was kind to do it, it was benevolent to do it, and he would do it again.'"

"It's pity," said I, scornfully, as I finished my interrupted breakfast, "that the man did not say what he had done and would do again."

"Squires of the Boar!" Pumblechook was now addressing the landlord, "and William! I have no objections to your mentioning, either up town or down town, if such should be your wishes, that it was right to do it, kind to do it, benevolent to do it, and that I would do it again."

With those words the Impostor shook them both by the hand, with an air, and left the house; leaving me much more astonished than delighted by the virtues of that same indefinite "it." I was not long after him in leaving the house too, and when I went down the High Street I saw him holding forth (no doubt to the same effect) at his shop door to a select group, who honored me with very unfavorable glances as I passed on the opposite side of the way.

But, it was only the pleasanter to turn to Biddy and to Joe, whose great forbearance shone more brightly than before, if that could be, contrasted with this brazen pretender. I went towards them slowly, for my limbs were weak, but with a sense of increasing relief as I drew nearer to them, and a sense of leaving arrogance and untruthfulness further and further behind.

The June weather was delicious. The sky was blue, the

larks were soaring high over the green corn, I thought all that countryside more beautiful and peaceful by far than I had ever known it to be yet. Many pleasant pictures of the life that I would lead there, and of the change for the better that would come over my character when I had a guiding spirit at my side whose simple faith and clear home wisdom I had proved, beguiled my way. They awakened a tender emotion in me; for my heart was softened by my return, and such a change had come to pass, that I felt like one who was toiling home barefoot from distant travel, and whose wanderings had lasted many years.

The schoolhouse where Biddy was mistress I had never seen; but, the little roundabout lane by which I entered the village, for quietness' sake, took me past it. I was disappointed to find that the day was a holiday; no children were there, and Biddy's house was closed. Some hopeful notion of seeing her, busily engaged in her daily duties, before she saw me, had been in my mind and was defeated.

But the forge was a very short distance off, and I went towards it under the sweet green limes, listening for the clink of Joe's hammer. Long after I ought to have heard it, and long after I had fancied I heard it and found it but a fancy, all was still. The limes were there, and the white thorns were there, and the chestnut-trees were there, and their leaves rustled harmoniously when I stopped to listen; but, the clink of Joe's hammer was not in the midsummer wind.

Almost fearing, without knowing why, to come in view of the forge, I saw it at last, and saw that it was closed. No gleam of fire, no glittering shower of sparks, no roar of bellows; all shut up, and still.

But the house was not deserted, and the best parlor seemed to be in use, for there were white curtains fluttering in its window, and the window was open and gay with flowers. I went softly towards it, meaning to peep over the flowers, when

Joe and Biddy stood before me, arm in arm.

At first Biddy gave a cry, as if she thought it was my apparition, but in another moment she was in my embrace. I wept to see her, and she wept to see me; I, because she looked so fresh and pleasant; she, because I looked so worn and white.

"But dear Biddy, how smart you are!"

"Yes, dear Pip."

"And Joe, how smart *you* are!"

"Yes, dear old Pip, old chap."

I looked at both of them, from one to the other, and then—

"It's my wedding-day!" cried Biddy, in a burst of happiness, "and I am married to Joe!"

They had taken me into the kitchen, and I had laid my head down on the old deal table. Biddy held one of my hands to her lips, and Joe's restoring touch was on my shoulder. "Which he warn't strong enough, my dear, fur to be surprised," said Joe. And Biddy said, "I ought to have thought of it, dear Joe, but I was too happy." They were both so overjoyed to see me, so proud to see me, so touched by my coming to them, so delighted that I should have come by accident to make their day complete!

My first thought was one of great thankfulness that I had never breathed this last baffled hope to Joe. How often, while he was with me in my illness, had it risen to my lips! How irrevocable would have been his knowledge of it, if he had remained with me but another hour!

"Dear Biddy," said I, "you have the best husband in the whole world, and if you could have seen him by my bed you would have—But no, you couldn't love him better than you do."

"No, I couldn't indeed," said Biddy.

"And, dear Joe, you have the best wife in the whole world,

and she will make you as happy as even you deserve to be, you dear, good, noble Joe!"

Joe looked at me with a quivering lip, and fairly put his sleeve before his eyes.

"And Joe and Biddy both, as you have been to church to-day, and are in charity and love with all mankind, receive my humble thanks for all you have done for me, and all I have so ill repaid! And when I say that I am going away within the hour, for I am soon going abroad, and that I shall never rest until I have worked for the money with which you have kept me out of prison, and have sent it to you, don't think, dear Joe and Biddy, that if I could repay it a thousand times over, I suppose I could cancel a farthing of the debt I owe you, or that I would do so if I could!"

They were both melted by these words, and both entreated me to say no more.

"But I must say more. Dear Joe, I hope you will have children to love, and that some little fellow will sit in this chimney-corner of a winter night, who may remind you of another little fellow gone out of it for ever. Don't tell him, Joe, that I was thankless; don't tell him, Biddy, that I was ungenerous and unjust; only tell him that I honored you both, because you were both so good and true, and that, as your child, I said it would be natural to him to grow up a much better man than I did."

"I ain't a going," said Joe, from behind his sleeve, "to tell him nothink o' that natur, Pip. Nor Biddy ain't. Nor yet no one ain't."

"And now, though I know you have already done it in your own kind hearts, pray tell me, both, that you forgive me! Pray let me hear you say the words, that I may carry the sound of them away with me, and then I shall be able to believe that you can trust me, and think better of me, in the time to come!"

"O dear old Pip, old chap," said Joe. "God knows as I forgive you, if I have anythink to forgive!"

"Amen! And God knows I do!" echoed Biddy.

"Now let me go up and look at my old little room, and rest there a few minutes by myself. And then, when I have eaten and drunk with you, go with me as far as the finger-post, dear Joe and Biddy, before we say good by!"

I sold all I had, and put aside as much as I could, for a composition with my creditors—who gave me ample time to pay them in full—and I went out and joined Herbert. Within a month, I had quitted England, and within two months I was clerk to Clarriker and Co., and within four months I assumed my first undivided responsibility. For the beam across the parlor ceiling at Mill Pond Bank had then ceased to tremble under old Bill Barley's growls and was at peace, and Herbert had gone away to marry Clara, and I was left in sole charge of the Eastern Branch until he brought her back.

Many a year went round before I was a partner in the House; but I lived happily with Herbert and his wife, and lived frugally, and paid my debts, and maintained a constant correspondence with Biddy and Joe. It was not until I became third in the Firm, that Clarriker betrayed me to Herbert; but he then declared that the secret of Herbert's partnership had been long enough upon his conscience, and he must tell it. So he told it, and Herbert was as much moved as amazed, and the dear fellow and I were not the worse friends for the long concealment. I must not leave it to be supposed that we were ever a great House, or that we made mints of money. We were not in a grand way of business, but we had a good name, and worked for our profits, and did very well. We owed so much to Herbert's ever cheerful industry and readiness, that I often wondered how I had conceived that old idea of his inaptitude, until I was one day enlightened by the reflection, that perhaps the inaptitude had never been in him at all, but had been in me.

CHAPTER 20

For eleven years, I had not seen Joe nor Biddy with my bodily eyes—though they had both been often before my fancy in the East—when, upon an evening in December, an hour or two after dark, I laid my hand softly on the latch of the old kitchen door. I touched it so softly that I was not heard, and looked in unseen. There, smoking his pipe in the old place by the kitchen firelight, as hale and as strong as ever, though a little gray, sat Joe; and there, fenced into the corner with Joe's leg, and sitting on my own little stool looking at the fire, was—I again!

"We giv' him the name of Pip for your sake, dear old chap," said Joe, delighted, when I took another stool by the child's side (but I did *not* rumple his hair), "and we hoped he might grow a little bit like you, and we think he do."

I thought so too, and I took him out for a walk next morning, and we talked immensely, understanding one another to perfection. And I took him down to the churchyard, and set him on a certain tombstone there, and he showed me from that elevation which stone was sacred to the memory of Philip Pirrip, late of this Parish, and Also Georgiana, Wife of the Above.

"Biddy," said I, when I talked with her after dinner, as her little girl lay sleeping in her lap, "you must give Pip to me one of these days; or lend him, at all events."

"No, no," said Biddy, gently. "You must marry."

"So Herbert and Clara say, but I don't think I shall, Biddy. I have so settled down in their home, that it's not at all likely. I am already quite an old bachelor."

Biddy looked down at her child, and put its little hand to her lips, and then put the good matronly hand with which she had touched it into mine. There was something in the action, and in the light pressure of Biddy's wedding-ring, that had a very pretty eloquence in it.

"Dear Pip," said Biddy, "you are sure you don't fret for her?"

"O no—I think not, Biddy."

"Tell me as an old, old friend. Have you quite forgotten her?

"My dear Biddy, I have forgotten nothing in my life that ever had a foremost place there, and little that ever had any place there. But that poor dream, as I once used to call it, has all gone by, Biddy, all gone by!"

Nevertheless, I knew, while I said those words, that I secretly intended to revisit the site of the old house that evening, alone, for her sake. Yes, even so. For Estella's sake.

I had heard of her as leading a most unhappy life, and as being separated from her husband, who had used her with great cruelty, and who had become quite renowned as a compound of pride, avarice, brutality, and meanness. And I had heard of the death of her husband, from an accident consequent on his ill-treatment of a horse. This release had befallen her some two years before; for anything I knew, she was married again.

The early dinner hour at Joe's, left me abundance of time, without hurrying my talk with Biddy, to walk over to the old spot before dark. But, what with loitering on the way to look at old objects and to think of old times, the day had quite declined when I came to the place.

There was no house now, no brewery, no building whatever left, but the wall of the old garden. The cleared space had been enclosed with a rough fence, and looking over it, I saw that some of the old ivy had struck root anew, and was growing green on low quiet mounds of ruin. A gate in the fence standing ajar, I pushed it open, and went in.

A cold silvery mist had veiled the afternoon, and the moon was not yet up to scatter it. But, the stars were shining beyond the mist, and the moon was coming, and the evening was not dark. I could trace out where every part of the old house had been, and where the brewery had been, and where the gates, and where the casks. I had done so, and was looking along the desolate garden walk, when I beheld a solitary figure in it.

The figure showed itself aware of me, as I advanced. It had been moving towards me, but it stood still. As I drew nearer, I saw it to be the figure of a woman. As I drew nearer yet, it was about to turn away, when it stopped, and let me come up with it. Then, it faltered, as if much surprised, and uttered my name, and I cried out—

"Estella!"

"I am greatly changed. I wonder you know me."

The freshness of her beauty was indeed gone, but its indescribable majesty and its indescribable charm remained. Those attractions in it, I had seen before; what I had never seen before, was the saddened, softened light of the once proud eyes; what I had never felt before was the friendly touch of the once insensible hand.

We sat down on a bench that was near, and I said, "After so many years, it is strange that we should thus meet again, Estella, here where our first meeting was! Do you often come back?"

"I have never been here since."

"Nor I."

The moon began to rise, and I thought of the placid look at the white ceiling, which had passed away. The moon began to rise, and I thought of the pressure on my hand when I had spoken the last words he had heard on earth.

Estella was the next to break the silence that ensued between us.

"I have very often hoped and intended to come back, but have been prevented by many circumstances. Poor, poor old place!"

The silvery mist was touched with the first rays of the moonlight, and the same rays touched the tears that dropped from her eyes. Not knowing that I saw them, and setting herself to get the better of them, she said quietly,—

"Were you wondering, as you walked along, how it came to be left in this condition?"

"Yes, Estella."

"The ground belongs to me. It is the only possession I have not relinquished. Everything else has gone from me, little by little, but I have kept this. It was the subject of the only determined resistance I made in all the wretched years."

"Is it to be built on?"

"At last, it is. I came here to take leave of it before its change. And you," she said, in a voice of touching interest to a wanderer— "you live abroad still?"

"Still."

"And do well, I am sure?"

"I work pretty hard for a sufficient living, and therefore— yes, I do well."

"I have often thought of you," said Estella.

"Have you?"

"Of late, very often. There was a long hard time when I kept far from me the remembrance of what I had thrown away when I was quite ignorant of its worth. But since my duty has not been incompatible with the admission of that remembrance, I have given it a place in my heart."

"You have always held your place in my heart," I answered.

And we were silent again until she spoke.

"I little thought," said Estella, "that I should take leave of you in taking leave of this spot. I am very glad to do so."

"Glad to part again, Estella? To me, parting is a painful

thing. To me, the remembrance of our last parting has been ever mournful and painful."

"But you said to me," returned Estella, very earnestly, "'God bless you, God forgive you!' And if you could say that to me then, you will not hesitate to say that to me now,—now, when suffering has been stronger than all other teaching, and has taught me to understand what your heart used to be. I have been bent and broken, but—I hope—into a better shape. Be as considerate and good to me as you were, and tell me we are friends."

"We are friends," said I, rising and bending over her, as she rose from the bench.

"And will continue friends apart," said Estella.

I took her hand in mine, and we went out of the ruined place; and, as the morning mists had risen long ago when I first left the forge, so the evening mists were rising now, and in all the broad expanse of tranquil light they showed to me, I saw no shadow of another parting from her.

"Today is my birth[day...]," implored her brot[her]

W9-AKU-773

"The big twenty-nine. The last year of your youth... So where the hell are you going with your life?"

Where the hell she was going with her life was back to Manhattan, if the damn train ever showed up.

"I don't want to meet your friend, Nicky. Okay?"

"Why not?"

"He's a dentist."

"Like this is a bad thing. I'm a dentist. Al's a dentist. Dad's a dentist. What's the problem?"

The problem was that Nicky, Al and Dad were dentists. Dentistry was the family trade, and her family's reaction, when she had militantly refused to take even a basic biology class in college, let alone anything that might smack of predentistry, was, "That's okay—she'll marry a dentist."

She had no plans to marry a dentist. It wasn't as though she was ever going to lose sleep over where her next plaque scraping was coming from. So what if she was everything her family feared: twenty-nine and single, with no prospects in sight, no suburban tract house and two point three kids in her foreseeable future.

But God, the pressure! Now that she was twenty-nine, it was only going to get worse. Loretta didn't respond to pressure well. When anyone—especially her blood relatives—applied it, she dug in her heels. As long as they pressured her about marriage, she was going to stay single....

Also available from MIRA Books and
JUDITH ARNOLD

LOVE IN BLOOM'S
LOOKING FOR LAURA

And watch for the newest romantic comedy from
JUDITH ARNOLD
Coming July 2004

JUDITH ARNOLD

HEART
ON THE
LINE

If you purchased this book without a cover you should be aware
that this book is stolen property. It was reported as "unsold and
destroyed" to the publisher, and neither the author nor the
publisher has received any payment for this "stripped book."

ISBN 1-55166-702-9

HEART ON THE LINE

Copyright © 2003 by Barbara Keiler.

All rights reserved. Except for use in any review, the reproduction or
utilization of this work in whole or in part in any form by any electronic,
mechanical or other means, now known or hereafter invented, including
xerography, photocopying and recording, or in any information storage or
retrieval system, is forbidden without the written permission of the publisher,
MIRA Books, 225 Duncan Mill Road, Don Mills, Ontario, Canada M3B 3K9.

All characters in this book have no existence outside the imagination of the
author and have no relation whatsoever to anyone bearing the same name
or names. They are not even distantly inspired by any individual known or
unknown to the author, and all incidents are pure invention.

MIRA and the Star Colophon are trademarks used under license and registered
in Australia, New Zealand, Philippines, United States Patent and Trademark
Office and in other countries.

Visit us at www.mirabooks.com

Printed in U.S.A.

This book is dedicated to the people who live in New York, and the people in whom New York lives.

ACKNOWLEDGMENTS

As always, I am grateful to my agent,
Charles Schlessiger, for his unwavering support
and encouragement. Thanks, also, to my editor,
Beverley Sotolov, and the staff at MIRA Books;
my family; and my writer friends.

One

Leaning out over the platform and staring down the tracks wasn't going to make the train arrive sooner. But Loretta leaned and stared anyway, and prayed for the 7:51 west-bound to chug into the station so she could say goodbye to Nicky, climb aboard and go home.

She wished she could tune him out, but she'd learned long ago that her family was un-tune-out-able. "It's not like I care or anything," he droned. "It's your life. You wanna throw it away, that's your choice. It's nothing to me."

"I'm not throwing my life away," she argued. "Come on, Nicky. Today is my birthday. Back off."

"Yeah, it's your birthday. The big twenty-nine, baby. The last year of your youth. After thirty, it's all downhill."

"Maybe in your case," Loretta needled him. "You've sure gone downhill in the past few years."

He ignored the dig. "We're talking about you. Where the hell are you going with your life?"

Where the hell she was going with her life was back to Manhattan, if the damn train ever showed up. She wished Al had driven her to the station instead of Nicky. As the oldest, Nicky seemed to feel a special obligation to lecture his wayward sister. He loved playing the role of the wise elder, although his propensity for dressing like Gilligan, in plaid shorts and inverted sailor hats, disqualified him for any mantle of wisdom, as far as she was concerned.

"All I'm saying," he continued as she gazed desperately down the tracks, "is, your first reaction shouldn't always be no."

"I don't want to meet your friend, Nicky. Okay?"

"Why not?"

"He's a dentist."

"Like this is a bad thing. I'm a dentist. Al's a dentist. Dad's a dentist. What's the problem?"

The problem was that Nicky, Al and Dad were dentists. Dentistry was the family trade, and her family's reaction, when she had militantly refused to take even a basic biology class in college, let alone anything that might smack of predentistry, was, "That's okay—she'll marry a dentist."

She had no plans to marry a dentist. It wasn't as if she was ever going to lose sleep over where her next plaque scraping was coming from. One of the reasons she'd become engaged to Gary had been that he was in advertising. A worthless occupation, according to her family, but what did she care? It wasn't dentistry.

So now her brother was trying to fix her up with a colleague. He thought Loretta would have a good time sharing drinks and dinner with some guy who got paid to stick his fingers into other people's mouths.

"Kathy vouched for Marty, didn't she?" Nicky reminded her. "She said he was nice."

"She said he was brilliant and he looked like Mel Gibson, only taller. Yeah, right."

"Are you calling my wife a liar?"

"I'm just saying maybe she was trying a little too hard to sell me on this buddy of yours. Tell me the truth. Does he really look like Mel Gibson?"

"Well..." Nicky considered. "He's taller."

The distant rattle of the train tickled her ears. She perked up with all the excitement of a dog hearing the whine of a can opener.

"Just this once, okay? Let me give him your number. It's nothing to me, but you could do worse. You *have* done worse. Not to mention any names, but *Gary*. Okay? Marty Calabrese is a nice guy."

"Gary was a nice guy, too," Loretta argued, meaning it. Her family would never forgive him for having broken up with her at a late-enough date that they'd had to sacrifice half the deposit they'd put down at the Roslyn Harbor Inn, but Loretta had forgiven him long ago. In fact, once she'd gotten over the shock, she'd realized she was grateful to him for figuring out that if they didn't love each other, getting married might not be the wisest option.

"You know," she added, wishing the train would glide up to the platform already, "I don't need my brothers soliciting dates for me. I can get dates on my own."

"Yeah? When was the last time you were on a date?"

"Wouldn't you like to know." He *would* like to know, she admitted silently. He'd love to know that it had been weeks, months—and going club hopping with Bob from work one evening when he'd been between girlfriends didn't really count as a date, because they were just pals. Nicky would love to know that she was everything her family feared: twenty-nine and single, with no prospects in sight, no wedding bells ringing on the horizon, no suburban tract house and two-point-three kids in her foreseeable future.

She wouldn't object terribly to having a husband someday, and even a kid or two. She wasn't too keen on the suburban tract house, but she was sure her parents would give her a pass on that if she'd do the marriage-and-children thing. But God, the pressure! They just wouldn't let up—and now that she was twenty-nine, it was only going to get worse. Loretta didn't respond well to pressure. When anyone—especially her blood relatives—applied it, she dug in her heels. As long as they pressured her about marriage, she was going to stay single.

Nicky peered down at her, all six brawny feet of him, and gave her a smile that displayed his extremely white teeth. He'd be handsome if he took off the dorky hat and did something about the paunch budding above his belt. "It's just that you're my sister and I care about you. And it bothers me that you won't keep an open mind about things."

She wouldn't keep an open mind? Nicky and the rest of her family were the ones who were close-minded. But the train was squeaking to a halt at the station, and she saw no reason to get into an argument about open minds with him. "Okay, look. I've got to go," she said, sounding much too relieved.

"Yeah, well, think about it, would you? He's a really nice guy. It wouldn't kill you to spend an evening with a nice guy."

"Uh-huh." She rose on tiptoe to kiss Nicky's cheek, then started toward the door, trying not to sprint.

"You got your ticket?" he called after her.

"Yeah, I got it. Bye, Nicky. Thanks again for the book."

"Kathy picked it out," he reminded her.

"Well, thank her again for me." She stepped onto the train and waved, then entered the car and let out a long, weary breath. Though the car wasn't packed, most of the bench seats held at least one passenger. The only unoccupied seat was the backward one just inside the door. She dropped onto the stiff upholstery, stifled a groan and closed her eyes so she wouldn't have to view all the passengers staring at her from the forward-facing seats.

The book Nicky and Kathy had given her for her birthday was called *The Secret to Success in Love*. Her brother Al and his wife had given her a book entitled *Two by Two: How to Find Your True Partner in Life*. Her parents had given her a simple gold bracelet with a small heart-shaped charm hanging from a link. She'd understood the message they were conveying with their sweet gift: poor Loretta didn't have a man in her life to present her with a romantic bracelet for her birthday, so her parents had to step into the breach.

The gifts had prompted her to request a refill on her wine. It was her birthday party, after all, and if she needed vast quantities of wine to survive the day, so be it. If ever she'd shared her family's yearning for her to have a boyfriend, it had been today; with a boyfriend, she could have begged off the family barbecue her parents had insisted on hosting in her honor. *Sorry, Mr. Wonderful is taking me out for dinner tonight,* she could have said, and they'd have been so ecstatic they wouldn't have minded that she wasn't spending her birthday with them. Or else she could have brought Mr. Wonderful with her to her parents' raised ranch in Plainview, and he could have been her ally. He and she could have exchanged amused glances whenever the discussion veered to tartar treatments or quadrant cleaning, or her mother aimed sly criticisms at her: *So, Loretta, are you ever going to get a haircut?* or *So, are people still threatening to tear each other limb from limb on that show you work for?*

But she'd attended the party alone because alone was her current social status. After faking delight over her presents, she'd dined with her family on grilled steaks and salad and bruschetta and more red wine, followed by a too-sweet

golden cake from Rocco's Bakery, the white frosting decorated with pink roses and the words *Happy Birthday, Dear
Loretta,* as if her family might need some help with the
lyrics when they sang the traditional birthday song. Nicky's
and Al's kids had run around the lawn after dinner, squeal-
ing and howling, while the adults had remained seated on
the deck, where they'd been dive-bombed by mosquitoes
that seemed passionately attracted to the pungent smoke
from the citronella candles her mother had lit and placed
on every available vertical surface. Her father had drunk
quite a few toasts filled with unsubtle hints: "Here's to my
grandchildren—the beautiful grandchildren I already have
and the ones Loretta will give me someday," he'd announce before taking a long chug of his Valpolicello. Or,
"Here's a toast to my birthday girl, whose beauty is so
overwhelming she scares the men away."

Loretta could think of plenty of things more overwhelming—and scary—than her beauty. Her family, for instance.

The train jerked forward twice, then started rolling
steadily down the track. Her seat was on the side facing
away from the platform, so she didn't bother to search for
Nicky as the station slid away. He probably hadn't waited
to watch the train's departure, anyway. She'd bet he was
halfway back to her parents' house by now, eager to grab
Kathy, Alyssa and Trevor—whom Loretta had nicknamed
"Terror" because at age four he was still deeply ensconced
in the terrible twos—and drive them home. Al and Cindy
and the twins were no doubt already back in Syosset, because Cindy lived by a strict schedule. Asked if she was
hungry, she always checked her watch before answering. If
the twins acted cranky and it wasn't nap time or bedtime,
she would blithely dismiss their fussing. "They can't be
tired," she'd say. "It's not seven-thirty yet."

The train picked up speed, clicking and rocking rhythmically as it carried its riders to Penn Station. Although it was only mid-June, Loretta guessed many of the passengers were returning home from weekends at their summer retreats on the eastern end of the island. The railroad's northern line was inconvenient to passengers from the Hamptons and Fire Island, but plenty of city dwellers maintained weekend properties on the North Shore. A few Sundays from now, this train would be even more crowded than it was tonight.

She didn't mind riding backward, except for having so many pairs of eyes aimed at her. She deliberately shifted her focus to the two passengers sitting directly across from her: a young, chichi woman with spiky platinum hair, skintight black apparel and an impractically small purse, and a man in faded and grass-stained blue jeans, a baggy gray T-shirt, scuffed sneakers and a scruffy day-old beard darkening his angular chin. His hair was tawny, the sort of pale brown that would probably fill with blond highlights over the summer. His eyes were downcast as he pored over some papers bound into a folder. A leather tote stood on the floor between his legs.

If she hadn't spent the better part of the afternoon being badgered by her parents, brothers and sisters-in-law about her pathetic single state, she might have considered the man attractive, his disheveled apparel notwithstanding. But she *had* spent the afternoon being badgered, and she refused to think about men at all.

She directed her gaze back to the platinum-blond woman across from her. The woman's sandals had such thick platform soles Loretta figured she would have been just as well off strapping a couple of wooden blocks to the bottoms of her feet. The instant the woman's eyes met hers, she glanced away.

A conductor shambled down the center aisle, and Loretta

produced her ticket for him. He asked to see a photo ID, and she showed him her driver's license, even though in the picture she had the pained look of someone trying to force out a sneeze. The conductor took her ticket, handed her license back and exited the car.

She rummaged through her tote—not a classy one like the man's leather model, but a beige canvas bag with Caribe Royale silk-screened on it, a souvenir from her parents' last cruise. Her mother had tried to give the bag to Loretta, but the last thing she wanted—with the possible exception of two books on how to capture men—was a cruise-ship tote. Her mother had insisted that she borrow it to carry the books home. "You can always return it, if you feel so strongly," her mother had pointed out.

Loretta felt strongly. She'd return it at the first opportunity—which would likely be within a week or two, when her parents decided to host another family barbecue to see if they could coerce her into accepting a blind date with Marty Calabrese or some other equally qualified dentist.

She pulled out *The Secret to Success in Love* and flipped it open. The table of contents was both pedantic and alarming: "From captivation to capture"; "The overlap of love and need"; "Power and empowerment in the love relationship"; "The twenty tricks of enthrallment." *Enthrallment?* If that was a real word, it shouldn't be.

She glimpsed the blond woman removing a tiny cell phone from her undersize purse. Loretta would have lifted her book higher, providing the woman with a little privacy for her call, but then everyone in the entire car would see the front cover and think she was a loser. Instead, she lowered the book to her knees, bowed her head and pretended to be engrossed in the twenty tricks. Trick number one was to be honest. Trick number two, she learned by skimming ahead a few pages, was to conceal the depth of one's interest in a potential lover. So much for honesty.

"Hi, it's me," the blonde said in a perky soprano. "Yes, it's me. Where am I? I don't know. I'm on the train." She paused, then said, "Yes, I know I'm on the train. I don't know where we are, though. Somewhere on Long Island. Maybe Westbury? Someplace like that. I don't know." Another pause, and she said, her voice a tad shriller, "Because I'm on the train. We left Hicksville and we haven't reached Mineola yet, so I'm guessing—well, I'm on the train."

Loretta lifted her gaze. The woman's lips were pursed and her forehead formed a cute little dent above the bridge of her nose. Her phone was small enough to fit inside her ear.

"Because the train is moving," she explained to the obviously dense person on the other end. "So we're not in Hicksville anymore. We left the Hicksville station about ten minutes ago. So we should be getting to Westbury soon, or is it Carle Place?... The Long Island Railroad," she clarified. "Yes, right now. I'm on the train this very minute."

Her voice wasn't that loud, yet it resonated in the little enclave formed by the facing bench seats. Loretta gritted her teeth and glanced toward the man in the grass-stained jeans. He glowered at the blond woman. Loretta noticed that his eyes were green and his eyelashes were surprisingly thick.

"Right now," the woman said. "The train is moving, so I don't know where we are. Maybe we stopped in Westbury already. I don't remember. Does Westbury come before Mineola?" She sighed. "I don't know. Maybe thirty miles an hour? Maybe forty? So I could be about ten miles from Hicksville, or maybe more. It could be less. I don't know. The train is moving, so even if I knew where I was right

this minute, by the time I told you, I'd be somewhere else...
Yes, I'm on the train. I think our last stop was Hicksville.
We haven't stopped since then. Right now we're moving.
So by the time I figured out where I was, I'd be somewhere
else.''

That struck Loretta as interestingly existential. Where
were they? Not where they'd been one minute ago, not
where they would be one minute from now. Then again,
she didn't care, as long as she wasn't in her parents' back-
yard.

''Hicksville,'' the woman said, her voice growing louder.
''Hicksville and Westbury. Somewhere. I don't think we
stopped in Westbury yet, but maybe we did. How should I
know? I'm just here, on the train. *Somewhere.*''

Abruptly, the man leaned toward the blonde, swiped the
miniature phone out of her hand and held it to his ear. In
a voice that was low but steely, each word carefully enun-
ciated, he said, ''She's on a moving train somewhere between Hicksville and Westbury.'' Then he hit the disconnect button, folded the phone shut and presented it to the
blond woman.

She gaped at him, her face clouding with shock and horror. He stared back. Greenish-gray, Loretta amended. His
eyes were classic hazel, those two muted colors flecked
with glints of silver and amber. He didn't frown, didn't
apologize, didn't explain. He just met the woman's gaze,
unflinching and defiant.

She let out a small huff, slid the strap of her purse onto
her shoulder and rose from the seat. The train lurched and
she bobbled slightly on her precarious platform sandals. As
soon as she'd steadied herself, she shot the man a fierce
look, then stormed through the door and out of the car,
letting the door slam shut behind her.

Loretta turned to the man. He shrugged.

"You did what you had to do," she reassured him, trying not to reveal how impressed she was by his gutsiness.

"It was either that or throw her damn phone out the window."

"The windows on these trains are always sticky. You might not have been able to open it." She gestured toward the drab suburban landscape rolling past the window that flanked their seats. "You don't suppose she's gone to find the conductor, do you?"

He shrugged again. "Who knows?"

"If they arrest you, I'll testify on your behalf," she promised.

"If they arrest me, I'll deal with it."

He sounded confident. Loretta wondered whether he was speaking from experience. Maybe he had an arrest record several pages long. Maybe he was an infamous criminal: the Cell Phone Bandit, a rogue who stole and silenced the mobile telephones of obnoxious users. Like Robin Hood, he might be the champion of common people everywhere, foiling cell phoners not just on trains but in boutiques and restaurants, on city sidewalks and on roadways where idiots negotiated million-dollar deals or screeched at the baby-sitter while barreling through rush-hour traffic in their un-wieldy SUVs.

Loretta's pulse picked up speed as she assessed him. This man—the Cell Phone Robin Hood—had definite possibili-ties. Not for her, but for the show.

He'd look great on TV, with those riveting eyes and that shadow of a beard. Maybe not Robin Hood—too medieval British. They could call him the Cell Phone Brigand. The Cell Phone Savior. The Cell Phone Superhero. A touch of alliteration would sell the concept. Becky would adore it.

"How would you like to be on TV?" she asked.

His eyebrows shot up. "What?"

"I work for Becky Blake." At his blank expression, she added, "You know, the *Becky Blake Show*? On TV? A talk show?"

He shook his head and smiled contritely. A dimple punctuated the corner of his mouth on one side. "I don't watch talk shows."

The train chugged to a halt at the Westbury station. Loretta wondered whether Blondie and her cell phone would detrain here, so she could give whoever she'd been on the phone with an accurate report on her location. Or maybe so she could round up some police officers to storm the train and drag the Cell Phone Superhero away in handcuffs.

Only one person boarded their car—a teenager lugging a weighty backpack—and he slouched his way past their seats and flopped down a few rows back.

"Becky Blake hosts a syndicated talk show," Loretta explained once the train started moving again. "In New York, the show is on the air weekday mornings at eleven. I'm one of the producers." Which was stretching the truth, but Becky always urged the staff to stretch the truth if it would benefit the show.

The man eyed her with bemusement. "Why would I want to be on TV?"

"Everybody wants to be on TV." Well, maybe not *everybody*. But Loretta was astonished by how many people were willing to act like buffoons, parade their neuroses and pretty much sell their souls for a few precious minutes of television fame. And God bless those neurotic buffoons. If not for them, she'd be out of a job.

"What I meant…" He cocked his head slightly. His hair was long, brushing against the ribbed neckline of his shirt in back. He seemed to be searching for something in her face, but she couldn't imagine what. "I guess what I'm really asking is, why would this show of yours want me to appear on it?''

"Because you took on an insufferable cell phone user. A lot of people would view you as a hero." A lot of other people—cell phone addicts, for instance—would view him as a villain. Controversy would ensue, and controversy made for great television, especially on talk shows like Becky Blake's.

He chuckled and shook his head. "I don't think so."

"You commandeered her phone and shut her up. Don't you think that's heroic?"

"Just a few minutes ago, we were hypothesizing about what we'd do if they arrested me."

Hypothesizing was a big word for a guy who looked as though he yanked weeds for a living. Then again, he had that fancy leather bag propped between his legs. If he was a gardener, he was a well-accessorized one. "You risked arrest to save us from the idiot cell phone yakker," she explained. "That would make you pretty damn special in a lot of people's eyes."

He didn't appear convinced.

She dug through her cruise-liner bag for her purse, and groped inside it for her business cards. Actually, they were "Becky Blake" business cards. Becky's name sprawled diagonally across each cream-hued rectangle in embossed violet. Loretta's name was cramped into the lower right-hand corner, along with the phone number she shared with the rest of the show's production team. "Here," she said, thrusting the card at him. "Think about it, okay? We'd really love to have you on the show."

He accepted the card, squinted at it and said, "You're Loretta D'Angelo?"

"That's right." She realized that nowhere on her card was she identified as a producer. But then, she wasn't identified as a hack staff member, either. He could assume whatever he wanted.

The train slowed, and the conductor poked his head into the car and shouted, "Carle Place!"

The man pulled his wallet from his hip pocket and tucked the card inside. Then he gave her another dimpled smile. "I'm sorry, but I don't think I want to be on your show."

She smiled back, refusing to accept defeat. "Think about it anyway. Maybe you'll change your mind."

He laughed, and tiny creases spread from the corners of his eyes. How old was he? From the neck down, he was dressed like a college kid. And his hair wasn't just long—it was unkempt. But his face... She couldn't tell.

Not that it mattered. The show had no age restrictions when it came to guests. This guy would look good on camera. That was the important thing.

And if he didn't agree to appear on the show, Loretta would survive. She'd come up with other ideas. She always did; that was why they paid her the not-so-big bucks.

Her smile relaxing, she settled back in her seat. Talking to this man had liberated her from the pall of having spent too many hours in the company of her family, whose idea of celebrating her birthday was to make sure she knew how disappointed they were in her.

The miles between her and her parents' house were multiplying, and the miles between her and her studio apartment on East 100th Street were decreasing. She was twenty-nine years old, and the closer she got to New York, the more grown-up she felt. By tomorrow, she would forget that her family viewed her as a pathetic spinster. She would forget her family altogether. She'd be who she was, only a year older, a year tougher, a professional who could converse with a good-looking stranger on a train without thinking, even for a moment, that he had the sexiest eyes she'd ever seen.

Two

Twenty minutes after stepping off the train in Penn Station, Josh Kaplan unlocked the door of his apartment on the northern edge of Greenwich Village. He flicked the wall switch that turned on a lamp in the living room, swung his briefcase onto the table in the dining area and pulled his wallet out of his hip pocket.

There it was: her card. Loretta D'Angelo.

As if he'd get in touch with her. Participating in a verbal slugfest on a trash-TV show was just his kind of thing. And gee, after he did his star turn on Loretta's show, maybe he could wrestle an alligator, rob a bank and swim across the ocean to Portugal.

Who the hell was Becky Blake, anyway? If she was inane enough to think that a guy taking action against an irritating cell phone user was an interesting topic for a television show, he didn't want anything to do with her. Or her show's producer.

Granted, Loretta D'Angelo had been a pleasant sight—a lot more appealing than the brief he'd pretended to read while he was in fact stealing glimpses of her. The Branford Arms Tenants Association deserved his full attention while he was working on their claim. But they didn't deserve every flipping minute of his life. He was allowed to put their suit against their landlord aside for a few minutes while he was seated across from a slim, wide-eyed woman with hair like a black waterfall, long and rippling, the sort of natural wonder a man could drown in.

He wandered into the kitchen to check his answering machine. Just one message: Solly reminding him of their weekly chess date tomorrow at noon. They'd been meeting every Monday at lunchtime for almost a year, and it was so much a part of Josh's routine he didn't even bother to make a note of it in his calendar. But Solly lived for their chess games, and if leaving Josh a reminder on the answering machine put his mind at ease, Josh couldn't object to the old man's nagging.

He pulled a Sam Adams out of the fridge, popped off the cap and returned to the living room. Sprawling out on the couch, he punched the remote's power button and surfed to CNN to find out if the world had ended while he'd been out on the island mowing his mother's lawn. Sections of the Sunday *New York Times* lay across the coffee table, and he rummaged through them until he found the weekly television schedule. Instead of checking to see if anything worthwhile was currently on TV, he scanned the daily listings.

Monday through Friday at 11:00 a.m. The *Becky Blake Show*.

He had better things to do than watch television on weekday mornings. Eleven o'clock usually found him at his desk, meeting clients, wolfing down a sandwich or heading over to the West Side Senior Center to play chess with Solly. Yet he stared at the listing for a surprisingly long time.

Loretta D'Angelo hadn't lied to him about her show. Even though she'd given him her business card, he hadn't been sure he believed she was actually a TV producer. She'd looked too young, and her hair, spilling wildly down her back, had seemed too unfashionable. Clad in dark-blue jeans and a knit shirt, she could have passed for a college kid, certainly not someone with a high-powered job in the big city.

Of course, the card she'd given him might not have been hers. She could have stolen it, or had a few fake cards printed up so she could impress strangers on commuter trains. She could be delusional. Compared with her, the blond dimwit with the cell phone who didn't know where she was might be the epitome of sanity.

New York teemed with crackpots and nutcases. Josh had surely met more than his share of them. His neighbor down the hall, Minka Colvitas, swore that in a former life she'd been married to Chester Alan Arthur. If she was going to allege that she was a reincarnated first lady, Josh wondered why she didn't claim a more highly esteemed president as her erstwhile husband, but he supposed she knew her past lives better than he did. His neighbor down the hall in the other direction, Colin Witt, bred and sold guppies as a hobby. He convinced guppy aficionados to spend hundreds of dollars on breeding pairs that were supposedly genetically elite. That people actually got excited about the pedigrees of guppies boggled Josh's mind.

All right, so the city was filled with lunatics. Maybe Colin and Minka would like to appear as guests on the *Becky Blake Show*. They'd be more entertaining than Josh, who considered himself far from scintillating talk-show material.

Tossing the TV listings aside, he leaned back into the couch's overstuffed cushions, propped his feet on the coffee table and took a long drink of beer. His mother never offered him a beer when he mowed her lawn. She didn't even offer him iced tea or lemonade. "I read in an article, it said the best thing to drink when you're exerting yourself is water," she lectured him every time he told her he was thirsty. Perhaps if he exerted himself less, she'd supply him with better beverages.

He really hated mowing her lawn, but he'd gotten sucked into the chore and couldn't seem to extricate himself. When he'd offered to pay a service to mow her lawn for her, she'd acted as if he'd suggested hiring an auto mechanic to remove her appendix. ''They don't know what they're doing, those lawn services,'' she'd declared.

''They know more about lawns than I do,'' he'd pointed out.

''They're total strangers. You want me to trust my lawn to a total stranger?''

That was exactly what Josh wanted, but his mother had guilt-tripped him into schlepping out to Huntington every Sunday to cut her grass. ''Your father would roll over in his grave if he knew I was letting a total stranger mow the lawn,'' she'd declared. Josh had considered arguing that his father would probably have been thrilled to hire a lawn service years ago, which would have allowed him to spend his Sundays watching football games in his air-conditioned den instead of shoving a sputtering lawn mower back and forth across the yard. Josh knew why his father had never hired a service: because Josh's mother would never have parted with the money to pay for one. Now that Josh's father was dead, she was refusing to let Josh part with his own money. ''Those outfits cost an arm and a leg,'' she'd complained.

Instead of an arm and a leg, keeping his mother's yard neat was costing Josh his Sundays.

Just for this year, he promised himself. Just for this summer, because his father had died last September and his mother was still pulling herself together. Next year she wouldn't have that excuse, and Josh wouldn't accept any other. Either she'd contract a service or he would.

He tapped the volume button so the TV would drown out the muffled din of traffic noises seeping through the window. Even when he could hear the broadcast, CNN had nothing exciting to tell him. The world was still intact. No one of note had been assassinated or indicted. Nothing had blown up or blown down. A teenager from Vancouver had set a world record in a Razor scooter race, and the Yankees had won.

Josh lowered the volume, closed his eyes and took another long swallow of beer. A vision of a woman with long, dark, wavy hair filled his mind.

He wasn't in the market for a woman. He already had one—even if she was currently living in Opa-Locka. He probably had a message from Melanie waiting for him in his e-mail inbox, an update on her current job along with her usual plaintive whines about how hot Florida was. If he wasn't so damn tired he'd go into the bedroom and turn on his computer. But right now he wanted the drone of the TV, the fizz of a high-quality lager on his tongue…and another minute or two to think about the Long Island woman with the cruise-ship bag and the Italian last name and the utterly goofy idea that his lack of tolerance for irritating cell phone users was a suitable subject for a TV talk show.

Just one more minute to think about Loretta D'Angelo, and then he'd go and download his e-mail.

Becky swept into the staff room Monday morning carrying a plastic plate containing what appeared to be a brownie with a lit white candle protruding from it. "Happy birthday, Loretta," she sang out in her trademark lilt. "They charge eight bucks an ounce for this stuff at La Pâtisserie Rondeau. I swear, illegal drugs are cheaper. Savor each bite." She set down the morsel at the center of the circular table around which the production team was gathered, then retreated to the sagging couch against the wall and reclined across it like a Victorian noblewoman taking a swoon.

"Aren't you going to have some?" Loretta asked.

"Are you kidding? It's fattening." With that, Becky became absorbed in the condition of her manicure.

Loretta sighed. That Becky wasn't going to partake of the birthday cake was probably just as well, because there was hardly enough to share with her three colleagues on the production team. Even at eight dollars an ounce, Becky could have afforded a larger piece if she'd cared about making her staff happy. But making them happy had never been high on her list of priorities.

Loretta blew out the candle and bowed with phony modesty as she accepted the applause of the others at the table, which sat in the middle of a small, windowless cell down the hall from Becky's much larger office and the studio where the show was taped. The room was drab—yet another indication of Becky's refusal to cater to her staff. Its decor featured the seedy plaid sofa where Becky currently lolled, a couple of travel posters featuring Athens's Parthenon and Rome's Colosseum, both photographed against an unnaturally blue sky, a telephone on a table beside the sofa and a large white board with different-colored markers resting in its tray. But the three people sharing the table with Loretta made the room welcoming. They were her partners, her office family—and generally easier to take than her real family.

"Dig in, folks," she said, gesturing toward the precious little pastry.

"Dig into what?" Bob asked, leaning over the table and squinting at the cake. "I can't see it."

"Eight bucks an ounce, huh." Gilda peered at the cake

and shook her head. "Becky, you're insane. No one should ever pay that much money for a cake. I mean, what? Flour is flour. Sugar is sugar. Chocolate is—"

"Manna from heaven," Kate declared, breaking off a corner of the cake and popping it into her mouth. Kate abandoned diets the way most people abandoned trash on the sidewalk. She had quit diets no one had ever heard of: the snake-meat diet, the lotus diet, the Mount Katahdin diet, the eggplant-and-egg-yolk diet. She wasn't even fat, no more than ten or twelve pounds overweight. But dieting was her religion and she was clearly on a mission from God.

Once Kate had assaulted the puny birthday cake, the rest of them dived in, scrambling for nibbles and stray crumbs. The cake was obscenely rich. Loretta managed to devour three moist, fudgy bites, which might have seemed greedy except that she was the birthday girl and deserved the largest portion.

Gilda licked a crumb from her finger, then settled back in her chair. "That was delicious," she called over her shoulder to Becky. "Grossly overpriced but delicious."

"Money is money," Becky said in a la-di-da voice, obviously mocking Gilda's claim that flour was flour and sugar was sugar. Gilda was Becky's mother. If Loretta's mother thought she wasn't always as respectful as she could be, she ought to see Gilda and Becky go at it.

In her mid fifties, Gilda was a firm, slate-haired woman with a fetish for elaborate earrings. Everyone on the team deferred to her not because of her parental link to their boss but because she was focused and shrewd. She was probably even aware that Loretta, Kate and Bob weren't particularly fond of her daughter. It didn't matter. All that mattered to Gilda was putting together successful shows. "Since you're still here," Gilda addressed her daughter dryly, "I assume it's because you have something to discuss with us."

"I do." Becky languorously rose from the sofa and approached the table.

"Wait a minute," Bob said. He took enormous joy in twitting Becky, acting as though she wasn't as important as she believed she was. Actually, Loretta wasn't sure exactly how important Becky was. In one sense, she was just the public face of her show. The team created each broadcast, put words in her mouth, made the whole thing possible. On the other hand, the show *was* called the *Becky Blake Show*. Without her, it would have to be called something else.

"I want to hear about Loretta's birthday presents," Bob said. Loretta shot him a quelling look. She didn't want to discuss her presents.

"Yeah," Kate chimed in. "What did you get? Anything exciting?"

"Some books and a charm bracelet," Loretta muttered.

Bob pounced. "A charm bracelet! How adorable! I didn't know you needed a bracelet, Loretta, but you could always use a little charm."

Loretta scowled. "Let's not waste Becky's time, okay?" She turned to Becky, trying to look eager. Bob made a kissing noise, quiet enough that only Loretta could hear. She swatted at him with her hand.

Becky stood at the table—since it was round, it had no head, but her position between her mother and Kate automatically became a head of sorts. Petite and impeccable, Becky was the personification of pastel: pink suit, blond hair, lavender-tinted lipstick and pale-blue eye shadow. Pastels might be innocuous, but the woman wearing them was not. Beneath her porcelain skin ran bitchy red blood.

"We have a problem, people," she announced. By *we,* she clearly meant that the production team had a problem.

Loretta glanced at Gilda. Her face gave nothing away. Apparently, Becky hadn't given her mother a preview of this talk.

"Our ratings are down," Becky said. "We did poorly in the May sweeps." This wasn't news; the team had discussed the drop in viewership. The ratings slump had affected other talk shows, too. Game shows had held steady and soap operas had spiked. These things were cyclical, worth monitoring but not mourning.

"The syndication company believes people don't want scuzzy shows anymore. We're in a more benign era. Harold wants us to do kinder, gentler shows."

"That's ridiculous," Loretta said. How benign the era was didn't matter. When people turned on the *Becky Blake Show,* they weren't looking for moral uplift. Harold might be the president of the syndication company that produced the show, but he wasn't a typical viewer.

Bob shook his head. "I thought we'd really hit a creative zenith with our 'I seduced my husband's gay lover' show. Or maybe with 'Pet affection—when does it cross the line?' Remember that woman who got turned on by biting her cocker spaniel's ears?"

Loretta's favorite recent show had dealt with a dentist who liked to fondle his female patients' feet when they were high on nitrous oxide. She'd almost phoned her parents and brothers and urged them to watch it, but a self-preservation instinct had kicked in. Since none of them ever mentioned the show, she assumed they'd missed it.

"Kinder, gentler," Becky repeated. "We don't have to avoid controversy, but Harold wants us to reduce the scuzz factor."

"The scuzz factor?" Kate asked, reaching for the empty cake plate and searching it for traces of chocolate.

"Those were his exact words," Becky told her.

"Fine," Gilda said, jotting something in her notebook. "Kinder, gentler. We can do that." Given her seniority and her bloodline, she usually had the final word, at least when Becky was in the room.

"There's more," Becky warned, leaning forward and pressing her dainty fists against the table. She couldn't look threatening if she tried. She was five-one and size two, a detail she often mentioned to the people she worked with. But Loretta and her colleagues knew better than to put any faith in Becky's appearance. If her desire was to scare them, their best recourse would be to tremble a little, just to keep her happy.

"The lower ratings mean lower ad rates, which mean lower income for the show and blah-blah-blah."

"In other words?" Bob pressed her. He didn't sound at all concerned, which Loretta considered more foolhardy than courageous.

"In other words, it's time to tighten belts."

"No raises," he summed up. "Oh, well. I guess I'll have to lay off the eight-dollars-an-ounce cake for a while."

"Layoff is right," Becky said, her voice chilly and her smile oddly smug. "We're going to have to reduce this staff by one."

"*This* staff?" Gilda exclaimed. "The production team?"

"Why don't you lay off Wally?" Kate suggested. Wally was the guy who warmed the audience up before the show. He'd point out the Applause signs and the Laughter signs, demonstrate his hand signals—"When I flap my arms like a rabid pigeon, it means *react!*"—and tell a few drastically unfunny jokes: "You hear about the fellow running for office right here in New York City? His name is Dreams

Come True. I hope he wins, so we can call him Mayor Dreams Come True.'' This joke was invariably followed by a great flapping of his arms so the audience would know they were supposed to *react*.

''Harold is evaluating other departments,'' Becky assured them, looking even more smug. She actually seemed to relish the prospect of giving a member of the team the boot. ''But as of right now, the odds are one of you will have to be let go. I feel terrible about this,'' she concluded with a smile bright enough to illuminate the Holland Tunnel at midnight. ''I'll keep you posted. In the meantime—'' she waltzed toward the door ''—remember...kinder, gentler.'' With that, she was gone.

Silence filled the room like a cold, damp fog. Loretta felt the final bite of her birthday treat rise back up into her throat and coagulate, making her want to gag.

She was going to be the one laid off. She knew it.

Gilda was Becky's mother, and no matter how contentious their relationship, Loretta couldn't believe Becky was nasty enough to fire her own mother. Kate had the most experience in television, having written for a children's show on PBS and a Sunday-morning shouting-pundits show before deciding to lower her standards and double her salary by working for Becky. Besides, she was the token African-American on the production staff. Bob was the token man. If they got laid off, they could charge discrimination.

But Loretta had no protection, no distinction, no tokens. Nothing to pull her clear of the ax's downward arc. Her first job out of college had been answering fan mail for a network anchorman. With a degree in English, she hadn't been particularly qualified to do anything, but she could write a damn good letter. After a year, she'd taken a secretarial position at the syndication company, and then one day Becky had plucked her from her desk and hired her to be a personal assistant. When it became clear that Loretta wasn't subservient enough for Becky's tastes, she'd been moved over to production, and she'd done a swell job there. She'd come up with one of the show's best concepts: a regular feature called "Wedding Bell Blues," which focused on disastrous weddings. And she'd instituted the makeover shows—she was quite good at getting plastic-surgery patients to appear on the program, and given her "medical background," as Becky referred to the D'Angelo family trade, she was adept at getting rhinoplasty and breast-enhancement specialists to discuss their work on camera. Plus, she'd put together the show on the foot fetishes of dentists, which had scored quite high in the ratings.

Still, she had less protection in this job than the others. She was neither a mother, an African-American nor a man.

"We're in deep shit," Bob announced.

"What do you mean, *we?*" Kate sighed loudly over the barren plate. "You guys are safe. She's going to fire me."

"Why would she fire you?" Loretta asked. "You've got such great credentials, such outstanding TV experience. You've put words in Big Bird's mouth."

"Like Becky gives a flying fuck about that. Sorry, Gilda—"

"Don't apologize to me," Gilda snapped. "She's probably going to fire me, just to get me back for all the times I grounded her in high school."

"Did you ground her a lot?" Bob asked, his eyebrows twitching with curiosity.

"No more than she deserved." Gilda shrugged. "So now she'll get her revenge. If I'm laid off, of course, her father will have to start paying me alimony again. He won't like that."

"He'll probably pressure her to keep you on," Kate pointed out. "You're safe, Gilda."

"I'm the one who'll go," Loretta declared glumly. "I've got the least seniority."

"Becky likes you the best," Kate told her. "You used to be her personal assistant."

"She moved me over here because she hated the job I did as her personal assistant."

"Are you kidding? You lasted longer as her personal assistant than anyone else. Most of them she chewed up and spat out. You, she gave a promotion to. You're golden, Loretta. You think she would have spent eight dollars an ounce on a birthday cake for you if she didn't like you?"

"Four dollars. That piece of cake couldn't have been more than half an ounce. And she probably gave it to me only to mislead me."

"She'll fire me," Bob predicted, "because I refused to sleep with her."

That shut them all up for a moment. Then Gilda opened her binder and said, "Until one of us gets fired—assuming Becky is serious about that—we've got shows to put together. And she wants kinder, gentler ideas. Does anyone have any?"

"I have a great idea for a show," Loretta said, shoving an errant lock of hair back from her face. "At least, it was a great idea yesterday. Today, I'm not so sure. It might not be kind and gentle enough." Everyone turned expectantly to her. "Obnoxious cell phone users," she said.

"What about them?" Kate asked.

"How we respond to them. How they're undermining the fabric of society, and how heroes among us are reclaiming the environment from the cell phone users." She recalled the man seated across from her on the train to New York City last night, and assured herself she was less excited by his bedroom eyes and wry wit than by the concept for the show. "There was this idiot cell phone user on the Long Island Railroad yesterday," she explained. "She was babbling on and on in a crystal-shattering voice, repeating herself, and suddenly the man sitting next to her—a total stranger—grabbed her phone and disconnected her caller. It was a true Zen moment."

"Did people on the train stand and cheer for him?" Bob asked.

"No, but I'm sure they would have if they'd been aware of how obnoxious the cell phone user was."

"If they weren't aware, maybe she wasn't that obnoxious."

"She was. I think people might not have realized that he was the one who'd shut her up. He was subtle about it. That was part of his magic. He silenced her without humiliating her."

"So, you're saying what?" Gilda grilled her. "His classiness was what made the deed impressive?"

"We don't do shows about classy people," Bob pointed out.

"If we've got to go kinder-gentler, perhaps that needs to change," Gilda argued.

"I'm not saying we should do a show about *him*," Loretta said. "I mean, yeah, he could be included. But I'll bet there are people who've tackled cell phone users in grocery stores. People who've grabbed someone's cell phone and thrown it through a window." Her train hero had considered that option, she recalled. "And then we could have some cell phone partisans up on stage, too, people who can't imagine how the world functioned before cell phones were invented. People who hate cell phone vigilantes. It could turn into a terrific fight."

Gilda, Kate and Bob exchanged looks. Gilda wrote

something in her binder. "They'd have to fight kindly and gently."

"We could have a police officer who describes an accident caused by careless cell phone use," Loretta suggested, pushing her concept further. "And a doctor who was able to save a life thanks to his cell phone. The show would leave people thinking instead of hyperventilating. There's nothing scuzzy about a doctor saving a life with his cell phone"

"I'm writing it down," Gilda said. "The idea needs tweaking, but maybe we can go somewhere with it. Do you know who this man is, the fellow on the train?"

"He didn't tell me his name," she admitted, "but I gave him my card."

"So, if he doesn't get in touch with you, you'd have to find other cell phone vigilantes for the show."

Loretta regretted this. She would have loved to have the show include *her* cell phone vigilante; he'd seemed awfully telegenic. But she had no way of reaching him. He'd had the opportunity to introduce himself when she'd given him her card, but he'd never mentioned his name. And she'd been demoralized enough by her birthday barbecue that she hadn't thought to ask him.

"I'm sure we could find plenty of cell phone vigilantes to come on as guests," she said. "We can broadcast an invitation." They often aired invitations to appear on the show just before the commercial breaks: *Are you sick and tired of people using cell phones in public places or behind the wheel of a car? Give us a call.* Some of the show's most entertaining guests had answered on-the-air invitations. "Or we can find people on the streets. Cell phone users are everywhere. I'll bet people who hate them are everywhere, too."

"I think a cell phone show has possibilities," Bob said.

''Personally, I hate my cell phone. But I always have it with me, and it's always turned on.''

''Why?'' Loretta asked.

Bob shrugged. ''You never know.''

''You never know what?'' Kate pressed him, but he only shrugged again. She gave him a minute to provide more of an answer, and when he remained silent she turned to Gilda. ''Could we do cell phones without having the show turn scuzzy?''

''We can do whatever we have to do,'' Gilda said.

''I've got another idea for a show,'' Kate said. ''Inspired by our own Loretta. Twenty-ninth birthdays. You've just turned twenty-nine, right?''

An icy ripple of dread shivered down Loretta's spine. She did not want to be the inspiration for a Becky Blake show, not even a kind, gentle one. ''My age is irrelevant,'' she said defensively.

''I was twenty-nine for many years,'' Gilda reminisced. ''Now I'm thirty-nine. I'll be celebrating my seventeenth thirty-ninth birthday in a few months. How old are you, Kate?''

''Twenty-nine, of course.''

Kate was lying. Everyone knew Loretta was the youngest person on the team. If she was twenty-nine, Kate had to be older.

''What is it about us that makes us want to land on an age that ends in a nine and stay there a while?'' Kate posed. ''How many of us fudge our age? Why do we lie about it? What's the underlying zeitgeist?''

''I don't lie about my age,'' Bob commented.

''No one asked you.''

''I'm just saying it would be a chick show.'' Bob gave them what they'd dubbed his token-man frown, a look of bemusement mixed with disgust. As the only male member of the production team, he occasionally labeled shows "chick shows," which meant he didn't think they'd appeal to men in the audience. But Becky Blake's demographic skewed heavily female, so Bob usually got outvoted.

"We could focus on women's hang-ups about their age," Gilda went on. "Age as a state of mind. Age as a social determinant. What does it mean when you're a woman facing your thirtieth birthday and you aren't married?"

Loretta held up her hands. "Stop. We're not going there." She'd gone there yesterday—and she'd hopped on the train and left. She had no intention of going back.

"I was married twice by the time I was thirty," Kate noted. "But being thirty and single is different from being thirty and married. Which is probably why women lie and say they're twenty-nine when they're single."

"I'm not lying when I say I'm twenty-nine," Loretta argued. "In my case, it's the truth."

"And what are you going to say next year?"

"I'll say I'm thirty."

"What if you're not married?"

Loretta rolled her eyes. Her job was worth worrying about. The fact that she was nearly thirty and happily unmarried was not. Annoyed, she pushed away from the table. "I'm getting a cup of coffee. Anyone else want some?" Thank God the coffee machine was in another room, so she could leave.

"I'll come with you." Bob shoved to his feet. "I'm single and I don't give a toad's fart about my age. Obviously, something's wrong with me. Maybe coffee will cure me."

Loretta managed a smile as she led the way out of the production staff room. The hall was a stark, straight passageway lit with glaring fluorescent ceiling lights. The only decorations on the walls were sporadically placed bulletin boards covered with flyers, memos and reminders. The coffee lounge was three doors down, past a bulletin board bearing a No Smoking sign, an ad for an Alicia Keyes concert and a poster about a fund-raiser for an ecological organization that promised to make the Hudson River once again safe for carp. Bob reached around Loretta and opened the door to the lounge for her.

"Did you really want coffee?" Loretta asked as she pulled the mug imprinted with her name from a shelf near the machine.

"Nah." Bob usually drank his coffee whipped, sweetened, laced with Baileys Irish Cream or otherwise doctored. Frappuccino was a current favorite of his. "I wanted to find out why you got all squirmy when Gilda started talking about age and marital status."

"I wasn't squirmy."

He grinned and lounged against the counter.

"Look. I'm about to lose my job—"

"You don't know that. We're all vulnerable."

"I'm more vulnerable." She hated the whiny undertone in her voice, and cleared her throat to get rid of it. "I'm in a lousy mood, okay?"

"Because you're twenty-nine and single?"

She might have disputed him, but in an odd way he was right. "I spent yesterday with my family," she said, then made a face. "They've got a nice Italian dentist they want me to meet."

Bob laughed. "He's probably a great guy," he said. "He'd probably spend the entire date analyzing your bite and discussing new products to combat gingivitis."

"I'd rather join a nunnery. In fact—" she filled her mug with coffee "—I'd rather get gingivitis."

"They've set up other blind dates for you, haven't they?"

Her scowl deepened. "They've tried. I've always resisted. But now, well, I'm *twenty-nine!*" She gasped melodramatically. "Maybe I'm supposed to be desperate. If I don't get married soon, all the nice Italian dentists will be snatched up."

"Some dentists are really nice," Bob said. Loretta couldn't tell if he was taunting her, but he seemed serious. "When I was a kid, my dentist had this big bowl filled with toys, and after a cleaning and fluoride treatment, I was allowed to choose a toy from the bowl. They were great—balsa gliders, yo-yos, whistles, stuff like that. My little brother screwed it up, though."

"How?"

"The fluoride treatments used to make him gag. Once, when he had one of those treatments, they brought him the bowl and he vomited into it. They never gave out toys after that. But Dr. Lunan was a nice guy. And I like the dentist I've got now. Dr. Wong. She's Asian and she doesn't speak English very well, but she's young and gorgeous, so who cares?"

"You ought to marry her," Loretta muttered. "You'd make my parents happy."

"I don't want to make your parents happy," Bob argued. "*You* don't want to make your parents happy. I don't want to make *my* parents happy." He lifted her mug. "Come on. If we hang out in the lounge too long, they won't just fire one of us. They'll give us both the ax."

A weary breath escaped Loretta. She felt weighted down, as if her clothing was wet and her shoes had lead soles. The pressures from her family were nothing compared with the pressure of having a pink slip dangling above her head. Why would she want to stay twenty-nine for the next ten years? This was her second day as a twenty-nine-year-old, and so far it was shaping up to be a rather grim age.

She followed Bob and her coffee down the hall. They arrived back at the staff room in time to see Kate running her fingers feverishly over the plate in search of one final crumb of cake.

Bob set the mug in front of Loretta's chair, then loped around the table to his own seat. "I've got an idea for a show," he announced.

Loretta eyed him suspiciously. Something they'd discussed in the coffee lounge had inspired him. She scrambled to figure out what. Not her, she hoped. She'd already inspired the whole twenty-nine-years-old-forever idea. She didn't want to be the inspiration for any others.

"Blind dates," Bob said. "Your worst blind date."

"It sounds scuzzy," Gilda observed.

"It could be, but it could also be funny. Think about it. I once went on a blind date with an acrobat from the Big Apple Circus. I thought, wow, flexible joints, this could be one hot date. It was awful, though. She spent the entire dinner lecturing me on kinesiology and the differences between circus trailers and trailer-park trailers. She hadn't read a newspaper in a year. She was the most boring conversationalist I ever met."

"But was she flexible?" Kate asked.

"I never found out."

"I've had some pretty bad blind dates, too," Kate remarked. "I made the mistake of marrying one of them."

"Well, here's an angle," Loretta said, relieved that this idea seemed to focus on Bob and Kate. "Maybe you two could go on the show and discuss your bad blind dates. Maybe we can even locate those blind dates and bring them on to get their perspectives. It *could* be funny," she added, because Gilda looked skeptical.

"I already know where my first husband is," Kate said.

"He lives in Piscataway and he still hits me up for money every now and then."

"Wait a minute." Gilda raised a hand to silence them, then jotted something in her notebook. Someday Loretta wanted to steal that notebook and leaf through it. It was probably filled with meticulous notes on every show idea and conference the team mentioned—but then again, it might not. It could be full of shopping lists or stream-of-consciousness erotica. Gilda never let anyone see the book—not even her own daughter.

She finished writing, clicked her pen shut and directed her gaze to Bob. "So we'd have poorly matched blind-date couples appear together on the set? How could we make sure that would be fun? Some of the guests might want to kill each other."

"It could be hilarious," Kate said. "It wouldn't have to lead to bloodshed if we set it up right."

"Blind dates from heck." Bob's eyes glowed like neon and he jiggled one of his feet, tapping the sneaker sole against the floor in a rapid tattoo. "Light and funny, no blind dates from hell. Then, to make it even cheerier, we could do a segment where someone is introduced to a blind date right on the show."

"There's the potential for embarrassment, but also the potential for true love." Kate beamed. "How warm and fuzzy can you get?"

"Fuzzy, not scuzzy," Bob quipped. "If the idea worked, we could do regular blind-date segments. I bet we'd have desperate single women lined up all the way to West End Avenue, begging for the chance to go on the show and meet a blind date."

"What about desperate single men?" Loretta suggested. She wasn't so enthusiastic about this idea. Becky Blake Sails the *Love Boat*? Yuck. But if everyone else on the staff loved the concept and she argued against it, she'd stick out. With the layoff threat looming above them, she didn't want to stick out.

"You know," Gilda said, "we've got a lot of singles on the show's staff. Not just in this room, but the technicians, the camera operators, Shirelle in makeup, Patrick, the stage manager—"

"He's gay," Kate reminded Gilda.

"Gay men go on blind dates, too." Gilda gave Loretta a smile that sent a chill down her spine. "We could start with you, Loretta. We could set you up on a blind date right on the show. Then you could come back a week later and report on how the date went."

"No way."

"Becky's going to love this," Kate said. "You volunteer for the first blind date, Loretta, and your job will be secure for life."

"You think so?" Loretta didn't want to believe her, but who knew? Maybe if she showed true courage and loyalty by letting Becky use her on the show, Becky might think twice about firing her. It was still a wretched idea…but she didn't want to lose her job.

"I'll talk to Becky about it. She's going to think it's cute," Gilda predicted. "Twenty-nine and unmarried, Loretta. You're our perfect guinea pig."

"I'm not a guinea pig," Loretta protested, wishing they weren't all gazing at her with such delight.

But Gilda was already on her feet. "I think this is exactly the kind of thing Becky is looking for," she said. "Topical, entertaining, but scuzzless."

Once she was gone, Loretta shuddered. "My parents warned me this was a terrible job."

"Sometimes parents are right," Kate said benignly, then

lifted the paper plate as if hoping against hope that one more crumb might be lingering on it.

"Not mine," Loretta insisted. If her parents had been right, she would have been married to Gary Mancuso right now, shopping for a split-level on Long Island and discussing when to start having babies.

"I wish I were single," Kate lamented. "I'd kill for a chance to win points with Becky. Loretta, you're going to appear on that show, find true love and get a promotion, while Bob and I are going to be vying for position on the unemployment line."

"Not me," Bob disputed her. "I'm the one who came up with this idea. If Becky likes it, I'm golden. In fact, I may volunteer to be a guinea pig, too. Maybe they'll find my dream woman—someone bright and pretty and double-jointed."

"Or maybe they'll find you a dentist," Loretta warned. If only she could guarantee that they'd find her a decent blind date, someone with whom she could spend a pleasant evening and report back to the show with amusing anecdotes about their time together. Someone with tawny hair and hazel eyes, maybe. Sexy eyes. And the guts to take on a cell phone twit.

Cleaner clothes, though. No grass stains. And clean-shaven. Loretta didn't like stubble.

Okay. She might just survive this, and wind up with her job intact. Twenty-nine, single and securely employed—was that really too much to ask for?

Three

Solly was waiting for Josh in the TV room at the West Side Senior Center, just a few blocks from the IRT station at Sixty-sixth and Broadway. Solly always dressed sharply, and today was no exception: in a pressed green polo shirt, khaki trousers and clean white sneakers, he looked ready to hit the links, the lanes or a Broadway matinee. He was short and trim, his face freckled but relatively unwrinkled and his eyes smiling behind stylish wire-framed glasses. Although he'd retired five years ago from his executive position at a retail apparel chain, Solly still knew how to put himself together.

Josh liked him—not just as a chess partner but as a friend. When they'd started their weekly games a year ago, Josh had viewed the routine as a charitable act. Melanie had asked him to come in and socialize with the old folks— "You're young and healthy and they're approaching the tail ends of their lives," she'd pointed out. So he'd journeyed over to the center one slow day to make nice with the neighborhood elders who gathered there to eat, socialize, attend lectures and play bridge. Solly had latched on to him and said, "You play chess? So come, show me what you can do." He'd proceeded to beat Josh in seventeen moves.

They didn't keep track, but Josh guessed they'd accumulated an equal number of victories and defeats over the

months of Mondays they'd faced each other across the battered wooden board in the TV lounge. Solly might be in
his seventies, but he'd lost none of his stuff, as he liked to
remind anyone within earshot. "I'm still all there," he'd
boast. "Up here—" he'd tap his index finger against his
brow "—and everywhere else, too."

Josh knew better than to question his claim. He'd clearly
lost none of his mental "stuff," if his skill at chess was
any measure. As for his "stuff" everywhere else, well, a
few female regulars at the center seemed prepared to testify
that he was all man.

One of them, Phyllis, greeted Josh with a lusty "Hi,
bubby!" and perched herself on the arm of Solly's chair as
soon as he and Josh settled themselves at the corner table
away from the TV and got to work arranging their pieces.
Phyllis was about Solly's age and a few inches shorter than
him, a compact woman with cropped orange hair and deep
creases stretching from her nose to the corners of her
mouth, giving her upper lip a triangular shape. She wore
bright lipstick and slim-fitting warm-up suits in colors so
vivid they strained Josh's eyes. Most of the rooms in the
center were furnished in drab neutral hues, but Phyllis ar-
rayed herself in hot pinks, loud turquoises and lime greens,
all of which clashed with her hair. "So, you boys want I
should get you some lunch?"

Solly eyed Josh above his row of pawns. "You hungry?"

Josh shook his head. On Mondays he usually grabbed
something on his way back to his office after the game—
a sandwich from the deli across from Lincoln Center on
Broadway, or a Sabrett's hot dog piled high with sauer-
kraut, and a cream soda—and ate at his desk.

"They made the pot roast today." Solly motioned with
his head toward the dining room. "They always overcook

it, so it's as dry as dead leaves, and then they drown it in gravy, as if that could bring the leaves back to life."

"It's fattening, the way they make it," Phyllis added. "That gravy, you can tell. High in fat. Who needs it? I could get you boys some fruit, though. You want a nice piece of fruit?"

"No, thanks," Josh said, waiting for Solly to make a move.

He glanced up at Phyllis. "You know what I'd like? A cold drink. You think maybe you could get me a spritzer? With a slice of lemon."

"I know how you like it." Phyllis patted his arm, then stood. She wasn't much taller on her feet than she'd been propped on the arm of the chair. "How about you, *bubbela?*" she asked Josh. "You want a spritzer?"

"A glass of iced tea would be good."

"Sweet? You want with sugar?"

"Just a slice of lemon would be great."

"My two boys, both with a slice of lemon. All right, I'll be back." She left the room, moving at a bouncy gait.

"She'll be back," Solly muttered, nudging his queen's pawn forward.

"You don't want her to come back?" Josh mirrored the move.

"Are you kidding?" Solly flashed him an easy grin. "A beautiful woman like that, leaning up against me while I play? Why wouldn't I want her to come back?"

"You tell me."

Solly contemplated the board, but Josh knew he was also contemplating the question. "She's a little aggressive, if you know what I mean."

"Yeah."

"She's looking for a commitment."

"And you want to play the field."

Solly shrugged and moved his knight. "It's a great big beautiful field. You get to be my age, Josh, you're alive, you're single, you don't drool, you know a few dance steps, you know the difference between Beethoven's Third and Beethoven's Eighth... Not to brag, but I'm a catch. And there are a lot of ladies out there, you know what I'm saying?"

Josh grinned. "I know, Solly. You're the stud of the West Side Senior Center."

"I'm the stud of the West Side, period. Now, are you gonna let me win today?"

"Not a chance."

Laughter and voices spilled out of the TV at the other end of the room. Two plump women sat on the sturdy plaid couch in front of the screen, but one was squinting over a needlepoint project and the other was thumbing through a magazine, so Josh doubted they were paying much attention to the show. He could probably change the channel without any objection from them—if he was interested in watching a particular daytime television show.

Of course, he had no interest in viewing the *Becky Blake Show*. It probably wasn't even on. It started at eleven and probably ran no longer than an hour, which meant that at— he glanced at his watch—twelve-ten, it would already be over.

Phyllis returned, carrying two plastic tumblers. She set them on the table. "Such a waitress I am," she said. "You should give me a tip."

Solly kissed his index finger and touched it to Phyllis's cheek. "There—the tip of my finger."

"You're so romantic!" She whacked him affectionately on the shoulder and settled back onto the arm of his chair.

"Listen, sweetie, I adore you, but I don't want you kibitzing while I play."

"You can't kibitz chess," she said. "You can only kibitz bridge."

"I never knew that. Is that true, Josh?"

Josh studied the board for a moment, then sent Phyllis an apologetic smile. "I think kibitzing is kibitzing, regardless of the game."

"Listen to him, Phyllis. He's a lawyer, he knows these things."

"All right, all right, I can take a hint," Phyllis grumbled, landing lightly on her feet. "I'll go. I'll leave you two sourpusses to your game. Just one thing, Josh. Have you heard from Melanie? How is our angel?"

Melanie used to be the director of the West Side Senior Center. A specialist in geriatric social work, she'd guided the program in its evolution from a sleepy little enclave one step removed from senior day care into a lively hub of programs and services. Authors gave readings at the center. Artists taught classes, and the multipurpose room was converted into a gallery several times a year to display the creations of the center's members. Yoga instruction and lectures on politics and health issues were offered. Students from Juilliard gave recitals. And—perhaps Melanie's most appreciated contribution—the hot lunches improved significantly. Except for the pot roast, according to Solly.

Melanie had done such a fabulous job of revitalizing the center that a retirement community in Opa-Locka, Florida, had dangled a huge contract in front of her. "I love New York," Melanie had told Josh. "I love my life here. But how can I turn my back on such an opportunity? Directing services for an entire retirement community. It's something I need to try. I owe myself the chance, don't I?"

No, Josh had wanted to say. *You owe yourself the chance to stay here with the Upper West Side folks who love you, and with me, who...* Perhaps if he'd said he loved her, she would have stayed. He was pretty sure he loved her; they'd been together for more than two years and things had been going smoothly. Her parents liked him, his father had liked her and his mother tolerated her, and the sex had been fantastic.

But if he'd said he loved her, she might have thought he was blackmailing her into staying. Emotional blackmail was one of those subjects the magazines Melanie read tended to dwell on, along with tips on eyebrow waxing and angst-ridden tales about people facing life-altering crises such as adult-onset acne and caffeine addiction. Emotional blackmail, as Melanie had explained it to him on more than one occasion, was manipulating people into doing what you wanted them to do based on your bestowing or withholding love.

If he'd told her he loved her, would he have been manipulating her into staying in New York? Probably.

He understood ambition. He himself brimmed with ambition—not to make a lot of money, but to accomplish things in the world, to change people's lives for the better. Melanie had that kind of ambition. It was one of the things he admired about her. If her ambition was luring her twelve hundred miles away, how could he keep her from going?

So there she was in southern Florida, bitching about the oppressive heat, and here he was in New York City, still making regular visits to the West Side Senior Center. Never in his wildest imaginings had he thought that a year after she'd asked him to sacrifice a couple of hours at lunchtime and do a good deed for a group of retired elders in a social club on the Upper West Side, she'd be gone and he'd still be hanging around.

Of course, there was nothing charitable about playing chess with Solly. Josh had no other time for chess in his life, and if it wasn't for these weekly contests, he'd never get to play. Besides, Solly played tough. Josh considered their games cerebral aerobics.

"Melanie is fine," he told Phyllis.

"She likes it down there?" Phyllis sounded dubious. Her geometrical upper lip curved in a sneer. "Florida is like a death sentence. It's where people go to die."

"She isn't dying," Josh assured her, not adding that Melanie's e-mails were full of ominous predictions about the killer heat and how she was doomed to perish from the humidity.

"She wasn't satisfied up here? What, she didn't like us?"

"She liked you a lot," Josh assured her, wondering how much she'd liked *him*. She'd left him, after all. She'd accepted the damn job.

"Because the new director, Francine, she's nice enough," Phyllis said, "but it's three months now and she's still messing up."

"Don't be so impatient," Solly scolded. "Give the girl a chance."

"All I'm saying is, she's no Melanie."

"She'll learn."

"Hosting a speech by that nudnick from Columbia University, the symbiotic expert—"

"Semiotics," Solly corrected her. "I thought he was interesting."

"He was full of crap. Melanie would never have asked a symbiotic expert to give a Friday-afternoon talk. She used to bring in art experts, that fellow from the Museum of Modern Art, remember him?"

"The Modigliani guy?"

"Right. With the paintings of the lounging nude ladies. Now, that was interesting. Symbiotics, what was he talking about? Here's a word, but it's not really a word—it's a picture that means a word... What a load of crap, forgive me. Thank God my granddaughter didn't get into Columbia, if that's the kind of cockamamy professors they've got teaching there.''

"It was very interesting," Solly whispered to Josh. "Who besides you knew what that man was talking about?"

"I think Francine did." Solly shrugged with feigned modesty. "What can I say? It took a higher level of intelligence to follow his arguments."

"Oh, *excuse* me," Phyllis said with a huff. Then she cracked a grin. "All right, so I don't understand a picture is a word. Common sense I've got plenty of. And I know good art. That Modigliani—now, *that* was a great lecture. One of his pictures is worth a thousand words."

"And a million bucks," Solly grunted.

Phyllis ignored him. "Francine needs to bring in more speakers like that. Speakers like Melanie used to bring us." She gave Josh's shoulder an affectionate squeeze that felt like a nutcracker crunching his bones. Rubbing the bruised area, he wondered what sort of megavitamins she was taking. "Of course, *you* miss Melanie for other reasons, poor *bubby*," she continued. "Don't you worry. She'll come back. She'll get sick of all that sun and the gorgeous beaches and those guys who wear the skimpy little swimsuits with their tushes hanging out, and she'll come home."

"Thanks." Whether or not Melanie came home wasn't keeping Josh up nights. Maybe it should have been, but it wasn't. He was usually so tired by the end of the day that nothing could keep him up, with the possible exception of a late Yankees game.

Solly drove his bishop forward, a move Josh had failed to anticipate. Phyllis had distracted him. Maybe having her hovering at their table and babbling about Melanie was some well-planned strategy on Solly's part.

Josh knew his theory was wrong when Solly glanced up, gave her a honey-sweet smile and said, "You're still kibitzing."

"I'm not kibitzing!" She held up her hands as if she'd just had a gun pointed at her, and backed away. "Excuse me! I'm leaving!" She made it as far as the door before hesitating. "You need anything, just give a holler. I'll be next door in the music room."

"Great," Solly muttered. "Go play music."

Josh waited until she'd vanished before he spoke. "I thought you liked Phyllis."

"I like her very much. Only not when I'm playing chess."

"And here I thought you wanted her to stick around and distract me." Josh captured Solly's rook. Solly let out a howl. "I know, Solly. It hurts me more than it hurts you."

"Bullfeathers." Solly ground a fist into his chin and scrutinized the board.

Another peal of laughter arose from the television set. Josh glanced toward it. He didn't expect to see a young woman with a Long Island accent and rippling black hair on the screen, but he still felt a twinge of disappointment at the sight of a blond woman in a spotless apron, aiming a handheld mixer at a nondescript man and turning it on, making the whisks spin. Was Loretta D'Angelo's show as stupid as that? he wondered. Wasn't all daytime television stupid?

Swiveling back toward the table, he saw a newcomer enter the room. She was round, her heavy bosom sloping down to her waist, and her hair was a cottony cloud of white framing her face, which was dominated by pudgy pink cheeks. Solly winced. *"Oy,"* he whispered.

She approached the table, carrying a paper plate. Josh was relieved that no aroma of pot roast arose from it. "Hello, Solly," she said, balancing the plate on the edge of the table. "I won't bother you. I just thought I'd leave these here for you."

The plate was filled with tawny cookies, irregular in shape and obviously homemade. Solly sighed, a sound both exasperated and blissful. "Dora Lee, you're going to make me fat."

"You're not fat. You're not even close. I was doing a little baking, and I thought, Solly likes molasses. So—enjoy. I won't bother you. I'll just leave these and go." She didn't go, though. She loomed above Solly, smiling expectantly.

"Dora Lee, this is very sweet of you, but—"

"Not so sweet. Hardly any sugar. I use molasses, a *bissel* honey, a *bissel* ginger. They're very healthy cookies. Just say thank-you and I'll disappear."

"Thank you," Josh said, not because he wanted her to disappear but because he was helping himself to one of the cookies. It was delicious, soft and velvety in texture and just sweet enough.

"Thank you, Dora Lee," Solly said, taking his cue from Josh. "You're too good to me, you know that?"

"It brings me pleasure." With a final, almost otherworldly smile, she turned and left the room, her large body swaying as she walked.

"That woman is spoiling me rotten," Solly confided, helping himself to a cookie as he pondered the game. "She does this all the time, Josh. She bakes these treats for me."

"You might try being gracious about it."

"I am gracious. I love Dora Lee. She's so generous." He chewed, swallowed and apparently realized that his knight was in harm's way. Moving the piece, he added, "She scares me a little."

"You mean, because she acts like she's a visitor from an alternate universe?" Josh had met Dora Lee several times before—usually when she was presenting Solly with a homemade confection. She always seemed to loom a few inches above the ground, even though Josh had peeked and seen her feet in contact with the floor.

Solly chuckled. "She doesn't do this for any of the other members here," he confided as he helped himself to a second cookie. "Just for me she does it."

"Maybe she does it for me," Josh teased, taking another cookie, too.

"I wish. No, I take that back," Solly contradicted himself. "Dora Lee is a sweetheart, and generous to a fault. If she wants to be in love with me, that's all right, I don't mind."

"You've already got Phyllis in love with you," Josh reminded him. As a matter of fact, Solly had more women panting over him than Josh did. The old guy was probably getting more action, too. Even if Josh weren't stuck in a long-distance situation with Melanie, he wouldn't have the time to meet as many women as Solly seemed to attract.

It was simply a matter of demographics. The city probably had ten widows for every widower in Solly's age bracket, and of those widowers, few were as "all there" as Solly was. Add to that the fact that Solly was retired, with plenty of free time and disposable income. He could go where he wanted, do what he wanted, linger as long at it as he wanted. For Josh, taking two hours away from his office for a chess game was an indulgence he paid for by working into the evening.

"So, what do you think of Modigliani?" Solly asked him.

Modigliani painted nude ladies. How could Josh not like him? "He's good," Josh answered, then sighed. "I can't remember the last time I went to a museum, Solly."

"Shame on you! You live in the greatest city on earth. It's full of museums, full of culture. The Met. The Frick. The Guggenheim. The Whitney. And what do you do all day? Defend tenants against their landlords?"

"Sometimes I defend tenants against developers or insurance companies," Josh said. "And sometimes I play chess with you."

"Maybe next week we should go to a museum instead of this."

"No. I like chess." He also liked paintings of nude women, but if Solly took him to a museum, for every painting of a nude woman he viewed he'd have to view a dozen paintings of ink splotches or dowdy, pasty-faced dukes or soup cans. "Tell me, Solly, how many girlfriends are you juggling these days?"

"Who knows? I can't help it, Josh—they throw themselves at me."

"I can see that."

"I wouldn't mind, except it gets awkward when Phyllis and Dora Lee are in a room together. Or Phyllis and anyone. She's very possessive."

"Have you talked to her about that?"

"I don't want to hurt her feelings," Solly said, sliding his bishop across the board. "Check."

Josh scowled. He'd bet the reason Solly didn't want to hurt Phyllis's feelings was that she was the best-looking of all the women throwing themselves at him. For a seventy-something lady she was in damn good shape. She had a lot of energy and an infectious laugh.

But Dora Lee was sweeter, mellower, easier to take. And Dora Lee baked molasses cookies.

He got himself out of check easily enough. He ought to concentrate more on the game, but he found his mind drifting. Thoughts of women should have led to Melanie, but they led, inexplicably, to Loretta D'Angelo, instead. He might not have time to meet women, but he'd met her, hadn't he? And Melanie was melting in the hot Florida sun, far, far away. If Solly could handle more than one woman, why couldn't Josh?

One reason was that he'd be cheating on Melanie. Another was that he had no idea who Loretta D'Angelo was, what she was like, whether she'd been interested in pursuing anything more from him than an appearance on her TV show. She hadn't provided him with her home number, he recalled. Just her work number. Surely that meant she wasn't looking for anything personal with him.

Since when had he become such a wimp, worrying about a long-distance girlfriend and struggling to interpret the signals of a pretty stranger on a train? He definitely needed to recharge himself. He needed sex, laughter, female companionship. He probably also needed a trip to a museum.

One thing he didn't need was help playing chess. "Mate," he said as he slid his deadly queen into place.

"Are these really cucumbers?" Loretta asked. Her eyes were closed; she could only go by feel.

"Of course they're really cucumbers," Donna retorted. "Whaddya think, I'd use onions?"

Loretta supposed that if Donna had put slices of onion on her eyes instead of cucumbers, she'd be weeping uncontrollably. Plus, the smell would overpower her. Right now she smelled only the garlic, tomatoes and pepper in the marinara sauce simmering on the stove.

She was seated in one of the ladder-back chairs in Donna's compact kitchen in the Bay Ridge neighborhood of Brooklyn, within shouting distance of the Verrazano Narrows Bridge, which connected Brooklyn to Staten Island. Loretta had no idea who Verrazano was, but her family had always taken inordinate pride in the fact that this very important bridge—not only the starting point of the New York Marathon but also the route that enabled people to drive from Long Island to New Jersey without having to go through Manhattan—was named after someone Italian.

Loretta's cheeks felt stiff and tingly from the creamy facial mask Donna had applied to her skin. "Trust me," Donna had said. "Nothing makes you feel better like a good facial."

Loretta had been trusting Donna pretty much from the day she was born. Two years her senior, Donna was her only female cousin, and at every family gathering, they'd stuck together, allies in a sea of testosterone. The boys—her brothers and Donna's—used to run around, behaving loud and obnoxious, knocking things over and devouring food like locusts gorging their way through a field of alfalfa. Donna and Loretta used to escape. When they were younger, they'd retreat to one or the other's bedroom to play with their Barbies, and later they'd retreat to one or the other's bedroom to listen to Tears for Fears and U2 CDs while experimenting with makeup and discussing what creeps boys were. Donna had never outgrown her love of makeup. She was a beautician, majority-owner of a salon three blocks away from the two-bedroom apartment she shared with her husband, Lou, and their two sons.

Loretta trusted Donna not only with her complexion but with her life. Perhaps she shouldn't. Donna had always demonstrated a wild streak. When they were in their early teens, she used to sneak Loretta cigarettes, which Loretta hated, thank God, because if her father had ever noticed a nicotine stain on her teeth—and he would have, given the

close attention he paid to that part of her body—she would
have been grounded for life. When they were in their later
teens, Donna had introduced Loretta to bourbon, which she
hadn't been crazy about but had felt extremely cool drinking, since she'd been way below the legal drinking age.
Donna had taught Loretta to stand up to people, not to let
her family bully her and never to settle down with a man
unless the sex was phenomenal. "Trust me," Donna used
to whisper, the voice of experience when she was all of
eighteen. "There's such a thing as bad sex. And it's *really*
bad."

No one else had ever told Loretta such a profound and
irrefutable truth. How could she *not* trust Donna?

"Okay, so explain this again—you're gonna lose your
job?" Donna asked.

Loretta caught a whiff of cigarette smoke mingling with
the spicy aroma of the pasta sauce. "I don't know, but it
looks that way."

"What's wrong with that bitch, anyway? She wants to
fire someone—whatsa matter, honey?" Donna suddenly
asked in a sweet, light voice.

With her eyes closed, Loretta couldn't see who'd entered
the room. She imagined it was Andrew, Donna's younger
son. Her guess was confirmed when he announced, in his
piping four-year-old voice, "I can't flush the toilet."

"Where's Daddy? Tell him to flush it for you."

"Okay!"

Loretta heard Andrew's footsteps scrambling against the
tile floor. Donna sighed. "What, am I the only person in
this family who knows how to flush a toilet? Okay, Loretta,
so that little blond bitch is gonna lay you off. You *think*.
It wouldn't be the end of the world if she did. You'll get
a better job. You're very qualified."

"Oh, yeah," Loretta groaned. "I'm very qualified. I'm

qualified to be a toll taker—no, too much arithmetic. I'm qualified to be a bagger in the supermarket. Not a cashier—too much arithmetic. I'm qualified to marry a dentist. There's a biggie.''

"You're a college graduate," Donna reminded her.

Her eyes felt sticky under the cucumbers, and the cream was growing heavy on her cheeks. "Big deal. I've got a degree in English from New Paltz. What good is that?"

"It was good enough to get you a hotsy-totsy job with that little blond bitch. Trust me, Loretta—something else'll come through. Something always does. Every time a door slams shut a window opens."

"But, wait, it gets worse," Loretta warned. "Before they fire me, they want to publicly humiliate me. Like during the French Revolution. They used to shave off a woman's hair and truck her around the public square in a dogcart before they cut off her head. It wasn't enough to decapitate her. They had to make her last minutes on earth miserable."

"So…what? They're gonna shave your hair off? I wish you'd let me do something with your hair, Loretta. I could take off a few inches, give it a little shape. Ten minutes. I could give you a new birthday coiffure."

"No, thanks. A birthday facial is plenty."

"So, what's the public humiliation they've got planned for you?"

"They want to do a show where they set me up with a blind date, right there in the studio."

"No shit?" Donna guffawed. "Sorry, Loretta, but that sounds like fun. Especially given the present I got for you. You want me to give it to you now?"

"I can't see anything."

"When I take the cucumbers off. I gotta give it to you when the boys and Lou aren't around. It's a girl gift, you

know? This pasta sure is taking its time. It's a new brand—
Gladys Caruso, I do her hair every Friday before she goes
for confession because she likes to look good for the priest,
go figure—anyway, she told me I should try this fancy
imported pasta. It costs twice as much as Ronzoni. But it's
taking forever to cook.''

"I'm in no hurry," Loretta assured her.

"It's a school night. I hate when the kids eat so late.
And after they eat some birthday cake, they're gonna be
bouncing off the walls from the sugar."

"Donna, your boys bounce off the walls from drinking
milk. Breathing air makes them hyper."

"They are *not* hyper," Donna defended her sons.
"They're normal boys. Better than your brothers or mine.
I'm raising them to be feminists. Don't tell Lou, okay?"

"It'll be our secret," Loretta vowed, suppressing a smile.

"All right, take the cukes off. I'll give you your present."

Loretta removed the cucumber slices from her eyes and
blinked a few times while her eyes adjusted to the light.
Her lashes felt damp and strange. "You want me to toss
these into the salad?" she joked.

"Toss 'em in the trash." Donna rose on tiptoe to pull a
flat, square box from the top of the refrigerator. She was a
good four inches shorter than Loretta, and as slim as a
teenager. People often wondered out loud how someone
like her could have carried two large babies to term, but
after meeting Donna's sons, they had proof that she was
their natural mother. Both boys looked exactly like her,
with curly black hair, smoky eyes and pointy chins. Lou,
of course, insisted that they both looked exactly like him.
"From the waist down, honey, they look like you," Donna
would say, and that usually shut him up.

She handed Loretta the box and grinned mischievously.

"Go ahead, open it. Fast, before those jerks come in and start asking when dinner's gonna be ready."

Loretta tugged the ribbon and lifted the lid. Buried within the folds of tissue paper was a lacy wine-red teddy. "It'll fit you perfectly," Donna promised. "I know how to size things. But you're gonna have to shave the bikini area when you wear this, okay?"

"Who am I going to wear it for?"

"Your blind date. Why not?"

"Oh. Of course. How silly of me not to think of that." Hearing tromping feet in the hall outside the kitchen, Loretta tucked the teddy back into the box and shut the lid.

"Wear it for yourself," Donna urged her. "When you want to feel sexy. That's the cool thing about underwear—you do it for yourself. No one else has to know."

"Thanks, Donna. It's very pretty," Loretta remembered to say. She couldn't imagine wearing such a meager scrap of lingerie for herself. What did she care if her breasts were tantalizingly visible through the delicate lace of the cups? What did she care if she was properly shaved in the bikini area? The only times she wanted to feel sexy were when she was in a position to act on that feeling, and that generally involved the presence of a man.

"Euww, Aunt Loretta, what's that stuff on your face?" Deuce bellowed as he bounded into the room. His name was Louis Barone Jr., but when the boy had been younger, Lou used to call him Lou the Second, and "Second" had somehow gotten shortened to "Deuce." The nickname suited him.

"That stuff is something so fancy, it would be a waste to use any on you," Donna told her son.

"Are you gonna wear it for Halloween? What's it for? What's it supposed to do?"

"It's supposed to make me feel better," Loretta told him. "It's supposed to make my skin all clean and smooth."

"It makes your skin look icky," Deuce informed her.

Donna broke in. "Where's Daddy and your brother? We might as well eat. This pasta is never gonna be any more done than it already is. You like it al dente, Loretta?"

"Better than al dentist," Loretta joked.

"What's al dentist?" Deuce asked.

"That's when the pasta's so hard you crack a tooth when you bite into it."

"It's not that hard," Donna assured her son, then turned to Loretta. "Go rinse off your face. Take a washcloth from the linen closet."

"I know where you keep them." Loretta ducked out of the kitchen before she had to come up with more answers for Deuce. He was seven, an age when children still believed there was an answer for every question if you asked it loudly enough.

She pulled a washcloth from a shelf of the linen closet, then shut herself inside the bathroom. A glance into the mirror above the sink caused her to shudder. Her face was slathered with peach-hued gunk, leaving only her eyes, nostrils and lips exposed. Deuce was right. She looked icky.

She twisted the X-shaped faucets on the old porcelain sink, soaked the washcloth and rinsed away the mask. She wasn't sure what she'd expected, but she was vaguely disappointed to discover her usual face under all that cream. After sitting for fifteen minutes with pink goop on her, cleansing her pores, tightening her connective tissues, rejuvenating her cells and all the other miracles facials promised, she ought to have emerged from the mask looking cleansed, tightened and rejuvenated, at the very least.

But she looked like Loretta D'Angelo. No different. Just Loretta, with a too-square jaw, too-thin lips, too-wide eyes and a few fledgling crow's-feet. She looked like a woman about to prove she was as big a failure as her family already believed she was. It was only a matter of time before she'd be lacking a husband *and* a career. She'd be a nearly-thirty-year-old woman teetering on a tightrope, without a safety net beneath her.

The prospect was so depressing she lowered the lid of the toilet—after making sure it had indeed been flushed—and sat on it. The bathroom revealed the apartment's pre-war charm: besides the pedestal sink, it featured black-and-white ceramic tiles on the walls, built-in soap and cup trays, a bulky tub with a curtain featuring playful bubbles all over it, and a floor of white-and-black hexagonal tiles that made Loretta think of soccer balls. The tub contained so many plastic tugboats, cups, balls and watering cans Loretta wasn't sure if there was enough room for the boys to take baths in it, and the cup tray held an assortment of toothbrushes featuring cartoon characters. Loretta imagined that brushing her teeth with Daffy Duck staring at her from the tip of the toothbrush handle would be an unnerving experience. But Deuce and Andrew were no doubt heavily schooled in proper toothbrush techniques. Donna was a D'Angelo by birth, after all.

Loretta didn't want to think about her family. She didn't want to think about her age—which she'd never had any qualms about. She didn't want to think about her marital status, which was her parents' hang-up, not hers.

But her job. Her career. She *loved* that part of her life. She loved working at the studio, wearing funky clothes to work if she wanted, following up on audience suggestions, flying to Louisville, Kentucky, or Omaha, Nebraska, to interview two sisters who were having affairs with each other's husbands or a lesbian dominatrix who could speak authoritatively about the subtext of leather, and deciding whether they'd make interesting guests for the show. She loved trading banter with Bob and Kate and Gilda. She loved the fact that, armed with a useless degree from a mid-tier state university, she was earning more than fifty thousand dollars a year, and she wasn't even thirty.

She loved her apartment, even if it could fit entirely inside Donna's living room with a few square feet to spare. She loved being able to go out for drinks with friends without worrying about maxing out her credit card, and shopping at Bloomingdale's without having to limit herself to the clearance racks. She wasn't extravagant, but she loved being solvent.

If she lost her job, she'd receive unemployment for a while, but it wouldn't cover her expenses and it wouldn't last forever. What would she do when she ran out of money? She couldn't ask her family for help. They'd tell her being broke was what happened to women who remained single too long.

Would accepting a blind date on the show really spare her from such a dismal fate? Or at least forestall that fate? Would it really be fun, as Donna said?

Now wasn't the time for pride, Loretta thought, standing and crossing to the sink again. She studied her reflection. No, she didn't want Donna to shape her hair. No, the facial hadn't turned her into Britney Spears. Hell, maybe the real loser in this blind-date show would be not her but the poor sucker they lined up to meet her.

She'd do it because she had to. She'd go on the blind date—not with her brother's dentist buddy but with someone the show set her up with. If that was what it took to save her job—because she loved that job, damn it, and she was good at it, and Becky was crazy if she thought the show could survive without Loretta's contributions, so for Becky's sake, to spare her from a disaster of her own making, Loretta *had* to keep this job—she'd go on the damn blind date.

But she sure as hell wouldn't wear her new birthday teddy for the occasion.

Four

Three days later, Loretta D'Angelo's card was still in Josh's wallet.

He wasn't a pack rat. He was in the habit of discarding whatever he didn't need. It kept clutter to a minimum and simplified his life.

But he hadn't thrown her card away. That had to mean something.

Seated at his desk, he let his gaze wander around his cramped but tidy office. He would have liked a more spacious workplace, but his law firm specialized in the kind of law that didn't earn huge fees, and a big, fancy suite would cost him and his partners more than they brought in. They represented tenants against landlords, consumers against chain stores, lowly citizens against vast, bureaucratic city agencies. Their client list didn't include society matrons from the Upper East Side, Hollywood escapees inhabiting million-dollar lofts in SoHo, Wall Street execs who knew what *zero-load* meant or the denizens of trendy cafés where glasses of bottled water went for three bucks a pop. Rather, Josh and his partners served the strap hangers, the broom pushers, the office workers who could juggle four incoming calls without disconnecting anyone and the food service workers who wore snappy paper caps and remained on their feet for hours at a stretch while they dispensed everything from hot pretzels at sidewalk stands to

three-buck glasses of bottled water at those trendy cafés—
in other words, the people who made New York City the
amazing place it was.

If Josh believed in schlock TV, he'd convince his partners to run cheap television ads in which they'd shout at
the viewer, *Are you at the bottom of the heap? Can't get
a fair shake? Let the attorneys of Finn, Kaplan and Reyes
represent you!* But Josh didn't believe in schlock TV.

So why hadn't he gotten rid of that damn business card?

Everything else in his office had a justification for being
there: the reference books lining the shelves, the chairs for his
unfairly shaken, bottom-of-the-heap clients to sit on, the utili-
tarian carpet, the mahogany pen stand his father had given him
when he'd quit his position at the city's Department of Consumer Affairs to form this partnership with Peter Finn and
Anita Reyes. The move had been risky and had involved a
drop in salary that had fortunately proved to be only temporary—since the Department of Consumer Affairs hadn't paid
much, either—but his father had been proud of him. "It's good
to get out of the bureaucracy and go somewhere where you
can do people some good," his father had said. "It's always
beneficial to work for yourself, Josh. That's the best way to
live—as your own boss." Josh's father had nursed some romantic notions about self-employment, and Josh suspected he'd
been a little disappointed when he'd seen the small, drab office
suite the newly created firm had rented near Union Square, in
a soot-caked building with plenty of age but no particular history. Josh's father had probably expected the office to contain
white carpets, leather furniture and a squad of secretaries who
looked like high-school cheerleaders, instead of a single secretary who looked like Howard Stern's older sister.

Ruth did her job well, and Josh had never found high-
school cheerleaders all that exciting, anyway. But given
that space was at a premium, Josh restricted what he kept

in his office to those things that served a purpose. Even the philodendron occupying his windowsill served the purpose of putting clients at ease. Ruth assured him it was impossible to kill philodendrons—"They're the hepatitis C of the potted-plant world," she'd explained—and many of his clients were people who'd never even talked to a lawyer before, so it was important for them to feel comfortable rather than intimidated when they entered his office.

All right. What was his justification for having Loretta D'Angelo's card? Why hadn't he thrown it out?

He was honest enough to know the answer. And it made him edgy.

Exactly how had he left things with Melanie? They were still a couple. "Our relationship can survive this," she'd insisted, and of course he'd agreed. What was twelve hundred miles between friends? She would have her wonderful professional experience, suffer from the heat for a while and come back to New York, and then they'd pick up where they'd left off.

Anita poked her head through his open doorway. "You're sitting second chair with me tomorrow, right?"

He slapped his wallet shut around the business card and blinked at her. "Refresh my memory."

"The Brunswick case. LaToya Brunswick is suing Equity Insurance Corporation for refusing to cover her medical costs after she was hit by a car. I want a white man sitting next to me, okay? From what I've picked up during the depositions, Equity's the kind of outfit that doesn't tremble in its boots in the presence of women of color."

"Everybody trembles in their boots in the presence of you, Anita," Josh told her. She laughed, even though he hadn't entirely been joking. Anita was short and voluptuous, with an infectious smile that made her appear harmless. But her staccato, slightly accented speech and her long fingernails, which were usually painted an aggressive shade of red, tended to put her opponents on the defensive. He couldn't believe she really needed him sitting at her side.

But she knew the case better than he did. He clicked the icon on his computer to call up his schedule for tomorrow. Sure enough, he'd marked off three hours of court time for her. "I'm on," he told her. "You want me to wear my white sheet and pointy cap?"

"Nah. But don't wear your Jiminy Cricket tie, either, okay? Dress like a Republican."

"The things I do for you," Josh muttered with mock annoyance.

"How's it going with the Branford Arms tenants?"

"We've got a hearing slated for next week. The bastard landlord keeps postponing, though. This is the third hearing we've set up. Thank God the court froze his assets. If they hadn't, he would have shipped them all offshore by now."

"He's got assets?"

"Millions of dollars. And he won't sink a penny into the building. The plumbing leaks in four units. All the units have electrical sockets that routinely cause short circuits, and other sockets that are completely dead. The radiators are sporadic, the stairwell lights aren't up to code and he keeps sobbing that he can't afford to make the repairs because of rent control. He knows he's going to lose if we ever get him into a hearing room, so he's stalling."

"Asshole," Anita summed up. "So what's up with you? You look worried."

He shrugged. "I'm fine."

"Women trouble," she deduced, stalking into the room, her hips shimmying in her snug-fitting skirt. "Whatsa matter, Melanie's giving you a hard time?"

"No," Josh said, which of course was part of the problem. If Melanie were giving him a hard time, he wouldn't

feel guilty about his current obsession with Loretta
D'Angelo's business card.

He wasn't neurotic or given to self-hatred. Thinking about
the dark-haired, dark-eyed woman on the train wasn't evil. It
wasn't even that disloyal, as long as he was only *thinking*
about her. And if he called her, it would only be to discuss
her TV show, so the whole issue of cheating was irrelevant.

"You wanna date someone else?" Anita guessed.

"No." Of course he wanted to date someone else. He
was lonely and horny, and Melanie was too far away, and—
just for example—Loretta had all that incredible dark hair.

"Okay, here's what I got to say to you." Anita leaned
forward, her expression hardening as she assessed him.
"You're a man. You think with your *cojones,* right? No,
don't apologize," she said, although he'd had no intention
of apologizing. "You can't help yourself. It's the way
you're wired. I know these things. I've been married, and
now I'm single, and there's a reason for that, right? I know
the way men's minds work."

"Your husband was a head case," Josh reminded her.

"He was a *nut* case," Anita corrected him. "And that's
what I'm talking about, okay? Men think with their nuts."

"Your powers of logic astonish me," Josh said dryly.

"So, you want to be a man? Come clean with Melanie.
Tell her your poor little nuts are going to shrivel up and
die if they don't get the proper attention immediately.
Maybe she'll come back."

Josh laughed. "Doubtful."

"Okay, then, take a long shower."

"A cold shower?"

"Cold, hot, what do I care? God gave you two hands,
Joshua. Use them. This is what I tell my son. I tell him
God gave him two hands so that he can stay a virgin until
he's twenty."

"Your son is seven years old," Josh reminded her.

"It's never too late. You know what the Jesuits say, right? Give us a child for the first six years and he's ours forever? What *I* say is, give me my son for the first ten years, and he's not gonna knock up some girl in high school and ruin his life."

"I wish you'd been my sex ed teacher," he said. "We spent three years learning about STDs and date rape. If only someone had taught us to get in the shower and jerk off, we would have all grown up a lot saner."

"You better believe it." Anita stood and nodded. "Now, don't you go stepping out on Melanie. She's not who I'd have chosen for you, but you chose her for yourself and you owe her something."

"She left me. She went to Florida."

"I didn't say you owed her a lifetime of celibacy, Josh. I said you owed her *something*. You don't need me telling you this. You're decent to a fault."

"Is that a compliment?"

"I don't know." She headed for the door, her high heels leaving indentations in the carpet. "Tomorrow morning, nine sharp."

"I'll be there," he promised.

Anita's departure left an almost smothering stillness in its wake. He leaned back in his chair and listened to the hum of his computer. His schedule disappeared behind his screen saver, which resembled the view through the Starship *Enterprise*'s windshield.

Anita could be a pain in the ass, but her most pain-in-the-ass trait was that she was so often right. She'd been right today—not her advice that he should masturbate in the shower, but that he owed Melanie *something*.

The question was, what did he owe her?

* * *

He still hadn't come up with an answer by the time he
arrived home around seven that evening. While he microwaved a wedge of spinach lasagna from the take-out department of the Greek-Italian deli at the corner of his block,
he checked the messages on his answering machine. He
carried his meal and a bottle of Sam Adams into the living
room and watched CNN while he ate. Today's reports
looked suspiciously like yesterday's, and he pondered the
possibility that he'd gotten stuck in a time warp and was
actually reliving the previous evening. No, he wasn't. Yesterday, he hadn't been mulling over what he owed Melanie.
Today, that question preoccupied him.

Loyalty. Of course he owed her that. Honesty—to a certain extent. Josh believed being honest with oneself was
vitally important, but with others, too much honesty could
be a bad thing. He'd learned that lesson from his mother,
who had drilled into him early and often that he must always be honest. When he was about nine, he told her, with
abundant honesty, that the kitchen wallpaper she'd chosen
was ugly. It was still hanging in her kitchen today, and it
was still ugly, bunches of green grapes scattered across a
background the color of intense piss. Her reaction to his
honest comment had taught him honesty was a potent substance that needed to be applied with extreme caution.

So while he didn't want to lie to Melanie, he wasn't sure
he owed her complete honesty, either. He did owe her sympathy, and damn, he'd been sympathizing via e-mail on a
nearly daily basis. She was hot. She was so hot she'd lost
five pounds since she'd moved to Opa-Locka, just from
sweating. The Miami area was so hot the asphalt melted
and sucked at her shoes when she crossed the street. It was
so hot she'd singed her finger to the point of blistering

when she'd touched the steering wheel of her car after she'd forgotten to place the heat shield across her dashboard. Her life consisted of racing from one air-conditioned environment to another.

Whenever he received one of her melodramatic e-mails, he invariably sent her a return e-mail overflowing with condolences. New York City got pretty damn hot in the summer, too, but he loved the city, so the sweltering weather didn't bother him. Even on the hottest, muggiest days of late July, the automobile traffic stirred the air, and breezes lifted off the rivers and whisked along the cross streets. Air-conditioning helped, but a person could combat even the most oppressive heat in New York by purchasing an Italian ice and sitting under a tree in Central Park.

So he gave Melanie sympathy. And loyalty, and imprecise but genuine honesty. He gave her support, encouraging her to pursue her career goals even though that pursuit had taken her away from him. He gave her his patience—a huge and precious gift, he believed.

Did he really have to give her his libido, too? Did he have to dedicate his nuts to Melanie? Did he have to resign himself to long, two-handed showers?

Shit. The part of his brain that wasn't located in his groin believed he did. And that was the wiser, nobler part. He couldn't ignore it.

Maybe if he heard Melanie's voice, its familiar sound would erase his awareness of all the other intriguing, available women in the city from the stupid, base part of his mind that was located in his groin. He'd feel more connected to Melanie. Surely she owed him something, too, and if they talked, their conversation would be a mutual reimbursement. His lasagna barely touched, he carried his beer to the bedroom, stretched out on the bed and pressed the memory dial for Melanie's number in Florida.

The phone rang four times before she answered, and when she did he was amazed she could even have heard the ringing. A fist of noise—voices and loud music—seemed to reach through the receiver and punch his ear. "Hello?" she shouted into the phone.

"Melanie? It's Josh," he shouted back.

"Josh! Hi! Hang on a minute—" she apparently turned away from the phone and hollered "—I'll be right back!"

"What the hell is going on?" Josh asked.

"I've got some friends over for dinner."

Some friends? It sounded as if she had half the city's population crammed into her apartment. And the music—what was it? Some woman wailing above a bouncy salsa beat. "Melanie—"

"I know, it's really loud." A pause, and then the sound was a bit more muted, as if she'd ducked into a closet and shut the door.

"What was that music?"

"The music? Gloria Estefan."

"Since when do you listen to Gloria Estefan?"

"Since I moved here. How are you?"

He hadn't been sure before he phoned. He was even less sure now. "I obviously caught you at a bad time. Maybe I should call back later tonight."

"I don't know, Josh. This party is going to last a while."

"It's a weeknight. Don't you have to work tomorrow?"

She laughed. "You sound like my mother. 'It's a school night, Melanie! Turn off that light and get some sleep!'"

"Well, yeah."

"God, it's so hot. I've got the air conditioner cranked up as high as it can go. My electric bill is going to kill me. I can't believe how hot it is."

Some of that unbelievable heat was probably body heat, Josh thought. She could cool her place down by sending her guests home. He didn't say that, but he couldn't seem to produce the sympathy she was fishing for. "Look, I'm sorry I called. We can talk some other time."

"No, Josh—I'm the one who should apologize. You obviously called for a reason. Please tell me. I can hear you if you speak up. Is something wrong?"

"Nothing's wrong. I just wanted…" *I wanted to hear your voice,* he almost said, but she would construe that as a romantic sentiment, and he wasn't feeling romantic at the moment. Quite the contrary, he was feeling ornery and impatient and uneasy. "I think calling you tonight was a mistake," he finally said—as honest as any words he'd ever spoken, including his critique of his mother's kitchen wallpaper. "We'll talk another time, okay?"

"Okay. I'm really sorry, Josh. It's just so loud!"

"I noticed."

"So, I'll talk to you later?"

"Sure."

"Bye, Josh!" She must have opened the door she'd been hiding behind, because he got bludgeoned by another explosion of noise, atop which her voice soared. "Here I am!" she bellowed to her guests just before the phone clicked down, disconnecting him.

Josh hung up, stared at the ceiling, took a long drink of beer and stared at the ceiling some more. What did he owe her now?

Not a goddamn thing.

He swung his legs off the bed, crossed to the dresser, lifted his wallet, unfolded it and checked. The card was still there, waiting for him.

Calling Loretta D'Angelo might mean having to appear on her TV show to discuss cell phones, but what the hell. For a chance to touch her hair, to find out if it felt as silky as it looked, to gaze into her eyes and remember that he was a normal, healthy man with normal, healthy urges, he could take a chance and call her.

Or else he'd call some other woman. Several other women. As many women as Melanie had dinner guests tonight.

Why not? As Solly said, there were a lot of ladies out there.

"Loretta," Bob announced, tossing the phone receiver onto the couch and beckoning her over from the table. The production team had one phone and they answered it themselves, but apparently even this economy would not be enough to spare their jobs. It didn't seem fair to Loretta. The team already operated on a tight budget, yet it was still slated to lose a staff member. Why not lay off one of the stagehands? Or that buxom script girl who made goo-goo eyes at all the guys and said "axed" instead of "asked." Or the fey young man listed in the credits as "Miss Blake's hairdresser," even though her hair wasn't at all dressed.

Of course, those people were all union, so it was practically impossible to lay them off. A union contract was an impressive thing.

At least Loretta didn't usually have to answer the phone. If Bob was in the room, he was the one to grab the call. He said he liked to hear the little hesitation whenever someone dialed and a man answered, that vestigial sexism that startled them. "In my next lifetime," he often joked, "I want to come back as a receptionist. Or maybe a stenographer. I want to sit on women's laps and take dictation."

"You'd crush their knees," Kate would point out.

"I'd sit delicately. And breathe in their ears, too."

Loretta was grateful to Bob for responding to the phone's ring that morning. She wasn't expecting a call, but whoever her caller was had to be at least marginally impressed that she didn't answer her own phone. She slid her feet into her sandals and crossed to the couch, a location that offered her a direct view of the white board. Gilda stood in front of it, writing a list of staff members from the show who were eligible for blind dates. She used different-colored markers to denote priorities. Loretta's name was at the top of the list, printed in red.

Sinking onto the couch, Loretta lifted the receiver to her ear. "Loretta D'Angelo here."

"Hi. It's Josh Kaplan."

She frowned at the unfamiliar name. "Who?"

"Josh Kaplan. We met on the Long Island Railroad."

The Cell Phone Renegade. Loretta blinked and leaned deeper into the cushions. On the white board across from her, Gilda had listed below her name, in blue ink, "Nancy—mail room. Lavonne. Patrick." Next to Patrick's name, she'd added "gay" in parentheses. To the right of Loretta's name, in green, she'd written "the dentist," because Bob had blabbed to everyone that Loretta's brother wanted to set her up on a blind date with Marty Calabrese, D.D.S.

She turned away from the white board and focused her mind on her caller. She'd given up on hearing from the cell phone guy. They'd met last Sunday and now it was Friday. Obviously, he was conflicted about whether he wanted to appear on the show.

She was conflicted, too. Becky had demonstrated great enthusiasm for the blind-date concept but had hedged on the cell phone concept, expressing concern about whether it would be kind and gentle enough for the "new" *Becky Blake Show* that Harold was demanding. Loretta had considered pushing for her idea but had decided not to. If she wanted to keep her job, she'd improve her odds if she supported concepts Becky was hot to do, not the ones she expressed doubts about.

But the hero of the Long Island Railroad had finally called, and she'd be a fool to brush him off. "Hi!" She must have sounded uncharacteristically spirited, because her three colleagues turned in unison to stare at her. "I'm glad you phoned," she added, surprised to admit how true that was.

"Well." He hesitated, then said, "Hi."

This was awkward. Kind of like a first date, she thought—or a blind date. The hell with "the dentist," in green or any other color. If she was forced to go on a blind date, she'd rather it be with someone like...*Josh Kaplan.*

Of course, she had no idea what kind of person he was. He did have those bedroom eyes...but he might also have a wife, or an array of bad habits. Or even a few illegal habits. Or—her eyes strayed to the white board again—he might turn out to be Patrick's type.

In any case, he'd called for a reason, and that reason undoubtedly had nothing to do with blind dates. "Have you decided you want to appear on the *Becky Blake Show?*" she asked. Hearing this, her colleagues turned from her, apparently losing interest in her caller.

"I think it's worth talking about," he said. "I'm at work right now—as I assume you are—but perhaps we could meet after work to discuss the idea."

Meet after work. She tilted her head, directing her gaze toward the Parthenon poster. *Meet after work* sounded like an overture.

It probably wasn't. He didn't want to talk right now because, as he said, he was at work. She shouldn't read more into his words than he'd intended. But it was fun to pretend, for just a minute, that he was interested in something other than attaining immortal celebrity by appearing on the show.

She'd have to choose a safe, public place for them to rendezvous, just in case he turned out to fall into either the bad or illegal-habit categories. Someplace not too cozy. Someplace that they didn't serve garlicky or oniony snacks, for breath reasons.

"What did you have in mind?" she asked, checking her watch. One-thirty. Damn. Now he'd know what a loser she was. Anyone with even a pathetically low-grade social life would have made plans for the evening by now.

But if they got together, she could make sure he understood that she'd squeezed him in that evening only because it was her job. She could spend half an hour with him and then swear she had to leave. Maybe she ought to be wondering how dead *his* social life was, since he'd been the one to suggest that they get together.

Of course, if he was married, his social life was dead by definition. If he was gay, the liveliness of his social life was altogether irrelevant to her. "I could spare a few minutes around five-thirty," she said, hoping she sounded terribly busy.

"Could we make it a little later? Would six be too late?"

She waited a minute, as if struggling to rearrange her life, and then said, "Six. Sure. Where should we meet?"

"My office is in Union Square."

And hers was in the West Fifties. "Someplace in Times Square?" she suggested.

"How about the Hilton? We can get something to drink, and talk."

A hotel bar sounded relatively safe. There would be lots of people around. "Okay," she said. "Six o'clock."

"I'll see you then. Okay?"

"Okay."

Another pause, a faint, almost bashful laugh, and he said, "Okay. Goodbye, Loretta."

"Goodbye." She hung up, took a deep breath and assessed that last little flurry of okays. A smooth operator he wasn't. If he was married, he didn't stray very much. If he did, he'd have skipped at least one of the okays.

She assessed what little she knew about him: he worked in an office—which wasn't a huge shock. The evening she'd encountered him on the train, he'd had that leather tote with him, so he was probably some sort of professional. And he had a name. Josh Kaplan. It didn't sound like the name of a psychopath.

"What was that all about?" Kate asked.

"Someone we might get on the show," Loretta said vaguely. She hadn't yet abandoned the cell phone concept. Just because everyone else—including Becky and, presumably, Harold thought the blind-date concept was marvelous didn't mean the show was going to become all blind date all the time. They'd need other ideas to fill in the days when people weren't being manipulated into falling in love with strangers.

Not just people, she thought with a sigh. Gilda had added a few more names to the list on the white board, but Loretta's was still on top, and still in red. She was still the number one sucker.

"What someone? What show? Is he a blind-date candidate?" Kate asked.

"No," Loretta said, refusing to reveal her thoughts about Josh Kaplan until she knew what those thoughts were.

"God, I'm starving," Kate announced, evidently done grilling Loretta for now. She and Loretta had eaten lunch downstairs in the courtyard of the building less than an hour ago, but Loretta wasn't surprised that Kate was hungry again already. She'd started a new diet, which involved eating only green foods. She'd consumed a salad of romaine lettuce, cucumber and celery, followed by a Granny

Smith apple and a lime lollipop. After a lunch like that, Loretta would be starving, too.

Gilda set down her markers and faced the others. Loretta remained where she was on the couch. If she returned to the table, Kate might interrogate her further about the man she was meeting after work, and she didn't want to talk about him.

Josh Kaplan. A man of action, a man of conviction, a man of broad shoulders and hazel eyes. A man she had not a scintilla of interest in, except in the context of the show.

Yeah, right. And a person could lose weight eating avocados and pistachio ice cream. They were both green, weren't they?

Five

Anxious was not part of Josh's repertoire. He did indignant very well, he could pull off ironic when necessary and dutiful was so deeply engrained in him he'd committed himself to mowing his mother's lawn every week this summer. He could manage courteous without breaking a sweat, and faced with a situation that demanded either fear or laughter, he chose laughter just about every time.

But as he sat in the lounge of the Hilton Times Square, one story above street level, watching guests and visitors mill about the spacious, amber-lit lobby, some dragging wheeled suitcases, others trailing porters who pushed brass carts laden with luggage, still others empty-handed except for a purse or briefcase, he began to suffer from a restlessness that felt an awful lot like anxiety.

It wasn't because he was "stepping out" on Melanie, as Anita would put it. He wasn't cheating on her. He hadn't arranged for this meeting hoping for love or sex.

Nor was the tension in his gut a reaction to the possibility that he'd end up on Loretta's TV program. He'd caught ten minutes of it that morning, after court had gone into recess because Anita's client suffered an asthma attack. Everyone had been cleared from the courtroom and sent down the hall to a musty waiting room where a TV set was tuned to the *Becky Blake Show*, of all things. Josh had stood at the rear of the waiting room, watching as a doll-like blond woman mediated a fierce dispute between two men who could have passed for professional wrestlers and who had a clear difference of opinion regarding a woman both were claiming as their wife. "Polyandry is not for Pollyannas," Becky Blake had intoned just before the commercial break.

Josh was not going to contribute to that show. He was not going to allow himself to be beamed into living rooms around the country while he engaged in a shouting match with some goon with a neck thicker than Josh's waist who believed Nostradamus had predicted that every person in the world was destined to own a portable communication device by the start of the twenty-first century. Worrying about appearing on the show was unnecessary. It wasn't going to happen.

So what *was* he worried about?

He drummed his fingers against the chilly marble surface of the table and watched the elevator doors, searching for Loretta D'Angelo. *She* was what he was worried about. For no good reason he could think of, waiting to see her was making him nervous.

What if she didn't show up? What if she showed up and was obnoxious? What if he had nothing to say to her? What if the sight of her long, luxuriant hair left him tongue-tied?

He was used to being one-half of a steady couple. He could converse with other women, relate to them, get friendly with them—but for the last two-plus years, all his encounters with women had occurred within the context of his being Melanie's significant other. The thought of meeting a woman without that identity to protect him caused a muscle to twitch in his thigh. He felt the tiny spasms, invisible beneath the khaki fabric of his trousers, a ticking that made him want to pace, or maybe go outside and kick a fire hydrant.

He saw her emerging from the elevator that linked the

lobby to the street entrance, and his thigh suffered a final sharp twinge before relaxing. Damn. She was prettier than he'd remembered.

He reminded himself that she produced an abysmally stupid show. He was a lawyer, and she worked backstage at a televised circus. Pollyanna polyandrists. How could he be daunted by someone like her, even if she was pretty?

They'd have a drink, they'd talk and then he'd tell her he wouldn't appear on her show. They'd part ways, and he'd go home and think some more about Melanie and sex and obligations and loud parties on weeknights. And maybe he'd call another woman and meet her for drinks, and that time he'd be immune to anxiety because he'd have had this experience to season him.

Loretta stood near the bell captain's station for a moment, surveying the lobby. She wore a pair of loosely draped gray slacks that made her legs look thin, and a sleeveless peach-colored top that made her bosom look thin. Her hair was bushy and her skin glistened from the heat outdoors. He wondered if she'd taken the subway or walked to Times Square. Either option on a hot June evening during rush hour was bound to make a person perspire.

After scanning the concierge desk, the check-in counter and the bank of elevators leading to the guest rooms, she turned toward the lounge area, spotted him and smiled. The impact of her smile pressed him back into his chair like a gust of warm wind. He must have seen her smile on the train last Sunday, but he couldn't recall responding the way he did now. Of course, last Sunday he'd been irritated by the dingbat with the cell phone and preoccupied by the Branford Arms depositions, and he hadn't been aware that Melanie was hosting weeknight Bacchanalia down in Opa-Locka.

Loretta had quite a smile. It emphasized her nearly horizontal cheekbones and flashed a row of teeth as smooth and shiny as ceramic bathroom tiles. As she approached him, he stood and returned her smile. His thigh muscle began to flutter again.

"Hi," she said, extending her right hand. He shook it, grateful for the businesslike greeting. Her palm felt damp, but he assumed that was due to the heat outside.

"Hi," he said, resuming his seat only after she'd dropped into the chair across the table from him. She swept a thick, frizzy lock of hair back from her face and let out a breath. "Would you like a drink?" he asked.

"I'd shoot my grandmother for something cold and wet." She closed her eyes for a minute, then let out another breath. "It's brutal out there."

He caught the eye of a waitress near the bar and she came over. Loretta requested a gin and tonic with lime, and he settled for a Pete's Wicked Ale when the waitress told him the bar didn't carry Sam Adams. She disappeared, leaving him to face Loretta. Her cheeks were naturally flushed, and she had no lipstick on, no makeup at all. It made her seem naked in a way.

Her feet were naked, too, he noticed as she crossed one long leg over the other. She wore sandals but no stockings. Sensible on such a hot day, but when he gazed at her bare pink toes, her sensibility was the last thing on his mind.

"So," she said when he failed to get a conversation going. "Have you assaulted any cell phone users lately?"

"I didn't assault that woman," he defended himself, although her grin informed him she was teasing. "All I did was get her to stop babbling."

"It was the highlight of that day for me," Loretta assured him. "The way you silenced her, no wasted motions, no apologies—it was a work of art." She smiled fondly at the memory. "As far as the show—"

"I've seen your show," he said, allowing privately that that was an exaggeration. He'd seen ten minutes of one show. "The *Becky Blake Show*. It was—"

"Which broadcast did you see?"

"This morning's. The woman with two husbands."

"Oh, gawd." Loretta shook her head. "Not only did she have two husbands, but they were both assholes."

"She deserves points for consistency," he said.

Loretta laughed. "We taped that show three weeks ago. It seemed like a good idea then. But I don't know if we'd do a show like that today."

"Why not?"

Loretta leaned back in her chair, shook her foot to adjust her sandal over her instep and smiled wearily. "Ratings."

Before she could explain, the waitress returned with their drinks. While she arranged the cocktail napkins, beverages and a bowl of what resembled trail mix on their table, Josh kept his gaze on Loretta. For some reason, his tension was draining away. This get-together was fine. Everything was cool. He was a man meeting a woman for a drink at the end of a workday. No problem.

As the waitress stepped away from their table, a couple emerged from the nearest elevator, the woman stalking ahead of the man, both of them glowering. "I told you never to touch me there when another man is in the room," the man snarled.

"That wasn't another man. It was room service."

"Well, he sure as hell didn't look like a maid from housekeeping."

"So next time, ask for the room-service guy to wear a sheer black pinafore," the woman snapped before storming into the hotel's restaurant. The man tore a leaf off a potted plant near their table in an apparent fit of rage, then followed her into the dining room.

Loretta observed the spat with the intensity of a scientist watching stem cells reproduce. Only when the couple was gone did she turn back to Josh. She lifted her drink and took a long sip through the straw.

"I bet you'd like to get them on your show," he said.

"The thought crossed my mind." Her eyes glowed. "I mean, consider the implications. They go to this hotel—a classy establishment right in the heart of Times Square—and if there's a cleaning lady in the room, the woman touches him. But if it's a room-service guy, she's not supposed to touch him."

"Not just touch him," Josh noted. "She's not supposed to touch him in a certain place."

"It's almost more interesting when you don't know the details." Her eyes remained bright with both amusement and fascination. "Where doesn't he want her to touch him? On his nose?"

"I don't like being touched on my nose," Josh joked. "Especially in front of other men."

She laughed. "Great. We've gotta get you on the show."

"You'd be better off using that couple," he said, gesturing toward the restaurant. "They're much more exciting than me."

She took another sip of her drink. "Actually, the sad fact is, we're not doing shows like that anymore. Our boss wants us to tone it down."

"Tone it down?"

"No more polyandrists for a while. No more wife swappers, no more teenage tartlets, no more men who like their lovers to touch their noses in front of other women but not in front of other men."

"So...the show is completely changing?"

"I don't know about *completely*." She lowered her drink and shrugged. "The thing about daytime TV—everything is cyclical. After the tower attack, we were told to do only uplifting shows about heroes and survivors. And we did. We did some absolutely gorgeous shows about firefighters, about EMTs, about this couple who lived in Battery Park City and couldn't go back to their apartment for a week, and when they got there their pet schnauzer was waiting for them in the foyer with his leash in his mouth—and he'd made all his poops on the kitchen floor because he'd remembered that he wasn't supposed to mess on the rug. One smart dog, I'm telling you. But eventually people wanted to go back to watching shows about incest and breast implants. Now I guess the pendulum is swinging again. Word from above is they want kinder, gentler shows."

"I see." He drank some beer and tried to figure out what the *Becky Blake Show*'s version of kinder and gentler would be. Women who divorced the first asshole before marrying the second? Breast implants that enlarged a woman to a C cup but not a D? A toy poodle instead of a schnauzer?

"In fact," Loretta continued, "I'm not sure the cell phone concept is going to make the cut."

He experienced an inexplicable pang of disappointment. Not that he'd ever intended to appear on her show, but he'd assumed that would be his choice, not Loretta's. "You don't think a cell phone show could be gentle?"

"It could be, but I'm not sure I can sell it to my boss that way. People get pretty emotional about cell phones, don't you think?"

"Some people, maybe." Josh thought he'd been pretty unemotional in his handling of the cell phone user on the train.

"No decision has been made yet," she told him. "I mean, nothing is black and white here. There's talk—I just don't know how serious it is. We're tossing around other concepts for programs, but there's nothing to say we couldn't do a kind and gentle cell phone show, right? Personally, I think a cell phone show would work. Others on the staff…'' She shrugged. ''Who the hell knows?''

''But you're the producer,'' he pointed out. ''Doesn't that give you the final say?''

She smiled sheepishly. ''I'm on the production staff,'' she confessed. ''There are four of us. And of course Becky gets a vote. Actually, she gets five votes. And Harold—the president of the company that owns the show—gets ten.''

That she'd overstated her professional status when she'd given him her card pleased him. It meant she'd wanted to impress him. It had worked—he'd been impressed—but he was gratified that she'd viewed him as someone worth impressing.

So she was one-fourth of a staff, and she'd floated the idea of a *Becky Blake Show* about cell phones to the rest of the staff, and although she hadn't quite come out and said so, he assumed her idea had been shot down. But she hadn't bothered to mention that when he'd phoned her earlier that day. She'd agreed to meet him, knowing a cell phone show wasn't likely to occur.

Maybe she wanted to size him up, to see if he could be kind and gentle, on the slim chance that she could push her idea past all those votes that were stacked against her. Or maybe…maybe she'd wanted to see him for some other reason.

He was getting ahead of himself, imagining this meeting was about something other than cell phones. His thigh muscle started to flutter again. He drank some beer.

''There's this other idea for the show that everyone is freaking out about,'' she said. ''In a positive way, I mean. They love this concept, for some reason.'' She uncrossed her legs and leaned forward to scoop a handful of the pretzel-peanut-Goldfish mix into her palm. ''Blind dates.''

He rubbed his thigh and waited for her to elaborate.

"The idea would be to have people meet a blind date on the show, go out with the date and then report back. It sounds kind of corny, but there's as much potential that the blind date would end in disaster as lead to romance. The premise has an element of suspense, which of course is very important for the *Becky Blake Show*. I don't know." She shrugged again. Her exposed shoulders were broad and slightly bony. She was just this side of skinny. He'd never been a big fan of women who counted calories and went into a panic if they gained an ounce. But she was eating the cocktail snack mix, popping nibble after nibble into her mouth, so he assumed she wasn't hung up on food. "To tell you the truth, the whole blind-date thing is not my idea, but Becky loves it, and she's got five votes."

"I see." Actually, he didn't. If Loretta wasn't aiming for him to go on the show and complain about stupid cell phone users, why had she agreed to meet with him?

She traced the rim of her glass with an unpolished nail, then smiled again. It was a different smile from her earlier ones, more hesitant, more questioning. "So anyway, the production team thought it would be fun for some of the blind dates to involve people who work on the show."

"Is Becky Blake going to go on a blind date?" He recalled the pert little blonde he'd seen refereeing the rival husbands on that morning's show. He wouldn't want to be her blind date. Everything about her had been too...*pink*.

Loretta shrugged again, her smile growing even more enigmatic. "As a matter of fact, the staff member they have in mind is me."

"You?"

"They think it would be great TV to set me up with a blind date on the air. Can you believe it?"

He drank some beer, buying time to sort out his thoughts.

Why was she telling him this? It wasn't about cell phones, but it was about him in some way. His inability to figure out where she was going with it vexed him. He prided himself on being an intelligent man—he could see through scumbag landlords and venal housing-authority drones without having to squint—but he couldn't seem to get a clear picture of this conversation.

His leg muscle relented, and he lost track of the hubbub around them, the clink of glassware and ice at the bar, the people swarming through the lobby, the potted plant from which that distressed man had torn a leaf on his way to the restaurant. His mind filled with only one notion, one question: Why was Loretta D'Angelo telling him about blind dates?

"So anyway, the thing is, I was thinking, assuming I'm stuck with this situation for the sake of my job and so on, you could come on the show as my blind date. And before you say no—" she held up her hand in anticipation "—you should hear me out."

Her blind date. Loretta's blind date on a nationally syndicated television show.

No.

But as requested, he would hear her out—because her smile was so plaintive and her eyes were so luminous, and what would he be doing that evening if he wasn't sitting in a hotel lounge, enjoying a drink with her? He'd be home, eating something he'd zapped in his microwave and watching CNN. Listening to Loretta present a crackpot idea was more fun than that.

"See, the thing is, *I* don't want to go out on a blind date. I hate blind dates. Blind dates are the pits. I've never had a good time on one in my life. I don't know about you, but my experience with blind dates has been uniformly sucky. My brother Nicky is driving me crazy, trying to set me up with this dentist named Marty Calabrese. I mean, I *hate* blind dates.''

''Yes, well—''

She held up her hand again. ''Just give me a minute, okay?'' She waited until he'd subsided, then went on. ''So anyway, I'm under a lot of pressure to do this blind-date show. I've got bills to pay, right? And it's not like they're asking me to exchange vows with a strange guy or anything, so I'm figuring, let me just get through it, be a good sport about it, and I'll win points with Becky and Harold. But as a member of the production team, I'm supposed to find guests for the show. That's part of my job. So why shouldn't I stack the deck a little? Why not make sure the blind date is someone who's personable, who shares my values—at least when it comes to cell phones—and who isn't going to expect this thing to end in a marriage proposal? You understand what I'm saying?''

''You don't want to fall in love with your blind date?'' Josh had always assumed the object of dating—even blind dating—was to find true love.

''Hell, no. And it's not as if I think I'm irresistible and whoever the show digs up to be my blind date is going to fall in love with me or something. But what if they find some man who takes the whole thing seriously? The way my family takes it seriously. My brother Nicky, with his buddy Marty—he's looking for a husband for me. My whole family is. But I don't want a husband. I like being single. All I want is to keep my job.''

''I'm still not clear how I enter into it.''

''As my blind date on the show. I'm telling you, Josh, you'd be a hell of a lot better than Marty the dentist.''

Josh wasn't sure how much of a compliment that was. ''How do you know I'd be better?''

She assessed him, her gaze narrowing, her confidence

flagging visibly. "Maybe I'm wrong, but I got a sense of your attitude on the train last Sunday. You seemed like someone who takes things seriously but not *too* seriously."

He hadn't expected such a frank answer, or such a perceptive one. He *did* take things seriously—but she was right. If he took things too seriously, he would have done something serious about his relationship with Melanie before she'd left for Florida. And he would have spent more time reading the files on the Branford Arms tenants than checking out Loretta on the train. And when he'd filled the second chair for Anita in the courtroom that morning, he would have done more than simply sit there looking stern and white and male.

He was flattered, not so much by Loretta's description of him as by her having reached such an accurate assessment of him, which implied that she'd paid awfully close attention to him when they'd met last week. An attractive single woman, not looking for love, had nailed down his personality on the basis of a single train ride into Manhattan. Melanie never even attempted to figure him out. She simply compared him with what her magazines claimed about men, and let him know how he measured up according to her experts.

"I can't," he said, surprised to hear the regret in his voice.

"You can't what?"

"I can't be your blind date."

She nodded, evidently having expected this response. She looked disappointed but not crushed. "You're married, right?"

"No, I'm not. But—"

"Oh, God—are you a dentist?"

"No." He wondered why she was so negative about dentists. With teeth like hers, she ought to be crazy about them. They'd obviously served her well.

"So, what's the problem? It wouldn't cost you any money. The show is going to pay for the date. We'd appear on TV, pretend we'd never seen each other before, act good-natured and jolly about the whole thing, and then go on the date. Then we'd return to the show after the date and explain that the chemistry was all wrong or something."

But what if the chemistry wasn't all wrong? Well, chemistry would never be an issue, he assured himself. He wasn't even going to venture into the lab with Loretta. She wasn't aiming to fall in love, and neither was he.

"I'm not married," he explained, "but I have a girlfriend."

Loretta nodded. "Yeah, okay, well, I guess that's not surprising. A good-looking guy like you. Of course you have a girlfriend."

Loretta thought he was good-looking. He tried not to smile.

"I'm probably keeping you from her right now," Loretta added apologetically, then took a long drink as if in a hurry to empty her glass and be on her way.

"No. She's not here. In New York, I mean. She's in Florida."

Loretta's eyes narrowed again. She was reappraising him. Taking him for a creep, no doubt, someone who'd met her for drinks because his girlfriend was out of town. Which, he supposed, wasn't that far from the truth. Should he mention that his out-of-town girlfriend hosted rowdy parties? That she'd taken to blasting Gloria Estefan through speakers that used to resonate with the New York Philharmonic and the Juilliard String Quartet, and occasionally, when Melanie wanted to cut loose, with Michael Feinstein?

Wait a minute. He didn't have to defend himself. For all Loretta knew, he'd agreed to meet her because he expected to discuss cell phones with her.

"Well, okay," she finally said, sighing dramatically. "It was just a thought. If I get dragged into this blind-date scenario, I'll just have to take my chances on whoever they dig out from under a rock."

She seemed resigned. He felt bad for her. As frustrating as his work sometimes was, no one ever demanded that he make a fool of himself on TV. "Do you really have to agree to a blind date?" he asked. "Can't they find someone else to appear on the show?"

"I really have to."

"I wish I could help out." He also wished she would smile again—even if he had a girlfriend and shouldn't be wishing for things like that.

"Hey, it's not your problem. Don't worry about it." She searched the bar for their waitress. "I'll take care of this," she said, gesturing toward the empty glasses on the table.

"Don't be silly." He reached into his hip pocket for his wallet.

"I'm not being silly. You came here because I wanted to talk to you about the show."

"I'm paying for the drinks," he insisted firmly.

"Josh, look. I dragged you here under false pretenses, I tried a bait-and-switch on you—"

"I'm paying for the drinks," he repeated, then thrust his credit card into the waitress's hand as she approached. "I'd like the check," he muttered, glowering at Loretta.

To his surprise, she laughed. "You're bossy."

"I am not."

"And argumentative."

"Absolutely not."

"I ought to count my blessings that you said no to the

blind date. It could have been really bad, someone as bossy and argumentative as you are…''

"It would have been terrific," he snapped, annoyed that she could laugh at him for acting like a gentleman. "I'd make a terrific blind date. Better than anyone else your show is going to find." His eyes met hers, and he suddenly felt trapped. She was still laughing, and to his dismay he couldn't keep a chuckle from escaping. "I didn't say I'd do it," he reminded her.

"You just said you'd do it better than anyone else."

"Not in those words." The waitress returned with the charge slip for him to sign. He stuffed his charge card and the receipt into his wallet and lifted his gaze to Loretta again. That smile of hers wouldn't die. It broadened her face, opened it up, made her seem a bit too smart and challenging. The way he felt at that moment was not unlike the way he felt whenever Solly checkmated him: annoyed but mostly appreciative, full of respect and admiration for a worthy opponent.

"A blind date on TV…" He shook his head. "It's crazy."

"But you want to think about it," she guessed.

He didn't want to think about the idea, but he couldn't help himself. "I really shouldn't be considering it."

"You'd make a terrific blind date. You said so yourself." Her smile was still smart and challenging, though there was an undertone of beseechment in it. She wanted him to do this, if only to protect her from Marty Calabrese, the dentist, or some creep the show would find under a rock.

He was weakening. *It's crazy,* he reminded himself. "Loretta…"

"I've got to have an answer soon. If it isn't you, we're going to have to line up someone else. God knows who they'll come up with. Someone who laughs like a horse. Someone with hair growing on his back. Someone who thinks smacking a woman's butt is an appropriate way of showing affection.'' She shuddered.

She was playing him for sympathy, but in such a comical way he laughed again. Damn it, he was allowed to make friends with an amusing woman.

Any alleged blind date he'd share with her wouldn't be about falling in love. She'd been quite clear on that score. How could Melanie object to his helping a friend out and having a little fun? Just this once, why not do something silly and meaningless and not entirely decent?

''Marty is probably your best bet,'' he said. ''But what the hell. I'll be your blind date.''

Six

"I'm going through schlock withdrawal," Bob moaned.

Loretta propped one leg across her other knee and noticed a couple of hairs near her ankle that she'd missed when she'd shaved that morning. She had on a pair of twill shorts with lots of pockets, which meant she didn't have to carry a purse. She always felt freer without a purse; her hands remained empty and she didn't constantly have to hitch her shoulder to keep the strap from sliding down her arm.

Central Park was crowded, even though a layer of clouds filtered out the sunlight. It failed to filter out the heat, but that didn't stop thousands of people from strolling through the park, in-line skating, bicycling, skateboarding, playing volleyball or boccie, lying on blankets and listening to music or dozing. People in Manhattan spent too much of their time indoors during the week, and on a Saturday they spilled into the park, preferring fresh hot air to stale conditioned air.

Loretta and Bob had met on the east side of the park near the entrance to the zoo, purchased ice-cream pops and settled on a bench that would have been in the shade had there been enough sunlight for the trees to create shade. He had phoned her a couple of hours ago and asked if she was up for an afternoon in the park. His girlfriend of the moment was in Washington, D.C., visiting her father, who was an assistant undersecretary of something, and anyway, he'd told Loretta, she wasn't a big fan of Central Park. "She says there are too many dogs and not enough pooper-scoopers," he explained.

Loretta considered that a legitimate complaint, but the problem didn't faze her. She was used to stepping in shit.

She hadn't stepped in any yet today. In fact, she was in a pretty good mood. She'd reached the fudgy core of her ice-cream pop without catching any drips on her T-shirt, and the pleasantly syncopated rhythm of African drumming drifted over the hill from the bandshell, where musicians and performers always congregated. The park's expanses of lawn were a vivid green, not the scorched yellow they'd be by August, and squirrels and pigeons swarmed the edges of the walkways, feasting on discarded popcorn, sunflower seeds and bread crusts.

Life could be worse, Loretta thought. It could be raining. Her ice-cream novelty could have been missing the fudgy core. She could have planted her foot in the wrong place and gotten dog turd all over her sandal. Josh Kaplan could have rejected her proposition last night, leaving her to the mercies of Becky Blake and the production team for her staged blind date.

Bob was clearly not in as good a mood as she was, however. He glumly licked his strawberry-shortcake ice cream and stared at the varied specimens of humanity wandering past the bench. Maybe he really, really missed his girlfriend, but Loretta didn't think that was the cause of his mopiness.

"What do you mean, schlock withdrawal?" she asked.

"Becky's wrong about the show," he said. "Harold's wrong. They're going to push us into becoming a smiley-face program, and we're going to lose even more audience share."

"Maybe they're not wrong," Loretta argued. "Maybe the world has finally grown sick of watching TV shows that feature tattooed, buxom women having catfights over beer-swilling bozos."

"Trust me, Loretta—women having catfights is something the world will never grow sick of watching. Especially buxom women." He scooped a blob of pink ice cream into his mouth with his tongue and swallowed. "Which of our shows had the highest ratings this year? The one about the Suburban Slut Society."

"That was a fluke," Loretta argued. "We blipped on the ratings because all the other stations were broadcasting the president's press conference. You know people care more about suburban sluts than about the president's latest initiative."

"People care more about suburban sluts than about a lot of things. I've been thinking about this, Loretta, and I believe Harold is steering us wrong. He just doesn't understand what we're all about. He doesn't even watch the show."

"How do you know? He could be the show's biggest fan." Actually, Loretta and Bob knew little about Harold at all. They saw him only once a year, at the annual Christmas party. He always remained removed from the festivities, hovering in one corner of the private function room at the restaurant where the party took place and allowing his employees to pay homage, to wend their way to his corner and thank him for allowing them the privilege of working for him. He was a large man in both height and girth, and he wore the same suspenders-and-bow-tie ensemble— bright red with white snowflakes embroidered on them— every year.

In addition to Becky's show, his syndication company produced two game shows, a cooking show and a home decor show. Loretta had watched *Home Sweet Home* once and found it about as exciting as watching paint dry—or, more accurately, watching wallpaper paste and grouting dry. The theme of that show had been renovating lavatories.

Amazingly, *Home Sweet Home* was performing better than the *Becky Blake Show*. Granted, the time slot for *Home Sweet Home* was Sunday morning at eight-thirty, when most people were either at church or asleep. Atheistic lavatory renovators apparently kept the numbers for *Home Sweet Home* up there.

But the game shows and the *Becky Blake Show* were Harold's cash cows. When the *Becky Blake Show* dropped in the ratings, the company felt the hit. Loretta supposed that Harold might panic under the circumstances. Heaven help his syndication company if it had to depend on *Home Sweet Home* and *Someone's in the Kitchen with Dinah* for the bulk of its income.

"We should do a show on moron bosses who manipulate their employees by threatening layoffs," Bob suggested.

Loretta gave him a look. "Now, Bob, that would not be a kinder, gentler show."

"Who the hell wants kinder, gentler, anyway? Wouldn't you rather put together shows with a high scuzz factor? Check it out," he murmured, indicating with a nod two curvaceous teenage girls sauntering past their bench in scanty tank tops and crotch-high shorts. Their exposed navels glinted with jewelry and their hair was highlighted with colorful dye—purple in one girl's case and green in the other's. "Suburban sluts," Bob observed. "Prime Paramus pulchritude. Look at how everyone is staring at them. They've got the highest ratings in the park today, am I right?"

"I wasn't staring at them until you pointed them out."

"Are you Becky Blake's typical demographic?"

"Of course not. I'm employed. I'm at my job when the show is on." She used her teeth to scrape the last of the ice cream from the stick, then tossed it into the trash pail next to the bench. "I suppose I'll be able to watch her show every day once I get laid off."

"You're not going to get laid off," Bob said, lobbing his stick in a hook shot over her head and into the pail.

"Of course I am. Last to arrive, first to depart. If anyone should be whining here, it's me." But she wasn't in a whiny mood. She was actually feeling hopeful—not about her job, but about next week. Whenever her future appeared ominous, Loretta's strategy was generally not to think more than a couple of days ahead. She'd meet up with those storm clouds lurking on the horizon soon enough. No need to keep focusing on them as they approached.

Right now, they were far enough in the distance that she could ignore them. The next few days ought to be okay, if she could enlist Bob's support.

"Listen, Bob, I've found someone to be my blind date on the show."

"What?" Twisting on the bench to face her, he scowled. If the afternoon had been brighter, the neon colors of his striped shirt would have hurt her eyes. Even in the gloomy light, the shirt was ghastly.

She kept her opinion of his apparel to herself. She required his help to make this date work, and insulting his sartorial taste wasn't the way to get it. "I don't want to be sandbagged on the show. I've been coerced into doing the whole blind-date thing on the air, but there's a limit to how much misery I can stand, especially since I'm going to wind up getting fired anyway."

"You don't know that."

"Well, just assuming. This guy I lined up to be my blind date is no one I actually know or anything. It's my cell phone guy. He's agreed to come on the show as my blind date instead of as the cell phone vigilante. I'm going to need you on my side when Gilda and Kate say it's cheating for me to know my blind date in advance.''

Bob studied her thoughtfully. ''Why? What I mean is, why him? You've got the hots for him or something?''

''No. That's just the point.'' She swiveled sideways on the bench and propped her feet on the green wooden slats. A gust of wind carried a musty scent their way from the vicinity of the zoo, a blend of old hay, soap and pachyderm. Loretta found the smell curiously pleasant, a combination of domesticated and feral that seemed appropriate to New York. ''I'm not looking for love,'' she explained to Bob. ''He's got a girlfriend. So we're both going into the date with our eyes open. It's really perfect. Neither of us has any desire to turn this date into the romance of the century. There won't be any hurt feelings, because there'll be no feelings at all.''

''If that was what you were aiming for...'' Bob pouted. ''You could've chosen me.''

''I didn't see you leaping to your feet to volunteer.''

''You didn't leap, either.''

''I got volunteered. Everyone at the show wants me to do it. You want me to do it, too. So fine, I'm doing it. I just don't want anyone's heart to get mixed up in it. That makes sense, doesn't it?''

Bob nodded slowly. ''I guess.''

''So you'll back me up when I propose Josh Kaplan to be my blind date?''

''It might work better if *I* propose him.''

It would work *much* better. ''Would you do that?'' she asked hopefully.

''Sure. This way you can pretend you don't know him. Josh Kaplan?''

"That's right."

"What's so special about him?"

"Nothing," Loretta said, although that wasn't entirely accurate. She'd enjoyed looking at him over her drink last night. His eyes were awfully expressive, a multitude of colors that signaled when he was going to smile and when he was going to frown. He had a nice build, the sort of body that looked equally comfortable in a business suit as in old jeans and a T-shirt. What made him most special, as far as she was concerned, was that he'd agreed to appear on the show, to have a little fun and not take any of it to heart—and that he wasn't being foisted upon her by her brother Nicky. "Like I said, he's got a girlfriend," she told Bob. "So I'm not exploiting him. He's not going to fall in love with me or anything."

"As if there was a serious risk of that," Bob deadpanned. Loretta threw her crumpled napkin at him. He caught it and rebounded it into the garbage pail. "All right, so how did I find out about this guy?" he asked. "How would I happen to suggest him?"

"I don't know." The strands of dark hair at her ankle annoyed her. She swung her feet off the bench and stood. "Let's walk. Maybe I'll get inspired."

"God help us all. You're dangerous when you're inspired." But Bob fell into step next to her. She held herself alert to the throngs filling the walkways, particularly the maniacs on skates, who moved fast but were less stable than pedestrians like her and Bob. She shifted out of the way of parents power-walking while pushing three-wheeled speed strollers, people slobbering over drippy cups of Italian ice and scruffy kids weaving among the crowds on skateboards. She tried to keep one eye peeled for dog droppings, too.

"Could I say he's a neighbor? Where does he live?"

"West Twelfth Street." Josh had supplied her with his address and phone number last night, scribbling the information on the back of a business card. "He's a lawyer."

"Oh, a lawyer." Bob curled his lip. "He's not going to be any fun at all."

"Don't be so negative." She tucked her arm against her side after an in-line skater sped past her, brushing her elbow. "I bet some lawyers are fun—sometimes." Josh Kaplan might be fun. He had a nice laugh.

"He's going to be too careful while he's on the show. He won't dare to say anything that could lead to litigation."

"Isn't that what Harold wants? A careful show?" Incredibly, the program had never yet been sued, not even by participants who'd been ambushed on the air. She remembered one fellow who'd threatened to sue after his wife announced on the air that she'd been born a boy and had undergone sex change surgery several years before he'd met her. Loretta never figured out on what grounds he could have sued the show, though. He must never have figured that out, either, because he didn't follow through on his threat.

"It's not as if Josh Kaplan is some sort of hotshot corporate consigliere," she added. She had no proof of Josh's lack of hotshotness, but he certainly seemed modest enough.

"Okay. I don't live near him, so I can't say he's my neighbor. Maybe I could say he handled some legal work for me. How does that sound?"

"Great." Loretta allowed an elderly man, heading in the opposite direction and clutching the hands of two children, to pass between her and Bob. "Think of some legal work he might have done for you," she suggested. "Kate's so nosy she's going to ask."

"What kind of legal work does he do?"

"How should I know? A lawyer is a lawyer. Maybe you were writing a will."

"Oh, right. Given the enormity of my estate, I really need a will." Bob snorted.

"You were having a problem with a neighbor," Loretta suggested. "Too much noise at one in the morning."

"Yeah, right." Bob grinned and shook his head. "I wish I had the kinds of neighbors who made noise at one in the morning. There's *never* a party going on in my building. Never."

"Maybe there are parties going on, but no one invites you," Loretta teased.

"Ah, that must be it." He landed a playful punch on her shoulder.

"Okay, so you went to him to discuss a neighbor problem and you thought, *Hey, he'd be a perfect blind date for Loretta.*" Walking had inspired her after all.

"Check it out." Bob halted and stared at a couple standing behind a pretzel kiosk, their bodies entwined in what would have been an X-rated pose if they'd had a little less clothing on. Their lips were locked, their arms tight around each other, one of the woman's legs wrapped around one of the man's, and their pelvises were grinding. They were more thoroughly knotted than the pretzels being sold at the booth.

"I guess seeing that must really make you miss your girlfriend," Loretta muttered sarcastically.

"Why can't we do shows with people like that?" Bob complained. "'I Like to Hump My Girlfriend in Public.' It would make a great show. More people would watch that than some show about you hooking up with a lawyer."

"I'm not going to hook up with him."

"Maybe you should. Maybe you should neck a little on the show, just for the sake of ratings." The couple continued to paw each other, and Loretta resumed walking. After lingering a moment longer, Bob caught up to her. "I think that's a good idea, Loretta—you and this lawyer sending some steamy signals back and forth on the show. You should imply that something's ready to explode between you."

"Nothing's ready to explode," Loretta insisted.

"Why? Is the guy a loser?"

"No. He's nice."

"And he looks good?"

"He looks fine."

"So why no explosion?"

"Because we have an understanding. We're keeping our emotions out of it. I wouldn't go through with this stupid blind date if there were any chance of someone getting hurt." She smiled. "Kind of like the schlocky shows, you know? The guests might throw tantrums and pull each other's hair, but no one ever really gets hurt. They do their bit, enjoy their fifteen minutes and then go back home to Woonsocket, Rhode Island, or Ypsilanti, Michigan, and resume their lives as kissing cousins or philanderers or transvestites." She ducked to avoid getting beheaded by an errant Frisbee. "Anyway, he's a lawyer. I'd never get anything going with a lawyer. They're almost as bad as dentists."

"Too safe? Too successful?"

"Too close to a profession my parents might approve of." She realized that probably made her sound adolescent—still rebelling against her parents—but what she was really rebelling against was her parents' insistence that due to her desperately advanced age, she needed to get married as soon as possible. She honestly didn't want to get married, though. She'd been much happier in the few months since Gary had ended their engagement than she'd been with her life so overwhelmed by wedding preparations she hadn't had a spare minute to breathe, let alone listen to her heart.

So she'd be a rebel. She'd fake a blind date to get everyone off her back. And when she was ready to take the plunge—and really, getting married seemed to her about as healthy as jumping off a very, very high cliff—it would be on her own terms and no one else's.

Josh didn't want to make this call. But the day was already shot—he'd had to mow his mother's yard in a drizzle, and the dampness had turned the grass slippery and limp. His mother had spent half the afternoon bitching about the plumber overcharging her when her powder-room sink had gotten backed up, and Josh had tried to explain to her that plumbers charged a lot and hers didn't seem out of line. His father used to take care of paying the plumber, so she'd had no way of knowing what a reasonable fee might amount to. Josh sympathized. But he could have done with a little less whining from her.

He'd caught a midafternoon train back to Manhattan, and if the stout old woman seated next to him had had a cell phone in any of her four shopping bags, she hadn't used it. But no one with long, rippling hair, wide, dark eyes and sleek legs sat across from him, so the trip was a wash.

He'd already phoned Solly to cancel tomorrow's chess game. Solly had sounded upset until Josh had explained the reason: he was going to be taping a TV show tomorrow. "It's a favor for a friend," he'd said.

"Friends I understand," Solly assured him. "Favors I understand. What kind of TV show? Something to do with tenants' rights?"

"It's a talk show," Josh had said vaguely. "I'll tell you if I find out more about it."

"So, maybe later this week if you've got a spare half hour, we can play chess."

"I'll have to get back to you, Solly. I'm taking the morning off from work to appear on the show. My partners aren't going to want me taking more time off for a chess game."

At least his partners didn't seem to mind his appearing on the show. Peter thought the idea was hilarious. Anita said, "Nobody watches daytime TV anymore, anyway. It's junk. Is this show you're doing junk?"

"It might be. I don't know. I'm doing a favor for a friend."

"What friend?" Sometimes Anita treated him as if he were her son. He expected her to grill him on who was going to be there, when he'd get home and whether chaperons would be present.

"Just a friend. I have to pretend to be her blind date."

"You're kidding." Anita pondered, then said, "That sounds like junk."

"I guess it does." Josh shrugged, hoping she'd take the hint and let the subject drop.

No such luck. "What about Melanie? Does she know you're pretending to be a blind date for this friend on junk TV?"

"I haven't told her yet."

"You haven't told her yet? What are you waiting for? You've got to tell her!"

"I know." He'd considered sending her an explanatory e-mail, but the trouble with e-mail was that if she reacted badly, he'd have no way of knowing. With a phone call, he'd hear her reaction immediately and initiate counter-measures if necessary.

She had no reason to react badly, though. All he was doing was a favor for a friend.

How Loretta had evolved into a friend he wasn't sure. But thinking of her as a friend made him smile. He had friends—a few old friends from high school still floating around the Greater New York area, friends from college and law school, friends from work, friends like Solly. But he hadn't made any new friends in a while, especially new female friends. Once he'd started dating Melanie, women related to him not as himself but as an adjunct of her. He met people not as an individual but as one-half of a couple. A new friend would say, "Let's get together," and Josh would say, "Sure, Melanie and I would love to make a plan with you," and it would turn into a couples thing.

Even Solly had gotten to know him as Melanie's boyfriend. That their friendship had developed on its own amazed him, but then, Josh couldn't imagine double-dating with Solly and Phyllis. Or Solly and Dora Lee. Or Solly and whoever else the man was juggling these days.

He had no reason to feel guilty or apologetic about having made a new friend since Melanie had left town. From the sound of things, she'd made new friends in Opa-Locka. A huge number of new friends, folks who listened to Gloria Estefan and crowded her apartment on a weeknight. He wondered if her new friends even knew of his existence. At least he'd told Loretta he had a girlfriend. He was already ahead on the honesty scale.

Armed with a Sam Adams, he trudged to the bedroom, kicked off his grass-stained sneakers, sprawled out on his bed and pressed Melanie's speed-dial button on his phone. When she answered, he heard no jumble of loud voices, no raging salsa beat in the background. "Hi," he said. "It's me."

"Oh—hi, Josh. Hang on a second..." She shouted away from the mouthpiece, "I'm on the phone."

"You've got company?"

"A couple of friends over for dinner. It's okay. Do I owe you an e-mail?"

"No." He stretched out his legs and tested the damp patches the drizzle had left on his jeans. Maybe he should have changed into something dry before he'd called. "I'm glad you're making friends down there," he said.

"Well, I'd be pretty lonely if I didn't make friends here. There are some very nice people in Opa-Locka. The place is crawling with displaced New Yorkers, so we have that in common."

"That's good." He drank a little beer for fortitude. "Listen, Melanie, I wanted to give you some warning. I'm taping a TV show tomorrow."

"Oh, wow! Really? Josh, that's so cool! What kind of TV show? Something about tenants' rights?"

Guilt gnawed at him. If he was going to be on TV, it ought to be a show about tenants' rights, not a cheesy charade about blind dates. "It's a favor for a friend," he explained. "It's a talk show. I'm supposed to pose as her blind date."

Melanie didn't say anything for a minute. Then, "*Her* blind date? *Whose* blind date?"

"A friend. Loretta D'Angelo."

"I don't remember any friend of yours named Loretta D—what?"

"D'Angelo. She needs to pretend she's going on a blind date for this TV show. I agreed to help her out. It doesn't mean anything. I just wanted you to know."

"If it doesn't mean anything, why did you want me to know?" Her voice sounded cold and brittle, like icicles snapping.

"Well, in case you turned on the TV and there I was on the show, pretending to go on this blind date."

"What are you talking about? What show?"

"It's called the *Becky Blake Show*. It's one of those day-time screamfests—I think. I've only seen about ten minutes of one broadcast, so I don't know that much about it."

"And you're going to appear on it? Why?"

"As I said, it's a favor for a friend." A friend with onyx-dark eyes and amazingly long legs, but mentioning that wouldn't improve the comfort level of the conversation.

"How come I've never heard of this person, Loretta D—whatever? This friend of yours."

"I know her from Long Island." It wasn't a lie.

"Oh, she's an old high-school friend?"

"Something like that." Not a complete lie. Teetering above the line, perhaps, but not an outright falsehood.

"When is the show going to air?" She sounded less shrill now.

"I don't know. Maybe never." *If I'm lucky,* he thought. For some perverse, inexplicable reason, he wanted to do the show. Perhaps he was looking for a little excitement, a change of pace, a morning of make-believe. But he wasn't sure he wanted every television viewer in the United States to witness him changing pace and making believe.

"And if people who know us see it and phone me and ask, 'How come Josh is going on a blind date with someone on TV,' what am I supposed to tell them?"

"That I'm doing a favor for a friend," he repeated.

"So it has nothing to do with us?"

"Nothing at all." No more than her having cacophonous parties and dinner guests had to do with them.

"It sounds like a silly thing," she commented. "You never do silly things, Josh."

He smothered his reflexive defensiveness. "Maybe I decided it was time for me to do something silly," he said calmly.

"Well." She said nothing for a minute. He pictured her,

one hand holding the receiver to her ear and the other arm crossing her chest, her hand hooked in the bend of her elbow. He pictured her strawberry-blond hair—had it gotten lighter from all the Florida sunshine? Or had she perhaps changed the color? Did she still wear it in a chin-length pageboy? She'd been gone more than three months; maybe she looked completely different. Maybe she'd gained a little weight, or lost a couple of pounds. Maybe every gram of excess fat beneath her skin had melted in the excruciating heat. Was she wearing the same style clothes she used to wear in Manhattan—unremarkable knee-length shorts and sleeveless tops that always seemed about to slide off her sloping shoulders—or had she traded in her old New York wardrobe for sparkly South Florida threads in bright colors, with feathers and ruffles?

Three months. She'd been gone three months, and while he had no difficulty visualizing her stance, her posture, the prim disapproval in her attitude, he was having a little trouble conjuring her face.

"Go ahead and open the wine," she called to someone in her apartment. It dawned on Josh that he ought to schedule a trip down to Florida to see her. Soon. Just so he could check out her new friends, friends around whom she felt comfortable enough to let them open her bottles of wine. For the sake of their relationship, they really needed to see each other.

But he'd rather do something silly. He'd rather go on TV and pretend to be Loretta D'Angelo's blind date.

He could visit Melanie later.

Seven

Donna arrived at the studio armed with a latched metal container that reminded Loretta of those toolboxes that hardware stores always advertised for sale before Christmas, filled with every tool you could possibly need to build a bookcase, a space shuttle or a suburban middle school.

Building Loretta's face into a thing of striking beauty was a project at least as challenging, but Donna had insisted on tackling it—I'm your cousin. I know you've got that makeup lady on staff, but we share blood, Loretta—and she'd arrived at the production team's windowless room equipped with her own supply of tools. She escorted Loretta to the third-floor ladies' room, just down the hall from the studio, and dragged a folding metal chair toward the sink counter, above which stretched a glaring fluorescent ceiling light. "Jesus. Your hair. What did you do to it?"

"I washed it," Loretta said. Her hair looked the way it always did: dark, shiny and chaotic. "What's wrong with it?"

"You really should let me shape it a little." Standing behind the chair where Loretta sat, Donna dug her fingers into Loretta's hair and lifted it. "See?"

"See what? I'm not one of your clients who wants to look pretty for confession, okay? My hair is fine."

Donna sighed. "You used to let me style it when we were kids."

"You were bigger than me then."

"All right. We'd better get started. I had to reschedule Annamarie Nardella's three-process highlighting and Mrs. Donofrio's perm so I could do this for you. And your hair…"

"Just do my face," Loretta insisted. "And don't make me look like a clown, okay?"

"Would I do that?" Donna pressed a hand to her chest and shaped her face into an expression of great indignation. "I am going to go a little strong, because TV washes you out."

"You're an expert on TV?"

"I'm an expert on cosmetics. Turn sideways—I need more light on your face."

Loretta obediently repositioned her chair, closed her eyes and tilted her face upward. She heard the click of Donna opening her tool chest, then felt pats of a damp sponge on her cheeks.

"I like the outfit," Donna said. "Is smoking allowed in here?"

"No."

"I've gotta go all the way downstairs and outside if I want a cigarette? Shit. Anyway, it's a good color on you, that dark green. Very elegant."

For her appearance on the *Becky Blake Show,* Loretta had donned a forest-green satin jacket over a lacy white camisole and tapered gray slacks. Elegant had been the look she was aiming for, but she didn't dare to smile at Donna's compliment, because she knew Donna would kill her if she moved her facial muscles while undergoing cosmetic resuscitation.

"So, this guy they're gonna hook you up with, you know anything about him?"

If Donna was going to ask her direct questions, she'd

have to move her mouth, cosmetics or no. "All I know is
that I won't run screaming from the set when I see him,"
she said. Everyone had believed Bob when he'd presented
himself as Josh Kaplan's acquaintance. Loretta wasn't going to risk revealing the truth, not even to her cousin.

"He's like, what? Older? Younger?"

"About my age, I guess."

"Try not to move your eyes when you talk."

"My eyes are closed."

"But they're moving." Donna had spent a bit of time
dabbing stuff under Loretta's eyes—to hide the shadows
and bags, Loretta guessed—and now she began her assault
on Loretta's eyelids. "Is he good-looking?"

"Bob says he is."

"So, what's Bob? An expert on good-looking men?
We're supposed to trust his taste in these things?"

"It's just a blind date," Loretta said, trying very hard
not to move her eyes. Donna applied something wet along
the fringe of her eyelashes—liner, no doubt. When Loretta
put eyeliner on herself, her fingers always twitched or her
eyelid fluttered and the line wavered and wiggled. But
Donna's motions were smooth and confident. She was a
pro, an artist. "Anyway, it doesn't matter what he looks
like," Loretta added. "It's not as if I'm planning to fall in
love with him."

"Nobody ever *plans* to fall in love. Not real love. Real
love sneaks up on you when you least expect it. Look at
me and Lou. Don't move—I'm doing mascara. Me and
Lou…I was hanging out with my girlfriends. I didn't want
to meet a guy. I'd had my fill of guys. I was taking a break
from the whole thing, right? And there we were at Coney
Island, and suddenly this guy is standing there in front of
me on the beach, wearing a big sweatshirt and these ugly
shorts, and I was like, holy shit, who *is* that?"

Loretta had heard the story of Donna's first sighting of Lou many times. Donna offered a few versions of it. In one, Lou's shorts were sexy. In another, his hair was so windblown she wanted to race across the sand to his side so she could run her best comb through it.

The moral was always the same, however: Love couldn't be planned or explained. It must simply be accepted.

"Okay. Open your eyes," Donna ordered her. Loretta did. Her lashes didn't stick together too much. "I'm not going overboard here, but you know, you've got great eyelashes. I was always envious of your eyelashes, even when we were kids."

"I was envious of everything about you," Loretta told her. "I'm still envious of your boobs."

"Have two kids. That'll make your boobs bigger. Are you gonna wear that teddy I gave you for your birthday on the blind date?"

"Of course not," Loretta said, glancing over her shoulder to check out her reflection in the wide mirror above the sinks. Her eyes looked enormous and sultry.

"You need some color on your cheeks," Donna told her, gripping her chin and twisting her head back to where it had been. "What do you mean, 'of course not'? Maybe you'll hit it off with this guy."

"Even if I hit it off with him, he's not going to see my underwear when all we've had is a blind date."

"It's for you, not him," Donna explained. "It's to empower you. It's to make you feel strong and sexy, like a real woman, when you're out on this blind date."

"Underwear's going to do all that for me, huh?"

"Do I know about this stuff, Loretta? Have I told you everything you ever needed to know about the opposite sex? Yes, underwear's going to do all that for you. There, a nice hint of blush. Now I'm going to do loose powder, and then your lips last of all. Think about what color you want your lips to be.''

''Not too bright,'' Loretta said. She didn't want her mouth to detract from the haunting darkness of her eyes.

''Dark Mocha,'' Donna announced. ''It's a great shade. Perfect for someone with your coloring. Red would be great too but you don't want bright. So, are you going to wear the teddy?''

''Sure,'' Loretta said, because it was easier than arguing with Donna. And what the hell—a bit of empowerment on a blind date, even if it wasn't really a blind date, wouldn't hurt.

''So, have you told your parents you're doing this?''

''I told Nicky. He called last night. He'll tell them.''

''Nicky?'' Donna plucked a Q-tip from her supplies and ran it under Loretta's eyes. ''Is he still acting like you're the old maid card in the deck?''

''Yeah. The jerk. He was pleased about this, though.''

''Really?''

''He thinks if I'm willing to do this I'll be willing to go out with his friend Marty.''

''Who's Marty?''

''Some dentist he knows. Marty Calabrese.''

Donna curled her upper lip into a tidy little sneer. ''How are your nails? Did you do them?''

Loretta folded her hands. ''No.''

''Shit. How much time do we have? I'll give them a quick coat. I've got some polish that's pretty close in color to Dark Mocha.''

''They won't dry in time,'' Loretta argued.

''Then you'll sit with your fingers spread open. You've got to have nail polish. I wish I had time to do a full manicure. Are they even, at least?''

''They're short.''

"I should have brought fake nails with me. Okay, we'll make do." She whisked a brush all over Loretta's face, dusting puffs of beige powder onto her cheeks, forehead and chin. Loretta sneezed. Before she could recover, Donna had hauled one of her hands out of her lap. "Spread 'em," Donna commanded as she shook a small bottle of nail enamel.

"No one's going to see my hands."

"And the blind-date guy isn't going to see your teddy. The key is, *you've* got to know your nails look nice."

"It's going to empower me?"

"You're catching on." She flicked polish onto each nail with a deftness that awed Loretta. One reason she rarely polished her nails was that polishing them was such an arduous process for her, one that usually left globs of enamel along her cuticles. She simply didn't have the patience or dexterity to do it well. If she had more money, she might splurge on a professional manicure every now and then, but given the exorbitantly high cost of living in Manhattan—and the looming possibility of unemployment—she couldn't waste money on such luxuries.

The room filled with the scents of perfumed powder and acetone. Loretta obediently extended her other hand to Donna, who slicked those nails. Abruptly, the door to the hall swung open and Kate stuck her head in. "Loretta, it's time."

"I've got to do her lipstick," Donna said.

"Yeah, well, it's time," Kate insisted.

Donna reared back and aimed her chin imperiously at Kate. "Becky Blake can cool her heels for a minute. Loretta's not going on TV without lipstick." To Loretta she said, "Keep your fingers still and shut your mouth."

Unlike Kate, Loretta knew better than to argue. She shut her mouth and Donna went at it with a lipstick brush,

smearing, smoothing, outlining and smoothing some more.
"Done," she said, standing back and appraising Loretta.
She ducked into a stall and returned with a square of toilet
paper. "Blot," she commanded.

Loretta blotted.

"Okay. You look good, except for your hair. If I had a
little more time—"

"You don't," Kate declared, for which Loretta was
grateful. Altering one's coiffure wasn't the sort of project
a person should rush into. It required contemplation.

Of course, if Loretta had engaged in any contemplation
lately, she wouldn't be going through with this at all. But
contemplation had never been her long suit, and here she
was. She supposed her hair ought to match her mental state:
disorderly.

"All right," she said, keeping her fingers splayed as she
stood and assessed her reflection in the mirror. She tilted
her head slightly and gave herself a Dark Mocha grin.
"God, I look fabulous."

"I'm not gonna argue," Donna agreed. "If you get a
chance to plug my salon on the air, don't hesitate." She
flashed a smile at Kate to indicate she was joking, although
Loretta suspected it wasn't really a joke.

"Kate, you've got a seat reserved for Donna in the audience, right?"

"Sure, if you two ever get your asses down the hall to
the studio."

Donna tossed her implements back into the metal case,
closed the latch and followed Kate and Loretta out of the
bathroom. They paused by the production-team room so
Donna could lock her supplies safely inside, then hurried
down the hall to the studio. "Break a leg," Kate whispered
to Loretta before whisking Donna away to her seat.

Loretta would indeed like to break a leg, preferably

Becky Blake's. She was willing to forgive Kate, Gilda and
Bob for pushing her into this ridiculous act; they, like her,
were operating under the threat of imminent unemployment. And Bob deserved extra credit for making sure the
blind date involved an apparently sane, decent-looking, intelligent and generally unobjectionable man.

But Becky... Instead of fighting Harold, Becky was going to offer up one of her essential staff as a sacrifice for
the supposed good of her show. Plus, she was a simpering
little twit who relied much too heavily on Easter-egg colors
in her wardrobe. She deserved some pain.

A monitor near the alcove where Loretta stood showed
the opening credits rolling for the show, and a speaker
above her blasted the sound track music, a jingle as cheery
and chirpy as the show was vulgar and sleazy. Maybe with
the show's new trend away from vulgar sleaziness, they
could come up with an equally misleading sound track.
Heavy metal would work.

"Welcome!" Through the speaker, Becky's voice
sounded tinny, but her spirited delivery was as bubbly as a
just-opened can of ginger ale. "We've got a very special
show for you today, something fun and romantic and oooh!
Well, who knows?" Watching the monitor, Loretta saw
Becky pound her small fists against the air in front of her
as if it were a door she was trying to break down. The
impression she gave was of such excitement she could
barely speak. Yet Loretta knew she was reading from the
meticulously crafted script Gilda, with extensive input from
the others on the team, had written last Friday. They'd
typed "...fun and romantic and oooh!..." because Becky
would be able to give such cute phrases an authentic lilt.

"You know we've often done shows about romances
that have gone rotten, romances where someone's cheating
on someone, where there's betrayal or heartbreak or re-

venge.'' The audience greeted this statement with lusty cheers. They sure did love to witness betrayal, heartbreak and revenge! Maybe today's show would bomb because, as Bob claimed, Becky's fans didn't want kind and gentle. They wanted vile and vicious.

But Harold wanted them to do kind and gentle, and he was the boss. Loretta only hoped that once she emerged onto the set, the audience wouldn't hoot and holler and hurl insults the way they did at the suburban sluts or the dentist with the fetish. She hoped they wouldn't roar as if this were a WWF match and she was the bad guy they hoped to see stomped and pummeled and tossed out of the arena by The Rock.

Her heart skittered upward, rattling against her rib cage as though it wanted to escape. The audience craved blood. They always did. This show was going to be a fiasco, and she was going to be that fiasco's star.

''To contribute to the happy part of love, the part that occurs before the lovers start looking for creative ways to destroy each other,'' Becky was saying. Loretta knew the lines better than Becky did. If not for her TelePrompTer, Becky would be paralyzed out there on the stage, staring silently at her studio audience, utterly tongue-tied. She would be a perky little Barbie doll dressed in a daffodil-yellow size two minidress, unable to come up with a single word to say.

''From our very own staff, right here at the *Becky Blake Show,* Loretta is a member of our show's production team, and she's single, and she's very, very eager to meet the blind date we've lined up for her. Come on in, Loretta!''

Loretta swallowed, forced a smile and strode from the dark wing onto the brightly lit set. She was *not* ''very, very eager'' for any of this. ''Very, very eager'' made her sound desperate. If Gilda had written that line into the script, Loretta would have edited it, deleting the *verys* and maybe even the *eager*. She would have written the line *Loretta is being a good sport about this whole ridiculous charade because she doesn't want to get fired.*

Holding her smile in place, she swept across the stage to where Becky stood. The set was smaller than it appeared on TV: a three-sided cream-colored wall angled like a paneled mirror in a fitting room, a sturdy gray carpet and several upholstered chairs that weighed enough to discourage infuriated guests from throwing them at one another. Today, a coffee table had been added, with a vase of red roses at its center. They were silk, but they'd look real enough on the tube.

"Here she is!" Becky welcomed her with a hug that startled Loretta. This wasn't the *Tonight Show,* for crying out loud. Becky had never hugged Loretta before—not on her birthday, not on the day she'd announced to everyone that she and Gary had called off their wedding, not when they'd found out that the dentists-with-fetishes show had kicked butt in the ratings. Becky wasn't a hugger. Loretta had never even seen her hug her mother.

Loretta hunched slightly, trying not to tower above Becky, and then took her seat in one of the chairs. Becky immediately moved into the audience, where she spent most of each show, allying herself with them against the guests. She held her cordless mike in front of her, and the lights brightened in the house, making it impossible for Loretta to ignore the one hundred twenty-four individuals she knew were seated in the tiered seats. "Loretta, why don't you tell us a little about yourself." Becky invited her in a deceptively gracious tone.

Loretta had been prepared for the questions—the team had scripted it, after all—but she hadn't written or rehearsed an answer. She had wanted to sound spontaneous.

She didn't feel spontaneous right now. Queasy was more like it. Her heart was still rattling against her ribs and her fingertips had gone numb with cold. She curled her fingers into her palms, effectively hiding her quickie manicure. "Well," she said, and her voice cracked.

"A little nervous, are you?" Becky seemed delighted. She swiveled her head back and forth to give the impression she was addressing the live audience and not the camera aimed at her. "Loretta works behind the scenes here at the *Becky Blake Show*. She's not used to being on camera."

Becky's words were true—and they were ad-libbed. Good for Becky, abandoning her TelePrompTer with such aplomb! Loretta thought. She swallowed, felt her cheeks struggle to maintain her smile and said, "I guess I am a little nervous. It's not every day I meet a blind date on national TV." *Not really a blind date,* she consoled herself. *It's just Josh Kaplan.*

"How about if we take some questions from the audience, then?" Becky said.

Loretta's abdomen tensed. She didn't want to take questions from the audience. Questions from the audience were likely to be hostile, nosy or silly. Hostile, nosy, silly questions defined the show—and people who'd had their breasts enlarged to 44-double-D or who'd slept with their sons' varsity basketball teammates deserved hostile, nosy, silly questions.

Loretta didn't.

A beefy, red-faced fellow in a tank top that displayed his assorted tattoos rose, and Becky steered her mike toward him. "I wanna know," he growled, "what's wrong wit' you, you can't get a date wit'out goin' on TV."

Great. Nicky must have planted this guy in the audience just to make Loretta feel like a loser. "I can get a date," she answered, clinging to her temper. "I'm just doing this for fun."

"And for romance!" Becky added. "Because the *Becky Blake Show* wants to contribute to some happy romance. Question? Over here." She climbed a few steps to reach a skinny, freckled woman wearing a multitude of gold and silver crucifixes on chains around her neck. "I've got two questions," the woman announced. "Number one, how old are you, and number two, how come you aren't already married?"

Another Nicky plant. Christ. If this show made it to broadcast, her family would give it a standing ovation. They'd videotape it for posterity. They'd make her watch it every time she went out to Long Island to visit them.

"Number one, I'm twenty-nine," she said, because if she lied Becky would correct her, and also because she didn't believe twenty-nine was an age that placed an unmarried woman on the threshold of disgrace. "And number two, I'm not married because right now I'm having too much fun being single." This answer inspired a chorus of yelps, whoops and whistles. Loretta wasn't sure whether they were supportive or jeering. On the *Becky Blake Show,* either was possible.

A third audience member, her hair a mass of flouncy platinum-blond ringlets and her blouse revealing prodigious cleavage, rose to ask, "Do you think it's harder for people in showbiz to find true love?" It took Loretta a minute to realize this woman believed *she* was a person in showbiz. She stifled a laugh. If working with the production team in that cramped back room was showbiz, the real glamour profession must be dentistry.

"I think it's hard for anyone to find true love," she said. "My cousin Donna always says real love sneaks up on you when you least expect it. And Donna knows what she's talking about. She owns her own beauty shop in Bay Ridge, Brooklyn—Salon Louis—named after her husband. She met him when she least expected it, and they're very happily married now, so that must prove something.'' Loretta didn't bother searching the seats for Donna; given the setup of the lights, she couldn't distinguish the faces of most of the people in the audience, and she didn't want to squint. She was certain, though, that Donna would be thrilled to pieces by the plug.

An earnest young woman with stringy brown hair rose and said, ''I just want to say that I've been on several blind dates, and they were the worst experiences of my life. They were really awful.'' Her eyes glistened with tears, caused— Loretta hoped—by the glaring lights and not by her agonizing memories of her blind dates.

''Can you tell us about them?'' Becky inquired in a hushed tone, her impersonation of tender concern.

''They were really awful.'' The woman's voice quivered. ''One guy took me to this very fancy French restaurant and told me to order whatever I wanted. And then, when we were finishing off our cognac and *fromage,* he announced that he was broke and I had to pay for the meal, or else we'd go to jail. I would never have ordered a cognac if I'd known he was going to do that.''

''I bet you wouldn't have ordered the *fromage,* either,'' Becky said sympathetically. Then she brightened. ''Well, we've got to take a break here, but stick around. When we come back, Loretta is going to meet her blind date!''

Music filled the studio, and Wally, the warm-up guy, bounded out from the wings, his scalp shining like a polished apple beneath the bright lights. ''You're doing great, honey,'' he whispered to Loretta before turning to the audience. ''What a fabulous audience! Becky, is this the best audience we've ever had here? I think so!'' He fluttered his hands and the audience applauded for itself. "Okay, folks—what do you get when you cross Rhett Butler with HBO? Clark Cable!" The audience roared with laughter. "What do you get when you cross Independence Day with *Star Wars*? May the Fourth be with you!"

Please, Loretta prayed, *fire him, not me.*

Becky tripped lightly down the aisle stairs and rejoined Loretta on the set. "This is great," she chirped. "It's not as gripping as the show we did on cannibalism last year, but it's really charming, don't you think?"

"I'm having a blast," Loretta muttered. Her hands had warmed up enough for her to unfurl them. One of her fingernails was smudged, she noticed. She must have touched it against something before the polish had dried completely.

"Are you ready to meet your blind date?"

"As ready as I'll ever be." Loretta reminded herself to look surprised when Josh Kaplan made his entrance.

The music cued up, the lighting adjusted itself and Wally retreated to one side of the set, out of camera range. One of the cameramen counted Becky down, and she beamed from the center of the set, as bright as spring sunshine in her adorable yellow dress. "Hi, everyone, we're back with Loretta, a member of the production staff here at the *Becky Blake Show*. Loretta is twenty-nine and single, and we're going to set her up with a blind date, right here on the show. After Loretta meets her blind date, they're going to spend an evening on the town, courtesy of the *Becky Blake Show*. Are you all as excited about this as I am?"

From his post at the edge of the set, Wally flapped his arms like a rabid pigeon. The audience reacted, shouting, "Yeah!" and "Aww-right!" and "Go for it, Loretta, baby!" That last exhortation seemed to come from the general vicinity of the tattooed man in the tank top.

"Well, then, let's meet Loretta's blind date!" Becky

gazed at the camera, where her script scrolled in a frame above the lens. "He's a lawyer, he lives right here in Manhattan and I bet he pays for his own cognac and *fromage*." Another ad-lib, and a good one at that. "Ladies and gentlemen, join me in welcoming Loretta's blind date, Josh!"

Loretta peered off to the left with Becky, and Josh materialized at the edge of the set. He wore a pale-gray suit—the same color as Loretta's slacks, she thought with a smile—over a black polo shirt. The lights brought out the streaks of blonde in his tawny hair, and his eyes were alive with glints of silver. He crossed the stage in an easy, long-legged gait and she rose instinctively, her hand outstretched and her smile feeling natural for the first time since Donna had finished painting her face. His smile appeared natural, too—a little surprised, a little hesitant but not at all phony.

"Loretta, I'd like you to meet Josh. Josh, Loretta," Becky said, back to reading her scripted lines.

"Nice to meet you," Josh said, shaking Loretta's hand.

"Nice to meet you, too," she said. She had to suppress the urge to giggle. This was so goofy, and he was being such a good sport about it.

Becky arranged them in chairs on either side of the table, so the vase of fake roses effectively blocked Loretta's view of Josh, and planted herself in the chair between them. "Tell us about yourself, Josh. You're a lawyer, right?"

"That's right," he said, then shot Loretta a quick look. Would that read the wrong way to the audience? Had it been a *knowing* look, or a curious one?

"What kind of law do you practice?" Becky asked.

"Tenants' rights," he said. Becky waited, as if expecting him to say more, but he only shot Loretta another look through the hedge of red rosebuds.

"And are you a New York native?" Becky asked.

"From the New York area, yes."

Laconic answers generally fell flat on a talk show, but Loretta was glad Josh wasn't running off at the mouth. Watching Becky struggle to keep a conversation going was so much fun. "Tell us, Josh, do you date much?" she asked, her effervescence taking on a slightly frantic edge.

He shrugged. "I think I date just the right amount," he said. "And you know what else? I hate cell phones."

That stumped Becky. Loretta swallowed a laugh and rescued her floundering boss. "Why do you hate them, Josh?" she asked.

"Most people use them for no good reason. They babble about nothing and irritate everyone within earshot. If you've got an emergency, that's one thing. But to call somebody in the middle of, oh, say, a train trip, just so you can tell the person on the other end which station you just left and which one you're approaching... I find that kind of thing really annoying."

"So do I," Loretta said.

"We've got a match made in heaven!" Becky sang out. "They both hate cell phones! Let's go out into the audience and take questions."

Josh found the questions, on the whole, inane. One woman asked if Josh had had his heart broken in the past, one man asked how he'd gotten roped into this—"It was a favor for a friend," he'd answered vaguely, figuring that if Loretta's superiors cared, he could explain that his friend was her colleague Bob—and one woman in a skintight shirt, with the sort of body that would be better served by a baggy sweater, asked if he was so hardup for female companionship that he visited prostitutes.

"No," he replied.

So it was inane. That had been the point, though, hadn't

it? He'd decided to do something silly as a favor for a friend.

And the friend—not Bob but his new "old friend," Loretta D'Angelo—looked fantastic. She was wearing a lot of makeup, but she didn't appear garish or tarty. Her eyes were uncommonly deep and mysterious, her cheekbones seemed sculpted and her dark, muted lipstick set off her brilliantly white teeth. Her outfit emphasized her slender height.

As he'd left his apartment that morning, he'd entertained second thoughts about the whole thing. Fifth or sixth thoughts, actually. He'd been wondering about the sanity of doing this show ever since he'd gotten off the phone with Melanie last night. But here he was, and damn it, he was enjoying himself.

Becky Blake reminded him of Tinker Bell, tiny and sparkly and impossible to view as a genuine human being. The audience could have been assembled from the parking lot of a discount department store, a police lockup or a casting call for extras in a postapocalyptic comedy starring Adam Sandler. The backstage folks had treated him compassionately, fetching him coffee, adjusting his jacket collar, smoothing his hair with a comb and loading him down with pens and a notepad embossed with the words *The Becky Blake Show* in gold.

But Loretta… Loretta amazed him. Her smile was wry, her gaze unexpectedly sensuous, and he found himself wishing they could flee the show and go on their blind date. He knew it was just a game, make-believe, but still…

No, he didn't need TV shows to solicit female companionship for him—and he didn't need prostitutes, either, thank you. He didn't need Loretta.

But the thought that she was his friend pleased him way out of proportion.

Eight

Solly's West End Avenue apartment was a residential manifestation of Solly: tidy, comfortable, displaying evidence that money had been spent but spent wisely. His furniture appeared old, not worn but well aged and settled, as if the prewar building had been built around it. The walls were covered with framed high-quality art prints. The kitchen equipment was dated; no Sharper-Edge gadgets, no coffee-bean grinder or carrot juicer. Just the basics—coffeemaker, toaster oven, microwave. A corner table in the living room held a chess set, meticulously dusted. The slightly filmy windows overlooked a street lined with shabbily genteel apartment buildings and brownstones and clogged with four double-parked cars.

"This is a terrific apartment," Josh commented once he'd taken a look around. They'd ended their tour in the kitchen, where Solly donned an unfortunately frilly apron and busied himself tearing romaine lettuce into a salad bowl.

"Rent-controlled," he boasted. "If they ever do away with rent control, I'll have to shoot up the state legislature. I'm counting on you to defend me, too, *boychik*. You said you liked chicken, right?"

"Chicken's great."

"Some people, they've got their vegetarianism, or vegan, whatever the hell that is. Or they're kosher, or they're low-salt, or they're low-cholesterol, or they're allergic to this and that. My wife, Edith, may she rest, had a friend who was allergic to garlic. Can you imagine such a thing? I'd kill myself if I couldn't eat garlic."

"Either that, or the vampires would kill you," Josh joked.

"Garlic was God's party favor to Adam and Eve as he was kicking them out of the Garden of Eden. 'Go,' he said, 'but take this with you. It can only help.' You ever eat a turkey that's made without garlic? Edith invited this friend of hers to join us for Thanksgiving one year, and then she made a turkey without garlic. 'Never again,' I said. 'You want Muriel to visit us, fine, but not on Thanksgiving.' A turkey without garlic is like a book without adjectives. It's a tragic thing. And now they're saying garlic prevents heart attacks. Or maybe it was Alzheimer's. One of those diseases."

"I take it there's garlic in the chicken?"

Solly gave him a guilty grin. "I don't know. Dora Lee made it. I'm just heating it up."

"That was nice of her." Josh tugged off his tie and tucked it in the pocket of his jacket. He'd come to Solly's apartment directly from work, accepting the dinner invitation to make up for the chess game he'd canceled on Monday. In all the months he and Solly had been facing off on opposite sides of the board, he had never been to Solly's home.

Perhaps Solly represented some kind of father figure for him now that his own father was dead. But Josh didn't think that was the basis of their friendship. He didn't relate to Solly the way he'd related to his father. He'd never felt like his father's equal, but he and Solly were peers. Advice and respect flowed in both directions. One of the things he loved about New York City was that anyone could be friends with anyone, even if forty years separated them.

Solly handed him an old-fashioned corkscrew, the kind with winglike levers that rose as the screw was twisted into the cork. Josh went to work on the bottle of chardonnay he'd brought. "Does Dora Lee cook for you often?" he asked.

"She likes to make home-cooked meals," Solly allowed. "She worries I should eat right."

"Does she visit you here a lot?"

"She comes and brings me food. Beyond that, none of your business." Solly's smile indicated he wasn't offended by Josh's probing. He turned off the oven, then carried the salad bowl to the alcove off the living room that served as a dining area. "Don't forget, Josh," he called over his shoulder, "I could ask you some questions, too."

"What questions?" Josh pressed down on the levers and pried the cork from the bottle.

"For instance..." Solly returned to the kitchen, grabbed a pair of pot holders and slid a Pyrex dish of chicken from the oven. "What's going on with you and Melanie?"

"She never makes me any home-cooked meals," Josh said.

"How could she, a million miles away in Florida? Come and bring the wine. Glasses are on the table."

Josh followed Solly out of the kitchen to the dining alcove and filled the goblets with the pale wine. Solly brought out a basket of rolls and gestured for Josh to sit. "Dora Lee made these, too," he said, indicating the basket. "Cheese rolls, she said. I don't see any cheese in them. Maybe it's baked into the dough."

"They look delicious. Everything does." A lot better than the prepared meals Josh wound up zapping in the microwave after work most evenings.

"So," Solly said, nudging the platter of chicken toward Josh, "Melanie doesn't cook meals for you. But this new lady, this blind-date lady you met on the television show, is she going to cook for you?"

Josh laughed. "Cooking is not on the agenda."

"This *Becky Blake Show,* Josh..." Solly shook his head and clicked his tongue. "I watched it a couple of mornings to see what it was like. *Oy,* what *tsuris!* People screaming at each other, calling each other terrible names. Everyone with a gripe, a bone to pick. Emotions boiling over. Resentments. Accusations. One show I saw, it was about women who'd lost their jobs for dressing inappropriately. And let me tell you, they were dressed inappropriately. Little skirts that came up to their *pupiks,* shirts with half their chests hanging out—and these ladies had office jobs. It wasn't like they were showgirls in Vegas. They were accountants, travel agents, teachers—if they bent over, you could see all the way to China. And the audience shouted and booed and called them terrible names."

"The show I appeared on wasn't like that at all," Josh assured him. "No one called anyone a terrible name."

"This I'd like to see. When is it going to be broadcast?"

"I don't know. In a couple of weeks, maybe. They told me they'd give me the date once they scheduled it."

"So, it wasn't *tsuris* on your show?"

"Not at all. They brought me out in front of the camera, and I met Loretta, my blind date, and the audience asked us a few questions, and then they outlined what our date would entail."

"And it's going to entail what?"

Josh tasted the chicken. A hint of garlic, along with other, less easily identifiable herbs. "This is delicious."

"Thank Dora Lee. All I did was heat it up. So, the date entails what?"

"Tomorrow night, Loretta and I are supposed to meet at six o'clock at a restaurant in the Times Square area. I've never heard of it, but I've got the name written down at home. A cameraman from the show is going to take some film of us at the restaurant. After dinner, we're going to a play. I don't know which one, but the show is providing the tickets."

"Don't look a gift horse…"

"Exactly. After the show, we're on our own. If Loretta wants, I'll see her home."

"Why wouldn't she want you to see her home?"

Josh shrugged and cut another forkful of chicken. "Paranoia. Maybe she wouldn't want me to know where she lives."

"You're a good boy. I'll vouch for you."

Josh grinned. "Anyway, there was some talk about whether we should go back on the show to report on how our date went, but that hasn't been decided yet."

"So, you get a free dinner and a free Broadway show out of these people, and you spend an evening with a lady, and that's that?"

"Basically."

"Well, for a good meal and a good play—"

"No guarantees on either, Solly. I have no idea what show the tickets are for. It might not even be a Broadway production."

"You're in Times Square for dinner, what else would it be?" Solly tore open a roll and took a bite. "Yeah, there's cheese in these. You can taste it. Cheddar. Try one, Josh."

Josh obeyed. "Definitely cheddar," he said after swallowing.

"Now, tell me. Melanie. How does she feel about all this?"

Josh sighed and took a swig of wine. The subject seemed

to warrant alcoholic fortification. He could copy Solly and say, "None of your business," but if he did, Solly would read much more into the situation than actually existed. Another slug of wine, and he admitted, "Melanie isn't crazy about it."

"She's upset?"

"No. Just not thrilled." He lifted his glass, then lowered it and peered at his friend. "Solly, you're juggling Dora Lee and Phyllis. How do you manage it?"

"Remember? It's more than Dora Lee and Phyllis," Solly informed him. "I've got other lady friends from outside the senior center, too. You've never met Olga, have you? A former ballet dancer. The posture on that woman is something to behold, Josh. I've never known a woman with such a straight back."

"You're juggling *three* women?"

"Why limit myself? I'm in demand." Solly spoke this as the simple truth, without a whiff of boasting.

"And the women don't mind?"

"Why should they mind? There's plenty of me to go around."

"They don't get jealous?"

Solly chewed thoughtfully while he mulled over the question. "Who knows? If they get jealous, they hide it from me. Olga, no, I don't think she's a jealous type. Sixty-three years old, she doesn't look a day over forty. You should see this lady, Josh. So straight, her chin always raised, her shoulders back..." He drew himself straighter in his chair as he described Olga. Josh sat straighter, too. "Olga has other men she sees, younger men. And she also sees me. We go to the ballet together. A lot of men won't go to the ballet—they think it's a *faygela* thing to do. Not me. I know who I am. I want to go to the ballet, I go. It's something Olga likes about me."

"I'm sure."

"As for Phyllis and Dora Lee... Jealous? I don't think so. A little playful rivalry, maybe, but what's the point of being jealous? It's not like I'm nicer to one than the other. I treat them both nicely because I like them both. What's to be jealous about?"

"Some would say it's human nature. A woman might want you all to herself."

"That's her problem, then. I'm not jealous of Olga, even though I know she's seeing other men. She gets something different from them than she gets from me, right? So let her see them. What's the big deal? None of us is married."

And Josh wasn't married to Melanie. She was more than a thousand miles away, hosting parties and dinners for her new Miami Sound Machine–loving friends. Like Solly, he had no reason to feel guilty.

Who ever said you had to have a reason to feel guilty?

And damn it, he *did* have a reason: Loretta. Her large, dark eyes, her sleek legs, her untamed hair and the little oval indentation at the base of her throat... Oh, yes, he had a reason to feel guilty.

Nothing was going to happen between them. She'd been clear about that. She wasn't interested. If she *had* been interested, he never would have gone through with the show and the date. That was the deal they'd made: Nothing was going to happen.

Yet he'd been thinking about her, the way she'd looked on the show in that pretty green blazer and the lacy top she'd had on under it—not exactly a shirt, not exactly lingerie but something in between. He'd been thinking about that not-exactly-whatever and the way it exposed the smooth skin of her upper chest, her collarbones and the delicate hollow between them. At inappropriate times—like in the middle of a deposition with the Branford Arms's

super, or at night in bed—Loretta had invaded his imagination, and he'd thought, *Fuck Melanie, fuck the deal Loretta and I made. I want her.*

He couldn't mention any of this to Solly, who had been
a huge fan of Melanie's long before he'd ever even met
Josh. Maybe Solly could juggle all his ladies—spunky
Phyllis, domestic Dora Lee and Olga of the magnificent
posture—without undue guilt because he was older.

Solly, a regular sex machine, satisfying those three and
countless other women, souped up on vitamins and the occasional Viagra. Maybe he didn't feel guilty because he
honestly believed his own words: *What's the big deal?
None of us is married.*

Josh realized Solly was watching him, measuring the
lengthening silence inch by inch. "It's not important," he
finally said. "I mean, this date with Loretta. It's just this
once. It doesn't mean anything."

"You're just friends, as the movie stars used to say."

"We're going to appear for a few minutes on a morning
TV talk show. We hardly qualify as movie stars."

"So it doesn't mean anything." Solly eyed Josh over the
rim of his glass as he sipped. "You'll have fun, you'll go
out with this lady one time, and no one should get jealous
about it."

Or feel guilty, Josh added silently, hoping he'd be able
to convince himself.

The teddy was absurd, but Loretta was running late and
didn't have time to change. She blamed Becky and the
production team for that. They'd demanded that she put in
a full day at work even though they knew she had to get
home, freshen up, change her clothes and race back downtown to Times Square by six for her stupid blind date. At
four-thirty, while Kate and Bob were engaged in a ludi-

crous argument over whether it would be ethical to invite some Rockettes onto the show and call them exotic dancers, Loretta had told them that no one who wore a little red Santa's elf costume and formed a kick line with live reindeer at Radio City Music Hall could be considered exotic, and left for home.

Two minutes in the shower. Five minutes to blow-dry her hair—Donna would have had a cow at how disheveled it came out. Ten minutes to don the teddy, a black silk blouse and a black Armani knee-length skirt that she'd bought on a whim during a postholiday sale at Barney's last January because she'd thought Gary would like it, but he'd broken off with her before she'd ever had a chance to wear it with him. Three minutes to remove the polish Donna had painted onto her nails, because a few of the nails had gotten chipped. Two minutes for makeup—a touch of eyeliner, powder and lipstick. Twenty seconds to pull her wallet and keys from her bag and stuff them into an evening purse. Two seconds to adjust the straps on the teddy, which were slack and drooping over her shoulders. One second to consider and reject the idea of switching the teddy for a regular bra and panties. A minute to resent everyone who'd pressured her into this ridiculous charade, and a lifetime to resent herself for having let them pressure her.

If the *Becky Blake Show* had had any class, a stretch limo would have been idling downstairs at the curb, ready to cruise her downtown to the Charter Beef House in Times Square. She'd never heard of the restaurant, but she figured that with a name like that, it would have to serve steak, a safe meal for a blind date. Not that this was a real blind date, but she would never risk eating boiled lobster or anything involving onions in the company of a man she hardly knew. Onions caused bad breath, and lobster took an hour to consume, plus you had to wear a dorky disposable bib. Not ordering anything with spinach in the company of anyone other than immediate family was also wise. Getting a shred of it caught in your teeth was on a par with losing your bikini top at a public beach—at least, if you were raised among dentists, where oral hygiene was next to godliness.

No limousine awaited her as she emerged from her building into the late-June heat. She would have treated herself to a cab, except that the rush-hour traffic was doing the exact opposite of rushing. The subway would get her downtown faster.

She walked the few blocks to the Ninety-sixth Street station, descended the stairs carefully, since she had strapped on sandals with two-inch heels, and tried not to gag on the subterranean air, which was flavored with assorted fumes—metallic scents from the trains and ripe organic aromas from some of the people sharing the platform with her. Three uptown trains stopped before a downtown train squealed into the station.

Loretta wedged herself into a car already packed with passengers. She grabbed hold of one of the vertical poles. Two other people sharing the pole with her were yakking into their cell phones. "We're just leaving Ninety-sixth Street," a man in a New York Giants jersey and a nose ring shouted into his phone. "The IRT, you asshole! East Side!"

I know just the woman for you, Loretta thought, remembering the ditzy blonde from the Long Island Railroad, the lady Josh Kaplan had silenced.

Josh Kaplan. Holy shit. She was going on a date with Josh. Why? Why was she doing this? Why was she doing it in that damn teddy Donna had given her?

The train shimmied and wobbled. The wheels screeched.

The air-conditioning couldn't compete with all the body heat steaming up the car. She could feel her hair tightening into springy strands of frizz. Her sister-in-law Kathy always complained that the city humidity was murder on a woman's hair. Loretta dealt with the problem by not caring how her hair looked. The rest of her was okay, and that ought to be enough.

Especially since this wasn't a real date, anyway. Just an attempt to bolster her job security. It was a weeknight and Josh had a girlfriend. This didn't count.

She reached Grand Central Station at five minutes to six and grabbed the crosstown shuttle, which was even more crowded than the last train had been. It was so jammed no one could use a cell phone, because to use one would require arm movements and the passengers were packed too tightly to budge. Loretta couldn't reach a pole, but it didn't matter. Even if the train came to a sudden halt, she was wedged in too snugly to fall. The bodies surrounding her provided protective cushioning. She only hoped no one was sweating onto her silk blouse.

The train reached Times Square, and she was swept along with the mob evacuating the car and ascending the stairs. Emerging into the pink twilight of early evening, she sucked balmy outdoor air into her lungs and pulled from her purse the scrap of paper on which she'd jotted down the address of the Charter Beef House. West Forty-third off Broadway.

Cars clogged Broadway and West Forty-second, drivers pressing on their horns because they couldn't press on their gas pedals. The air vibrated with summer and energy and dozens of clashing sounds. Pedestrians wove through the stagnant traffic, dressed in business suits, in tank tops and shorts, in athletic Lycra, in floral-print sundresses and hospital scrubs and, in one case, a long black robe and a conical hat. People in Plainview never left home dressed like witches. This was why Loretta lived in Manhattan.

From the corner of Broadway and Forty-third, she spotted Josh and Glenn Santos, a cameraman from the show, lurking outside what appeared to be a seedy tavern. Josh looked fresher than she felt, clad in khakis and a greenish-gray shirt about three shades darker than his eyes. Next to the door, which was festooned with beer stickers, hung a small sign reading Charter Beef House.

A shudder passed through her. But Josh was smiling, and that helped to soothe her bristling nerves. She had nothing against seedy taverns, after all. She'd spent some of her most forgettable nights in them.

"Hey, Loretta," Glenn greeted her as she crossed Broadway and joined them. "You're late."

"It's—" she checked her watch "—6:02. Becky made me work late today." She sent Josh an apologetic smile. "Hi."

"Hi."

She eyed the restaurant and shuddered again. "Seems the show robbed a bank to pay for this elegant dinner."

Before Josh could offer an opinion, Glenn said, "Let me get a shot of you two, okay?"

"You might want to pose us in front of a classier joint," she suggested. Becky's audience probably would expect them to dine somewhere glamorous. Of course, Becky's audience might view the Charter Beef House as more glamorous than the eateries they usually patronized. Becky's audience was Becky's audience, after all.

"No, no, this is fine," Glenn assured her. "Just stand like this…" He arranged them so they blocked most of the beer-label signs. "Look like you're happy. Look like you're falling in love."

"Oh, so now we've got to act, too?" Loretta sent Josh a wry glance.

"We can fake happy, don't you think?" Josh teased, then slung an arm around her shoulders. He didn't hug her close, just held his arm loose and light. She smiled and realized she wasn't really faking it.

Glenn filmed them in that pose, then urged them to enter the restaurant while the tape continued to roll. Josh held the door open for Loretta and she stepped inside.

The place was only moderately seedy, she reassured herself. It was too dark, and the bar that occupied the front half of the room was lined with beefy men in denim work clothes accessorized by leather tool belts and orange hard hats, enjoying an after-work beer and heckling the baseball players on the small television screen roosting on a shelf above a row of whiskey bottles. The air was infused with a hot-oil fragrance that implied the fried dishes would be swimming in grease. Loretta would avoid the French fries, along with fried or any other onions and spinach. She doubted lobster would be an issue at a dive like this.

Glenn followed them inside. "They've got Guinness on tap here," he said, as if that would make her think more highly of the place. The hostess, a bony pink-haired woman chomping on a large wad of gum, acknowledged their arrival with a bored nod, and Glenn explained that Loretta and Josh were the blind-date couple from the *Becky Blake Show*. Her face lit up. Maybe she was a fan of the show.

"So, I'll meet you two outside at seven-fifteen," Glenn instructed them. "I'll have the tickets for you, and we'll get some shots of you heading into the theater."

"Any idea what show we'll be seeing?" Josh asked Loretta as they followed the hostess through the gloom to a wood-sided booth against one wall.

"None whatsoever." She smiled her thanks to the hostess, who handed her a menu, and then turned back to Josh and smiled again. No, she didn't have to fake happy. Her smile was real.

"I don't suppose it's one of those hits that's been sold out for months," he guessed, his gaze circling the dining room, lingering for a moment on the TV as the batter fanned out, then on the wall's array of autographed photos of second-string athletes and performers he'd never heard of.

She laughed. "Who knows? Maybe this restaurant is actually Le Cirque 2000 and we're just having a simultaneous hallucination."

"You think?"

He had a nice smile. Not too pushy, not too cocky. It was a smile that said, *We're in this together, and we'll make the best of it.* She smiled back, then opened her menu and lost her smile. They were definitely not in Le Cirque 2000. The entrées included fried chicken, fried sole, fried pork chops and seven different kinds of hamburger. "These prices aren't even that cheap," she complained. "I know some fantastic Italian restaurants that don't cost any more than this."

"Maybe we could sneak out to one of them," Josh whispered.

"There's a place around the corner and down a few blocks on Eighth Avenue. My nona's cousin Carlotta once had an affair with the owner. It was a big scandal in both families. I still remember going there as a little girl when we made a trip to the city. I was supposed to call the owner Uncle Vinnie. Best calamari I ever ate."

"Calamari is one of those disgusting dishes, right?" Josh asked hesitantly.

"It's squid. What's disgusting about that? Cooked right, it's..." Closing her eyes, she reminisced about Uncle Vinnie's calamari, so tender inside its delicate breading, with spicy marinara drizzled over it. "It's wonderful," she finally said, aware the word didn't do her memory justice. "One day, when I was about seven, Uncle Vinnie's wife chased Cousin Carlotta around the kitchen with a boning knife and Cousin Carlotta left Uncle Vinnie and went back to her husband, Alfredo. I don't really remember him, but Nona always said he had the brains of a *fico*—a fig. Anyway, we weren't allowed to eat Uncle Vinnie's calamari after that."

Josh grinned. "My family's nowhere near as interesting as yours."

"My family's boring," Loretta assured him. "At least, my generation is."

"You aren't."

She chalked his comment up to good manners, not a genuine compliment. "My brothers make up for me," she told him.

The waitress approached, armed with a sharp pencil and a pad. Loretta ordered a mushroom burger and whatever was on tap. Josh opted for a bacon cheeseburger and a Sam Adams beer. The waitress took their menus and left.

Neither of them said anything for a minute. Loretta wondered whether he thought she talked too much—as if she cared. She wasn't under any obligation here; the plan wasn't for her to make a marvelous impression on him. He already had a girlfriend, she reminded herself as she observed the strong line of his jaw and the appealing blend of color in his eyes. Realizing that she was staring, she turned to study the photo on the wall above their booth, which featured someone in an unfamiliar hockey uniform whose autograph was nearly indecipherable. Below the scribble his name was printed: Sven Blute.

"So," Josh said.

This was why she hated blind dates. They were so awkward. No one ever knew what to say, other than "So." It was either "So" or a long-winded saga about her grandmother's cousin's adultery. Blind dates made everything stilted and weird. "I hate blind dates," she said.

"Do you go on them a lot?"

"No. I hate them."

"Why don't we pretend we're not on a date?" he suggested. "Let's pretend we're just old friends who haven't seen each other in a while."

She grinned. "Okay. Say, Josh, it's great to see you. You've lost some weight, huh?"

He seemed momentarily taken aback, then realized she was joking. "About eighty pounds," he played along.

"So...the evening we met on the train, what were you doing on Long Island?" Since that Sunday marked the start of their old friendship, she figured they might as well begin there.

"I was visiting my mother in Huntington. How about you?"

"Visiting my family in Plainview."

The waitress arrived with their beers, and he waited until she was gone before saying, "You're from Plainview? I think we played you in football."

If Josh was a rah-rah hometown boy, madly in love with the suburbs, this old friendship probably wasn't going to last very long. "I didn't go to football games when I was in high school," she said before taking a sip of her beer.

Josh shrugged. "Neither did I."

He wasn't rah-rah. The friendship could be saved. "Actually, I'm not a big fan of Plainview," she elaborated. "I mean, it's a very nice town and all, but...my parents live there. It's so..."

"Long Island," he supplied.

"Exactly." Their eyes met and he and she both laughed. "Are your parents divorced?" she asked. He'd said he'd been in Huntington to visit his mother.

He shook his head. "My father died last year. My mother still needs a lot of hand-holding."

"I'm sorry."

He shook his head, dismissing her concern. "It's all right."

"Are you the only hand-holder, or do you have brothers and sisters?"

"I'm it." He drank some beer and reflected. "I don't think she really needs hand-holding. What she needs is someone to mow her lawn and take care of all the chores she assumes a man should do. I change lightbulbs for her, tighten the screws on the handrail for the basement stairs, check the oil in her car, that kind of thing."

"She's a real feminist, isn't she," Loretta muttered sympathetically.

"She believes she is. She claims feminism means women can do anything men can do, but men still have to mow the lawn and check the oil. So, you have brothers?"

If she didn't know better, she'd think they were on a blind date. The conversation certainly fit. But it also fit two old friends who hardly knew each other and were trying to change that. "Two, both older," she answered. "Dentists."

"Dentists?"

"Both of them. My father, too. The D'Angelo trade is dentistry."

"You're not a dentist."

"I'm the black sheep."

"Well, working for the *Becky Blake Show*—compared with that, dentistry is a holy mission."

She would have taken offense if she hadn't noticed his

teasing smile. "You think the *Becky Blake Show* is unholy?"

"Look where it's gotten us. On a fake date in a cheap restaurant."

"There's a Broadway hit show in our future," she reminded him.

"A Broadway hit. Right. And this is Le Cirque 2000."

The old friendship was looking more and more viable. Josh not only had those sexy eyes—which she appreciated only in a detached way—but he also possessed a sense of humor, which she appreciated in a far-from-detached way. She was a real sucker for guys with a sense of humor, even more than guys with sexy eyes.

"So," she said, deciding a reality check was in order, "tell me about your girlfriend."

The waitress materialized with their food, and he fell silent while she slapped down their plates and a plastic bottle of ketchup and then disappeared. He stared long and hard at his hamburger. Loretta didn't see anything all that riveting about it, but he studied it as if it were a rare artifact. "Her name is Melanie Gruber, and she's in Florida right now," he said. It took Loretta a moment to realize he wasn't talking about the burger.

"What, did she clear out of town when she found out you were going to be on the *Becky Blake Show*?"

"No. She's been gone a few months. She's got a job down there," he said, his voice clipped and the laughter gone from his face. He gazed at his burger a minute longer, and something inside him seemed to soften. "Do you know what a thrill it is for me to eat a bacon cheeseburger?"

Clearly, he didn't want to talk about his girlfriend. Okay. Talking about food could be more interesting than talking about romance. "What kind of thrill is it?"

"I grew up kosher. Well, not exactly kosher—kosher-style. My mother kept kosher in our house, but we went to restaurants and ate at other people's houses. She wasn't fanatical about it. But we never had cheeseburgers when I was growing up. Or bacon. I still get this wicked thrill whenever I have a bacon cheeseburger. It's breaking two laws at once. It's not just speeding but speeding in a stolen car.''

Loretta made a big show of glancing past him and checking behind her. ''I don't see any police cars. I think you're going to get away with it.''

He grinned, his humor apparently restored. ''I'm not kosher.''

''Obviously.'' Loretta waved at his burger.

''But it still feels wicked.''

''Sin away. I won't tell.''

He took a bite, swallowed and let out a contented sigh. ''Not great, but it'll do.'' He lowered his burger and nodded toward hers. ''How is that?''

''Not particularly sinful.'' Actually, it was pretty bad. The meat had a flannel texture and the mushrooms were drenched in a gloppy gravy. ''In my family, the real sinful food is Gummi Worms. When I was a kid, I loved them, but my dad said they destroyed children's teeth. I used to have to sneak them when he wasn't looking.''

''Those sticky jelly candies? They're gross.''

''Yeah. But they were forbidden, so I loved them. Like bacon for you.''

''Your father must have done something right. You have great teeth.''

She tried not to bask in his compliment. She knew she had great teeth, but it wasn't the sort of thing most people paid attention to. That Josh had noticed was oddly flattering.

While they ate, they lapsed back into blind-date talk. He

told her about his work, about how often tenants got ripped off by their landlords. She didn't doubt it; the partnership that owned her building was about as compassionate as Hannibal the Cannibal but lacked his charm. He told her about his colleagues and about how hard they worked for the clients they represented, even the idiots who deserved to be evicted because they threw their trash out the window instead of into the compactor chute, or because they thought playing Marilyn Manson at maximum volume at 3:00 a.m. was their God-given right. She told him about the *Becky Blake Show,* about how it had traditionally wallowed in sleaze but the staff was currently under orders to elevate it to a more civilized level, and she and Josh were pioneers in that effort.

She wanted to ask him more about his girlfriend, but she didn't dare.

They were just finishing up their food when Loretta spotted Glenn entering the restaurant. He parked himself next to the pink-haired hostess—judging by their body language, Loretta suspected he was flirting with the woman. She made a note to propose Glenn for the next blind-date show Becky orchestrated. Assuming Glenn was single, of course. He could be married and still flirting.

"We've got to go," she told Josh, who was polishing off the last of his sin burger. She'd given up on hers halfway through, when the bulk of it settled in her stomach like a block of granite. As they stood, their waitress hurried over—for the first time since she'd delivered their food. "I know, I know, your TV show is paying your bill," she said, "but I don't think they're covering the tip."

"They are," Loretta assured her, refusing to let a waitress who'd spent the past hour ignoring them con tip money out of them. "If they don't, have your boss get in touch with the *Becky Blake Show* directly." Josh nodded as if he'd been about to say the same thing, and he touched the small of Loretta's back lightly as he ushered her through the tavern to the door. Glenn had his camera aimed at them. Josh must have spotted the camera and put his hand on her back so they'd look as though they were falling in love.

"How was dinner?" he asked enthusiastically as the three of them exited the restaurant.

"The food sucked," Loretta said.

"Great," Josh answered simultaneously.

"Well, I hope you enjoy the show." He led them away from Broadway toward Eighth Avenue. They passed the marquees of a Tony Award–winning musical and a Pulitzer Prize–winning drama, both with eager throngs swarming around their doors—and then drew to a halt at an abandoned-looking theater with a sign in front of it reading *Three Dead Corpses*.

"Is this the play we're seeing?" Loretta asked dubiously.

"Harold says it's terrific," Glenn insisted, handing Josh the miniature envelope that held the tickets. "These are excellent seats, too."

Loretta gazed around at the absence of any other theatergoers. She suspected she and Josh would have their choice of any seat they wanted once they went inside.

"Is there such a thing as a live corpse?" Josh asked.

"It's a comedy," Glenn explained. "Let me film you going in."

Josh and Loretta exchanged a look. He wasn't smiling, but his eyes were bright with laughter. She couldn't control herself. She started to giggle. *"Three Dead Corpses,"* she mouthed.

"A comedy," he whispered back. "I can hardly wait." With that, he tucked her hand around the bend in his elbow and escorted her into the pathetically empty theater.

Nine

Josh rarely attended the theater. If *Three Dead Corpses* represented the current Broadway crop, he wasn't missing much.

About thirty audience members occupied seats scattered discreetly throughout the orchestra section. The actors performed valiantly, but given the material—a musical comedy about cadavers—their efforts were in vain. When one of the actors climbed out of his body bag and belted out a showstopper about how dying cured his migraines, Josh started feeling a little suicidal himself.

The highlight of the show was the intermission, and not only because during those fifteen precious minutes the stage was empty and silent. When the houselights came up and he and Loretta stood to stretch, her *Playbill* slid from her lap to the floor. She and Josh both bent over to pick it up, and when she leaned down her blouse gaped at the neckline. He glimpsed wine-red lace beneath her blouse, and the sight sent a bolt of electricity sizzling through him.

He told himself this was not a big deal. So she was wearing something sexy under all that black. Why shouldn't she be? She was an attractive woman. What she wore against her skin was none of his business.

But throughout the second act, as the dead rose to sing and dance and crack jokes about weight loss and never having to file income taxes again, Josh couldn't stop thinking about Loretta's underwear, trying to picture it, trying to picture her in it and nothing else. While a petite female corpse stood center stage and sang a syncopated ditty about how "being dead meant no more sex, no more studs with flexing pecs," Josh contemplated the fact that he wasn't dead, and his having not had sex since Melanie's move to Opa-Locka was not a healthy situation.

His morality reared back and shouted down those thoughts. He might not be a corpse, but he wasn't a maniac, either. Surely it wasn't unhealthy for a man to remain chastely loyal to his faraway girlfriend.

His faraway girlfriend who had collected a whole new circle of friends in her faraway home. Who might, for all Josh knew, be seeing other men. And wearing lacy wine-colored underthings while she was with them. And removing those lacy wine-colored underthings while she was with them.

So why the hell was he being such a good boy? Guilt might be one of the mainstays of Jewish culture, but celibacy wasn't.

Yet he didn't want to think of Loretta in sexual terms, not only because of Melanie and loyalty and guilt and morality and all those other weighty concerns, but because of Loretta herself. He liked her. He liked talking to her, having a beer and a burger with her, getting to know her. And she'd told him she wasn't interested in a romance. If thinking about her in terms of lingerie was going to screw up their budding friendship, he'd better stop.

After what felt like ten hours but was only a little more than two, the play ended and the cast took its bows to the accompaniment of sparse, forlorn applause. The lights came up and Josh's mind once again filled with thoughts of friendship and lace. "How about a cup of coffee?" he sug-

gested as he and Loretta edged down the row of seats to
the aisle. "Or do we have to film more stuff for the show?"

"I think Glenn's done taping us. He's probably home by
now, watching reruns on TV."

"Reruns would have to be better than a corpse kick
line," Josh muttered. "So... Coffee?"

"The *Becky Blake Show* won't pay for it," Loretta said.
"All they included was dinner and this." She pointed toward the stage.

Josh grinned. "Call me a big spender. I'll pay for the
coffee."

She eyed him curiously, as if searching for ulterior motives. "Okay," she said after mulling over the invitation
far longer than it deserved.

"Do you know any cafés around here? Someplace that
serves espresso."

"I'm sure there are cafés, but I don't know Times Square
too well. I know of some places up near where I live, but
that's out of your way."

"Up near where you live is fine," he said. If they traveled to her neighborhood, he could see her safely home
after they were done with their coffee. Solly would approve.

Outside the theater, he flagged down a cab and helped
her in. "Ninety-sixth and Third Avenue," she told the cabbie, then settled back against the cracked upholstery and
sent Josh another curious look.

Was she waiting for him to make a move? Some women
expected men to take charge, to ignore whatever rules and
limits they'd established and force the issue. Other women
considered such men Neanderthals. One of the nice things
about being in a long-term relationship was that you didn't
have to worry about expectations. You didn't have to figure
out whether aggression was called for, whether a woman

secretly wanted you to come on to her or whether she'd slap your face or knee your groin if you made a pass. After two years with Melanie, Josh knew when she wanted him to take the lead and when she wanted him to back off.

With Loretta he knew nothing, except that romance wasn't supposed to be a part of this evening. So where did burgundy lace fit into the picture?

"Was that the worst play you've ever seen?" she asked once the cab had battled through the crosstown traffic to Park Avenue, where a car could actually hit twenty miles an hour between lights.

"Possibly." He thought. "I once had to sit through an excruciating amateur production of *Annie* because a friend of mine owned the dog playing Sandy."

"Did it have a kick line of corpses in it?"

"You're right. This was the worst."

Park Avenue slid by his window in a blur of apartments, potted flowers and pedestrians ambling along the sidewalks. Even on a weeknight the city was busy and buzzing, people congregating at every corner, young men on bicycles delivering takeout to the posh addresses of the Upper East Side. Was Loretta rich? Did the show pay her enough to live in this ritzy neighborhood?

The driver hung a right at Ninety-sixth, drove two long blocks east and deposited them on the corner of Third. Josh paid the fare while Loretta climbed out of the cab.

"There's a decent place right across the street," she said once he'd emerged from the cab and stuffed his wallet back into his pocket. "It's got some outdoor tables, but the service stinks if you sit outside."

"Then let's sit inside." He wasn't crazy about sidewalk cafés. Their primary purpose seemed to be public display, making pedestrians envious of the lucky patrons getting waited on and having a grand time in full view of the world.

Outdoor tables were more likely to be dirty, pigeons prowled underfoot in search of crumbs and people had to shout over the noise of passing cars and buses and idiots on cell phones.

The café she led him to might require shouting inside, too. As they entered, they were swamped by music being pumped out of hidden speakers, an overwrought tenor half sobbing, half singing the famous aria from *I, Pagliacci*. Josh wasn't an opera fan, but his mother had schooled him in classical music because she'd felt it was important for his cultural development. She used to borrow opera records from the library, play them for him and narrate the story to him. All the stories seemed to end in death and/or despair. He used to sit glumly in the living room, listening to her describe Mimi's death from consumption, or Carmen's death at her lover's hands, and he'd wish he were in the den with his father, watching football on TV.

Other than the music, though, the café was nicely atmospheric, with brick walls, small, round tables and muted lighting. He and Loretta took a table in a cozy corner. Settling into her chair, she crossed one leg over the other and Josh's spirits rose considerably.

A waiter came over, a thin young man with a goatee. Loretta ordered an espresso. "And you, sir?" the waiter asked.

"Do you have decaffeinated espresso?"

"Decaffeinated?" Loretta snorted.

"I don't want to be awake all night."

"Wuss," she muttered.

He accepted her teasing with a smile. "Would you like something to eat?" he asked. "A pastry?" She'd eaten only half her burger at dinner, and he'd noticed some interesting-looking desserts in a glass showcase near the front door.

She mulled over the question. "Want to split a cannoli with me?"

"Sure." He hesitated, then confessed, "I've never had a cannoli before."

She looked stricken. Clicking her tongue and shaking her head, she peered up at the waiter. "We'll have two cannolis to share. One plain, one chocolate. Lots of sugar."

"Okay." He swept away from their table, his posture elegant enough to make Josh think he might be a dancer, like Solly's sweetheart Olga.

"You've never had a cannoli?" Loretta asked him.

"I'm afraid not."

"What kind of life have you been living? A deprived life," she said, answering her own question. "You don't know calamari, and now you say you've never had a cannoli. You're, what, thirty years old?"

"Thirty-two."

"Thirty-two years old, and you've never had a cannoli. God." She shook her head again, as stunned as if he'd told her he'd never read a book.

He felt the need to defend himself. "Have you ever had kasha varnishkes?"

"Kasha varnish—what?"

"See?" He sat straighter, prouder. "You haven't lived, either. How old are you?"

"Twenty-nine, and what's kasha...whatever?"

"Kasha varnishkes. Kasha—it's buckwheat groats steamed into a kind of porridge, mixed with noodles. Bow ties are best. My mother serves them with pot roast and pours the meat drippings on the kasha."

"Yuck." Loretta grimaced. "Where I come from, we know how to make noodles—and we don't make them with buckwheat. And meat drippings? Eeuw."

He laughed. Being teased by Loretta was surprisingly enjoyable. "So, are you really twenty-nine?" he asked.

"As opposed to thirty-something and lying? No. I don't lie about my age. As a matter of fact, I just turned twenty-nine. The day we met on the train? That was my birthday. My family had invited me out to Plainview for a wake."

"A wake on your birthday?"

"My birthday *was* the wake. They think my being twenty-nine and single is pathetic."

"Pathetic?" For a moment, he thought she was teasing him again, but her expression was resigned, no hint of amusement in it. "Why would they think such a thing?"

"Because I'm twenty-nine and single." The waiter arrived with two tiny cups of thick, steaming coffee and two plates, each containing a pastry tube oozing a creamy filling and dusted with a heavy layer of powdered sugar. Josh watched as Loretta took the lemon peel garnishing her cup and rubbed it around the rim, then dropped it into her espresso. He'd never been sure what to do with the lemon, and he'd always tucked it discreetly onto the saucer and ignored it.

All right, so he didn't know how to drink espresso. Or how to eat cannolis. One bite would probably cause all that powdered sugar to puff into the air like a radioactive cloud. But none of that interested him as much as her statement that her family thought she was pathetic.

There was absolutely nothing pathetic about Loretta, from her lush hair to her luscious legs—and her mind, he added virtuously. Her mind, her personality, her smile... "You are not pathetic," he said.

Her smile widened. "Yeah? Well, you are. Never had a cannoli?"

"That's about to change," he said, gazing warily at the pastries. "Is there a way to eat that without it exploding?"

"No," she said simply, lifting the chocolate-filled one and taking a delicate bite. It didn't explode. The edge crumbled a little, and she picked up a slick of sugar on her upper lip—which looked unfortunately erotic, especially when she licked it off with the tip of her tongue. "Try that one first," she said, gesturing toward the untouched cannoli. "That's a cannoli in its purest form."

He lifted it and took a bite. The crunchy tube of pastry cracked and the rich, sweet filling oozed onto his fingers. He didn't care. It tasted great. Significantly better than kasha varnishkes.

"Okay," he said once he'd licked the bulk of the cream from his thumb and wiped the rest on a napkin. "Explain to me what's wrong with your family."

She stared at him for a minute, then laughed. "Besides their being dentists?"

He noticed a spot of sugar on the tip of her nose, but he thought he might embarrass her if he mentioned it. Anyway, it looked kind of cute there. "There's nothing wrong with dentists," he said.

"You've never met my family." She leaned back in her chair, affording him a better view of her legs, and sipped her espresso. "You're right. Dentists in and of themselves are fine. They perform a necessary service. They fight in the front lines in the battle against tooth decay and gum disease. God bless them." She sighed. "As for my family, they want me married and settled down, that's all."

"And you don't want that?"

She shrugged. "Right now, I'm pretty happy with my life the way it is."

"And you're not looking for a romance," he reminded her, quoting her own words. "If you were, you wouldn't have wasted this opportunity on me."

"What opportunity? This blind date, you mean?" She

laughed again. "Imagine if I'd gone out with someone I had big hopes for. *Three Dead Corpses* would have sure spoiled the mood. I mean, would you want go someplace and make love after watching people jumping out of coffins and singing—what was that horrible song about how the spirit was willing but the flesh was nonexistent?"

Well, actually, yes, he would want to go someplace and make love—right now, even after two hours of *Three Dead Corpses*. He'd like to kiss that speck of sugar off Loretta's nose, and then get an up-close look at whatever she had under her blouse...and he'd want to feel guilt-free afterward.

He wanted the impossible.

"You must have plenty of boyfriends," he said.

"Millions. Billions." She took another bite of the chocolate cannoli, then swapped plates with him.

Was she pulling his leg about the billions of boyfriends? Or did she really have a wild social life? In which case, why had she lassoed him into this blind date? Why not choose one of her billions?

"Okay, so maybe not billions," she said, answering his unasked questions. She bit into his cannoli, managing not to make a bigger mess of it. "Truth is, I was supposed to be getting married this month."

It was his turn to lean back, to regard her in a new light. Almost married? Had some bastard shattered her heart? Josh suddenly felt gallantly protective of her.

"My fiancé broke up with me on Valentine's Day." She didn't seem particularly sad about it.

"That's terrible."

She shrugged again. "Actually, it was great. A little messy, sure. We'd already lined up the church, reserved the place for the reception. I hadn't bought my dress yet, but I had my bridesmaids lined up—my cousin Donna was going to be my matron of honor, and my two sisters-in-law were going to be in the party, and my three nieces were all going to be flower girls because heaven help us all if someone got left out, and Gary's brother was going to be the best man. We'd done a real good job of focusing on the details and missing the big picture.''

"Gary." Josh appreciated having a name he could attach to the villain in this story.

"Gary Mancuso. He wasn't a dentist, but he was a good Catholic boy from Neapolitan stock and he was willing to marry me, so my parents adored him. I liked his parents, too. They were very nice." She sipped her espresso and smiled. "In fact, everything about it was very nice. Then, on Valentine's Day, I made a romantic dinner for Gary— three-cheese lasagna and a beautiful antipasto, and a bottle of Salice Salentino—and he brought me flowers and Perugina chocolates, and everything was nice. And suddenly he said, 'We've got a problem, Loretta. I don't love you.'"

"Tact wasn't his long suit," Josh commented.

"He was honest." Loretta sucked some sugar from her index finger. "And you know, when I thought about it, I realized I didn't love him, either. We were just going along with everything, living according to everyone else's expectations, doing what everyone assumed we should do. I was getting up there in age, according to my family, and I'd been dating Gary for a while, so what the hell, why not? He was getting the same kind of pressure on his end. We got so caught up in it, we forgot to think about what *we* wanted." She toyed with a crumb of cannoli shell. Her fingers were longer than he'd realized; with her nails cut short, they had seemed kind of blunt, but they were like her legs, like all of her—long and slender. "The closest I ever came to loving him was that Valentine's Day. He saved us both from a very boring marriage—or a very trite divorce.''

"So I don't have to find this guy and beat him up for you?"

Her smile was sweet and warm and slightly surprised. "If you want to beat people up for me, I'll give you a list. But not Gary. He's okay in my book. You remind me of him a little."

"I do?" Josh wasn't sure if she meant that as a compliment.

"You seem like the kind of guy who'd be better at honesty than tact."

"I'm not sure about that." In fact, he didn't think he was particularly good at either.

"You're both funny, and you're willing to take chances. And you both have gorgeous hazel eyes." She dropped the crumb and sipped her espresso. "Of course, to Gary, eating a bacon cheeseburger would not be a sin. To him, a sin would be, for instance, committing adultery."

"He committed adultery?"

"No, I'm just saying. Catholics have a pretty straight-forward system of sin. Lent is the only time food is in-volved—and you get to choose which foods you're going to give up then. And if you fall off the wagon—say, if you eat a cannoli during Lent, for instance—it's not a sin. It's just a lapse, no big deal. If you commit a sin—adultery, for example—you go to church, confess, do your penance and the slate is wiped clean. You're good to go."

"Catholicism is a lot more user-friendly than Judaism."

"Plus, we get Christmas." Her smile widened, causing her eyes to glitter. "You might want to consider convert-ing."

"I'll just stick with sneaking the occasional bacon

cheeseburger," he said. "So after this debacle with Gary, you decided to swear off men?"

"No. What I've sworn off is getting panicked about not having a man in my life. I don't want a serious love affair. I don't want my family nagging me about how I have to get married before it's too late."

"Too late for what?"

"Who the hell knows? I like my life the way it is. I just want them to leave me alone about it."

"I don't blame you." He lifted his cup and was disappointed to discover it empty. Only debris from the cannolis remained on the plates. The clock above the café's entry indicated that it was nearly eleven.

He had work tomorrow. So did Loretta. He signaled the waiter over and requested the check. The waiter took his credit card and vanished. "Do we have to appear on the show again?" he asked Loretta.

"To recap our date? Becky hinted that she might want us to do that." She gazed into his eyes. "Do you want to?"

"Appear on the show again?" he asked. The way she was looking at him, he wasn't sure exactly what she was asking, or what he wanted.

"Because I can probably talk them out of it, if you'd rather skip. You've been a good sport about this, but—"

"I'm not a good sport," he said. "I didn't do this because I'm a good sport."

"Why did you do it?"

"Because…" He pondered his answer, searching for the right words, wondering whether honesty would win out over tact. "I decided it was time to take a chance."

She studied him, apparently unsure of what he meant. He hoped she wouldn't question him further, because he didn't want to clarify his answer. He didn't want to explain his uneasiness about Melanie, about their relationship and his own restlessness. If Loretta asked, he'd have to lie. This was one of those occasions where tact trumped honesty.

Fortunately, she let his answer stand unchallenged. "So, you wouldn't mind going back on the show?"

"I don't know. Why don't you find out what they want us to do, and then we can figure out whether we want to do it?"

"Okay." The waiter returned with a receipt for Josh to sign. He took care of it, then stood and offered Loretta his hand.

"This has been great, Josh," she said. "I mean it. One of the more pleasant evenings of my life."

"Because it wasn't really a date," he reminded her.

"Yeah, but I had fun, too."

"So did I," he said. "It's always fun getting together with an old friend." She caught his smile and returned it. "Where do you live? I'll walk you home."

"It's just a couple of blocks from here. And you've got a long trip home, yourself—"

"My friend Solly will kill me if I don't see you home."

"Solly?" she asked as he ushered her to the door and outside, into the balmy night.

"Solly is a long story," Josh warned. "If you want to hear about him, we're going to have to save it for another time."

"I want to hear about him," Loretta said. Their gazes met, and he understood. This wasn't a date, it wasn't romance, but they were going to see each other again.

They headed north, leaving behind the bustle of Ninety-sixth Street for the quieter residential blocks. A few pedestrians cruised the sidewalks, accompanied by dogs on leashes; a few folks sat on front stoops chatting, or stood huddling in the glow of a street lamp. But the neighborhood was clearly winding down for the night. Josh was doubly glad he'd insisted on escorting Loretta home. She would probably be safe without him, but she was safer with him.

"So, what are you going to tell your colleagues at work tomorrow?" he asked her.

"About tonight? I'll tell them to avoid *Three Dead Corpses* and the Charter Beef House."

He grinned. "That's all?"

She poked his arm. "Fishing for compliments? I'll tell them this was the best blind date I've ever been on."

How much of a compliment that was depended on how bad her previous blind dates had been. He chose to be flattered anyway. He couldn't remember the last time he'd been on a blind date, either—it might have been his freshman year at Penn, when his roommate's girlfriend dragged a friend along with her from Bryn Mawr and they'd attempted a double-date weekend. Compared with that episode, this was the best blind date he'd ever been on, too.

Even in delicate dress sandals, Loretta walked with a strong, purposeful stride. The heels added a few inches to her height, bringing the top of her head in line with his ear. When light struck her hair, it took on a silver sheen, like tiny flashes of lightning rippling through the black waves.

"This is where I live," she said, pointing to a stodgy brick apartment building. She dug into her tiny purse and pulled out a key ring. "Thanks for making this whole fiasco bearable."

"It wasn't a fiasco," he said. "Except for the play."

"That was definitely bad." She smiled up at him.

God, she really was pretty. Guilt, schmilt. She'd pointed out, and he'd agreed, that he was willing to take chances. He might as well live up to that assessment.

He bowed his head and touched his lips to hers.

When she didn't pull away, he grazed her lips with his

again, a little more firmly, not pushing but asserting himself, making sure she understood that this was no accident, no meaningless gesture. Making sure she knew he wanted her.

Her mouth was warm and soft and not at all resistant. She didn't touch him, didn't reach for him and pull him to her. But she didn't reject him, either. She let his mouth linger on hers for a long, sweet moment, then sighed and parted her lips just enough for him to steal inside.

A tiny sound, half a gasp and half a moan, escaped her, and she pulled back. ''What was that about?'' she asked.

''That was about me kissing you.''

Her eyes were wide and dark; her lashes, as thick as mink. She contemplated him, her lips pressed together, as if to keep him from kissing her again. That one kiss had felt too good. Not because it had been months since he'd kissed a woman but just because. Because he and Loretta were new old friends. Because she was beautiful and funny and smart.

''I thought...'' She cleared her voice and started again. ''I thought we had an understanding.''

''No romance.'' He held up his hands, palms forward, as if to demonstrate that he wasn't armed. ''Yes. Understood.''

''So you're just—what? Kissing me? For no reason?''

''Do you really want me to list the reasons?''

''All I'm saying is, if you expect me to invite you upstairs—''

''I don't expect that at all,'' he swore. ''If you invited me, I'd say no.'' He considered that for a minute, then decided that honesty was more important than tact. ''Who am I kidding? If you invited me upstairs, I'd definitely say yes.''

She looked as if she was trying not to laugh. She failed, and a faint chuckle escaped her. "I'm not inviting you."

No surprise there. He brushed a stray hair back from her cheek, just so he could touch the silky strands. "Look," he said, letting his hand fall to his side. "I'm out of line. I'm sorry. I know you're not interested—"

"Who says I'm not interested?"

He thought about the dark-red lace caressing her skin under her blouse. Damn. Maybe she *was* interested. Maybe she was just jerking him around. "Are you interested?" he asked carefully.

"Josh." Her smile took on a hint of disappointment. "Come on. You think eating a bacon cheeseburger is a sin, but you don't think there's anything wrong with coming on to me when you've already got a girlfriend?"

Guilt swept over him, not guilt-schmilt but the real thing, as damp and heavy as a wave crashing against the sand at Jones Beach. "You're right," he confessed. "I'm a son of a bitch."

Her smile brightened. She shook her head, gave his arm a squeeze and pulled open the outer door of her building. "I'll call you," she promised before letting the door swing shut behind her.

He stood staring through the glass at her silhouette in the vestibule as she used her key on the inner door and then vanished inside. She'd said she would call. She'd implied that she was interested. She hadn't outright agreed with him when he'd said he was a son of a bitch.

She hadn't disagreed with him, either. He *was* a son of a bitch.

But he was grinning as he turned and strolled to the corner in search of a cab.

Ten

Nicky phoned at 7:00 a.m. He wasn't her first post-blind-date call; Donna had buzzed her a few minutes before midnight last night. Loretta wished she'd been able to sleep during the seven intervening hours, but she'd had a restless night reliving Josh's kiss in her mind, over and over, recalling the warmth of his mouth, the erotic foray of his tongue. She'd been drifting into a desperately needed slumber when Nicky's call jolted her awake.

"What?" she growled into the mouthpiece. Anyone rude enough to phone her at such an ungodly hour didn't deserve courtesy.

Nicky probably didn't expect courtesy from her, anyway. "Hey, Loretta! How'd it go last night?"

"How did what go?" Tucking the receiver against her ear, she sank back into the pillows and shut her eyes. Morning light filtered through the curtains, but with her eyes closed she could pretend it was still dark.

"Your big blind date. We're all dying of curiosity here. How'd it go?"

She pictured Nicky, bright and chipper in his crisp white medical jacket, crepe-soled shoes and inverted sailor hat, standing in his sun-filled kitchen and drinking water because coffee might stain his teeth. The kids would be clamoring around him, throwing Cheerios and raisins at each other, and Kathy would be hovering nearby, pretending not to eavesdrop on the conversation. One good reason Loretta was in no hurry to get married and become a parent was that people who got married and became parents wound up wide awake at seven in the morning.

"The blind date was fine," she said.

"What was the guy's name again? Joseph or something?"

"Josh. Joshua, I guess."

"Joshua? What kind of name is that?"

In the background, Loretta heard Kathy say, "It's biblical, Nicky."

"So the date went well?" Nicky said into the phone.

"It was fine. I'm tired."

"Why? Were you out late with him? Jesus, Loretta— he's not there with you now, is he?"

"Of course not," she retorted, wondering whether hanging up on Nicky would precipitate a major family crisis.

"All right, well, I was just asking. I mean, you're a single girl in the city, am I right? A man might make assumptions. But if he took advantage, you know? He'd have to answer to me. I'm not kidding."

"What's your point, Nicky?"

"Okay, okay—" He seemed to be addressing Kathy, but then his voice returned stronger. "So, you had fun?"

"Do we really have to talk about this now? It's seven in the morning. I'm not even up yet."

"I wanted to catch you before you left for work. Everybody wants to know how the date went. Mom, Dad, Kathy, Al..."

"You all need a life. Maybe you should organize a family outing to see a movie. Then you can talk about that, instead."

"The thing is, you survived, right? You survived this blind date."

She wasn't sure where he was heading, and given that this was Nicky, she wasn't sure she should follow him there. "And?" she said cautiously.

"And, I was thinking, why not try another blind date? With Marty this time. I'm telling you, Loretta—"

"Whatever you're telling me, I'm not interested. Okay? I agreed to go on a blind date just this once because my job was at stake. Your friend Marty can do nothing to help me keep my job. So there's no reason for me to go on a date with him."

"There are plenty of reasons," Nicky argued. "He's good-looking."

"Yeah, right. Mel Gibson, only taller." The brightening sunlight seeped into her apartment and pressed against her eyelids. She rolled onto her side, facing away from the window, and again toyed with the idea of hanging up on her brother. She could say they got accidentally disconnected. She could blame it on technology.

"And he's Italian, Loretta, you know? Calabrese. A *paesano, capisce?*"

Oh, great. Now Nicky was going to do his *Godfather* routine. For Christ's sake, he'd grown up in Plainview, not Palermo. "I'll let you in on a secret, Nicky," she said. "I hate your friend Marty. I've never even met him, but I hate him because you keep pushing him on me. See? It's *your* fault I will never go on a blind date with him."

Nicky clearly didn't know what to say to that. He laughed. "That's a joke, right?"

"I've got to go," she grumbled. "Give Alyssa and Terror a hug from Aunt Loretta. I'll see you later."

"Yeah, okay." He paused. "That was a joke, right?"

"Goodbye, Nicky." She hung up the phone.

Silence surrounded her—New York silence, which was actually fairly noisy. Loretta could hear the whoosh of running water as her upstairs neighbor took a shower, the hum of her refrigerator's motor, the distant rumble of traffic and the metallic stutter of a jackhammer outside. But compared with Nicky's yammering, these were soothing sounds, sounds that left her mind free to slip back into unconsciousness—or into those dark thoughts that lurked in wait when a person lay in bed, too tired to escape.

She didn't want to slip into those thoughts again, but there they were, as unavoidable as the mud puddle at the bottom of a slide in the playground on a rainy afternoon when you're halfway down the slide and accelerating. You know you're going to hit the puddle and splatter water everywhere, and probably ruin your sneakers, too, but you can't stop your descent.

She couldn't stop descending into thoughts about Josh Kaplan. Specifically, thoughts about the last couple of minutes she'd spent with him, when he'd kissed her.

He'd called himself a son of a bitch, and he'd been right. How could he *do* that to her? How could he kiss her so briefly, so casually, yet leave her so totally hot and bothered?

She'd been simmering and squirming last night when Donna had phoned. "Did you wear the teddy?" Donna had asked, making Loretta angry with herself that she had. Maybe if she'd stuck to her boring cotton underwear, his kiss wouldn't have had such an impact on her.

Or maybe her underwear had been irrelevant last night. Maybe Josh's kiss would have done it to her even if she'd been wearing a prison jumpsuit. Maybe she'd responded not because wearing the damn teddy made her feel womanly, but because Josh was so manly.

What was it about him, anyway? He wasn't macho. He wasn't cool. He wasn't a movie-star-caliber hunk, although those beautiful eyes of his... Well, okay, so he had spectacular eyes and a nice build and a contagious smile. But he wasn't the sort of guy who'd freeze women in their tracks so they could gawk at him.

And he really shouldn't have kissed her. Loretta wasn't a prude; she'd read a book on situation ethics in college, and she believed that how individual couples worked out their fidelity issues was none of her business. But she personally wouldn't choose to start anything with a man who had a girlfriend. She and Josh had discussed not looking for romance. They'd had an understanding.

So why had he kissed her?

She knew why: He'd let his testosterone do the thinking for him. The real question was, why had she kissed him back? Why had she felt so incredibly aroused standing outside the door with him, reveling in the heat and pressure of his mouth on hers? Why had it taken all her willpower to stop him when what she'd wanted was to go further, deeper, to find out how he kissed when he wasn't holding back, to find out how he did everything else when he wasn't holding back?

It could be that she was just plain horny. She and Gary had broken up in February, and now it was nearly July. She was twenty-nine, which, her family's opinion notwithstanding, was not the same thing as being dead.

If her response to Josh was only due to horniness, she could solve that problem with any reasonably decent man. It didn't have to be Josh Kaplan—and it shouldn't be, since he had a girlfriend. Nor could it be Bob, because not only did he have a girlfriend but Loretta worked with him. Maybe Marty Calabrese would fit the bill.

Ugh.

She didn't want to get naked—or even wear her teddy— with Nicky's friend Marty. Or with Bob. She'd known him for a long time, spent many hours with him both in and out of the office, and never felt the least twinge of excitement in his presence. Whereas with Josh...with his bedroom eyes and his quiet laugh...

Her alarm clicked on, filling the studio apartment with Alanis Morissette's cat-in-heat howling. She slapped the button on her clock radio to turn it off, then sat up and rubbed the sleep from her eyes. The hell with it, the hell with everything. She was never going to wear the teddy again. She was never going to kiss Josh again. In fact, she might never phone him again, even though she'd promised him she would. She was never going to spare him another thought, because thinking about him gave her *agita*.

She'd done what she had to do. Now Becky Blake had better not fire her.

Kate was eating baby carrots when Loretta entered the staff room. "Those aren't green," she said.

Kate stared at her Ziploc bag of carrots for a minute, then shrugged. "I'm not on the green diet anymore. It didn't work. I discovered this stuff called grasshopper pie. It was green and I gained three pounds eating it. But enough about me. How did the date go?"

Loretta sighed and edged back toward the door. "Fine. Who wants coffee?"

"Bob will get coffee," Gilda announced. She stood at the white board, writing lists, her earrings glittering in the brassy overhead light. Bob was sprawled out on the sofa, but he sat up at Loretta's entrance. His impish smile unsettled Loretta.

"I don't mind getting the coffee," she said.

"Bob will get it," Gilda commanded. "You will sit down and tell us about your date."

"I want to hear about her date, too," Bob complained. "I don't want her spilling all the juicy details while I'm in the lounge spilling the coffee. After all, Josh Kaplan is my lawyer." He sounded persuasive, as if he'd come to believe this fib himself.

"Fine. Then she'll wait for you to get the coffee. The sooner you get it, the sooner we can all hear about her date."

Bob didn't seem pleased. "Sure, I'll get the coffee. They don't even have any mocha latte up here," he grumbled as he strode out of the room.

"You want a carrot?" Kate extended the bag to Loretta.

She shook her head. She'd had a hard enough time forcing down a dry bread stick and a glass of orange juice at home. Carrots at nine-thirty did not strike her as appetizing. "I'm not hungry."

"I think she's in love," Kate said to Gilda.

"Think again," Loretta snapped.

Gilda nodded solemnly. "Either she's in love or she has PMS. The symptoms are similar."

"What symptoms?"

"That pallor," Gilda said, pointing in the general direction of Loretta's cheeks.

"The grouchiness," Kate added.

"An apparent lack of adequate sleep. You've got bags under your eyes."

"You look bloated," Kate said.

That was a patent lie. Loretta looked the way she always did—the bags under her eyes were fast becoming a permanent fixture—and her stomach was no puffier than usual. She did not have PMS. What she had was an overactive imagination that circled relentlessly around her memory of kissing Josh outside her building last night. "The evening went well," she reported, "but we didn't fall in love."

"Wait." Gilda held up her hand to silence her. "Wait until Bob gets back. Josh is his lawyer, after all."

With another sigh, Loretta turned to stare at the Parthenon on the wall poster.

Bob returned to the team's room, balancing three full cups in his large hands. He set them on the table and Loretta reached for one. "Now, tell us about last night," he ordered her.

"It was fine." She kept her voice as even as possible so no one would detect any emotion. She wasn't in love; of course not. Kate was crazy if she thought such a thing was possible. But Loretta allowed that she might just be a little bit in lust, and if her colleagues figured that out, they'd cause her all kinds of grief. They'd probably come up with a new topic for the show—twenty-nine-year-old single women in lust—and make her appear on it.

"Just fine?" Gilda pressed her.

"The restaurant was lousy. And the play was worse. They got us tickets for this thing called *Three Dead Corpses*."

"That's supposed to be hilarious," Bob noted.

"It sounds pretty morbid for a first date," Kate remarked.

"Harold probably got the tickets for free," Gilda added.

"That's my guess," Loretta said. "Corpses—it was horrible. Then we went out for espresso and then Josh walked me home. And that was it."

"No good-night kiss?" Kate pried.

Loretta felt her cheeks grow warm. She hid behind her coffee cup so she could blame her sudden feverishness on the steam rising from it. "I hardly even know the guy."

"So? You still could have kissed him. He was pretty cute for a white boy."

"He was very cute," Gilda agreed.

The door burst open and Becky waltzed in, a summery

vision in peach and ecru. "Loretta! How was your date?" she asked.

"They didn't kiss," Kate said, eyeing Loretta as if she wasn't sure she believed this assertion. "But the consensus is, they should have."

"That's your consensus," Loretta muttered.

"If I'd gone out with him, I sure would have kissed him," Bob deadpanned.

"He seemed like a very nice man." Becky flitted around the room like a peach blossom on a breeze. "A little prickly, and what was that all about? His odd fixation with cell phones. But he was good-looking. His eyes were amazing. I've viewed the tapes, and they look very green on the monitor."

"That's why I would have kissed him," Bob murmured.

"Those amazing green eyes." Loretta forced a laugh, but his comment cut way too close for comfort.

"Harold was very impressed with what he saw. We're going to push up the broadcast date to next Monday. He wants us to get started with the kinder, gentler shows, and he thinks this'll be a terrific launch."

Good. Maybe I won't get laid off, Loretta thought.

"He wants to see the audience response to this before we attempt any more blind-date programs. But in the meantime, we need to decide whether to have a follow-up show with Loretta and Josh."

"And his amazing eyes," Bob said, shooting Loretta a conspiratorial look. She realized he was allying himself with her and mocking Becky. She appreciated his support, even though every time he mentioned Josh's amazing eyes she spun back in time to last night and Josh's amazing kiss.

"First off, Loretta," Becky said, positioning herself so the light would wash evenly over her smooth features, "I need to know how the date went."

could surround himself with air-conditioning and drink a beer. He had a suspicion he was going to wind up one-for-two.

"I don't have any beer," his mother said, fulfilling his expectations. "I've got some Diet Coke."

Cold and wet. It would do. He swung open the refrigerator and inspected its contents, most of which were sealed inside plastic containers in a variety of shapes and sizes. He spotted a can of soda—some no-name diet cola. "This isn't Diet Coke," he complained as he slid the drink off the shelf.

"It's the same thing," his mother told him.

He was too thirsty to argue with his mother. He popped the top, tipped the can against his lips and guzzled half its contents without even tasting the soda.

His mother watched, her mouth pursed. She was taller than average but gave the impression of being small. Something about the way she held herself, her shoulders hunched inward, her ash-blond hair close-cropped, her face usually pulled into a slight scowl, diminished her. He would blame her forbidding expression on residual grief from her husband's untimely death, but she'd been forbidding long before his father had died. She wore an attitude of chronic resentment, believing she'd been slighted by life, denied her full allotment of pleasure but making the best of it— reading the right books, listening to opera, raising her son to be obedient and respectful. Maybe, someday, the grand scales of destiny would recalibrate themselves and she would receive her due. God would make it up to her somehow.

As far as Josh could see, she hadn't been slighted, at least not financially. She lived in a lovely brick ranch house on a half acre, fully paid for. She'd never had to work outside the house—his father, an economics professor at the state university at Stony Brook, had earned a good living—and she'd never lacked for the finer things. Her kitchen had Corian counters and solid-oak cabinets. The diamond on a gold chain around her neck was a full carat. Careful investing, a solid pension and a whopping life insurance policy left her a comfortable widow. Yet she acted as though she feared waking up one morning to find herself destitute. She would never buy Diet Coke if Cheapo-Cola cost ten cents less. She would never hire a lawn service if Josh was available to cut her grass.

"Listen, Mom, I've got to tell you something," he said once he'd drained the can, a project that took less than ninety seconds.

"Oh my God." His mother collapsed onto one of the oak captain's chairs at the table. Josh leaned against the counter near the sink. The chairs had gingham seat cushions tied onto them, and he knew his mother would blow a gasket if he got sweat stains on the fabric. "What?" she asked. "It's something horrible, right?"

"No. I just wanted to warn you—"

"Oh my God. What? You're in trouble?"

"I'm going to be on television tomorrow."

"Why? What did you do?"

He was beginning to think the worst thing he'd ever done was to launch into this conversation.

"What I did," he said, his patience straining, "was a favor for a friend. She works for a TV show called the *Becky Blake Show*. It's a low-rent talk show. Anyway, she needed to pretend to meet a blind date on the show, and I agreed—as a favor to her—to pose as her blind date."

"What friend?" his mother asked.

"Just a friend. I have friends." He admitted privately that this was a slight exaggeration. He did have friends, of course, but most of them had been friends for years and his mother would be familiar with their names. Loretta was the first friend he'd made since Melanie's departure.

"And she works on that show? That schlock?"

"You know about the *Becky Blake Show*?"

"With people screaming at each other, throwing things, getting bleeped every other word? Of course I know about the *Becky Blake Show*. Everybody knows about the *Becky Blake Show*."

Josh hadn't known about it until he'd met Loretta.

"So you have a friend who works on this show? How did you ever meet her? You're not going on the air and getting bleeped, are you?"

"No. I didn't say a single bleepable thing when they taped the show." He wanted another soda, but the no-name brand had left a bitter aftertaste on his tongue. What he really wanted was a beer. And he wanted to be drinking it in his own apartment.

Better yet, he wanted to be drinking it with his friend Loretta.

She'd phoned him yesterday morning to tell him the show was going to be broadcast on Monday. He'd appreciated the heads-up, but more than that he'd appreciated her having phoned him at all. He hadn't been sure she would.

Not that he'd done such an unforgivable thing. One kiss. A small kiss. A kiss that could be overlooked if they stayed focused on the friendship angle. A man couldn't have too many friends, Josh always believed.

So he'd asked if he could see her, as a friend.

She'd said she would have to think about it.

Okay, maybe the kiss hadn't been that small. Maybe it couldn't be overlooked. He knew—and no doubt she knew, too—that if they saw each other he might want to do a whole hell of a lot more than kiss her.

What was that line from the *Three Dead Corpses* song about how being dead meant having no more sex? "I've lost my flesh, my fresh skin tones, and no one wants to jump my bones..." He wanted to see her not so he could jump her bones but so they could reminisce about that song, about the show. It was a significant part of their shared history.

"So should I call your aunt Rhea and uncle Maury and tell them you're going to be on this show?" his mother asked. "Should I call Grandma Dodie? It'll probably kill her, seeing you on a show like that."

Josh forced his attention back to his mother. Her eager tone implied that she wanted her mother-in-law dead. "The show was very civilized and pleasant. Nobody got bleeped or threw anything. I only pretend to be a single guy willing to go on a blind date with this friend of mine."

"You *are* single. Unless—oh my God, you didn't marry Melanie, did you? You didn't marry her behind my back?" She clutched her chest.

He was too exasperated to laugh. "When would I have married Melanie?"

"Some morning when I wasn't looking. How should I know? If you're not married to her, then you're single. This is very simple. Single—" she held out her right hand "—and married—" she held out her left. "Two separate things. You can't be both."

"I'm not married, but I am..." He searched for words that wouldn't cause her to clutch her chest again.

"You're what?"

"In a relationship."

"But you're not married. Until you're married, you're not married."

He hated to admit it, but she had a point.

The aftertaste faded from his mouth. His mother's face

couldn't have softened any in the past ten minutes, but his vision softened, making her appear almost maternal, the kind of mother who would defend her son and offer him guidance and make him realize that he had no reason to feel guilty. In other words, the exact opposite of the kind of mother she actually was.

He savored the moment, the sudden rush of gratitude he felt toward her. Any mother who could erase her son's guilt deserved unlimited love.

"You'll have to set up the VCR for me," she said, "so I can tape this show you're going to be on, with all the bleeping. That VCR." She clicked her tongue and shook her head. "I don't know why your father bought it. It's too complicated, and I don't know how to program it, and now I'm stuck with it. He spent a fortune on it, too." She pushed away from the table, still shaking her head, obviously tormented by the existence of the machine. "A fortune. He didn't even buy it on sale, and now I'm stuck with it. Thank God I've got you to program it for me. Without you, what would I do?"

Josh's gratitude faded as quickly as the soda's aftertaste. All right, he loved her. She was his mother. And sometimes she came through for him, however inadvertently.

But she still was a pain in the ass.

Eleven

Solly had invited Josh to meet him at the senior center early so they could watch the *Becky Blake Show* while they played chess. He could have stayed at his office and caught the show on the small TV he and his partners kept in the conference room for reviewing videotaped depositions and the like. But he believed that sitting in the conference room with Anita, Peter and their glum-faced secretary, Ruth, and watching himself pretend to be an unsuspecting, unattached man-about-town would be more awkward than sitting with Solly in the senior center lounge and distracting himself from the broadcast with a challenging game of chess.

A couple of silver-haired women occupied the sofa, working on elaborate needlepoint projects while the TV droned in front of them. "We're watching a special show," Solly announced as he led Josh into the room. The women reacted with a flurry of coos and clucks and fussing with their fabric and colored threads. Solly had already dragged the chess table across the room to be closer to the screen. He bounced around on his sneakers, moving chairs, appropriating the remote control and setting up the chessboard as if he were Josh's personal roadie. "This is so exciting," he said. "I can't believe it, our Josh on TV. It's so exciting!"

Josh didn't think it was so exciting. He felt a little queasy, actually.

He'd phoned Melanie yesterday evening, once he'd arrived home from his mother's house after programming her VCR to tape the show—and also fixing one of the glass sliders that led out from the den to the back patio; the door was sticking in the track, and he cleaned out the dirt and dead bugs and rubbed a little mineral oil on it to lubricate it—and replacing a dead bulb in the strip light above the mirror in her bathroom, and telling her that if the toilet in that bathroom kept running after it was flushed, she was going to have to bring in the plumber to repair it, because even Josh's handyman skills had limits. He'd listened to his mother fulminate over the plumber's hourly rate, but he'd refused to buckle. He was not going to fix her toilet. He did offer to pay the plumber's bill, and she'd insisted that wouldn't be necessary. "I can just jiggle it," she'd said. "I don't need the plumber. A little jiggling, and it stops running."

In any case, he hadn't been in the best mood to call Melanie and rehash the whole blind-date thing with her. But he'd had to alert her that the show was going to be broadcast tomorrow. He probably should have phoned her earlier in the week, or sent her an e-mail, but he'd been procrastinating.

She hadn't been home late Sunday afternoon. He'd left a message on her machine, mentioning the show and feeling as if he'd dodged a bullet.

The bullet must have been a smart bomb, because it had circled back and found him later that evening. "Josh? I got your message," she'd said, her voice fighting through a faint hiss on the line. Had she called him from a cell phone? She'd never used a cell phone in New York. "Am I going to be upset when I watch this show?"

"I don't see why you should be." Bullshit. Of course he'd seen why she should be upset: She was going to watch her boyfriend hook up with an attractive young woman on a nationally syndicated television show. "It was just a favor I was doing for Loretta," he'd reminded her.

"I understand that, Josh. I just wish I knew who this Loretta person was."

"If you watch the show tomorrow, you'll see her," Josh had said, and then had sworn under his breath. Why encourage her to watch the show? If she did watch it, she'd see Loretta, all right. She'd see that Loretta was a leggy, dark-eyed beauty with incredible hair.

On the other hand, suggesting that Melanie watch the show proved he had nothing to hide. If he'd urged her not to tune in, she would have had grounds for suspicion. But he was being open about the whole thing, totally aboveboard.

"It's just—hard," she'd said, a tiny whimper rippling through her voice. "You're so far away from me..."

No, you're so far away from me, he'd wanted to argue. *She* was the one who'd moved to Opa-Locka, after all. He was exactly where they'd both been until a few months ago.

"And you've got friends I've never even met—"

"So do you," he'd pointed out. She had friends who crowded into her apartment on weekday evenings and shouted to be heard above the salsa strains of Gloria Estefan. "We can't stop living just because I'm in New York and you're in Florida. It doesn't mean anything's changed between us, but..."

"Of course things have changed between us. I'm always hot. You're not hot."

"I'm very hot," he'd argued. Especially after mowing his mother's lawn that afternoon. Just remembering how hot he'd been had caused a fresh layer of sweat to glaze his skin. "We do have summer in New York. Surely you haven't been gone long enough to forget that."

"I know you have summer, but it's nothing like what we have here, Josh. You're in another world. You're living a life that has nothing to do with me. You have friends I've never met. I have no idea what you eat for dinner anymore."

That last comment had taken him aback. "I eat the same stuff I used to eat on the nights we weren't together when you lived here," he'd said, recalling that when she'd lived in New York, they'd been together nearly every night. She used to come to his apartment because it was bigger than hers, and prepare chicken a dozen different ways, only all the preparations had tasted the same. She'd experiment with her grandmother's recipes: latkes, kugel, chopped liver that he would still be digesting days later. She'd been a lousy cook, as he'd recalled. His microwave meals were a culinary step up.

Maybe she'd cooked for him because she'd been vying for a marriage proposal. And maybe she'd abandoned him for Florida because that marriage proposal hadn't been forthcoming. Maybe it was his fault she was so far away.

And maybe he was sliding back into the guilt trap again.

"Look, Melanie, the show was just a gag. It doesn't mean anything. Loretta needed to go through with it for the sake of her job, and I helped her out. I'm only mentioning the program to you in case you want to watch it. But it's stupid. It's a very stupid show."

"You didn't use to do stupid things when we were together."

"We still are together," he'd insisted, then sunk back into the pillows on his bed, pondering what he'd just said. Were they still together? Did he want to still be together with her?

Of course he did...but he couldn't stop thinking about Loretta, and her legs and her eyes and her hair, her throaty laugh, her concept of sin, her strength and humor even after having been jilted a mere four months before her wedding. And her soft, sweet lips.

"I'll be at work tomorrow," Melanie had broken into his thoughts. "I don't know if I'll be able to catch the show. I guess I should tape it, just in case."

Just in case what? "It ought to be good for a laugh," he'd said, hoping to communicate that she shouldn't take it seriously. "You can tell me if you think my nose looks big on TV."

"Why should your nose look big? It doesn't look big in real life."

"I'm just saying," he'd emphasized, "that it's a joke. It's nothing you need to take seriously. *I* don't take it seriously."

"Okay, well, maybe I'll watch it."

"Great." Once he'd said goodbye and hung up, he'd closed his eyes and concluded that "great" was the most dishonest word he could have come up with. What about this was great? His girlfriend distrusted him, Loretta didn't want him, he hadn't done anything and he felt guilty as hell.

Solly found the right channel and stepped back to assess the reception. Because the set was connected to cable the reception was fine, but he was of the generation that used to fine-tune every show and manipulate the dials with each channel change. Cable couldn't alter certain habits.

"*Nu,* what is this?" one of the needlepointing biddies on the sofa asked.

"A very special show," Solly announced, then indicated Josh with a flourish of his hand. "My friend Josh Kaplan is starring in it."

"What kind of show? With song and dance?"

"Just talk," Josh said modestly. "It's a talk show."

"Has it started yet?" a familiar voice bleated from the doorway. In hurried Phyllis, her gait as bouncy as Solly's, her sneakers as thickly treaded. She was wearing athletic shorts, and Josh was surprised by the muscle tone in her legs. He wondered if she'd been a gym teacher in her youth. She had that bulldog personality he always associated with girls' gym teachers. Also the short hair, the pugnacious chin and the assertive personality. "Josh! *Bubbela!* This is so exciting, you being on TV!"

He cringed. Maybe watching the show at the senior center hadn't been such a wise idea. Of course, Anita, Peter and Ruth would have given him a hard time if he'd watched it at the firm, but they wouldn't have called him *bubbela*.

"It's not on yet," Solly said, checking his watch. "Five minutes. We can get in a few moves, Josh. You want to be white?"

Josh settled at the table. Solly took his seat across from him and Phyllis planted herself on the arm of the sofa behind him. She gazed over his shoulder to study the board. "Such a complicated game," she murmured. "I like checkers. Every piece moves the same way. Are you boys hungry? I don't think they're serving lunch yet. It's early."

"I'm fine," Josh said, sliding his queen's pawn forward.

"It's too early for food," Solly added. "Besides, Dora Lee will probably have some goodies for us."

"Dora Lee," Phyllis muttered, as if the name were a curse. "All that noshy stuff she bakes, Solly, it's full of fat. It's no good for you. She's going to kill you."

"Then I'll die happy. Have you ever tasted her peanut butter cookies? Next time she bakes them, make sure you try one. They're magnificent."

"How can a cookie be magnificent? A cookie is a cookie."

''Shh,'' Solly silenced her, turning his chair toward the television. ''Look—it's starting!''

Josh rotated his chair for a better view. He wished he could shift it back a few inches, or a few feet, or perhaps into another room. He probably should have gone home to watch the damn show so he could have wallowed in his embarrassment alone, not surrounded by the beaming smiles of enthusiastic friends.

The screen filled with a montage of photos of Becky Blake, all pink and perky, against a flat blue background. The photos dissolved as the words *The Becky Blake Show* materialized on the screen, and then the words dissolved into a shot of the set. He remembered that arrangement of chairs, the table, the vase filled with fake roses, the thin, putty-colored carpet. The set appeared much larger and grander on television than it had in person.

Becky was reciting her introductory speech. He remembered hearing it through a speaker in the room where he'd been held until his entrance, a small, undecorated chamber with a counter, a couple of folding chairs, a ceiling speaker through which Becky's voice emerged and the lingering scent of stale coffee and marijuana. He remembered thinking, as he was summoned from the room and led down a glaringly lit hall with cinder-block walls and linoleum floors that would have seemed appropriate in a medium-security prison, that TV was a lot less glamorous than most people realized.

Now Loretta was on-screen. Solly let out a wolf whistle, and Phyllis punched him in the arm. ''What?'' he asked innocently, rubbing the spot she'd pummeled.

''You whistled at her.''

''I know. I was here. I heard myself whistle.'' Solly rolled his eyes at Josh. ''She's a good-looking lady. A man is allowed to notice. What's the big deal?''

"Is that your friend?" one of the biddies on the couch squawked at Solly. "That girl? She's your friend on the show?"

"*Meshuga,*" Phyllis whispered, just loud enough for Solly and Josh to hear. "She talks to herself, that one. I've heard her."

Josh ignored Phyllis and focused on the broadcast. He'd set up his own VCR to tape the show, in case he wanted to torture himself by watching it again, so there was no reason to concentrate so raptly now, as if he had to memorize it.

No, there *was* a reason, an irrational one: By watching this show, watching Loretta and him through the distance of time and the barrier of a glass screen, maybe he would be able to figure out what he wanted from her, and from Melanie. Maybe everything would start to make sense after a viewing of the broadcast.

"I saw this show once," the previously silent biddy suddenly piped up. "It had skinheads on it. Nazis." She made a spitting noise. "They should die in horrible ways, those people shouting that this is a Christian nation and anyone who doesn't like it should leave! *Ach!*" She made another spitting noise; fortunately, as best Josh could tell, nothing sprayed from her mouth when she did it. "Evil, those people."

"And the folks in the audience, shouting," her friend recollected. "I remember that. Very noisy."

"This is a different episode," Solly informed them.

Phyllis drew a circle in the air next to her ear to indicate that the women on the couch were crazy.

"It's boring," the first biddy said. "With all those Nazi skinheads shouting, it wasn't boring."

"They're very evil, those skinheads," her friend observed.

"Look!" Solly erupted. "There's Josh!"

Indeed, there was Josh on the small screen, entering the set. He seemed more relaxed than he'd felt at the time, which wasn't to say he seemed particularly relaxed. His chin was raised defensively, and his fingers were curled halfway into fists. He'd been tense that morning, braced for disaster, for Loretta to double-cross him, for Becky Blake to trip him up, for—why not?—skinheads to burst out of the audience and shout obscenities.

The show had gone smoothly and peacefully, though, and he could watch it without seizing up. He could watch Loretta smile and cross her legs, and smile even more when he launched into his speech about cell phones. He hadn't planned to do that, but after a few minutes of the stilted chitchat and the blinding lights, he'd succumbed to a mischievous impulse. Becky appeared as nonplussed today as she had the day they'd taped the show, but Loretta... He hadn't noticed how much she was smiling then. He noticed now.

He just wasn't sure they could be friends. In theory a platonic relationship ought to work. They enjoyed each other. They had no trouble conversing. Cell phones exasperated and amused them in the same ways. Surely this was a valid definition of friendship.

But could he be friends with a woman he'd kissed the way he'd kissed Loretta? He was a guy. Friendship shouldn't include kissing like that. It shouldn't even include thoughts about kissing like that.

"So, did you go out with this woman, Josh?" Phyllis asked, leaning around Solly as if afraid he wouldn't hear her otherwise. "You took her on a date? What was she like?"

"She's great," he said. That misleading word again, not exactly dishonest in this case, but weasely. Loretta had been

MIRA

YOUR PARTICIPATION IS REQUESTED!

Dear Reader,

Since you are a lover of fiction – we would like to get to know you!

Inside you will find a short Reader's Survey. Sharing your answers with us will help our editorial staff understand who you are and what activities you enjoy.

To thank you for your participation, we would like to send you 2 books and a gift – **ABSOLUTELY FREE**!

Enjoy your gifts with our appreciation,

Editors,
The Best of the Best™

P.S. And because you are important to us, you'll find something extra inside ...

**SEE INSIDE
FOR READER'S
SURVEY**

HOW TO VALIDATE
YOUR
EDITOR'S FREE
THANK YOU GIFTS!

1. Complete the survey on the right.

2. Send back the completed card and you'll get 2 "The Best of the Best™" books and a gift. These books have a combined cover price of $11.98 or more in the U.S. and $13.98 or more in Canada, but they are yours to keep absolutely FREE!

3. There's no catch. You're under no obligation to buy anything. We charge nothing—ZERO—for your first shipment. And you don't have to make any minimum number of purchases—not even one!

4. We call this line "The Best of the Best" because each month you'll receive the best books by some of today's most popular authors. These authors show up time and time again on all the major bestseller lists and their books sell out as soon as they hit the stores. You'll like the convenience of getting them delivered to your home at our special discount prices, and you'll love your *Heart to Heart* subscriber newsletter featuring author news, horoscopes, recipes, book reviews and much more!

5. We hope that after receiving your free books you'll want to remain a subscriber. But the choice is yours—to continue or cancel, anytime at all! So why not take us up on our invitation, with no risk of any kind. You'll be glad you did!

6. Don't forget to detach your FREE BOOKMARK. And remember... just for completing the Reader's Survey, we'll send you 2 books and a gift, *ABSOLUTELY FREE!*

YOURS FREE!
We'll send you a fabulous surprise gift absolutely FREE, simply for accepting our no-risk offer!

Visit us online at

www.mirabooks.com

® and TM are registered trademarks of Harlequin Enterprises Limited.

great, but she'd been better than great. Riskier than great. More threatening than great.

"So what about Melanie?"

"Melanie is Melanie," Josh told her. "As for Loretta and me... We're friends." Saying those words felt good, even though he knew, as soon as he uttered them, that he and Loretta could not be friends. Not given the way he'd kissed her.

Loretta joined Donna at the sink to offer her assistance with the dishes. Her thigh muscles were cramped because Andrew had insisted on sitting on her lap for the final ten minutes of dinner, and he was so adorable she couldn't say no to him.

Deuce was not quite so adorable. He'd spent most of the meal critiquing Loretta's TV appearance in a much louder voice than necessary. "Why did you wear pants? Girls are supposed to wear dresses on dates. My friend Anthony told me. He knows about stuff and he said girls are supposed to wear dresses on dates. I thought the guy was weird. I think cell phones are cool. When I grow up, I want my own cell phone..." On and on he went, making Loretta wish her show had been aired a month ago so Deuce would have been in school during the broadcast hour and thus would have been unable to see it. With summer vacation in full swing, though, he'd been home—and apparently glued to the TV set.

Lou said little during the meal. He rarely spoke. He was a smart man; he knew when to keep his mouth shut. He'd even kept his mouth shut when Andrew had asked if he could sit on Loretta's lap. Donna had told Loretta she didn't have to say yes, but Loretta was a sucker, especially when it came to four-year-old boys in cute little OshKosh overalls.

As soon as it was time to do the dishes, of course, Andrew didn't want to sit on Loretta's lap anymore. Nor did Deuce want to dissect the *Becky Blake Show*. The menfolk vanished at the first spurt of water into the sink, leaving Loretta and Donna to fend for themselves.

"The osso buco was great," Loretta remarked. "How do you find the time to cook stuff like this?"

"I made the osso buco Friday," Donna told her as she swabbed the dishes with a sudsy sponge. "We had a little then, but it didn't taste as good as it did today. It needed to sit a couple of days. That's the thing about osso buco—it's got to sit. Three days is about right."

"So you made it Friday." Loretta took the first clean plate from Donna and dried it. "My mother would freak out at the thought of serving veal for dinner on a Friday."

"Why, because it's meat?" Donna snorted. "Hello? The pope did away with meatless Fridays before you and I were born."

"But not before my mother was born. She never accepted the change."

"Really? You never ate meat on Fridays?"

"Not when I was growing up. We ate fish sticks with lots of ketchup on them. They were gross. You want to do penance? Go meatless. You want to *really* do penance? Eat my mother's fish sticks."

Donna handed her another damp plate, then stared at her and frowned. "What's that smile?"

Loretta hadn't realized she was smiling. "Just remembering my mother's fish sticks," she said.

"No. It was a different smile," Donna said, returning her gaze to the mounds of soap bubbles in the sink. "Definitely not a remembering-mom's-fish-sticks smile."

Loretta's brain seemed as foamy as the sink's contents. Somewhere beneath the bubbles lurked something substantial—a bowl, a fork, an actual thought. "Oh, I know," she said, then felt the smile spreading her lips. "I was thinking about how Josh told me eating a bacon cheeseburger was like a double sin."

"Why?"

"He's Jewish. So it's doubly unkosher—meat and cheese, and then bacon. It's like an expressway to hell."

Donna laughed. "He's Jewish, huh. What did your parents think of that?"

"I don't know if they figured it out. Josh Kaplan—it's not exactly an Italian name, you know? Not that it matters." She methodically dried a serving spoon, blinking as it reflected the overhead light into her eyes. "I didn't talk to my parents after the show was aired. We were too busy at work, and I came straight here afterward."

"So you think there's going to be a message from them waiting for you when you get home?"

"At least one message. Probably several." Nicky might have called again—or Kathy might have called to extol the virtues of Marty the dentist. Al might have called, if he could fit a call into the twins' schedule. And her mother... no question. Her mother would want to discuss her outfit with her: "That jacket, where did you get it? You know, you should do your shopping out here on the island—the sales tax in the city is so high." She'd want to discuss Loretta's hair—Donna had wanted to discuss that, too, but Loretta had silenced her—and then, most important, she'd want to discuss Josh. "Nicky told me he talked to you after the date, but he didn't ask you the essential questions. So I've got to ask, Loretta. Was this person a gentleman? Did he treat you with courtesy? Did he show respect? Did he see you home?"

Oh, yes, he'd seen her home. She cut off her roving mind before it could amble too far in that direction.

She wasn't going to think about kissing him. She was going to think only about how much she'd enjoyed talking to him. She and Gary had never talked about bacon cheeseburgers. She couldn't actually remember what they *had* talked about. Wedding plans, for one thing. Whether her brothers should be Gary's ushers. Whether they should go for a buffet dinner or a sit-down meal—prime rib, Gary wanted, although Loretta argued for the buffet so vegetarians and people who wanted traditional Italian fare could find something to eat. They'd talked about the damn dinner a lot, as she recalled. And the flowers. She'd wanted lots of flowers, and he was appalled at the thought of spending so much money on something that would be dead in two days.

"You know," Donna remarked, "Josh Kaplan was cute. I saw him live, and then I saw him again on TV today. So what if he can't eat bacon cheeseburgers? No one says you have to marry him. You ought to try out that teddy with him. He's cute and you're single, am I right?"

He's not single, Loretta almost blurted out.

"I mean, I'm married—I love Lou with my heart and soul, you know that—but if I had a friend who looked like Josh Kaplan, I'd wear a teddy."

Deuce chose that moment to barrel through the kitchen. He probably didn't know what a teddy was, though, other than a stuffed bear. "We need cookies!" he shouted as if racing from a fire and announcing that he needed a ladder and hose.

"You don't *need* cookies," Donna corrected him. "You *want* cookies."

"That's what I said. We want cookies!"

"There's a package of chocolate chip cookies in the cabinet. Loretta will open the package for you. My hands are all wet."

Deuce located the bag and handed it to Loretta. "What do you want the cookies for?" she asked.

"We're watching this cool show," Deuce reported. "*BattleBots*. These remote-control robots are beating each other up. There's collisions and explosions and everything. It's so cool. It's makin' us hungry. This show… It's more interesting than the show you were on."

Loretta didn't take his criticism personally. Until recently, the *Becky Blake Show* had featured collisions and explosions, too. Deuce probably would have loved the vulgar screamfests that used to be a staple on the show. He probably wouldn't have understood what the screamfests were about—infidelity, polygamy, kinky sex, suburban sluts—but he would have adored the level of violence.

She eased apart the seal of the cookie bag without tearing it, then handed it to Deuce, who grabbed the package and charged across the room. At the doorway he caught himself and spun around. "Thanks!" he yelled in the general direction of the sink before he vanished.

"What an obnoxious child," Donna muttered. "If I were his mother, I'd tell him to shape up fast."

"He's a terrific kid."

"He thought you should have worn a dress."

"And you thought I should have worn the teddy." *I did,* Loretta thought. *I wore it on the date. Maybe if I hadn't, that kiss wouldn't have happened.*

"So, are you going to see him again?" Donna asked. "Josh, I mean. Not Deuce."

"I don't know." She dried another serving spoon. In its shiny bowl, she saw a distorted reflection of herself. "We might have to go back on the show another time to describe our date."

"Oh, God. You can't talk about that play on TV, what was it? *Two Dead Bodies*? The way you described it to me—if you talked about it that way on TV, you might get sued for slander or something.''

"It's *Three Dead Corpses*...and Josh is a lawyer. He wouldn't let me say anything libelous.''

"So, besides the show, are you going to see him again?''

No. She couldn't see him again. Maybe she wanted to—the way Deuce wanted cookies. It wasn't necessary, it wouldn't make the robots collide and explode any more effectively, but Loretta would like to keep her friendship with Josh going. She'd like to introduce him to other Italian treats—had he ever had zabaglione? Or tiramisu—the good stuff, not the fluffy, booze-free pastry every third restaurant was offering these days, but dense, one-hundred-proof tiramisu. The hell with the Charter Beef House; she wanted to take him down to Little Italy and let him discover what real food was all about. If he was going to sin, it shouldn't be with a bacon cheeseburger.

There was sin and there was *sin*. Food was one thing, but seeing a man—even if he was only a friend—and wishing he would kiss you the way he'd kissed you once before, knowing full well he had a girlfriend...

In Loretta's book, that was a sin.

"No," she answered Donna. "It was just a put-on for the show, you know? Just so maybe they won't fire me. There's no reason for me and Josh to see each other again.''

No reason at all.

Twelve

"**M**om, I'm at work," Loretta grumbled into the phone.

The rest of the production team were gathered around the table in their windowless cell, bickering about whether to pitch Becky a show on fashion faux pas. Gilda thought the topic was kind and gentle; Bob thought it was dumb-assed beyond belief. His use of the term *ass* had inspired Kate to propose a variation: bringing a fashion designer and several normal women—women who wore size twelve—onto the show and having the women interrogate the designer on why designers always created clothes that looked good only on anorexics with silicone-enhanced breasts and no asses whatsoever.

Loretta had liked Kate's concept. But while she'd brainstormed with Kate on the possibilities of a face-off between the fashion industry and real women, the phone had rung. Loretta had been closest to it, so she'd leaned back on the rear legs of her chair, tilting the seat until she could snag the receiver.

Hearing her mother's voice, she'd suffered a twinge of dread and leaped to her feet. Her mother never phoned her at work. "Oh my God. What happened?"

"Nothing happened. Everything's fine. You think I only call you when something is wrong?"

Releasing her breath, Loretta reminded her mother of where she was.

"I know you're at work," her mother said. "You think I don't know what number I dialed?"

"What I meant was, I'm *working*," Loretta emphasized, stretching the phone cord as far as she could to put distance between herself and the table. "This isn't a good time to talk."

"Last night would have been a good time to talk," her mother noted. "Last night I called you and left a message on your machine. You never called back."

"I was at Donna's," Loretta explained. Just as she'd predicted, a message from her mother had been awaiting her when she'd arrived back at her apartment, her stomach lazily digesting osso buco and her mind shaping certain vows about the extremely limited conditions under which she would ever again wear the wine-red teddy. "I got home late and I was exhausted." It hadn't been *that* late, and she hadn't been so exhausted she couldn't have returned a phone call. But a phone conversation with her mother would have exhausted her even more than she'd already felt. Especially a phone conversation on the subject of Josh Kaplan and the blind date.

Apparently, that particular phone conversation was going to take place now, while she was staring at the Colosseum poster and trying not to be distracted by the quarrel behind her—"The *fashionistas* have made life unbearable for every realistically proportioned woman in America, and that would include Becky's prime demographic," Kate was lecturing in a clarion voice.

Gilda whispered something in response, but Loretta couldn't make out the words above her mother's: "He was a nice-looking young man. What kind of name is that, Kaplan?"

"Jewish," Loretta said.

"Oh." A long pause as her mother regrouped. "Well, that's okay. He could always convert."

"Mom—"

"I'm just saying, if there's going to be a wedding, it should be in the church."

"I'm not going to marry him, Mom."

"He's nice-looking. And a lawyer, that's not so bad. A dentist would be better, but lawyers make good money."

"How much money he makes is irrelevant. I'm not going to marry him."

"Why not? Other than the religion problem—which you could work out, we could talk to Father Joseph about it, he'd know what to do. They even have these weddings. My friend Sonia went to a wedding for her niece who married a Jewish man and they had both a priest and one of his people, a rabbi. They did the service together. Sonia said it took a little longer, all those extra prayers, but she said it was a very nice service. And the reception afterward was stunning, she said. Flowers everywhere, the air so thick with the smell of blossoms, and the table settings—"

"Mom. I'm at work."

"Right, right. I'm sorry, you're busy. But how often is my daughter on TV? You looked very nice on the show, Loretta, but I think maybe you should have worn a dress."

"You and Deuce," Loretta muttered.

Her mother didn't hear her. "Pants on a woman can come across as masculine sometimes. You're meeting a man for the first time, you don't want to come across as masculine."

"Are you saying I seemed masculine on TV?" Loretta asked. All conversation at the table ceased. She gritted her teeth, aware that the others found her half of this conversation more interesting than the fashion industry's efforts to undermine the confidence of the average-size woman.

"No, you looked lovely," her mother assured her. "I'm just saying. So, when are you going to see this nice lawyer again?"

"I don't think we're going to see each other again," Loretta said. "It's not going to work out."

"Loretta! Give it a chance. You're twenty-nine years old. You can't just toss this fellow aside because he happens to be Jewish."

"His religion has nothing to do with it, Mom." *His girl-friend, on the other hand, has plenty to do with it.* "We had a pleasant evening, but there was no chemistry." *Except for that one kiss, which I'm not going to think about.*

"Big deal, chemistry. I'm not saying you should open a laboratory with him, Loretta. Just go out with him a couple of times. He dresses nice—he's not a *sporcaccione,* am I right? So you'd get to know him a little bit. It wouldn't kill you."

"Maybe he doesn't want to go out with me." *And if he does, he's a son of a bitch and I don't want to go out with him.*

"Why not? A beautiful girl like you? But you have a way of putting people off, you know that? Putting men off. You send out these waves, Loretta—are waves chemistry?"

"Physics, I think."

"That's what I like, a smart girl. You know your science. But you send out these waves of 'Don't come too close. I'm not interested,' and it puts men off. This is why you're twenty-nine and all alone."

"Maybe I'm twenty-nine and alone because I choose to be," she snapped. A glance over her shoulder revealed that her colleagues were leaning forward, eavesdropping. "Mom, I've got to go. I've got work to do. I don't expect to hear from him again, so there's really no point in discussing it."

"If you're not going to hear from him again, you ought to let Nicky set you up with his friend Marty. A nice Italian boy, a dentist, and you wouldn't have to deal with the whole rabbi thing at the wedding."

"I've got to go, Mom," she repeated. "Talk to you later. I love you. Goodbye." She hung up before her mother could say anything more.

"See?" Gilda said after a moment of silence. "She's twenty-nine and alone because she chooses to be. That's how I thought it was supposed to work. Lots of women are twenty-nine and alone because they choose to be. There's a potential show there."

"Please, no." Loretta held up her hands as if she could fend off Gilda's suggestion with her palms. "I've already been a guinea pig for a show. I'm not doing it again unless Becky offers me a contract renewal chiseled in granite."

"With a raise," Bob suggested.

"Right. A huge raise."

"I've been married twice. I deserve two raises," Kate declared. "Let's get back to the business at hand—women's apparel designed for toothpicks with tits."

"We could bring on a designer of plus-size fashions and a designer of toothpick fashions," Loretta said, eager to immerse herself in work and eradicate all remnants of her conversation with her mother. "They could discuss their different theories of women and size, and then we could take questions from the audience."

"Why would anyone want to spend an hour talking about women's apparel?" Bob asked.

"Go get coffee, Bob," Gilda ordered him.

He was rolling his eyes and shoving away from the table when the phone rang again. "If it's for me, I'm not here," Loretta said, diving into her chair at the table and pressing her hands to her ears.

Since Bob was already halfway to his feet, answering the phone became his task by default. "Hello?" He listened for a minute, his gaze zeroing in on Loretta. "She said to tell you she's not here."

"Oh, God," Loretta groaned. If it was anyone from her family, *anyone,* even her sweet little niece Alyssa, who spent most of her time on the telephone nodding or shaking her head so the person on the other end had no idea if she was there, Loretta was going to kill Bob.

"Sure, I'll get her," he said generously, then extended the receiver toward Loretta. "It's for you."

"I hate you." She pushed herself out of her chair and trudged around the table. "I hope a pigeon dumps a load on your head the minute you leave the building today."

"You're so cute when you're angry," he teased, handing her the receiver. "I'll go get coffee."

"Spill it on yourself, why don't you," she snarled, then lifted the receiver to her ear, took a deep breath to brace herself and said in a falsely cheery voice, "Hello?"

"Loretta? It's Josh Kaplan. Did you really not want to talk to me?"

"No, I—" She took another deep breath, not to brace herself this time but to compose herself. Josh. Josh, who had kissed her. Josh, who her mother believed should convert to Catholicism, although they could work around that if necessary. "I've gotten other calls here this morning that I didn't want to get," she explained to him. "I just… If the call was from someone else, I wouldn't want to talk to them. But you, I mean… You're not someone I don't want to talk to." That didn't sound right. In fact, nothing she'd just said sounded right. Nerves were making her babble, and she resented that he could make her nervous. "So," she said briskly. "So. How are you?"

"I was wondering if you might be free for lunch today?"

He was asking her out for lunch. Like a date. "What about your—" She cut herself off before saying "girlfriend." If Gilda and Kate hadn't been in the room, openly eavesdropping, she would have completed the question. "What's going on?" she finally asked.

"I want to talk to you. That's all."

"None of that other stuff?"

"You mean, like my kissing you?" Simply hearing him say it caused her toes to curl against the straps of her sandals. "No. I just need to talk."

"About what?"

"I have a situation."

"A situation?"

"Can we meet for lunch?"

Loretta twirled her finger through the coils of the phone cord. That he wasn't asking her out on a date should have appeased her, but it disappointed her, as well. And it shouldn't. She shouldn't want to go out on a date with him.

But her alternative would be to sit in one of the pocket parks and watch Kate eat something green—or not green, depending on her current weight-loss diet. And she had to admit she was a bit curious about what Josh's "situation" might entail.

"All right," she said. "Why don't you meet me downstairs in the lobby at noon."

"You don't want me to come up to your office?"

"No," she said emphatically. If he came up, Gilda and Kate would fuss over him. So would Becky, if she found out he was in the vicinity. Bob might blow the fiction they'd concocted about how Josh had helped him with a legal dilemma. It wasn't worth the risk. "I'll meet you downstairs."

"All right. Noon."

"Fine."

''I appreciate this, Loretta,'' he said before hanging up. His words whetted her curiosity further. What did he appreciate? Why? Did his ''situation'' have something to do with her?

Those questions continued to circulate through her gray matter as she resumed her place in the discussion on hefty women and skimpy fashion. She nodded when Bob suggested that women dress to impress other women more than they dress to impress men, and told Kate she was a paranoid idiot when Kate insisted that most fashion designers were involved in some sort of plot to make women hate themselves, and gave an impassioned defense of the late great Versace, even though she'd never be able to afford anything with that label inside it, and all in all did a pretty good job of convincing her colleagues that her mind was a hundred percent on her job and not at least seventy percent on her impending lunch with Josh.

At a few minutes to twelve, she bolted from the staff room. She stopped in the ladies' room long enough to finger-comb her hair and make sure her bra straps hadn't slid out from beneath the slightly wider straps of her tank top. She dabbed a layer of lipstick onto her lips, then scolded herself for caring how she looked. This wasn't a date. He had a girlfriend. If she kept repeating these truths often enough, she might accept them.

Josh loitered near the newsstand by the main door; she spotted him among the throngs of workers teeming in the lobby almost as soon as she stepped off the elevator. He looked hot—not hot like the kind of guy who could make a woman's toes curl merely by mentioning a kiss they'd shared, but hot like the kind of guy who'd been trudging through a muggy summer day in the big city. His hair was limp, his tie loose, his jacket draped over one shoulder and his shirtsleeves rolled up to his elbows.

Actually, he looked the other kind of hot, too. Which was really a shame, because Loretta was never going to curl her toes over him again.

He noticed her just seconds after she noticed him, and his face brightened. That was bad. She didn't want him to be happy to see her.

But he obviously was. Wending his way through the crowd, he shoved his hair back from his face. "Where can we go?" he asked once they were close enough to hear each other over the echoing din of conversation in the vaulted lobby.

"There's an okay place around the corner," she suggested, leading him toward the door. The restaurant she had in mind was in fact a bit nicer than okay. Not that she was turning this into a date, but if they were going to discuss his situation, they might as well do so in pleasant surroundings, eating food a step above.

He willingly followed her out into the steamy air, down the sidewalk to the corner and into the shade of the side street. Droplets of water flicked onto her head from the air conditioners above her, and the pavement baked the soles of her feet through her sandals. How did men survive in suits during the summer? How did women survive in stockings? Her first job after college had required "office attire"—dresses, sleeves, panty hose—and she'd been miserable. Today, clad in a knee-length skirt and no stockings, she could just about bear the heat.

Cool air blasted them as they entered the restaurant. The place was already pretty full, but the hostess found them a table in a dim corner near the kitchen. They sat and Josh gazed around, taking in the tasteful green wallpaper, the black lacquered tables, the genuine cloth napkins. "This looks more promising than the Charter Beef House," he said.

"It smells more promising, too."

"Yeah. Remember that greasy aroma?" He grinned and skimmed the menu.

She felt her resistance eroding a little. The truth was, they did have a date in their shared history. She saw no point pretending that date—the mediocre dinner, the ghastly musical, the espresso and cannolis, the kiss—had never happened. If she could learn to laugh about it, his kiss would lose its power over her, and she could probably be friends with him.

They ordered—a turkey sandwich for him, a tuna wrap for her and iced tea for both. The waitress vanished, leaving them at their dark little table. Josh studied her for a long moment, then said, "This is going to sound strange, Loretta, but…as I said, I've got this situation, and I needed to talk to someone about it. And the person I thought of, the person I wanted to talk to, was you."

"Okay." She tried not to feel flattered.

"It's about my friend Solly," he said. "I mentioned him to you the other day, remember?"

"He wanted you to walk me home," she recalled. Perhaps she ought to blame this Solly character for Josh's having kissed her.

"Solly is in his seventies, a great guy, smart and in excellent physical shape."

"Uh-huh." Josh had a friend in his seventies? Why was he telling her this?

"Solly's got a few girlfriends," Josh continued.

Fortunately, the waitress arrived with their drinks, sparing Loretta the need to respond. A seventy-something friend of Josh's with a few girlfriends. At least Josh had only one girlfriend. Or so he'd told Loretta. Maybe he and Solly were good friends because they both believed in having more than one girlfriend at a time. Maybe they went cruising together and covered for each other.

"Solly phoned me last night and asked for my legal expertise," he said.

She struggled to figure out why *she* was the someone he wanted to talk to about his old friend's legal difficulties. "Is he having a problem with his landlord?"

"No. It seems one of his girlfriends attacked another one. Physically."

Whoa. They'd veered into strange territory here. "How old are his girlfriends?"

"Around his age, I'd guess. I don't know exactly, but we're not talking about bimbos and trophies. The two girlfriends I know—the ones involved in this mess—are both members of Solly's senior center."

Two old women beating up on each other over an old man. This went way beyond strange. Loretta ought to be horrified, but she'd been working for the *Becky Blake Show* too long. This was right up her alley.

She leaned forward, intrigued. "Was anyone hurt?"

"As a matter of fact, yes. Dora Lee was pushed—or else she fell—into the path of a moving car. Fortunately, it was traveling very slowly. She suffered a broken leg and a chipped tooth. She's in the hospital, but it could have been worse."

"Jeez." Loretta tried to look stricken. But honest to God, two elderly ladies beating each other up? One of them landing in the hospital? Damn, this would make a great show. Septuagenarian warrior women entering into battle over a septuagenarian stud! If only Harold wasn't stuck on his kinder, gentler concept.

"Phyllis—the girlfriend who allegedly pushed Dora Lee—was arrested and charged with assault," Josh continued. "I spent last night at the precinct house helping Solly to arrange her bail. She claims she's innocent. She says Dora Lee tripped on the curb and fell. According to her, it was an accident.'' He shook his head, obviously dismayed. The waitress appeared with their sandwiches, and he acknowledged her with a nod. Once she was gone, he murmured, ''The whole thing is just so…so…''

''Strange,'' Loretta supplied, pleased by how concerned she sounded.

''Yeah. Strange.'' He lifted the top slice of whole wheat bread from his sandwich to inspect the filling, evidently liked what he saw and lowered the bread into place before picking up the sandwich to take a bite. Loretta tasted her wrap. It was cold and moist, as refreshing as her iced tea. ''It's just so…strange. I saw them all yesterday morning. Solly, Phyllis and Dora Lee. I watched our blind-date show with Solly at the senior center, and Phyllis was with us for the entire broadcast. Dora Lee showed up about twenty minutes into it. She had cookies.''

''Cookies.''

''She's a phenomenal cook. She bakes cookies for Solly all the time.''

''So Phyllis felt threatened by Dora Lee's domestic talents and decided to do her in.''

''I don't know if Phyllis pushed her,'' Josh argued. ''Dora Lee might have tripped and fallen. It could happen. She isn't exactly agile.'' He sipped his tea. ''On the other hand, Phyllis can be kind of bitchy, so I wouldn't put violence past her.''

''Which one is Solly's favorite?''

''He likes them both. He's got at least one other girlfriend I know of, but she doesn't go to the senior center. She's a former ballet dancer. I wouldn't believe a story about her tripping on the curb. But Dora Lee is kind of— I don't know, lumbering.''

"Why were *you* at the senior center?" she asked. "Isn't that an odd place for you to watch the show?"

"I meet Solly every Monday to play chess," Josh explained. "It's a long-standing tradition. Yesterday was a Monday, so we decided to play and watch the show at the same time. Phyllis was there, kibitzing and gossiping, and then Dora Lee lumbered in with her cookies. They were wonderful. They tasted like *hamantaschen*."

"Like what?"

"The Jewish answer to cannolis."

A giggle bubbled up from her throat. She tried to swallow it down. A woman was laid up with a broken leg in the hospital, possibly put there by her rival. Loretta should be ashamed for finding anything amusing in this.

But she was amused. Okay, so she was a terrible person, unforgivable, shameful, but the thought of two women—two old ladies with coarse features and odd hairs sprouting from their faces like Nona and Cousin Carlotta, and shrieky, raspy voices, and cardigans with pills all over them, and orthopedic shoes—engaging in a geriatric wrestling match over a seventy-year-old guy—how could she not be a little amused? "Josh, why are you sharing this with me?" she asked.

"I needed someone to talk to," he said bluntly.

"Why me? I mean, okay, you didn't want to discuss the situation with your friend Solly—he's already living it. But you've got other friends." *You've got a girlfriend,* she thought. *Why not tell her about it?*

"You're easy to talk to," he said. "I feel good talking to you. I trust you. I couldn't just talk to anyone about this. It's so…"

"Strange," she repeated.

He nodded. "These are people I care about. Solly and I

have known each almost a year. I know Phyllis and Dora Lee, too. The whole thing is tragic.''

"No, it's not," she assured him. "No one's dead. You need someone dead for it to be tragic."

"All right, then. What is it?"

Strange, she thought. "You want the truth? It's the kind of thing that keeps the *Becky Blake Show* in ratings heaven."

"Why? It's such a sad situation."

"People in love fighting over each other? Two girl-friends coming to blows over the same boyfriend? I'm salivating here, Josh. It's stories like this that made Becky Blake a household name."

"Old people aren't supposed to act that way," Josh argued. "You can't imagine how weird it was to have to bail out Phyllis on an assault charge. I mean, Christ. Solly mumbling in Yiddish, and the cops eyeing him up and down, trying to figure out what sort of magic he's got that he can satisfy two women at his age."

"What sort of magic has he got?" Loretta asked.

"A good heart? A sharp mind? How should I know? I'm not a woman."

"I'd like to meet this guy," Loretta said, grinning mischievously. "He's obviously got *something.*"

"If you were seventy, you'd appreciate what he's got. I suspect healthy, sane, unattached gentlemen are hard to come by in that age bracket."

"Like they're so easy to come by in my age bracket," she muttered.

He grinned sheepishly. "You're right. Healthy, sane gentlemen are a rarity across the board."

Especially unattached ones, Loretta thought, then decided to bring it out into the open. "What about your girl-friend?"

He seemed surprised. "What about her?"

"Why didn't you talk to her about this instead of me?"

He considered his answer before speaking. "She would have viewed them as clients, not people. She's a social worker specializing in geriatrics. She works with folks like Solly and Phyllis and Dora Lee. She sets up programs for them, makes sure they're taking care of themselves and then forgets them the minute she leaves work for the day. They're a job to her. And don't get me wrong—she's an excellent social worker. She used to work at the West Side Senior Center, which is how I met Solly and Dora Lee and Phyllis. They loved her there. She created wonderful programs for them. But she'd approach a case like this clinically. She'd do what had to be done, file her reports and put it out of her mind."

"She sounds a little cold," Loretta remarked.

Josh shrugged. "Maybe she has to be cold in order to do her job. She can't get too involved with her clients. She has to maintain objectivity."

"As a lawyer helping Solly, don't you have to maintain objectivity, too?"

"I'm not his lawyer. He doesn't even need a lawyer to handle this. He needs a friend, and I'm that. As for Phyllis, I gave him the names of some professional acquaintances to pass along to her. She needs someone who specializes in criminal law." His sandwich gone, he settled back in his chair and stirred what was left of his iced tea with his straw. "I appreciate your listening, Loretta. This has been eating at me all morning, and…I needed to talk."

"I'm a great listener." Actually, she wasn't, but if Josh thought she was, she didn't mind. "You're a softie, you know? I thought lawyers all had hearts of stone."

"We do. It's just that when it comes to my friends, if

they're going through hell...I guess that stone surface has a few fissures running through it.''

She wondered if he considered her enough of a friend that his stone heart would crack a little if she were going through hell.

"So, what do you think? A lot of *meshugas*?''

"You really want to know what I think?'' she said. "I think we should do a show about Solly.''

His smile faded. "A show?''

"A *Becky Blake Show*.''

"Don't be silly.''

"I'm serious. It would be fantastic.'' Better than a show on skinny women's fashions. Much better than a show about a fake blind date.

He scowled. "I don't want these people getting any more hurt than they already are. Phyllis and Dora Lee are nice women. Solly likes them both.'' His frown intensified as he mulled over the idea.

"Who says the show would hurt them?''

"You'd be exploiting them.''

"Did I exploit you? Of course not,'' she answered herself, refusing him the opportunity to say yes. "We could approach the story gently. And kindly. With lots of consideration for everyone's tender feelings. That's the way we're doing the program these days. No more chaotic stuff, no more screaming and shouting.'' A little screaming and shouting wouldn't hurt, she thought, but even without it, Solly's love triangle could make for a fabulous show. "We could approach this story as an exploration of late-in-life passion.''

Josh scowled. "It sounds exploitative.''

"I'm not talking about sexual passion,'' she clarified. "Although we could deal with that, too. I'm talking about the sort of passion that would make a woman shove her rival in front of a moving car. These sorts of things happen all the time, but not among seventy-year-olds."

"Women shove their rivals in front of moving cars all the time?"

"You know what I mean. Lovers compete. They get jealous. Sometimes violence erupts. Add the element of this happening among senior citizens, and we're talking about a ratings knockout." They were talking about Loretta keeping her job, too. Maybe getting a promotion.

"I don't know why I wanted to share this with you," he grumbled. But he wasn't tossing down his napkin and storming away.

"Because I'm so easy to talk to," she reminded him. "Look, Josh—" she impulsively reached across the table and took his hand, just to make sure he wouldn't bolt "—I wouldn't do anything your friends felt uncomfortable about. But they might *want* to come on the show. Lots of people want to come on the show. And this show wouldn't be vulgar or nasty. Nothing about the show was vulgar or nasty when you and I were on, right?"

"Well…" He appeared to be groping for words. But he didn't pull his hand away. "They're fragile. One of them is in the hospital and another is facing criminal charges. And Solly is an emotional wreck."

Okay, so Solly was an emotional wreck. Emotional wrecks were the *Becky Blake Show*'s middle name. This trio would be perfect for the show. Becky could approach the story earnestly, let the people talk, let them reveal to the viewing public that even older people could suffer the vicissitudes of love. Ratings. Promotion. It was perfect.

If only she could convince Josh. "The show would be tasteful," she promised. "It would make people view their grandparents in a whole new way. We tend to think of old people as—as folks you shut inside a seniors' home and forget about, right? By putting Solly and his girlfriends on the show, we could open people's eyes to the complexities of late-in-life romance.''

Josh's eyes softened slightly, as if they, too, had fissures running through them. His fingers stirred against her palm, a light, hesitant stroke. He didn't say anything.

She dug deeper into her arsenal. "You mentioned that Dora Lee chipped a tooth?"

The question appeared to startle him. "Yes. She hit her mouth, and a front tooth—"

"I happen to know some dentists who would do a magnificent job capping that tooth for her."

He arched an eyebrow. Could he tell she was bribing him? Was her bribe going to work? "You wouldn't by any chance be related to these dentists, would you?"

"My father and two brothers could give her a smile like a movie star's."

"Loretta, I don't know if she's got insurance, if there's going to be a criminal trial—"

"And in the meantime poor Dora Lee is going to walk around looking like a hillbilly every time she smiles."

"She can't walk around. She's got a broken leg."

"She needs top-notch dental treatment," Loretta argued. "I can get it for her. Maybe even for free." She'd twist Nicky's arm. Or Al's. She'd promise him and Cindy some free baby-sitting. Or she'd tell him fixing this poor old woman's tooth would be an altruistic act. Al loved to think of himself as saintly.

"Would this be a *quid pro quo* thing? Free dental work only if she agrees to appear on your show?"

"Of course not!" she said, forcing indignation into her tone. "I'm just trying to be helpful. The show would be a totally separate issue. But if we did it," she pressed on, "you have my word that it would be sensitive and respectful of all the people involved. It would address issues. It would be educational.''

"The *Becky Blake Show,* educational.'' He snorted.

"Of course we're educational. Thanks to us, more people know about transsexuals and fetishists than ever before.''

Josh laughed reluctantly. "Why did I think it would be easy to talk to you?''

"Because it is,'' she told him. "Because I'm your friend.''

He was still clearly entertaining doubts, although his smile held on. "A man is heartbroken, a woman is in the hospital and another woman may wind up in jail.''

"Or else they'll work it out and make peace on the *Becky Blake Show.* Trust me, Josh. This my area of expertise.''

"Tawdry human scandal.''

"People who put their hearts on the line,'' she corrected him. "Can I talk to my colleagues about the idea? Can I see if there's some way we could turn this into a beautiful, healing show?''

He sighed again, deep and long. "I never quite figured out how you talked me into the blind date, either.''

That was as good as a yes. Suppressing a triumphant smile, she gave his hand a reassuring squeeze. "I can make this work for Solly and his ladies, okay? I can make it come out beautifully.''

"I want to believe you,'' Josh said. "I don't know why, but I do.''

"And I wasn't kidding about the dental work. Seriously. If Dora Lee doesn't have insurance, I'll get my father or one of my brothers to do it as a professional courtesy.''

"They do good work?'' he asked.

"What do you think?'' She grinned broadly, revealing her well-tended, sparkling-white teeth.

His smile was both resigned and appreciative. "Okay, they do good work."

She relaxed. Life was looking better. Delivering a show like this to Becky would definitely help to save her job. Getting Dora Lee's tooth repaired would be a good deed. Working with Josh...well, that could be positive or negative. She decided to assume it would be positive.

His girlfriend was out in the open; they'd talked about her. No one was going to pretend she didn't exist. So what if he had a girlfriend? One of those fissures in his heart of stone had Loretta's name on it.

Thirteen

"**Y**ou're looking piqued," Anita declared.

Josh scrubbed a hand through his hair and forced a weary smile. Anita had a way of surprising him, sometimes speaking with an earthy vulgarity and other times using effete terms like *piqued,* as if she'd escaped from a Victorian novel and gone undercover as a *zaftig* Hispanic New Yorker. She liked keeping people off balance. She always wore frilly blouses when she was facing a particularly gruesome courtroom battle, and dressed in severe conservative suits when she was heading off to meet a new client. Josh would have thought the reverse would be more effective—dressing like a tough warrior for court and like a gentle lady for meetings with easily intimidated clients. But doing the opposite seemed to work for her. He didn't understand why.

Then again, he didn't understand plenty. For instance, he didn't understand how Loretta managed to talk him into things. First he'd agreed to go on a phony blind date with her. And now he'd agreed to talk to Solly about appearing on the *Becky Blake Show.*

Why had Josh said yes to Loretta? Probably for the same reason he'd asked her to have lunch with him. He felt comfortable with her. He could unburden himself to her. They were on the same wavelength. He *liked* her.

"I'm not piqued," he told Anita as she sashayed into his

office, a glint of thigh visible through the side slit of her skirt. "I just got a call from the lawyer representing the Branford Arms landlord. He wants to work out a settlement."

"No shit?" Apparently, Anita was no longer slumming in Victorian-language territory.

"He knew he was going to lose at the hearing," Josh explained. "He decided to get real."

"Joshua, that's great! You should be singing. And instead, you're looking like your dog died."

"I don't have a dog. And I'm not sad. Just...bewildered."

"Why should you be bewildered? You're good at what you do. I'm not surprised you brought that Branford Arms landlord to his knees."

He shook his head. "It's not the Branford Arms thing. It's..." He sighed, unsure how much to tell Anita. Too little and she'd nag him to tell her more. Too much and she'd lecture him on his foolishness. "A friend of mine is in the hospital," he said, then realized that wasn't exactly accurate. Dora Lee wasn't actually his friend. Of the Solly trio, she was the one he knew the least.

He knew her cooking, though. He'd eaten her chicken and her cookies, including those wonderful pastries stuffed with poppy seeds and honey that she'd brought to the center yesterday. That alone was enough to qualify her as a friend.

"Oh, I'm sorry!" Anita slipped into maternal mode, circling his desk and wrapping her arms around him, nearly gouging his neck with one of her lethal-weapon fingernails. "I'm so sorry. Is it serious?"

"A broken leg and a chipped tooth. I've got another friend with dentist connections, though. The tooth is going to be all right. I assume the leg will eventually be all right, too." He decided not to go into detail. The story was too weird—and for some reason, he'd been more able to discuss it with Loretta than with Anita, whom he'd known a whole lot longer. "It's left me a little rattled."

"Of course it has. I still remember when my son fell off his tricycle and popped out a front tooth. He was only four, thank God—it was a baby tooth. But it hadn't been ready to come out, and he had this awful gap right in the front of his bite for two years until the second tooth finally came down. Those bike helmets, they ought to be designed with a tooth guard."

Anita could hardly compare her son's tumble off a trike with a violent encounter between two elderly women. But like Anita's son, Dora Lee would recover, especially with the dental therapy Loretta was promising.

Why did he trust Loretta? Why had he said yes?

Why did the thought of bringing her and Solly together hold an odd appeal? Because they were both his friends? Because when he liked two people he wanted them to like each other? Or had Loretta simply cast a spell on him?

No, it wasn't a spell. If it had been, he would have wanted to kiss her once they'd walked back to the massive granite building that housed the production studios a block from Rockefeller Center. But he hadn't wanted a kiss, other than in the most general, male-hormonal-reflex way. She was attractive, he was a guy; so sure, kissing her would be terrific. But he wasn't looking to start a *relationship* with her. That much seemed pretty clear.

"So this friend of yours," Anita said, "does he need a lawyer? Are there insurance issues? Those insurance companies inflict more pain and suffering than they pay for."

"I don't know." Josh didn't bother to note that his friend was a she and not a he. He'd supplied Solly with a list of criminal lawyers' names for Phyllis; maybe he should supply him with a list of lawyers who specialize in settling insurance claims for Dora Lee. If Solly held both women as equals in his heart, Josh ought to dole out the lawyers' names equally.

"Joshua, honey, your friend is going to get better. Save your grief for a funeral, okay?"

"Okay." He managed a smile to prove he wasn't grieving.

Anita headed for the door, then paused and turned to him. "Did I ever tell you I hate that tie?"

He glanced down. He was wearing one of his more modest ties, a dark red with a paisley pattern. He knew Anita hated his Jiminy Cricket tie and his tie with the *South Park* characters on it. What could she possibly find objectionable about this one?

As if he'd voiced the question, she answered, "It's boring," then sauntered out of the office, her hips zigging and zagging with each step.

Solomon Hirschbaum was an inch or so shorter than Loretta, but he had charisma. She could feel it the moment she entered his cozy, well-furnished living room. Josh had let her in and greeted her with a quiet smile, but her attention quickly shifted to the slight, silver-haired man hovering near the row of windows that overlooked Amsterdam Avenue. He turned at her entrance, and she saw his misery in his eyes and the tension around his mouth.

Yet even miserable—and short—he seemed like a pretty cool guy for someone in his seventies.

If only her widowed nona could meet a guy like him... Although then they'd have to have one of those weddings with the priest and the rabbi, because Nona would insist on a wedding. And besides, Josh's friend might not be such a terrific catch, given that he was already stringing along a bunch of other women, one of whom had sent a rival to the hospital.

"Mr. Hirschbaum," she said, extending her right hand. Sometimes older men felt funny shaking hands with women, but he gripped hers without hesitation. "I'm Loretta D'Angelo. I'm so glad you were willing to meet with me. Josh has told me a lot about you."

"If he's told you a lot about me, he should've told you to call me Solly." His eyes were a caramel brown behind his glasses, and his chin was strong. The hell with Nona; Loretta wanted him for herself.

Not really. He was cute but not so cute she'd risk assaults by his other sweethearts. And she didn't think he'd go over too well with her family. Nicky would phone her day and night to harangue her for getting involved with such an inappropriate man. He'd haul his friend Marty into the city and handcuff Loretta to the guy.

"If I'm calling you Solly, you have to call me Loretta," she said.

Solly assessed her thoughtfully, then glanced at Josh. Loretta wasn't sure how to interpret his look; he was communicating something to Josh, but she didn't know what. Nor did Josh reveal anything. His expression remained pleasantly noncommittal.

Solly turned back to her. "You want something to drink? Vodka, sherry, schnapps..."

"No, thanks." If this worked out, she'd treat Josh to a celebratory drink afterward.

And she truly hoped it worked out. When she'd run the idea past the team that afternoon, the air in the room had practically crackled with electricity. "Old farts beating up on each other!" Bob had hooted. "I love it!"

"We've got to keep it kind and gentle," Gilda argued. "Nobody can beat up on anyone."

"I think they're all done beating up on each other for now," Loretta told them. "I see it as a sweet show. Elderly lovebirds, vulnerable to all the same insecurities and jealousies as young lovebirds."

"And then we can follow it up with middle-aged lovebirds," Kate suggested as she nibbled on sunflower seeds—some new diet of hers. "Not that I'm middle-aged. I'm twenty-nine. Right, Gilda?"

"We're all twenty-nine," Gilda replied. "Except possibly Bob."

"Bob is two," Loretta said. "Maybe two and a half on a good day. What I was thinking," she continued, "was that instead of bringing this old man and his rival girlfriends onto the show, we could take a mobile cam and film them where they are. In their senior center, for instance." She'd have to check with Josh whether such a thing was possible. "Or in the hospital. Or in their homes. Becky could interview them, show them living their lives, you know? I think it could be very classy and tasteful."

"But what about the studio audience?" Kate asked. "We always tape in front of an audience." The growing pile of sunflower shells on the table in front of her smelled like mulch.

"The studio audience would be goading them," Bob noted. "Enough audience input, and we'd have the geezers rumbling live and on the air."

"Which is exactly why we can't do it in the studio," Loretta pointed out. "Becky won't allow rumbling geezers on the new, improved show. Or Harold won't allow it. Or whoever's calling the shots these days. If we take the show out of the studio, we could avoid the whole goading aspect."

"If we took it out of the studio, who'd ask the questions?" Gilda wanted to know.

"We could show a tape of Becky's interviews to the studio audience, and then open the floor to discussion," Loretta explained. She'd given this a lot of thought in the time since she'd returned from lunch—only ten minutes, but she'd holed up in the bathroom until she could work out the whole thing. She'd locked herself inside one of the stalls, ignoring the two secretaries from *Someone's in the Kitchen with Dinah* who were camped out by the sinks, fixing their hair and arguing over the odds that Tupac Shakur and Aaliyah would hook up in heaven—the *Becky Blake Show* had done a show on recently dead rock stars just last year—and figured out how to pitch Solly's story so it could be produced in a kind, gentle way.

"Just a discussion?" Kate asked skeptically. "What would they talk about?"

"We could have a social worker who specializes in geriatrics come into the studio to address some of the issues," Loretta said. A social worker like Josh's girlfriend, she thought, although she'd prefer someone else. *Anyone* else.

"I think we should try to convince the central parties to appear on the show," Gilda said. "The old man and his ladies."

"Do you think we should risk having a group of seventy-year-olds sitting on the set while tattooed thugs in the audience ask them sleazy questions about their sex lives?" Loretta asked.

"The scuzz factor," Kate murmured portentously.

"If they got asked enough scuzzy questions, maybe the old ladies would go into the audience and start beating up on the tattooed thugs," Bob said rather too eagerly.

"Look, I don't know if I can pull this off," Loretta reminded everyone. "I'd have to meet with the people first."

"Let's run it by Becky," Gilda said. The team phoned down the hall to Becky's office to ask her to visit them.

Gilda was the only member of the team allowed to enter Becky's office with any regularity. If the rest of them needed to see her, she came to them. When Loretta had been Becky's personal assistant, she'd been in the office quite often, and there was nothing so special about it that the production staff needed to be barred from it. It was big, it was bright, it was pastel. It was the architectural equivalent of Becky's ego. But Becky liked her little power plays, and one of them was keeping the production staff out of her office. Her mother was the only team member for whom Becky opened her door.

Becky asked Gilda to come to her office to pitch the idea. They returned to the team room together less than two minutes later. "I want this show," Becky announced, steely-voiced and clad in a pistachio shift. "Loretta, can you get me this show?"

"I can try."

"Do better than just trying. I want this show."

If Loretta could get Solly and his girlfriends for the show, her job would be more secure than a tenured professorship. So she called Josh and asked him to introduce her to Solly.

And there she was, just hours later, in Solly's attractively decorated living room, politely declining his offer of schnapps.

"Josh, you want anything?" he asked.

"I'll take a beer if you've got one."

"Of course I've got one. I've got more than one. Loretta, honey, you want a beer?"

Not really, but she didn't want to offend him by refusing his hospitality. "Okay, thanks."

Solly bounded out of the living room, apparently delighted that he'd gotten her to accept a drink. He wore jeans, sneakers and a polo shirt, and he looked much younger than seventy. His age showed in the creases framing his eyes and mouth and the brown age spots on his hands and arms, but he exuded vigor. That was definitely part of his charisma.

"Is he a good chess player?" she asked, noticing the board displayed on a corner table.

"Damn good," said Josh. "How about you? Do you play?"

"I know the moves, but not the strategy. My brother Al tried to teach me, but then my brother Nicky would always come in and interrupt us. He liked to be in charge. He didn't like Al and me doing something he wasn't in charge of."

"He sounds obnoxious."

"He is." She grinned. "Al's obnoxious, too—in different ways."

"It's a family trait, huh?" Josh asked, then smiled.

She smiled back, then jabbed him in the side with her fist. He made an *oof* sound and grabbed her hand, as if afraid she'd punch him again. "I've got brothers," she reminded him. "They're obnoxious, but they taught me how to defend myself."

Solly entered the living room with three brown bottles of beer, their necks wedged between his fingers. "Here we go," he said, passing out the bottles. "Sit, Loretta. Right there—that couch is the most comfortable."

She obeyed, sinking deep into the sofa's cushions, which were too soft. Josh sat next to her and Solly settled into an easy chair. "I saw you on TV," Solly informed her, then added to Josh, "she's prettier in person."

"I think so," Josh agreed.

"Pretty on TV, too, but in person..." Solly nodded. "So, you had a nice date, you two?"

"It was fine," Loretta said, then hurried ahead. "I came

here to talk to you about appearing on the *Becky Blake Show*.''

"I know, Josh told me. And I know that show, Loretta. When Josh told me he was going to be on it, I started watching. Such *tsuris!* Does she know what *tsuris* means?'' he asked Josh.

"It means fussing and heartbreaking drama," Josh informed her.

"Oy," Solly continued. "This one hating that one, that one swearing at the other one, this one sleeping with that one, that one sleeping with everyone in the county."

"Our show is moving away from that," Loretta assured him. "We're doing less...what was the word? *Tsuris?* Less of that and more uplifting stories."

"Like your blind date."

"Right. Did you see today's show? It was about people who rescue abandoned pets. They have networks and pet adoption services, and they try to place the animals in good homes. It was really inspiring."

"And these people who rescue the pets, do they sleep with each other?"

Loretta smiled. "If they do, it didn't come up on the show. Tomorrow's show is going to be about recovering alcoholics—people who've been sober for at least three years. Also very inspiring." And boring as hell, but Harold had expressed his pleasure with the show's new direction.

"So where's the *tsuris?*"

"As I said, we're getting away from that. We thought your story—being a mature single man with women fighting over you—could lead to an interesting discussion on dating and romance among older people."

"Let me tell you something, Loretta." Solly leaned forward and patted her hand. "My life at the moment—it's *tsuris*. Dora Lee ending up in the hospital and Phyllis behind bars... Now, there's your definition of *tsuris*.''

"Did you talk to Phyllis about doing the show?" Josh asked.

"She's thinking about it." Solly seesawed his hand through the air, implying that Phyllis was undecided about the idea. "I told her to come over and meet Loretta, but she said not yet, she doesn't want to meet anyone. She spent several hours in a holding cell yesterday. A holding cell, like on TV, like on *Barney Miller*. You remember *Barney Miller* or was that before your time?"

"I remember the show."

"That Hal Linden, very talented," Solly observed. "He also had pipes on him. You ever hear him sing? Like a cantor, that one. Okay, but we're talking about Phyllis," he said, steering himself back on track. "She was traumatized. And today—" he clicked his tongue "—she learned that she can't go back to the senior center until the situation is resolved. Those were her exact words. Until the situation is resolved. Francine is being very strict about this." He drank some beer. "Francine is the social worker who runs our senior center," he explained. "She's not as nice as Melanie, who was—" he exchanged a quick glance with Josh "—the social worker before Francine."

"Josh's girlfriend?" Loretta said helpfully, to convince Solly she was on top of things.

"She knows?" Solly asked Josh.

"There's nothing to know," Josh said.

"Josh and I are friends, Solly," Loretta added.

"Uh-huh." Solly appeared unpersuaded. "You're friends. Very modern."

"We really are," Josh insisted.

"Uh-huh. A beautiful lady like this—" he gestured with

his beer bottle toward Loretta "—and you're just friends. If Loretta were *my* friend, we wouldn't be just friends."

She laughed. So did Solly. God, she really liked the guy. Why couldn't she have an uncle like him? Or even a great-uncle. Or a stepgrandfather, if Nona was interested.

She sipped some beer, then explained to him how she and her colleagues had envisioned the show they would produce about him and Phyllis and Dora Lee. "We could interview each of you separately. Dora Lee and Phyllis would never have to be in the same room."

"That sounds like a good idea." Solly nodded.

"We'd explore their feelings. If Phyllis was willing, we could discuss how she was treated in police custody. It's not every day they arrest a woman like her. If she's got some gripes about the way that happened, we'd be happy to air her complaints."

"It sounds as if you've got more than enough material for one show," Josh commented.

"We could spread the story over a couple of shows," Loretta said. "Becky Blake's enthusiasm was huge."

"I never thought of myself as a TV star," Solly murmured. "Sid Caesar, *that's* a TV star. Or Hal Linden."

"I've got to tell you, Solly—if you go on TV, you're going to be more than a TV star. Women all over the country are going to start fan clubs in your honor. You're going to wow them."

"Me?" His shock seemed genuine.

"You bet." Now that she'd met him, she was absolutely certain. He would be fabulous on the air. Maybe she would found the Manhattan chapter of his fan club.

He shrugged. "I think I can talk Phyllis into doing it. She's got an ego like the Empire State Building. Dora Lee, I'm not so sure. She's very shy. And she's in such pain. I spent a couple hours with her at the hospital today. They're giving her morphine. Morphine! A narcotic, like she was some kind of drug addict.''

"It's what they use," Josh reassured him. "She won't get addicted."

"They say in a day or two she can go home. But what's she going to do at home? She lives by herself and she's got a cast on her leg. She can't be alone. I'm thinking I'll bring her here so I can take care of her."

"She could probably get a day nurse to stay with her," Josh suggested.

Solly hissed through his teeth. "A day nurse, a total stranger? I'll take care of her." He gazed at Loretta. "Josh tells me you know people who can do something about her tooth? It's in front." He pointed to his own upper incisors. "It's bothering her. She needs something, I don't know what."

Loretta nodded. "I've got three dentists in my family, Solly. If she'd like, I could ask one of them to do the work."

"They'd do that for you?"

"They'd make me pay," Loretta said with a grin. "Not in money but in…I don't know, what's that word again? *Tsuris?* It doesn't matter. They owe me some favors."

"You don't even know Dora Lee. Why do you want to use up your favors on her? To get her on the show?"

"If it helps to get her to agree to appear on the show, why not? But even if she decides not to do it, I could twist some arms."

"You're a very sweet girl for someone who works on a cockamamy show," Solly said, patting her hand again. "Josh, she's beautiful *and* she's very sweet."

"I noticed."

"I'm also obnoxious," Loretta pointed out.

"No. You're very sweet," Solly insisted. "You'd never push Melanie in the street, would you?"

"Now, Solly, Phyllis insists she didn't push Dora Lee," Josh reminded him.

"And maybe she didn't. I don't know. I wasn't there. It's such a situation." Solly sighed and shrugged again. "Who would have thought? I like them all, you know? Phyllis and Dora Lee and Olga. Is that a crime?"

"Not as long as you don't assault anyone," Loretta said. "Who's Olga?"

"The ballet dancer. She's another whole situation," Josh informed her. "She's not a part of this situation."

"I'll talk to Phyllis and Dora Lee," Solly promised. "I'll see what they have to say about this television show."

"Thank you." Her bottle still three-quarters full, she set it down on the coffee table. "I won't take up any more of your time—"

"Please. It was a pleasure. But I know, I know, you and Josh want to go off somewhere and be friends. No problem."

Josh lowered his bottle, too. "I'll be in touch, Solly."

"We'll talk." They shook hands. When Loretta presented her hand to Solly, he took it, drew her closer and kissed her cheek. "A beautiful lady, forgive me but shaking hands is insufficient. Now, go, you two. Go be friends."

"Are we being friends?" Loretta asked.

They'd wound up at the Lincoln Center plaza, eating pizza. Josh's slice was too limp; the tip kept drooping like a clock in a Dali painting. Loretta had her slice curved in such a way it remained stable. Manipulating a pizza slice successfully must be some inborn Italian talent.

Her question puzzled him. "What do you mean?"

"Solly said we should go and be friends. Is that what we're doing?"

"It sure feels that way to me."

She nibbled on her pizza and swallowed. "Do you think Phyllis and Dora Lee are going to say yes to the show?"

He licked a strand of liquid cheese from his thumb and leaned back on the bench they were sharing. "You're the expert. What do you think?"

A car honked on Broadway, inspiring several other cars to honk in response, as if the vehicles were talking to one another. On the sidewalk, two men quarreled loudly in a Slavic language. Pigeons swarmed around a child tossing puffs of popcorn onto the ground for them. A model-handsome man and woman were calling each other vile names just a few yards away from the bench where Loretta and Josh were sitting. The air was surprisingly crisp for June, cooled by the rhythmic spray of water in the fountain at the heart of the plaza.

"Some people love coming on the show because they're exhibitionists, or because they've got an ax to grind," Loretta answered. "I don't know these women, though."

"That's not what I meant." He rearranged his slice, propping it up with a napkin. "You're a woman. I figure you know better than I do why women would come to blows over a man."

"Many women would not come to blows over a man. A lot of women would say no man is worth it." She looked serious when she said this, as if she was one of those women. "But you know these two ladies, Josh. Do you think either of them is unbalanced? Or passionately in love with Solly?"

"Unbalanced, I can't say. Phyllis does strike me as kind of aggressive." He recalled her muscular legs and her feisty personality. "And Dora Lee is kind of...vague."

"Vague?"

"She floats in and out, bearing platters of food, like something out of T. S. Eliot. I can't get a read on her." He shrugged again. "Apparently, she feeds Solly very well."

Loretta sighed and stretched, extending her legs and resting her head against the bench's back. "God, it would make for a fabulous show. They might even let me keep my job if I can deliver this."

"Keep your job? Is your job in danger?"

Loretta shrugged. "Probably. They've warned us they might have to lay off someone from the production staff. I don't know whether they mean it or they're just making threats to keep us on our toes. But a show like this—I'd be golden. They'd never fire me if I could put it together."

"If you lost your job, would you find work at a similar type of show?"

"If I lost my job, I'd grab anything that paid a living wage and allowed me to keep my clothes on while I worked. I'm not the most employable person in the world, Josh. I kind of stumbled into this job. But I really like it— and I'm good at it. If they fire me...I'd be seriously pissed."

A lock of her hair slid forward, nearly dipping into her pizza, which she held just below her chin. He brushed the strands away, tucked them behind her ear and leaned back. "I bet you could talk your way into a lot of other jobs. You're very persuasive."

"Oh, yeah?"

"Look what you've talked me into. Twice."

"That's because you're too easy."

"I'm very hard," he argued, squaring his shoulders and deepening his voice.

"Admit it. You're a pushover." She tossed the remains

of her pizza into the trash can beside their bench and gave him a challenging look. "I can't talk my family into anything, but I can talk you into two things. That must mean something."

He rose, aware that she was daring him but not sure why—or why he was so eager to rise to the dare. "Maybe you caught me at a weak moment."

"Two weak moments."

"First you call me easy, and now you call me weak?" He told himself not to take her taunts seriously, but she was pushing buttons. And like an idiot—like a man, he supposed—he was responding exactly the way she wanted him to. He was easy *and* weak, at least when it came to Loretta.

"Now, Josh," she murmured, giving him a conciliatory grin. "All I said was—"

"Weak," he concluded. "You called me weak."

She must have sensed his manly pride rearing up, building into a physical threat, because she let out a little laugh that sounded like a hiccup, lurched off the bench and started to run across the plaza.

He chased her, passing an older couple licking ice-cream cones, passing a young couple pushing a stroller, passing a gaggle of ballet dancers emerging from the New York State Theater, their hair smoothly lacquered against their scalps and their toes pointing outward like penguins' feet. She raced toward the fountain, but he easily caught up with her, grabbed her and hoisted her into the air. "Who are you calling weak?" he asked, dangling her over the gushing water of the fountain.

"No! Don't!" she shrieked, although she was laughing.

"Don't what?" Chlorine-scented water jetted skyward, cooling them with mist.

"Don't throw me in the fountain!" Clinging to his neck, she laughed even harder.

"How could I throw you in the fountain?" He dangled her precariously above the water. "I'm so very, very weak."

He pretended to lose his grip on her, and she slipped down. "Josh! Josh, don't! You're not weak! I swear."

He began to laugh then, too. His heart was beating a little too hard—from the running, the teasing, from how damn good she felt in his arms. Slowly, pretending great reluctance, he lowered her to her feet, safely beyond the fountain's edge.

"Okay," she conceded, sounding out of breath. "I take it back. You're not weak."

Yes, I am, he thought, gazing into her face, her cheeks flushed and glittering with drops of water, her eyes bright with laughter. He was strong enough to be able to lift her without the slightest strain, but he was weak enough to want more than her friendship. Friendship was all she'd ever agreed to give him, all he deserved under the circumstances, and he was weak enough to resent that he couldn't have more.

But she kept smiling, a warm, more-than-friendship smile, and he let himself revel in her nearness. Stray droplets rained down on them, and the rush of the water whispered around them, and Josh decided that lust and guilt did not mix well at all.

Fourteen

"Oh, come on, Loretta—don't you want to at least sleep with him?" Donna babbled through the phone.

Loretta heard the click of the call-waiting signal but ignored it. One of these days she was going to discontinue her call-waiting service because interrupting one caller to check out another struck her as terribly rude, right up there with inappropriate cell phone use. "I really don't want to sleep with him," she told her cousin. "He's attractive, but we've got a friendship going here. I don't want to ruin it."

"Why would sleeping with him ruin it? Granted, sex ruins a lot of things…" Donna paused, and Loretta heard a sharp hissing sound through the wire. Evidently Donna was lighting a cigarette. "But, come on. You watched the Fourth of July fireworks with him, right? That's practically the same thing as getting naked with a guy."

"It is?" Loretta hadn't known that. Josh had joined her and half the tenants of her building up on the roof to watch the city's fireworks display. They'd had a couple of beers— she remembered that he liked Sam Adams, so she'd bought a six-pack—and one of her neighbors had played Billy Joel's "New York State of Mind" and Bruce Springsteen's "Born in the U.S.A." on his boom box. Once the final pyrotechnics arced down through the sky in glittery threads of light, she and Josh had gone back downstairs to her apartment and split a pint of Ben & Jerry's Aloha Maca-

damia. The evening had been remarkably pleasant. Very
friendly. Sex had never entered her mind. Well, almost
never. He was a good-looking guy, after all, and she knew
from experience that he could kiss, but other than that...
Really, they were friends.

This friendship thing she had going with Josh was special. She had plenty of other friends, even male friends.
Bob, for instance. Like Josh, Bob had a girlfriend, the one
with the political family in Washington. Maybe Loretta's
new role in life was to be the pal of guys who got their
rocks off elsewhere.

And that was all right with her. Romance meant messes
like her near-miss wedding to Gary Mancuso, or her parents' hysteria about her old-maid status, or Nicky driving
her nuts about his friend Marty. She experienced none of
those horrors with Josh. No pressure, no panic, no demands.
Surely a night of sex wasn't worth jeopardizing what she
and Josh had.

She heard the click again. "Someone's trying to call
you," Donna noted.

"Yeah, so they can try me later."

"No, that's okay. I've got Andrew yanking on my leg.
I've gotta get him into bed. But listen, Loretta, don't be a
prig. A little nookie, just for fun, never hurt anybody. I
know this woman—I do her hair, blond highlights, a three-
step process so it takes a while. Anyway, she decided she
wanted to be a virgin when she got married. And there she
was, twenty-five years old and still a virgin—I'll be right
with you, honey," Donna said in a high, sweet voice, obviously to her son. "Go find Daddy. I'll be right in... Anyway—" she resumed her normal voice "—so this woman
was twenty-five and horny as hell, but she'd made a vow
to God she was going to stay a virgin until she got married.
And wouldn't you know, she said yes to the first guy who

asked her to marry him, just so she could lose her virginity already. It was a terrible reason to get married.''

''I'm not a virgin,'' Loretta reminded her.

''I'm just saying.''

''So, does that woman have any regrets?''

''No regrets. She got married, lost her virginity and got a divorce. She was a redhead then. That might have had something to do with it.''

''Probably,'' Loretta said. She heard the click again. ''Okay, I'm getting off. Give Andrew a big juicy one from me.'' She tapped the button to disconnect her from Donna and connect her with her incoming call.

''Hi, Loretta. It's Josh.''

She smiled and sank into the lumpy cushions of her sofa. She'd bought it at a Salvation Army outlet on Long Island, and Al had generously rented a van and hauled it, along with all the other Salvation Army furniture she'd purchased, to her apartment. Her father had offered to help with the move, but she knew he'd be griping about backaches after lifting a few cushions, so she'd said no, thanks. Nicky hadn't offered at all. He'd thought she was crazy remaining in Manhattan after her roommate had moved out and taken all the furniture with her. ''You can't afford that apartment on your own,'' Nicky had scolded.

''Actually, I can,'' she'd told him, silently adding, *barely*.

''You're crazy. You should live out here with your family.''

''Now, *that* would be crazy,'' she'd retorted.

Thank God Al wasn't quite as much of a busybody, and he liked to be a do-gooder, so he'd helped her move in her new furniture. She'd draped a slipcover over the couch, which made it look better than it felt, and she'd used a pretty circle of beige linen to cover the nicks and dings in the surface of the small dining table she'd purchased. A Japanese screen blocked off the sleeping alcove, and her parents had generously bought her a color TV for her birthday, back when she was twenty-seven and not yet in danger of dying an old maid. The rocking chair she'd found on the street, dragged home, cleaned and polished and piled with embroidered pillows. It looked perfect, nestled into the corner by a window. Unfortunately, it was the most uncomfortable chair she'd ever sat in, so she regarded it more as decor than actual furniture.

If only the rocker were more comfortable, she'd be curled up in it right now. Instead, she curled up on her couch. And smiled. She and Josh talked to each other just about every night, sometimes for five minutes and sometimes for fifty. If pressed, she would have been unable to remember three-quarters of what they'd talked about. It didn't matter.

Today's subject apparently mattered. "I've got news," Josh reported. "First, Phyllis said she doesn't care what her lawyer says, she wants to do the show."

"Great!" Phyllis's lawyer had been opposed to her appearing on the *Becky Blake Show,* worried that she might say something that would come back to haunt her if she had to stand trial on the assault charges. But Loretta had met Phyllis, and she was stubborn and fierce. If Dora Lee was going to go on TV and say Phyllis had pushed her into traffic, Phyllis was determined to go on TV and point out that Dora Lee was a liar.

"And my other news is, Dora Lee was released from the hospital and moved in with Solly."

"She's living with him? That must've yanked Phyllis's chain."

"Phyllis is on the warpath. Solly sent her flowers, but she's spitting fire."

"We'd better get this show in the can before that fire burns itself out," Loretta said.

"Loretta." Josh's tone held a warning. "You said this was going to be a gentle exploration of passion among older people. Spitting fire is not gentle."

"I know, I know. And the show *will* be gentle, I promise. But it'll be more dramatic if Phyllis and Dora Lee are pumped."

"Dora Lee is never pumped."

That was probably true. Loretta had also met Dora Lee—at the hospital—and found her oddly detached, almost ethereal. Her flutelike voice didn't match her bulky body, and she smiled even when a smile wasn't appropriate. Loretta had chalked that up to painkillers, but Josh said that even when she wasn't on a morphine drip, Dora Lee had a tenuousness about her.

Becky wanted this show. Harold wanted this show. Loretta had the impression they'd want the show even if Phyllis were spitting ice instead of fire, if the entire show consisted of Solly explaining that he loved both women, if the show turned into one big group hug, if Phyllis and Dora Lee decided they didn't need Solly and instead ran off together to the island of Lesbos. Harold and Becky would especially want *that* show.

"If Dora Lee's at Solly's place, we can interview her there," Loretta said. "Solly wouldn't mind, would he?"

"Solly's up for it. God knows why. I sure don't."

"News flash, Josh—you aren't God," she pointed out.

Josh laughed. "So, when do you think you'll do this?"

"The sooner the better. Do you want to be there for the taping?"

"If I'm going to be there, you'll have to schedule the interview in the evening. I work during the day."

"All those poor, abused tenants you've got to save,"

Loretta teased, although she thought Josh's work was truly noble. So many people went into law for the money. He was idealistic enough to have gone into it to change the world, at least the world of abused tenants. "Tell me, Josh, does anyone ever use the word *lessee* in speech? I've seen it in rental contracts, but it always makes me think, 'Lessee…can I really afford this rent?'"

Josh laughed again. She heard a gap in his laughter, almost a hiccup, and realized she had another call coming in. It wasn't Donna—Loretta had just gotten off the phone with her.

"Are you still there?" The call-waiting clicked again, creating an odd little pause in the middle of the word *still*.

"Yeah, I'm here," she assured him.

"I heard a clicking noise."

"It's the FBI. They wiretap my phone all the time," she joked, then said, "It's call waiting. Ignore it."

"What if it's important?"

"What if it's someone calling me on their cell phone to tell me they're somewhere between Westbury and Carle Place on the Long Island Railroad?"

"Good point," Josh conceded. "So what should we do about Phyllis and Dora Lee? Should we set up a time for you to come to Solly's apartment to tape interviews?"

"I'll have my people call your people," Loretta said grandly. "Any chance we could get Phyllis to Solly's apartment for her interview, too?"

"I don't think that would be a good plan. The last time Dora Lee and Phyllis were in the same place at the same time it led to bloodshed. Speaking of which, are you going to do something about Dora Lee's chipped tooth?"

"I've got to talk to my brothers," Loretta answered. "Has Dora Lee seen a dentist in town yet?"

"Not that I know of. I'll check with Solly. He said he

doesn't think she has any dental insurance. I don't know if Medicare covers something like this. That clicking is really getting annoying."

Loretta didn't mention that he'd caused similar clicking during her phone conversation with Donna. "Do you want to hang on while I find out who's calling?"

"Sure."

She thumbed the button on her phone. "Hello?"

"Loretta? It's your mother."

She should have ignored it. "Mom, I'm on another call. Can I get back to you?"

"I've been trying to reach you for hours," her mother said. An exaggeration; Loretta hadn't been on the phone that long. "We want you to come out to Long Island on Sunday. Dad is going to throw some steaks on the grill."

"Oh, I—"

"The boys and their families will be there. We want you to come. It's not your birthday, so you don't have to worry about us reminding you how old you are."

"Wonderful," Loretta muttered.

"Nicky says he and Kathy are bringing a friend. We thought—"

"Marty? They're bringing Marty the dentist?" Loretta's voice emerged in a near shriek. "I'm busy Sunday. I can't make it."

"Loretta, be reasonable. He's a friend of Nicky's. If you wanted to bring a friend to our house, I wouldn't object."

"Fine. I'll be bringing a friend," she said, thinking fast.

Her mother hesitated. Evidently, she hadn't expected this. "What friend?"

"Josh Kaplan. My blind date." *Please, Josh, be free on Sunday,* Loretta prayed silently.

"Your blind date? From the TV show?"

"Yes."

"He was a nice-looking boy. And—what was he, a banker?"

"A lawyer."

"Right. I knew he wasn't a dentist." Faint disapproval tinged her mother's voice. "I thought he was nothing special to you."

"He's very special." That much wasn't a lie. "As a matter of fact, Mom, I'm on the phone with him now."

"Oh, so that explains why you weren't answering your phone. That call-waiting thing. Your phone kept ringing and ringing. If you weren't home, I knew the answering machine would pick up. All those gadgets you've got."

"Yeah, well, can I call you back, Mom? I don't want to leave him hanging for such a long time."

"Of course. A lawyer. Well, I guess that's something. If you're bringing him to our house on Sunday, I'll have to let Nicky know."

"Please do. I'll call you back, Mom. Goodbye." She disconnected before her mother could say anything more. Then she sucked in a deep breath, sent another prayer heavenward and tapped the button on her phone. "Josh, you still there?"

"I finished the *Times* crossword puzzle while I was waiting for you."

"I'm sorry. It was my mother. Listen, Josh, you've got to do me a huge favor."

"Shit." She heard amusement in his voice. "If it has to do with the *Becky Blake Show,* I'm saying no."

"It doesn't, so you'd better say yes."

"Shit," he muttered again, this time through his laughter. "What?"

"Come to my family's house with me on Sunday. They're hosting a barbecue."

"Oh." He sounded surprised. "Why would that be such

a huge favor? Are they going to be serving pickled pigs' feet?''

''No, but I think the goal of this get-together was to set me up with my brother Nicky's friend Marty, the Italian Long Island dentist. I don't want to be set up with him. So I told my mother I was bringing you.''

Josh spoke slowly. ''As a date?''

''I didn't exactly put it that way.''

''But you left her with that impression.''

She winced and dug her bare toes into the lumpy upholstery. ''I know it's a big favor, Josh. It's just that they've been trying to cram this guy down my throat—well, that sounds obscene. They've been trying to introduce me to him, and I don't want to be introduced. I don't want to be treated like a desperate spinster that my family has to rustle up Italian Long Island dentists for. So I thought, if you came with me...kind of like my beard...''

''Your what?''

''You know—when a gay guy has a female friend hanging from his arm so people will think he's straight, the woman is called his beard.''

''Ah. So you want me to hang from your arm so your family won't realize you're gay.''

''Will you do it, Josh? Will you be my favorite person in the whole world and go to the barbecue with me?''

''Only if you promise they won't serve pickled pigs' feet.'' He ruminated for a moment. ''When did you say this was? Sunday?''

''Yeah.''

''I've got to mow my mother's lawn first.''

''Why?''

''Because I always mow my mother's lawn on Sunday. The world would come to an end if a Sunday passed without me mowing her lawn. But I could get myself to your parents' house afterward, I guess. I'd be out on the island anyway.''

"Oh, God, I love you," she blurted out. She meant it, too. She loved Josh for being the kind of friend who would rescue her from her family's matchmaking attempts. "I owe you big-time, Josh."

"Yeah. Maybe you should mow my mother's lawn for me.''

"Okay! I mean it. It's been years since I mowed a lawn." Actually, the closest she'd ever come to mowing a lawn was when she pushed her father's mower into the garage after he was done mowing. Nicky and Al used to mow the lawn, a chore for which they got paid decent money, she recalled. Her chores—emptying the dishwasher, stuffing ricotta into manicotti shells, lugging laundry baskets downstairs, to the corner of the basement where the washing machine stood—never earned her a dime. When Al left for college and she was the only D'Angelo child left at home, she'd begged to mow the lawn so she could pocket some extra cash. Her father had told her that mowing the lawn was hard work requiring brute male strength. She couldn't believe it required any more strength than hauling tons of her brothers' smelly socks and wet towels down the stairs to the washing machine.

"No, you won't mow my mother's lawn," Josh said. "But here's an idea—we can rent a car, drive out to my mother's, I'll mow the lawn and then we can drive on to your parents' house and convince them you don't need to get set up with any dentists, and then we can drive home."

"No Long Island Railroad? What a luxury."

"Then let's do it. I'll be your beard, and you can be my mustache.''

"It's a deal," Loretta said, deciding that Josh was indeed her favorite person in the whole world.

* * *

Josh paid no attention to the voice inside him nattering that this was not a good idea. What was bad about it? Friends did stuff together. They went to each other's houses, met each other's parents, mowed lawns and ate grilled burgers, if not pigs' feet. The whole plan was so unremarkable he didn't even bother mentioning it to Melanie when he e-mailed her about the developments with Solly, Phyllis and Dora Lee.

Of course, she was interested in that little soap opera. She knew the cast of characters from her time working at the West Side Senior Center, and she'd e-mailed him several long paragraphs on sexuality in older people. "In this age of Viagra and hormone patches, people's libidos don't fade away," she'd written. "It's certainly an issue I've been dealing with down here in Florida, where there are four widows for every widower. They often become very possessive partners. No one wants to die alone."

Josh had never thought about it that way. Solly, Phyllis and Dora Lee all seemed so vital he couldn't contemplate their deaths in any but the most abstract terms. But he could understand their need for companionship. Loneliness didn't confine itself to certain age groups.

Amazing, but he hadn't suffered a moment's loneliness since he and Loretta had transitioned to friendship. That first week, when he wasn't sure what he wanted with her, he'd been acutely aware of his solitude. He'd reflected obsessively on her legs, her mouth, her hair, the elegant angle of her jaw. He'd reflected even more obsessively on the emptiness of his bed. But once he'd gotten past that, once he'd relaxed into the relationship, he hardly *saw* her anymore. She was laughter, words, energy, crazy ideas, huge favors. She wasn't a beautiful woman.

Well, she *was* a beautiful woman. He'd have to tear out

his eyes to ignore that fact. But he didn't think of her that way.

She was looking particularly beautiful—all right, so he noticed—as she emerged from her building to join him in the car, which he'd rented a few blocks down on Madison Avenue. He'd had to double-park in front of the building because no spaces had been available; he'd abandoned the car only to dash into the vestibule and signal her on the intercom, and then bolted back out before the vehicle could be ticketed and towed. Watching her smile, stride to the car and let herself in, he admitted that she was indisputably beautiful in her tan cargo shorts and sleeveless black shirt, a purse slung over her shoulder and her hair slightly frizzy from the July heat. As usual, she wore little makeup—a touch of something that made her eyelashes look darker, and a layer of tawny lipstick not far removed from the natural color of her lips. She'd hooked a pair of sunglasses over the neckline of her shirt, and when she folded her long legs into the car, he caught a whiff of a tangy shampoo.

"This car is so bourgeois," she murmured, adjusting the side vent to blow air-conditioning directly into her face.

"It's a Buick," he said, starting the engine.

"I know. My father drives Buicks." She evidently didn't see this as a positive thing.

"It was what the rental place had. I could have chosen this or a Mercury Sable."

"This'll do," she assured him, stretching her legs under the glove compartment. "It's not a Porsche, but what the hell."

"It's better than the Mercury, at least."

"In what way?"

He steered to the corner and waited for the light. He rarely drove in Manhattan, but he relished the challenge of it. Sharing the roads with so many crazy drivers was like solving a puzzle or winning a tricky negotiation with a recalcitrant landlord. Every block he drove without getting cut off or honked at or flipped the bird represented a small victory.

"Mercury is made by Ford," he explained. "Jews don't drive Fords."

"They don't?" She eyed him curiously. "Why not?"

"Because Henry Ford was an anti-Semite."

Her eyes grew round and she let out a laugh. "Henry Ford? Like from a hundred years ago?"

"More like seventy years ago, but Jews have long memories. I was raised to understand that Jews didn't drive Fords, period."

"So, there are no old Nazis in Buick's closet, huh."

"None that I know of." Another couple of blocks. The Buick cruised smoothly, silently, very much the sort of car someone's father would drive. His father had been partial to Oldsmobiles, but they were pretty much the same thing as Buicks.

"Okay, so I shouldn't sing the praises of Henry Ford in front of your mother. Anything else I need to know?"

"She's a *kvetch*."

"A *kvetch*." Loretta struggled over the word, lending it an extra syllable.

"She complains. Behind every silver lining she sees a cloud." Josh steered onto the Fifty-ninth Street Bridge. It was probably the ugliest bridge in the city, which was part of its charm. Heavy, rusty-looking girders slanted on either side of the roadway, and the upper deck closed off the sky above them. But once they crossed the East River to the other side, the world opened up around the shorter, sparser buildings of Queens. The sun glared through the windshield, and he reached for his own sunglasses, which he'd tucked into the pocket of his T-shirt. He had dressed in his usual lawn-mowing apparel but had packed some fresh clothes in a knapsack, so he could shower and change before heading over to Loretta's house and pretending to be her boyfriend.

He was actually looking forward to the charade. Of all the adventures Loretta had talked him into, this one struck him as potentially the most fun. Because they were just friends, he could pretend affection and devotion without getting into trouble. He could wrap his arm around her shoulder or kiss her cheek or maybe even nuzzle her hair, and she wouldn't misinterpret his moves. She'd welcome them. They would be part of the show.

It would be exactly what he'd hoped for when they'd gone on their fake blind date: a hint of sex without any expectations or emotional repercussions. He wasn't betraying Melanie, because this outing was meaningless playacting, nothing more than a favor for a friend. Like the blind date, only with touching.

The Long Island Expressway wasn't a huge improvement over the Long Island Railroad, which moved slowly but at least moved. The expressway presented long stretches of stagnation, too many cars squeezed onto too little asphalt, too many frayed tempers confined within too many vehicles. Loretta noodled with the radio until she found a progressive-rock station. As long as she didn't choose opera, he had no complaints.

"You do this every week?" she asked. "You're such a good son."

"Racking up points for heaven," he told her.

"Your mother shouldn't be...what was it? A *ka-fetch?*"

"*Kvetch.* You're right. She shouldn't be. But she can't help herself. It's programmed into her genes."

"Am I going to have to know Yiddish to talk to her? As

of now, *kvetch* is about the limit of my knowledge. *Kvetch* and *tsuris*."

He laughed. "She speaks English. Am I going to have to know Italian to converse with your parents?"

"Nope. They were both born in America. And they're going to love you."

"What makes you so sure of that?"

"You're a man." She shrugged. Her shirt revealed the strong curves of her shoulders. Did her brothers have shoulders like that? Would they beat him up if they found out his intentions toward their sister didn't incline toward the matrimonial?

He could survive this one afternoon. Then he'd never see them again—except, perhaps, at Loretta's wedding. He would like to think he and she would remain friends even if she met her ideal partner and got married. He would like to think that if that ever happened, he wouldn't become even the slightest bit envious when that ideal partner wrapped an arm around her, kissed her cheek and nuzzled her hair the way he was planning to as he performed the role of her boyfriend today.

Of course he wouldn't be envious if she got married. He'd be happy for her. Friends were happy for their friends. No problem.

Still, he couldn't help stealing glimpses of her as he wove through the stop-and-start traffic of the highway, and admiring her smooth cheeks and the pugnacious tilt of her chin, and imagining how much fun pretending was going to be. He couldn't help thinking he was going to be a method actor today, throwing himself into the part, living it…letting her parents believe, for a few precious hours, that their spinster daughter had snared herself one hell of a guy.

Fifteen

"That wasn't so bad," Loretta said three hours later as Josh helped her into the car. Freshly showered, he smelled of a lime-tinged soap, and he wore a lightweight cotton shirt in a quasi-Hawaiian print and clean jeans faded to a soft blue. His hair was still damp, but the late-afternoon heat would dry it quickly enough. It looked darker wet, but she could see a few sun-bleached highlights glinting through the waves.

"It was ghastly," he refuted.

"Your mother was interesting."

"She spent the entire afternoon filling you in on every bonehead thing I've ever done in my life."

Loretta grinned. "I liked that story about the time you brought your ant farm to school and it broke and the cafeteria was overrun with ants."

"That was an accident," Josh grumbled.

"And the time you took out a chunk of the garage door, a week after you got your license."

"I did all the repairs and painted the whole damn door. She didn't have to mention it."

"But I'm so glad she did." Loretta gave him a sweet smile. "And I never would have guessed you'd be the type to get suspended for writing an editorial in the high-school newspaper."

"I stand by that editorial," he muttered. "The principal *was* a honking dweeb."

"And all those bar mitzvah pictures! Christ, she must have showed me a million bar mitzvah pictures of you. Two whole albums, plus the framed enlargements. You hardly had any nose when you were thirteen."

"Amazing that I was able to breathe." He slid his sunglasses onto his adult-size nose and backed the Buick down the driveway, then steered to the corner of the tidy suburban cul-de-sac on which his mother's brick ranch house stood. Her lawn was quite possibly the greenest and most neatly groomed on the block. Obviously, Josh took good care of it.

"You looked so cute in that navy-blue suit. Actually, you looked like you were outgrowing it. Your wrists stuck out."

"I grew three inches in the month before my bar mitzvah. One month after my bar mitzvah," he added, "my nose grew three inches."

"It did not. It's a very nice nose." Loretta studied his profile and nodded in approval. "Just the right size for your face. I don't think your mother liked me," she added in passing. She wasn't sure exactly what the pinched, thin woman with the perpetually downturned mouth had thought of her. She hoped Josh would enlighten her. Not that it mattered, not that she'd ever see Mrs. Kaplan again, but she was curious.

"My mother liked you fine."

"She kept talking about the importance of Jewish traditions. During that marathon tour of your bar mitzvah photo albums, she went on and on about how the world was running out of Jews and it was essential to create more Jewish babies."

"Lucky for you the world isn't running out of Catholics," Josh noted.

"I think your mother was hoping I'd convert to Judaism and create babies for the cause. When I didn't leap up and volunteer my womb, she put a black mark next to my name."

"In my mother's eyes, everybody has a black mark next to their name. You'd better give me directions to your parents' house, or we're going to spend the rest of the afternoon cruising Route 110 and getting nowhere."

"Get back on the L.I.E.," she instructed him. "Another reason I think your mother didn't like me was, she wouldn't give me anything to drink. I was dying of thirst and she didn't offer me anything. If you hadn't come in from the garage looking like a sweatball… What was that word she used?"

"*Farschvitzed.* It means looking like a sweatball."

"Yeah. Well, if you hadn't come in all *farschvitzed*—" she labored to wrap her lips around the word "—and asked me if I wanted a glass of water when you got one for yourself, I might have withered away to dust in her kitchen. Which is very yellow, by the way."

"She likes yellow. No, she doesn't," he contradicted himself. "She doesn't like anything. And she never offers me anything to drink, either. So if that means she doesn't like you, I guess she doesn't like me, either."

"Well. Her lawn is beautiful."

"Thank you." He shot her a look. Even though his eyes were hidden by his sunglasses she could picture them dancing with amusement. She smiled. Three hours in the company of his dreary mother couldn't diminish the pleasure she felt in spending her Sunday with him. He was so easy to talk to, so easy to laugh with.

"Did she like your father?" Loretta asked.

"Hmm?"

"You said she doesn't like anything. Did she like your father?"

He pondered his answer for a minute. "I think she might have," he decided.

"But she doesn't like you?"

"She never gives me anything to drink, for what that's worth."

"Why are you such a good son? Why do you cut her grass for her?"

He shot her another look, then smiled. "I'm a nice Jewish boy. Don't you know anything about nice Jewish boys?"

"Obviously I don't know the important stuff." She combed her memory. "I dated a Jewish guy in high school for a while. He was incredibly smart. He went on to MIT. I think he went into medicine."

"Maybe he's a dentist," Josh suggested.

"Nah. He's probably a brain surgeon. Or an AIDS researcher. He was too smart to be a dentist. I don't remember him being a devoted son, though. I don't think he ever cut his parents' grass. His parents didn't let him do chores because they wanted him to spend all his free time studying. They didn't like me much," Loretta recalled.

"Because you weren't Jewish?"

"Because I wasn't smart enough for him." She reminisced for a minute. Stuart Krupnik had been a dazzling student, but she didn't recall their conversations centering on heavyweight subjects like calculus or astrophysics or the philosophy of Wittgenstein. Mostly, they'd talked about Pearl Jam and *Saturday Night Live*. "I don't think he cared one way or another about my brain," she said.

"You have a wonderful brain," Josh pointed out. "It's one of your best features."

Her smile reflected warmth deep inside her. No one had ever complimented her brain before, not even Gary when he'd asked her to marry him. She knew she was smart, no whiz-kid genius but no dummy, either. Yet the men she'd dated in her past had never commented on her intelligence. They'd been turned on by her long legs, or they'd found her Long Island accent amusing, or they'd considered dating someone who worked on the *Becky Blake Show* cool. Her brainpower had never been the stuff of male fantasies.

Maybe Josh liked her for her brain because they were just friends. Friends didn't have to be a certain height, or have a certain size bosom or a certain color of eyes. Their minds, their attitudes and inclinations took precedence.

She wanted to thank Josh, but she was afraid she'd sound mawkish. So she said, "We'll be taking the next exit."

Silence settled over them for a minute. "What are you thinking about?" he asked.

She'd been thinking about Josh's affection for her gray matter, and about how he mowed his mother's lawn and put up with his mother's negativity Sunday after Sunday. He'd lost his father just as surely as his mother had lost her husband, but unlike his mother, he had vitality, a sense of humor and generosity. As much as Loretta admired his brain, she admired his heart even more.

"You *are* a nice boy," she finally said. "Not only do you take care of your widowed mother, but you also take care of tenants who are getting ripped off by their landlords. You do the kind of work that makes the world a better place. And your girlfriend is a social worker—also the kind of work that makes the world a better place. And what do I do? Come up with ideas for a TV show about women who seduce their daughters' boyfriends and guys suffering from steroid psychoses, and suburban sluts, and con artists who've been permanently banned from the Atlantic City casinos. Nothing important. Nothing with redeeming value. Crass commercial shit.''

"Suburban sluts?"

"One of our more successful shows."

"But you're making different shows now," he reminded her. "Shows about how older people navigate the shoals of love."

"'Navigate the shoals of love,'" Loretta echoed. "That's so poetic. Can we use that phrase in the show?"

"If you want."

"See? You're poetic, too. A devoted son, a champion of the oppressed and a poet."

"What is this, your sales pitch for your parents? Don't worry. I'll win them over."

Loretta was certain he would. As he steered through the neighborhoods of her hometown, through newer and older subdivisions, past split-levels, ranches, Cape Cod houses and mock colonials, all of them set on tree-shaded third-of-an-acre plots marked by mature hedges of yews, forsythia, lilac and arborvitae, Loretta imagined him wowing her parents to the point where they'd ban the mere mention of Nicky's tartar-scraping bachelor buddy at family gatherings.

"That's it," she said, pointing to the raised ranch sitting on a curving stretch of Eton Lane. The developers of the subdivision she'd grown up in had given all the streets pompous British-school names—Eton Lane, Harrow Drive, Oxford Road, Cambridge Circle—as if that would impart class to the neighborhood. But there was a limit to how classy any house with aluminum siding could be, even if it sat on Rugby Avenue.

Her parents' house was one of the larger models, with a two-car garage and a front porch trimmed with a wrought-iron railing that Loretta thought of as overwrought-iron, its painted white vertical bars adorned with rococo curlicues and vining leaves. The window boxes were filled with brightly colored fake flowers. This year her mother had chosen ersatz daffodils the same garish yellow as the walls in Josh's mother's kitchen. The planters flanking the front porch contained real flowers, at least—pink and white impatiens, the petals spilling over the lips of urn-shaped pots that looked like tacky reproductions of relics from ancient Rome. The double-width driveway held Nicky's Explorer and Al's Windstar van—both Ford models. She hoped Josh wouldn't take this to mean that her brothers were Nazi sympathizers.

She directed him to park alongside the curb. "I didn't bring anything," he said belatedly. "I should have brought a bottle of wine or something."

"You brought me," Loretta reminded him. Her father would probably consider her well aged, too. Fast approaching the vinegar stage. She shoved open the door and climbed out. "And I brought my mother's cruise-liner tote," she added, reaching into the back seat for the canvas bag her mother had sent her home with on her birthday. Josh locked the car and joined her on the sidewalk. "We may as well go straight around to the back—everyone's going to be out there. They won't even hear the doorbell."

They walked up the driveway, circumventing her brothers' hulking vehicles, and passed through a break in the forsythia hedge that grew flush with the front facade of the house. As soon as they'd reached the other side, Josh folded his hand around Loretta's. A nice touch, she thought, sending him a grin as they strolled around to the backyard.

Everyone was there: Nicky, in his inverted sailor hat and baggy shorts; Al, with his manicured mustache; Kathy, in a sleeveless sundress; Cindy, in a matching shorts-and-shirt outfit in vivid lime green; Trevor and Alyssa and the twins, who were flopping around in a freestanding wading pool on the grass beyond the deck, which extended off the back of the house. Loretta's father presided over the gas grill, an apron inscribed Don't Forget To Floss tied around his thickening middle, and her mother fussed with the color-coordinated paper plates, plastic utensils and nylon table-cloth covering the picnic table, which stood beneath a red-and-white-striped umbrella on the deck. And—oh, God—Loretta's grandmother was ensconced in a woven-plastic chair occupying a corner of the deck. No one had warned her that Nona would be here.

As soon as Loretta said, "Hi," everyone froze in a tableau, even the kids in the pool. They all gaped at her, at Josh, at their clasped hands.

Then, in unison, it seemed, they exhaled and came back to life. "Loretta!" her mother shrieked a bit too enthusiastically. She set down a cup filled with red plastic forks and swooped toward them, her arms outstretched, as Loretta ushered Josh up the steps to the deck. Fortunately, her mother's kamikaze approach didn't intimidate him. He let her gather his hand in hers and didn't flinch as she exclaimed, "I'm so glad you came! This is such a special occasion, Loretta bringing a boyfriend!" So special even Nona had made an appearance, dressed as usual in basic black without looking the least bit stylish: black blouse, black skirt, black canvas sneakers and dyed black hair pulled severely back from her face, her dour expression and gloomy attire combining to suck some of the sunshine out of the afternoon. Loretta tried to recall ever seeing Nona in a color other than black. Even at her brothers' weddings, Nona had dressed for a funeral. "It's practical," Nona always said. "It doesn't show stains."

Josh handled the introductions with aplomb, shaking hands, nodding, repeating names, nodding again as Cindy explained painstakingly how to tell Jennifer and Lauren apart. "They're actually not identical," Cindy informed him. "They're fraternal, but they look so much alike that people take them for identical. You'll notice that Jennifer's hair is a shade lighter than Lauren's—can you see that? Well, no, you can't right now because their hair is wet from the pool, but trust me. It's lighter. Lauren's voice is higher pitched than Jennifer's, too. Lauren usually does everything five minutes ahead of Jennifer, which makes sense since Lauren was born five minutes ahead of Jennifer."

Josh absorbed this lecture with a tolerant smile. "Does that mean that if Lauren kicks me, Jennifer will kick me five minutes later?"

Cindy bristled with indignation. "My twins don't kick."

"So, what are you drinking, Josh?" Loretta's father asked. "What can I get you?"

"Have you got any beer?"

"Have I got any beer?" Her father eyed Nicky. "He wants to know if I've got any beer."

Loretta thought this would be a good time to leave, but no such luck. Her father hauled Josh away, bellowing rhetorical questions about beer, and Nicky dragged her to the edge of the deck, where Kathy leaned against the railing, keeping an eye on the children in the pool. "This is him?" he asked. "This is the guy you think is better than a dentist?"

"He *is* better than a dentist," Loretta said.

"He looks different than on TV."

"He looks better," Kathy piped up. "He's taller."

"He's definitely taller than Mel Gibson," Loretta said, gazing around at the familiar yard, the familiar trees, the familiar people. "How come no one asked me if I wanted a beer?"

"If you want to make a nice impression on your guy,

don't drink beer," Kathy advised. "It's not ladylike." Kathy, Loretta observed, was drinking lemonade.

"Josh has already seen me drinking beer," Loretta told her. "It's too late. The damage is done."

"Loretta, *cara mia,*" Nona called from her chair. "How serious is this? This man, is he gonna marry you?"

"Marry me?" Loretta blurted out, then lowered her voice, embarrassed that Josh might have heard. She moved closer to her grandmother and clasped her hand. "I don't know, Nona. We only just met."

"So, you're still open to a date with Marty?" Nicky asked.

"I've never been open to a date with Marty." She turned her back on Nicky. "How are you, Nona?"

"How am I? Your mother said it's serious with this man."

"I don't know how serious it is," Loretta hedged. "We like each other."

"And he's not Catholic?"

Loretta resisted the urge to wrest her hand from her grandmother's. Nona must have sensed this, because she tightened her grip. "We're not serious enough to worry about religion," Loretta said.

"Then why am I here? Your mother said this was serious."

"Tell her she should go out with my friend Marty, Nona," Nicky coached her.

"This Marty—he's Catholic?"

"As Catholic as the pope."

Loretta decided it was time for a beer. "I'll be back," she promised Nona, then set out on a quest for one. Before she got far, she spotted her father leading Josh out of the house through the sliding doors. Josh was carrying two open bottles of beer. Not Sam Adams, but his having thought to bring her a drink made her wonder whether she might just want to marry him after all.

Sipping his own beer, Josh patiently listened to her father describe the wonders of the new drills he'd purchased for his office. "I bought three of them, one for me and one for each of my boys," he said. "We've got three chairs in our practice, three rooms. Did I tell you about the new drills, Nona?" he shouted past Josh. "Three air abrasion systems. I'll tell you, these Mach-5 babies are like nothing you've ever seen before—or felt before in your mouth. Drilling with them is like driving a Porsche, only you don't have to worry about a cop pulling you over. Did Loretta tell you that Nicky, Al and I are all in a practice together?"

"No, she didn't mention that. It must be nice, working as a family."

"We've got room for a fourth chair. I had hoped maybe—who knows?—Loretta might go into dentistry. I'm a liberated man—I'm aware women become dentists, *capisce?* But no, she majored in something useless. What did you major in, Loretta?"

"English."

"Like I said, something useless." He shot Josh a conspiratorial glance. "So I figured, what the heck, maybe she'll bring home a dentist and say she's marrying him, and we'll take him into the practice. Why not? All in the family."

"I see."

"Dad," Loretta broke in, "Josh has a friend in New York City—actually, a woman who was injured and needs some dental work. She has no dental insurance. She's in her seventies. What do you think?"

"Has she got Medicare? Medicaid? Tell you what, sweetie, have her call Florence. Florence is my office manager," he told Josh. "A wonderful girl, she's practically family herself, been with me since before Nicky started college. I love it that she's named after a city in Italy, right? She'll figure it out. She knows all those insurance things— Medicare, Medicaid. This friend of yours, can she come out here? Can she get herself to Plainview?''

''She's got a broken leg, so she isn't too mobile,'' Josh answered.

''No problem. We'll work something out. Have her call Florence.''

''That's very kind of you,'' Josh said. He casually arched his arm around Loretta's shoulders, a jolting reminder that he was supposed to be her boyfriend. She tried not to react visibly to his unexpected gesture, or the warmth of his hand against her bare upper arm. When she glanced over her shoulder she noticed Nona's scowl. She supposed this wouldn't be a good time to describe to her grandmother the bar mitzvah photos she'd viewed at Josh's mother's house.

The air filled with the sizzle and scent of roasting meat as her father forked onto the grill enough sausages and Delmonico steaks to feed a bloodthirsty *Becky Blake Show* audience. Her mother shuttled in and out of the house, carrying platters filled with garlic bread, green salad, tortellini salad and sliced tomatoes and arranging them on the table. ''No pigs' feet,'' Josh whispered, bending close to Loretta's ear and grazing her temple with his mouth. She felt heat where his lips had touched her, and more heat flooding her face when she noticed Nicky's intense observation.

She cleared her throat.

''Am I overdoing it?'' he murmured.

Not just that, but you're enjoying yourself too much, she almost said.

This little make-believe kiss meant even less than last week's kiss did. Melanie hadn't sailed off to the Bahamas with a dashing drug runner in the past few days. She was still in the picture. And Loretta was still happy to be single. Josh was just adding these affectionate flourishes for show.

Still, he *was* enjoying himself too much. So, for that matter, was she. She edged away, abruptly determined to help her mother unload her tray of condiments: ketchup, steak sauce, salt and pepper, napkins in a specially weighted outdoor napkin holder. Cindy and Kathy rounded up the kids and wrapped them in oversize towels. Al and Nicky pitched in by getting themselves fresh drinks.

"You like grilled steak?" Loretta's father asked Josh. "Because I sure like grilling it."

"It looks delicious," Josh said politely.

Trevor reached the deck and raced across it, weaving among the adults and splattering water from the pool in his wake. Loretta noticed a large splash staining the denim on Josh's shin. "Hey, slow down, Terror," Loretta scolded her nephew. "You're getting Josh wet."

"It's okay," Josh assured her.

"Leave him alone—he's a good boy," Nona added, reaching for a napkin and wiping water from her skirt.

Ignoring them, Trevor piled a plate with tomato slices and careered back to the stairs and down to the lawn. "You can guess why I call him Terror," Loretta murmured.

"Obnoxious little SOB, isn't he," Josh whispered back, smiling so no one besides her would realize what he'd said.

Loretta laughed, which helped to overcome the tickling heat of his breath against her ear. "If you like tomatoes, you'd better grab some fast. He'll eat them all."

"He can have them. I'll hold out for a steak."

Lauren piled her plate high with garlic bread and tortellini salad five minutes before Jennifer did, and they joined Trevor on the grass. On the deck, adults found seats where they could—a chair here, a railing there. Without discussion, Loretta's family left the two-seat glider for her and Josh to share.

He wasn't fat; he could have provided her with more space on the cushions. But he encroached on her half of the glider, his hip pressed to hers. While he sawed at his steak with the inadequate plastic cutlery, he genially fielded questions from her parents, brothers and sisters-in-law about his work, about his high-school years in Huntington, about how he'd felt appearing on the *Becky Blake Show*. "It's a silly show, you'll forgive my saying," Loretta's mother opined. "People screaming at each other over nonsense. Tattoos! Drugs!"

"It's disgusting," Nona added.

"The show is undergoing a change," Loretta told her, not bothering to add that even if the show on Solly and his lady friends came out well, she still might find herself no longer working for the silly, disgusting show by the end of the year. Her family was worried enough about her marital status. If she got laid off, they'd probably hog-tie her and drag her to church to marry someone—dentist or not, as long as he could support her. Someone from Long Island, so she wouldn't live in the city anymore.

Hell, they might just cheer if she lost her job.

Josh's knee rested against hers. The fabric was worn as soft as flannel. She was glad he had on long pants rather than shorts; if his bare knee had touched hers, she probably would have jumped out of her skin.

It was all a performance, she reminded herself. An Oscar-worthy performance. She was awed by his congeniality, his willingness to answer her parents' nosy questions about his education and his father's death—"a heart attack, *aaiiee*, Josh, such a tragedy—so, is a bad heart something that runs in your family?"—and to laugh at her brothers' stupid remarks—"This patient of mine, she says she broke her bicuspid on a piece of peanut brickle. I say, 'It's peanut *brittle,* not peanut *brickle.* What country are you from?' and she says, 'The Bronx!'" Josh ate two small steaks, praised her mother's tortellini salad, indulged in a second beer under heavy pressure from her father and winced but didn't yelp when first Lauren and then Jennifer stomped on his foot in their eagerness to grab biscotti from the dessert plate her mother brought out to the table. The light began to fade, the voices grew louder, Cindy checked her watch and decided it was time to light the citronella candles, and the children ran in circles on the lawn, chasing one another, making themselves dizzy, screeching and convincing Loretta she wasn't ready to become a mother yet, unless she could be guaranteed her child wouldn't behave like her nieces and nephew.

"Should I make espresso?" her mother asked. "If I make it, who's having? Josh, you'll have some, right?"

Josh looped his arm around Loretta and whispered, "Is she going to make it with lemon peel?"

She remembered the café they'd gone to after *Three Dead Corpses.* The espresso was the only part of their blind date not mapped out by the TV show. That and his kiss, and her subsequent realization that yeah, Donna was right, she could truly enjoy having sex with Josh—if only he weren't already claimed. If only Melanie didn't exist.

"She doesn't make decaffeinated," Loretta whispered back, bowing her head toward his, enjoying the intimacy. "She doesn't believe in it. Her espresso is really strong. It'll put hair on your chest."

"My chest is hairy enough. I'll skip," he murmured, leaving her to wonder how hairy was hairy enough. She didn't like a lot of body hair on a man, but a little could be quite attractive. He had a great build, but what if he had hairy shoulders? A hairy back?

Not that it mattered. She was only curious.

By seven o'clock, a sliver of moon had grown visible in the sky. Josh had skipped the espresso but obediently downed a biscotti, and her father had brought out a bottle of Amaretto. "I'm sorry," Josh declined, holding up his hands to halt him, "but two beers are my limit. I've got to drive back to the city."

"In fact, we really should be hitting the road," Loretta chimed in. Her task was accomplished. Thanks to Josh, she'd convinced her parents that she could find male companionship without any assistance from Nicky. They ought to clear out before the evening deteriorated. Alyssa was fussing. The mosquitoes were beginning their aerial maneuvers. Cindy was checking her watch again, announcing that she and Al were going to have to leave in twenty minutes to keep the twins on their schedule. Nona wanted to know if *Sixty Minutes* was on.

"Yeah, I think we should be heading off," Josh agreed. He endured a flurry of handshaking and backslapping, and recited heartwarming lines about what a pleasant evening it had been and how happy he was to have met all the D'Angelos. Loretta kissed her parents and grandmother, and then she and Josh broke free, descending the deck steps, holding hands, shouting more farewells as they strolled around to the forsythia hedge and out to the front yard.

Crickets chirped in the descending night, accompanied by the hiss of a neighbor's sprinkler. The scent of grilled meat hung in the air, as did the muffled chatter of her family. But the night on this side of the hedge was tranquil, darker without the deck light and the citronella candles, calmer without the crush of smothering relatives.

Josh didn't let go of her hand.

"You are the best sport in the world," Loretta declared

as he led her to the curb and unlocked the Buick. "I owe you so big—"

"And I'm going to rack my brain trying to come up with a way for you to repay me," he warned, smiling mischievously.

She navigated him through the British prep-school streets and onto the expressway. He turned off the air-conditioning and opened his window, and the car filled with heady gusts of real air. Before them lay a chain of red taillights; to their left a chain of white headlights, sparser because fewer cars were traveling east. Loretta settled into the upholstery, with its leathery new-car scent, and felt all the tension drain from her body.

"Thanks," she said after a while.

"You already thanked me."

"That was an impulsive burst of gratitude. This is the real thanks. You were good. I think my parents are in love with you."

"Your grandmother isn't. She didn't smile at me once."

"Because you aren't Catholic. Don't worry about it."

"How about your brothers? Did I wow them?"

She grinned. "Hard to say. Nicky will never forgive you for not being a dentist."

"So…what's going to happen when you tell your family we aren't a couple?" Josh asked. "Are they going to come after me with a shotgun?"

She opened her window, too, so the warm wind could blast her from both sides. "I don't know about a shotgun. They might come after you with their Mach-5 air abrasion systems."

Josh shot her an alarmed look.

"No, they won't. They'll come after me. They're convinced it's my fault Gary dumped me."

"How could it be your fault?"

"They think I'm too—I don't know. Too stubborn. Too independent. I don't go to church, I'm not ladylike enough, I work on a silly, disgusting TV show... They give me guidebooks on how to catch a man. They think I don't know how."

"They're crazy," Josh said. The wind blew back his hair, allowing her to admire the perfect proportion of his adult nose in profile. "If you wanted a boyfriend, you'd have eligible guys lining up around the block."

She snorted. "Oh, of course."

"The only reason guys aren't lined up around the block is that you don't want them to be. You make it clear you're not interested in a big romance. So maybe your parents are right," he added thoughtfully, "and it *is* your fault."

The traffic thickened as they approached the city. Everyone who didn't take the Long Island Railroad home from weekend places in the Hamptons or on Montauk or Fire Island or Shelter Island took the highways home. Still, she considered riding home in a car a luxury. No idiots with cell phones could get to her here.

And she had Josh all to herself. Just the two of them, talking, enjoying the bracing night air, relaxing after an overloaded afternoon.

He crossed the bridge into Manhattan. They were only fifteen minutes from her apartment, and it was still early. "How about, let's drop off the car and go back to my place?" she said. "I've got a pint of Ben & Jerry's Concession Obsession in the freezer."

"That sounds better than those cookies your mother served. What's Concession Obsession?"

She shrugged. "I bought it for the name. I think it's got M&M's in it."

He cruised uptown on Third Avenue, and the sounds of the city flooded into the car through the open windows. No hiss of a lawn sprinkler here, no twittering of crickets. These were the sounds Loretta loved: horns blaring, people shouting, the jagged pulse of hip-hop booming from a portable radio. No split-levels on Third Avenue, no aluminum siding, no third-of-an-acre lots. No suburbs. Just the city in all its noisy joy.

Josh settled up at the rental office, refusing to let Loretta contribute toward the cost of the car. "It was a treat for me," he pointed out. "I don't get to drive very often, so this was a thrill." Then they set out toward East 100th Street. Josh took her hand again, just as he had at her parents' house. He had no one to impress here, no one to con into thinking they were a couple. Yet holding hands seemed appropriate. They'd survived an ordeal today, or maybe two ordeals if she counted the time they'd spent at his mother's. She felt triumphant. No one was going to nag her about her love life for at least the next few weeks.

At her building, they halted while she dug her key from her purse. Josh stood close to her, closer than she would have expected. He'd had to release her hand so she could rummage through her purse, but he hovered just inches from her, casting a shadow over her in the pool of light that spilled from the fixture above the door. She could practically feel his breath in her hair.

The city was hotter than Long Island had been. The tall apartment buildings tended to hug the heat, and the subways underground sent more heat upward...and none of that had to do with the prickly warmth she felt having Josh so close. She thought about ice cream and her window-unit air conditioner, and her fingers closed around the jingling metal of her key ring.

Josh cupped his hands over her shoulders. More warmth, his palms so warm against her upper arms she flinched. "Loretta."

She peered up at him and tamped down her concern. She trusted Josh. He was her friend, her loyal accomplice. Nothing was going on here.

"I've got to go," he said.

He looked so solemn she laughed. "It's not that late. Only—" she twisted her arm to check her watch, and his fingers flexed in response "—eight-fifteen."

"That's not it. It's just…" He sighed. His eyes resembled green crystals. "If I go upstairs with you, I'm not going to want ice cream."

She could fill in the blanks a lot of ways. She opted to fill them in the safest way. "I could give you a beer. A Sam Adams, not that stuff my dad foisted on you."

He smiled slightly and shook his head. "I shouldn't even be thinking this way. We've got an understanding."

"You've got a girlfriend," she reminded him.

Relief flickered across his face at her acknowledgment that they weren't discussing ice cream versus beer. "It's just—all day, getting into the role, living it, I…" He sighed. "I'm sorry. I've been thinking…"

"You've been thinking what?" she asked when his silence stretched too long.

"You know what I've been thinking. If you tell me you're not thinking the same thing, I swear I'll turn around and go home and drink my own beer. I know I'm out of line here, but—"

Yes, she knew what he was thinking. Yes, she was thinking the same thing. Not because Donna had nagged her about it, not because she hadn't had sex since Valentine's Day, not because her parents wanted her in a romance, but because Josh was such a true friend, and she felt so good around him, and *damn it, he had a girlfriend.*

"You *are* thinking it," he said.

And his girlfriend was, what? More than a thousand

miles away? And no one would ever even know, and he'd been living the role of her boyfriend in a big way all day, touching her, sending her amorous gazes, kissing her cheek, toying with her hair, acting like her lover...and they were both thinking it. He was so right about that.

"Just this once," he said. "It doesn't have to destroy our friendship, Loretta. That's fundamental. That's not going to change. It means too much to us, so we won't let anything undermine it. But just to, I don't know, get it out of our systems. And then we can have some ice cream."

"Just this once," she echoed.

His eyes met hers. His smile was both hopeful and resigned, as if he was braced to accept whatever she decided.

"Just this once," she said again, half in warning and half in capitulation. He smiled as she opened the door.

Sixteen

Naturally, she wasn't wearing the silky burgundy teddy. If she'd known how this day might end, she would have chosen her underwear more carefully. But she'd dressed for comfort, donning high-cut panties and a plain white cotton bra. At least they matched.

The funny thing was that, all in all, the paltry seductive quotient of her underwear didn't bother her. This was Josh. It was a onetime thing, devoid of profound meaning. They were going to make love because they really, *really* wanted to, and the hell with moral qualms or fears about the long-term repercussions. It was just sex, just once, a little fun between friends, possibly more pleasurable than Ben & Jerry's ice cream—and possibly not. The act might just disappoint them both. But that would be okay, too. They'd still be friends afterward.

She led Josh into her apartment, past the slipcovered sofa and the uncomfortable rocker and around the screen to her bed. It was the one piece of furniture she'd actually bought new, after her mother had badgered her for several days, citing the dubious scientific fact that a person could catch something by sleeping on a used bed. "You don't know where a used bed might have been," she'd scolded. "You don't know what might have been done on it."

Murder? Loretta had wondered. The filming of a porn flick? Trampoline practice? But she'd yielded to her mother's wishes and blown the money she'd been saving for a weekend in the Berkshires on a new Posturepedic double bed, which was delivered sealed in sterile plastic. A single or twin mattress would have fit better into the nook of her L-shaped studio apartment, but Loretta figured she'd be spending more time in that nook sleeping than strolling around, so she wedged the bed into the cramped space and did her best to avoid stubbing her toes when she had to walk to the closet or the bathroom.

She doubted Josh cared that she'd bought the bed new. He spared it only a glance before turning her toward him and lowering his mouth to hers.

This kiss was nothing like the kiss he'd given her outside her building after their blind date. It wasn't tentative; it wasn't asking. It was telling, announcing, celebrating. It was lusty and hungry and unabashed. It was his breath filling her, his teeth gently tugging on her lower lip, his tongue sliding deep.

Oh, God, he could kiss.

After a long minute, he drew back. His beautiful hazel eyes were glazed; his breath, shallow. "Do you—?"

"Yeah."

"Because I didn't—"

"It's okay." She'd gone on the Pill when she and Gary started getting serious, and she'd stayed on it after they'd broken up because she'd loved what it did for her complexion. She was pretty sure she had a box of condoms in her night table drawer. Besides, Josh didn't seem like a high-risk guy. A nice Jewish boy, she thought, although his kisses, which had moved from her mouth to her throat and shoulder and the edge of her earlobe, weren't exactly "nice." But…oh, she was feeling nice, very nice as he slid his hands down her back and tugged her shirt free from the waistband of her shorts. Very, very nice as he moved his hands up underneath, as he caressed the warm skin there, as he lifted his mouth back to hers.

She was greatly relieved, when he shed his shirt, to discover that his chest wasn't terribly hairy. Just a small patch of tawny curls along his sternum. He could have guzzled her mother's espresso without turning into King Kong—but if he'd had some, he might have been jittery from the caffeine, and she didn't want him jittery. She wanted him exactly as he was: purposeful but relaxed, almost leisurely as he stripped off her clothes, her boring underwear and then his jeans and boxers.

They were friends. This *should* be relaxed. She'd never made love with a friend before, but she liked the lack of emotional neediness in his touch—and in her heart. She liked the absence of unspoken promises. This was what it was and nothing more. Just one final scene at the end of a successful performance, an epilogue for the enjoyment of the players alone.

They sprawled out on the bed, kissed some more, touched, tangled. He wove his legs through hers, ran his hands all over her, ran his mouth all over her. Through the arousal that filled her with a shimmering heat, she managed to notice that he had a gorgeous physique. Not surprising; the very first time she'd seen him, clad in old, grass-stained work clothes as he rode home from his weekly mowing chore, she'd figured him for a great body. The reality was every bit as attractive as she'd assumed. What she couldn't see in the dim light she could feel—the sleek surface of his back, the knotted muscles of his butt, the breadth of his shoulders and the taut plane of his abdomen. But there were surprises, too. His hair was much softer than she'd expected, cool and silky against her fingers. And his arms were strong, taking the bulk of his weight so he wouldn't crush her, even when he was on top of her.

She liked having him there, his hips settled between her thighs, his shoulders bunched as he held himself above her. She liked gazing up into his face and glimpsing his smile just before he bowed his head to kiss her breasts. He kissed lower, and she liked that even more. Oh, God…she would be his truest friend until her dying day if he just kept kissing her like that.

He slid back up her body, replacing his mouth with his hand between her legs as she reached down for him. He smiled again when she stroked him, groaned a little, sighed when she abandoned him to dig through her drawer for a condom, then let her guide him in. And suddenly she didn't feel like his friend anymore.

Well, yes, still his friend but…*more*. All the neediness, all the possessiveness, all the promises they hadn't dared to acknowledge flared to life inside her. With each thrust, she recognized what a mistake this was, what a fool she was, what a disaster this would turn out to be…because nothing in her entire life had ever felt as magnificent, as honest, as *right* as having Josh inside her.

She came in a great, shuddering rush, clinging to him and closing her eyes, hoping he wouldn't see the love bursting open like a ripe blossom inside her. He kept moving and she came again, feeling bits of her soul shatter and drift beyond her reach. Tears burned her eyes, but he wouldn't see that, either, not as long as she kept her lids slammed shut.

He let go, his body wrenching and his tension escaping in a moan. She wrapped her arms tightly around him and pulled him down, keeping her face turned from him so he wouldn't notice the few stray tears that leaked through her lashes.

He lay still for a few minutes, then stirred, twining his fingers through her hair. His legs relaxed against hers, his breathing slowed and he let out a long, weary sigh. *Don't say anything,* she pleaded silently. *Don't make jokes, don't ask me for ice cream, don't mention your girlfriend, don't say we're friends. Don't do anything until I've had a chance to recover.*

But he didn't wait for her to recover. He straightened his arms to prop himself up and stared down into her face. "We're in trouble, aren't we," he murmured.

She batted her eyes and bravely attempted a smile. "What trouble?"

"This was too good."

"Just a little too good," she said.

"A lot. A hell of a lot. Damn." He looked away, and she realized he regretted the whole thing as much as she did, for precisely the same reason.

Why did he have to reach the same conclusion she had? Why couldn't he have thought nothing special had just occurred? Then she could have labeled him a jerk and put some emotional distance between them. But no—he had to agree with her. It had to be too good for him, too, and its too-goodness had to bother him the same way it bothered her.

He rolled off her and settled onto the bed beside her. Because it was a firm, high-quality mattress, it didn't sag under his weight, and she didn't slide toward him. He rectified that by pulling her into his arms, guiding her head onto his shoulder and resting his chin against her hair.

"What are we going to do?" she asked.

"Make love again."

"How is that going to help things?"

"I don't know if it's going to help, but it sure won't hurt."

"Josh." He didn't seem to be taking the situation as

seriously as she was. She couldn't decide whether that pleased or irritated her.

"Until you kick me out of your bed, I'm not going anywhere," he said. "Okay? You want to kick me out, go ahead." He made that challenge impossible for her by circling her breast with his hand, fondling it, teasing the nipple with his thumb until she was hot and restless, wanting him again.

"No fair," she whispered. She started to push his hand away, but wound up only covering it with hers, holding him to her.

"The damage has already been done, Loretta. We can repair it now or later. I vote for later."

"There might be more damage later."

"I don't think so." He moved his hand down her belly, her hand going along for the ride because she didn't want to let go of him. "We've screwed things up—"

"Literally."

"But they're not going to get any more screwed up than they already are." He raised himself so he could see her. "Are you kicking me out?"

How could she kick him out? He looked as worried as she felt, as apprehensive, as passionate. She doubted he was falling in love with her, but she was more than falling, she was plunging, tearing through the atmosphere like *Apollo 13* and watching her protective heat shield burn away. Nothing he could do or say would keep her from crashing.

His hand crept lower, and she knew she couldn't kick him out. Not with fingers like his. Not with eyes like his. Not with his shy, bewildered smile and his mouth capable of performing wonders, and his hard, lean body with its perfect complement of hair. A stronger, wiser woman would kick him out, but she'd already admitted to herself that she was a fool.

Resolving to worry about the damage later, she dug her fingers into his hair and pulled him down to her.

Kate had abandoned sunflower seeds for wedges of pineapple, which she'd brought to the production team room Monday morning in a Ziploc bag that failed to contain their cloying tropical fragrance. Bob arrived with a jumbo frappaccino. Gilda arrived with bottled water. Loretta arrived with a headache.

"What happened to you?" Bob asked.

"Nothing."

"Big weekend, huh." He was so chipper she wanted to smack him.

"Can we get started?" She turned plaintively to Gilda. "I've got some new kind-and-gentle ideas for the show." In fact, she'd been inundated with ideas over her coffee that morning. Ideas for the show had flooded into her mind, as if to fill the vacuum left behind by Josh's absence. Most of the ideas had been stupid: people who talk in their sleep, fanatics who write hundreds of letters to the editor every week. One idea—sex between friends—had seemed downright toxic. But a few of them had been keepers. "How about women who create their own clothes out of nontraditional materials?" she suggested.

Bob pretended to gag. "Oh, God, where's my cyanide pill?"

Ignoring him, Loretta went on, directing her comments to Gilda. "How about diets that really work? You know that show'll get ratings."

"As if there *is* such a thing as a diet that works," Kate snorted, then popped a chunk of pineapple into her mouth.

"How weather affects our moods."

Bob faked a noisy yawn.

"The hidden costs of sleep deprivation."

"That's a good one," Kate said, perking up. "Just looking at Loretta, I can see the costs of sleep deprivation written on her face. Not quite hidden, are they?"

Loretta scowled. She looked bad, but not *that* bad. So she hadn't gotten more than maybe thirty minutes total of sleep last night. She'd thought about sending Josh home, but she wouldn't have slept any better without him in her bed, so she'd let him stay—and they'd wound up going at it all night long. As Josh had said, the damage had been done—and as he hadn't said, but they'd both understood, they were never going to get naked in each other's company again. So they'd taken advantage of their one idiotic night together and made love until they were beyond exhaustion, until the sheets were humid, until Loretta believed she'd be walking like a cowboy for the rest of her life. Josh had arisen at six, claiming he needed to go home so he could shower and put on a suit for work. She'd remained in bed for another hour, trying to gauge just how much damage had been done.

More than Josh knew. She loved him—the bastard—and he had a girlfriend. She was disgusted with herself and furious with him. *We're in trouble, aren't we*, he'd said, and she'd lain awake, her eyes stinging, and calculated exactly how much trouble she was in.

"Not bad," Gilda said, crossing to the white board and jotting down Loretta's ideas. "With the sleep deprivation one, we could get a medical expert on the show for expert commentary."

"And people who've suffered due to sleep deprivation," Kate suggested.

"Like Loretta," Bob added, then sent her a quick smile. "We could show mangled cars from accidents caused by folks who fell asleep at the wheel."

"Yuck," Kate grunted.

"That would increase the scuzz factor," Gilda observed. "We could do something tasteful about sleep deprivation. It would appeal to both men and women."

"As opposed to a show about women who design their own clothes out of—what, nontraditional materials?" Bob muttered. "Tinfoil? Duct tape?"

Gilda surveyed what she'd written on the white board. "I'll take these ideas to Becky. They're good, Loretta. You're inspired today."

"What happened this weekend?" Bob asked, sounding genuinely curious.

"Nothing."

"You come in here looking like shit and full of good ideas. This is not you, Loretta. It's the exact opposite of you. You usually look good and are full of shitty ideas."

"You know, if I wind up getting fired, I'll really have to force myself to miss you," Loretta retorted.

"I'm the one who's going to get fired," Kate predicted. "I haven't had a good idea since I stopped eating grasshopper pie. Now, *there* was a diet that didn't work."

"In the meantime, Loretta—" Gilda crossed back to the table and flipped through her notebook "—you're scheduled to go out with Becky this afternoon to tape interviews with Solomon Hirschbaum and Dora Lee Finkelstein."

"They want me there?"

"Becky's going to need you with her. She's never done this kind of fieldwork before."

Loretta almost blurted out that she'd never done it, either, but she decided to project herself as professional and competent. Such an attitude might buy her a few points when it was time for Harold to pick someone to cut from the payroll. "Glenn Santos will be your cameraman," Gilda continued. "The three of you will be heading over there this afternoon, once we're done with postproduction on to-day's show.''

"What *is* today's show, anyway?" Bob asked after taking a sip of his frappuccino. A tuft of white foam clung to his upper lip. "What kind-and-gentle show is she taping today?"

"Men with body image problems."

"That was my idea," Kate remembered, beaming. "Maybe I won't get fired after all."

"Oh, and one other thing," Gilda said, homing in on Loretta. "Becky wants you and your blind date to tape a follow-up show."

"No."

"She's gotten lots of positive feedback on the original show. Not just from Harold, but from fans. They loved it. They want you and—what was his name? John?"

"Josh." His name emerged from Loretta on a faint groan.

"Right. You and Josh. They want you to come back and tell what happened on your blind date. And afterward."

"Nothing happened," Loretta said rather too vehemently. She realized the other three were staring at her, and she subsided in her chair and took a deep breath. One not-so-hidden cost of sleep deprivation was that her nerves were frayed and exposed. She lacked the energy to disguise her mood. "Really, nothing happened. We had a pleasant time and saw the worst play in the history of Western drama. But there were no sparks." Like hell there weren't. Last night she and Josh had generated enough sparks to ignite conflagrations in drought-ravaged forests from here to California. And if she went on TV, the world—or at least that portion of the world addicted to the *Becky Blake Show*—would see for themselves just how many sparks were arcing between them.

"Becky and Harold think it would make a terrific show, either way," Gilda insisted. "You and Josh appealed to the audience."

"Let her fire me," Loretta said, too tired to argue. "I'm not going to do it."

"Great," Bob said, giving Loretta an encouraging poke in the arm. "Let her fire Loretta."

"We'll discuss it further," Gilda announced, pursing her lips. "Meanwhile, be prepared to visit your friend Mr. Hirschbaum this afternoon."

"What do you mean, you're leaving?" Anita asked.

As long as she stood blocking his office door, Josh wasn't leaving. He tugged loose his tie, which featured a pattern of tropical fish. Melanie had sent it to him shortly after she'd moved to Opa-Locka. He'd thought wearing a gift from her today would help him straighten out his head. Instead, he'd felt as if the tie were a noose, choking him.

He met Anita's disapproving gaze. "It's three," he said. "I'm supposed to be at Solly's by three-thirty. I've finished scheduling depositions for that Haitian family whose landlord keeps threatening to get them deported, and I've reviewed the settlement papers for the Branford Arms case. I'm getting my job done, okay?"

"Well, don't bite my head off, hey? Do I look like a jalapeño to you?"

"If you were a jalapeño, I definitely wouldn't bite your head off. Jalapeños make me sick."

"You're a grouch today, Joshua. Very testy. You know what I tell my son when he acts this way? I tell him, no more video games."

"I'll remember that," Josh promised.

"You didn't sleep well, right? I can tell. Shadows under your eyes, and that nasty temper."

"My temper is fine!" he exploded, then sighed. Even loosened, his tie pressed into his windpipe. Melanie's extended reach, he thought. She'd make him pay for last night by strangling him long distance with this Sea World tie.

Anita entered his office, frowning as she studied him. "What, you got problems with your love life?"

"My love life is fine, too," he lied. Christ. He'd gotten home at six forty-five that morning, showered, changed into business clothes and stared at his computer, all set up on a worktable in his bedroom. There would probably be a note from Melanie among his e-mails. She hadn't left a phone message on his answering machine, so she'd likely have sent him something via the computer, an electronic epistle informing him that her bones had melted into sludge from the heat and questioning him about where the hell he'd been all night.

Why bother with the e-mail? He could save time and effort by simply killing himself with the tie. *Loretta. Guilt.* He was in deep shit.

"Would you like this tie?" he asked, waving the tails at Anita, two strips of turquoise silk with manta rays and marlins and sunfish floating across them. He doubted the tie would choke Anita. If Melanie had imbued it with black magic, its voodoo properties would attack only him. "Look, I'm sorry about my temper. I've got to go. Everything is under control."

Anita shook her head and shrugged. "Suit yourself, Joshua. I think you're in trouble, but what do I know? I'm just your partner, your friend, someone who cares about you."

"I promise I'll stay away from video games," he said, scooping his jacket from the back of his chair and following her out of his office.

He caught the subway uptown and emerged from the

station near Solly's building to discover that a warm drizzle had begun to leak from the low, gray clouds. It matched his mood, which—as bad as Anita had considered it—was getting worse by the second. He suspected Loretta was going to be at this taping, and she was the last person he wanted to see.

No, that wasn't true. He did want to see her. Desperately. The way he'd seen her last night, and yesterday. The way he'd seen her at her parents' house and his mother's house, with her wry humor and her determination, her refusal to knuckle under to her family, her insistence on following her own heart.

He wasn't being fair to Melanie, he wasn't being honorable, but damn it, if he followed his heart it would lead him straight to Loretta. All the loud weeknight bashes, all the Gloria Estefan CDs, all the mysterious friends and dinner parties Melanie had been hosting didn't justify the fact that while she was away, he'd fallen for another woman. If he hadn't slept with Loretta last night, it might have taken him a little longer to figure this out. But after last night...

Christ. Merely thinking about seeing Loretta at Solly's apartment gave him a hard-on. He was so hot, just from the knowledge that he'd be in her presence in a few minutes, that he half expected the raindrops to hiss as they struck his skin.

But he couldn't let Loretta know he still wanted her. Last night had been a one-shot deal. Well, maybe half a dozen shots—he hadn't been counting—but not the start of something big. They'd both agreed to those terms, and he'd better not forget it.

Steeling himself, he marched down the street to Solly's building, identified himself to the doorman and gained entry. Riding the elevator, he prayed for the air-conditioning to cool him down. He was here not to see Loretta but to hold Solly's hand. A favor for a friend, that was all.

A favor necessary because Loretta had conned him into this whole stupid show about passionate senior citizens.

Solly responded to his doorbell almost immediately. "Oh, Josh, thank God you're here," he said, ushering Josh inside. "It's a madhouse."

Not quite a madhouse, but the living room was a bustling scene. The cameraman who'd filmed his blind date with Loretta was there, a large camera balanced on his shoulder and coils of black cable covering the floor at his feet. Becky Blake waltzed out of the bathroom, her face cosmetically polished and her hair buoyantly blond. Dora Lee sat in a wheelchair, dressed in a skirt and an embroidered cotton sweater, her right leg propped up and encased in a molded plastic brace. Her mouth was open, and she was prying her lips apart to display her teeth to Loretta, who nodded sympathetically. "That's really small," she assured Dora Lee, then glanced over toward Solly to see who had arrived. She flashed Josh a brief, noncommittal grin and turned back to Dora Lee. "It looks like a chip, not a crack. That's a very easy repair. They just fill it in with some porcelain. The trick is to get the porcelain to match your tooth enamel. But it's not a big job at all. Not like a cap or a crown."

"It feels funny, is the thing," Dora Lee said modestly. "My tongue just keeps wandering over there. Like this." She demonstrated, sliding her tongue over her front uppers.

"Well, once it's fixed that won't be a problem." Loretta straightened up, shot Josh another hesitant smile and then addressed everyone. "Okay, I think we should get started. Solly, I'm going to need you to leave the room. We're going to have Becky interview Dora Lee alone first, and then interview you alone, and then we'll see about getting you two together."

"What are you saying? I'm an exile in my own home?" Solly asked. He attempted a smile, but his eyes churned with worry.

"Just for a few minutes," Loretta assured him. "Could you wait in another room? Would that be really bad?"

He shrugged. "I could go in the den. I've got lots of *Seinfeld* reruns on tape, I could watch one. Josh, you come with me. We'll watch an old *Seinfeld*, okay?"

Josh didn't want to watch an old *Seinfeld*. He wanted to watch Loretta, who spoke with such authority and seemed so marvelously in control. He didn't feel the least bit in control, and he resented that she was apparently suffering no aftereffects from last night.

But he'd come here for Solly, and if Solly wanted him to watch *Seinfeld* reruns...well, what were friends for? Reluctantly, he followed Solly into the apartment's second bedroom, which had been converted into a den. Solly fussed with the VCR for a few minutes, mumbling about the episode in which George's fiancée died from licking the glue on envelope flaps. Josh wandered to the doorway and peeked out into the living room.

Becky sat on a chair next to Dora Lee. The cameraman stood about ten feet away, with Loretta positioned next to him. She'd armed herself with a large spiral-bound pad, which she held up so Becky could read something on it.

"Is the lighting okay, Glenn?" Loretta asked the cameraman.

"Lighting's fine. I'm gonna need the lady in the wheelchair to speak a little louder, though."

"Can you do that, Dora Lee?" Loretta asked. "Can you speak a little louder?"

"I don't know." Dora Lee sighed heavily. "I have a broken leg."

"Well, that shouldn't affect your voice," Loretta said, her tone gentle.

"And my tongue. It just keeps going to that tooth."

"Well, do your best." She held the pad higher and Becky began reading from it in her effervescent voice.

"Here it is," Solly called to him from the depths of the den. "The one where George's girlfriend drops dead. A very funny episode."

Josh nodded but remained where he was at the doorway. "Other than your leg and your tooth, Dora Lee, how do you feel?" Becky asked while Loretta scribbled furiously on the pad and then flipped it over for Becky to see.

"Other than my leg and my tooth, how should I feel?" Dora Lee responded.

Becky's smile hardened. "Now, you've said Phyllis Yellin pushed you into a car."

"I haven't *said* it," Dora Lee corrected her. "It's what she did."

Loretta scribbled some more, and held the pad up. "Why do you think she did it?"

"Why? Because I cook for Solly. She doesn't like I should cook for him."

"You think she pushed you into a car because you cook for Solly?" Becky blurted, not bothering to read the cue card Loretta had written for her.

"She wants Solly all to herself. She can't stand it that, God forbid, he might like my cooking." Dora Lee flicked her tongue over her front teeth. "It feels funny," she explained, then added, "I'm a better cook than Phyllis."

"If she were in the room right now, Dora Lee," Becky read off the pad, "what would you say to her?"

"I would say, 'Go away.'"

Becky's expression implied that she considered Dora Lee's answer reasonable. Josh did, too. His gaze drifted back to Loretta, her hair thick and slightly frizzy, her shoulders, arms and fingers in perpetual motion as she simultaneously absorbed Dora Lee's statements and jotted new questions for Becky to ask. She was amazing.

Hell, even if she hadn't been feeding Becky lines she'd be amazing.

We're in trouble, aren't we, he thought, then turned to see Solly lounging in a leather sling chair, guffawing over something on TV. "This is hilarious, Josh! You ever see this episode? George is all set to marry this girl, and she—"

"I know." Josh had indeed seen the episode, and he managed a smile for Solly. As he recalled the show, George didn't really want to marry the woman, but he was committed to her, and then she had an allergic reaction to the glue on the envelopes for their wedding invitations, and she died. And George, whose secret wish had come true, felt pleased and guilty all at once.

Josh didn't wish Melanie dead. Of course not. They'd known each other for over two years, shared significant chunks of each other's lives, understood each other, practically lived together until she'd moved to Florida. Josh wanted only the best for her. He was an honest, upright guy. Nothing like George.

He peeked through the doorway once more, in time to see Loretta brush a heavy lock of hair back from her face. He glimpsed her jawline, her throat, the smooth surface of her cheek. And he felt pleased and guilty, all at once.

Oh, yeah, he was in big trouble.

Seventeen

Wasn't this cute. She and Josh, facing each other across a tiny round table in an overcrowded bar with sticky-sweet Enya music and the eager chatter of prowling singles clogging the air, Josh in possession of a Sam Adams, and Loretta a gin-and-tonic. Their surly waitress couldn't be bothered bringing them any bar snacks, so Loretta was stuck fiddling with her straw, repeatedly poking the wedge of lime in her glass below the surface of the bubbly liquid and watching it bob back up.

She'd agreed to have a drink with him once they'd finished taping at Solly's place. Of course she had—why wouldn't she? They were friends, weren't they?

Never before had the concept of friendship made her so uncomfortable.

The glass-front wall of the bar was streaked and smudged from the drizzle outside. The sidewalk glistened. Her hair felt like a bale of hay on her neck, coarse and scratchy.

Josh picked at the label on his bottle with his thumbnail. He looked as uncomfortable as she felt. Why had he asked her to join him for a drink if he had nothing to say?

As it turned out, he did have something to say—only what he had to say she didn't want to hear. "About last night—"

"No." She all but pressed her hands to her ears to block out his voice. "I don't want to talk about it. I don't want to think about it. It's past, it's over, it's old news. It doesn't matter. Forget it.''

His eyes widened slightly, but she'd managed to shut him up. Now she was stuck with silence. She struggled for something to say. She ought to be able to share a pleasant conversation with him without having her stomach launch into a gymnastics routine. She and Josh were supposed to be *friends,* after all.

''So,'' she said, recalling the early stiltedness of their alleged blind date. This was worse—probably because there was nothing blind about it. She'd seen him. She'd seen every square inch of him, naked and aroused and vulnerable. A little blindness would have come in handy right about now, if it could have kept her from remembering how wonderful he'd looked last night.

''So,'' he echoed, obviously feeling as awkward as she did.

''So I'm figuring we'll tape Phyllis tomorrow,'' she said. ''I don't know if Solly's going to want to be there. I do know her lawyer is. He doesn't want her to appear on the show, but since she insisted, he decided he ought to be there. We're taping in his office.''

''That won't be very homey.''

''It won't be homey at all. But those were the terms. We're lucky to get the interview at all.'' She sipped some of her drink. The tonic left a bitter aftertaste on her tongue. ''Then I want to do some filming at the senior center. For context, and also to get some observations by people who know all the involved parties.''

''That sounds like a good plan,'' Josh said woodenly.

If he was sulking—and he seemed to be—she would be royally pissed. It was all his fault they couldn't be lovers, after all. He was the one with the goddamn girlfriend. Sure, Loretta had sworn to him that she wasn't in the market for a romance, but she might have reconsidered that policy after making love with him—if Josh had said anything about reconsidering his relationship with Melanie. But he hadn't. He apparently wasn't interested in ending that relationship. So okay, fine, he and Loretta wouldn't be lovers. They were still *friends,* though. That had been part of the deal last night, as she'd understood it: that no matter what, they'd still be friends.

If he wanted to remain her friend, he'd better not sulk, that was all. She hated sulkers.

He took another sip of beer, then said, "I've taken on a new case." He seemed to be exerting himself, shaping each syllable carefully, but at least he was talking, forcing the words past his mood.

"What's it about?"

"The Charnier family is from Haiti. They complained to the landlord about the lack of hot water and he threatened to have them deported."

"That sucks."

"So I took the case. The landlord is a turd. I'm going to have fun cutting him to bits."

"Bits of turd," Loretta pondered. "Yuck."

"That's what he'll be saying when I'm through with him. Yuck."

The conversation was flowing more smoothly now. They were talking the way they always talked. Loretta relaxed in her chair—not easy to do, since the chair's back was too short and the upholstery was about as thick as the gauze square at the center of a plastic bandage strip. But listening to Josh describe Henri Charnier and his wife, his two sisters, his mother and his three daughters made up for the uncomfortable seating. "He's the only man in the house," Josh said. "Not that I'm a sexist or anything, but he told me the bathroom reeks of perfume and hair spray, and the air is always vibrating with high-pitched voices, all talking at the same time. He said he wanted to buy a male dog, but the landlord would deport him if he did.''

''So, what? He hangs out with his buddies somewhere else?''

''As best I could gather—given his accent, he's sometimes a little hard to understand—he locks himself into the master bedroom every day and turns on ESPN so he can hear men's voices. He's not into sports—he asked me what the point of football was, and I had to tell him it really didn't have a point. But he just loves those announcers.''

They sipped their drinks. They talked about another case Josh had handled, and about Solly and Dora Lee and how Loretta thought the afternoon's taping had gone: ''Really well, all things considered. Becky can read almost as fast as I can write.''

''You were great, feeding her all those lines,'' Josh said, a genuine smile warming his face.

''Oh, please. They were such basic questions, I don't know why she couldn't have thought of them herself. I mean, come on! 'What happened?' 'Why do you think it happened?' Pretty basic stuff.''

''She needs you,'' Josh declared. ''She couldn't possibly fire you. She'd fall apart without you.''

Loretta scowled. ''Anyone could have scribbled questions for her today. Of course, Kate's questions would have all been about the kind of food Dora Lee cooks for Solly. Kate's obsessed with food. And Bob would have written questions about how far Dora Lee and Solly had gone, stuff like that.''

''That would have embarrassed Dora Lee.''

''Bob can be a jerk.'' Her straw made a slurping sound as the level of liquid in her glass approached the bottom.

"So...speaking of the show, they want you and me to go back on."

"Go back on Becky Blake's show? What for?"

"So viewers can see how we turned out. Apparently, a lot of viewers have been inquiring."

Josh eyed her cautiously, his smile gone, his head tilted slightly. "Do you want us to go on?"

"No. Do you want to go on?"

He looked relieved. "God, no. I was afraid you were going to talk me into it, though."

"I don't talk you into things," Loretta protested.

"Right." He snorted a laugh. "You talked me into the original blind date, and helping you create a show around Solly and his harem, and pretending to be your boyfriend for your parents."

That last item might have been a mistake, but Loretta wouldn't apologize for the others. "I don't talk you into things you don't want to do," she argued. "Whatever I talked you into, it was just what you deep down really wanted to do, anyway."

He opened his mouth and then shut it, rethinking his response. "Maybe," he admitted quietly.

"Then we won't do the show."

"What about your job? If we don't go back on, will they fire you?"

Who knew? She'd proven her value that afternoon, simply by writing out elementary questions on the fly for Becky. If Becky recommended her for the ax after she'd helped to create this amazing show about Solly and his women, whether or not she and Josh made a follow-up appearance was irrelevant.

After all, what would they say if they *did* reappear on the show? "Our blind date was a success. We wound up sleeping together." Or: "Our blind date was a disaster. We wound up sleeping together.'' Or: ''We wound up sleeping together and we're never going to do it again, because Josh is a cheating bastard and I'm his accomplice, and isn't that the basis for a solid friendship?''

The world did not need to see her and Josh sharing a TV screen again. The sooner everyone forgot she and Josh had ever been linked, the better.

The sooner she and Josh forgot, the sooner they could get back to being the friends they used to be.

Maybe.

Josh entered his apartment, swung open the refrigerator and realized he didn't want a beer after all. He'd just had a beer with Loretta, and it had satisfied him about as much as a glass of unfiltered New York Harbor water might have. He was listless and tired—understandable, given how little sleep he'd gotten the night before. His head hurt. So did his heart.

The message light on his answering machine flashed, but all he heard on the tape were two hang-ups. Had Melanie tried to phone him, or were those messages the usual crap, strangers thinking he'd actually consider investing in un-monitored stock funds and Colorado steaks simply because they'd favored him with an unsolicited sales call?

He yanked off his tropical-fish necktie and stalked to his bedroom. Time to suck it up and check his e-mail. He turned on the computer, pried off his shoes and unbuttoned his shirt.

Three e-mails awaited him. One was from an old college buddy, just catching up. One was an invitation to view horny housewives in real time, if his software was Java-enhanced. And one was from Melanie.

He dropped onto his chair and opened her note:

Hi, Josh. Not much happening here. One of the Iglesiases is performing in Miami tonight and I'm going with some friends. I wish I could remember which Iglesias it is, but the heat is so bad here I'm convinced my brain has melted to the consistency of Vaseline. Is Iglesiases the plural of Iglesias, or do you think it might be Iglesii?

No accusations. No *Where were you last night?* Melanie was simply heading off to a concert by yet another musician she'd never listened to before she'd moved to Florida.

Did she miss Josh? Did she care? Was she as torn up about her flourishing social life as he was about his? Did her social life include anything resembling the night he'd spent with Loretta?

He was going to have to do something. He couldn't just keep things as they were. Simply going out for a casual drink with Loretta had been excruciating. But she'd made it quite clear that they couldn't return to where they'd been last night. And as far as he was concerned, not seeing each other at all wasn't an option.

With a groan, he dived onto his bed, pried off his shoes and listened to the hum of the air conditioner. After a minute, he picked up his phone. He needed to talk to a friend, one who'd been where he was now.

His call was answered on the second ring. "Hello?" said Solly.

"We've got to play chess," Josh announced.

"Josh! Chess, yes. That would be great. Today, with the filming, all that showbiz *meshugas,* right in my apartment, no less... Maybe we could play tomorrow? Or Wednesday? I could meet you at the center."

"What about Dora Lee? Can she be left alone?"

"Either that, or I'll bring her with me. It doesn't matter. What matters is, you and I need some chess."

"Tomorrow," Josh said, not bothering to check his schedule. If he had appointments, he'd cancel them. Chess was more important, especially if Solly mixed a little wisdom in with his moves. "Let's do it tomorrow."

"Cut it all off," Loretta said.

Donna's scowl bounced off the mirror and into Loretta's eyes. Loretta was seated in one of the chairs at Salon Louis, wrapped in a voluminous smock of silver plastic that made her feel a little like a ham swaddled in aluminum foil, ready for roasting. Donna stood behind her, fluffing her hair and frowning, as if Loretta looked even worse to her than she did to herself. "You're joking, right?" Donna asked.

"I'm sick of it. Just do something."

"You walk in here on a Saturday morning, no appointment, and you tell me to cut off all your hair? What, you've got PMS? I never change a client's hairstyle when she's got PMS."

"I don't have PMS."

"What have you got?"

Loretta sighed. "All right. Don't cut it all off. Just trim it or something. Fix it so that when you're all done I'll feel better about my life."

"Let's start with a shampoo." Donna slapped her on the shoulder, a little harder than necessary, and headed for the shampoo sinks at the rear of the salon. Loretta climbed out of the thronelike chair and followed her. The abundance of silver—wallpaper, fixtures, chrome trim and other clients, all as foil-swaddled as she was, made her dizzy. The air even smelled silvery, laced with a combination of lilac, ammonia, cinnamon, coffee and cigarette smoke. Smoking wasn't allowed in the salon, but the aroma clung to Donna.

"Sit," she ordered, shoving Loretta into a chair in front of a sink.

"Why are you mad at me?"

Donna nudged her head backward and blasted it with a spray of hot water. "Who says I'm mad at you?"

"If you're not mad at me, why are you parboiling my scalp?"

Donna begrudgingly adjusted the spray to a milder temperature. "I'm mad at you because you never listen to me."

"I do listen to you. You said I should cut my hair, and here I am, asking you to cut my hair."

"You're almost thirty years old," Donna reminded her. "And I bet you haven't done a damn thing with that cute Jewish lawyer."

I have so done a damn thing with him, Loretta responded silently. "We're friends."

"Friends! I gave you that teddy for a reason, Loretta." She plowed her fingers through Loretta's hair, massaging citrus-scented foam into it. Tiny bubbles of shampoo popped in Loretta's ears, sounding like crinkling paper. "You wanna be single all your life? You've got a live one on the line and you just want to throw him back in? What's wrong with you?"

"You want to know? Nothing's wrong with me. He's the one who has something wrong with him."

"From where I sit, he hasn't got a single damn thing wrong with him."

"He's got a girlfriend," Loretta retorted. Dumping some of her frustration on Donna felt good. More bubbles popped in her ears, a sharp, crunching sound. "Keep the shampoo out of my ears, would you?"

"He's got a girlfriend?"

"Yeah."

"Two-timing shit. Why did he agree to go on a blind date with you if he's got a girlfriend?"

"She lives far away. I guess he was lonely." Loretta didn't add that she'd twisted his arm, that she'd wanted him to do it *because* he had a girlfriend. Donna seemed annoyed enough at her as it was.

"Two-timing shit," Donna repeated, rinsing the shampoo out of Loretta's hair with a spray that was actually a comfortable temperature. "Okay, so you like him? You gotta go after him."

"Why?"

"Why should his girlfriend have him? You've got just as good a claim."

"No, I don't."

"Why not? He's not married, is he?"

"No."

"So you're not a home wrecker. If he wanted to be with her, he'd marry her. He didn't marry her because he's not sure. Go after him."

"What if I don't want him?"

Donna leaned over so she was staring straight down into Loretta's face. "You don't want that guy? With those eyes? And that body?"

"Donna—"

"And I'll tell you another thing." Donna leaned back and squirted something with a different citrus scent into Loretta's hair, grapefruit instead of orange. By the time Donna was done with her, she'd be smelling like fruit cocktail. "I've heard Jewish guys make the best lovers. Don't tell Lou I said that."

Loretta's personal experience with one Jewish guy supported Donna's assertion, but she didn't mention that. "Why do they make the best lovers?"

"I'd say it was because they're trimmed, you know?"

Loretta felt her cheeks warming at Donna's crude description. "But lotsa guys are trimmed, so that can't be the reason. What I think it is, is Jewish boys are raised to take care of women. It's like part of their culture."

"How do you know this?"

"Look where I work." She waved her sudsy hands around. "What do you think I do all day?"

"Style people's hair?"

"Listen to women bitch to me about their husbands. And I'm telling you, the Jewish women, they get taken care of. Their husbands take care of them, they take care of their mothers, they take care of their aunts, and they won't let any boys near their daughters unless they're absolutely positive that those boys will take good care of their precious little girls. Think about it. Did your father ever corner Gary and say, 'You gonna take care of my precious little girl?'"

"I would have killed him if he had."

"It doesn't matter. He wouldn't have done it. He looks at you and says, 'First single male willing to have her, I'll pay for the wedding.' Am I right?"

Donna had a point. Her father was more concerned with finding Loretta a husband than with finding her a considerate, honorable husband.

"So Jewish men make good fathers—"

"And they make good lovers," Donna insisted. "They take care. They do what they have to to make you happy. This is what all my Jewish clients tell me."

"Okay, so even assuming Jewish men make good lovers, why does it have to be Josh? Why can't I find another Jewish man?"

"A bird in the hand, honey." Donna nudged her upright and draped a towel around her wet hair. "A bird with a great body. Now, you don't really want me to cut it all off, do you?"

"No," Loretta admitted. "Just do something with it."

"I'll make you look so gorgeous Josh won't be able to resist you."

Loretta sighed and forced a smile as she followed Donna back to the chair, leaving a trail of water drops behind her on the silver-and-gray tiled floor. She was already irresistible to Josh—except that he'd managed to resist her. But that was her doing. She'd been the one to say no more, and he—being a truly considerate, protective representative of the Chosen People—was honoring her request.

Their friendship wasn't back to where it had been before, but it was improving. They talked on the phone. Josh had called her the evening after she'd produced Becky's interview with Phyllis Yellin, and they'd spent an hour discussing what a feisty lady Phyllis was. "She reminded me of one of those fighting roosters," Loretta said.

"She's the wrong gender to be a rooster."

"Yeah, but she's got the personality of one—ready to snap at opponents, and it was so easy to ruffle her feathers. She kept squawking, too. Her lawyer kept telling her not to talk, but she's got a real squawky voice."

"So when are you going to film at the senior center?"

"Maybe over the weekend. We've got to work all this in around our regular shows. And after we've got all the tape, I'm supposed to help Glenn edit it."

"Do you know anything about editing?"

"I didn't know anything about trash TV before I took this job. I didn't know anything about scripting on-the-fly interviews. I'm learning."

"You're doing great," Josh had said, although he'd had no basis for such a claim. It had just been the sort of encouraging statement friends told one another.

Another night, while she'd munched on ice cream, he'd regaled her with news about his client Henri Charnier. Apparently, the man had formed an all-Haitian-American doo-wop quartet so he could surround himself with male voices. They wanted to practice in the basement of the apartment building, in a room adjacent to the laundry room. The land-lord was threatening to deport them all. Henri believed that if his singing group could get a gig at the Apollo, the land-lord would be so impressed he'd leave Henri and his family alone. "Maybe you could get his group to appear on the *Becky Blake Show*," Josh had joked, but Loretta hadn't laughed. She'd thought it was a damn good idea, actually.

Being friends was easy enough when all they did was talk on the phone. If they couldn't see each other, if they weren't in touching distance, they could handle it. But she missed him. Eating Ben & Jerry's by herself wasn't as much fun as sharing it with him, two spoons digging into one container.

Thursday night he'd called and told her he was going to Florida. "I'm flying down on Saturday," he'd informed her.

"You're going to visit Melanie?" She'd kept her voice as smooth and cool as the ice cream she'd been shoveling into her mouth.

"Yeah."

A long silence ensued. What was she supposed to say? "Have fun! Don't forget to pack your rubbers!"

Damn it, he was going to see his girlfriend and patch things up with her. And if Loretta was as good a friend to him as she claimed to be, she'd wish him a safe trip. She'd be happy he was traveling all that way just to make sure everything was copacetic with his sweetie. She'd told Josh to forget about any romance between them, and that was what he was doing, and she ought to be glad.

"It's going to be hot there," she'd said.

"That's all Melanie ever tells me about the place."

"You'd better bring a swimsuit. And sunblock." *And your rubbers, you asshole.*

"I'm not—I don't know how much swimming I'll get to do. She doesn't live on the beach or anything. And really, I'm going down there because she and I need to see each other, face-to-face."

So you can kiss. So you can do to her all those wonderful, wicked face-to-face things you did to me. Loretta had never considered herself a jealous person, but suddenly she was drowning in jealousy, being sucked down by it as if it were a treacherous riptide. She'd once gotten caught in a powerful undertow at Rockaway Beach, but a beefy, sunburned lifeguard had spotted her getting dragged away from the shore and had raced out into the water with a boogieboard. She'd gripped it, then gripped him, and he'd kept shouting, "Put your feet down, put your feet down," and to her surprise she'd discovered the water was only about four feet deep.

Jealousy seemed much more dangerous. Jealousy because some other woman was going to wind up with the man you'd turned away was not only dangerous but stupid.

Perhaps getting her hair cut was stupid, too. Perhaps it was dangerous. But Donna knew what she was doing, at least when it came to hair. When it came to advice for the lovelorn, Loretta wasn't so sure.

"I'm only going to give it a little shape," Donna assured her. "Nothing drastic. I never do anything drastic when a client's got PMS."

"I *don't*—" Loretta cut herself off. Let Donna think she had PMS. It was better than having her think Loretta was an idiot for wishing Josh a *bon voyage* as he flew down to Opa-Locka to see his girlfriend.

She ought to act like Phyllis, she thought, strutting around like a fighting cock, sharpening her beak and wearing a blade on her leg. Or like Dora Lee, blunt and unaffected, stating exactly what she meant and requesting exactly what she wanted.

Right. She could be like Phyllis and Dora Lee, settling for half of Josh the way they each settled for half of Solly Hirschbaum. Forget that. She'd rather have nothing than half.

Although nothing seemed pretty pathetic. She was twenty-nine, she was single, she had turned away the best lover she'd ever had and tried to convince herself his friendship would be enough to satisfy her.

God, she was stupid, she thought as Donna lifted her scissors and snipped.

Eighteen

Christ, it was hot. To say it was hotter than hell would be euphemistic. It was hotter than hell multiplied by the temperature at the core of the sun.

The air rippled before him as he stood outside the terminal in the waiting area for cabs. Melanie had explained why she wouldn't be able to pick him up at the airport, but the heat burned away his memory of her reason. If pressed, he might remember his own name, but not much else.

It wasn't just hot. It was wet-hot. Within ten seconds of his stepping outside, a layer of damp sealed his skin like cellophane wrap. He could scarcely breathe. If a cab didn't come along soon—an air-conditioned cab—he would suffocate. No, he would *drown*. He would get poached like an egg. They'd find his soggy, scalded body under the concrete awning, the shade of which failed to moderate the air temperature or humidity. His last meal would have been an unevenly microwaved chicken breast, smaller than a playing card and served on dried rice with red things in it—pimento, the flight attendant had claimed—and the last thing he saw would have been the precariously tilting royal palms at the far end of the driveway leading away from this terminal of Miami International Airport.

A cab pulled up to the queue, and a lanky fellow with a Spanish accent markedly different from the Spanish accents that abounded in Manhattan waved him over. "You want a cab, *señor*?"

Josh wanted an igloo, but he managed a nod and wheeled his carry-on over to the cab. The windows were shut. A promising sign.

He swooned into the back seat, slammed the door behind him and gulped in the cool air. *Thank you, God,* he murmured, although he supposed the cabbie deserved some thanks as well. It took him several deep breaths to recover enough to read Melanie's address off the index card he'd tucked into the chest pocket of his polo shirt.

"Opa-Locka? Shee', you goin' all the way to Opa-Locka?" the cabbie grumbled. He was a skinny, jive guy with elaborately braided hair. His shirt was constructed of a shiny fabric so brightly colored it hurt Josh's eyes. Unfortunately, his sunglasses were packed into his carry-on and he lacked the energy to unzip it.

"Yes. I'm going all the way to Opa-Locka," he said.

"Well, okay, I guess. We got these rates, see—"

"Just take me there, okay?"

"I wanna get it straight up front. We got these rates."

"I understand. I have every intention of paying those rates."

"All right, then." The cabbie pulled away from the curb and into the traffic circling madly around the terminal.

I have died and gone to hell, Josh thought as more palm trees loomed into view. Did people actually think palm trees were attractive? They looked like something Dr. Seuss might have designed while under the influence of bad drugs.

In Florida less than a half hour, and already he was homesick—and not just for the trees of his hometown. What he missed most were the people back in New York. One person in particular. All he had to do was close his eyes and a vision of her face filled his mind. Her face and her long legs and her dark, dark eyes. Judgmental eyes. Condemning eyes. And a mouth that had told him, more than once, that she was not interested in a romance.

He was doing the right thing, damn it. He was here to see Melanie, to tell her he'd met someone else—who might have no interest in building a relationship with him, but that didn't change his understanding of the fact that his relationship with Melanie was over. Any other man would have sent her an e-mail or left a phone message—or not left any message at all, just cut off all communication. Any other *sane* man would have handled it that way. But Josh had chosen to be honorable.

Actually, he hadn't really had a choice. He'd been so swamped with guilt that the only way he could end his relationship with Melanie was the hard way. It had to be inconvenient for him if it was going to count. It had to be painful. If breaking up with her didn't make him at least as uncomfortable as a case of weeping poison ivy, he'd never be able to overcome his guilt.

The cab cruised past stucco buildings, shotgun shacks, low, rectangular structures that sat in clusters along the highway like the landscape painting of a cubist who'd run out of every color of paint except the palest pastels. It cruised past tall palms, short palms, scruffy palms and shrubby palms. It cruised past grass that had shriveled in the heat, past vivid turquoise swimming pools, past billboards featuring pictures of towering hotels beside curving white beaches, and restaurants offering early-bird specials, and voluptuous women in swimsuits so skimpy the models must have sunbathed nude to avoid tan lines.

Did Melanie wear skimpy bikinis like those on the billboards, with push-up bras and thong bottoms? Did she sunbathe nude? Might he see her, glowing an even, all-over

copper, and forget what he'd come to Florida to do? He
was only human, after all. He was only a man, which
placed him among the lower order of Homo sapiens. A sexy
woman with a gorgeous, sun-darkened complexion—in a
thong bikini—well, he might not be able to control himself.

He closed his eyes against the merciless midday sunshine, rested one arm atop his suitcase to keep it from sliding into him as the cab zigged and zagged through highway
lanes, and tried to remember everything Solly had told him.
"Everyone here," he'd said, gesturing toward the others
sharing the lounge with them at the senior center, where
they'd been playing chess, "they all love Melanie. They
adore her. And no question, she's a fine girl. She did a
wonderful job when she was here. Speaking of which, remember Phyllis has been banned from the senior center,
pending? She's very upset about this. You think you could
pull some strings?"

"Me? What strings could I pull?"

"You and Melanie were an item, Josh."

"But Melanie isn't here anymore. She doesn't make the
rules."

"You could talk to the new director, Francine, and tell
her maybe she could let Phyllis back in."

"Why would Francine listen to me? I've never even met
her."

"One, you're a lawyer. Two, you and Melanie. I should
warn you, Josh, you don't want to move your knight there.
You move it, and you'll regret it for the rest of this game—
which won't last much longer."

Josh gave the board intense scrutiny and released his
knight without moving it. He already regretted enough in
his life. "I don't know what I'd say to Francine."

"Say something legal. Heretofore. *Nolo contendre.*
You'll think of something."

"Do you really think Phyllis should be back at the center? She nearly killed Dora Lee."

"Assuming she pushed her. This is America. Innocent until proven guilty."

"Wait a minute." Josh leaned back in his chair and gave Solly even more intense scrutiny than he'd given the chessboard. "You're living with Dora Lee and defending Phyllis. How can you play both sides so easily?"

"Who said any of this is easy? My heart is breaking, Josh." Solly looked about as heartbroken as Roger Clemens after pitching a shutout. "Two wonderful women, and I care for them both."

"Not to mention your ballerina friend."

"Not to mention her," Solly agreed. "I'm not playing both sides. I'm playing no sides. I want all my women to be happy." Solly smiled sadly. "What do you think? I'm a *meshugena* old man?"

"I don't think you're a *meshugener*. I think you've got some unrealistic goals."

"And you're a realist?"

"Yeah."

"Then get real, as my grandson would say. You want Loretta, am I right? One look at you and I see it oozing out of you, all this want. You're crazy about her."

"I like her," Josh allowed. He couldn't bring himself to admit he was crazy about her. He'd cop to crazy, period.

"She's a fine girl, too, that Loretta. Not Jewish, am I right?"

"No, she's not."

"There are worse things in this world. When I was a young man, my father always said, 'Those *shiksas*—woo-woo!'"

"Woo-woo? Your father said woo-woo?"

"I knew what he meant. You know what he means, too."

Unfortunately, Josh did. And while he wasn't sure "woo-woo" described Loretta D'Angelo, it came pretty close to describing the way he felt about her.

The cabbie performed a death-defying pass before veering off the highway and down a ramp. A red light stopped him, and Josh had to cling to his suitcase to keep it from slamming into the back of the driver's seat. "What's that address again?" the driver asked.

Josh read it, his voice betraying none of his tension.

"I gotta tell you, man, I don't know Opa-Locka real well."

"Neither do I," Josh muttered.

The light turned green, and the cab rolled through the intersection. Not knowing Opa-Locka real well apparently wasn't going to stop the driver from traveling its roads. As he steered, he pulled a cell phone from his pocket and punched in a number. "Tito? Hey, 's me. Yeah. Hey, man, you got a road map of Opa-Locka lying around? I need some navigational assistance here."

Josh glowered at the cell phone. He should be grateful the driver had one; with Tito's guidance, the guy might actually deliver Josh to the apartment complex where Melanie lived. But still, on principle... A professional driver ought to know his way around Opa-Locka. If he didn't, he shouldn't be licensed to operate a cab.

The driver babbled into his cell phone. "You sure? A right turn? Looks like a one-way street to me..." followed by gales of laughter. Josh wished he could share the driver's mirth, but he was entertaining visions of a head-on collision in the middle of that one-way street. He had visions of a head-on collision with Melanie, too. The longer the driver meandered along the steaming roads of this Miami suburb, the more time Josh would have to prepare what he was going to say to Melanie.

Which was...what? *Hi, I'm here to break up with you.*

Hi, you're looking great, I'm glad you're happy, I'm here to break up with you.

Hi, I'm pretty sure I loved you, but you left New York and I met someone else, so have a good life—and the plural would be Iglesiases.

Hi, it's great to see you, I've missed you, I slept with another woman, but hey, I'm here, it's been a long trip so what the hell, right? Just this once, for old time's sake...

Damn. Maybe he ought to have the cabbie turn the car around and bring him back to the airport. Then he could fly home and break up with Melanie the way a sane, guilt-free person would: by e-mail, long-distance, without eye contact.

He couldn't do that, though. It wouldn't be right. If he felt guilty now, he'd feel twice as guilty ending their relationship the coward's way.

Besides, there was a chance—a small chance, but still—that he'd see her and remember why he'd come so close to using the word *love* with her as recently as a few months ago. Right around the same time Loretta was getting ditched by her fiancé, Melanie was contemplating whether to accept the job offer in Florida and Josh was contemplating whether to convince her not to accept it by using that four-letter word. Something real had existed between them then. He couldn't deny it. And he had to see her, in person, in the flesh, to make sure it didn't still exist.

"You kiddin'? Okay, I'll do that," the driver said into his cell phone. "I'm at the corner now. There's a Mickey D at the corner—that's right."

I'm somewhere on Long Island, maybe Westbury. Josh recalled that dimwit on the train, pinpointing her location to the nearest railroad tie for the benefit of someone on the receiving end of her cell phone call. He remembered Loretta sitting across from him during that Sunday evening ride, the wild ripples of her hair, a book open in her lap and her expression a mixture of exasperation and amusement. He recalled thinking, *This cell phone ninny is irritating her as much as she's irritating me. I bet that dark-haired woman would be impressed if I took action.* So he'd taken action.

And look where that had gotten him: trapped in the back seat of a cab driven by a cell phone ninny.

More sprawling stucco buildings. More minimalls and traffic lights. Then the driver cruised onto a driveway that led into a complex of two-story buildings nestled among palm trees and palm shrubs and bushes with obscenely red blossoms erupting from their branches. "This is it," the driver announced.

Josh paid the driver an outrageous sum, hauled his bag out of the vehicle and walked up to the door that bore Melanie's address. He rang the bell, felt heat roasting his back and glimpsed a skinny brown lizard skittering across the red tile walkway. He was used to mice, cockroaches and pigeons. Lizards gave him the creeps.

The door swung open to reveal a woman he recognized as Melanie. Not the Melanie who'd left New York three months ago, however. A different Melanie. An Opa-Locka Melanie.

She must have paid a visit to the local Salon de les Marines, because her fluffy blond chin-length hair had been shorn into a buzz cut. He'd never before realized how long her neck was, but now it was naked, exposed to the elements. So were her earlobes, which bore more holes than he'd remembered. Last year for Hanukkah, he'd given her diamond stud earrings. Given how much they'd cost, he was glad she'd only had two holes to fill back then.

Her eyes hadn't changed much, but her eyebrows had

been plucked and shaped so they arched thin and high, lending her a startled appearance. Her smile was the same, though. He used to love kissing those lips.

Now he watched them shape words: "Josh! Hi! Did you have any trouble finding the place? Come on in—get out of the heat."

That sounded like a great idea. He stepped inside and she shut the door behind him. The cool interior air sent a chill down his sweat-damp back and he struggled not to shiver.

He continued to study Melanie. There was a lot to see, since she was dressed rather scantily in a filmy minidress with a halter top. She was still slim, but her skin was a bit darker. Not as dark as that of the models in the thong bikinis on the billboards, but getting there. Her feet were bare, and she'd painted her toenails green.

"Hello, hello!" she said so perkily he suffered a fresh surge of guilt. She seemed pleased to see him. He ought to pretend he was pleased, too.

"You look great," he said, not sure how much of a lie that was. Just so she'd believe him, he kissed her cheek and then presented her with a smile.

She smiled back. "You hate my hair."

"There's not much of it to hate." He cautiously lifted one hand to touch her crew cut. It felt bristly, like indoor-outdoor carpeting. "No, really, you look good."

"How was your flight?"

He shrugged and followed her into a living room decorated in a tropical motif—rattan furniture with floral-patterned cushions, potted plants, strawlike matting on the floor and a swirling white-bladed ceiling fan that might have been a leftover prop from the set of *Casablanca*. A stack of magazines sat on a corner table. Josh could only hope they wouldn't come into play during his visit. He could just imagine her reading him some magazine article about two-timing SOBs, or about women's castration fantasies, as a way to facilitate their dialogue.

"My flight stank," he said honestly. "And it's so damn hot here—"

"I've been telling you," Melanie reminded him. "You want something cold to drink?"

"I'll take a Sam Adams."

She cringed, then smiled sheepishly. "I haven't got any, Josh. I forgot. Would you like a Michelob?"

Michelob? He never drank Michelob. How long had they been together? She knew Sam Adams was his drink, and he'd traveled all the way from New York City to see her, and she hadn't even thought to pick up a couple of Sam Adams beers. If she'd traveled to New York City to see him, he would for damn sure have stocked up on Beringer Chardonnay for her.

Michelob. Well, if her haircut hadn't proven that she'd changed beyond redemption, her failure to have a bottle of Sam Adams on hand did.

Reluctantly, he followed her into her efficiency kitchen. While she pulled a beer out of the refrigerator, he scanned the small room: Formica counters, the usual complement of appliances, a huge bowl of oranges, grapefruit and bananas beside the toaster, a tube of sunblock on the windowsill, a wall phone. Was that where she'd talked to him when he'd called her during her midweek party? How far would the phone's cord stretch? Into the vestibule, maybe. All that rattan furniture had been filled with yakking guests, and the components of her small but apparently effective stereo system stood on a series of shelves in the living room, visible because a counter was the only barrier between the kitchen and living room, one section of which formed a dining nook. As soon as he had his beer, he ought to check out her CD collection, to see how many Ricky Martin CDs she'd added in the past three months.

After prying open the cap on his beer, she fixed herself a rum-and-pineapple-juice. Not chardonnay. In New York...

Forget New York. She wasn't in New York anymore. Josh had journeyed all this way to ascertain that, and now he knew.

"I came here to break up with you," he blurted out.

She spun around to face him. Her bare feet squeaked on the tile floor and her eyes looked doubly large without any hair framing her face. "You did?"

He couldn't tell if she was upset or simply surprised. Or maybe only surprised that he'd stated his mission so bluntly. Maybe the actual mission didn't surprise her at all.

They went back into the living room. Melanie gravitated to the stereo; Josh, to the window that overlooked the grassy courtyard, around which stood apartment buildings nearly identical to Melanie's. The grass was the same color as her toenail polish. Would it blend in if she walked barefoot outside, creating the illusion that she had holes at the tips of her toes?

"I thought you were coming down to see me," she said.

"I am. I did. I'm here."

"So you think we should break up?"

He felt guilty for having stated his case without couching it in gentle terms and flattery. But if he'd resorted to soft touches and compliments, he'd have felt guilty for beating around the bush. It was clearly a no-win situation for him, guiltwise.

She stared at him, looking neither thrilled nor despairing. In fact, she looked kind of pretty, her hair glinting like a gold velvet swimming cap. "Why the hell did you come all the way down here to tell me that? I mean, haven't you ever heard of the telephone?''

"Well—"

"Or e-mail?"

"I thought of that, Melanie. But given our history, I thought the least I owed you was to do this in person."

"And maybe—" she approached him, her footsteps making crunchy sounds on the straw rug "—you thought you should check me out one final time and see if there was anything left between us."

Melanie wasn't a social worker for nothing. She could read people's motivations the way most people read the newspaper. She was probably right about his decision to travel to Florida. He had to see her one more time to be sure.

Her insight caused his resolution to falter slightly. Her intuition had been one of the things he'd admired about her. Her knowing smile—the smile she was wearing right now—was another. Her willingness to call it as she saw it was another. Her hair... Well, that would grow back.

But she was in Florida. She seemed to have embraced the place, if her home decor and that summery little sprite dress were anything to judge by. "Are you planning to return to New York?" he asked.

"Of course. My folks live in Westchester."

"I don't mean for visits. I mean to live."

She shrugged. "How should I know? I've only been here a few months, Josh. I'm just beginning to get used to it. Except the heat. I'll never get used to that."

"But you like it here? You must. You've made friends."

"Well, duh. Was I supposed to not make friends?"

"You weren't *supposed* to do anything. Or not do anything. All I'm saying is, your life is here now, and my life is still in New York."

"And you wouldn't be interested in moving down here?"

"To live around all those palm trees?" He made a face. "They're disgusting."

Melanie frowned. "What's disgusting about palm trees?"

"I don't know. They're so—Mesozoic."

"Mesozoic? Josh." She laughed in disbelief. "Only you."

"Only me what?"

"Only you would use Mesozoic in casual conversation like that. Okay, look." She closed the distance between them, slung an arm around his waist and smiled up at him. "You're a very sweet man, you know? Coming all the way down here on a flight that stank just to tell me you want me out of your life—"

"I never said—"

"Which, as it happens, I already pretty much am."

"That was never my choice."

"It's your choice now."

"Because you dumped it on me. You took this job. You left."

"So it's my fault?"

Insinuating that he blamed her was an effective way of stoking his guilt. "No, it's not your fault," he said quickly, fending off the rush of remorse. "It's nobody's fault. It's just what happens when two people live twelve hundred miles apart."

"Right. No argument." She hugged him. She wore some exotic scent—he didn't know enough about perfumes to identify it, but it was fresh and fruity. "So here we are. Breaking up."

"I'll always think of you as a friend," he said, because he thought he should.

She laughed. "Don't quote clichés to me. Give me a kiss for old time's sake."

He did. They'd been lovers, after all. They'd been in love, practically. One kiss—he owed her that much.

It turned into quite a kiss. He kept his eyes open, and they crossed slightly as he focused on her half-inch hair, but even without long tresses for him to twine his fingers through, she still kissed with exquisite effectiveness. One thing that hadn't changed was her tongue, which had been, arguably, his favorite of all her organs. Given the way she was kissing him, it remained at the top of his list.

God, it was hot in Florida.

"You have a problem?" she murmured, leaning back and peering up at him.

"Yeah," he said. He probably shouldn't have opted for honesty, but he hadn't journeyed all this way to lie to her. His problem got worse when she leaned farther back and angled her pelvis into his. "I don't want to do this, Melanie."

"Sure you do."

"Sure I do," he agreed, drawing as far back as he could. She still had her arms around his waist, and it would be rude to wrench himself out of her embrace. But they didn't need all that groin contact. It wasn't helping matters at all. "We already know what that's about, Melanie. We were good together. But we're not together anymore."

"Well, I don't know about you, but I haven't had sex in three months. And if you really think of me as a friend—"

At that moment, a friend was the last thing he thought of her as. Fresh guilt washed over him like a massive wave on one of those nearby beaches—the ones filled with sharks. Melanie hadn't had sex in three months, but he had. Oh, yes, he most definitely had. And that was one of the reasons he was here right now.

Ah, the irony. This attractive—except for her haircut—woman whom he'd known for years and whom he'd at one time even considered in the context of marriage wanted to use him sexually, and he was feeling like a put-upon virgin desperate to protect his chastity. Yet he was the one who'd made love to someone else. She was the chaste one.

"Look, Melanie, let's just…" Carefully, gradually, he extricated himself from her.

"Let's just what?"

"Be friends. Talk. You can give me the grand tour of Opa-Locka. You can show me where you work. I'll take you out for a very nice expensive dinner. Whatever you want. But let's not fall into bed, okay? I came here for a reason. Don't derail me."

"Is that what I was doing? Derailing you?" She seemed to think this was hilarious. Buoyant laughter spilled from her lips. "Okay, I'll give you the grand tour, and you can spend a fortune wining and dining me. If we wind up in bed tonight, it won't be because we fell. How does that sound?"

Not as definitive as he would have liked. But he didn't want to argue with her, he didn't want to defend his non-existent virtue to her, and he definitely didn't want to get into a discussion of how he'd happened to have sex within the past three months, how he found himself, just minutes after kissing Melanie, wishing he were with Loretta.

"It sounds fine," he mumbled, promising himself that during the grand tour, he would find a clean, safe-looking motel and book himself a room for the night.

Central Park felt like a carnival to Loretta—too many people, but they kept moving and they seemed friendly enough. The usual midway attractions abounded: jugglers, step dancers, a blues guitarist, a semiorganized Ultimate

Frisbee game, dogs wearing bandannas, men wearing do-rags, women sunbathing on blankets on the grass, skate-boarders and in-line skaters gliding by.

Loretta wondered how protective of Solly she should be. He was significantly older than most of the people enjoying a sunny Saturday afternoon in the park, but he was light on his feet. Coming here had been his idea, and he didn't flinch or cower as younger, stronger, faster people swarmed around him on the winding asphalt path.

She'd spent the noon hour with Glenn at the senior center, filming. She'd write a voice-over for Becky to read later, a monologue about the importance of the center as a social nexus for older people, a place for them to congregate outside their homes. "Context," she'd explained to Becky, who'd thought the extra filming would be fine as long as she didn't have to be present. Glenn didn't mind meeting Loretta at the center—he was union and got time-and-a-half for working on Saturday. They'd finished taping a half hour ago, and Loretta had sent him on his way. That was when Solly had suggested that she take a walk with him in Central Park.

Why not? She had nothing better to do that afternoon. If not for a walk in Central Park, she would be sitting at home, pigging out on Ben & Jerry's—a habit she was really going to have to get under control—and feeling sorry for herself. She could feel just as sorry for herself here in the golden July afternoon, surrounded by humanity and in the company of one of humanity's finest specimens, Solly Hirschbaum.

"Did I mention, your hair looks nice?" Solly asked. He wore a New York Fire Department cap, a short-sleeve cotton shirt, knee-length shorts and dark sunglasses. His legs were thin but not bony, his arms muscular. Loretta hoped she'd look as good in shorts when she reached his age—with less hair on her legs, of course.

"I got it cut this morning. My cousin Donna is a hair-stylist."

"I like it. Not too short," Solly assessed. "But a little breezier. It's got more life in it. A pretty girl like you, you don't want to hide behind all that hair, you know what I mean? There we go," he said, nudging her toward an Italian-ice vendor. "You're an Italian girl, so this is the treat for you. What flavor do you want?"

"Oh, Solly…" She was about to decline but realized she was hungry. She hadn't eaten since the bagel she'd wolfed down on the subway en route to Donna's salon that morning. "Can I treat?"

"Don't insult an old man. Besides, I got more money than you. What flavor?"

"Lemon," she acquiesced.

He bought a lemon and a cherry Italian ice, grabbed a few napkins from the dispenser perched on the shelf above the freezer compartment and pocketed his change. "There. A lemon for you. Eat. Enjoy."

"Thanks." They resumed their stroll, licking the cold, sweet mounds of flavored ice in their pleated cups. "So, Solly, what do you think of showbiz? Any regrets about letting us film your story?"

"It's not my story. It's Dora Lee and Phyllis's story. I'm just the guy in the middle of it."

"Did you enjoy the filming?"

"I don't know. Frankly, I was a little surprised the center let you film there today. It's not a religious place, but most of the members are Jewish, and today being Shabbat…"

"Shabbat?"

"What you call Sabbath. Friday sundown to Saturday sundown, nobody should be taking movies. Of course, if you're not Jewish, I don't suppose it matters much. Not like I'm a Hassid or anything. If I was, I couldn't have paid that man for the ices. Money exchanges aren't allowed on Shabbat.''

''I didn't know that.''

''You'll have to learn these things if you're going to wind up with Josh. Not that he's a religious man. He's not. But it's good to know each other's culture, don't you think?''

''I'm not going to wind up with Josh,'' Loretta muttered, her mood descending like an elevator with a broken cable.

Solly halted so abruptly in the middle of the walkway a teenage skateboarder nearly crashed into him. ''Watch it, ya dumb asshole!'' the kid shouted as he veered past Solly. His voice hadn't even changed yet.

Loretta considered shouting back at the kid, but he vanished into the crowd. ''Are you all right?'' she asked Solly.

''Me? I'm fine. I wonder, though, he called me a dumb asshole. That seems redundant, doesn't it? You ever hear of a smart asshole?''

Loretta laughed. She wasn't in a laughing mood. She hadn't been in one all day, not when Donna had restyled her hair, not when she'd led Glenn around the center like an arty Hollywood director, demanding that he shoot this and shoot that and linger for a minute on the table in the TV room, which Solly had identified as the site of his chess games with Josh. She still wasn't in the mood to smile, let alone laugh, but Solly had gotten to her. No wonder Josh counted him as a friend. She'd like to think he was her friend, too.

Could they be friends if Solly liked Josh and Loretta hated Josh's guts?

Why did she hate his guts, anyway? It was her own fault that he'd flown to Florida to see Melanie. Loretta had banned all further intimacy with him. She'd said no more lovemaking, just that once was it, and she wanted them to be nothing more than friends. If she were truly his friend, she wouldn't be fuming over the fact that he'd left town to visit his sweetheart.

"You know what?" Solly gazed at her. His lips had turned red from his Italian ice. "I'm not so dumb. So let me tell you something. Josh is crazy about you."

"No he's not," she said automatically. "We're friends, but—"

"But he's crazy about you. I can tell. He's oozing with it."

Not the most glamorous image. Not a true one, either. Did Solly even know where Josh was right now?

Thinking of him down in the Sunshine State, probably peeling an orange for Melanie right this minute and letting her eat the dripping wedges from his fingers, plunged Loretta's mood even lower. Josh had a girlfriend. That had always been the bottom line.

"He's in Florida," she told Solly.

"Yeah, he told me he was going. He told me he might have to cancel our usual Monday chess game if he wasn't back by then."

"So I think," Loretta said, resuming her amble along the blacktopped path, "if he's oozing over anyone, it's Melanie."

"That's what you think," Solly intoned. "You think that, huh. Well, let me tell you something, Loretta. You're the dumb one."

"What makes you say that?"

"I got twenty-twenty vision, that's what."

"You wear eyeglasses, Solly."

"I'm talking about here." He thumped his chest with his fist, then squeezed some slushy ice from the bottom of his cup. "I'm talking about what the heart knows. Life is short, Loretta. Josh is crazy about you. And you're crazy about him, and you're both *nudnicks,* thousands of miles apart when you should be together."

"I'm not crazy about him," Loretta insisted. She wasn't sure what a *nudnick* was, but she doubted being called one was a compliment.

"How can you not be crazy about him? He's smart, he's handsome, he's a gentleman, he's a lawyer, he does good in the world—what's not to be crazy about?"

"He's got a girlfriend."

"She's there. You're here."

"*He's* there."

"So get him back. What's stopping you?"

"A thousand miles," she muttered. "Airfare. Melanie."

"Airfare is just money. Miles is just miles."

"And Melanie is a fantastic human being, from what I've heard."

"But not for him. I never saw between them what I see between him and you. Life is short," he repeated. "Let him know you love him."

"But I don't," Loretta argued, wishing her voice carried more conviction.

"Right. You don't love him like I'm a dumb asshole. Look at me, Loretta. Do I look like a dumb asshole to you?"

"Of course not!"

He nodded, evidently satisfied that he'd made his point. "You love him. He loves you. Somebody's gotta be the smart one. Since Josh isn't around, it better be you."

"Why do I have to be the smart one?" she complained. She drained the last of the ice from her cup. Her mouth felt rounded out inside, tart and tangy from the bittersweet lemon flavor.

She didn't want to be the smart one. She wanted to pout and mope and wallow in misery until Josh returned to her, swearing he had to have her and no one else would do, not even Melanie the noble social worker. She wanted him to beg her, to insist she was the only woman in his life now and forever, and then she wanted him to make love to her the way he had last week, only she wouldn't want him racing off in the morning.

And she didn't want him to say one word about how old she was, or how she'd better grab him and hang on tight because she was pretty much over the hill. She wanted him to say he thought she was the perfect age—and, while he was at it, the perfect woman.

"You have to be the smart one," Solly explained, "because you're the one I'm talking to. I know about love, sweetie. I had a wonderful marriage to a wonderful woman, and I know what that's like. You don't ignore it. You don't say, '*Oy*, the airfare.' If you're smart, you go after love and claim it."

Going after Josh seemed like an extraordinarily stupid move.

Yet hadn't Solly just said she was dumb?

Nineteen

"**W**hat do you mean, you want to borrow money from me?" Nicky bellowed through the phone.

"Not 'money.' Just fifty bucks," Loretta wheedled. She had enough of a balance on her credit card to cover a round-trip ticket to Florida. But a loan from Nicky would enable her to sleep tonight, if there was any chance in the world she'd be able to fall asleep now that she'd gone ahead and booked a flight to Miami, which, according to the Delta ticketing agent, was the airport closest to Opa-Locka.

"This is the stupidest thing you've ever done," Nicky railed. "You're telling me that guy of yours, that absolute turd, is in Florida visiting his *girlfriend,* and you want to go chasing after him?"

"It's not his girlfriend," Loretta fibbed. "It's his old girlfriend."

"*I'll* go," Nicky volunteered. "Let me go, instead. I'll knock his teeth in."

Coming from Nicky, who believed dental health was next to godliness, that was quite an offer. "I don't want you to knock his teeth in," she insisted. "If you want to do anything with teeth, you should fix Solly's girlfriend's tooth. It hardly needs anything. Just a little touch-up on the enamel. It wouldn't take you more than a half hour."

"You want me to do a half-hour job on this lady *and* lend you fifty bucks?"

"I'll pay you back," she promised. She hated begging, but she didn't have much choice. If she'd had a choice, she wouldn't have called Nicky—and even without a choice, she probably shouldn't have. She should have blown her budget on the damn ticket and resigned herself to living on a diet of oatmeal and chewing gum for the rest of the summer. Or else she should have asked Donna for a loan, except that Donna was always broke *and* she'd undercharged Loretta for the haircut that morning, which was a gift right there. She could have asked Al, except that Al would have subjected her to a lecture on fiscal responsibility, and then he would have turned her down. Nicky would rant and rave for a while, but he'd say yes, which was why he was her favorite brother, even if he was what her nona would call a *rompicogliono*—a pain in the ass.

"I tell you what," she continued when he didn't say anything. "You can lend me fifty bucks and Al can fix Solly's girlfriend's tooth."

"You know what? I've had it up to here with people's girlfriends," Nicky fumed. "I hate the word *girlfriend*. None of this would have happened if you'd listened to me and let me set you up with Marty Calabrese."

"You're right, Nicky." He *was* right. None of this would have happened, but she also would have missed out on something incredible. The possibility of missing out on something incredible was what had compelled her to splurge on the ticket to Miami. If it turned out that she and Josh weren't meant to be, she'd wind up a few hundred bucks poorer—including the fifty dollars she was borrowing from Nicky—and maybe with a shattered heart. But not going, not finding out, not taking a chance... She'd wind up with the same shattered heart.

She wouldn't be hitting her brother up for money, though. She'd have a shattered heart but not the heartburn Nicky gave her.

"How am I supposed to get this loan to you?" he asked.

"I'm flying out of LaGuardia tomorrow at noon," Loretta told him, tamping down her hopes. He hadn't said yes yet. "I'll be at the Delta terminal around ten. We could meet there."

"Right." Nicky didn't sound thrilled. "I'm supposed to miss church for this?"

As if he'd never missed church before. "I'm sure God will forgive you," she wheedled. "You're helping out your sister—who happens to be fast approaching her thirtieth birthday and still single. And here's this terrific guy, this live prospect, within her grasp—"

"Who happens to be in Florida visiting his *girlfriend*," Nicky broke in.

"His old girlfriend, who may or may not be his girlfriend anymore. But I have to find out, Nicky. I have to know for sure if Josh and I should be together."

"You love this guy, huh?"

"How can I not love him? He's smart and funny and handsome, and he devotes himself to helping the less fortunate."

"He isn't a dentist."

"I consider that a plus."

Nicky sighed. "So, how are you planning to get to LaGuardia?"

"I was figuring I'd take a cab."

"A cab is gonna cost you fifty bucks right there," he pointed out.

"Why do you think I'm trying to borrow some money?"

He sighed again. "All right. Look, I'll pick you up at

your apartment. At 9:00 a.m. Be ready to roll. I don't feel like looking for a parking space."

This was why she put up with Nicky—because beneath his silly Gilligan sailor hat, beneath his bombastic exterior and his bossy, critical attitude, he was an angel. "I'll be outside at quarter to nine."

"This guy better be worth it," he grumbled. "Promise me one thing, Loretta."

"Anything."

"If he turns out to be a son of a bitch, I want you to give me permission to knock his teeth in."

"I'll knock them in myself," she assured him. "Nicky, I owe you big."

"You owe me fifty and a favor. I'll see you tomorrow."

She hung up, sank into the lumpy couch cushions and let out a long breath. Fifty dollars wasn't much, but fifty dollars and a free ride to the airport added up. She might be able to pay Nicky back, if she didn't lose her job.

Her job. Shit. How could she take time off from work when the threat of layoffs hung over the production team's collective head? Well, she deserved a day or two. She'd knocked herself out on the Senior Center Love Triangle story, filming nearly every day that past week after putting in her regular hours with the team at the studio. She'd even spent weekend time today filming at the center. Surely Becky couldn't begrudge her a couple of personal days.

And if Becky couldn't, if this trip to Florida was going to cost her her job, well, fuck it. Loretta had never done anything for the explicit purpose of promoting her career, and now didn't seem like a particularly good time to start.

She crossed to her refrigerator—a grand hike of six steps—and swung open the door. She was too jittery for ice cream, even Ben & Jerry's S'mores. Instead, she pulled a Sam Adams from the door shelf and rummaged in a drawer for her bottle opener. She'd bought the Sam Adams for Josh, but he was far away. Somebody ought to enjoy the beer.

She took a long sip, but she didn't enjoy it. Drinking Josh's favorite beer made her realize how far away he was, and not just in miles. What if seeing Melanie had completely erased Loretta from his mind? What if he decided, as any normal human being would, that a social worker who specialized in helping older people lead productive, healthy lives contributed more to the world than a hack who specialized in helping older—and younger—people make jackasses of themselves on a syndicated TV show? What if Loretta's trip to Florida was a huge mistake? What if she'd gotten herself in debt to MasterCard and Nicky for nothing?

Too late. She'd already bought the ticket. She was going.

She carried her beer back to the sofa, flopped onto it and dialed Bob's number. He answered, panting, on the third ring. "I'm interrupting something," Loretta said contritely.

"Loretta?" He breathed for a few seconds. "No problem. What?" he said, obviously to someone not on the phone. "It's Loretta. I work with her. A colleague... No, I haven't..." He exhaled wearily, then addressed Loretta. "We seem to be having a little snit here."

"It's my fault. I'm really sorry, Bob. Put her on the phone—I'll assure her I've never seen you naked."

"That's all right. She'll get over it."

"Is this the one whose daddy is the deputy undersecretary of something?"

"Yeah... Honey, it's *work*, okay?" he said to his companion. Then back to Loretta, "We'd better make this fast. Someone needs a lot of attention right now."

"Okay. I just called to let you know I'm not going to

be at work Monday. So if you could tell Gilda, I'd appreciate it.''

''What's up?''

''It's just a family thing.'' That wasn't a lie; Nicky's involvement made it a family thing.

''Is someone sick?''

''Physically, no. Mentally, the jury's still out. Anyway, will you cover for me on Monday?''

''Sure. When will you be back?''

''I don't know. Tuesday, maybe.'' Tuesday, with her tattered heart on her sleeve and Nicky's lectures about how she should have let him set her up with Marty the dentist echoing in her skull. ''Tell them I've got a lot of stuff to work with on the Solly show.''

''The what show?''

''Solly. Tell them that if they fire me while I'm gone—no, don't plant any ideas. Just say I'll get back as soon as I can.''

''They'll probably fire me for being your messenger. I'd better go. Little Miss Patriot is turning into a Patriot missile.''

''Apologize to her for me,'' Loretta said.

She hung up, took a long pull of beer and gazed around. Her apartment seemed to have shrunk. She almost felt as if she could stretch out her legs and kick the rocker at the opposite end of the room, or even the wall behind the rocker. She could stretch her arms and slam her palms against the ceiling. She was going to lose her job, she was going to decimate her savings account and she was going to wind up evicted because she couldn't afford the exorbitant rent on this minuscule apartment, and she wouldn't be able to seek the assistance of the only lawyer she knew who could help her renegotiate her lease, because he'd pledged his troth to a Florida social worker—all because

Solly had bought her a lemon ice and spoken with the wisdom of Yoda, and she'd decided to follow his advice.

Was this the sort of behavior typical of desperate twenty-nine-year-old single women? No. She hadn't wanted to fall in love. She hadn't been even remotely interested in it, let alone eager to get married.

She was doing this because Josh was Josh. Because he was her friend. Because sex with him had been incredible, their bodies connecting as smoothly and naturally as their minds did. Because a woman had to do what she had to do, whether or not it made any sense.

Crazy or not, she'd better pack. She had a plane to catch tomorrow.

Josh staggered off the airplane and into the terminal. Flying had never been his favorite activity, but it definitely seemed to be more unpleasant these days. The man seated next to him had boarded the plane, settled into his seat and whipped out a cell phone, into which he'd yakked nonstop until the plane taxied away from the gate and the flight attendant threatened to take the cell phone from him if he didn't put it away. The gist of his conversation, which Josh had been forced to listen to, was that a security guard in the airport had confiscated the plastic sword-shaped skewer that had held an olive in the martini he'd drunk before boarding. He'd been extremely fond of that skewer. It had been cuter than words could say. A pirate's sword, three inches long and green. "Like I could've hijacked the plane with this cocktail toothpick," he'd whined into the phone.

But it didn't matter. Josh was home. He'd ended things with Melanie, cleanly and honorably, and when she'd insisted that he spend the night in her guest room he had, literally. He'd heard her moving around her bedroom, heard her showering, heard the creak of her bed as she'd climbed into it—and he'd thought, *Tomorrow I'll be back in New York, convincing Loretta that even if she'd rather not have a romance in her life right now, she's stuck with one.*

The air-conditioning in New York felt better than the air-conditioning in southern Florida. Less implacable, somehow. And the foliage! He was home, where trees were trees and women—at least the woman he wanted to sleep with—had hair. He was home, safe in the knowledge that Melanie hadn't been terribly shocked or hurt by his decision to end things, that she'd seen their relationship was fading and she appreciated his having made the move to end it.

Now all he had to do was force his way into Loretta's heart.

If he owned a cell phone, he'd be speed-dialing her apartment right now, instead of roaming the terminal, pushing past people staggering under heaps of luggage and nattering in fifty languages, in his search for a pay telephone. That was another reason he hated cell phones: thanks to them, pay phones were scarcer than oxygen on the moon. He reached the exit without spotting a pay phone and decided to call Loretta from home.

The cabdriver he got spoke in a language that wasn't English, but he knew how to get to Greenwich Village. Josh settled into the upholstery, closed his eyes and mapped out his evening. He'd call Loretta first, and talk her into having dinner with him. Then he'd call Henri Charnier and make sure he and his family hadn't been deported in the past twenty-four hours. Then he'd shower. Then he'd see Loretta.

He smiled.

Forty minutes later, the cab delivered him to his address. Outside the elevator on his floor, he ran into his neighbors, Minka Colvitas and Colin Witt, engaged in an animated conversation about a guppy Colin had just sold. ''This guy's a collector,'' Colin gushed. ''He'll pay anything just to get his hands on the right guppy. I'm telling you, one little fish is going to buy me that leather jacket I saw at Prada.''

Josh nodded a greeting to them and let himself into his apartment, dragging his wheeled overnighter behind him. Without breaking stride, he headed for the kitchen to grab the phone. His message light was flashing.

Loretta, he thought hopefully. She'd called him to tell him how much she missed him, to insist that he phone her the instant he arrived home.

Or maybe Melanie. His smile faded. Maybe Melanie had shed her civil veneer now that he was gone, and she'd phoned to curse his puny soul to hell. And to complain about the heat. Although now that he'd experienced it himself, he would cut her some slack on that.

Bracing himself, he hit the message replay button. ''Josh? It's your mother. The grass is so long. I know you said you couldn't come and mow it today, but it looks terrible. The blades are supposed to stand up straight, but they're drooping. Totally limp. When are you going to come and cut it?''

He'd assured her that skipping one week wouldn't damage her lawn. The grass might actually appreciate a week's respite from the mower. Josh knew he'd appreciated the week's respite.

He'd overdosed on guilt during his time in Florida. He wasn't going to give in to it now. Let his mother despair over her totally limp grass. It wasn't his fault, and it wasn't his problem. He refused to feel bad about it.

After rewinding the message tape, he punched in Loretta's number. Her machine answered, and he decided he hated answering machines as much as he hated cell phones. ''Hi, Loretta, it's Josh,'' he said to her machine. ''I'm home and I'd really like to see you. Please call me as soon as you get in.'' *I missed you. I'm free and clear and I want you. I want to spend the evening with you, and the night, and tomorrow, and the day after tomorrow, and the day after that, and the day after the day after...and all those nights, too. Okay?*

He didn't say it. But he thought it so loudly he could practically hear the words in his voice. How long had he been involved with Melanie, and he'd never said things like that to her. He hadn't said them to Loretta, either. But right now, his thoughts were shouting.

He looked up Henri Charnier's number and dialed it. One of the multitude of females in the apartment answered, and she informed him Henri's singing group was rehearsing in the basement—and in fact, they planned to perform in a talent show at a Haitian-American social club later that week, if Josh would like to attend. He jotted down the information on a square of paper towel. Maybe Loretta would come with him. Maybe she'd wind up producing a show for Becky Blake about musically talented Haitian immigrants in Brooklyn.

He lugged his bag down the hall to his bedroom, unpacked, stripped, showered, dressed. His phone didn't ring. He returned to the kitchen, inspected the contents of his freezer and found nothing to whet his appetite, pulled a beer from the fridge and stared at his silent phone, praying for it to ring.

As if unable to resist the force of his will, it rang.

"Hi," he said in his most seductive tone. He lounged against the counter and grinned in anticipation of hearing Loretta's voice.

"Josh? It's Solly. Are we on for tomorrow?"

"Solly?" He straightened up and coughed to clear his throat.

"Are we on for tomorrow? Chess. Because I want to ask a favor of you. Phyllis organized a petition to get permission to return to the center. All these people want her to come back, and they signed her petition. They like her. And it's not like anyone's convicted her of anything."

"So she'll return to the center."

"But I promised Dora Lee I'd bring her to the center tomorrow. Her first time back. It's wheelchair accessible."

Josh was tired, he was lonely, he was horny—*he wanted to talk to Loretta*. He could hardly wrap his brain around Solly's dilemma. "Maybe they'll see each other and kiss and make up," he suggested.

"And maybe I'll grow a third eye. I want you there, just in case. Okay?"

"Do you want me to throw myself between them if they start whaling on each other?"

"They won't. Not if you and I are both there. I can make sure Dora Lee doesn't have her cane within reach." He let out a weary breath. "It's a mess, Josh. Somehow, both women are angry with me. Dora Lee is angry because I signed Phyllis's petition. Phyllis is angry because Dora Lee is staying with me until she's able to take care of herself. I'm trying to do right by both of them, and they're both angry with me. I don't understand it."

"Women can be that way," said Josh, as if he were an expert.

"So we'll play some chess and keep the women from killing each other—or me. Can I count on you?"

"I'll be there," Josh promised.

"Now, tell me—how was your trip? Did you see Loretta?"

Solly was allowed his momentary confusion. It didn't mean he was going senile. "I went to see Melanie, not Loretta," Josh gently reminded him.

"I know, I know. And then Loretta went down to see you."

"What?"

"She went to see you. You didn't see her?"

"No!" Josh jerked upright. "You're telling me she's in Florida?"

"She said she was going to see you."

"Why? What did she want to see me there for? She can see me here."

"I guess she wanted to see you while you were with Melanie, just to set things straight."

Oh, shit.

The kitchen was too small for a table and chairs, so he had no place to sit except the floor. He slid down until his butt hit the tiles, and rested his head against the walnut door of the cabinet where he stored his dishwashing soap and empty coffee cans.

Loretta had wanted to see him with Melanie? To set things straight? She'd flown all the way to Florida to witness him and Melanie together. Maybe she'd figured she would catch him in Melanie's arms—and he *had* shared that one smoldering kiss with Melanie. Not that it had led to anything—but damn, the guilt was cascading onto him like Niagara Falls, dragging him under, drowning him.

Loretta had gone to Florida to see him with Melanie.

But he was here, and she was there.

With Melanie.

What was it Solly had just said? Something about trying to do right by both women, and winding up with both of them angry with him. Something about how it was a mess. It was a mess the way Mount Everest was a hill. "Solly, I've got to go."

"So, I'll see you tomorrow, right?"

"I don't know." He couldn't think about chess or Phyllis

or Dora Lee. All he could think about was Loretta showing up on Melanie's doorstep, surrounded by lizards and those demented palm trees and her hair all bushy from the humidity, and Melanie inviting her in, and...*oh, shit*. He couldn't begin to guess what they'd talk about—although he felt safe in assuming the main topic of conversation would be him. "I'll get back to you, Solly, okay?"

"Is something wrong?"

"Just about everything. I'll talk to you later." He hung up, feeling an extra bucketful of guilt wash over on him for ending the phone call so rudely. Then he dialed Melanie's number. The phone on her end rang four times, and her machine picked up.

Shit on top of shit. "Melanie? It's Josh. Listen, a friend of mine, a woman named Loretta D'Angelo... I just found out she's in Florida, and I think she might be looking for you because she thought I was with you and she was looking for me." He took a deep breath and tried to slow down. "If she shows up at your place, could you have her phone me? I'm at home. I appreciate it." He thought for a minute, realized that on top of deranged he sounded dictatorial, issuing commands as if he viewed her as his secretary. He had to humanize the message. "It was great seeing you, by the way. I'm glad things are going well for you. And that restaurant was great. A lot cheaper than any restaurants in New York. Well, anyway. Thanks for having Loretta call me. If you see her, that is."

He hung up and buried his face in his palms, accidentally banging his head against the beer bottle in his hand. He didn't even want the beer. What he wanted was a new life. A simpler one.

One that had Loretta in New York City rather than Opa-Locka.

Twenty

Loretta had been to Florida before—Orlando, with her family, when she was nine. The D'Angelos had done Walt Disney World. Loretta had hazy memories of wandering around the park wearing a Goofy hat, eating ice-cream pops shaped like Mickey Mouse, accusing a performer in an oversize Chip costume, or maybe it was a Dale costume, of not *really* being Chip—or Dale—because on TV the characters were much cuter, and experiencing what was probably the preadolescent equivalent of an orgasm on Splash Mountain, when the log-shaped car she and her brothers were riding in plummeted down the flume chute in a blur of screams and splashes.

But she didn't really remember Florida. She didn't remember the lushness of the plants, the heaviness of the air, the sultry warmth of the wind.

She hadn't come to Florida to play tourist this time, and she doubted her confrontation with Josh and his old flame was going to resemble any sort of equivalent of an orgasm. She'd had two entire flights—from LaGuardia to Atlanta and from Atlanta to Miami—to contemplate the foolishness of having traveled all this way. Fighting for the love of a man didn't come naturally to her.

Still, she'd come. That had to mean something. Whether it meant she was in love with Josh or in the thrall of a manipulating old man or else just too stupid to live, she had traveled many miles and many hours to reach her current position, standing on the welcome mat outside the door of Melanie's garden apartment. Solly had gotten Melanie's address for her from Francine, Melanie's replacement at the senior center. Loretta wasn't sure how or when he'd finagled it out of Francine, but if he could talk Loretta into chasing Josh to Opa-Locka, he could probably talk anyone into anything.

She rang the bell, psyching herself up for the possibility that the man and woman on the other side of the door might right this minute be involved in an activity that didn't require clothing. If Josh and Melanie were going at it for old time's sake—or for new time's sake—Loretta would handle it. She'd come to Florida not to judge Josh, not to beseech him or to brain him with a skillet but to let him know she loved him.

If he still loved Melanie, Loretta would feel pretty foolish. But she was feeling pretty foolish anyway.

The woman who answered the door was fully clothed—or as much clothed as a person could tolerate in southern Florida in July: She was clearly braless under a pale cotton tank top, and her shorts ended at midthigh. She had hardly any hair, which took Loretta aback. Staring at the woman's delicate features beneath her nearly bald scalp, Loretta wondered whether Melanie had recently undergone chemotherapy. But no, what hair she did have lay short but thick on her head, like the fur on a lion's back.

If the poor woman had been fighting cancer, surely Josh would have thought to mention that minor detail to Loretta.

Melanie was not sick but shockingly chic. The selfless angel of the geriatric social-work world was making a statement with her hairstyle, a much louder statement than Loretta made with the trim Donna had given her yesterday morning. If she'd known she would be traveling to the tropics, she might have asked Donna to take off more. Her hair felt as heavy as a woolen scarf against her neck in the muggy evening.

The woman stared at her, frowning. Loretta realized she needed to say something. "Hi. Is Josh here?"

"Josh?"

Damn. Did Loretta have the right address? "I'm Loretta D'Angelo," she introduced herself. "I thought a friend of mine, Josh Kaplan, might be here." Her voice curled up at the end, turning the statement into a question.

The woman on the other side of the threshold tilted her head slightly to size Loretta up. "Loretta. Loretta from the TV show. Josh's blind date. I thought you looked familiar."

"Right." Loretta smiled weakly. Where was Josh? Hiding naked in a closet somewhere?

"You're Josh's old friend."

"I'm not that old."

Melanie laughed, as if she thought Loretta had made a joke. "Well, come on in. This seems to be my weekend for visitors from New York City." She stepped aside so Loretta could enter.

The apartment was cool, furnished in soft greens and ambers. A piquant fragrance arose from the kitchen, which was visible on the opposite side of a counter lined with rattan stools. The apartment seemed spacious and airy, much larger than anyone living on a social worker's salary could afford in Manhattan.

Melanie wasn't what Loretta had expected. She was petite and gaminelike. Her hairstyle was terribly daring—Loretta wondered whether Josh's taste would accommodate such an extreme coiffure. He didn't seem to like the multiple-ear-piercings type, either, but Melanie had three holes per ear, one hoop, one gold stud and one diamond stud adorning each lobe. On her feet were tacky sandals with plastic daisies attached to the straps.

"I love your sandals," Loretta said, meaning it.

"They're fun, aren't they?" Melanie swung around the counter into the kitchen. "I just got home ten minutes ago. I picked up a seafood stew at my favorite Cuban restaurant. You want some? I've also got rice and beans."

"Oh—you don't have to feed me. Is Josh here?"

"No. He left this morning."

"You're kidding." Loretta slumped against the counter and let the strap of her mini-duffel slide off her shoulder. The bag hit the floor with a thud. "He left?"

"He flew down here, broke up with me, spent the night and left this morning."

Broke up with me resonated inside Loretta's skull. So did *spent the night*. "You're kidding," she repeated.

"Nope. That's what he did. You look stunned. Are you okay?" She whirled around the kitchen, busying herself, fussing with plates and plastic take-out containers, every now and then glancing at Loretta, who sank onto one of the stools.

"I guess I am a little stunned."

"What a shame, your traveling all this way and he isn't even here. He probably landed at LaGuardia about an hour ago—" she glanced at the clock built into her wall-unit oven "—or maybe an hour and a half. I don't remember his itinerary. You want something to drink?"

"What have you got?"

Melanie pulled a bottle of pineapple juice from the re-frigerator. "I used to be a chardonnay drinker, but I've gotten hooked on rum-and-pineapple-juice since I got here. It's like a piña colada without the coconut. Coconut is so high in cholesterol, and it's never too soon to pay attention to that. Would you like one? I'm going to fix myself one."

"Thanks." Loretta gave her head a dazed shake. What was she doing here? Josh was back in New York. *But he'd spent the night.* With Melanie? What kind of breakup was that?

As if Loretta had any right to be jealous. He'd spent the night with her before he'd broken up with Melanie.

And Melanie was so *nice*! Chattering as though she and Loretta were bosom buddies, offering her food and a drink, making her feel welcome. What was up with that?

Of course Melanie was nice. Would Josh have been involved with her if she wasn't?

But she didn't seem like a saintly social worker. She was too hip. And she drank rum-and-pineapple-juice and wore kicky sandals.

She splashed rum into two tumblers, tossed in some ice cubes from the freezer and topped them off with pineapple juice. "I didn't mean to interrupt your dinner," Loretta said, although what else could she have expected when she'd shown up at Melanie's apartment at six-thirty? "You don't have to feed me," she repeated.

"It's way too much for me. The portions at Hector's are always big enough for three meals." She gazed at the containers lined up on the counter. "We can reheat them in the microwave when we're ready to eat. The stew's kind of spicy. I hope you don't mind."

"Spicy's fine," Loretta conceded, figuring she might as well go with the flow. She accepted the tall, cool glass Melanie handed her and lifted it in a silent toast. Then she tasted the beverage. It was shockingly sweet. But given how much Ben & Jerry's she'd been eating lately, she'd developed a high tolerance for cold, sweet foodstuffs.

Melanie circled the counter and motioned with her head for Loretta to join her in the living room. "Mind if I put on some music?" she asked.

"Go right ahead." Loretta abandoned the stool for the upholstered wicker sofa near the window. Unlike her own, Melanie's furniture looked new.

"This is the Buena Vista Social Club," Melanie said as she slid a disk into her CD player. "I've really gotten into Latino music in a big way since I moved down here."

"That makes sense," Loretta said. "When in Rome…"

Once the syncopated rhythms of the first song spilled out of the speakers, Melanie flopped into an easy chair, kicked off her sandals and folded her legs under her. Loretta had never minded being tall, but she felt Amazonian next to Melanie. And absurdly hirsute.

"Okay, so tell me—what's your real agenda?" Melanie asked.

So much for bosom-buddy patter. Loretta took a slug of her drink. The rum sizzled through the pineapple juice, briefly numbing her throat. "My agenda?" she croaked.

"Why did you come here? You didn't have to come all the way to Opa-Locka to see Josh. You can see him in New York."

"Yeah, well, I wasn't seeing him there." Loretta saw no reason to lie. Melanie had already said she and Josh had broken up, regardless of what might have occurred last night. Last night was history. Loretta was going to pretend it didn't matter. "I mean, he and I were sort of avoiding each other, because…" While she didn't want to lie, she didn't want to come right out with the truth, either.

"Because?" Melanie goaded her.

"There was an attraction," Loretta said delicately. "And Josh was still involved with you."

"Oh, Josh. Such a gentleman." Melanie shook her head and laughed. The short strands of her hair glittered in the light from the bulb in the ceiling fan, which whirred slowly and atmospherically. "He was keeping his distance because he was afraid that if he saw you he'd jump you?"

"Something like that," Loretta mumbled.

"That still doesn't explain why you're here." Melanie sipped her drink and flexed her toes. Her toenails looked like baby peas, all lined up and polished green.

"Well, this guy—actually, I think you know him. Solly Hirschbaum."

"Solly!" Melanie's smile grew nostalgic. "How is Solly?"

"He's got women fighting over him."

Melanie chuckled. "He's something, isn't he."

"I'm not joking. They're literally fighting over him. Phyllis Yellin may have pushed Dora Lee Finkelstein into traffic. Dora Lee broke her leg. We're doing a story about it on the *Becky Blake Show.*"

"You're kidding. Shame on those two hussies." Melanie shook her head. "Violence? No man is worth that."

"You don't think so?"

"Have you ever met a man worth going to jail for?"

Loretta thought. Josh, maybe…if the legal situation had something to do with one of his clients—those poor folks at the Whatever Arms, or that Haitian family he was working with now. If a huge principle was at stake, sure, she'd go to jail for Josh. But she couldn't imagine getting into a shoving match with Melanie over him. Melanie was too nice. And the drink she'd given Loretta was heavenly.

"So what does Solly have to do with this?" Melanie asked.

Loretta explained. "He figured out that I was, well, there was this attraction," she hedged, not about to announce to Melanie that she was in love with Josh. "And I knew Josh had gone to Florida to see you. I assumed he'd gone to

Florida to revive your relationship, to make sure you and
he were still tight. And I thought—actually, Solly thought—
I should come down here and make my case before you
and Josh...I don't know...did something permanent.''

"Well, hell. We did do something permanent, I think.''
Melanie ran her fingers over her head, leaving her hair in
tiny, spiky tufts. "I still love the way that feels,'' she said,
stroking her head a second time. "I just got scalped a few
days ago. I've been down here, living in a state of permanent *schvitz*—''

Loretta nodded, remembering that word. Josh's mother
had used it.

"So I finally cut my hair. It feels so good not having
that hair weighing on my neck.''

"I just cut my hair yesterday,'' Loretta commented. "It's
still weighing on my neck.''

"You could get it off your neck by pinning it up in a
ponytail,'' Melanie suggested. "It's long enough for that.''

Loretta suppressed a laugh. Was this going to turn into
a pajama party, with the two of them getting tanked on rum
drinks and fixing each other's hair? "I should have brought
some barrettes with me. I didn't think of it.''

"Okay, so here's what I don't get,'' Melanie said, steering them back to the previous subject. "What would you
have done if you'd come down here and found Josh and
me—I don't know, screwing our heads off, or pledging
eternal devotion to each other? I mean, what was your plan
B?''

"Plan B? I didn't even have a plan A,'' Loretta admitted,
this time allowing a laugh to slip out. A plaintive, self-
derisive laugh. "I would have done something, though.
You've got to understand, Melanie, I work for the *Becky
Blake Show*. I spend every day coming up with ways to get

a group of opponents together on set, in front of cameras, and having them interact."

"Having them scream at one another," Melanie said. "I've seen the show a few times. My clients down here love it. They loved the show you and Josh were on, but they also love it when the show's guests try to tear one another's heads off."

"I wasn't going to tear anyone's head off," Loretta assured her. "But I figured, maybe we'd all shout awhile, and when the air cleared I'd have a better idea of where I stood. Maybe it would have been—is the word *cathartic*?"

"*Cathartic* is a good word." Melanie grinned. "You're in love with Josh, aren't you."

"I—" Damn. She couldn't lie, not about that. "It looks that way."

"He's quite a guy. A bit self-righteous."

"You think so?"

"And overflowing with guilt. Guilt is his middle name. Have you met his mother?" Melanie settled back in her chair, took a long drink as if it were fuel and then launched into a monologue about how Josh had taken care of everything for his mother when his father had died—the will, the insurance, the arrangements with the synagogue and the funeral home, the sitting *shivah*, whatever that was—*everything*, because his mother insisted she couldn't do anything. She told Loretta about the time Josh invented an excuse to miss a young cousin's bar mitzvah and then felt so guilty, he spent the entire day moaning about the importance of family and ritual. She explained that she'd gotten him to come to the senior center the first time by reminding him that he had his youth and his health and many of the center's participants didn't. "He's the only guy in the world who can feel guilty for being young and healthy," Melanie said.

"Maybe he was just being nice."

"I'm telling you—you want anything from him, play the guilt card," Melanie instructed her. "You want a special birthday present? Remind him he didn't take out the garbage. You want to go out for dinner? Mention some evening when he didn't help you with the dishes. His guilt gene'll kick in and he'll be helpless to resist."

"What else can you tell me about him?"

Plenty, it turned out. As Melanie heated and divided the seafood stew, as she and Loretta ate, as they polished off their drinks and refilled their glasses with more rum-and-pineapple-juice, Melanie told Loretta about Josh's weakness for butterscotch, his fervor when it came to his clients, his desire to win at games. "Don't ever play bridge as his partner," Melanie warned. "If you make a mistake, he'll never let you forget it. It's better if he's playing chess, because then he's got only himself to blame if he loses." She described his loyalty to the New York Yankees, his laundry habits—"he likes to tie his clean socks together, one knotted around the other. He never rolls his socks. It's like a religion to him"—and his reading tastes. "Mysteries. His grandfather gave him *The Complete Sherlock Holmes* when he was a kid, and that was that." She mentioned his vices, which included a frequent indulgence in sarcasm, an impatience with what he considered unnecessary high-tech gadgetry, an unfathomable fondness for *Saturday Night Live*—"even now, when it's not funny anymore"—and his apathy toward parties. "I like parties, especially hosting them. He didn't mind going to them every now and then, although he prefers socializing on a small scale, you know, maybe two couples. I love a crowd, but he never did. One thing he does love is Sam Adams beer."

"I know about his thing for Sam Adams," Loretta noted.

"And sex. He loves sex."

"Is that a problem?" Loretta asked cautiously, focusing on the stray grains of rice on her plate so she wouldn't have to look at Melanie.

"Well, it's not like he ever forces a situation. Sometimes I just wasn't in the mood, though, you know? Like when I had my period. He didn't care about it. His attitude was that I was a woman and women get their periods, it's natural, not a problem."

"That sounds pretty evolved," said Loretta.

"I guess. And...well, he's very good, so it was never a big deal. His wanting sex, I mean. Even if I wasn't in the mood, he managed to get me in the mood. He was good at that. Very good."

Loretta had little difficulty imagining this. To be sure, she had more difficulty imagining herself not in the mood to have sex with him. Even if she had her period.

The stew was filling, the black beans and rice even more so. She shoved back her plate and drained her glass. The rum, combined with a long day of travel and the inundation of information from Melanie, left her brain pleasantly fuzzy. "Why did you leave him?" she asked.

Melanie reached for the rum bottle, which stood on the table between them. She splashed a little in each of their glasses. "I got a job offer here in Opa-Locka."

"You could have turned it down. You must have known that accepting it would cause problems for you and Josh."

"I suppose." Melanie added some pineapple juice to their glasses—the ratio of juice to rum seemed to have decreased over the course of the evening, but Loretta didn't bother to point this out to Melanie. "It was a great job. It involved more responsibility, a big increase in pay and some new challenges." She sipped, then shrugged. "I knew leaving New York would cause problems with Josh...but I thought about it and I really wanted the job. That must mean something. As much as I cared for Josh, I wanted the job.''

More than she'd wanted Josh. Loretta understood. She hadn't broken them up; she wasn't some evil Other Woman who'd shredded the healthy bonds of a deeply committed couple. Melanie had wanted the job more than she'd wanted Josh. In a way, she'd broken up with him long before he'd come to Florida to break up with her.

"This rum-and-pineapple stuff is really good," Loretta said.

"Isn't it?" Melanie sipped and smiled. "Now, tell me what it's like working for a TV show. Is Becky Blake really as perky as she seems on TV?"

Loretta laughed. "Oh, boy. Don't get me started on Becky."

"I just did." Melanie gestured toward the bottle of rum, which was still half-full. "Tell me everything. Is she a diva? Is she a tyrant? Is she as cute as a button?"

"All of the above," Loretta said, glancing at the bottle and deciding it contained enough rum to keep her and Melanie going well into the night.

The shrill ringing of Josh's telephone at a few minutes past midnight jerked him upright. He hadn't been asleep, but he'd been in bed, brooding. Even if he hadn't been brooding, though, the blare of a phone at such a late hour rarely boded well.

He clicked on his bedside lamp and lifted the receiver, bracing himself for news of some catastrophe. "Hello?"

"Josh? It's Melanie."

Christ. She'd finally gotten around to returning his call now? After midnight? Where the hell had she been all this time?

More accurately, where had she and Loretta been? What

he'd been brooding about was the notion of the two of them together. What had they said to each other? What had they done? Why hadn't Melanie returned his call?

Well, she had. Finally. At an unforgivably late hour. He scraped his hand through his hair and blinked his eyes into focus. "Do you know what time it is?"

"Oh, I'm sorry," she said, sounding not the least bit apologetic. "The answering machine is in my bedroom, you know? And I turned off the beeper on it—it's so annoying—so I didn't realize I had a phone message until just now, when I was getting ready for bed."

No sense complaining to her about the time. He had more important matters on his mind. "Did Loretta D'Angelo visit you?"

"She certainly did." Melanie laughed. "As a matter of fact, she's here right now."

"There? With you?"

"She heard your message. She's spending the night. I've got a guest room. Oh, right—you already know that."

"So she's with you? Now?"

"Of course she's with me now. Isn't that what I just said? Hey, Loretta," she called away from the phone, "isn't that what I just said?"

He heard laughter in the background. It made him very uneasy for some reason.

"We've been having a great time," Melanie told him. "We just finished watching *Moonstruck*. It's very Italian. Loretta is Italian, did you know?"

"Yes, I knew."

"You want to talk to her?"

"I'd love to," Josh said grimly.

He heard the muffled thumps and rustles of the phone changing hands, and then Loretta's voice. "Josh?"

"Loretta. What the hell are you doing in Florida?"

"Drinking rum," she told him. "Rum-and-pineapple-juice. I feel so tropical."

Oh, God. It was worse than he'd thought. She and Melanie had spent the evening watching a chick flick and getting drunk. "Loretta." He used his sternest voice. "Why are you in Florida?"

"Well, I thought I wanted to see you. But now I'm not so sure. I've been having such a great time with Melanie, I'm thinking maybe I came down to see her."

"You can't change your reason *ex post facto*."

"What's that? You sound like a lawyer." She laughed. "She's been telling me all about you, Josh."

Shit. "What did she tell you?"

"You love sex."

He closed his eyes, leaned back into the pillow and took a deep breath. Hell, yes, he loved sex—with the right woman. With Loretta, for sure. But why was she discussing that with Melanie? What was the context? And why did he feel a little sick to his stomach?

"Listen, Josh, it's very late and I'm tired. So I'm going to say good-night now. Okay?"

"When are you coming home?"

"I don't know. Eventually, I guess. I'm going to say good-night now."

"Fine," he snapped. "Say it."

"Good night. Oh, Josh? I got a haircut."

Hell, shit and damn. Had she gone and scalped herself like Melanie? Her hair would grow back, he consoled himself, but the thought of Melanie without her long, lustrous mane dismayed him. "How short?"

"I think you'll like it."

"How short?"

"Donna did it yesterday, while you were down here with Melanie."

A revenge haircut? A panic haircut? How bad could it be? Why wouldn't Loretta tell him?

"I'm going to say good-night now," she announced again, then hung up the phone.

Josh lowered the receiver to its cradle and recited a juicy string of blasphemies. The thought of a tipsy Loretta and Melanie hanging out together, discussing his sexual appetites, was enough to make him want to swear off women forever. Except that he loved sex. Swearing off women didn't seem a palatable option.

Maybe he'd just swear off two women. He'd broken up with one and he loved the other. Maybe, for the sake of his sanity, he should simply forget that either one of them existed.

The next day he decided he'd have to swear off more than two women. Specifically, he wanted to add Dora Lee and Phyllis to his swear-off list.

Phyllis lay in wait for him outside the senior center when he arrived there after spending the morning ascertaining the status of Henri Charnier's visa, updating a grant application for a foundation that helped support his law firm and sitting next to Anita while she took a deposition from a witness who'd seen a rat while visiting his friend Hubie up in Washington Heights. Hubie was Anita's client, and according to Hubie's friend, the rat was happily ensconced on the fire escape outside the kitchen window, "looking like a frigging cat, I'm telling you. This mother was huge."

"Don't exaggerate, Mr. O'Neal. I need you to tell the truth here."

"I'm tellin' the truth! That rat was on steroids. That rat coulda fit Hubie's entire granddaughter in its mouth. We're talking the Jaws of the rodent world."

After a deposition like that, Josh was hardly in the right

state of mind to deal with Phyllis, the Jaws of the senior center. She spotted him as soon as he turned off Amsterdam Avenue, and started haranguing him before he'd even reached the front door of the center. "Solly is in there with Dora Lee. He promised me he'd get Francine to let me in. I haven't been convicted of anything, Josh. I've got signatures and everything!" She waved a petition in front of his face. "*Bubbela*, you've got to help me!"

If he closed his eyes he would picture Loretta and Melanie passing a bottle of rum back and forth like sorority sisters, singing dirty songs and cursing Josh's soul to hell. Not because he'd done anything worth damnation but because no good could come of a former girlfriend and a future girlfriend getting drunk together. He willfully kept his vision focused on Phyllis. Her skin seemed tighter across her face, pulled sharp with tension. "All right," he said wearily. "Let's go inside."

"I can't. Francine said I can't."

"We'll work it out. We'll get you inside and work it out."

"But Dora Lee is in there."

"I'm not going to ask her to leave. If you want to go in, let's go." He opened the door.

Phyllis hesitated a couple of seconds, then entered the building.

The foyer was empty, thank God. Fluorescent ceiling lights illuminated the cinder-block walls and the broad bulletin boards tacked with announcements of poetry readings, aerobics classes and duplicate-bridge tournaments. Voices and the salty aromas of turkey and gravy flooded the hall from the dining room to the left, and from the right came the staccato crackle of the television.

If they could get to Francine's office without running into anyone, Josh would consider it a major victory.

Instead, he faced a major defeat. He and Phyllis were perhaps three steps from the door to the administrative offices when the hall suddenly filled with curious people, some approaching from the dining room, with corn-bread crumbs and cranberry sauce clinging to their mouths, others from the TV lounge. Among those from the lounge was Solly—pushing Dora Lee in her wheelchair. Obviously, all the others had come to witness the showdown.

"What's she doing here?" Dora Lee asked.

"Now, Dora Lee," Solly murmured gently. "Give her a chance."

"You're a klutz," Phyllis shouted at Dora Lee. "You're trying to ruin my life because you happen to be a klutz."

"I'm not a klutz," Dora Lee defended herself in her breathy little voice.

"You fell and I wound up arrested. Tell me—" she seemed to be addressing everyone within earshot "—is this fair? Is it reasonable? A lady falls and I'm accused of pushing her?"

"Is that fair?" one woman from the lounge murmured to another. Josh recognized them as the needlepointers who often watched TV while he and Solly played chess.

"Is it reasonable?" the other murmured back.

"You pushed me," Dora Lee maintained.

"Please!" Solly positioned himself between the wheelchair and Phyllis. "No arguing! It won't solve anything!" To Josh, he added, "Get her into Francine's office."

"You know," Josh said, and everyone turned to gaze at him. Was it because he was a lawyer or because he was younger than the others by at least thirty years? He didn't care; they were listening. "You have a situation here in which two women have created a feud where none needs to exist. Solly likes you both. At this point, he isn't looking for an exclusive relationship with either of you. Whether or not you fight isn't going to change that. Now, in the law, we have what we call settlements. We try to iron out differences and negotiate a compromise without dragging the courts into it. Whether or not Dora Lee and Phyllis learn to get along, Solly is going to stay friends with you both— and he's not in any rush to marry either of you. So you two ladies are going to have to figure out a way to live in peace.''

The silence that ensued lasted long enough for Josh to wonder if anyone had even understood what he'd said. He was pretty sure he'd been speaking English, so they should have grasped the gist of it. He wanted them to comprehend that whether Phyllis and Dora Lee hated each other, tolerated each other or loved each other had nothing to do with Solly. It was a choice they had to make themselves, without involving him.

Melanie and Loretta had managed to become friends, hadn't they? Josh had adored them both, he'd slept with them both—and damn it, they seemed to be getting along just swell. Why couldn't Phyllis and Dora Lee accomplish that? There was so much less at stake for them, because in Solly's case, marriage was not an issue at the moment.

God, what was he thinking?

He was thinking of Loretta. And marriage. Loretta for the rest of his life. Loretta making him laugh, making him think, making him horny. Loretta talking him into doing all sorts of things he didn't want to do—and then making him glad he'd done them.

Phyllis and Dora Lee continued to glower at each other. Dora Lee repeatedly ran her tongue over her front teeth, creating a strange bulge under her upper lip. Phyllis stared down at her imperiously, evidently pleased that for once she stood taller than her rival. Solly planted his hands on his hips and eyed Josh questioningly. "Will you talk to Francine?" he asked. "Phyllis has a petition."

"She's going to hurt me," Dora Lee warned.

"I'm not going to hurt you," Phyllis told her. "If you weren't such a klutz, we wouldn't be here now. Do you know how much *tsuris* you've caused me?"

"She's not going to hurt you, Dora Lee," a man from the dining room said. He had a spot of gravy on his polo shirt, and his eyeglasses were so thick he seemed to be peering out from behind two small, clear bowls of water. "How could such a thing happen, with all of us watching?"

"You could try mentioning to her," a short, plump, whiny-voiced woman commented to Phyllis, "that you're sorry she hurt her leg. She was in the hospital, you know. A little sympathy, it wouldn't kill you."

"If Solly ever remarries," a woman whose incongruously auburn hair framed a face of prunish wrinkles, "it'll be to me, so the two of you should just give up."

Who was that? Did Solly have yet another girlfriend? Josh glanced at Solly, who shrugged but looked distinctly intrigued, gazing above the heads of the people crowded around Dora Lee and Phyllis to see who his admirer might be.

"Okay, so we've established there aren't going to be any assaults, any violence, any nonsense, right?" Josh said.

"I've got a petition," Phyllis added.

"Then let me talk to Francine and see what I can do."

"My tooth feels funny," Dora Lee piped up.

"We'll deal with your tooth later. Loretta D'Angelo will take care of that." *If she ever sobers up and comes home,* Josh almost added.

"Okay," Dora Lee grunted.

"Okay," Phyllis muttered, thrusting her petition into

Josh's hand. "If Solly isn't going to marry either of us, what's the point?"

"You cook for a man and what does he care?" Dora Lee added.

"He likes us both," Phyllis grumbled, "but so what? He won't put his money where his mouth is."

"I made him so many cookies," Dora Lee lamented. "And for what?"

Josh realized that one way to end a dispute was to get the warring factions to unite against a common enemy. Solly, standing between them like a barricade, had suddenly become their common enemy.

Was that what Melanie and Loretta were up to? Had they formed an alliance against him?

He couldn't bear to think about it. So he concentrated on pleading Phyllis's case before Francine. He'd never met Francine, he had no idea what she was like, but if necessary, he'd toss around terms like *heretofore* and *nolo contendere,* just as Solly had suggested. By the time he was done, Phyllis would be pushing Dora Lee's wheelchair, and Dora Lee would be baking Phyllis cookies.

Patting Solly on the shoulder, he knocked on the office door. "Set up the chessboard," he ordered Solly. "I'll be out as soon as I can." They'd need that chess game, too—two men plagued by romantic disasters. Two men who could figure out a way to checkmate a lot more easily than they could figure out a strategy for pleasing the women in their lives.

Twenty-One

Loretta could understand why Melanie had accepted the job offer in Opa-Locka. Unlike the senior center on the Upper West Side, here she was working in a huge residential complex, complete with condos, assisted-care apartments, art studios, rec rooms, an Olympic-size swimming pool and an entire community of golden-age New Yorkers who'd happily retired to warmer climates. Melanie had a staff of three and an office with wall-to-wall carpeting, a desk as big as a Ping-Pong table and a window overlooking a courtyard filled with viney, jungle-looking plants.

She'd brought Loretta with her to work Monday morning. Loretta had found a seat on a late-afternoon flight out of Miami, and given the choice of hanging out at Melanie's apartment, hanging out at the airport or hanging out at the complex where Melanie worked, Loretta had voted for the third option. If she'd brought a swimsuit she could have gotten a workout in the pool, but even without swimming laps, she had plenty to keep her occupied while Melanie attended to her job. The library was stocked with old paperbacks—Agatha Christie and Barbara Cartland seemed to be favorites—and one of the rec rooms had a billiards table. Nicky had taught Loretta how to play pool when she was twelve. She was probably a bit rusty, but she doubted anyone at the center could beat her.

She parked her duffel in Melanie's spacious office and

wandered the grounds. The heavy air didn't do much to clear the hangover fog from her brain, but the people she stopped to chat with were friendly and sounded like home, their noo-yawk accents thick and comforting. She played a cutthroat round of shuffleboard with a bald, portly man who had liver spots on his arms, smoked an overripe cigar and called her sweetheart. She observed an aerobics class populated by a lot of compact, intense, silver-haired women who reminded her of Phyllis Yellin. She caught a catnap in a lounge chair in the shade of a royal palm and woke up sweating from the heat.

At noon, she returned to Melanie's office so they could have lunch together. Melanie looked less fatigued than Loretta felt. "I'm used to staying up late," she told Loretta.

"You must be used to rum, too."

"I guess," Melanie said, divvying up the containers of yogurt and snack packs of crackers, the Diet Pepsi colas and the bananas she'd brought for their lunch. "We could eat outside, but it's too damn hot," she said. "That's the one thing I really hate about being here. The heat."

"You don't hate losing Josh?" Loretta asked. A lot had been said last night, but much of it had vanished in the rum-scented miasma that was Loretta's memory of yesterday. A lot had been said about Josh, and about men in general. But Loretta couldn't recollect what Melanie had specifically said about her breakup with Josh.

"You know something?" Melanie swirled her plastic spoon through her yogurt, stirring it until it turned pink from the strawberries at the bottom of the cup. "If Josh had ever told me he loved me, even once, I probably would have stayed in New York. But he never said it. He was a great guy, and we had a great relationship, but he never used the word *love*. I knew him for nearly three years. We'd met each other's families. By the end we were practically living together—and he never even hinted at making it legal. And I realized, he's one of those commitment-phobic types. He just can't take it to the next level. So what was I going to stick around for?"

"Did you want to marry him?" Loretta couldn't recall Melanie saying anything that revealing last night, but again, she couldn't recall much of anything from last night.

"It's not like I wanted to get married," Melanie emphasized. "But if I'm going to be with a guy for as long as I was with Josh… It had reached the point of shit or get off the pot, you know? He was clearly constipated."

Loretta tried not to choke on the bite of banana in her mouth.

"How about you?" Melanie asked. "Are you looking for marriage? If you are, consider yourself forewarned. Josh is a great guy, but if that's what you want, you're not going to find it with him."

"Good," Loretta said, wishing she sounded a little more positive.

"You don't want to marry him?"

"I don't want to marry anyone," Loretta insisted. "My family keeps pushing me to get married. I'm twenty-nine, and they think that if I don't have a wedding at least in the planning stages by the time I'm thirty, I might as well slash my wrists, because my life won't be worth living."

Melanie nodded sympathetically. "My parents wanted me to stick around and force a proposal out of Josh. But it just wasn't going to happen. I don't know—he's very responsible, very decent, but he couldn't even bring himself to think about it. I finally realized that was the way he was, and the proposal wasn't going to happen. I'm fine with it," she added. "My mother's still in mourning, but I'm fine."

I'll be fine, too, Loretta told herself. She wasn't dreaming of a proposal from Josh. All she wanted was his love. If she'd been eager to get married, she would have placed her fate in her family's hands. She would have gone out with Nicky's friend Marty. She would have twisted Gary's arm last Valentine's Day, when he'd told her he didn't love her. "Who needs love?" she would have argued. "We get along okay. We could make our families happy. And let's face it, we don't want to lose the deposit at the Roslyn Harbor Inn, do we?" Gary might have ultimately come to see things her way, and she would have been Mrs. Gary Mancuso for a whole month by now.

No, she didn't need a commitment from Josh. She didn't need promises he wasn't prepared to make. If she managed to create a relationship with him and it lasted three years—well, she'd be thirty-two then, way over the hill, and her mother would be saying novenas and lighting candles for her, and Nicky would probably corral Al into kidnapping Josh and taking him to a cabin in the Poconos and feeding him nothing but raw calamari until he agreed to make an honest woman of their sister.

"I should phone my brother," she said abruptly. "Just to let him know I'm going home today." She'd actually be able to pay him back his fifty dollars the next time she saw him, too. Because Melanie had insisted on her spending the night at her apartment instead of at a motel, this trip had wound up costing Loretta less than she'd anticipated.

"Sure." Melanie nudged her phone across the desk. "Dial nine for an outside line. I'll be in the bathroom." She stood, smiled and headed for the door, giving Loretta privacy she didn't really need for her phone call.

Nicky would be at work now, but probably on a break. In fact, right about now—she checked her watch—he'd be brushing and flossing his teeth to remove any residue from the meatball sandwich Kathy would have packed him for lunch. Loretta punched in the office number, waited for the receptionist to pick up and asked to speak to Nicky. "Who may I say is calling?" the receptionist asked prissily.

You may say anyone you damn well want, Loretta thought, but she only gave her name. Nicky might not stop flossing for just anyone, but he'd stop flossing for her.

After a few seconds on hold, she heard a click and then her brother's voice: "Loretta? Did you nail the son of a bitch?"

"No. I didn't even see him. He's back in New York," Loretta answered, then hurried ahead so Nicky wouldn't have a chance to ask her how she'd managed to botch things so magnificently, missing Josh in Florida by mere hours. "I just wanted to let you know I'll be home tonight, too. And it turns out I didn't need your money, so I'll pay you back the next time I see you."

"You're getting home tonight?" Nicky mulled that over. "In other words, you're going to wind up spending less time in Florida than in airplanes."

"Not quite. I'm glad I came, Nicky. It wasn't a wasted trip."

"Even though you didn't see the son of a bitch?"

"He's not a son of a bitch." Loretta didn't consider this an appropriate time to explain that Josh had broken up with Melanie—and that Loretta and Melanie had become friends.

"So what time are you getting in?" Nicky asked.

"Around quarter to eleven."

"That's too late. You can't come in to LaGuardia that late."

"Delta Air Lines seems to think I can. They found me a seat on a plane that gets in then. I'll be all right, Nicky."

"I'll come pick you up."

"No," she said quickly. This trip had been weird enough. She needed time alone, beyond the reach of her

family, to digest the experience, to assess what she'd
learned about Josh and his commitment phobia and his love
of sex. "Ten forty-five isn't that late." It sounded a lot
earlier than quarter to eleven.

"You can't take a cab that late, Loretta."

"I won't." She thought fast. "Josh is going to pick me
up."

"He is?"

"Yes. See? He's not a son of a bitch." There. She'd
killed two birds with one little white lie. She'd redeemed
Josh's reputation and fended off her brother's concern
about her arrival time at LaGuardia.

"Okay, then." Nicky thought for a minute. "Is he going
to marry you?"

"Give it a break, Nicky. He's going to pick me up at
the airport. That's romantic enough for me." She almost
believed that—and she almost believed Josh was picking
her up at the airport. But he wasn't, of course. He had no
idea she was returning home tonight. She hadn't secured
her seat on the 5:25 out of Miami until that morning. And
anyway, he'd sounded so pissed last night, when Melanie
had finally gotten his phone message and called him back,
that Loretta wouldn't have dared to ask such a favor of
him.

She hadn't done herself much good with this trip. True,
she'd made a new friend, she'd discovered a new mixed
drink, she'd played hooky from work for a day—which
might just be enough to lift her to the top of Becky's layoff
list, although if Becky could fire her after she'd created
such a fabulous show with Solly and his rival lovers, the
Becky Blake Show didn't deserve her. She'd learned some
important things about Josh. She'd learned that he'd ended
his relationship with Melanie, and that he wasn't in the

market for marriage, which was really what she wanted, since she wasn't in the market for marriage, either.

Yet that knowledge loomed above her like her own personal cloud, blocking out a patch of light in her soul. She wasn't in the market for marriage, but Josh... She loved him. She loved him enough to wish he were the sort who would pick her up at the airport late at night, and get down on his knees, and...

Damn. What was wrong with her? Her family wanted that for her, but she didn't want it for herself. Right?

Melanie reentered the office, and Loretta said goodbye to Nicky. Then she plastered a bright smile across her face. "You have to get back to work. I'll go find someone to play shuffleboard with. I met the greatest guy this morning. He called me 'sweetheart.'"

"That would be Bernie Gertz. He calls everybody sweetheart. He's the biggest flirt in the place."

"And here I thought he was madly in love with me," Loretta joked, gathering the trash from her lunch and tossing it into the wastebasket beside Melanie's desk. "Thanks for having lunch with me. Now, I'll go and stay out of your hair."

"I haven't got any hair," Melanie reminded her. "Be back here by three the absolute latest. We've got to take off then for me to get you to the airport in time."

Loretta left the office, strolled out of the building and felt the heat of the sun slam against her skin. But still there was that patch of gray hovering over her heart. No, she didn't want to get married. She wanted to stay single forever, or at least until she'd reached her thirtieth birthday, if only to prove that she didn't buy into her family's bullshit about unmarried women of a certain age. She wanted to share ice cream with Josh and misbehave at the Lincoln Center fountain with him, and listen to him describe his cases to her, and bounce her ideas for the show off him. She wanted to expose him to amaretto cannolis, and fresh pasta with fresh pesto. And she wanted to have sex with him every night, for as long as he'd have her.

And if he never made a commitment? She could handle it. Sure she could. It was what she wanted.

Just like she wanted that little blot of shadow stealing the light out of her life.

"There's a call for you," Ruth intoned in her chronically sullen voice. "Line two."

"Who is it?" Josh prayed it wasn't Solly—or Phyllis, or Dora Lee, or Francine. He'd worked out a truce among the warring parties, but a glance at the international news pages of the *Times* on any given day was all it took to remind him of how fragile most truces were.

"A new client, maybe?" Ruth guessed. "He said his name was Nicholas D'Angelo. Actually, he said *Dr.* Nicholas D'Angelo, so he's probably too rich to become a client of ours."

Josh's heart lurched. Loretta's brother Nicky? Why would he call, unless something was terribly wrong? "Thanks," he said, then hit the button for line two and said, "Josh Kaplan," in the calmest voice he could muster when his mind was conjuring up images of Loretta sick, Loretta hurt, Loretta lost.

"Josh? It's Nicky D'Angelo," Loretta's brother boomed. He sounded friendly enough, but his voice had an edge to it.

"Nicky. Nice to hear from you."

"Yeah, well, if you really wanted to hear from me, you would have given me your phone number. I had to jump through a few hoops to get it."

"We're listed in the Yellow Pages," Josh pointed out.

"Not under Kaplan. Besides which, there are only something like two million attorneys-at-law named Kaplan in New York City. You didn't think of that, did you?"

"Actually, no."

"So I called Loretta's place of business and said I was trying to reach you. You know that guy she works with—Bob? Someone said he was a client of yours, and he gave me your number."

"Right." Bob had indeed posed as a client of his. By pretending to be a client, Bob had connived to get Josh onto the show as Loretta's blind date. And now Loretta was in Miami, becoming best friends with Melanie while Josh was fielding calls from Loretta's big lug of a dentist brother. Sometimes life really sucked. "Well, I hope the effort was worth it," he said pleasantly. "What can I do for you?"

"I'm just checking to make sure you're picking Loretta up at LaGuardia tonight."

Josh clamped his mouth shut before blurting out anything that would expose his complete ignorance. She was coming home tonight? He was supposed to pick her up? When was she intending to inform him of this?

"Um, yeah," he said carefully. "I think that was the plan." *What flight? What time? Jesus, did she think he was clairvoyant?*

"Because I hate the idea of her getting in so late and not having anyone there waiting for her. You know? A woman alone, it's just not safe."

How late is she getting in? "LaGuardia's pretty safe," Josh assured him.

"I told her I'd pick her up, but she said no, you were taking care of it."

Josh fit the pieces together: Loretta had lied to Nicky so he wouldn't greet her at the airport. "That's right," Josh played along. "You don't have to worry about Loretta. I'll be picking her up. Let me see, what flight was it...?" He pushed some papers around his desk. "You know, I think my secretary misplaced the flight information. Do you remember what flight she was coming in on?"

"Great. This is who she trusts to pick her up," Nicky muttered. "Someone with a stupid secretary."

"Never mind." Josh labored to sound peeved. "My secretary isn't stupid. I'm sure she has the information at her desk."

"Loretta didn't tell me the flight number," Nicky relented. "It's Delta, because I took her to the airport to fly down there—to see *you*, I thought. Like any of this makes any sense at all. But I figure, if she flew down on Delta, she'll be coming back on Delta."

"Of course."

"Eleven o'clock? Sometime around then, I think she said."

"Yes, that's right." Josh scribbled "Delta—eleven" on the corner of a photocopy of Henri Charnier's lease.

"Look, Josh." Nicky lowered his voice to an intimate tone. "I don't know what's going on with you two. If I asked Loretta, she'd say it was none of my business. And maybe you'd say the same thing."

"That's a good bet," Josh said.

"But she's my baby sister, if you catch my drift. The last guy she was involved with, if I had my way he'd be singing soprano right now. You know what I'm saying?"

"You're coming through loud and clear. But Loretta's an adult. She gets to make up her own mind."

"She didn't make up her own mind with that last boyfriend of hers. A real *cazzo*. You know what that is? A prick. He dumped her."

To her great relief, Josh recalled.

"My sister doesn't deserve that. Okay? She's a pain in the ass, but she's also my sister. You treat her badly, I'm going to get you."

"Nicky—"

"And I'll bring my brother, Al, with me to hold you down. You see what I'm saying?"

"I love your sister," Josh said. "If anyone dumps anyone, it sure as hell won't be me dumping her."

"Yeah, well, she's almost thirty years old. She can't afford to dump anyone at this point. So—" Nicky altered his voice once more, ridding it of its intimidating edge "—how's that old lady with the funky tooth? Loretta says it's a half-hour job, just a little resurfacing."

"I wouldn't know."

"Give us a call next week. My brother or I will free up some time for her."

"That's very kind of you."

"And don't be late at the airport tonight," Nicky demanded. "I don't want her standing around all by herself for a minute. A lot can happen to a woman who's alone in an airport late at night."

"Don't worry. I'll be there." Josh said goodbye, hung up and let out a groan.

Had he actually told Nicky that he loved Loretta?

A little dishonesty was sometimes necessary, he reassured himself. When dealing with Loretta and her family, a little dishonesty seemed to be standard operating procedure. With Nicky threatening castration—as a dentist he probably had all the equipment he would need to perform such an operation right in his office, starting with the high-powered drill his father had bought for him—Josh would have said anything to calm the guy down.

But it hadn't felt like a lie when he'd said it. In fact, as the words had flowed from his mouth, he'd been thinking,

Why am I telling her brother this? Why am I not telling her?

Because she was down in Opa-Locka with Melanie, bonding over a bottle of rum and an old Cher movie. Because Melanie was probably stuffing Loretta's head with ideas about Josh, negative ideas about the man who'd not only broken up with her but refused her suggestion of a friendly fuck for old time's sake. Because from the start, Loretta had been forthright about her desire to steer clear of love.

But he loved her.

And damn it, he'd better be at the airport to meet her tonight, or Nicky was going to come after him with a sharp object.

He logged on to the Internet, called up the Delta Air Lines home page and checked the schedule for incoming flights. He found no direct flights from Miami, but a connecting flight from Atlanta was scheduled to land at 10:46. He'd aim for that one. If she wasn't on it, he'd sit around and wait for the next flight. And if she wasn't on that one…

He'd fly down to Miami and get her himself.

Loretta was beat. She'd bought a soft pretzel during her layover in Atlanta, and now it sat in a congealing lump in the pit of her stomach. The salt on it had made her so thirsty she'd downed three bottles of water on the airplane, and her bladder had swelled like a water balloon during the thirty-minute approach to LaGuardia, when the flight attendant announced that passengers were to remain in their seats with their seat belts on until the plane was safely at the gate.

She'd made it to a lavatory inside the terminal—just barely. Her head hurt, her cheeks stung from a touch of sunburn—that Bernie Gertz sure did like to play a lot of shuffleboard in the hot afternoon sun—and she wanted to go home, curl up in bed and swear to God that she'd approach rum with greater caution from here on in.

She rinsed her hands, splashed water on her cheeks and examined her reflection in the mirror above the sink. The trim Donna had subjected her hair to had done nothing to protect it from the vicissitudes of southern Florida heat and humidity. It looked like a fuzzy black rug. Melanie had had the right idea when it came to hairdos.

Melanie had had the right idea about a lot of things. Like cutting her losses with Josh when it became clear that he wasn't going to make a commitment. Loretta was going to have to decide for herself whether to be satisfied with what Josh could give her and expect nothing more, or to end whatever relationship they had now, before he broke her heart. Because of all the stupid things she'd done recently, the stupidest had been to fall in love with him after claiming that love was the one thing she didn't want from him.

She left the rest room and joined the flow of human traffic heading from the gates to the baggage claim area. Nearly 11:00 p.m. She hoped she wouldn't have to wait long for a cab. Through the security gate, down the escalator...

"Loretta."

She halted, then glanced around. People swarmed in all directions around her, mothers dragging cranky children, young couples clinging to each other as if one of them had just returned from a war, businessmen with garment bags slung over their shoulders, strutting and jabbering importantly into their cell phones. *I don't know where we are... Somewhere on Long Island.* Wasn't that what the babbling blond nitwit on the train had said? The Sunday evening when Loretta had first laid eyes on Josh Kaplan and—

"Loretta," someone spoke more firmly, in Josh's voice.

She spun around, feeling dizzy and disoriented as people pushed past her to get to the baggage carousel. She saw a bearded man in a broad-brimmed hat, one of those very religious Jews who could pass for Amish. She saw a barrel-chested skinhead in a T-shirt reading This Could Be Your Lucky Day. She saw a kid scarcely out of puberty, with acne scars pocking his cheeks and a lovelorn sorrow in his eyes. She saw an enormous bouquet of flowers, enough flowers to fill the back of a hearse at a funeral. Somewhere behind the bouquet was a person; human hands were holding the bouquet around the stems.

The hands looked familiar. She'd seen those hands before—gripping a bacon cheeseburger. Holding a bottle of Sam Adams. Weaving into her hair and angling her face for a kiss.

The bouquet shifted lower, and Josh's face appeared above the array of blossoms. "Loretta."

She felt even more dizzy and disoriented. What the hell was he doing here? Other than meeting her, which he wasn't supposed to be doing, even though she'd told Nicky he was. She'd never believed in the power of lies before.

"Who died?" she asked, focusing on the flowers until she regained her equilibrium. The blossoms represented the full spectrum of color, bunched with dark-green leaves and brighter stalks that resembled chives.

"What do you mean, who died?"

"No one gets flowers like those unless they're dead."

"You can be the first live person to get flowers like these. They're for you," he said, presenting them to her.

She gathered them into her arms and nearly staggered under their weight. "What are you doing here?" she finally asked. "How did you know I'd be arriving now?"

"Your brother Nicky called me to make sure I'd be picking you up. He made it pretty clear what would happen to me if I wasn't here when you got off the plane. Frankly, I don't think either of us would want him to do what he was threatening.''

She gazed into Josh's beautiful hazel eyes. They held laughter but other emotions, too. Panic—perhaps reflecting his response to Nicky's warning. Hope. Dread. Something else—something she couldn't decipher.

''You cut your hair,'' he observed.

''Donna cut it. It looks like shit.''

''It looks beautiful.''

''You like it?'' She was thinking his hair looked beautiful. Tousled, windblown, honey-blond streaks shimmering in the terminal's bright lights.

''It looks great.'' He studied her for a minute. ''You're not going to go much shorter, are you?''

''You mean, like Melanie's hair?''

He didn't smile. ''I like to be able to run my hands through a woman's hair.'' His expression became grimmer. ''Not just any woman's hair. Yours.''

And she liked his being able to run his hands through her hair. That still didn't explain why he'd let Nicky browbeat him into making her lie come true. ''What are the flowers for?''

''I thought you'd like them. I...'' He sighed. ''I love you, Loretta.''

''What!'' Josh didn't say things like that. Melanie had told her.

''I love you. I know you're not looking for love, so all right. We'll deal with that. We'll start with flowers and work our way up.''

''We'll work our way up to what?''

''I don't know.'' He shrugged helplessly. ''A ring? A wedding? Whatever you wind up talking me into. You know you can talk me into anything, Loretta. You've already talked me into blind dates and TV appearances and God knows what else.''

She felt really dizzy now. Seriously disoriented. This wasn't supposed to happen. She'd just spent the past twenty-four hours preparing herself for the fact that it would never happen. Yet there she stood, in the middle of a bustling LaGuardia Airport terminal, her arms aching around the bulk of the flowers, her shoulder sore from the strap of her duffel, and the man she loved, a man who was supposed to be commitment-phobic, was talking about rings and weddings.

Weddings. With photographers and reception halls and Alyssa and the twins as flower girls. In a church—or in a synagogue? Oh, God, how were they going to work that out? One of those hybrid ceremonies like the one her mother's friend Sonia had gone to, with the clergymen enacting a bad joke: *A priest and a rabbi walk into a wedding...*

"I wasn't expecting this," she said.

"Great. You told your damn brother I was supposed to be here. Now you tell me you aren't expecting this."

"I'm not talking about your being here. I wasn't expecting that, either. But the rest of it."

"The flowers."

"And the other things."

At last Josh touched her. He cupped his hands beneath her elbows, helping her bear the weight of the bouquet. "I wasn't expecting those other things, either." He gazed at her through the multicolored petals and spiky green stalks. "So what happens now? You tell me you don't want a relationship? You break my heart?"

"I'm not going to break your heart, Josh."

"Promise?"

"Promise."

He pressed through the flowers to kiss her. She heard stems rustling and snapping between her body and Josh's, and smelled the heavy perfume of the blossoms pluming around them. She felt the warmth of his mouth on hers, the sweet glide of his tongue against her teeth, and the dizziness this time came from a surge of pure lust.

"My parents are going to want more grandchildren," she whispered when, after a shamelessly long time, he drew back.

"This minute?"

"No, I'm just saying."

"We wouldn't want to disappoint your parents."

"No, we wouldn't." She smiled.

He smiled, too, then touched his lips to hers. "Why did you go to Florida?"

To tell you I love you. She'd answer his question later, as many times and in as many ways as he wanted her to. But some of the ways she wanted to answer that question were not appropriate for two people standing in the middle of the LaGuardia Airport terminal. So she said, "I wanted to pump Melanie for information about you."

"That's what I was afraid of."

"I know everything about you now," Loretta warned him as, keeping one hand on her elbow, he led her past the baggage claim area to the taxi stand outside. "She said you're self-righteous and overwhelmed by guilt."

"Lies. All lies," he protested with a laugh.

"She said you're sarcastic and fanatical about your socks."

"She doesn't know what she's talking about."

"She said you love sex."

"She… Well, okay. We'll let that one go." He ushered her through the sliding glass door and into the balmy dark. No palm trees swayed along the driveway here. No steambath humidity hugged the pavement. This was New York, her home, and she was with the man she wanted to come home to. She had Josh, and a starlit night, and more flowers than she'd ever know what to do with.

Okay, so maybe she'd get married before she turned thirty. It wouldn't be the end of the world.

A beautiful novel about desire, healing
and the most powerful medicine of all—love

USA TODAY bestselling author

SUSAN WIGGS

Isabel Fish-Wooten has spent most of her life on the run.
Blue Calhoun runs a thriving medical practice while raising
his son alone after an unthinkable tragedy.

When Blue is forced at gunpoint to save Isabel's life, her rescue
comes with an unexpected price. He is drawn to her fragile
beauty and the mystery that surrounds her. She is touched
by this remarkable man and his son.

From danger-filled back alleys to the glittering ballrooms of
high society, Isabel and Blue confront the violence and
corruption that threatens their newfound passion. Theirs is an
unforgettable quest to discover a rare and special love, and the
precious gift of a second chance at happiness.

"Wiggs has a knack for creating engaging characters, and her
energetic prose shines through the pages."
—*Publishers Weekly* on *Enchanted Afternoon*

A SUMMER AFFAIR

Available the first week of August 2003 wherever paperbacks are sold!

Visit us at www.mirabooks.com

MSW710

USA TODAY **Bestselling Author**

JODI THOMAS

Apart from sharing the same zip code, Randi Howard,
Anna Montano, Meredith Allen, Helen Whitworth and
Crystal Howard have absolutely nothing in common.
But on a blistering day in early autumn a tragedy binds
the women closer together than a lifetime of friendship.

As they gather at the hospital, waiting to learn who
among them will not have to bury her husband, they
turn to one another for support, beginning a journey
of faith, of strength, of tears and of love.

THE WIDOWS OF WICHITA COUNTY

"Jodi Thomas will render you breathless!"
—Romantic Times

*Available the first week of August 2003
wherever paperbacks are sold!*

MIRA®

Visit us at www.mirabooks.com

MJT715

MIRA®

USA TODAY bestselling author

SUSAN WIGGS

brings you four classic historical romances
that will touch your heart.

"Susan Wiggs delves deeply into her characters' hearts
and motivations to touch our own."
—*Romantic Times*

"Wiggs' synergistic blending of historical authenticity,
complex multifaceted characters, and riveting plot
makes for an exquisite romance."
—*Booklist*

**Look for these heartwarming novels along with
Susan's new release, *A SUMMER AFFAIR*, the first week
of August 2003 wherever paperbacks are sold!**

Visit us at www.mirabooks.com   MSW758

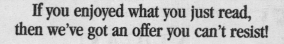

If you enjoyed what you just read,
then we've got an offer you can't resist!

Take 2
bestselling novels FREE!
Plus get a FREE surprise gift!

Clip this page and mail it to The Best of the Best™

IN U.S.A.
3010 Walden Ave.
P.O. Box 1867
Buffalo, N.Y. 14240-1867

IN CANADA
P.O. Box 609
Fort Erie, Ontario
L2A 5X3

YES! Please send me 2 free Best of the Best™ novels and my free surprise gift. After receiving them, if I don't wish to receive anymore, I can return the shipping statement marked cancel. If I don't cancel, I will receive 4 brand-new novels every month, before they're available in stores! In the U.S.A., bill me at the bargain price of $4.74 plus 25¢ shipping and handling per book and applicable sales tax, if any*. In Canada, bill me at the bargain price of $5.24 plus 25¢ shipping and handling per book and applicable taxes**. That's the complete price and a savings of over 20% off the cover prices—what a great deal! I understand that accepting the 2 free books and gift places me under no obligation ever to buy any books. I can always return a shipment and cancel at any time. Even if I never buy another The Best of the Best™ book, the 2 free books and gift are mine to keep forever.

185 MDN DNWF
385 MDN DNWG

Name		(PLEASE PRINT)	
Address		Apt.#	
City		State/Prov.	Zip/Postal Code

* Terms and prices subject to change without notice. Sales tax applicable in N.Y.
** Canadian residents will be charged applicable provincial taxes and GST.
   All orders subject to approval. Offer limited to one per household and not valid to
   current The Best of the Best™ subscribers.
® are registered trademarks of Harlequin Enterprises Limited.

BOB02-R   ©1998 Harlequin Enterprises Limited

She had everything to lose.
Now she must risk the only thing worth saving…her heart.

SILENT
WISHES

Sylvia Hansen, newly appointed CEO of Harcourts International, N.Y.,
is at the top of her game when crisis strikes: a traitor has divulged
the decor company's new product line to the competition.

Despite her misgivings, she joins forces with Jeremy Warmouth,
head of Harcourts' European operations, in an attempt to uncover
the source of the leaked information.

But when a silent stalker declares war on Sylvia, quietly tormenting
her with his knowledge of her past that for years she has desperately
kept hidden, she believes her carefully crafted world is about to
collapse. Now, if the truth becomes known, will all her
achievements and buried dreams be destroyed?

FIONA
HOOD-STEWART

"This huge, action-packed saga is a feast for anyone
who yearns for a long, rich read."
—*Romantic Times* on *The Stolen Years*

Available the first week of September 2003, wherever paperbacks are sold!

Visit us at www.mirabooks.com

MFHS728

USA TODAY bestselling author

Sherryl Woods

Even when it's the last thing you expect...
Home is where the heart belongs.

Welcome to Flamingo Diner, where friends and family come first.
It's also the family business that Emma Killian has spent her life
trying to avoid.

Now her father's tragic death has brought her home to Winter Cove,
Florida, to face a mountain of secrets, debts and questions about
how her beloved father died. As she grapples with her out-of-control
family and the responsibility for keeping Flamingo Diner afloat,
Emma finds support from an unlikely source—onetime bad boy
Matt Atkins, who is now the Winter Cove police chief. Matt has
always had a penchant for trouble and an eye for Emma. Now it
seems he's the only one who can help her discover the answers
to her questions...and give her a whole new reason to stay home.

**"Clever characters and snappy, realistic dialogue add
zest...making this a delightful read."**
—*Publishers Weekly* on *About that Man*

*Available the first week
of September 2003,
wherever paperbacks are sold.*

Visit us at www.mirabooks.com

MSW722

Visit a new address
in Cedar Cove:

311 Pelican Court

New York Times **bestselling author**

DEBBIE MACOMBER

Rosie Cox
311 Pelican Court
Cedar Cove, Washington

Dear Reader,

Everybody in this town knows that my husband, Zach, and I recently got a divorce. Everybody also knows that the judge decreed a pretty unusual custody arrangement. It won't be the kids moving between my place and Zach's. *We're* the ones who'll be going back and forth!

But the *really* big gossip has to do with the dead guy—the man who died at a local bed-and-breakfast. Who is he? Roy McAfee, our local private investigator, is absolutely determined to find out. I hope he does—and then I'll let you know! See you soon....

Rosie

"Macomber is known for her honest portrayals
of ordinary women in small-town America, and this
tale cements her position as an icon of the genre."
—*Publishers Weekly* on *16 Lighthouse Road*

*Available the first week
of September 2003,
wherever paperbacks are sold!*

MIRA®

Visit us at www.mirabooks.com   MDM719

JUDITH ARNOLD

66918	LOVE IN BLOOM'S	___ $6.50 U.S.	___ $7.99 CAN.
66828	LOOKING FOR LAURA	___ $5.99 U.S.	___ $6.99 CAN.

(limited quantities available)

TOTAL AMOUNT	$_____
POSTAGE & HANDLING	$_____
($1.00 for one book; 50¢ for each additional)	
APPLICABLE TAXES*	$_____
TOTAL PAYABLE	$_____
(check or money order—please do not send cash)	

To order, complete this form and send it, along with a check
or money order for the total above, payable to MIRA Books®,
to: **In the U.S.:** 3010 Walden Avenue, P.O. Box 9077, Buffalo,
NY 14269-9077; **In Canada:** P.O. Box 636, Fort Erie, Ontario
L2A 5X3.

Name:_____
Address:_____ City:_____
State/Prov.:_____ Zip/Postal Code:_____
Account Number (if applicable):_____
075 CSAS

  *New York residents remit applicable sales taxes.
  Canadian residents remit applicable GST and provincial taxes.

MIRA®

Visit us at www.mirabooks.com   MJA0803BL